BELLS *of* LOWELL

TRACIE
PETERSON

JUDITH MILLER

BELLS *of* LOWELL

BETHANYHOUSE
MINNEAPOLIS, MINNESOTA

Published by Bethany House Publishers
11400 Hampshire Avenue South
Bloomington, Minnesota 55438

Bethany House Publishers is a division of
Baker Publishing Group, Grand Rapids, Michigan.

Printed in the United States of America

Library of Congress Cataloging-in-Publication Data

Peterson, Tracie.
    Bells of Lowell / Tracie Peterson and Judith Miller.
        p.   cm.
        ISBN 978-0-7642-0483-8 (hardcover : alk. paper)
    1. Women—Massachusetts—Fiction.   2. Women textile workers—Fiction.   3. Textile industry—
Fiction.   4. Lowell (Mass.)—Fiction.   I. Miller, Judith, 1944-   II. Title.

    PS3566.E7717B45   2007
    813'.54—dc22   2007033735

TRACIE PETERSON is a popular speaker and bestselling author who has written over seventy books, both historical and contemporary fiction. Tracie and her family make their home in Montana.

Visit Tracie's Web site at: *www.traciepeterson.com.*

JUDITH MILLER is an award-winning author whose avid research and love for history are reflected in her novels, many of which have appeared on the CBA bestseller lists. Judy and her husband make their home in Topeka, Kansas.

Visit Judy's Web site at: *www.judithmccoymiller.com.*

Books by Tracie Peterson

www.traciepeterson.com

A Slender Thread
What She Left for Me
*I Can't Do It All!***

ALASKAN QUEST
Summer of the Midnight Sun
Under the Northern Lights • *Whispers of Winter*

BELLS OF LOWELL*
Daughter of the Loom • *A Fragile Design*
These Tangled Threads

LIGHTS OF LOWELL*
A Tapestry of Hope • *A Love Woven True*
The Pattern of Her Heart

DESERT ROSES
Shadows of the Canyon • *Across the Years*
Beneath a Harvest Sky

HEIRS OF MONTANA
Land of My Heart • *The Coming Storm*
To Dream Anew • *The Hope Within*

WESTWARD CHRONICLES
A Shelter of Hope • *Hidden in a Whisper*
A Veiled Reflection

LADIES OF LIBERTY
A Lady of High Regard

SHANNON SAGA‡
City of Angels • *Angels Flight* • *Angel of Mercy*

YUKON QUEST
Treasures of the North • *Ashes and Ice*
Rivers of Gold

*with Judith Miller   †with Judith Pella   ‡with James Scott Bell
**with Allison Bottke and Dianne O'Brian

Books by Judith Miller

www.judithmccoymiller.com

BELLS OF LOWELL*

Daughter of the Loom

A Fragile Design

These Tangled Threads

LIGHTS OF LOWELL*

A Tapestry of Hope

A Love Woven True

The Pattern of Her Heart

FREEDOM'S PATH

First Dawn

Morning Sky

Daylight Comes

POSTCARDS FROM PULLMAN

In the Company of Secrets

Whispers Along the Rails

*with Tracie Peterson

DAUGHTER
of the LOOM

1

I will not fail," Lilly Armbruster whispered into the early morning dawn. Setting one foot in front of the other, slowly, methodically, she continued onward until reaching the bridge over the Hamilton Canal, the bridge that would take her into the Appleton textile mill.

How different life might have been if only Lowell could have remained unchanged. How different her life might have been if only Matthew had remained unchanged, as well. Lilly tried to dispel the memory of the only man she'd ever loved. He was her enemy now— as clearly as the others who had marred her beautiful East Chelmsford with their monstrosities of brick and iron. Even worse, they had renamed it *Lowell*! She shuddered at the thought.

"Progressive industry," Matthew had called it, pleading with her to understand. "It will be to the betterment of everyone concerned," he'd promised. But it hadn't been to her betterment—nor to her father's.

The sun was beginning its ascent into the gray eastern sky as Lilly crossed into the mill yard by the only open gate, the one that would permit her entry into the fiefdom of the Corporation, a fiefdom that had been carefully planned and cultivated by a group of Bostonians, now referred to by the locals as the Boston Associates or the lords of the loom. Powerful men—men with money, connections, and an unrelenting passion for the creation of the mill town they had named after their visionary, Francis Cabot Lowell. These same men had given special attention to every detail, completing their architectural wonders with moats, fortified walls, drawbridges, and serfs—many, many serfs.

Step by step, Lilly moved farther into the mill yard, her attention now drawn toward the dull, rumbling noise seeping through the thick brick walls of the taller buildings that formed the outer perimeter of the fortress. She had never noticed the sound before, but she had never been this close to the mills before, either. The reverberating din seemed to be pounding out a message of doom.

Despite a chill in the morning air, a rivulet of perspiration trickled down the small of her back. Swallowing hard to gain control of the bile that now rose in her throat, Lilly paused momentarily to deposit her bags before entering the building. There was no sense in dragging them along with her, especially since she was already exhausted from carrying them all this way.

She took a deep breath and smoothed down the pleats of her bodice. Her gown wasn't very fashionable or stylish, but she couldn't imagine that would matter to the men inside. Squaring her shoulders, Lilly knew the moment of truth had arrived. She had to go through with her plan. She had to see this through, no matter how distasteful.

A middle-aged man was perched at a desk near the doorway; probably a clerk or bookkeeper, she decided. He looked up from his papers, gave her an agitated glance, and nodded toward a single chair near his desk. With her fingernails biting into the flesh of her palms, she seated herself and waited while the clerk continued writing in his ledger.

What would Father think if he could see me in this place? She pictured him cupping large worn hands to his mouth, calling out from the gates of heaven and warning her against such folly, shouting that she didn't belong among these evil men who had lied to him, breaking his heart with their wicked schemes.

Lilly watched as the clerk laid down his pen and scratched his balding head before giving her his attention. "Applying for a position, I presume?"

Lilly forced herself to look him in the eyes—brown, wide-set, beady-looking eyes that sent a dark message. "Yes." It was all she could manage. Her heart raced in a maddening staccato. It seemed to beat out the words *You fool! You fool! You fool!*

In a slow, lingering manner, the man let his gaze travel the full length of her body. "How old are you, girl?"

Lilly knew her slender figure and petite frame often caused people to believe her years younger than her actual age. "I'm twenty," she said, straightening her shoulders. She wished silently that she'd pinned her hair up instead of leaving it in a single braid down her back. Then, too, her bonnet was at least five years old and much too childish for a young woman.

"Twenty, eh?" The man looked as if he didn't believe her.

"Yes, I'm twenty." Lilly stood her ground, offering nothing more.

The man gave a *harrumph*ing sound, then shook his head. "We have no openings. Did one of the boardinghouse keepers send you?" he asked, glancing about the room while giving her a smirk that revealed uneven yellowing teeth.

"I'm applying for a position as a weaver or perhaps a drawing-in girl. My name is Lilly Armbruster, and I think if you'll check with Mr. Boott or Mr. Appleton, there may be a position available for me." Her confidence swelled. She would not let this man deter her.

His lips curled into a mocking sneer, his beady eyes now narrow slits in a too-thin face. "Well, since Mr. Boott and Mr. Appleton aren't in the immediate vicinity, why don't you tell *me* why you think one of them would be willing to create a position especially for you, Miss Armbruster?"

She struggled to maintain her decorum, wanting to reveal neither her fear of this leering man nor her abhorrence for seeking employment in one of the mills. "Mr. Boott attended my father's funeral last week. While at the cemetery, he told me there would always be work at the mills for our family." She paused, giving him what she hoped was a look of complete innocence. "Do you think he was insincere, merely making consoling remarks to a bereaved family?" she asked, intoning concern.

The clerk shifted in his chair and shoved a bony finger under the soiled collar of his dingy white shirt. Exhaling deeply, he shoved his chair away from the desk and excused himself. Lilly watched as he scurried off and whispered in the ear of an older man across the room. Wagging his head first in one direction and then the other, he occasionally stole a glance at her from under hooded eyelids, his appraisal making Lilly feel somewhat less than human. Finally, the older man turned back to his work, obviously bringing the conversation to an end.

The clerk returned to the desk and settled into his chair. "Mr. Nettles tells me there will soon be an opening in the spinning room and you can begin a week from now. Come with the others at the first bell. Report to me, and I'll take you to your assignment. I'm also to tell you that there's an opening at Adelaide Beecher's boardinghouse, number 5 Jackson Street. Mr. Nettles has sent one of the doffers to advise Miss Beecher of your arrival. She'll be expecting you."

His smug look had vanished. "And *your* name, sir?" Lilly inquired, putting her innocent act aside.

"Arnold. Thaddeus Arnold. I'll have your contract ready for signature when you arrive next Monday."

"Thank you, Mr. Arnold." She lingered for a moment, watching as he took up his pen and went back to his ledgers. "Good day, Mr. Arnold, and again, my thanks for your kind attention." When his head snapped up to meet her eyes, she knew she had failed to keep the bite of sarcasm from her reply.

"It's not wise to make enemies of those in authority, Miss Armbruster." His thin lips barely moved as he hissed the words across the desk at her.

A tingling sensation coursed through her body, and she could feel his glowering stare follow her every move as she rose from the chair and exited the building. Though her instincts told her to run and never come back, she held herself in check, straightened her back, and raised her head high until she was out of his sight.

Gathering her luggage, Lilly moved away from the mill and the disgusting man. Once she'd rounded the corner of the building, she stopped and leaned against the cool brick wall. Would she never learn to control her tongue? There was no changing things now, but perhaps it would be wise to try and make amends with Thaddeus Arnold next Monday. For now, she'd best gather

her wits and make Miss Beecher's acquaintance. The boardinghouse was just down the street, and a friendly face and a cup of tea would be welcome.

A row of three-story brick boardinghouses flanked by smaller white frame houses at each end lined both sides of Jackson Street. A few children were playing outside one of the houses at the end of the square, and Lilly paused momentarily to watch their carefree antics. Had she ever been so young and lighthearted? It seemed impossible to recall such a time.

Trudging down the street, she paused momentarily in front of number 5 before ascending the two steps and firmly knocking on the front door. The door opened, and a plump woman with a winning smile stood before her. "Welcome, welcome, welcome, my dear. Do come in and let's get you settled." Wasting no time, the older woman took Lilly's satchel and started toward the parlor. "Don't stand there gathering flies, dearie. Bring the rest of your belongings inside, and let's get acquainted. I'm Adelaide Beecher."

Grabbing her bandbox and a small trunk, Lilly entered and shoved the door with her backside. She nodded in satisfaction at the clicking sound as the door latched. "Mr. Arnold sent me. I'm Lilly Armbruster. Where to?" she asked as the plump woman moved aside, permitting an unobstructed view of two long dining tables surrounded by what looked like as many as thirty chairs.

"This way, dearie. We've several flights of stairs to climb, so you may want to make two trips," she warned.

"No need. I'm accustomed to hard work, Mrs. Beecher," Lilly stated firmly, knowing her small frame might suggest otherwise.

"Suit yourself. And it's Miss Beecher. I've never been married. The girls call me Miss Addie—you do the same. Unless my sister's around, of course," she giggled. "Then they call me Miss Adelaide. My sister's name is Miss Mintie Beecher. She's a bit of a stickler for formalities and barely suffers the use of our given names. She's the keeper at number 7 across the street. She houses some of the men, so her quarters are off limits for my girls."

Lilly smiled and nodded as she continued trudging up the stairway. "How much farther?" she panted. The first flight of stairs hadn't been so bad. They were slanted at an easy angle, and she'd hardly lost her wind. But this flight was steeper and narrower. Her feet seemed to barely get a decent toehold before striking the back of the step, threatening to topple her backward.

"Almost there. Just one more," Miss Addie cheerily called back over her shoulder. "You can leave one of those satchels and come back for it if you're having difficulty. The next flight is a bit steep."

Lilly heeded the warning and dropped her bandbox at the foot of the stairs. It was a wise decision. The ascent seemed never ending, and Lilly had truly despaired of reaching the top when Miss Addie finally announced, "Here we are."

"I guessed this might be it. We couldn't have gone much farther unless you planned to put me out on the roof," Lilly jibed as she touched the rafter with her outstretched hand. Instantly she worried that her words had been spoken out of line. She looked to Addie to ascertain if she'd offended her, but the woman merely smiled back at her.

"I like your sense of humor, Lilly. A sense of humor is a true gift from the Lord. I don't know how I would have survived the last six months without mine. I must admit, however, some of the girls don't share my opinion, so don't be surprised if you hear some of them say they're looking to change boardinghouses. Seems no sooner do I get a new girl than I lose another. Which does bring to mind the fact that two girls moved out yesterday, and I didn't need to bring you clear to this attic room after all," she admitted with a chuckle. "Unless you'd prefer to be up here by yourself?"

"I'm not sure," Lilly panted, still winded. The lumpy mattress sagged in protest as she dropped onto one of the four beds sandwiched into the tiny, airless room—there was barely room to store her baggage. Two small chests were wedged into the small space on either side of the two narrow attic windows. It appeared that opening the top drawer of either chest would be impossible without hitting the wall, and she had to turn sideways to walk between the two beds.

"You get two drawers in one of the chests, and you'll share the bed as new girls move in. The previous keeper told me she sometimes had eight or nine girls up here, but most times just six or seven."

Lilly laughed. "I like your sense of humor, too, Miss Addie! Eight or nine girls. Why, there's not room for more than four in this room at best. It's not so bad in here right now, but the heat in summer and cold in winter would most likely be dreadful."

"I'd like to tell you that I'm joking with you about the accommodations, miss, but what I've told you is truly the way it is. 'Course, if my cooking doesn't improve, there may never be more than one or two up here. These girls put great store in having good food and plenty of it. But I'm afraid my cooking isn't quite up to the boardinghouse standard yet."

Lilly gave her a wilted smile. "Let's take a look at the second floor."

Miss Addie nodded and led the way back downstairs, stopping in one of the two large bedrooms on the second floor. Lilly glanced about the room. It, too, had four beds, and the chests that lined the wall were similar to those in the upper room. However, this space was larger, and she determined that not having to contend with sloping rafters was a distinct advantage. "How many girls in each of these rooms?"

"Eight—two to a bed and two drawers in the chest. There's a bed open in this room. Well, at least half a bed is open." She grinned. "Nadene lost her bedmate and will probably be glad for the company. It can get rather cold up here at night."

Lilly had no idea who Nadene was. It seemed strange to be agreeing to bed down with folks she didn't even know, but apparently that was how things were done in the mill boardinghouses.

"I think I'd prefer to be down here," Lilly stated. "I'm afraid Mr. Arnold didn't give me much information regarding the boardinghouse. I have no idea how much you charge for room and board."

"The Corporation pays me twenty-five cents, and you pay me one dollar and twenty-five cents per week. Washing your bed linens is included in the price. I've a list of the boardinghouse rules downstairs that each girl must agree to abide by. Remind me to have you read it over and sign the contract. I'm rather forgetful about keeping up with the paper work." She looked over her shoulder as if to ascertain if anyone else would overhear her before adding, "That's frowned upon, don't you know," she said in a hushed voice.

"I'm not sure I can afford to pay before I begin working at the mill. I can ill afford to spend the little money I have," Lilly reported.

Holding a finger to her pursed lips, Miss Addie creased her brows in contemplation. "That does present a problem. I don't suppose you know how to cook for a crowd of hungry girls, do you?"

"*That* I can do," Lilly replied, untying the ribbons to her bonnet.

Miss Addie chortled and clapped her hands together. "Can you teach me?"

Lilly carefully removed her bonnet and placed it atop the dresser. She ran her hand through the chestnut curls that had escaped her braid, knowing she must look frightful. "I'm not sure I can turn you into an expert cook in six days, but I can certainly help you on your way. And you can always ask me questions after I've begun to work at the mill."

Miss Addie's rounded cheeks took on a rosy hue, and her deep blue eyes sparkled. "I think we've solved the problem of your room and board. I knew we were going to be great friends the minute I laid eyes on you. Come along. You need to begin my lessons. The girls will be coming home for dinner in two hours, and my preparations are far from complete. You can unpack after dinner while I wash dishes and clean the kitchen," she instructed, already three-fourths of the way down to the first floor.

Lilly followed along obediently, listening intently as the older woman explained that the largest meal of the day was served at noon and that the girls would arrive at five minutes past the hour. "The food must be on the table when they arrive. They have only half an hour to get from the mill, eat their meal, and return. Their schedule demands that the boardinghouse run smoothly in order for them to eat and return to work on time. I do have one little doffer who helps serve—I don't know what I would have done without her—but there's still more work than I can manage. I'm hoping that once I get all the beds filled, I'll be able to hire someone to help a little more, especially with the meals. But for now, I'm on my own."

"This shouldn't be much different from cooking for the farmhands during harvest," Lilly replied. "How many are you feeding?"

Addie hesitated a moment. "Fifteen, including us."

Lilly nodded. "That shouldn't be too hard. Show me what you've already done."

Two hours later the pealing of the tower bell that had tolled over the city for the past five years announced that midday had arrived. Lilly placed the last bowl of food on the table as the front door flew open. Twelve young women had soon crowded their way into the dining room, with chairs scraping, silverware clanking, and voices competing to be heard above each other as they called out for bowls or plates to be passed. The noise was deafening after the preceding hours of quiet camaraderie in the kitchen with Miss Addie. For a moment, Lilly found herself staring at the group of girls. Instead of exhibiting the manners of genteel young ladies, the girls wolfed down the meal with little attention to etiquette or polite conversation. There was no time for such social amenities here.

"This is so-o-o good," one of the younger girls commented, her mouth still full of rice pudding. "You've been holding out on us, Miss Addie. This is the best meal I've had in ages!"

Several others nodded in agreement and one took a moment to ask, "How'd you do this, Miss Addie?"

All gazes were fixed on the older woman, some faces filled with amazement, some with doubt, and some with what appeared to be undying devotion. "Save your praises. It wasn't my doing; I merely helped. It's our new boarder you have to thank. Meet Lilly Armbruster."

"You've hired a cook? Isn't that what *you're* supposed to do?" Prudence Holtmeyer inquired.

"Indeed, it is one of my duties, but I'm hoping to become more skilled, and Lilly has agreed to help. However . . ."

Before she had completed her explanation, the girls were pushing their chairs away from the table, grabbing their cloaks and bonnets, and rushing toward the door. Several took an extra moment for one last bite of the rice pudding before scurrying off. Minutes later, all was once again silent. Lilly glanced over the table in amazement, for she'd never seen anything like it. Even the farmhands that she and her mother had cooked for took longer to relax and eat the noon meal. These girls were like a colony of locusts swarming in, devouring everything in their path, and moving on. There was one difference, however: the girls would be returning in only a few short hours to repeat the routine.

"I was certain we'd prepared too much food," Lilly commented to herself. She'd thought Miss Addie a bit touched when she'd continued to pull food from the cupboards as they prepared the noon meal.

"Oh, dear me no," Addie replied, already reaching for two empty serving bowls. "The work is terribly hard. They build a powerful appetite, which is why they grow most discontent when their meals are tasteless or ill-prepared."

Lilly thought of the hard work and tried to imagine herself joining the girls at such large meals. The idea struck her as almost amusing. There was no possible way she could ever eat as much food as those girls had eaten. Why, her waist would get as thick as . . . as thick as Miss Addie's! Matthew had always liked her tiny waist.

Matthew! How he seemed to plague her mind at the most awkward of times. Lilly knew she wouldn't mind it half so much if the ache in her heart wasn't yet so pronounced. *I cannot allow myself these feelings,* she told herself, pushing aside the chance to relive her girlhood dreams of becoming Matthew's wife. There was no sense in remembering the ivory satin wedding gown her mother had promised to make. There was no need to dwell on the way her heart fluttered whenever Matthew flashed her a smile. Lilly sighed and forced her attention back to the job at hand.

Addie seemed not to notice Lilly's contemplation. Already she was humming a tune and making order out of the mess. "I'll clear the table and wash the dishes. You go upstairs and unpack. There's fresh water in the pitcher so feel free to freshen up. I'm sure someone as pretty as you is used to being able to see to her appearance, but around here, you have to grab what opportunity presents itself. When you've finished, we can decide about supper."

"Perhaps we should plan the menu first. It doesn't appear there's much bread remaining. I'll need to start now if it's to be ready in time for supper. By the way, what time is supper?"

"The girls will be home at six-thirty. The lighting up doesn't occur until September 21. Then supper will be later, not until seven o'clock," Miss Addie explained.

"The lighting up?"

Miss Addie smiled. "Mercy, but you have a lot to learn. September 21 marks the date when the winter hours begin. Work commences a half hour later in the morning, but you make up for it by working a half hour later in the evening. Folks call it the lighting up because it's dark in the morning when you go to work and dark in the evening when you return home—the lamps become necessary both morning and evening. Then, come March 21, there's what they call the blowing out. The days start becoming longer once again and the lamps aren't needed so much."

Lilly nodded and reached for one of the dishes. She scraped the remnants of dinner from the serving platters into an empty serving bowl. "Seems like a sensible plan." But Lilly reminded herself that if her own plan went well, the mills wouldn't even be around come March 21.

Miss Addie clucked in agreement as she took hold of Lilly's thin wrist.

"Oh, but that's not the best part. Sit yourself down for a minute while I tell you."

Lilly seated herself on one of the dining room chairs while Miss Addie poured a cup of tea, added several spoons of sugar, and began to vigorously stir. After taking a sip of the brew, the older woman leaned forward and spoke in a hushed tone. "The very best part is the balls. There's a Lighting Up Ball and Blowing Out Ball. Very, very fancy, I might add. Not like the parties I knew in Boston, mind you, but very tastefully done for a town the size of Lowell."

Lilly began to rise, but when Miss Addie motioned her down, Lilly plopped back into the chair. "I really should start clearing off the dishes, Miss Addie. I'm not interested in balls or parties, but I do thank you for explaining the lighting up."

"Well, you may not be interested right now, but you will be come the twenty-first day of September. Attending the ball is a must for all the mill girls. It's required. Well, perhaps *expected* is a better word. Those two balls are the only time when there's socializing among all the people who work at the mills. Why, the supervisors dance with all the girls, even the little doffers. Those are the little girls who sometimes hire on for lesser jobs like helping in the boardinghouses or removing empty bobbins in the mills."

"Children work in the mills?" Lilly asked in stunned disbelief.

"Well, the doffers don't work all that much. No more than fifteen minutes or so at a time. They're usually the daughters of women who work there, and they have plenty of playtime and still attend school. They benefit from the money they earn, for usually it helps their family a great deal."

"Still, they're just children. They shouldn't have to work in the mills." *I shouldn't have to work there, either,* Lilly thought.

"Oh, don't you concern yourself about it." Addie continued, "Let me finish telling you about the balls. They're quite the event. Mr. Boott makes an appearance, along with some of the other Boston Associates. The girls look forward to those two dates all year long. You mark my words—after you've listened to the girls talk about the balls, you'll be ready to don your prettiest dress and dancing slippers when the time comes."

Miss Addie obviously expected her to become smitten by the whole affair. Any further denial of interest was only going to cause additional delay in the cleaning-up process, so hopefully a neutral answer would suffice. "We'll see, Miss Addie. We'll see."

Addie nodded and rose from her chair. Each of the women skillfully balanced an armload of dirty plates and bowls and headed toward the kitchen. While Addie put the dishes to soak, Lilly began to take stock of the larder and what they might prepare for supper. Her thoughts ran rampant.

I'm actually here. Here, where God can use me best, Lilly reasoned. Although she had struggled in her spiritual walk, even going so far as to give up her Bible readings and church, Lilly knew God had a purpose in bringing her here to the mills. He would use her to make right the very thing that had brought such tragedy to her family.

Then everything shall be better, Lilly assured herself. *I will find a way to drive the mills out of Lowell, and God will reward me and bless my life.* Lilly looked over her shoulder, almost fearful she'd spoken her thoughts aloud. Addie was nowhere in sight.

Lilly breathed a sigh of relief to find herself alone. Addie would never understand Lilly's feelings. Addie didn't know what it was to have the Association come in and destroy the land she'd come to love—demolish her father's hopes—steal her inheritance. Had Lilly truly not felt led of God to come here to the mills, there was no telling what might have become of her. Women without protectors suffered greatly.

Well, it is certain the mills will offer me no protection, Lilly reasoned. She picked up a bag of flour and balanced this with a can of lard. "I can do this," she whispered. "I can do whatever I have to, to make it all right again."

"Did you say something, my dear?" Addie questioned, popping into the room.

Lilly smiled. "I was just saying that I've found the ingredients to make bread. Come and I'll show you what's to be done."

Scooping heaping cups of flour into a bowl, Lilly then began measuring lard and scalding milk. "Why in the world did you ever take this position if you don't know how to cook, Miss Addie?" she inquired while continuing to prepare the ingredients for a half dozen loaves of bread.

Addie wiped her hands on her apron, then blotted the hem against her perspiring neck. "It's a long story. Suffice it to say, our father managed to die while owing more creditors in Boston than either my sister or I knew existed. Mintie and I were reared in a family of privilege and position—Boston society," she explained proudly. "But when the Judge—that's what we always called our father—died, the creditors came calling, and there was no stopping them until we'd sold our home and almost all of our belongings. Suddenly Mintie and I found ourselves not only penniless but friendless. People of class want nothing to do with you once you've lost everything. We had to find some way to support ourselves, and we read in the newspaper that they needed boardinghouse keepers, as the mills were expanding. Of course, the Judge had once been against the mills. He figured them to be full of spies. In fact, he wouldn't have anything to do with them."

"Would that more men were like him," Lilly muttered.

Addie didn't seem to hear the remark and continued with her explanation. "Mintie sent a letter of inquiry to Tracy Jackson, one of the Boston Associates. He and the Judge had been friends, and I think he took pity on us. In any event, after receiving Mr. Jackson's reply, Mintie decided it was a magnificent opportunity for us to take employment here. She said it would be a job of great virtue for two spinsters. She's very practical, you know." Then with a twinkle in her eye, the older woman added in a hushed, almost ominous tone, "She also thought it a good way to keep an eye out for British spies."

Lilly couldn't help but giggle. The very thought of anyone harboring such ideas was amusing. The war had been over for a very long time, and England was now considered an ally. How strange that Addie's sister should still be worried over such a thing.

"During our years at home, Mintie was always in the kitchen helping cook and run the Judge's household. Like I said, she's very practical. She's tried to help me with my cooking, but she has twenty men to cook, clean, and wash for in her own boardinghouse. So she's busy all day and most of the evening," Addie confided. "Sometimes that's a relief and other times it leaves me quite lonely."

A mixture of sorrow and pain lingered on Adelaide's face. Lilly wondered if her memories of the past, mixed with her present failures at the boarding-house, caused Miss Addie undo grief. "You don't need to explain further, Miss Addie," Lilly whispered, giving the older woman a reassuring smile. "I find myself in much the same predicament."

Addie nodded and wiped away a stray tear that had managed to escape and roll down her plump cheek. "You'll not have long to suffer, I'm sure. With your beauty, I don't know how you've managed to remain single this long. You'll no doubt be married before you're even here a year. You're such a pretty little thing, so young and full of life. Why, you've just begun to live. Now, Miss Mintie and I, that's a different story. At our age, we don't have men lining up at the door anxious to pledge their devotion."

"Neither of you ever married?" Lilly blurted, immediately wishing she could take back the words as a look of sorrow once again returned to Addie's face.

"I was betrothed years ago, but father insisted that I wait to marry until Mintie found a proper suitor. He argued that the eldest should marry first. Unfortunately, a proper suitor didn't come along, and my young beau tired of waiting. Not that I blame him. He was quite a handsome man, my Charles, even if I do say so myself. We were well suited. Both of us enjoyed laughter and wanted lots of children. Last I heard, he and his wife had seven children and a multitude of grandchildren." She hesitated for a moment and sighed. "Now, why don't you tell me about all the beaux who must have come knocking on your door, Lilly. I'll wager we don't have enough hours remaining in the day for the telling of those tales."

"Quite the contrary, Miss Addie. In fact, I've had only one beau; and much like your courtship with Charles, my relationship with Matthew

Cheever was destined for failure." She paused, transfixed for the briefest of moments. "But no matter," she continued. "We've chosen our separate paths." Silence hung in the room, creating an emptiness that needed to be filled, a void that too closely resembled her barren heart.

2

Boston, Massachusetts

Matthew Cheever watched closely as Nathan Appleton glanced toward his wife at the end of the table. Appleton nodded his head and the couple rose in unison. "Shall we adjourn to the library, gentlemen? I believe there are cigars and a fine bottle of port that need our attention. Ladies, I'm certain my wife has some new piece of needlework or a book of poetry she wishes to discuss with you in the music room."

The two groups took their respective cues, the men following Nathan to the library and the women trailing along behind Jasmine Appleton in customary fashion. The meal had been superb, but it was obvious the men now longed to be done with the formalities so that they could finally get to the business at hand—the *real* reason they had gathered: to report and discuss their successes and formulate their plans for the future. Men's business. Aside from obvious social impropriety, their wives' total inability to comprehend matters dealing with business forbade any interesting discussions at supper. They had managed a brief conversation regarding their good fortune in escaping the disastrous results of the depression that had devastated many of their friends. But with their money invested in the Lowell project, none of them had been adversely affected. When Jasmine realized her husband was discussing such a disturbing topic while their guests were being served crème brûlée, she had lovingly chastised him and called a halt to their conversation.

"Finally, gentlemen," Nathan remarked as he offered a humidor filled with an array of pungent imported cigars. The men stroked the tightly wound tubes of tobacco between their fingers, sniffing them the way their wives inhaled the sweet aroma of summer's first rose. Finally, after much ceremony, each of them clipped off the cigar's end and settled back to puff on the aromatic offering.

Matthew felt enthralled by the scene unfolding before him. It was difficult to believe that he could find himself among this group of influential men. Strange, he thought, how opportunities arise from the most unexpected circumstances.

"Listen and learn," Kirk Boott instructed in a barely audible tone.

Matthew nodded, chiding himself for getting caught up in his own thoughts, even if only for a few moments.

"As I was saying at supper before my wife cut me short, we've been most fortunate, gentlemen. Many here in Boston have been suffering great losses, and I fear they will continue for at least the remainder of the year. Not a major depression, perhaps, but certainly those who have invested at the wrong time and in the wrong places have suffered dramatically. Fortunately for all of us," Nathan commented, surveying the room filled with men, "we've experienced nothing but profit. Our project has been every bit the success we had anticipated."

"That's true enough, Nathan," Tracy Jackson remarked, "and with the Appleton Mill opening just last month and three other mills slated for opening next year, we'll see even greater profits in the years to come. Textiles will be our future and fortune. My only regret is that Francis didn't live long enough to see his plan to fruition."

"Agreed, Tracy, but your brother-in-law will never be forgotten. I can think of no greater honor we could have paid than to make the town his namesake."

Tracy nodded his head. "That's true, although I think perhaps some of the locals resented the town's name being changed to Lowell. It appears they're now becoming accustomed to the change, and with the daily influx of newcomers to the town, I believe the name has taken hold."

"I'm not so sure the old farm families have accepted the renaming of East Chelmsford just yet," Matthew interjected. A wave of embarrassment washed over Matthew as he realized he'd spoken the words aloud. He was here to listen and learn, not to necessarily voice an opinion.

All heads turned toward him, making his embarrassment even more complete. Kirk Boott gave him a slight smile before turning to the others. "I believe all of you know Matthew Cheever. He has strong ties to the Chelmsford farming community. He keeps me abreast of any unrest that may be stirring among the locals. Most of it has been settled by now, of course, but Matthew can tell you that many of the old East Chelmsford landowners still resent us—particularly those of us involved in purchasing their land."

Tracy Jackson swirled the deep purple liquid in his snifter. "Don't tell me they're still contending they were duped."

Boott looked to Matthew. "Go ahead," he encouraged.

"I'm afraid so," Matthew responded, feeling strengthened by Boott's approval. "Many say you deceived them."

"How so? They were paid a fair price," Appleton retorted.

"It's not the money, although they do believe they were underpaid," Matthew replied. "Those landowners truly believed the land would continue to be used for agrarian purposes. They sold their acreage based on that belief and say that Mr. Boott told them he planned to plant crops and raise sheep. Now they deeply resent the industrialization of their land."

"Surely they didn't believe Kirk was going to become a country squire,"

Tracy jibed. Several of the men chuckled. "What they're angry about is the fact that we've been able to put their land and water rights to profitable use."

"Since Mr. Boott is the visible member of the Boston Associates, the one with whom the locals have had personal dealings, their anger toward him runs deep. They have even gone so far as to make up a song about Mr. Boott," Matthew replied.

Tracy Jackson shook his head and laughed. "Ah, you've been memorialized, Kirk. I hope they haven't portrayed you too shamefully. Why don't you sing it for us, Mr. Cheever?" Jackson encouraged.

Kirk shifted in his chair. "If it's a musical offering you're wanting, Tracy, I'm sure the women have something to offer in the other room."

"Come now, Kirk. It can't be all that bad," Tracy taunted. "Give us the gist of it, at least, Matthew."

Kirk nodded his head. "But no singing," he admonished his young protégé.

Matthew made a show of himself, clearing his throat as he walked to the center of the room. Gone was all hint of embarrassment. The other men applauded in delight as he gave an exaggerated bow. "No singing," he promised as he turned toward Boott and received what he knew to be a forbidding glance. "Besides, I'm afraid my voice would send the gentlemen running out the front door. Now, let me see if I can remember a verse or two of that little ditty.

> "There came a man from the old country,
> the Merrimack River, he happened to see.
> What a capital place for mills, quoth he,
> Ri-toot, ri-noot, riumpty, ri-tooten-a.
> And then these farmers so cute,
> They gave all their lands and timber to Boott,
> Ri-toot, ri noot, ri-toot, riumpty, ri-tooten-a."

A thunder of applause filled the room while he gave a slight bow and returned to his chair. Matthew sensed that Kirk was carefully observing him. He didn't want to do anything to estrange their relationship, yet truth be known, he was enjoying the attention of these powerful men.

"You have the boy well trained, Kirk. I notice he ceased his recitation and came running back to his chair the moment you appeared bored by his presentation."

Matthew ignored Paul Moody's remark but was somewhat surprised when Boott nodded, gave his friend a wry smile, and said in a voice loud enough for all to hear, "Let's hope so. I believe I've earned my reputation among my business partners as well as the Lowell community." The comment irked Matthew, who was no child. At twenty-five he was no one's trained boy.

Nathan leaned forward and offered Kirk more port. "The last I heard, they were referring to you as the tyrant-in-residence."

Holding out his glass to accept the offered drink, Kirk shook his head. "I'm not sure it's quite so bad. I may be quick to exact punishment, but I believe I am fair."

"And what of that young boy who felt your riding whip upon his back last week? Would he believe you to be fair?" Nathan asked.

"Ah, word does travel quickly, doesn't it? Just remember, gentlemen, none of you wanted to live in Lowell and create civilization out of mayhem. You willingly granted me the position of tyrant-in-residence, and I believe the town is better for it. That boy was an impudent scoundrel who needed to feel my whip. And in the event you haven't heard, I fired a foreman last week for disobedience. If any of you have a grievance with my methods, please speak out," Boott challenged.

A silence fell over the room as each man cast sidelong glances at the others. Matthew could hardly agree with all of Boott's methods, but he admired his ability to lay everything out on the table. Leaning back in his chair, Matthew crossed his arms and waited to see if anyone would take Boott to task.

Nathan broke the silence. "Now, Kirk, you know we have nothing but praise for your efforts in Lowell." Matthew smiled to himself. He might have known Appleton would rise to the occasion and smooth any ruffled feathers. Nathan Appleton knew the importance of keeping Boott content in his position. As Boott had mentioned, no one else wanted the job of turning chaos into order.

Nathan continued when no one else joined in to comment. "There's not a man here who would challenge your ability. After all, we chose you in large part because of your demanding personality. You have the paternalistic temperament necessary to manage the town. None of us is equal to the task, nor do we want it."

Boott placed his arm around Matthew's shoulder, breaking the tension that had filled the room. "Well done, my boy. Now that we've been entertained, let's get down to business. Nathan, would you like to begin?"

Matthew breathed a sigh of relief as they waited for Nathan to settle behind his large walnut desk and then begin rummaging through a stack of papers and drawings. "Well, gentlemen, as you know, the textile mills are expanding at the approximate rate we had planned, and the profits have exceeded our expectations. As these additional mills are constructed, we're going to need more girls to operate the looms. Kirk, why don't you tell us what you're doing in that regard? You might also give us a bit of information regarding the Irish. Have you been able to keep them contained?"

"Hiring more farm girls won't be a problem. The girls themselves spread word of their good fortune through their letters and occasional visits back home. Their friends and relatives come to Lowell seeking the same opportunity to earn money. However, I did take an added precaution and hired two men to travel farther north into New Hampshire, Vermont, and even Maine, spreading the word and bringing back any girls that may be ready to come. We still have openings at the Appleton, and then there are always those that want to go home for vacations or leave due to illness—the usual turnover.

"As for the Irish, don't concern yourselves. Although they are the one thing we seem to have overlooked in our planning, aren't they?" Kirk questioned as he glanced about the room.

Matthew knew only too well the concern Boott and the others had in regard to the Irish. Ignorance of Irish culture, beliefs, and attitudes made this necessary element of laborers an unneeded worry. But they'd brought it on themselves. The Irish provided dirt-cheap labor—men who would break their backs from dawn to dusk, day after day after day, for a quarter of the pay other men would demand.

Paul Moody raised his hand to the back of his neck and smoothed down the fringe of hair that circled his balding head. "I guess I always thought they'd return to Boston. Of course, I didn't consider the fact that as we continued to build, we'd need them in Lowell digging the canals and helping construct the mills. We should have realized they'd begin to bring their families and squat on some of the land. Not much we can do about that now."

"They're a necessary evil, and that's a fact," William Thurston concluded. "Dirty bunch of beggars for the most part—heathens, the whole lot of them."

"They're papists, William, not heathens," Nathan interjected.

"Same thing. More witchcraft than Christianity, as far as I'm concerned. Superstitious miscreants. You'd think so, too, Nathan, if you'd take some time and go down into that mess of shanties they've patched together on the Acre. It's a blight to our fair city, and so are they."

Nathan's lips curled into a wry grin. "Really, William. I didn't know you were spending so much time among the Irish, but since you've become such an authority, perhaps you've devised some sort of plan. What solution do you propose?"

Irritation crossed William's face as he pulled a linen handkerchief from his pocket, wiped his forehead, and moved away from the blazing fireplace. He stuttered momentarily as all eyes shifted in his direction. "I didn't mean to give the impression that I spend inordinate amounts of time with the Irish over at the Acre. I visit only when it's necessary to question Hugh Cummiskey and assure myself things are progressing when I make my occasional trips to Lowell."

"I guess the rest of us rely upon Kirk to give us that assurance," Nathan put in. "After all, he's the one that we've charged with the task of building and supervising the operation of the mills and canals—a monumental task, I might

add, Kirk. It's no wonder you're in need of an assistant." Nathan allowed his
gaze to rest upon Matthew for a moment. "Ah, well, I digress. You still haven't
told us your solution, William."

William had moved to a chair across the room from the fireplace, but the
pinkish-purple flush continued to splotch his cheeks. "I don't have a solution,
but that doesn't negate the fact that there is a very real problem. Left
unchecked, the situation will only worsen," he replied, his remark tinged with
irritation.

Matthew watched intently. It was apparent William Thurston was upset
with the lack of support among the Associates, though Boott stroked his chin
while giving Thurston his exclusive attention. A look of gratitude washed over
Thurston's face when he realized he had been successful in garnering Boott's
attention. Finally Kirk rose from his chair and sauntered toward Nathan's desk.
Slowly he turned toward William and casually leaned against the oversized
desk. "I agree with your observation that the Irish presence in Lowell was
unplanned, William. We must always keep in mind, however, that although
I've been successful in luring men away from the farms and out of Boston to
work as mechanics and in the offices of the mills, there are few men willing
to perform the heavy, dirty work of mucking out the canals, clearing the land,
and constructing the buildings. I need pure brute labor to accomplish this
work—not just animals, but men, too. The Irish may not offer much in the
way of skilled labor or intelligence, but they've strong backs and, more importantly, they're hungry. Even if I could find others willing to do the manual
labor, the Irish tolerate lower wages. In that regard, it seems prudent to continue employing the Irish."

"Hear, hear," Tracy Jackson replied, holding up his glass toward the others.
"Kirk is doing an excellent job protecting our investment. Don't forget, William, you're a major stockholder. I would think you'd be more interested in a
good rate of return on your money than the plight of the Irish. Besides, they're
a pitiful lot of humans who have low expectations from life, especially from
England and her descendants. Why not let Kirk take care of dealing with the
Irish in Lowell? You'd serve us all better by remaining in Boston overseeing
the banking business. I'm sure it would make your wife happier if you weren't
off to Lowell every week or ten days," he added, giving William a perceptive
glance.

William patted his linen handkerchief across his forehead. It appeared he
didn't quite trust himself to speak. Matthew watched closely, knowing that
wisdom required Thurston to align himself with Boott and the Associates. But
why was Thurston so hesitant? It was obvious he was a minority of one. Continuing to argue would only cause a breech—a breech that would cause problems for the other Associates, and one that Thurston surely couldn't financially
survive.

"You're right, gentlemen. We need the Irish and they need us. So be it," William finally replied. "I thought perhaps Daniel would be joining us this evening."

Kirk smiled, nodded, and then leaned toward Matthew. He held his hand over his mouth and spoke quietly. "Mr. Thurston's an intelligent man. He knows when to fight for a cause and when to give it up. Changing the subject was an intelligent tactical decision on his part."

Tracy Jackson blew out a long, spiraling curl of smoke before answering William's question. "Daniel was detained in Washington but hopes to be in Boston by mid-October. He sends nothing but good reports and continues to spread word among Congress that our venture is successful. Fortunately, our backers in Congress remain supportive—and Daniel assures me the federal funds will continue. Good news to all of us since that reduces our risk considerably."

Matthew glanced around the room, his questioning gaze settling on his mentor.

"My young friend hasn't been privy to information regarding our financial windfall and, I believe, is a bit perplexed by your comments, Tracy," Kirk commented.

Nodding in agreement, Matthew turned toward Tracy Jackson as he stated, "Nothing difficult to understand, my boy. One learns early on the importance of choosing a lawyer who is not only well versed in the law but who has the proper connections. The Boston Associates decided on Daniel Webster. Daniel is well connected to members of Congress and a close friend to several of us."

"An excellent lawyer, too," William Thurston added, the ash on his cigar turning bright orange as he inhaled deeply.

"Absolutely—Harvard educated!" Tracy agreed. "When we were in the early stages of planning our textile revolution here in New England, each member of the group agreed to pledge personal funds toward the financial stability of our plan. Of course, additional financial security was a concern. It was Daniel who relieved us of that worry. He managed to secure a million-dollar windfall from Congress, which is being paid out over the course of our development of the Lowell project." Tracy leaned back and blew a grayish-blue puff of smoke, a slow smile creeping across his lips as he watched the cloud inch upward into a circle and then rise toward the ceiling.

Matthew took a deep breath and slowly exhaled. Had anyone other than the principal stockholders of the Boston Associates told him that the Congress was financially involved in this venture, Matthew would have denounced the revelation. There was, however, no sound reason for him to question the truth of what he was told. In fact, he found the information intoxicating. That he, the product of an East Chelmsford farm family, was sharing drinks with men who had the ability to influence the spending of Congressional dollars was surely one of his finer moments. A sense of power washed over him, and he wondered if Boott ever had such feelings. The improbability that he should be sitting in the midst of the Boston elite was mind-boggling, and there was no doubt in Matthew's mind that he would find a way to make this situation beneficial to himself. He glanced toward Boott and was met by his steely gaze.

———

Later, as they prepared to make their way to the carriage, Boott spoke. "You remind me of myself in many ways, Matthew. I could almost hear your brain at work trying to determine how best to capitalize on your newfound place among these men of power and position."

Matthew felt the heat rise in his cheeks. "I count you foremost among these men, Mr. Boott."

Kirk gave Matthew a wry grin as he slapped him on the back. "I'm sure you do, my boy. I'm also sure that you bear watching."

Matthew knew the words were not spoken in jest. Boott would be watching him very closely in the future. If he was going to achieve his goal and become a member of the Boston Associates, he must be careful to do nothing that would cause Boott discomfort or concern. He chided himself for taking center stage earlier in the evening. He would need to remain low-key in the future, he thought as he followed behind Boott, shaking hands and offering his thanks and farewell to the men and their wives as they left the Appleton residence.

Soon they were settled into the carriage that would return them to Lowell. "It was obvious you enjoyed yourself this evening," Kirk remarked.

Matthew leaned forward with his arms resting across his thighs. "Absolutely! I feel rather the fool for not realizing what an important role the government could play in a private business venture."

"It's merely your youth and inexperience that prohibited you from gaining such knowledge—coupled with the fact that such information isn't bantered about among strangers. As a matter of fact, I was rather surprised when Nathan broached the subject in front of you. On another note, however, I'm interested in what thoughts you might have on Thurston's comments regarding the Irish. Do you view the situation as problematic?"

Matthew leaned back in the coach and thought a few moments before answering. "I believe there are some valid concerns. Although Thurston was speaking of the larger settlement, there really are two separate groups settled in fairly close proximity to each other. But I'm sure you're aware of that."

"No, I don't spend any time in that area. Hugh Cummiskey is my contact with the Irish workers. When necessary, I've sent one of the men from the machine shop to fetch him. So the Irish are squatting on more land than any of us realized, and there is a problem. Is that what you're telling me?"

"I'm not certain the Irish occupy any more land than you surmise. I merely wanted to point out that there are two Paddy camps on land located slightly outside the edge of town. Two groups that do not get along very well, I might add. Depending upon how you plan to enlarge the mill community, it appears those Paddy camps could end up in the middle of town. On the other hand, you can't build without the Irish laborers. It's become evident the young farm boys are interested in becoming mechanics and working for Mr. Moody on the locks and canals, but—"

"But they'll not count themselves among the lords of the spade. Not that I blame them, of course," Boott concluded. "The infighting . . . now, that could present a challenge. The Irish have always been a factious sort—my years in England taught me that much. If they want to survive, they need to out-grow that clan mentality they've brought with them."

Both men remained silent as the coach continued to lumber through the countryside, swaying both of them back and forth—unmercifully at times. Matthew would have much preferred Nathan Appleton's offer that they remain in Boston for the night and depart the next morning. Boott, however, had adamantly refused, obviously convinced the mills and newborn community could not survive without him. Although Boott verbalized trust in his managers' judgment, Matthew knew that he never gave them the opportunity to exercise much authority.

Finally Boott broke the silence. "John Farnsworth will be arriving from England within the week. Of course, I'll be meeting with him upon his arrival, but I would like for you to be present also. In the meantime, make arrangements for him at one of the better boardinghouses. I'm sure he'll expect a house to himself, but we can negotiate that after his arrival."

"Farnsworth. He's the expert you hired for calico printing, isn't he?"

Boott nodded his head, a wry smile crossing his lips. "Quite a negotiator. Did I tell you about my meeting with him in England?"

Matthew leaned forward, his eyes alight with interest. "No, I don't believe so."

"When we first discussed the possibility of calicos, Francis—Mr. Lowell—mentioned the talented artisan he had met when he toured the mills in England. Said the man was one of the most brilliant craftsmen he'd ever had the pleasure of meeting. When we ran into difficulty producing our calicos, the Associates agreed that I should attempt to locate Farnsworth."

"And he was obviously willing to leave England."

"After a bit of dickering about his wage. When I asked what wage he would require, he told me five thousand dollars a year."

Matthew's jaw dropped. He couldn't believe his own ears. "He was joking, of course."

"I'm afraid not. When I told him that was more than we paid the governor of Massachusetts, he replied, 'Well, can the governor of Massachusetts print?' I had to tell him the governor could not and that I needed him more than I needed the governor."

"The Associates agreed to a salary of five thousand dollars? That's difficult to believe."

Kirk reached for the small cushion he carried with him whenever he traveled. "It's bad enough that my back gives me problems when I sit in a comfortable chair, but riding in these coaches is going to be the total ruination of my spine," he stated, pushing the support behind his back and settling farther into the seat. "Where was I? Oh yes, discussing the merits of John Farnsworth's wages. 'Tis true the man will be paid more than any of us, and that was a difficult pill to swallow—harder for some than others. However, we came to the conclusion that he will be worth that figure ten times over once the Merrimack is producing quality prints."

"I don't doubt you've made a sound decision."

"There isn't a man among the Associates who would doubt the validity of the man's worth. After all, if there was anything that Francis Cabot Lowell knew, it was the looms and textiles."

"I'm sorry I didn't have the opportunity to meet Mr. Lowell before his death."

Kirk stared out the coach window for several minutes, seemingly lost in his thoughts. Matthew had settled back, the motion of the coach beginning to lull his senses, when suddenly Kirk leaned forward, slapped Matthew on the knee, and issued a challenge. "Well, my young friend, if you were the agent in charge of this project, how would you reconcile the problem of the Irish? Would you remove them from the land? Order them to quit their fighting or suffer the consequences?"

Matthew cleared his throat. "I would work through their religion. As Mr. Appleton pointed out earlier this evening, they're all papists. No one has more influence over the Irish than a Catholic priest. If you could somehow manage to have a priest assigned to them, it could help. Many of the men now have their families with them. A strong religious leader could keep the men in line and possibly alleviate the feuding."

"I *knew* you were bright. I believe you have an idea worth exploring. I'm personally acquainted with Bishop Fenwick. I believe I'll send an invitation for him to visit in the near future—or perhaps I should travel to Boston and pay him a visit myself. Excellent idea, excellent."

Matthew basked in the adulation for only a moment before Boott fired another question in his direction. "Is there anything else you learned this evening that we haven't discussed?"

Matthew thought of a great many things he'd tucked away for future reference. He had no desire to share them with his employer just yet, but of utmost importance was the earning of Boott's trust. Not only that, but Matthew hoped that by cultivating their working relationship with sound judgment and positive initiative, Boott would soon come to see him as an invaluable asset.

"Well, it did appear there is a hierarchy among the stockholders, but I wasn't certain. I thought perhaps there was deference shown due to those men holding more stock." Boott nodded and motioned for him to continue. "I learned it's imperative to cultivate influential friends."

"Absolutely!" Boott exclaimed, slapping Matthew on the leg. "Think about the fact that there is no single member of the Boston Associates who was powerful enough to influence Congress, but several of us doggedly pursued our friendship with Daniel Webster. It has reaped a multitude of benefits. You must keep this lesson in the forefront of your mind, both in your business *and* personal life. If you do, you'll go far, my boy. A wife must be chosen with no less intelligence and cunning than one chooses a lawyer or business partner."

Matthew grinned. "I would imagine that to be true enough, but I never have cared for the way my lawyer wears his hair or fashions."

"Looks can be deceiving," Boott said, sobering. "Just remember that. Things are not always what they appear to be, and this is especially true when dealing with people."

~❦ 3 ❦~

Lilly trudged up the narrow stairway and made her way down the hall. Her back ached, and she longed for quiet and the comfort of a good night's sleep. Carefully, she turned the doorknob, fearful she might awaken the other girls with her late arrival to the room.

"Welcome to our humble abode," the girl known as Marmi greeted in a none-too-quiet manner. Six girls sat gathered together on one bed.

"Shhh!" Prudence Holtmeyer warned. "Keep your voice down, Marmi."

"Sorry, I always forget," she replied. "Lilly, in case you haven't met everyone, this is Katie, Sarah, Beth, and Franny. Nadene's asleep, but I think you met her earlier."

Lilly smiled as she closed the bedroom door. "Thank you for the welcome," she said in a low voice. "I thought you would all be asleep by now. I was afraid I'd awaken you coming in this late."

"Not us—we always stay up late chatting, except for Nadene," Katie replied.

"She's the early-to-bed girl. You needn't worry about waking her. She falls into bed after supper, and nothing seems to interrupt her sleep," Franny added.

"We rearranged your things closer to your bed," Prudence said. "Hope you don't mind, but we thought it would make it easier for you when you're getting ready for work in the morning. You won't have to crawl across the bed to get to your clothes."

"Thank you again," Lilly replied. She had half expected the girls to act aloof since she really wasn't one of them, at least not yet. Apparently they weren't given to drawing class distinctions among themselves.

Marmi bounced across the bed. "There I went and made all the introductions, and we haven't been formally introduced. I'm Margaret Mildred Tharp, but everyone calls me Marmi. I know you met Prudence earlier at supper."

She pointed toward the figure cocooned in a log-cabin patterned quilt. "Nadene is from Vermont. Prudence and I hail from New Hampshire, and the others are from around the state. Whereabouts do you come from?"

"I suppose if we're making proper introductions, I should say that my name is Lilly Armbruster, and I'm from right here, East Chelmsford—that would be Lowell to you."

Prudence raised her eyebrows ever so slightly. "The girls that hail from Lowell usually live at home."

"It saves them the cost of room and board," Beth threw in as if Lilly couldn't discern that for herself.

"Why did you decide to live in a boardinghouse?" Prudence questioned.

Marmi glanced toward Prudence and shook her head. "You don't have to answer any of our questions you don't want to. We all tend to be a bit inquisitive."

"Nosey's more like it." The cocoon had spoken. All the girls turned to peer at the multicolored quilt. A tangle of copper-colored hair appeared, followed by two light blue eyes and the palest complexion Lilly had ever seen. "They'll be asking you questions until sunrise if you don't put a stop to them early on," Nadene said, nodding her unkempt curls toward the ensemble. "I'm Nadene Eckhoff. We're to share a bed."

Lilly smiled. "Pleased to make your acquaintance."

"What are you doing awake, Nadene? You usually sleep through no matter how noisy we get—and we're talking quietly tonight," Prudence quickly added.

Nadene slipped her legs over the side of the bed and pulled on a thin cotton wrapper while shoving her feet into a pair of broken-down work shoes. "Need to go to the outhouse," she answered.

"Want me to go with you?" Marmi offered.

Nadene shook her head. "It's you that's afraid of the dark, Marmi, not me. But thank you anyway." The girls stared after Nadene as she trudged out the door carrying a flickering candle.

"She has beautiful hair—and her skin, it's so pale it's almost translucent," Lilly whispered.

Prudence nodded. "She's sickly, that's why. No matter how much sleep she gets, she's always tired—and pale," she added.

"Maybe it's just her natural coloring," Lilly offered.

"No. One of the other girls who came at the same time as Nadene told me Nadene had color in her cheeks and was healthy looking when she first arrived at the mills. I think she's gotten worse since they transferred her over to the Appleton. She used to work at the Merrimack, but when they opened the Appleton, they took some of the most experienced girls and moved them over there to teach the new hires. Nobody can match Nadene when it comes to spinning, so it didn't take long for the supervisors to decide she should become an instructor at the Appleton. They're working her too hard," Prudence explained.

Marmi nodded in agreement. "That's probably true enough, Pru, but Nadene doesn't take care of herself, either."

Franny added, "She doesn't keep herself warm enough in winter and won't even go see the doctor when she needs to."

"She doesn't keep enough of her money to pay for a doctor visit," Beth declared. "She sends it to her family."

Sarah, the quietest of the group, shook her head. "I think it's nice she sends her pay home to help her family, but she carries it too far, never willing to use any of her wages to care for herself."

"Her money, her choice," Prudence replied.

Footsteps quietly echoed on the stairs and Marmi put a finger to her lips. "Talk about something else," she whispered.

"You never answered my question about why you're living in the boardinghouse," Prudence remarked, turning back toward Lilly. All the girls seemed to await her answer in great interest.

"My parents are both deceased. We lost our farm when the Associates decided to make East Chelmsford the site of their industrial community."

Nadene turned sideways as she wove her way through the narrow aisle between the beds and dropped onto the lumpy mattress. "You never give up with your questions, do you? Now look what you've done—you've caused Lilly to dredge up sad memories. Now she'll never get to sleep," Nadene scolded, pointing toward the gloomy expression etched upon Lilly's face.

The girls glanced in Lilly's direction. "We're sorry," they chorused in unison.

"And don't you tell them it's all right, Lilly, or they'll just keep on with their unending questions until they've learned and repeated every detail of your life," Nadene interjected.

The girls giggled. "She's right. We don't know when to stop asking questions."

Lilly glanced toward Nadene, then chose her words carefully before answering. "Your apology is accepted."

Nadene nodded her approval.

"We truly do appreciate your cooking skills," Prudence said, obviously not wanting to go to bed. "I'm only sorry you can't remain here at the house and be our cook. We all like Miss Addie, but she's a poor excuse for a culinary artist."

"Oh, listen to you, *culinary artist*," Marmi mimicked, causing all of the girls to giggle.

"Do you know where you'll be assigned once you begin at the Appleton?" Franny inquired.

"I've been told the spinning room, but I'm sure that it's subject to change since I haven't actually signed a contract yet. The thought that we're required to sign a contract seems to imply that the owners don't believe women will keep their word. As if women might not be responsible employees, don't you think?" Lilly inquired, hoping to elicit the girls' attitude toward their employer.

Nadene leaned back against her pillow and tucked the quilt under her chin, obviously willing to remain awake a bit longer.

"They require contracts from *all* employees—the men, too," Prudence replied. "I think the contracts are a good thing. That way there's no misunderstanding. We're all given the same information about the rules and what is expected of us."

Most of the girls nodded in agreement. Nadene didn't respond.

"So you don't mind any of the rules?" Lilly ventured.

"Some of the regulations may seem harsh—we're certainly expected to give a long day of hard labor for our pay, but that's to be expected. At least the Corporation has eliminated the required pew rent at St. Anne's Episcopal," Nadene stated.

Lilly was aghast at the remark. "Pew rent?"

Nadene nodded. "Thirty-seven and a half cents a month."

Franny added in a conspiratorial whisper, "They held it out of our pay, but we raised enough of a ruckus that they finally stopped."

Nadene continued. "The pew rent was an easy way for Kirk Boott to recover the cost of building his Episcopal church. My feeling was that if he wanted an Episcopal church, that was fine, but why should I pay for it? I'm a Methodist."

Lilly folded her arms across her chest. "Such behavior by Mr. Boott and the Boston Associates shouldn't come as a surprise to me. Every one of those men is self-serving, set upon nothing but the almighty dollar. Not one of them has any concern for others. Those men and their greed have caused untold suffering to the farmers of East Chelmsford. I have no doubt they'd sell their souls to the devil to turn a profit."

Prudence's mouth dropped open. "How can you say such things, Lilly? Why, the Boston Associates are forward-thinking men who have finally given women an opportunity to be of value in this country. I personally applaud what they've accomplished. Perhaps you haven't given thought to how you would have supported yourself upon the death of your parents if these mills hadn't been here to provide you a job," she countered.

Lilly clenched her fists, her expression hardening as she fought to control her voice. "If the Boston Associates hadn't invaded this countryside, my father would still be alive, and if he weren't, I'd at least have a farm to provide my living, Prudence. You'll not convince me that those evil men have done me any favors. Had they ventured into New Hampshire and stolen land from your family, I'm sure you might think differently."

Lilly knew she'd gone too far. Exhaustion made her vulnerable and free with her thoughts. Why couldn't she be sweet spirited like her mother? *Mama would be so ashamed of my attitude.*

Marmi placed an arm around Lilly's quivering shoulder. "I'm sorry for what's happened to your family's land, Lilly, but the mills are here to stay, and if you're going to work in them, you need to forget the past. If you can," she added quickly.

Lilly took a deep breath before exhaling slowly. She was alarmed that such random conversation could elicit her anger so quickly. It was obvious she'd made a spectacle of herself the very first night. The girls were all staring at her.

Forcing a smile, she glanced about the room. "I see my performance has left you all in awe. My father always said I was born to be an actress. Do tell me more about all these fees for church pews."

Marmi, Prudence, and the others visibly sighed in relief while Nadene appeared to be calmly evaluating her behavior. It was apparent that Nadene was not easily deceived.

"One thing about the fee at St. Anne's: you were told when you were hired that you had to pay. At least the Corporation didn't steal the money like old Elder Harley over at the Freewill Baptist," Marmi said, once again taking up the banner for the Associates.

"Same thing as far as I'm concerned," Nadene replied. "Neither one of them had consent to take the money."

"Yes, but at least Mr. Boott used it for the church," Beth said, her eyes wide as if she suddenly knew a great secret. "I heard Elder Harley did unspeakable things with his ill-gotten gains."

Prudence laughed. "Who knows what Elder Harley did with all the money the girls donated to him."

Lilly curled her legs beneath her, listening to the tales, surprised at how sheltered she had been from this information while living so close. "Whatever are you talking about? Did one of the preachers steal money from the mill girls?"

Marmi's head bobbed up and down. "Indeed, he did. He told the girls he needed funds to build a church, which would be a good thing for the community. In order to raise the money, he offered the girls interest on any funds they loaned him. All of the Baptist girls as well as girls from other denominations loaned him money. Then he absconded with their funds, having never laid a cornerstone."

"Cornerstone! He never even turned a spade of dirt," Prudence chimed in.

"I heard he had a mistress," Katie offered.

"Katie! That's gossip, pure and simple. The rest of this we know firsthand," Franny admonished.

"Are you planning to attend St. Anne's?" Marmi inquired. "That's where most of us attend church."

"I haven't attended in a long time. I'm not sure that I'll be going to church, at least not in Lowell," Lilly replied.

The girls gasped in unison. Nadene merely gave her a wry smile.

"Why are you smiling at me like that?" Lilly asked.

"You'll attend. It's in your contract. All mill employees must regularly attend church or be subject to dismissal. And yes, they do check with the boardinghouse keepers to assure themselves of our attendance. You may get by with staying abed for a Sunday here and there, but be assured, such behavior will not be tolerated frequently."

"Besides, why wouldn't you want to go?" Sarah asked softly.

Lilly had so long been troubled in her spirit that she'd given up trying to understand it. She wanted to do the will of God, but at the same time, God's will seemed very uncertain—very unclear. It was almost as if He were playing a game with her. Testing her. Teasing her.

"I was very sad throughout my father's illness," Lilly said, reluctant to confide her true reasons. "I haven't felt like going to church and being around a lot of our old friends."

"Well, that makes perfect sense," Marmi said, patting Lilly's hand. "But now you'll have all of us and you shan't be sad for long."

Lilly wished that were true. If only she could know for sure that her plans were what God wanted. At times she felt confident—almost as though God had written them out on a tablet like He'd done for Moses with the Ten Commandments. Then other times she felt so confused, wrestling whether or not God even heard her prayer—whether He saw her misery.

"I don't know about the rest of you, but I must get up early in the morning. I think we should all get some sleep," Nadene remarked. Without waiting for a reply, she snuffed out the candle, sending the room into immediate darkness.

Lilly quickly realized there was nothing to be done but prepare for bed. She slipped into her nightgown, thankful she had removed it from her trunk while there was still candlelight in the room, then crawled into the empty space beside Nadene. She could hear the other girls settling in for the night, the swishing of sheets and the groaning protests of the bed frames breaking the silence.

Lilly clung to the edge of the uncomfortable mattress. Never in her life had she shared a bedroom, much less a bed, with another person. She attempted to relax, but it seemed her body had stiffened into a rigid column, unwilling to yield to her command. Sounds of deep, relaxed breathing soon turned to soft snores, interrupted by an occasional mumbled, unintelligible word. Yet sleep would not come. Thoughts of pew rent, stolen church funds, contract signings, and beady-eyed clerks skittered through her mind until she finally sat up along the edge of the bed, holding her aching head in her hands.

"You'll get used to it after a while," Nadene whispered before breaking into a deep racking cough.

"I'm sorry I wakened you. I tried to be quiet, but I'm not accustomed to sleeping in a room with anyone else."

"You didn't waken me, Lilly. The girls don't realize that the reason I'm so tired is because I'm awake for long periods of time every night. This cough won't let me sleep, so I come to bed and get rest when I can. Strange thing is, my cough never seems to bother them."

"Why don't you see a doctor? Perhaps there's an elixir that would help."

"There's no elixir going to help me. My lungs can't seem to bear up under the humid conditions at the mill. I suppose one day it will be the death of me, but for now, it's salvation for my mother and brothers."

Lilly turned toward Nadene, stunned by her cavalier attitude. She could barely make out Nadene's form in the darkness, but somehow she knew Nadene was awaiting her response. "Life is a precious gift from God, Nadene. I think we're meant to protect it as best we can. Death won't serve you or your family well," she whispered in reply. She felt Nadene's weight shift the bed. "I promise I won't spend my time telling you what you should do, Nadene. I know how tiresome that can become. Let's just agree to look out for each other. Would that be all right?"

Nadene reached out and took Lilly's hand. "Yes, Lilly, that would be all right. I think you and I are going to get along just fine."

"I hope so, because I surely could use a friend. I wouldn't tell the others, but I'm frightened about going to work in the mills. I'm used to being out-doors, coming and going at my pleasure. I fear being cooped up all day. Is it terrible?"

"It's like most things, Lilly—after a while you get used to it. But I won't tell you there aren't times when I truly long for the quiet of home. I can remember thinking that a colicky baby was more noise than I could bear. Now I know different. The sounds of a crying baby would be a mere lullaby com-pared to those clamoring machines in the mill. And heat—I'd be happy to stand over a wood cookstove for the rest of my life if I didn't have to suffer the mugginess that they create for us to breathe."

"I don't understand, Nadene. There are windows in the buildings—I saw them. Why don't you open the windows and let fresh air circulate in the room?"

"Ha!" The remark sent Nadene into another fit of coughing. When the hacking finally ceased, she leaned against the headboard of the bed, gasping for air until finally her breathing returned to normal. "The windows, dear Lilly, are nailed shut. If the air in the room is dry, the threads break. Too many broken threads make for a shabby piece of fabric. On the other hand, moisture in the air helps prevent broken threads. Since a good product is more impor-tant than the health of the employees, our windows are nailed shut. After all, workers can be replaced. The reputation of the Corporation rests upon the fabric we produce."

"So you dislike what's going on here as much as I do," Lilly ventured.

"Probably not. I need the work, so I'm thankful for a job that pays well. Were it not for the mills, my family would be starving. I dislike the fact that the conditions are unhealthy—at least for me. Some of the girls seem to have no problem working in the humidity. Now you'd better try and get to sleep. My guess is that you have to be up even earlier than the rest of us in order to help Miss Addie with breakfast."

"Thank you, Nadene."

"For what?"

"Offering me your friendship," Lilly replied simply. She pulled the sheet across her shoulders and tried to adjust the meager pillow. But no matter how much she plumped the ticking, the bundle of feathers inside fell flat. Finally she quit struggling with the pillow, laid her head down, and began to pray.

4

Only the continual pumping of John Farnsworth's right hand over-shadowed Kirk Boott's verbal welcome as he ushered Farnsworth into the vestibule of the Boott residence. Matthew stood back watching the exchange, studying both men as they eyed each other. They could have passed for brothers, both tall and lanky with thick wavy hair, both exuding an air of confidence. And while Farnsworth was the elder by at least ten years, his physical agility belied that fact. There was a vibrant assurance in his step and an obvious eagerness to greet life's many challenges.

"I hope you don't mind that we're meeting here in my home rather than at the Merrimack," Kirk said as he led the men into his office. His large walnut desk stood in front of two large windows overlooking the flower garden. Boott's prized mums, goldenrod, asters, and dahlias, all dressed in their autumn finery, were in full view. "Sit down," he requested, gesturing toward one of the leather-upholstered chairs opposite the desk. "Tea will be here momentarily," he continued while ringing a small gold bell.

Although Kirk hadn't invited him to be seated, Matthew lowered himself into the chair alongside Farnsworth who, at the moment, appeared somewhat nonplussed by Boott's fawning behavior.

Farnsworth settled into the chair and turned his attention toward his host. "I generally find the meeting place of little concern. Rather, it's the outcome of such interaction that is of interest."

"Exactly! I couldn't agree more. However, I find that information discussed at the mills sometimes makes it way through the entire Corporation before I've left the building. Consequently, when I want to assure myself of privacy, I conduct business meetings here at home."

"Ah, I see. Well, perhaps it's not the place where you hold your meetings but the trustworthiness of the employees who attend those meetings?" Farnsworth suggested.

Matthew glanced up as a mobcapped maid entered the room. Boott pointed to a spot on his desk and then watched as the woman dutifully placed the tea service where he had indicated.

Massaging the back of his neck, Boott directed a steely look at Farnsworth. "You may be correct, Mr. Farnsworth. If so, I hope you won't prove to be one of those gossiping employees."

"I can give you my word on that, Mr. Boott, but only time will prove if you have my loyalty," Farnsworth replied as he took the cup of tea being offered.

Matthew turned his attention toward Boott, who hesitated a moment. "That's a fair enough answer, Mr. Farnsworth. Truth be told, people never know about loyalty until it's put to the test, do they?"

Farnsworth nodded his agreement and took a sip of his tea. "This is your meeting, Mr. Boott. What would you like to discuss?"

"Most important, the improvement of our calicos. After that, we'll need to discuss arrangements for your housing and detail your position at the Merrimack. I believe we have any number of matters that must be resolved prior to your first day on the job. And, of course, you need to sign your contract."

"I'm pleased you didn't include my salary as one of those items under discussion, Mr. Boott. Otherwise, I would be looking askew at *your* sense of loyalty," Farnsworth replied, with the corners of his mouth turning up ever so slightly.

"If there is one thing I learned from the Englishmen who arrived before you, it is to settle salary negotiations before paying for passage to this country."

"Did my English brothers give you a bit of trouble when bartering for their wages?"

Boott nodded his head in agreement. "They gave me more than a bit of trouble. They decided that unless I met their salary demands *and* provided them with housing that met their specifications, they wouldn't work for me. I thought they were bluffing and told them I wouldn't agree to their requirements."

"I take it they called your bluff?"

"They did. I turned and walked away, thinking they'd knuckle under. Instead, they loaded back into their wagons and left town. I thought they would merely go a short distance and make camp, thinking I would come running after them."

"And?" Farnsworth asked, his eyes sparkling.

"They were well into New Hampshire by the time we found them. They had no plans to return. I met their every demand as well as a few extra incentives in order to convince them to turn around. That is why I insisted we agree upon your wages prior to your departure from England. You'll recall that I expected you to drive a hard bargain—and you didn't disappoint me in that respect. I am, however, pleased that the matter of your wages was settled while I was in Lancashire."

Farnsworth rose from the leather-upholstered chair and shoved his hands deep into his pockets. "We came to this country at great risk. You know very well that the law was against us. We weren't to divulge information or bring drawings related to the mills under threat of great penalties. The money had to be worth our while. After all, it would be very hard for us to return home once word got out that we'd aided the competition. I, for one, would fear the consequences."

Matthew heard the bitterness edged with sorrow in John's voice. He knew the man spoke truthfully. England wanted to keep America dependent upon her for textiles. The fact that Americans had taken the initiative to plan their own textile mills had not gone over well at all. The matter of Frances Lowell touring the English mills and walking away with the knowledge embedded in his memory was even more distressing.

Farnsworth put the matter behind him and pressed a question. "Why don't we begin by talking about the calicos? I know you've hired me to improve the quality of your prints. How would you say they currently compare to English imports?"

Matthew glanced toward Boott, and the two of them laughed. "I apologize, Mr. Farnsworth. It's just that when anyone asks about the quality of our calicos, we're reminded of the story that frequently circulates about the city," Matthew said.

"If the story gives you cause for laughter, I would enjoy hearing it," Farnsworth responded.

Kirk nodded at Matthew. "It is said that one of the female residents of Lowell purchased a piece of Merrimack calico, intent upon making herself a new frock for special occasions. She worked diligently until she had completed her sewing. The following Sunday morning she appeared in her new dress, expecting her family to be duly impressed. Her brother, however, took one look at her and advised that it was good she was planning to wear the costume to church because that dress was certainly holier than she could ever hope to be."

Farnsworth nodded his head in recognition but didn't laugh. "You do have a problem, gentlemen. If the best you are currently producing is a piece of cloth that is full of holes and you're passing it off as calico, we have much to accomplish. But accomplish the task, we will. By the time we've fine-tuned the Merrimack's machinery, we'll be producing cloth that will make the English envious."

Boott leaned forward, focused upon Farnsworth's words. "That's the attitude I want to hear," he said, slapping his hand upon his knee. "I knew you were the right man for this corporation the minute I laid eyes upon you."

"Well, I thank you for your confidence, Mr. Boott, but there's much work to be done before we'll actually overtake the English. It will take your continual cooperation—and the funds for necessary changes to the equipment."

Boott rose from his chair and came around the desk. "You'll have no problem with either of those items. I'll make myself available to you at any time."

"Thank you. I'll remember that promise. Now, I believe you mentioned something about housing earlier. I would like to get settled before taking a tour of the Corporation's holdings. I trust you've made arrangements for my accommodations?"

Boott appeared to squirm at the question. "I believe I may have mentioned there is an area of housing known as the English Row. It is, however, full at this time. Since I wasn't sure what you might prefer in regard to housing, I took the liberty of seeking out a room in our best boarding-house."

Farnsworth was silent for a moment. Kirk pulled a linen handkerchief from his pocket and pressed it against his forehead. The room was apparently becoming uncomfortably warm for him.

"A boardinghouse will suffice until a house can be provided, but I suspect it would be best if we address housing in my contract so that there is no misunderstanding."

"Of course, of course," Kirk quickly agreed.

"My father has agreed to come to America when his health improves. I would want to have adequate accommodations prior to his arrival," Farnsworth added.

"We can begin plans for a house as soon as you tell me what you'll need. We can add another house to the English Row—or build something else, if you prefer."

John smiled, a faraway look in his eye. "I find it unnecessary to live alongside my English brothers. In all honesty, I'd prefer a house that had a bit of land around it for a garden such as you have out there," he replied, gesturing toward Boott's backyard. "Though perhaps a bit smaller. We wouldn't want folks to think I'm trying to outshine the Corporation's agent."

Boott laughed, but Matthew sensed he was not completely pleased that Farnsworth wanted a home apart from the English Row. It was obvious, however, that Farnsworth's request would not be denied.

"I have your contract here in my desk if you'd like to sign it," Kirk offered, pulling the paper from a drawer.

John carefully folded the pages and tucked them in his coat. "Why don't I take this with me and read it over. I'm sure it's in proper order, but I prefer to read binding legal documents several times before signing them. I'm sure you understand."

"Of course, of course," Boott concurred. "We can meet again tomorrow—if that will give you ample time," he quickly added.

"Tomorrow morning should be fine. Eight o'clock?"

"Yes, eight o'clock. Why don't we meet here at my house? Once the contract has been signed, we can go down and walk through the mills."

John nodded and rose from his chair, then hesitated. "What about a horse and carriage? I'll be in need of transportation from time to time."

"I can make arrangements at the livery. You'll be able to use a carriage any time you desire," Kirk said with a smile.

John furrowed his brows ever so slightly. "Quite frankly, I was thinking more along the lines of the Corporation furnishing me with my own horse and carriage. Of course, you could board them at the livery stable until my house is constructed. Perhaps young Matthew and I could take a look at what they have available at the livery on our way to the boardinghouse."

"Certainly. Matthew, why don't you stop at Kittredge's and see if he has any good horseflesh available? Check about a carriage while you're there, also."

Boott and Farnsworth exchanged their good-byes with Farnsworth once again agreeing to read his contract before returning the next morning. Kirk stood on the portico watching after them as they rode off in the carriage, his earlier exuberance seeming to have waned. Matthew could only imagine what thoughts were now flying through his mentor's mind.

The carriage had barely begun to move when Farnsworth emitted a chuckle. "Well, my boy, how do you think our meeting went?"

Matthew glanced at his companion. He wasn't sure how to answer the question. He didn't want to offend Farnsworth in any way—after all, he was an important asset to the Corporation. On the other hand, he didn't want to appear disloyal to Boott. "I believe it went quite well, Mr. Farnsworth," Matthew cautiously replied.

Farnsworth laughed a thunderous, reverberating guffaw that seemed to begin at the bottom of his feet and work itself upward until it exploded into the crisp autumn air. "Good for you, Mr. Cheever. It's a wise man who guards his tongue with a stranger. Now, let's see if Mr. Kittredge has any horses."

Matthew yanked back on the reins, pulling the horses to a halt in front of the combined hardware store, wood yard, blacksmith shop, and livery stable. "The livery stable's out back," Matthew announced, leading Farnsworth toward the rear. "Would you look at that—what is it, I wonder?" he asked, pointing toward a huge pile of black rocks.

"Quite a mess, I'd say," Farnsworth replied.

They could hear a number of voices in the blacksmith shop, the noise escalating as they grew nearer. "Appears you threw away forty hard-earned dollars, Kittredge," one of the men hollered. The comment was followed by boisterous laughter.

Matthew and Farnsworth stood to the rear of the crowd, watching as

Jacob Kittredge ignored the guffaws and remained intent on the task at hand. Curious, Matthew edged his way a bit farther in. Moments later he returned to where John was standing. "He's trying to set fire to some of those black rocks—doesn't seem to be working."

Kittredge appeared undaunted as he remained focused upon the task at hand. Soon the observers lost patience and began leaving the building, which allowed John and Matthew adequate space to move closer. The black rocks were piled in an open grate, where Kittredge was doggedly attempting to set them on fire.

"You ain't never gonna get them things to burn," Henry Likens called from the back of the shop. "You shoulda never believed that lawyer from Salem."

Kittredge didn't acknowledge the remark. In fact, he acted as though he were alone in the room. Matthew strode back to where Henry stood. "Why's he trying to burn those rocks, Henry?"

"Some lawyer from up in Salem told him about black rocks from Pennsylvania that are supposed to burn. Said they could be used for fuel instead of wood. So ol' Jacob, he ordered two tons—forty dollars worth. Now he can't even get a spark going with 'em. He would have gotten more heat from setting his money afire."

When Matthew returned, Farnsworth was standing beside Jacob Kittredge, using a hammer to break up the black rocks. Jacob was now starting a fire with tinder and several larger pieces of wood. Once the fire was going, Farnsworth and Kittredge began placing the broken black rocks upon the fire until they'd covered the wood fire with two bushels of the small rocks. Matthew was amazed as he watched the rocks begin to take on a reddish-orange glow, the fire growing hotter by the minute. The horses, obviously sensing the fire and increasing heat, became skittish, kicking at their stalls, snorting, and neighing until several men rushed to get water to douse the hot coals. Still the fire continued. Finally Henry directed the men into a bucket brigade, and after several attempts they were able to exact enough water to calm the coals from a raging fire to glowing embers.

"What kind of rocks are those?" Matthew's voice was filled with amazement.

"Coal," Farnsworth simply replied. "Quite a fuel. My guess is that one day it will replace wood. Now, then, do you suppose Mr. Kittredge might be able to assist us with a horse since the excitement has died down a bit?"

"I'm certain he would be pleased to do so. After all, you certainly came to his rescue when the others were willing to stand back and laugh."

By the time Matthew and John Farnsworth left the livery stable, John was the proud owner of a fine black mare and a carriage that any man would be pleased to own. He was also the recipient of Jacob Kittredge's abiding loyalty.

"You can rest assured that your horse will receive the best of care, Mr. Farnsworth. Anytime you want your horse and carriage, you just send someone down here to tell me. I'll make sure it's ready at the appointed time. You've got my word on that, sir," Jacob said as he walked alongside his departing customers. "I can't thank you enough for helping me out. I was beginning to think I had been bamboozled out of my money. I fear the townsfolk wouldn't have permitted me to live down such an error."

"You are welcome, Mr. Kittredge, but I'm sure you would have finally compared the coal to tinder and wood, realizing that the smaller chunks might burn more easily. It appears as if you made a sound investment."

Kittredge nodded. "Thankfully so. And you've made a sound investment in that mare. She's a beauty."

Farnsworth shook Kittredge's outstretched hand and hoisted himself into the carriage while Matthew took up the reins. "I feel certain that by nightfall the good citizenry of Lowell will be well acquainted with the name of John Farnsworth," Matthew said as they moved down the street.

"Notoriety is the last thing I'm seeking," Farnsworth muttered. "Where are we off to now?"

"Number 7 Jackson Street. It's the boardinghouse operated by Miss Mintie Beecher. We selected Miss Beecher's house as she is reputed to operate the best boardinghouse in the city of Lowell. I'm told there are men who have offered to pay a handsome sum for room and board with Miss Mintie."

"In that case, how does it happen that there's a space available?" John inquired with a twinkle in his eye.

"One of the men was willing to give up his bed."

John's eyebrows arched and his lips gathered into a thoughtful pucker. "Really? In exchange for what?"

"A tidy sum of money, combined with the promise he would receive the next available opening at Miss Mintie's."

"I see. Well, then, let us hope that it won't take too long for my house to be completed. After all, I don't want to be the cause of a man being forced to give up his bed."

"There was no forcing involved, Mr. Farnsworth. The gentleman understood it would most likely be a good span of time before he returned to Miss Mintie's. All of the men are aware that boarders just don't leave her house, and I was forthright in explaining that the Corporation had not yet begun construction of your house."

"All the same, we'll see if we can't rush things along. Right, my boy?"

There was no doubt that Farnsworth's figurative use of *we* was directed at Matthew. "Yes, sir, I'll do my level best."

"And call me John. 'Mr. Farnsworth' is a bit formal for the two of us, wouldn't you agree?"

"If that's your preference, Mister, uh, John," he quickly corrected.

Farnsworth grinned and nodded his head. "That's my preference. I've been thinking it might serve us well if I deposited my trunks at the boardinghouse, and then you and I could take a short tour of the area. You could point out land that might be suitable for my house."

Boott hadn't discussed the possibility of such a tour with either of the men. And, Matthew concluded, Farnsworth hadn't mentioned his idea of a tour with Boott before departing, either. He didn't want to overstep his boundaries with Boott, yet he didn't want to appear unwilling to assist Farnsworth. After all, Boott would be unhappy if Farnsworth conveyed any displeasure with his welcome to Lowell.

"It appears I've caused you a bit of a quandary," Farnsworth said as they arrived at Mintie Beecher's boardinghouse. "The tour can wait until you've had an opportunity to seek Mr. Boott's approval."

"I'll . . ."

Farnsworth held up his hand. "No need to apologize, my boy. Your first loyalty must be to Mr. Boott and his instructions. I understand. Now, let's see what the Beecher boardinghouse has to offer."

Each of the men lifted a trunk out of the carriage and placed them near the front step. Matthew rapped on the door and waited. Moments later he was greeted by Mintie Beecher. To say it was a warm welcome would have been untruthful, for the woman's welcome was meager and aloof. She stared in unabashed curiosity for several moments.

"Miss Mintie Beecher," Matthew introduced, unable to deal with the silence, "this is Mr. John Farnsworth."

"Well, at least you're prompt," she said, frowning. Her pinched expression led Matthew to believe she was less than pleased with this change to her orderly home.

"Well, bring your things," she said as she turned and headed for the stairs.

Matthew noted that she didn't even wait to see if they were following. He hurriedly lifted the trunk at his feet and threw an apologetic glance toward Farnsworth. "Guess we'd better get to it."

Farnsworth chuckled and hoisted the other trunk to his back. "It's clear she's the no-nonsense sort."

"To say the least," Matthew murmured, fighting to balance his load and clear the door.

Miss Beecher led the way to the upstairs bedrooms, pointed out Mr. Farnsworth's bed, chest, and allotted floor space for his trunks, then retreated back down the steps. The men placed the trunks along the wall and quickly followed behind. It seemed the expected thing to do.

"This is the parlor," Mintie announced. "You can have guests until ten o'clock in the evening, but no women on the second floor. Dining room," she said as she continued marching them through the house. "Dining chairs are not assigned. Pick whichever one is available. I expect my boarders to use proper manners, and I'll not tolerate any profanity in my house. No spitting on the floor. No boisterous talk or crude stories. No singing, unless of course we're having a musical night, and then you're allowed to sing in the parlor but nowhere else." She gave Farnsworth a stern, almost reprimanding look, as though the man had already sinned against the rules.

Matthew would have laughed out loud at the sight of this tiny but very determined old woman laying down the rules and regulations to a man twice her size, but he knew it would only serve to aggravate the situation.

Miss Beecher continued, "The house supplies clean sheets. If you want any other laundry done, you'll have to pay extra like the rest of my boarders. I'll expect you to take a bath at least once a week. I won't have smelly men stinking up my house."

"Yes, ma'am," Farnsworth replied. "Seems quite reasonable."

The older woman paused and assessed him momentarily. Again she eyed him, as if trying to ascertain some deep, mysterious truth. "The other house rules are posted by the door." She pointed a bony finger toward the front of the house, then proceeded to push up the wire-rim spectacles that now rested on the tip of her beaklike nose.

"If I didn't know better, Miss Mintie, I'd swear that you just got off the ship from England, too," Farnsworth said as he tried out one of the wooden dining room chairs before moving to another.

Mintie's eyes opened wide at the remark. "My name is Miss Beecher, and that's the most preposterous thing I've ever heard," she sputtered. "I've never set foot on the soil of England and shall never do so!"

"Really? You have that same disquieting aloofness so many of my countrymen hold dear. I thought you surely must have deep roots in the homeland."

Matthew watched as Mintie's cheeks flushed bright pink. He thought for a moment she might actually have a spell of apoplexy. She hesitated only a moment, however, before regaining her composure.

"In that case you should feel right at home, Mr. Farnsworth. I'll make every attempt to maintain my temperament so that you may continue to feel as though you're still in the bosom of your motherland," she replied, her features strained into a tight frown.

Farnsworth's face crinkled into a bright smile as he pulled a pipe from the pocket of his wool jacket. "Of that I have no doubt, Miss Mintie . . . excuse me, Miss Beecher."

✳ 5 ✳

Mintie Beecher pulled back the heavy drapes that covered the dining room windows. There was just enough time to finish dusting the remainder of the downstairs rooms before preparing the noonday meal. Adjusting her spectacles, she peered across the street and smiled in satisfaction. Her sister hadn't pulled back the drapes in number 5. Mintie prided herself on being an efficient woman. It had served her well as her father's hostess in their Boston home, and although assuming the position of a boardinghouse keeper in Lowell wasn't to her liking, efficiency had continued to serve her well in this new post.

On the other hand, she seriously doubted whether Adelaide would ever develop any of the necessary skills to operate a smoothly run boardinghouse. Having carefully dusted the windowsills, Mintie began to move away from her vantage point. A blond-haired girl, bonnet askew and satchels in hand, was moving toward Adelaide's front door. *Another one!* How many chances would her sister receive? It was one thing when boardinghouse vacancies occurred due to circumstances beyond the control of the keepers. It was quite another when the tenants departed due to the ineptness of a keeper. And depart from Adelaide's house they had, like mice fleeing a fire.

Mintie had warned her sister of the consequences of her lackadaisical attitude. Of course, Adelaide continually insisted she was doing her very best, but Mintie knew better. Adelaide had never attended to the important duties of running the Judge's household, always running off to a piano lesson or dress fitting. The work had always fallen to Mintie. The Beecher sisters had been the Martha and Mary of Lexington Street, at least from Mintie's martyred perspective.

Unfortunately, there wasn't time for her to both personally investigate the new boarder at Adelaide's house and have the noonday meal on the table as planned. Curiosity was one vice that Mintie had failed to overcome—that, along with giving unsolicited advice. Still, she thought, someone of wisdom and etiquette should be available to advise those who were less knowledgeable. Helping one's neighbor could hardly be seen as a vice.

Putting the matter behind her, Mintie called out, "Lucy, come here this minute."

The child came running on spindle-thin legs, jerking herself to an abrupt halt directly in front of Mintie's freshly starched white apron.

"How many times have I told you not to run in the house?" Mintie nodded with satisfaction when the child visibly shrunk back at her words. "It's beyond me how you manage to work as a doffer in the mill. It's a wonder you haven't been mangled by one of those machines. You absolutely *never* follow instructions."

"I'm supposed to run at the mill, Miss Mintie—the faster, the better. Then, when I come to help you serve meals, I have to remember to slow down. Sometimes I have trouble remembering."

"Well, that much is obvious. I want you to go across the street to my sister's boardinghouse. Tell Miss Beecher I need to borrow some darning thread."

"I saw some in your sewing basket just yesterday. I'll run and get it."

"Lucy, I said *I need to borrow some darning thread.* I don't give two whits what you saw yesterday. While you're there, you may discreetly inquire as to any new boarders. Now get yourself across the street!"

The child snapped out of her wide-eyed stare, turned on her heel, and rushed toward the door. The corners of Mintie's mouth turned up ever so slightly. *I'll get that girl trained if it's the last thing I do!*

The potatoes had been peeled and set to boil when the front door slammed, quickly followed by Lucy rushing into the kitchen. Leaning forward to catch her breath, the child extended her hand upward. A piece of limp thread dangled in midair.

An exasperated *hurrumph* escaped Mintie's lips. "She sent you back with that little piece of thread?"

Lucy nodded and extended her hand just a bit higher. "Miss Beecher said to tell you that she didn't bother to send more than a snippet because she knew you didn't really need the thread," Lucy panted.

Mintie could feel the heat rise in her cheeks. "What did you say, young lady? You told her I had thread in my basket, didn't you?"

"No, ma'am. Miss Beecher said you pride yourself on keeping stocked. She said she's never known you to run out of anything and that you just send me over there when you're snooping for information. She said to tell you that you're invited for a cup of tea this afternoon if you'd like to meet one of her new boarders."

"Boarders? How many new girls has the Corporation sent her?"

The child shrugged her shoulders. "Two or three, I think," she replied.

Mintie dismissed the child with a wave of her arm and turned back to her dinner preparations. How dare her sister pass such acerbic words through a mere serving girl? It was no wonder the Judge hadn't trusted Adelaide with the supervision of servants. Well, she would go to tea this afternoon—of that there was no doubt.

An hour later, the scraping of chairs and sound of footsteps announced that the men had finished their noon meal and were heading back to the mills. The older woman nodded at Lucy, and the two of them entered the dining room and began removing the dishes. Mintie glanced up from the table as John Farnsworth paused and turned her way.

"I was wondering if you might help me with a matter, Miss Mintie. I've been so busy since my arrival from England that I've not had time to go into town and visit the stationery shop. I promised to write my aging father back in the homeland, and I hoped that you might be willing to make such a purchase for me. I placed the money on my bureau. I would be most willing to reimburse you for your time and inconvenience."

Mintie frowned, drawing her brows together as she was known to do. She felt the tightness in her face and hoped her look relayed her displeasure. He'd called her by her first name, but instead of reprimanding him, she decided to let it pass. "I suppose I could put it on my list, but I won't be going shopping until tomorrow."

Mr. Farnsworth took a step backward and nodded. "Quite all right. I won't have sufficient time to write a proper letter until Sunday afternoon."

Lucy's eyes danced with anticipation as the door closed behind Mr. Farnsworth. "I'll go into town for you, Miss Beecher."

"I'll just bet you'd like to do that. I'm paying you to serve meals and clean up afterward, not go prattling off to town wasting valuable time on that Englishman. You best move along or it will be time for you to get back to the mill before you've finished your work here. You can be certain I'll not pay you for a shoddy performance of your duties. I'm going upstairs, but I'll be back down to check on your progress."

Mintie watched the child hasten into action and then hurried up the steps to the room occupied by John Farnsworth and five other men. Hesitating momentarily, she glanced up and down the hallway before silently chastising herself. Whom was she expecting to see lurking in the corners? There was nobody in the house except Lucy. Besides, Mr. Farnsworth himself had told her the money was on his bureau. She turned the knob and pushed open the door.

Entering the upstairs rooms on a Wednesday, she felt oddly out of place. Monday mornings and Thursday afternoons were the times she normally entered the rooms occupied by the men. Mondays for stripping the beds and gathering other laundry, Thursdays for dusting and scrubbing floors. Unlike the girls who worked in the mills, these men were more than willing to pay for cleaning chores that weren't included in their monthly rate for room and board—which was precisely why Mintie had taken the position as keeper of the men's boardinghouse. Across the street, Adelaide had enough difficulty maintaining some semblance of order with the few girls she had. How could she ever possibly manage a house that was completely full, plus the extra chores for the men?

Observing the coins, Mintie hesitated only a moment before sweeping them into her palm. Making a quick survey of the room, her gaze fell upon a tattered envelope lying atop Mr. Farnsworth's trunk. Instinctively, she reached for the missive but stopped herself. Instead, she leaned forward until her nose nearly touched the aging paper as she carefully read the name and address inscribed on the letter.

"Miss Beecher, are you still up there?"

Startled, Mintie jumped back, rushed out of the room, and hastened down the stairway. "What do you want?"

Lucy's upturned lips and sparkling eyes were quickly replaced with confusion. "Did I do something wrong, Miss Beecher? You said I'm to tell you when I complete my chores and to never leave without first telling you."

Mintie felt heat rising in her cheeks. "You did nothing wrong. Are you leaving now?" That was as much of an apology as Mintie would make to a servant.

"Yes, ma'am. I'll be back later."

Mintie nodded. Why did the child make that same remark every time she left the house? They both knew she would be back later. Lucy's family needed her earnings, and although it was a concession not easily made, Mintie needed Lucy's assistance. Still, it would do the child some good to learn proper manners and speech. Perhaps if time permitted, Mintie could further instruct the girl. There was no sense in allowing the child to turn into a hoyden.

Lilly tucked the porcelain teapot into a cozy and placed it on the dining room table beside a small silver tray of shortbread, teacups, and saucers. "I can complete the meal preparations, Miss Addie. I want you to enjoy your tea and have a nice visit with your sister."

"I never enjoy visits from my sister. She comes over here to snoop and feed her own ego, and that's a fact. Each time she spies a new boarder arriving or hears that one has departed, she shows up on my doorstep with her admonitions. After she's had her tea and enumerated my list of failures, she flies back across the street, leaving me to feel even more inadequate than when she arrived."

Lilly patted the plump woman's shoulder. She'd come to care about Addie in the few days since her arrival. There was something motherly in the woman, and it caused Lilly to miss her mother more than she realized. Though sometimes she remembered her mother doing little things—dusting the furniture, tucking a handkerchief in her sleeve, pouring tea—Lilly's favorite memories were of the times when she'd prepare for bed and her mother would come in and brush Lilly's long hair while they talked of the day.

"Sometimes," Addie confided, "I think sisters are merely a nuisance."

Her comment roused Lilly from her memories, and she shook off the sadness that threatened to ruin her day. "I always longed for a sister. But perhaps it wouldn't have been so much better than a brother."

Addie gave her a soulful smile. "Mintie is fifteen years my senior. She's always believed that age alone gave her the authority to manage my life," she replied. "But tell me more about your family. You have a brother? I'd like to hear about him—and the rest of your family. We have time before Mintie arrives."

Addie was difficult to refuse. The woman reminded her of a ray of sunshine, always lighting up the room, so Lilly heeded her request and sat down. "My brother, Lewis, is nine years older. We were never close. Oh, I attempted to win his affection as a little girl, but nothing seemed to work. Soon I learned to keep my distance. Lewis resented having another child enter the family circle. For some reason, which I fail to understand, he believes our parents ceased to love him when I was born."

" 'Tis true that some children can't seem to comprehend the fact that their parents have enough love to spread among all of their children."

"I suppose so, but I don't believe my parents could have been any more obvious in showing their love and affection for Lewis. Even after their deaths, he continues to despise me. He grasps at every opportunity to make my life miserable."

"Surely he's not quite that bad, my dear. You know, Mintie can sometimes make my life miserable with her callous remarks and rigid behavior, but deep down I know she loves me."

"Miss Addie, Lewis does not love me. From the time I could toddle, he took great pleasure in pulling my hair, pinching me, and even tripping me as I passed by him. When I was six years old, my dear brother held me upside down over the bank of the Merrimack River. Had Jonas and Matthew Cheever, neighbor boys who lived on the adjoining farm, not happened along that particular day, I'm certain Lewis would have dropped me over Pawtucket Falls and into the rushing waters of the Merrimack River."

"Now, now, don't think such a thing. Boys are prone to outrageous pranks—or so I've been told. Of course, that does seem a bit extreme. Perhaps he didn't realize the seriousness of his actions."

"He was fifteen years old, Miss Addie. And now that our parents are dead and he's made off with everything they ever owned, I suppose he doesn't care whether I'm alive or dead. He gave absolutely no thought to what would become of me after Father died." Pain stabbed at Lilly's heart with the realization of how absolutely alone she felt.

Addie clucked her tongue and slowly shook her head back and forth. "I know it can be difficult to think good of someone who has hurt you so deeply, but I don't believe your brother wishes you dead. You're much too lovely a girl for anyone to wish you harm. I'm sorry to hear you've lost your parents, child. How long since their . . . ?"

"Mother's been gone five years, but my father was buried just last week," Lilly said with a tremble in her voice. She swallowed hard, hoping to hold back the tears that were forming and threatening to spill at the mention of her father's death.

The older woman leaned forward and wrapped Lilly in her embrace. "I had no idea. Why, you should still be allowed to mourn his passing. Seems just terrible that you should lose him and your home at the same time. But don't you worry. You're going to be just fine, Lilly," she whispered. "I can feel it in my bones. You have a home here now."

Lilly wiped at her eyes and tucked a stray curl behind her ear. "Thank you for being so kind. I didn't mean to become so emotional." Addie's kindness made it easy to give in to her sorrow and memories.

Lilly watched the older woman's face tighten into a grimace as the clock chimed. "Mintie." Addie breathed the word as if it held some mystical spell over them.

The forbidding announcement was followed by a sharp knock at the front door. Before Lilly had an opportunity to exit the dining room, Mintie Beecher swooped down the hallway, entered the room, and seated herself at the table. "Are you going to take my cape and bonnet, or must guests hang them up themselves, Adelaide?"

"I'd be pleased to take your cape and bonnet," Lilly offered.

"May I assume you are one of the new boarders?"

"She is," Addie replied. "What other questions have you come to ask me?"

Mintie's eyes grew dark as she wagged her finger up and down in front of Addie. "Watch your tone, young lady. You seem to forget whom you're speaking to."

"How could I forget when you constantly rush over here to remind me, Mintie?"

"I don't know what's gotten into you. I merely came by for a nice cup of tea. A brief respite in a week of drudgery. Now you've succeeded in ruining even that small ray of sunshine. Why must you be a torment to me when I only seek to maintain civility and unity for the sake of the Judge and our sisterhood?"

Lilly watched as Addie's face began to etch with concern at her sister's words. It was apparent that Mintie knew how to control Addie's every emotion. "I'll leave you ladies and be off to the kitchen," Lilly announced once she'd hung Mintie's cape and bonnet.

"No, I want you to join us."

Mintie Beecher's words were a command, not a request, and Lilly hesitated for a moment before speaking. "I thank you for the kind offer, Miss Beecher. However, I work for Miss Adelaide until I go to the mills, and she's instructed me to complete preparations for the evening meal. I can ill afford to take orders from another."

Addie patted the chair beside her. "Why don't you join us for a few minutes, Lilly? Then you can finish your work."

Lilly nodded and seated herself beside an obviously grateful Addie as Mintie poured the steaming tea. "How is it you're working for my sister?" Mintie's thin eyebrows rose in unison as she looked over her spectacles and awaited a reply.

Lilly studied the stern-faced woman momentarily. Her gray-brown hair had been pulled back into a tight and orderly bun. Not a single strand of hair dared to be out of place. Her gown was just as simple and no-nonsense. The dove gray cloth had been done up in a very plain fashion without benefit of trim or embellishment.

"Well? Are you tongue-tied?" Mintie questioned.

Lilly held back a sharp retort. "I don't begin my employment at the mills until next Monday, and we were able to reach a mutually satisfactory arrangement."

Mintie waited. An uncomfortable silence shrouded the room as the older woman sat staring across the table, first at Lilly and then Addie.

Addie drew in a breath to speak but paused momentarily before proceeding. "I understand *you* have a new boarder, Mintie. I hadn't realized you had any vacancies until Mrs. Wilson gave me the news while she was measuring me some yard goods yesterday."

"Is that what she's telling folks? That I had a vacancy? How dare she? I had no vacancy. That young Mr. Cheever sent word, asking that I take on Mr. Farnsworth as a boarder."

The mention of the Cheever name caused a tightening in Lilly's chest. No doubt it was Matthew to whom Miss Mintie referred. He was a part of this nightmare that had been brought to Lowell by the Associates. His participation had forever put a wall between them. It had destroyed their love for each other—their plans.

Miss Mintie continued to ramble on. "He said he knew I had no openings, but Mr. Griggs agreed to move to another house so that I could take on Mr. Farnsworth."

"Seems odd to move one man out so another can have his place," Addie commented.

A look of pride washed over Mintie's face. Squaring her shoulders, she lifted her chin and elongated her neck until she resembled a matriarchal ostrich. "Well, Mr. Cheever's note said that he had been informed my board-inghouse was the best run in the city and that when he had questioned the men with regard to where they would live if given the opportunity, my house was the most highly recommended. He went on to explain that the Associates wanted Mr. Farnsworth to experience only the best that our boardinghouses had to offer."

"Cheever. That name sounds familiar," Addie remarked, glancing toward Lilly.

Lilly frowned. *Please don't ask me, Miss Addie. Please don't ask.* Lilly quickly turned her attention to Mintie. "What's so special about Mr. Farnsworth?"

"I'm not sure, but I can tell you that if I had known he was straight off a ship from England, I wouldn't have agreed to take him. He's probably a spy, and those Associates are too foolish to realize it."

Addie chuckled and leaned forward to pour another cup of tea. "Good-ness, Mintie! Will you never get over thinking the English are continuing to plot against us? If the Associates were bright enough to stake out and build these mills and this community, I'm sure they're capable of choosing loyal employees."

"Spoken with a complacency the English would love to hear, dear sister. They've brought this Farnsworth over to help them with their calico prints, I've been told. Seems he brings with him the expertise to improve that fabric the mills are passing off as calicos at the present. Who is to say if that man is coming here to spy on us and send word back to England? If a man says he's willing to turn on his own country, he bears watching. Why, just today I saw a missive on his trunk bearing the imprint from a Lancashire factory. You'll not soon convince me he's come to aid this country in its bid toward industri-alization."

"You were searching through Mr. Farnsworth's personal belongings?" Before she'd had time to think, the words had escaped Lilly's lips. She now had the full attention of both sisters. "I'm sorry, this is none of my concern. Please—disregard my question."

"I am not a snoop!" Mintie ignored her sister's raised eyebrows and turned her full attention to Lilly. "That letter was sitting out in plain sight. I was in Mr. Farnsworth's room at his direction. He asked me to purchase some sta-tionery. He told me there were coins on his bureau to pay for the supplies. I did nothing improper."

"I'm sure you didn't, Miss Beecher. I didn't mean to question your pro-priety. In all likelihood, however, I doubt Mr. Farnsworth would send you into his room if he had anything to hide."

"I can see you'll do quite well with my sister. You two make a fine pair. Neither of you can see beyond the tip of your nose. Just remember how the Judge believed that there would never be an end to war with England until we put an end to them. The Judge was seldom wrong, Adelaide."

"He was wrong about his finances. If he had invested with the Associates, we'd still be living among Boston society. Instead, we're boardinghouse keepers in Lowell. I don't think there's any more to your Englishman than meets the eye," Addie replied.

"Well, Mr. Cheever certainly is interested in Mr. Farnsworth. He personally came to interview me and inspect my house before Mr. Farnsworth arrived."

Addie gave her sister a puzzled stare. "What does that have to do with your suspicions?"

"Nothing, I suppose. Well, except that Mr. Farnsworth must be important or Mr. Cheever wouldn't take such pains regarding his welfare. Mr. Cheever is an excellent young man—a man of quality, as the Judge would say. Quality and breeding always show. I trust that he would know if this Mr. Farnsworth were up to something. But then again, Mr. Cheever is very young."

Eventually, the sisters' conversation became nothing more than background noise to Lilly. The mention of Matthew Cheever and his involvement with the Associates sent her thoughts scurrying back to the summer after he'd completed his second year at Harvard. He'd returned to the family farm. For the remainder of that summer, she and Matthew had thoroughly enjoyed each other's company. Matthew's mother had even hinted to Jennie Armbruster that perhaps more than boundary lines would unite their adjoining farms. Lilly had blushed when her mother repeated the statement. And even though Matthew had gone off to Harvard University to further his education, he had pledged to maintain the family farm. He'd hinted at other pledges, as well. But those promises—those dreams—had been rapidly forgotten with the arrival of Kirk Boott.

"You hail from these parts?" Miss Mintie inquired, her shrill question breaking into Lilly's thoughts.

"Yes. East Chelmsford is my home." Mintie leaned in more closely to hear the voice that was barely a whisper.

"East Chelmsford? East Chelmsford no longer exists. This is Lowell," Mintie retorted, her voice carrying that same rebuking tone she had taken with Addie only a short time earlier. "Chelmsford was no doubt an English name."

Lilly shifted only slightly in her chair as she gazed back at Mintie with the same determination she had seen in the older woman's eyes. "This will always be East Chelmsford to me. Kirk Boott and his lords of the loom can name it whatever pleases them, but that doesn't mean it changes in my mind or heart."

"What has Kirk Boott ever done to you that you speak his name with such disdain?" Mintie inquired.

Lilly silently scolded herself. Confiding in Miss Addie was one thing—she was a person who could be trusted. But Miss Mintie was a woman to be reckoned with, one to whom you gave as little information as possible. "I'd best be getting to my chores, Miss Addie. Nice to make your acquaintance, Miss Beecher. Please excuse me," she replied, scurrying from the room before Miss Mintie could lodge her objections.

"Well, I never! Such rudeness—and she calls you by that awful alteration of your name."

Lilly heard the older woman's exclamation of surprise as she exited the room. She half expected Miss Mintie to follow behind, switching at her legs with a sapling branch. Lilly grinned at the thought, but her smile soon disappeared. Miss Mintie's harsh words were drifting into the room like storm clouds on a sunny day. She strained to hear Miss Addie's reply, surprised by the younger sister's lighthearted retorts. Amazingly, Miss Addie's cheerfulness was meeting with success; the conversation soon calmed to a normal level.

Almost an hour had passed when Addie bustled into the kitchen carrying the tea tray. "I thought she would never go back across the street. I apologize for my sister's rude behavior. She shouldn't have questioned you like that. Unfortunately, Mintie feels she has a right to ask anything she wants to know, but heaven help the poor soul who invades *her* privacy."

The two women laughed in unison. "She does have a way about her," Lilly remarked, sending them both into gales of laughter once again.

"I am glad you held your ground with her, Lilly. It didn't seem to affront her. As a matter of fact, she's invited the two of us for tea a week from Sunday. Perhaps more people need to confront her."

Lilly turned to face Miss Addie. "And what of *you,* Miss Addie? Have you ever confronted your sister?"

Addie furrowed her brow for a moment. "I have on one or two occasions. I remember one time in particular. It was probably five years ago. I had gone to the dressmaker's shop early in the day and picked up a new gown that I had specially ordered. It was a beautiful creation. That evening I donned my new dress for dinner. Mintie came downstairs and saw me. She accused me of being half-dressed, insisting I should wear a pelerine to cover my neck and shoulders. I refused."

Lilly stared wide-eyed at the rosy-cheeked woman. "What did she do?"

Addie frowned. "She continued on her tirade, saying the dressmaker had no sense of fashion placing such a tight band on my plump waist."

"That was a cruel remark."

Addie nodded her agreement. "She did say she would be praying that I would come to my senses before I died and ended up in the fiery caverns of hell. I told her I would appreciate any supplications she made to the Almighty on my behalf, but I still did not intend upon wearing dreary, ill-fitting garments. You see, my dear, I still held out hope that I would find a husband. In fact, I still do," she confided in a hushed whisper.

"There's nothing wrong with continuing to pursue your dream, Miss Addie. And finding a husband is an honorable dream. Certainly nothing you need to hide," Lilly replied.

Addie lifted a stack of plates from the shelf. "I know, but Mintie always chided me for such thoughts. She thought me ungrateful for wanting to leave the Judge's household. She said a husband would merely attempt to squander away the Judge's fortune. Fact is, he didn't need anyone else to help him do that. He managed to lose everything without any assistance whatsoever."

"And what of that new dress you wore? Was the Judge aghast at the sight of you sitting down to dinner without a cape about your neck?"

Addie giggled. "Mintie always discussed the business of the day with the Judge. That particular day he had been at a meeting with some business acquaintances concerning the growth of the textile industry and the fact that several of these men were going to invest in the creation of an entire community based upon the mill industry."

Lilly was mesmerized by the thought of it. A group of men sitting down to plot how they could purchase land with ample waterpower in order to make themselves wealthy. It was mind-boggling. The daughter of a man who had been privy to all of the information surrounding the plan to dupe the residents of East Chelmsford now stood before her.

"What else did the Judge tell you about the plan?" Lilly urged.

"He didn't support the idea."

"Why not?"

"The Judge was certain the British were somehow involved in it. The plans for the loom had been smuggled out of Britain, and he was sure there would be repercussions. The Judge became upset with me when I questioned the validity of his fears about the English and told me I was speaking like a Tory. Of course, I assured him I would never do such a thing. In any event, my dress—"

"So he thought the plan folly? Did he feel these business acquaintances were taking unfair advantage of the landowners?"

"He determined that the textile industry might prove to be a good investment—if, and only if, the British could be kept out. He intended to keep the matter under surveillance as a possible future investment. Of course, that never occurred. We would still be living among the society of Boston had he set aside his fears of the British and invested his money. As to the landowners, he never made mention of that, although he knew the purchase of land near Pawtucket Falls had already begun. Why all these questions about the landowners? I thought you wanted to hear about my dress."

"Oh, I do, Miss Addie. Please tell me what the Judge had to say about your dress."

"We had just begun eating our fresh strawberries. They were covered with sweet cream," she added, her eyes glazing over as though the sumptuous dessert might reappear with the telling.

Lilly waited as Addie licked her plump lips. "What happened?" She could wait no longer.

"Oh yes. Well, the Judge took a bite of his strawberries, then looked at me and said, 'Addie, that is a beautiful gown you're wearing this evening. It would make me proud if you would wear it when we go to dinner at the Whitneys' next week.' It was all Mintie could do to hold her tongue. Of course, I immediately told the Judge I would plan to do that very thing. When the Judge had taken his leave to go over some pressing paper work, Mintie told me I would gain an unseemly reputation if I entertained such a foolish notion. But I did it anyway," she said, her giggle once again returning.

Lilly laughed along with her. "It doesn't appear they ran you out of Boston."

"No. In fact, I had many compliments that evening, and Mintie in her brown frock received not one word about her attire. I don't believe I will ever forget that evening.

"Mercy! Look at the time. The girls will be home for supper in no time."

When six o'clock arrived, Lilly still hadn't made it upstairs to finish the unpacking she'd started days earlier, but Addie had successfully turned out four loaves of bread on her own. In between preparing fried potatoes, baked beans with pork, turnips, parsnips with horseradish sauce, and a sweet plum cake, they had managed to wash the dishes and once again set the table. It hadn't taken long for Lilly to realize that Miss Addie didn't comprehend the need to prepare in advance. With some menu and meal planning, the older woman could save valuable time. She had enjoyed their afternoon of visiting, but in the future they would need to devote such time to working on the basic skills of household organization.

Lilly enjoyed it when the girls returned home for the evening. They didn't rush into the house in one large cluster as they did for the noon meals. Instead, they entered in twos and threes, visiting with each other as they sat down for their meal at a more leisurely pace. Rather than the clamoring rush of the noonday meal, they seemed to actually enjoy the evening repast, savoring the smells and tastes of the culinary feast, as well as each other's company.

"I can't tell you how pleased we are you're teaching Miss Addie to cook," Prudence commented as Lilly placed another bowl of horseradish sauce on the table. She winked at Lilly as though they were great conspirators.

Addie smiled, not in the leastwise offended. "I'm trying hard to learn my lessons. After all, Lilly's going to work in the Appleton next Monday. She agreed to help me in the kitchen until then, but after that I'm on my own."

There were groans all around the table. "You mean we'll be going back to scorched stew and bread that's heavy as a rock?" Eva Medley soulfully inquired.

Lilly noticed Miss Addie's shoulders visibly slump and her bright smile disappear. "I think you're going to continue to be pleasantly surprised, even after I begin working at the mill. Miss Addie is doing a wonderful job in the kitchen. She's an exceptionally quick student. In fact, that bread you're eating is her creation. As is the plum cake," Lilly quickly replied. "And she also prepared those baked beans and pork you're so heartily eating. She simply needed a bit of guidance on seasoning and cooking time. By the time I start work at the mill she'll be more than capable."

"This bread is very good—and the beans, too, Miss Addie," Eva remarked. Several of the girls nodded their heads in agreement. "I haven't tried the cake yet, but it looks wonderful."

Nettie Smitson gave Addie a warm smile. "You keep this up, Miss Addie, and we may have the best boardinghouse in town by year's end."

A smile returned to Addie's lips, and her shoulders straightened a bit. "Thank you for your vote of confidence, girls. I'll do my best."

Lilly already felt a burgeoning affection for the plump boardinghouse mistress. Addie was kind and considerate—almost motherly in her attention toward her girls. However, as the evening wore on, Lilly noticed Addie's mood begin to change. She had been almost jovial as she clucked about the room, waiting on the girls and listening as they related the day's events and stories of home. But as the young ladies wandered off and settled into small clusters or drifted upstairs, she took on an air of dejection.

After watching Addie for several moments, Lilly took up a piece of writing paper. Lilly didn't know what sorrow had overcome the boardinghouse keeper, but perhaps a change of routine would help. "Shall we begin some menu planning, Addie?"

Addie nodded in agreement as the two of them walked into the kitchen. "Best squeeze in as much teaching as possible in the next couple of days," she commented.

"The girls seem like a friendly group. I've hardly had time to spend with any of them. Either I'm busy down here with you or they're well on their way to sleep by the time I get to our room."

"They're mostly a good lot. But they can be demanding—and unforgiving, too. Perhaps it comes from working in the mills and having to meet the demands that are placed upon them. They have very few hours of freedom from their work, and they expect to have their needs met when they come home. They'll take few excuses. The men over in my sister's house are more accommodating, especially when Mintie's ill. But the girls expect their meals on time, their laundry done, and the house in order, no matter what my circumstances may be. Oh, there are a few who understand, but the rest are quick to complain and tell me they'll soon move if I don't meet their expectations.

They know how the Corporation works, and I realize their remarks are little more than veiled threats that they'll report me and I'll receive my discharge papers."

"Oh, Miss Addie, don't worry so needlessly. I promise I'm going to be here to help you. By the time I leave, you're going to have girls begging to get in this house."

Addie gave her a faint smile. "You're talking about leaving and you haven't even begun your work at the mill. You've got plans, haven't you?" Addie asked, the twinkle beginning to return to her eyes. "You'll most likely be taken for a wife before you've been with us even a year. Which reminds me, is the Mr. Cheever that Mintie mentioned earlier *your* Matthew Cheever?"

6

Lilly sauntered back down Merrimack Street, her arms heavy with the groceries she had purchased for Miss Addie's girls. It was her first real outing since she'd arrived at the boardinghouse—if one considered grocery shopping an outing. Addie had awakened that morning with a swollen foot, a flare-up of gout, she had explained while asking if Lilly would consider going to the market. It had been an apologetic entreaty, at least until Lilly assured the older woman she would enjoy a walk in the fresh air. And she had enjoyed every lighthearted step as she made her way to the market. A crispness of autumn hung in the September air, yet a vibrant golden sun shone down, vying for one last surge of summer's warmth.

Lilly relished the feeling. It took her back to happier times—days that seemed so long gone that they blurred in her memories. With a sigh, she picked up her pace. Nothing could be gained by living in the past. Walking briskly, she made excellent time and, after finishing her marketing, decided she could allow herself a few extra moments to survey the array of new bonnets in Wellington's Millinery Shop. Perhaps with her first paycheck she would purchase a more grown-up creation.

Standing in front of the bonnet-filled window, Lilly felt a tap on her shoulder. Glancing around, she met Julia Cheever's warm smile. Julia, her deceased mother's dearest friend. Julia Cheever—Matthew's mother.

Julia pulled Lilly into a warm embrace. "I'm so sorry about your father, Lilly. We were out of the city when he passed away. Matthew mentioned that Lewis returned home for the funeral. I wondered if you had gone to New Hampshire with him. But now I see for myself that you're here."

"Actually, Lewis was a day late. He missed the funeral, but thank you for your concern," Lilly murmured. Pulling away, she offered Mrs. Cheever a weak smile. "I'm sorry. I must go."

"Nonsense, I've only just found you. You must tell me what is happening in your life. Where are you living? Am I amiss in my information regarding your brother living in New Hampshire?"

Lilly didn't want to tell the woman that she had no idea where her brother had taken himself. "I'm not sure about Lewis. I'm living on Jackson Street."

"Are you staying with friends?"

Lilly stiffened. "I really have to go. I have a great deal to do. I'm sorry." She made every attempt to hurry back to her secret hiding place at the boardinghouse. Of course, now it wasn't quite so secret.

"You'll not escape so easily, Lilly. I insist you come for supper this evening. And I'll not take anything but yes for an answer!" Julia insisted.

Fearing Matthew's participation in the meal, Lilly was loath to agree. "That could be rather uncomfortable for Matthew," she finally said.

Julia shook her head. "He won't be there. He's out of town on business."

Lilly made other protests. "I'm in mourning. It wouldn't do to have me partaking in dinner parties."

"Nonsense," Julia retorted. "We're practically family, and this would hardly be a party."

Lilly felt awash in defeat. Each of her arguments was met by Julia's counterattack. No escape could be had, so she finally smiled as sweetly as possible. "Just tell me what time and I'll be there."

"Very good." Julia gave her the information, then added with a hint of amusement in her voice, "If you don't make your appearance, I'll send Mr. Cheever to fetch you."

Now, as Lilly watched Julia depart, she wished she had stood her ground and refused the invitation. Mrs. Cheever, the picture of refined elegance, glided down Merrimack Street, her skirt swaying like a bell. No doubt it was of the latest fashion and fabric. The Cheevers hadn't frittered their fortune away. Lilly swallowed hard. A dinner party at the Cheever home would bring nothing but discomfort and humiliation.

The older woman's parting words still echoed in Lilly's ears as she watched Julia disappear into one of the shops. *If you don't make your appearance, I'll send Mr. Cheever to fetch you.* It sounded every bit a threat.

Lilly turned and hurried toward Jackson Street with unwelcome memories of the past invading her thoughts. It had been at Matthew's urging that the Cheevers sold their adjoining acreage some five years earlier and built a home in Lowell. Although Lewis had visited the Cheevers' new residence when he had made his occasional visits home, Lilly had never so much as seen their new house. Of course, Julia had invited her on many occasions when she'd come to the Armbruster farm for a visit, but Lilly had resisted. In fact, she'd gone out of her way to avoid even a glimpse of the new mansion. Seeing the Cheevers in another home would solidify their absence and force her to admit they were never coming back to tend their orchards or their flocks of woolly sheep.

"Of course, Father's death has assured that fact for me, so it truly doesn't matter anymore," Lilly told herself. She only wished it wouldn't hurt so very much.

Miss Addie was seated in the kitchen peeling potatoes and scraping vegetables for the potpies, her foot propped on a wooden stool. "You're back in no time at all. Did you run all the way?"

"No, of course not," Lilly replied, forcing herself to return the woman's jovial smile.

"I forget those young legs can carry you much more quickly than these worn-out old stubs. Did Mr. Lacy have everything we needed?"

Lilly nodded as she continued unpacking the basket, her back to the older woman. She continued searching her mind for some way she could avoid supper at the Cheever residence. A cheery Miss Addie tapping on her arm interrupted Lilly's solitary thoughts.

"I've been meaning to ask you again, Lilly, was the Matthew Cheever Mintie spoke of your long-lost beau? You went scampering out of the room like a mouse after cheese when I inquired about him earlier."

This time there was no escaping Miss Addie's question. "Yes. My, it appears you've made excellent progress on the potpies," she stated, hoping the change of subject would put an end to the investigation.

Her strategy, however, failed to work with Miss Addie. "And now he's Kirk Boott's protégé? It would appear you let a good thing get away from you, Lilly. If that young man has captured Mr. Boott's attention, he's sure to go far with the Corporation. Whatever caused the two of you to go your separate directions?"

"His affiliation with Mr. Boott and the Boston Associates."

"Why, that makes no sense, child. A man who loves you is establishing himself in the business world, and you find fault with him?"

"Perhaps it makes no sense to you, Miss Addie, but it's reason enough for me," Lilly replied as she crimped the dough she'd placed atop one of the chicken potpies that now lined the worktable.

"Well, are you going to explain it to me?" Addie inquired while scooting forward on her chair.

"It's a long story."

Addie gave her a broad smile. "I've got nothing but time to listen while we're fixing dinner, and I love to hear a good story."

Lilly shook her head. There was no escaping this time. "It's not such a good story. Matthew and I were friends throughout our growing-up years. You may recall I mentioned he once saved me from drowning in the Merrimack River the day Lewis held me over Pawtucket Falls."

"That's right! I do remember," Addie agreed, her blue eyes sparkling at the realization.

"It wasn't until the year before Matthew went off to Harvard that we pledged our love. Matthew talked of the day when he would be in charge of his family's farm. Jonas, his older brother, had no interest in the land, but Matthew was like me—he had a desire to maintain his family's acreage. I cherished the idea of marrying a man who would work the land and keep me close to family.

"Anyway, it was his final year at Harvard when he began to change. He had been involved in discussions regarding the industrialization of our country in his classes at Harvard, and he began talking about proper utilization of the land and how it could serve more people—things that were completely foreign to his earlier beliefs.

"Then on one of his visits home, he told me he was no longer interested in farming, that he had convinced his parents to sell their acreage and hoped our family would do the same and that it would be best for us to do so. He said my father's health would soon prevent him from farming, and with Lewis's obvious lack of interest in the property, it only made sense to sell." Lilly looked away and tried to shake off the strangling sorrow that welled up in her heart.

"He had become a stranger to me. When my father resisted, someone wrote to Lewis telling him there was a good price to be had for our land. Needless to say, my brother returned home, and the land was sold. That was five years ago, in 1823."

Confusion imprinted Addie's plump face. "Five years ago? Where have you been since then?"

"On the farm, tending the orchards and caring for my father. The Associates knew they wouldn't need our land until the mills began to expand, so the contract contained a clause that we could continue to cultivate and live on the land for five years. As the day for our departure grew nearer, my father's health worsened. I believe he died of a broken heart. He had already lost my mother, and he couldn't face the possibility of beginning a new life away from everything he held dear. He died a week before we were to vacate our homestead.

"Lewis arrived the day after my father was buried—he was detained in a game of cards with some gentlemen in Nashua, New Hampshire. It seems he was on a winning streak and couldn't force himself away from the gaming table. Of course, he lost all of those winnings before he arrived back in East Chelmsford. Upon his appearance, he laid claim to the remaining gold pieces my father hadn't already given him. He then proceeded to sell everything of value that remained in the house before he rode away. In all likelihood, he gambled away his remaining inheritance before the week had ended."

Addie shook her head. "It appears that Lewis needs to be introduced to the Lord. Perhaps then he would change his ill-advised ways."

Lilly shrugged her shoulders. "The only way that will happen is if there's a revival in one of the taverns or brothels he frequents."

The color heightened in Miss Addie's cheeks as she shook her head again. "The Lord works in mysterious ways, Lilly. Don't sell Him short."

The corners of Lilly's mouth turned upward and formed a soft smile. "I would never do that, but I believe Lewis has already committed his soul. Unfortunately, not to God."

"I've seen some hardhearted characters change their ways. Perhaps we should pick a special time each day and pray for him," Addie offered with a sense of excitement filling her voice.

Lilly's smile faded as she finished preparing the last of the potpies and set them to bake. Wiping her floured hands on the white cotton apron, she turned toward Adelaide. "You are a truly kind woman, and I appreciate your offer, but I don't believe I could pray for Lewis—I'm not at all sure I care what happens to him."

Addie took hold of Lilly's hand. "Well, then, I'll just set aside some time each day and I'll be praying for the *both* of you. We'll see if God has something to say in the matter of Lewis and his evil ways."

"And *me,* Miss Addie? What are you looking for God to do with me?"

Addie gave her a wink and smiled. "Just a bit of softening on that heart of yours—I'm afraid it's beginning to harden at much too early an age. You're a good girl, and I just thank the Lord you've come into my life. I wish there was something more I could do for you, aside from your bed and board."

"There is one favor you could do for me."

"Anything. You just tell me what it is."

"I'm invited to a supper this evening—not until half past seven," she quickly added. "Would you give permission for me to attend?"

"Why, of course, Lilly. You don't need my permission to go out. The girls go out shopping and visiting every evening. However, it would be nice to know where you're going," Addie replied, giving her a grin. "Or am I being too meddlesome?"

Lilly couldn't help but laugh. Addie's deep blue eyes were alight with curiosity. "Julia Cheever, Matthew's mother, spotted me on Merrimack Street when I was shopping today. She insisted I come to supper this evening. I attempted to refuse her invitation, but she wouldn't hear of it. She threatened to send Mr. Cheever if I'm absent."

"It would be more interesting if she sent Matthew," Addie replied with a mischievous grin.

Lilly met Addie's lopsided grin with a stern frown. "Matthew won't be in attendance. Rest assured that I would never have accepted the invitation under any other circumstance. I'm certain Mrs. Cheever would never intentionally cause such an embarrassing situation for either of us."

"It is amazing what a mother will do for the well-being of her child," Addie whispered as she lifted her foot from the stool.

~ 7 ~

Matthew smiled at his reflection in the large oval mirror that hung over the ornately carved mantel in his parents' parlor. He adjusted his cravat ever so slightly, then glanced out the front window. Pulling a gold watch from the pocket of his double-breasted waistcoat, he decided he could wait only five minutes longer. If his mother hadn't returned by then, he would ask Mary to deliver a message. But moments later, she entered the front door, a basket containing the morning's purchases hanging from her arm.

"Matthew, what a pleasant surprise," she greeted as he met her in the hallway. "I'll be with you as soon as I unpack these things. They had such fine produce at the market this morning, it was difficult to decide what to buy. Sit down," she urged.

"I can't stay, Mother. In fact, I'm already late."

"But since you're already here, I was hoping you'd stay for supper. I'm having guests."

"I couldn't possibly do that," Matthew replied.

"But, Matthew, this is the third time in recent weeks that we've invited you to join in our dinner party. I've already invited other guests and I am short one male escort. What is so important that you must create this last-minute disorder for me?"

Matthew squared his shoulders, his chest swelling as he spoke. "Mr. Boott wants me to accompany him to Boston for a meeting with Bishop Fenwick."

A startled look crossed Julia's face. "You've come at the last minute to tell me you are not attending my dinner party in order to go with Kirk Boott and meet with some Catholic priest? What's gotten into you, Matthew, that you think fraternizing with some papist is more important than attending my party?"

"Mother, I'm sorry if I've caused you inconvenience. However, this meeting is important to my future with the Boston Associates. Perhaps you could ask Jonas to bring along one of his acquaintances."

An exasperated sigh escaped Julia's lips. "Boston Associates," she remarked with a hint of disdain. "You have a Harvard education, Matthew. There are any number of businesses that would be pleased to employ you. Without, I might add, requiring you to travel so often that you can't partake in a supper engagement at your parents' home."

"At the moment, I don't have time to argue the benefits of working with Mr. Boott, but suffice it to say that I'm willing to make any necessary sacrifice in order to become a valued employee of the Associates."

"*Any* sacrifice, Matthew?" Julia pulled a lace handkerchief from her sleeve and began dabbing at her face. "I pray that remark isn't true."

"Please, Mother, you need not attempt to convince me you're going to faint over an offhand remark. I promise I won't sell my soul to the devil, but I am going to Boston with Mr. Boott."

"Well, do as you see fit. I'm sorry you'll miss my special guest. You'd better be on your way. I wouldn't want to detain you further," she replied as she began walking out of the parlor.

His mother's game playing was exasperating. She knew he wouldn't leave until the unnamed guest was revealed. When he had been a little boy, she could always entice him with a secret—she still could. Julia enjoyed the game and he knew it. Yet, his curiosity forbade departing without knowing the name of her mysterious guest.

"You have my promise that I will be here for dinner a week from Sunday," he coaxed.

Julia stopped, turned toward him, and placed a finger against her pursed lips. "And that you'll be in attendance at Sunday services?"

"I'll be sitting alongside you and Father in the fourth pew," he answered.

"Now, don't take that peevish tone, or I'll be forced to require a greater sacrifice."

His mother held the trump card. They both knew it, and time was growing short. Accordingly, he gave her his most winsome smile. "I shall be pleased to attend church with you next week. Now, who is your surprise guest?"

"If you had more time, I would oblige you to guess," she coyly replied. "But since time is of the greatest import, I shall tell you. It is Lilly Armbruster."

Without thought, Matthew lowered himself onto the sewing chair behind him. "Lilly?" His voice was a hollow whisper. He stared up at his mother, feeling the blood drain from his face.

"Yes. I thought you would be pleased," she ventured. "Are you feeling ill, Matthew? You've lost your color."

"Where? How? Why did you do this?"

"I love Lilly. Just because the two of you are no longer—shall we say, betrothed—doesn't mean I don't want to spend time with her. Her parents are both dead. She has no family, unless you consider that scoundrel Lewis—which I don't. I wanted to reach out to her in some way but wasn't sure how. Then, as I was strolling down Merrimack Street this morning, I saw her in front of the millinery shop. I offered my condolences and explained that we had been out of town when her father passed away. I inquired about her welfare and asked if she would come to supper. She was as close to a daughter as—"

"But she *isn't* your daughter, Mother, and I am your son. You knew it would create an uncomfortable situation for me, but you went ahead and invited her. I can't believe you would do such a thing—or that she would accept."

Julia's attempt to appear composed fell short. She was wringing her hands, and tiny beads of perspiration had formed across her upper lip. "Don't think harshly of Lilly. She asked if you would be in attendance. I told her you were out of town on business. And you will be," she quickly added. "Although, I had hoped—"

Matthew rose from the chair. "Hoped what—that we'd renew our relationship? That we'd become engaged again? She's in mourning, Mother. Her father just passed on. How appropriate would it be for me to suddenly appear on her doorstep with ring in hand?"

"Well, granted, there are proprieties to be held to. However, if you feel the same way about her . . ."

"I don't want to discuss this further. It appears my trip to Boston will make an honest woman out of you, Mother. However, you will do nothing but cause pain for Lilly and me if you continue to interfere. Our relationship is over. And please remember it was Lilly who terminated our liaison. I didn't drive her off."

"If you hadn't taken up with Kirk Boott and that group of Bostonians, she'd still be at your side."

"You and Father didn't object to my association with them when it fetched you a better price for your land than that of the other East Chelmsford residents," he retaliated.

Julia shook her head in denial, her cheeks growing flushed. "That was *your* doing, Matthew. You convinced your father to sell the acreage."

"Your life has never been better than here in Lowell."

"There is no doubt my life is easier, but don't try to disguise the truth with that argument. You wanted to impress those men with the fact that you were an East Chelmsford resident who could give them an advantage dealing with the locals as they attempted to purchase the land. You started with your own family in order to impress them. Now, I'm not saying what you did was in any way improper. And I would venture to say that most of the original landowners are doing well, even though they feel misrepresentations were made to them. Unfortunately, Lilly Armbruster is *not* one of those people who has benefited. And it breaks my heart."

"The fault lies with her brother, not the Boston Associates. The Armbrusters received more than most."

Julia nodded her head. "Perhaps. But the coins that line Lewis Armbruster's pockets do nothing to help his sister. This discussion will do nothing to change Lilly's circumstances.

"You best be going, Matthew, for I'm sure Mr. Boott is anxiously awaiting your arrival."

He wished now that he had merely sent his regrets. The conversation with his mother had completely ruined the excitement of traveling to Boston and meeting with Bishop Fenwick.

"Give my regards to Father," he said as he opened the front door.

"You may do that yourself next Sunday. I haven't forgotten your promise. I'll expect to see you promptly at ten o'clock. And don't think I haven't noticed your absence in church the past two weeks, young man."

Matthew could only nod in agreement as he bounded down the front steps. His mother had succeeded in ruining his journey into Boston, yet there she stood on the wide front porch, waving her lace handkerchief after him as though she were bestowing some unspecified blessing upon him.

He rushed down the street, turned the corner, and hastened toward the Boott residence. A sigh of relief escaped his lips when he saw the carriage had not yet departed. As Matthew drew closer, he observed the legendary tyrant-in-residence pacing back and forth along the pillared entryway to his mansion, a look of annoyance etched upon his face. Quickening his step, he rushed onward, his pounding heart threatening to explode within his chest. Sights fixed on Boott, Matthew watched as his mentor turned toward the street and headed for the awaiting carriage. Matthew raised his arm, waving it back and forth above his head. He didn't have breath enough to call out a greeting.

"You are seventeen minutes late," Boott stated in a measured voice. "I loathe tardiness, Matthew. You should remember that in the future."

Matthew gasped for air. "Yes, sir. I apologize. I stopped to say hello to my mother—"

Boott held up his hand. "Please—don't give me an excuse. As far as I'm concerned, there is no excuse for tardiness. If you're finally prepared, let's be on our way."

A deafening silence permeated the carriage. Matthew determined he would await Mr. Boott's opening comment. He certainly wasn't going to cause himself further embarrassment—at least not if he could help it. The pastoral countryside prepared for autumn, a hint of rustic color beginning to tinge the green landscape, and Matthew settled his gaze out the carriage window. Passing the farms and orchards, his thoughts returned to the conversation with his mother. Somewhere deep inside him, he longed to be sitting at the supper table this evening, filling his senses with Lilly and her charming laughter, touching her chestnut curls, and gazing into her golden-flecked brown eyes.

The warmth of the sun beating upon the carriage coupled with the beauty of the countryside served as reminders of times spent with Lilly. He missed their long walks and the simplicity of plucking an apple from a tree in the orchard or reading poetry by the river. But most of all, he missed sharing his dreams with Lilly. Why did she have to be so unyielding? They could have shared a wonderful life together, if only she would have opened her eyes to reality. No matter that he had presented valid, intelligent arguments for selling the farmland. She could not be convinced that East Chelmsford's future lay in manufacturing, not farming. His thoughts were entirely focused upon Lilly when Boott's words broke the silence.

"Since our supper at Nathan's earlier this week, I've given further thought to your ideas regarding the Irish. Although there is merit to meeting with the bishop, I don't want to appear overly zealous about the possible role of the bishop or the Catholic Church in Lowell. When we meet with Bishop Fenwick, I will do the talking. Unless I specifically direct a question to you, you will say nothing other than proper formalities. Is that understood?"

Matthew nodded his head in agreement. "Absolutely."

"I can only hope you'll perform this task more efficiently than your late arrival this morning." The comment was laced with sarcasm. Boott's sardonic grin followed the biting remark.

"You can depend on me, Mr. Boott," Matthew reiterated, his palms growing moist.

Boott ignored the assurance. "Let me give you a bit of background about Bishop Fenwick. Before his assignment to Boston, he held an appointment in New York. Fenwick's not as popular as his predecessor, at least not among the Protestant elite of Boston. However, he does understand his need for assistance from them if the Catholic Church is to continue prospering in his diocese. Right now they're struggling, with Holy Cross being their only strong parish."

"Then you think he'll be pleased with the prospect of offering religious instruction to the Irish in Lowell?"

"I'm told he has only five priests for the entire diocese. I don't know what will or will not please him, but I do know he's a shrewd man. The last thing I want to do is appear vulnerable. He would consider us easy prey."

Matthew stared across the coach and met Boott's steely gaze. "Prey? How could a man of the cloth victimize the Corporation? And why would Bishop Fenwick even entertain such a notion?"

"Don't underestimate the clergy, Matthew—especially the papists! There's nothing they covet more highly than a nice piece of acreage. Always in the name of the church, of course. I'm willing to donate to their cause when a favor is needed, but the amount and kind of donation will be on *my* terms, not those of Bishop Fenwick. Or any other clergyman, for that matter."

The messages were clear. Keep your mouth shut, keep your ears open, keep your mind sharp, and be careful where you place your trust.

And by all means, be punctual.

Impressed with Boott's knowledge of Bishop Fenwick and the Catholic Church, Matthew, at the same time, was thankful that Boott hadn't inquired if he had gathered any information for their meeting with the bishop. Leaning back against the leather-upholstered carriage seat, Matthew wondered if Bishop Fenwick had been carefully preparing for their arrival, scrutinizing Kirk Boott's heritage and business acumen. If so, this meeting could prove even more interesting than he had anticipated.

S everal carriages lined the drive in front of the Cheever house on Pawtucket Street. Lilly determined it fitting that there should be a street named after Pawtucket Falls and that the Cheever home should be located on that particular street. Of course, the Cheever family truly belonged on their acreage adjacent to Pawtucket Falls, just as she belonged on the Armbruster farmstead. *If only the Boston Associates had begun their fancy manufacturing dreams in some other place—New Hampshire or perhaps Vermont,* she thought as she approached the house.

There was still time to turn and go back to her room on Jackson Street, and she hesitated a moment. Would Matthew be in attendance after all? Surely not—she could trust Julia Cheever's statement that he was out of town. Besides, the thought of Randolph Cheever appearing at the front door of the boardinghouse to fetch her would give rise to questions from the other girls.

Straightening her back and taking a deep breath, Lilly walked up the front steps and knocked. Her heart began to race when the door opened and a man stood beside Mrs. Cheever, his back toward her as he talked with a group of guests. When he turned, she felt a rush of relief—or was it disappointment? Before her, extending his hand in greeting, stood Matthew's older brother, Jonas.

"Well, if this isn't quite the surprise," Jonas exclaimed. "How good to see you, Lilly. So this is our surprise guest. Mother has been taunting us all afternoon."

"Us?" It was all Lilly could manage for the moment. All eyes were turned in her direction.

"Father and me," Jonas replied. "We've suffered an afternoon of pure torment, both of us guessing until we'd exhausted everyone we could possibly think of. Won't Matthew regret that he couldn't attend this evening?"

"Didn't I say you would be surprised? I was right, wasn't I?" Julia questioned. Her eyes were dancing with delight as she pulled at her husband's arm.

"Absolutely correct," Mr. Cheever replied.

"How nice to see you again, Lilly," greeted Sarah, Jonas's wife.

"Lilly, it's been too long," continued Mr. Cheever. "Hopefully your arrival means my wife will now serve supper." He grasped her hands in greeting and bent down to whisper, "I'm famished."

Lilly smiled at the remark. She remembered that Mr. Cheever's favorite greeting when coming home from the fields had been, "I'm famished—when do we eat?"

"You couldn't possibly be famished, Randolph. You've been in the kitchen sampling food all afternoon," Julia countered. "Come along, Lilly. I'm going to seat you next to Jonas and Sarah."

The meal consisted of a multitude of courses, beginning with a delectable lobster bisque, and all were served with an expert ease and graciousness that caused Lilly to marvel. Julia Cheever was no longer the farm wife serving dozens of workers during harvest season; she was now the accomplished society hostess entertaining refined guests. How had the transition been exacted in such a short time, she wondered.

"Do tell us what's going on in your life since moving from the farm, Lilly. Where are you living?" Jonas inquired as a server offered Lilly a heaping platter of mutton.

Prying questions. She had known they would be asked. Why had she placed herself in this prickly situation? "On Jackson Street," she replied, offering nothing further.

"Jackson? I thought Jackson was nothing but boardinghouses for the mills," Sarah stated. She grimaced ever so slightly and shuddered.

"So it is," Jonas remarked. "Are you certain it's Jackson Street?" he asked, turning back toward Lilly.

Had the question not been so insulting, Lilly would have laughed aloud. She wasn't sure what bothered her more, the fact that Jonas was actually questioning if she knew her own address or that she was being confronted with the realization that working in the mills diminished her social acceptability. She remained silent. All eyes were turned in her direction, a sense of discomfort suddenly permeating the room.

"Sometimes Jonas doesn't think before he speaks," Julia finally said, breaking the silence. "Nor does Sarah," she quickly added. "But they meant no harm, dearest Lilly. Hasn't the weather been unseasonably warm for this time of the year?"

With the expert ease of a perfect hostess, Julia had changed the conversation and set her guests at ease. Once again the room was abuzz with meaningless small talk as Lilly attempted to devise some plan of escape.

"Come along, everyone," Julia instructed. "We're going to play charades, and I don't want any of you men sneaking off to smoke cigars or talk business."

Randolph laughed as he and two of his colleagues turned in their tracks and returned to the parlor. "We wouldn't think of running out on a game of charades," he teased.

"I really must be leaving," Lilly whispered to her hostess. "We have a curfew."

"Nonsense. Randolph will escort you home and explain that you were with us. I'll not hear of you running off this early in the evening," Julia replied, her voice growing louder and more insistent when Lilly began to shake her head in disagreement. "I absolutely refuse to permit your departure!"

Lilly winced as the other guests began to look in their direction. "Fine. I'll stay for a little while. But I really must leave within the hour."

"We'll see," the unrelenting woman replied, giving her a smile. "All right, let's number off into teams. You begin, Randolph. You're team one," she instructed as she continued around the room assigning each guest a number.

In spite of her misgivings, Lilly joined the others, shouting out possible answers as guests performed their antics, laughing and cheering for several hours, forgetting the drudgery of her life and the tiny, airless bedroom she shared with seven other girls.

The Cheevers were standing at the doorway bidding their guests farewell as Lilly approached. "Ready, my dear?" Randolph inquired as he offered his arm.

"I can walk home alone. I don't want to take you away from your remaining guests," Lilly replied.

Randolph shook his head. "I'll hear of no such thing. It's a beautiful night, and the fresh air will do me good. Besides, I'll be back home before Julia has an opportunity to miss me," he quipped as he winked at his wife.

Lilly didn't argue. It would be wasted breath and she knew it. "Thank you once again for a lovely evening," she said, kissing Julia's cheek.

"You must promise you'll return to see us soon."

Lilly merely nodded, knowing she wouldn't soon return to socialize among the elite of Lowell.

"I've missed you, Lilly," Randolph stated. "I'm genuinely sorry things didn't work out between you and Matthew."

"And I've missed you and Mrs. Cheever, but time goes on and our lives change," she replied in a feeble attempt to appear philosophical about her station in life.

Mr. Cheever patted the hand she had tucked inside his crooked arm. "It's true our lives change, Lilly, but sometimes I think we do better to look at life in smaller slices, a change at a time, perhaps. Sweeping generalities sometimes tend to diminish those minor changes. We need to take time and realize that sometimes good comes along with bad."

"I'm not sure I understand what you mean, Mr. Cheever. My life has been turned upside down—nothing is the same. East Chelmsford no longer exists. Lowell has overpowered and smothered the life out of East Chelmsford."

He smiled and shook his head. "I disagree. The name has changed and the town has grown, but East Chelmsford and her people are still alive and vibrant. Lowell didn't smother us. We've been cultivated and nurtured so that we could change and grow into a larger, more productive community. Sometimes I think we humans just don't want to give in and think that any good can come from change. Could you agree with me on that?"

"I suppose. But it's difficult to find good that has come from all of this so-called industrialization. Our beautiful farmlands are now ugly brick buildings and canals. I miss the tranquility of the countryside, the pride of orchards producing bountiful crops, and the pleasure of seeing herds of woolly sheep roaming about."

"I see. And do you miss the years of drought when we broke our backs attempting to eke out a living on the few crops we could produce? Don't forget the bad as you remember the good, child. Otherwise, you paint yourself a false picture. There were good things about those days, but there were just as many hard times. One must keep events in perspective. Change is always going to be a part of our lives. If we don't grow and change, we stagnate and die. Perhaps you should attempt to see Lowell with the unbridled enthusiasm of a newcomer. I believe you would find it exciting and, dare I say, quite lovely."

Lilly looked up at Mr. Cheever and was instantly reminded of Matthew. Although Jonas was marginally handsome and well spoken, it was Matthew who had inherited not only his father's good looks but his gift of persuasion. It was indeed a formidable combination. She feared she still hadn't succeeded in obliterating Matthew from her memory after all.

~ 9 ~

Boston, Massachusetts

Matthew tugged at his waistcoat as he and Kirk Boott followed closely behind a tranquil, black-clad priest. After traversing several hallways, the cleric rapped on a carved oak door, waited for a response, then opened the door to Bishop Benedict Fenwick's private office.

The rotund man rose from a cushioned red velvet chair and came out from behind his desk, his dark-eyed gaze fixed on Boott. His upturned lips and the dark curly locks that surrounded his forehead and cheeks gave the bishop a youthful appearance. A stiff gold braid trim surrounded the edge of his unbuttoned collar, thus permitting his sizable double chin to rest upon a layer of soft white fabric. Matthew noted that the row of black buttons aligned down the front of the bishop's jacket strained against the man's expansive bulk.

"Good to see you once again, Mr. Boott," Bishop Fenwick greeted, stretching his arm in welcome.

Kirk grasped the proffered hand and then turned to Matthew. "May I introduce Matthew Cheever, Your Excellency. He has recently been hired by the Boston Associates to assist me with my duties in Lowell. I decided to reward his hard work with a trip to Boston."

"A pleasure," the bishop replied, extending his ring-adorned hand to Matthew. "Always good to meet with men who have the best interests of our citizenry at heart. Sit down, sit down," he offered, gesturing toward two dark blue brocade chairs opposite the large walnut desk.

Matthew and Kirk seated themselves, remaining silent as the bishop circled the desk and lowered his expansive body into the velvet-upholstered chair. The walls behind the desk were lined with matching walnut bookcases, each shelf crowded with volumes of leather-bound books. Across the room, an ornate silver tea service rested upon a marble-topped serving table. At the ring of a small gold handbell, a priest entered the room. He carried a tray of small cakes that he placed on the table before silently pouring tea into three china cups and exiting the room as noiselessly as he had entered.

"Tea, gentlemen?" The words were formed as a question, but both men knew what was expected.

They drank the spiced tea with lemon and ate the layered cakes Bishop Fenwick offered. They exchanged pleasantries, discussed the weather, and inquired into one another's health. It was the way of genteel, well-bred people. It was also the way of far-reaching men hoping to gain advantage and power.

When Bishop Fenwick had finally eaten his fill, he leaned back in his chair, reaching his arms across the expansive girth of his belly. His thick fingers barely met. Boott leaned forward ever so slightly, obviously awaiting some signal that the cleric was ready to move their conversation into a more serious vein.

"I assume you gentlemen haven't made an appointment to see me merely to inquire about my health," the bishop stated. He leaned deeper into the chair, his eyes hooded by thick black lashes.

Matthew remained silent as Boott leaned forward, a look of concern now crossing his face. "Indeed, we do have a matter of importance to bring before you, Your Excellency. Not a matter that will be easily resolved, but a problem I believe we can eventually solve if we work together. Reasonable men can always benefit each other. Don't you agree?"

The bishop's eyelids opened wider. Matthew noticed an obvious spark of interest in the cleric's dark eyes. "Unreasonable men have been known to become quite reasonable when the stakes are high enough, Mr. Boott. Just what is it that you perceive as our mutual problem?"

"Simply stated, the growing Irish population in Lowell," Kirk replied. "Not that the Irish themselves are a problem," he quickly added when the bishop unfolded his hands and gave him a look of obvious displeasure. "I take responsibility for this whole situation. It's my lack of planning—not giving thought to the permanency of our Irish brothers in the community. To be honest with you, Bishop, I didn't expect they would want to remain in Lowell. I always assumed they'd want to return to Boston and live among—"

"Their own?"

"Well, yes, if you want to put it that way. However, we have an ever-increasing number of Irish in Lowell who appear to be setting down roots. I don't want to sound disparaging, but the Irish tend to be a clannish sort of people. You'd agree with that, wouldn't you?"

The bishop nodded and stroked his plump red cheek. "They find comfort in that which is familiar. Not unlike most of us, Mr. Boott. However, the Irish do bring with them a deep sense of loyalty to the clans of their homeland and align themselves accordingly. In that regard they are somewhat different from other immigrants."

"Right," Boott chimed in, vigorously nodding his head up and down. "Well stated, Your Excellency." He hesitated for a moment before continuing. "Another thing that I've observed about the Irish is their deep regard for the church."

"For a moment there, I thought you were going to say their deep regard for a pitcher of ale." The bishop gave Kirk a serious stare but then snorted as he attempted to hold back his own laughter. "It was a joke, good fellow— you're permitted to laugh."

Kirk's nervous laughter mingled with Bishop Fenwick's snorting noises for what seemed several minutes. Matthew sat quietly, observing the interchange, a smile emerging on his lips when the bishop finally gazed in his direction. "And what do *you* think of our Irish brothers, Mr. Cheever?" The bishop's question brought the laughter to a startling halt.

Matthew glanced toward Boott, who nodded his head ever so slightly. "I agree with Mr. Boott's assessment, sir."

"Not much of an independent thinker? I'm surprised Mr. Boott would hold you in such high esteem," the bishop rebutted.

Matthew knew he was being baited. His words must be carefully chosen. He dared not fail a second test in one day. "I don't believe the fact that I agree with Mr. Boott's assessment gives credence to your judgment of my ability to evaluate a given situation. It merely affirms the intelligence of my employer's evaluation of this particular circumstance. I, too, believe the Irish hold the church in deep regard," he replied in a measured voice.

The bishop laughed aloud. "Well put, my boy. Don't know if I could have done better myself in such formidable circumstances. Isn't that right, Mr. Boott?"

A forced smile formed upon his mentor's lips. "That's exactly right, Excellency."

"Well, then, we all agree the Irish hold the church in high regard. So what is your problem?"

"They have no church in Lowell, no place to worship, no church leader to marry or bury them, no priest to hear their problems or direct them down the path of righteousness," Boott replied.

The bishop's face was stoic, unreadable. "I'm going to guess that since you've determined there is a problem, you've also devised some type of solution."

"I've given thought to several ideas, but nothing concrete just yet," he lied. "That's what I want to discuss with you. Surely you have some knowledge of the increasing problems the Irish face in Lowell. After all, they are your people," Boott said, obviously hoping to lead the matter into a discussion where he could further ascertain the cleric's stance.

"You're right that they are Catholics, and in that regard, they are my people. I would agree that all Catholics need spiritual leadership. However, Mr. Boott, they are your people also. They are in Lowell because you could find no others willing to perform the grueling labor of digging your canals and building your factories. Now that they have decided to remain in Lowell, you have a dilemma. You find them difficult to control, yet you need them close at hand to continue constructing your growing community. It is truly a troublesome situation."

Bishop Fenwick was obviously enjoying himself as he rose from the chair and moved aimlessly about the room, stopping directly in front of Boott and forcing him to look up into the bishop's face as he continued the assessment. "As I see it, you need the Irish—at least the men. However, you don't want them living in Lowell, mucking up the tidiness of your well-thought-out progressive community. So now you've decided the Catholic Church should come to your rescue. Would that be what prompts your visit to Boston?"

Matthew had become increasingly uncomfortable as Bishop Fenwick spoke. The cleric had painted the Boston Associates, and particularly Kirk Boott, as tyrannical, abusive men who had shamelessly abused the Irish population of Lowell. It was ludicrous. Yet Boott seemed undaunted by the turn of events. Instead, he smiled at the bishop and helped himself to one of the remaining cakes sitting on the marble-topped table. Seeming not the least disquieted by the silence, he finished the cake, carefully wiped his mouth with a linen napkin, and waited until Bishop Fenwick had finally seated himself in the velvet chair.

"Now, then, let me see if I can adequately respond to your summation. First of all, I didn't go rousting about hunting for Irishmen to work in Lowell. It was Hugh Cummiskey that led a group of his fellow clansmen from the Boston docks to Lowell seeking me and asking for work. I doubt you will have any difficulty verifying that fact. Once Cummiskey and his men were working, word spread that there was work available in Lowell. I never advertised, encouraged, or lured any immigrants, Irish or otherwise, into the community. Those who chose to come and work have been paid a fair wage. I have no control over how they spend their money or where they place their values. However, I believe the church should have a vested interest in their eternal souls, and I'm sure you could find use for a bit of their earnings if they cared to give a portion to the church."

The bishop gave a hearty laugh. "I always enjoy a good sparring event with you, Mr. Boott. Now, let's get to the heart of the matter. We both know the Irish are beginning to form settlements in Lowell, and we both know they get out of control from time to time. What is it you want from me?"

"Short term, I'd like to have you assign a priest to serve the Catholics. Long term, I'd like to see you build a Catholic church that would serve to unify the Irish who settle in Lowell."

The bishop once again stroked his flushed cheek. "To a man unfamiliar with you and the goals of the Boston Associates, that would appear to be a plan cultivated to fulfill the needs of your fellow citizens. However, we both know that this proposal is made more for your benefit than that of the Irish people of Lowell, and I'm sure you also know I have a shortage of priests.

Simply put, I don't have a priest I can send to Lowell, much less the funds to purchase land and build a church."

Matthew watched the unfolding scene. It was a methodical exchange, a game of chess played with words rather than pawns and kings. Both men retained their composure. It was Kirk's move, and Bishop Fenwick waited patiently.

"Would additional funding assist you in securing another cleric for the diocese?" Kirk ventured.

"Perhaps. But I would need to present a long-term plan, something of substance, to my superiors if I were going to assign a priest to Lowell. After all, we have a more urgent need for priests in larger cities."

Kirk nodded, acknowledging it was his move. Matthew was enjoying the discourse. It was obvious his employer would need to raise the stakes if they were going to make any progress.

"There is a piece of land, large enough for a good-sized church. It lies directly between the two Irish settlements. Possibly it could draw them together, become a source of unity. I think I could convince the Associates to sell it at a very reasonable price, perhaps even donate it to the church. I feel certain your parishioners would be more than willing to donate their labor once you've enough funds to begin building."

Bishop Fenwick's lips turned upward, and he rubbed his large hands together. "I believe I could take this information to my superiors with the expectation of a satisfactory result for all concerned. Why don't you write a figure on this piece of paper that we could expect to receive if another priest were assigned to the diocese? Oh, yes, and why don't you jot down the address of the property you're going to assign to the church. It would make my discussion with the church more, shall be say, *profitable* to all concerned."

Kirk accepted the outstretched pen and dipped it into the ink before writing the requested information and returning the pen. The bishop slid the paper back across the desk and placed a pair of spectacles across the bridge of his nose before reading the inscribed words. After reading, Bishop Fenwick nodded his head, rose from his chair, and extended his hand to Kirk.

"I'll be in touch with you once I have something definite to pass along."

"Always a pleasure visiting with you, Your Excellency," Kirk responded.

"If not a pleasure, at least profitable," Bishop Fenwick replied as he rose from his chair to dismiss them.

The same priest who had earlier admitted them now escorted the two men down the maze of hallways and out the front doors. There was a note of finality to their visit as the cleric pushed the heavy doors closed behind them.

"The meeting went well, don't you think?" Boott inquired as the two of them stood waiting in the lobby of the Brackman Hotel a short time later. "Hope you don't mind mixing a bit of pleasure with our business," he continued, without waiting for an answer to his first question.

"No, of course not," Matthew replied. "I thought the meeting—"

"Ah, here they are now," Kirk interrupted as he walked off toward the two women entering the front door.

Matthew watched the exchange from a distance. Both ladies had the same aquiline nose, wide-set eyes, and broad shoulders of their male relative. Unfortunately, the features that created a rather striking appearance in Kirk Boott failed to have the same effect on the female members of the Boott family.

"This is the young man I've been telling you about," Kirk announced as he pulled Matthew forward. "Matthew, this is my sister, Neva Locklear. And this," he said, wrapping his arm around the younger woman, "is my lovely niece, Isabelle. I know you'll find it difficult to believe, but she's every bit as bright as she is comely."

Matthew felt the heat rise in his cheeks. He had assumed they would dine with some of the Boston Associates for supper. What was it that Kirk had said as they'd followed the priest down the hallway? Something to the effect that he had made reservations for supper and hoped the evening's discourse would prove as fruitful as their meeting with Bishop Fenwick. Yes, those were his words. There had been nothing about dining with his relatives. Matthew silently chided himself. While he had been looking forward to supper and a lively discussion with the Associates, Boott had been anticipating a reunion with his sister and niece. A liaison that, for some unknown reason, caused a prickling sensation to course down his spine.

"I hope you don't mind, Matthew, but I took the liberty of posting a letter to my sister setting forth all of your many virtues. He's everything I promised, isn't he, Neva?"

Matthew watched the shrewd glance that passed between Kirk and Neva. This was more than meaningless chitchat. No matter that Boott was lively and engaging, that he appeared the carefree host entertaining guests for the evening; there was purpose to every word being uttered.

"He is absolutely delightful. Don't you agree, Isabelle?" Neva inquired, placing her hand atop Isabelle's unadorned left hand.

Eyes cast downward, Isabelle nodded her head in agreement.

"Speak up, Isabelle. We can't hear you with your head down," Neva persisted.

"Yes, he is everything you promised, Uncle Kirk."

Matthew's head jerked up and he looked at his employer. Boott's comment several days earlier echoed in his mind. *"A wife must be chosen with no less intelligence and cunning than one chooses a lawyer or business partner."* Was this then the intelligent, cunning choice that Boott had in mind for him?

"Look at this," Nadene said, jabbing Lilly with her elbow. "The book of John has Jesus saying, " 'I am the way, the truth, and the life: no man cometh unto the Father, but by me.' " She pointed to the verse in the fourteenth chapter. "Then look here," she added, "My granny has written a note that says, " 'God will make thee provision. He will make a way even when it seems impossible.' " She turned and looked at Lilly. "Jesus said that He's the way. Do you suppose that's what my granny was talking about?"

Lilly was chilled and wanted only to slip under the covers and go to sleep. The sole reason the candles were still burning was the fact that Pru and Sarah had taken a last-minute trip to the necessary. "I suppose it could mean that," Lilly finally answered. "Although the Bible is full of examples where God used people to fulfill His plan." She thought of her own mission. Surely God had put her plans in motion as surely as He had sent Jonah to warn the people of Nineveh.

Lilly wanted only to change the subject and scooted down in the covers. "Did your grandmother always write notes about Bible verses?"

"Oh my, yes." Nadene replied. "It's one of the reasons I cherish this Bible so much. It was the one thing Granny left me when she died. Just look here. Sometimes she wrote her thoughts alongside the verse—right on the same page. A great many times, however, she wrote on a scrap of paper and just stuck it in between the pages. When I need to understand a particular passage, I often find Granny's words help."

Nadene closed the Bible and put it aside. She blew out the candle and then settled back on her pillow. Only the candle from Pru's bedside still shone. The other girls seemed to have fallen asleep, mindless of Lilly and Nadene's discussion.

"I take my Bible with me to the mill," Nadene told Lilly in confidence. "I like to pull it out and read it when I have a moment."

"I've heard some of the other girls say they tape up bits and pieces of articles and books. Seems a shame to tear something apart just in order to read while you work."

Nadene sighed. "I could never tear up Granny's Bible, though I've seen some girls do just that. I suppose it gives them comfort in the midst of their trials, so I cannot fault them."

Lilly knew it had been some time since she'd concerned herself with reading the Bible. Even the small portion shared by Nadene pierced her heart and conscience. *I am the way,* Jesus had said. Lilly had heard that verse even as a child. It was a convicting statement—one on which she didn't want to dwell at the moment.

I know God has brought me here with a special purpose, Lilly reasoned. The turmoil in her heart churned while her mind mocked her for the traitor she was. How could she be certain of anything God wanted? She wasn't exactly listening to Him these days.

10

Lilly's trembling fingers fumbled with the strings of her bonnet. More than anything, she wanted to awaken to discover that this was nothing more than a bad dream. She wanted to be back in her cozy room at the farm, where she could smell the scent of burning wood in the fireplace and feel the coolness of an autumn morning on her windowpane. Rather than join the ranks as an anonymous mill girl rushing off in the early morning darkness to toil in the Appleton, she wanted to escape to the peaceful countryside of East Chelmsford—even more, she wanted her identity back.

"You're going to do fine today. There's no doubt that once you've mastered your tasks in the spinning room, the overseer is going to wonder how the mill operated without you," Addie encouraged.

"I wish I shared your confidence," Lilly replied, still groping with her bonnet strings.

"You'll be back here in no time, eating your breakfast and telling me your fears were misplaced. Just remember that I have your name on the top of my prayer list today. Now off with you—you dare not be tardy on your first day."

Lilly attempted to smile. It proved impossible. "I can use as many prayers as you can squeeze into your schedule."

Miss Addie's words echoed in Lilly's mind—at least temporarily. It was more likely the overseer would rue the day he hired her, she decided. Once outside the door, the other girls surrounded her, and as they made their way to the mill, girls from the other boardinghouses joined them. Lilly was swept along with the momentum, no longer in control of her destiny, the force of the bustling girls now carrying her along toward a worrisome future.

A short time later two of the girls abruptly broke off and hurried toward No. 1 of the Appleton, their void quickly filled by others, all rushing toward No. 2. They hurried through the gate, across the yard, and up the winding staircase. Lilly stopped short and turned into the counting room. She breathed a long sigh of relief. Thaddeus Arnold was nowhere in sight. Instead, a rotund middle-aged man with a balding pate and cherry red cheeks occupied the chair. He smiled in her direction. Lilly glanced over her shoulder expecting to find someone behind her. There was no one, yet she was somewhat surprised to see the man still sporting a smile when she turned back in his direction. He crooked his finger, beckoning her closer. Taking a hesitant step forward, Lilly was buoyed by his broadening smile, so she continued onward until she was standing directly in front of him.

"You must be Lilly Armbruster." His tone was deep and resonant, much like her father's voice.

"Yes, I was to report to Mr. Arnold—Thaddeus Arnold—but I don't see him."

He motioned her toward a wooden chair. "I am Lawrence Gault, and I've replaced Mr. Arnold. He has been promoted to another position with the mill." Mr. Gault gave her another broad smile, his cheeks puffing into the shape of two rosy apples. "I fear you'll be forced to complete your employment papers with me."

Lilly issued a silent prayer of thanks. At least she didn't have to begin her day dealing with that pompous, beady-eyed Mr. Arnold. Returning the man's smile, she dropped into the empty chair beside his desk. "It will be a pleasure, Mr. Gault."

She sat quietly as Mr. Gault slid a neatly stacked pile of papers toward her then pushed his wire-rimmed spectacles onto the bridge of his nose. "Now, then, this is your employment agreement. You should read the terms, and if you have any questions, we can discuss them. While you're reading the agreement, I have some other papers I must complete, but please interrupt me if you find something that you don't understand."

Lilly nodded and returned his smile. This man was certainly a refreshing change from her initial interview with Mr. Arnold. After scanning the first paragraph relating to duties of the overseer, she slowed down and began reading more carefully. She found the rule one of the girls had mentioned. It stated that she must agree to stay for a minimum of one year, and all employees intending to leave employment of the company must give two weeks' notice of such intention to the overseer or their contract would not be considered fulfilled. She scanned the paragraph requiring she be at work unless the overseer determined her unable to attend due to illness.

The rule regarding church attendance, the one Nadene had mentioned, was next. It stated that regular attendance at public worship on the Sabbath was necessary for the preservation of good order and that the Company would not employ any person who was habitually absent. Did the Boston Associates truly feel it necessary to include church attendance as one of their rules? Perhaps she should ask Mr. Gault. On second thought, perhaps she should not. It would be foolhardy of her to be labeled as a troublemaker on her first day. Yet she wondered about such personal matters being regulated by an employer.

"I trust you read the last paragraph regarding your wages—you'll be paid the last Friday of each month. Any questions?" Mr. Gault inquired when she glanced in his direction.

Heeding her better judgment, Lilly moved her head back and forth. "No, the contract appears to address much more than I could have ever imagined."

If Mr. Gault noticed the sarcasm in her voice, he gave no indication. Instead, he dipped his pen into an inkwell and thrust it toward her while pointing at an empty line at the bottom of the page. Lilly wavered for only a moment before carefully affixing her neat signature to the page. Her fate was sealed. She knew it, Mr. Gault knew it, and God knew it—and of course, following the Lord's plan was the primary reason she was here. She was now positioned to become the instrument of God—ready to mete out rightful retribution upon Kirk Boott and his wealthy associates for the many wrongs they had inflicted upon the farm families of East Chelmsford. Her mission had just begun.

Her stomach churned. *I am doing the right thing,* she assured herself. *This has to be what God has required of me.* A momentary confusion swept over her. What if she'd misunderstood? What if God wasn't bringing her here to rid East Chelmsford of the mills? She handed the papers back to Mr. Gault then pressed her hands against her temples. *This has to be the right thing to do—there simply aren't any other options.*

Mr. Gault finished reviewing the papers and removed his spectacles. "Follow me. I'll show you where you'll be working," he said, rising from his chair.

Together they walked from the agent's office and crossed the mill yard, Mr. Gault waving and calling out hellos to several of the men pushing carts of cotton that would soon be devoured by the carding machines.

The white tower with its huge clock cast a shadow across one of the brick-lined flower gardens that centered the yard. The bright, colorful blooms of spring and summer were gone, replaced by fading, dried stalks, providing evidence of the changing season. Lilly followed Mr. Gault to the narrow winding stairway that ascended one end of the mill. The enclosure covering the stairway jutted out from the structure, giving the appearance of a misguided afterthought.

They entered the stairwell and began their upward climb, the clamoring of the pulsing machinery growing louder with each turn. Lilly instinctively wrinkled her nose at the stale, fetid air. By the time they had passed the second-floor landing, Mr. Gault had slowed his pace, and when they finally stopped outside the third-floor doorway, his breathing had turned shallow and labored. Lilly balanced herself on the narrow top step as he hesitated and grasped the doorknob with his right hand.

"Fortunately, we need climb no farther," he said, his words bursting forth in short gasps. He gulped another breath of air. "I'll take you in and introduce you to your supervisor." The words were barely out of his mouth before he stopped with a look of recognition on his face. He gulped two more breaths. "Thaddeus Arnold is the supervisor of the spinning room," he said in an apologetic tone before pushing open the door.

The blood drained from Lilly's face, leaving her pale and shaken. This must be a cruel joke—the thought of facing toady little Thaddeus Arnold every day. Being forced to tolerate his infuriating pomposity was surely more than she could bear.

Mr. Gault waved to someone across the room. Lilly fixed her attention on the room, allowing the scene to tug her back to the present. She was greeted with Mr. Arnold's leering gaze. Despite the intense heat and humidity that hung in the room, a shiver ran up her spine, and she quickly glanced downward. Lint was already clinging to her dark chambray dress. *I should have listened to Miss Addie and worn my faded old work dress,* she silently chastised herself. Had it not needed laundering, she would have taken the older woman's advice. Instead, she had gone to bed. Now she would pay for her laziness.

Mr. Gault mouthed his good-bye before making a hasty departure out of the room and back down the stairway.

Lilly stood mute before Mr. Arnold, the humidity and his leering stare dampening her hair and her spirits in synchronized accord. He slithered off the stool and motioned for her to follow. They walked past Mary Albertson, who had a room across the hall at Miss Addie's boardinghouse. None of the other operators looked familiar, but several of them extended a welcoming smile as she followed Mr. Arnold down a narrow aisle, attempting to keep her distance from the machinery that was spinning thick white ropes of cotton onto tall bobbins.

Lilly placed a finger to her ear. How could anyone be expected to spend her waking hours in these horrendous conditions? And yet, the other girls seemed oblivious to the thundering noise that surrounded them. They moved on cue, shifting to and fro in time with the machines, carefully unknotting any errant thread that dared tangle before gliding back in place to continue their vigil. Silent sentries, they guarded over the metal monsters that thundered and pounded as they produced the thread-laden bobbins.

Without warning, Mr. Arnold's fingers closed around her wrist, startling Lilly to attention. She pulled free and met his beady-eyed glare. Mouth turned upward in a half smile, his touch lingered on her arm while his defiant look dared her to say a word. Finally he stepped aside.

"This way," he shouted, pointing toward several frames that stood idle at the end of the row. She followed, relief flooding her soul as she spied Nadene. Mr. Arnold motioned Nadene to join them. "Nadene Eckhoff," he screamed into the lint-filled air.

Lilly nodded. "We board in the same house," she screamed back.

"Get to work!" he commanded before walking away. Lilly tried to hide her relief as she turned to face Nadene.

Nadene rewarded her with a bright smile as she pointed toward the handle.

She grasped Lilly's hand in her own and together they pulled the handle, sending the machine into motion, adding yet another level of noise to the already deafening racket. The two of them watched the machine momentarily, and then Nadene pulled Lilly toward another frame.

"This one is yours, also. It's not difficult; just watch that the roving doesn't twist or snarl. Mr. Arnold comes around every hour to assure himself our work is satisfactory, so be mindful your bobbins are filling evenly. He always looks at the bobbins. The other day he threatened to reduce Mary's pay because he said she was daydreaming and her bobbins weren't filling uniformly. He's new to his position, and several of us think he's hoping to impress his superiors by increasing our workload. We don't like him much," she added, pulling the handle and causing the second machine to move into frenzied gyrations. "If the roving goes awry, I'll come help you if need be," she promised as she moved back to her own frames.

Lilly nodded and mouthed a thank-you before beginning her wearisome vigil over the metal beasts. It was mindless work, with nothing to break the monotony except the occasional skewed roving or unevenly wound bobbins. The clamor of the machinery was deafening, but the other girls seemed unaware. Curiously, they appeared to be in a trancelike state, each having escaped to some unknown place—somewhere far beyond the walls that surrounded and held them prisoner. She wished that *she* could escape into their dream world, but the noise prevented her departure. It held her captive, a slave to the torturous din.

She startled at Mr. Arnold's touch. He had come up behind her, placing his hand on the small of her back. Stepping away from the machine, she backed into his awaiting arms. He held her in a viselike grip, his acrid breath assailing her nostrils as he leaned in close to her ear, his fingers squeezing her flesh. "Your bobbins are not winding properly," he said, slowly releasing his hold. He held up a bobbin in front of her face. "Unacceptable!" he screamed. His beady eyes gleamed grotesquely as he grabbed her by the arm. "Watch after those machines," he screamed as they passed Nadene. Lilly turned to look back at Nadene as Mr. Arnold pulled her along, back out the door and into the stairwell, then pushed her into the corner. "Do you want to maintain your position in this mill?" he snarled. His yellow teeth were bared like an animal attacking its prey.

Lilly turned her head as he moved in closer. His arms pinned her on either side. She ducked beneath his arm and then held up a warning finger. "Don't touch me, Mr. Arnold, or you'll live to regret it," she shouted. Quickly, she turned the doorknob then rushed back into the room, down the aisle, and to her position at the machines. She didn't look up until she heard the faint sound of the breakfast bell. It grew louder as the girls quickly slammed their machines to a halt and began rushing toward the doorway. Nadene shoved the handle back on one of Lilly's frames and motioned for her to quiet the other one.

"Hurry or you won't have enough time to eat breakfast and get back here on time," Nadene said as she headed toward the door.

The other girls were already moving into the stairwell as she made her way down the row of machines. A strange noise caused Lilly to look over her shoulder. She swallowed hard. Thaddeus Arnold had another girl backed into a corner. She appeared to be smiling and nodding in agreement, although Lilly couldn't be sure. Edging closer to the door, Lilly continued watching, unable to tear herself away from the unfolding scene. Arnold's hands were around the girl and his head was bent forward. It was impossible to see if they were talking or if he was kissing the girl. The thought was repugnant. His head came up as he stepped back and allowed the girl to move away. Lilly shivered as she watched Thaddeus pat the girl's backside. Silently, Lilly slipped into the stairwell, her hands quivering as she wondered just what liberties Thaddeus Arnold might be taking with the girls employed at the Appleton.

At each level, additional operatives poured into the stairwell, each group seemingly more harried than the last, until they finally reached the bottom. Rushing forward to greet the crisp, bright morning, Lilly inhaled deeply. Her dress was damp with perspiration, and suddenly the cool air was more enemy than friend. She drew her cloak tight around her body, looking neither to her right nor left as she hurried down Jackson Street. She couldn't drive from her mind the scene of Thaddeus Arnold with the girl. What if he approached her again?

Suddenly someone took hold of her arm and Lilly whirled about. "I'm sorry. I didn't mean to startle you," Nadene apologized. "I wanted to tell you that you did a grand job this morning. You've nothing to worry about." Nadene matched her step to Lilly's.

"Thank you. I didn't expect you to wait on me. You're wasting precious time when you could be eating your meal."

"Some things are more important than food. I was concerned about you. Did Mr. Arnold give you a difficult time this morning?"

Lilly hesitated. "He told me if I didn't do a better job he'd be required to terminate me."

Nadene didn't seem overly surprised. "He did that with the other girl who just started yesterday. I think Mr. Arnold's afraid *he'll* be terminated if he doesn't do well in his new position. After he's more secure, perhaps he'll stop his bullying behavior."

"Has he said anything to you?" Lilly inquired.

Nadene gave a small giggle. "I don't think he would dare. Mr. Boott himself transferred me to the Appleton because of my abilities in the spinning room at the Merrimack. I doubt Mr. Thaddeus Arnold would say one word to me. And don't you worry; he won't fire you, not with me for a teacher."

"Why should you care whether I succeed?"

Nadene smiled. "That's easy. I care because you're my friend."

Four or five girls were already eating breakfast when they arrived at the boardinghouse, and several others were reaching for bowls of food as they seated themselves. Lilly had been at work for only two hours, yet it seemed an eternity. Dropping onto one of the dining room chairs, she sat idle as the ravenous girls around her continued their feeding frenzy. Josephine nudged her with an elbow. "Pass the potatoes," she sputtered, her mouth still filled with half-eaten food. She grabbed the potatoes from Lilly's hand and swallowed. "You had better get some food on your plate, or you're going to go hungry."

Lilly nodded and put a mound of the potatoes on her dish when Josephine returned the bowl to her. It was the first time since her arrival that Lilly had been seated at the dining room table. It didn't feel proper, Miss Addie serving breakfast without any assistance, but the older woman appeared to be doing very well on her own. The meal was hearty and on time, which was no small task for someone who only a week ago had served her boarders bread that would sink a ship.

In spite of a throbbing headache and upset stomach, Lilly poured a dollop of cream on a small bowl of pumpkin mush and forced a spoonful into her mouth. She swallowed hard, forcing the protesting lump downward, then clutched her midsection as the orange glob settled heavily in her stomach. Had Miss Addie not been watching, Lilly would have avoided breakfast altogether. Instead, she added a portion of fried cod, a biscuit, and a small wedge of cheese to the potatoes already congealing in grease on her plate. What was she thinking? It would be impossible to force another bite into her mouth, yet she didn't want to offend Miss Addie. Using her fork, she pushed the food around her plate, occasionally feigning a bite or two. Busy with their own plates, the other boarders didn't seem to notice. Within fifteen minutes, the girls began scurrying away from the table, some of them grabbing a biscuit to eat as they rushed back to the mill. Hoping she would go undetected, Lilly cautiously scraped her remaining food back onto the large serving platters and issued a silent thank-you when no one seemed to notice.

"Breakfast was splendid," Lilly whispered to the older woman as she prepared to leave.

Addie blushed at the praise. "I know you haven't time to visit, but did everything go well this morning?"

Lilly nodded. "As well as could be expected in such a place. I'll tell you more this evening," she promised.

"Yes, of course. Hurry along. I'll see you at dinnertime. By then, you'll be an old hand at operating your machinery."

Lilly didn't respond. She tied her bonnet, walked out the door, and joined the group rushing off toward the mill—all seemingly happy they had this opportunity to support themselves. Lilly cringed at the thought of spending years inside the walls of the towering brick fortress. Already she longed to return to a life where she could walk outdoors whenever she pleased. Thankfully, she told herself, she would be here only long enough to carry out God's plan of retribution.

～ 11 ～

Matthew bounded up the steps to the Cheevers' front porch. He had left work an hour early, so his mother would undoubtedly be surprised at his arrival. The thought pleased him. After all, he had promised to come to dinner on Sunday, but that visit would be bound by duty rather than choice. Arriving unexpectedly at a time when the two of them could relax and enjoy their time together would be like old times, he decided.

Entering the front door, he called out, "Mother, where are you?"

"You needn't yell. I'm right here," Julia replied. She was seated in her tapestry-covered sewing rocker, her fingers deftly pushing and pulling a thread-laden needle in and out of a delicate piece of embroidery.

Matthew smiled, walked to where she sat, and kissed her cheek. "You don't act surprised to see me," he remarked, seating himself opposite her chair.

"You forget I have a clear view of the front street. I saw you coming long before you reached the door. I've even had several moments to contemplate why my son would be paying me an unexpected visit."

There was a lilt to her voice. She no doubt already suspected why he had come. He might succeed in fooling himself but never his mother. She continued her sewing while he settled into the chair, contemplating his reply. Should he come right out with it, or should he attempt to convince her there was no ulterior reason for his visit? Matthew settled into the chair, elongating his body as far as possible, then propped his feet on the matching footstool.

"Do sit up correctly, Matthew. You're going to crush your tailbone or pinch a nerve in your back sitting in that ungentlemanly position. You're just borrowing future medical problems when you don't use proper posture. Ask Dr. Barnard. He'll confirm the truth of what I'm telling you."

"I don't want to talk to Dr. Barnard about crushed tailbones or pinched nerves, Mother. I've come to hear all about your supper party," he said.

"Truly? That's a bit odd, since you generally tell me that all supper gatherings are dull and unimaginative." She gave him a wry grin before continuing. "Well, it goes without saying that the meal was delightful. I served the most delectable lobster bisque, and the mutton was beyond description—so tender it nearly melted in my mouth. And then there were baby peas with caramelized onions and parsleyed potatoes. Oh yes, and cherries jubilee, one of your favorite desserts. See what you missed? Positively a gastronomical delight, as your father would say," Julia gloated.

Matthew watched his mother's animated face as she delightedly recounted the details of each culinary offering. He remained patient as she explained the placement of her centerpiece and stemware, knowing she was baiting him to interrupt her once again. He would not. She would only prolong the agony by detailing each of the gowns worn by her female guests, or worse yet, the details of some latest piece of stitchery the women had discussed in the music room.

He pushed his chair back onto its rear legs and then quickly let it back down when his mother snapped her fingers. Obviously his mother was going to force him to ask questions. Perhaps if he told her about his trip to Boston, she would give him the information he truly sought. Might as well wade in and test the waters, he decided. "I had an interesting time in Boston. Mr. Boott and I met with the bishop and then had supper with some of Boott's relatives. His niece, Isabelle, joined us for supper. She's quite lovely. Boott seems to think she'd be a good match for me." He hesitated only a moment and then added, "I trust you enjoyed delightful conversation during supper?"

Too late he realized he had said more than his mother could tolerate. Mentioning Isabelle was a mistake. Julia's posture had turned rigid at the remark. She appeared ready to do battle as she placed her sewing in the basket beside her chair and turned to give him her full attention.

"So Kirk Boott has entered the matchmaking business? Well, you can give him a message from your mother. Tell him that when we find ourselves in need of a matchmaker's assistance, I will personally come calling."

"Now, Mother, don't get upset. He knows I'm not seeing anyone at the moment and made a casual suggestion. I'm certainly not obligated to call upon his niece in order to maintain my position with the Corporation."

She leveled a stare directly toward him. "Are you *absolutely* sure about that?"

"Preposterous! How could you even think such nonsense?"

Julia stood up and stared into the mirror above the mantel. Pulling a small decorative comb from her hair, she tugged at several strands before tucking the comb back into her coif. She turned and looked down at her son. "Matthew, you would be surprised at how cunning people can be. Don't deceive yourself. You would make a fine catch for Boott's niece—a nice addition to his family, and having you as a member of the family could do nothing but help his cause as he ascends upward in the Corporation. You could be the son he never had. I'm sure he wishes his daughter were old enough to marry; then he could truly take you on as a son. Don't you see what he'll do?"

"I'm sorry I mentioned the supper. And that's all it was, Mother—supper."

Julia's lips turned upward in a sardonic smile. "You think that's all it was?

Just remember that I've warned you. His niece will soon appear in Lowell, and you will be expected to be her escort. Mark my words."

"I was hoping for a pleasant afternoon of visiting, Mother. Would it be possible to change the subject? I'd wager the women were begging to know the secret ingredients for your cherries jubilee."

Julia picked up her embroidery and once again began to stitch. "The supper party was delightful, and lest you think you've succeeded in changing the subject without my realization, be aware that I know what you're doing."

Matthew responded with a hearty laugh. "Yes, Mother, I'm well aware that we'll not change topics unless you choose to do so." He took a deep breath before proceeding. "Did all of your guests attend?"

She graced him with a demure smile. "All except you. Why don't you ask what you really want to know, Matthew?"

He shook his head in resignation. "All right, Mother. Did Lilly attend?"

Julia nodded in satisfaction. "I knew that was why you came to visit. Yes, Lilly attended and she looked stunning. I dare say, that girl becomes more beautiful with each passing minute. She inherited both her mother's charm and her father's intelligence. You let a good thing slip away, Matthew. In my heart, however, I do believe you could win her back if you would set your mind to the task."

Matthew tugged at his collar as he rose from his chair. He didn't want to speak in haste. No need to intentionally become the target of his mother's ire. He would speak calmly, rationally. He cleared his throat and turned. "Please try to remember, Mother, that it was Lilly who terminated our relationship. As you may recall, I was planning to ask Mr. Armbruster for Lilly's hand when she became consumed with anger regarding the Boston Associates purchasing the farmland."

Julia waved her lace handkerchief in his direction. "Don't make excuses, Matthew."

"I'm not making excuses. I'm reminding you of what occurred. Lilly said she wouldn't consider continuing our relationship unless I promised to remain a farmer and disengage myself from the Boston Associates."

His mother shrugged her shoulders. "Did you even consider her wishes?"

Matthew stared at her in disbelief. His mother was talking utter nonsense, yet he dared not confront her with such a remark. "You realize we are discussing the choice I made for my life's work? Lilly wanted me to bend to her will. Think about what a precedent that would have set for our married life. I didn't want to begin married life having my wife dictate my professional choices. Think how Father would have rebuffed such an idea when you two were contemplating marriage. What if you had told him you wouldn't marry him unless he gave up farming and became a banker? I think he would have reconsidered marriage. Even God's word substantiates my position—a wife is to be subject to her husband."

"Don't begin quoting the Bible to me, Matthew, for it also says a man will love his wife above himself. Lilly is a fine girl. Your Mr. Boott will find none that will even begin to compare. You can't imagine the sorrow I felt for that child, knowing she's lost every member of her family, and now she's relegated to working in the mills."

"She's working at the mills?" he asked without thinking.

His mother gave a self-satisfied smile. "Yes. Poor child. There was nothing left to do."

Matthew tried to compose himself. He didn't want the matter to get out of hand any more than it already had. "You exaggerate, Mother. Lilly has not lost every member of her family. Lewis is still alive, and if she's working in the mills . . . well, it's because she chose to work in the mills. I didn't force her to take a position in the mills. And please don't forget the fact that there are girls who come from all over the countryside, anxious for such an opportunity."

"Don't even mention Lewis Armbruster in the same breath with his sister. Lewis was a mean child, and he's grown into a despicable man. I'm told he left Lilly penniless, gambling away all of the family's money. It would have been better for Lilly had she been left without Lewis. He's served only to make her life more miserable. As for working in the mills, we both know how distasteful that must be for Lilly."

"I agree Lewis is a poor excuse for a brother. He is, however, a living member of Lilly's family. And although Lilly may find working in the mills distasteful, it was apparently her choice to seek employment with the Associates. I might also remind you that Lilly is no stranger to physical labor. She grew up working on the family farm, which is certainly more taxing than operating machinery in the mills."

His mother was looking past him, staring out the front window toward the dusk-filled skies, a smile beginning to form upon her lips. He would say nothing further. Obviously he had made his point.

"I believe your father is home," Julia remarked, the front door opening as she spoke.

"Look who I've brought home for supper, Julia," Randolph called out from the entryway. His broad smile faded, however, as he walked into the room with Lilly. "Son, I didn't realize you would be . . ." His voice faltered as he looked toward Julia, obviously hoping she would rescue him.

Julia rushed toward Lilly, pulling her into a warm embrace. "What a delightful surprise—two of my favorite people for supper. Let me take your cape, dear."

Matthew watched in awe as his mother released Lilly, unfastened her cape, and removed it from the girl's shoulders before there was time for any objection. It was difficult to ascertain whether Lilly was angry or merely perplexed to find herself in his presence. He watched the color rise in her cheeks as she reached for her cape.

"I told Mr. Cheever I should go back to the boardinghouse, but he insisted. I really must be leaving," Lilly said.

"Nonsense. Of course you'll stay. Supper will be ready in no time at all. Let me go see how things are progressing," Julia stated while moving toward the kitchen. "Randolph, you bar the door if she attempts to escape."

Matthew stood transfixed. His mother was right. Lilly appeared to grow more beautiful each time he set eyes upon her. He struggled for a moment to gain his voice. "Don't leave on my account, Lilly. I'll go," Matthew croaked, his voice suddenly foreign to his ears.

Julia whirled about. "Nobody is going anywhere. We are going to have supper—all of us—together, like the civilized people we are. Now sit down and visit while I see about the preparations," she commanded.

Julia marched out of the room as they seated themselves. Lilly folded her hands and stared at the floor; Matthew leaned back and cupped his folded hands around his knee. Randolph pulled his pipe from his pocket, tapping it gently in his hand. Silence reigned.

"How was your trip to Boston, Matthew?" Randolph finally asked.

"It went very well. Thank you for asking, Father. How was your day, Lilly?" Matthew ventured.

"Hot and tiresome," she replied without looking up.

"Hot? I've been in Lowell all day and the weather has been beautiful. Where have you been that you consider it so hot?"

"In the Appleton Mill, where the windows are nailed down. Unlike you, I didn't have the opportunity to walk about town enjoying the beauty of the day. You should pay a visit to one of the weaving or spinning rooms. Perhaps then you would understand my reply," Lilly stated, her gaze now riveted in his direction.

"Supper is ready," Julia announced, a bright smile on her face as she came back into the room. "I can't begin to tell you what a joy it is to have servants preparing meals, Lilly. It is such a change for me. Come along now and tell me what you three have been discussing."

As the evening wore on, it seemed that Matthew irritated Lilly at every turn. It wasn't his intent. In fact, he had valiantly endeavored to find neutral topics of discussion throughout supper. However, with each attempt, the conversation returned to the mills and Lilly's discontent. To his amazement, Julia appeared to navigate the conversation toward Lilly's circumstances at every opportunity.

"Matthew!"

Julia's voice brought him back to the present. "Yes?"

"Lilly must return to the boardinghouse. I've insisted you escort her. Of course, she objected, but I told her I would brook no argument—from either of you. Hurry. She's in the hallway with your father," Julia insisted in a hoarse whisper.

He met his mother's steely stare. There was no use arguing, for it would only result in additional embarrassment for all of them. "Ready?" he inquired, nearing the front hallway.

Lilly nodded in his direction. It appeared, however, that Julia was intent on prolonging the farewell. Matthew waited patiently as Julia hugged Lilly several times while attempting to elicit the girl's promise to return soon. He noted Lilly's careful choice of words as she sidestepped the issue and made her way down the front steps.

"Mother hasn't lost her knack for manipulating people's lives," Matthew remarked as they walked down the street.

"So it would seem. I am truly amazed by her transition from farm wife to fashionable hostess. Her party last Saturday evening was exquisite."

"No doubt. You probably were never told that my mother's family was both influential and wealthy. She grew up accustomed to elegant parties and expensive belongings. Her parents were aghast when she married my father. Needless to say, her life changed dramatically. The transition to farm wife was much more difficult than what she has experienced returning to a life of advantage."

"I would have never suspected, but it certainly explains her ability to entertain in fine fashion. I must admit that I'm surprised. I always thought your mother was content as the wife of a farmer."

"She was very content with her life on the farm. However, she was delighted to return to a more leisurely lifestyle. Given the opportunity, I believe most women would do the same."

Lilly stopped and looked up at him. "But not all. There are still women who prefer farm life."

"Yes, Lilly, I am well aware of your opinion," Matthew replied as he took her elbow and began to lead her across the street.

She tugged her arm from his grasp. "I can find my way back to the board-inghouse, Matthew. We're out of your mother's vantage point, and I promise she'll never hear from my lips that you didn't escort me all the way home."

"I'm afraid you'll have to put up with me a while longer, Lilly. There's no way I dare leave you. My mother will subject me to a multitude of questions at her first opportunity. Moreover, I would suffer her wrath should she discover I left your side before reaching the door of the boardinghouse."

"You can tell her—"

Matthew placed his finger on her lips. "Please don't encourage me to tell her a lie. It's impossible. From the time I was a little boy, she always knew when I was lying."

Lilly backed away. Matthew couldn't quite figure her mood, but she seemed almost fearful of him. "You're an adult now, Matthew. You've become an expert at deceit. I'm sure that once you set your mind to the task, your mother won't suspect a thing. And, as I said, I certainly wouldn't tell her that we parted company before reaching the boardinghouse."

Her words stung. While he considered himself truthful and straight-forward, she thought him cunning and deceitful. He had never lied to her, never hidden his desire to succeed in the business world. Surely she didn't think he should hold to a childish promise to farm the rest of his life. Those words had been spoken long before he entered college and realized the scope of what the world had to offer. He had explained all of this to her, but she had closed her ears, unwilling to plan a future unless it was solely on her terms. "I didn't realize your hatred ran so deep," he finally replied.

She didn't respond, so they continued onward, an uncomfortable silence threatening to smother them, until they finally arrived outside number 5 Jackson Street.

"Hello, Lilly," Josephine Regan greeted as she and Jenny Dunn approached from the opposite direction.

Lilly nodded her head. "Hello."

The two girls waited. "Aren't you going to introduce us to your *friend*?" Jenny finally asked.

Lilly's teeth were clenched together, her jaw forming a hard line. "He is *not* my friend; he is Matthew Cheever. Matthew, these are two more of your employees, Josephine Regan and Jenny Dunn. Good night, ladies. Good night, Mr. Cheever."

Matthew watched as she turned, walked inside, and left him staring after her. *"He is not my friend,"* she had said emphatically. The words rang true, and the emptiness left in their wake devastated Matthew's sense of well-being.

"Where have you been, Lilly? Nadene wouldn't tell us anything except that you'd been invited to supper," Marmi squealed as Lilly walked in the bedroom door.

"Shhh. You'll waken the others," Lilly cautioned.

Marmi and Prudence sat up in bed, their attention focused on Lilly. "Tell us, then, or we'll continue to get louder until you do," Prudence warned.

"You have no shame, either of you! I have nothing exciting to report. I had supper at the Cheever household and came home."

The girls' disappointment was evident, but they quickly recovered. "We spent most of the evening deciding on dresses for the Lighting Up Ball. I think we're going to trade dresses this year. Pru is going to put new lace on my dress, and I'm going to refashion hers just a bit. We're hoping no one will realize. Do you have something special you plan to wear?"

The color had heightened in both girls' cheeks. Just talking about the dance had obviously given them great pleasure. Lilly wasn't sure how they could become excited over something as trivial as a dance, but she would never tell them her true feelings. "I don't plan to go," she replied simply.

Their gasps echoed through the room. "Not going? But you must. We all go—it's . . . well, it's expected. The ball is one of the nice things that the Corporation does for us," Marmi explained while Prudence bobbed her head up and down in affirmation.

"If it's one of the *nice* things the Associates do for us, surely they won't mind if I don't take advantage of their kindness. I think what they want are hours of drudgery in the mills, not the opportunity to hold us on the dance floor."

The two girls giggled. "That's true for most of the men, but there are a few who find it enjoyable to pull a girl or two close," Prudence replied. Once again the girls began their chortling.

Lilly glared at them. "You find that kind of repugnant behavior humorous?"

Immediately the girls sobered, Marmi appearing on the verge of tears. "Several of the girls have managed to find husbands at the mills," Marmi whimpered. "Is it wrong to giggle about that? We all want to find a husband. The Lighting Up Ball is a good opportunity to meet some of the men."

Lilly silently chided herself. Prudence and Marmi didn't know about Thaddeus Arnold and his disgusting activities; they were merely excited about having an evening of fun squeezed into their monotonous existence. She was spoiling the small ray of sunshine in their lives. "You're right, Marmi—the ball is an excellent place to meet some of the men. Please accept my apology. I'm tired and didn't think before speaking."

Immediately Marmi's mood lightened and she bounced across the bed. "That's all right, Lilly. Do you have a special dress you can wear?"

There was a soft knock. Prudence climbed across the bed and stood whispering through the door, "Who is it?"

Instead of a reply, Josephine and Jenny pushed open the door. Josephine folded her arms and plopped down on the bed opposite Lilly. "Just *who* are you, and how is it you know the likes of Matthew Cheever?" she demanded.

Lilly was silent. How could she answer Josephine's questions? Matthew Cheever was from another time and place. A time and place that no longer existed, that had slipped away and would never return.

12

Restlessness plagued Lilly's sleep. Images of her father and Lewis arguing were mingled with a woman's screams. Lewis was counting coins at a table in front of the fire while her father mumbled indecipherable words.

The scream again. Lilly's eyelids fluttered and then closed. Lewis was riding off at full gallop on a chestnut mare.

Another scream.

Lilly bolted upright in her bed. A loud crash followed by a piercing cry and a man's muffled voice filled what should have been a silent night. She looked about the darkened room, her heart pounding. The other girls slept soundly; even Nadene's cough was silent tonight. Something crashed against the wall, followed by a heavy thud.

"Please don't," a woman begged, her voice shrill.

Lilly grasped Nadene's arm. "Wake up, Nadene," she whispered. "Please wake up!"

"I didn't hear the bell," Nadene muttered.

Lilly leaned close to Nadene's ear. "The bell hasn't sounded yet. There's something going on next door. Listen!" The man's voice grew louder. A dull thud reverberated, then sobbing followed a woman's shriek. "Did you hear that?"

Nadene nodded. "These row house walls are not very thick. I hear it almost every night."

"You do? Why haven't you mentioned it?"

Nadene wriggled upward in the bed, leaning her back against the headboard. Lilly sat beside her, both of them staring toward the wall separating them from the sickening sounds.

"I decided there was nothing we could do. Losing sleep isn't going to benefit Mrs. Arnold, and it certainly isn't going to do us any good, either."

Lilly's mind reeled at Nadene's words. She turned in the darkness and looked toward Nadene. She could barely make out her friend's features. "Mrs. Arnold? Mrs. *Thaddeus* Arnold? Is that who lives there?"

"The Arnolds moved in last week after he became supervisor of the spinning room. That's when the noises began. We never had any of these disturbances when Mr. Hester and his family lived next door in the supervisor's quarters."

"Do you think Thaddeus Arnold is beating his wife?"

"Think about it, Lilly. Who else could it be?"

Lilly heard the words, but her mind raced, thinking of the times she'd seen Mrs. Arnold outdoors. On those occasions when Lilly had walked nearby, Mrs. Arnold had turned her back or rushed indoors. Surprised by the older woman's reactions, Lilly had decided Mr. Arnold didn't want his wife associating with the hired girls. Now Lilly feared that Mrs. Arnold had become reclusive in order to hide her bruises. An involuntary shiver coursed through her body. How could that poor woman endure living with Thaddeus Arnold? she wondered.

"We must do something, Nadene. I can't bear to sit here and listen to her suffer."

"What do you suggest?"

Lilly remained silent for several minutes, just long enough for the noises to resume. "I'm going to knock on the wall so he knows we can hear them," she finally replied. "If Mr. Arnold knows someone can hear them and that we know what he's doing, surely he will stop."

"I don't know if that's wise. Sometimes it's best to stay out of other people's business."

"Wouldn't you want someone to help *you*, Nadene?"

Nadene began coughing raspy, croaking sounds from deep in her chest. Finally able to get her breath, Nadene wiped her nose and once again leaned back. "Of course I would. But Mr. Arnold's our supervisor. If we get into the midst of his family problems, it could lead to more trouble than you or I could ever imagine."

At that moment Mrs. Arnold's voice pealed out in a desperate cry for help. Lilly bounded off the bed, grabbed her heavy work shoe, and began pounding on the wall. Again and again she beat against the wall, all the while praying that her feeble effort would somehow rescue poor Mrs. Arnold. Her hand and arm ached when finally she ceased her efforts. She dropped the shoe and turned back toward the bed. All was silent. Prudence and Marmi were huddled beside Nadene, where a candle now flickered on the bedside table. Katie, Sarah, Beth, and Franny had all joined together on one bed. Their faces were etched with apprehension and fear.

Prudence finally broke the silence that hung in the room. "Have you gone mad?"

"I don't think so," Lilly replied with a nervous giggle. "I think Mr. Arnold may have gotten the message."

"What message?" Marmi's wide-eyed innocence reminded Lilly of a small child.

"That we can hear through the walls, Marmi. That we know he's beating his wife. I'm hoping Mr. Arnold realizes that if he doesn't stop his ugly behavior, there will be repercussions."

Prudence folded her arms across her chest and shook her head. "You may find that the repercussions are directed at us rather than Mr. Arnold. That man could cause more problems than any of us can conceive."

"If Mr. Arnold takes steps to persecute any of you, I'll take the blame. What occurred is my doing. I'll absolve you of any involvement," Lilly promised.

Katie motioned to Sarah. "Come on, we need to get to sleep." Sarah slipped into bed first since she slept against the wall. Katie joined her while Beth and Franny went to their own bed.

Prudence squirmed between the beds and plopped down beside Lilly. "It's not that we disagree with you, Lilly. But we all need our jobs. He has the power to make things happen. We don't."

Lilly nodded. "We may have more power than you think, Prudence. Either way, I can't ignore his behavior. He's a vile man who apparently has no respect for women, even his own wife. But for now I believe we had better try to get some sleep. I've kept everyone awake long enough," Lilly said as she snuffed the candle and settled back into bed.

"What you did was a good thing," Marmi whispered into the darkness.

"Thanks," Lilly replied. She closed her eyes and tried to pray. Instead she found herself questioning God, wondering why such horrible things happen to people. Why, she wondered, didn't God make life any easier?

The events of her own life flooded her thoughts. God had allowed her to suffer at the hands of her brother. God had taken her parents just when she needed them most. It all seemed so unfair. *I tried to live as a good Christian girl,* Lilly reasoned. *Did I do something so very wrong that God had to punish me?* She pushed the thought aside. God was good and loving, just and fair. She had to believe that.

But if God was good and fair, then why had she come to this place in her life?

You have a mission, she reminded herself. *God was even harsh with Jonah when he avoided the job God had given him to do. When I complete my mission, God will smooth the way for me. He will be pleased with me then and make things right again.*

Perhaps she had become privy to Thaddeus Arnold's behavior in order for God to reinforce the need for retribution against the Boston Associates. Tonight's incident was one more reason that she must remain strong in her determination to mete out justice against the greedy men and their selfish motivations. Once again sleep came, this time filling her mind with dreams of an idyllic countryside filled with bountiful fruit trees and sheep drinking from streams of crystal clear water.

Thaddeus Arnold's icy stare had remained fixed upon Lilly for several days. At first she hoped it was merely her imagination. But when he slithered off his chair and began walking near her machines several times each day, she realized he was playing a game, stalking his quarry as he watched and waited. His beady eyes appeared to dance with pleasure when he noted her discomfort.

Lilly could only assume Mr. Arnold was hoping to find fault with her work as he strutted back and forth checking her bobbins. He would draw close, his breath hot on her neck as he stood behind her, and then silently he would retreat. That is, until yesterday when he approached from behind, leaned in, and allowed his body to come up against her while he pretended to examine her roving, telling her he expected her to be present at the Lighting Up Ball.

She had remained silent, giving no indication of the repulsion that raged within her. The incident, however, was catalogued among Lilly's memories, now added to her mounting list of grievances against the Associates. By week's end, Thaddeus had apparently grown bored of the game and was once again settled on his perch, a vulture carefully eyeing his prey.

Lilly knew deep thankfulness when Saturday finally arrived. As she and Nadene left the mill yard at the end of another long day, she took satisfaction in knowing she need not face Thaddeus Arnold the next day. "He knows it was me," Lilly said, locking arms with Nadene as they walked down the street.

"No he doesn't. There is no way he can know for sure. He can't see through the walls. He doesn't even know where you sleep—only that you board with Miss Addie."

Lilly stopped in her tracks and pulled Nadene to a halt. "Haven't you been watching him this week? The way he's been coming around me? And those evil beady eyes, always watching me. He knows. One day he'll say something. I'm sure of it."

Nadene giggled. "I'm sorry, but you sound so dramatic. You need to put this whole thing out of your mind."

Anger welled up inside Lilly. "You would think it was serious, too, if he constantly watched you." She hesitated a moment. "Yesterday he leaned up against me. Do you think I should overlook that, also?"

Nadene's mouth dropped open, and her eyes widened in astonishment.

"I don't know why you would be surprised by his actions; he's always handling other girls. He said I'd best be in attendance at the Lighting Up Ball. I'm sure he will find some way to humiliate me if I do attend the ball. If I don't make an appearance, I'm certain he'll find a reason to have me terminated."

Nadene looped her arm back through Lilly's as they began walking once again. "I'm so sorry. I shouldn't have laughed at you. I didn't think Mr. Arnold would take things so far. Why don't you talk to Matthew Cheever and see if you can be transferred to the Merrimack? Surely he would help you."

"Ask Matthew to bestow a favor upon me? I think not." Lilly cringed inwardly at the thought. She'd told Nadene a little about her past with Matthew. Nadene thought there should be a reconciliation between them, and no doubt she thought this would be a good way to rekindle their communication.

"You can ill afford to become filled with pride right now," Nadene cautioned. "If Mr. Arnold has become bold enough to—"

Lilly stood squarely in front of Nadene, blocking her entry into the boardinghouse. "I don't want anyone else to know about what's happened at the mill. Promise you won't tell."

"I promise, but I think you're making a big mistake," Nadene replied. "Why not talk to Miss Addie at least? She would keep your confidence, and perhaps she'd have some ideas."

Lilly shook her head as they entered the house. "No, I don't want her to think I'm depending on her to resolve the problem with Mr. Arnold, because I'm not. Besides, she'd worry herself sick."

"Well, who are you relying on?" Nadene whispered.

Lilly placed her bonnet and cape on one of the hooks beside the front door. "God, Nadene. I'm relying on God."

13

Making her way down the steps and into the kitchen, Lilly smiled at Miss Addie, who was carefully assembling a plate of cookies.

"I thought it might be a nice gesture if I took some cookies to Mintie when we join her for tea," Addie remarked. "Did you enjoy the church services this morning?"

"The church services were fine," Lilly replied without much enthusiasm. "Taking cookies is a lovely idea, Miss Addie. I'm sure your sister will beg for the recipe once she's tasted them."

Addie beamed at the praise. "I know you'd prefer to spend your afternoon visiting with the girls or going for a walk. You're always so kind and generous."

Lilly blushed. If only Miss Addie knew her private thoughts regarding Thaddeus Arnold and the Boston Associates, she'd not think her either kind or generous. "Taking tea with Miss Mintie won't consume my whole afternoon. Besides, there will be ample time for a walk or other frivolity later in the day. Let me carry the plate," Lilly offered.

Mintie greeted them at the door, her smile fading somewhat as she glanced toward the plate of cookies. "Did you think I wouldn't provide you with a proper tea?"

Before Addie had an opportunity to reply, Lilly thrust the plate forward. "Addie was certain you would prepare a sumptuous tea tray, but I insisted we bring the cookies. My mother taught me it was good manners to take a small hostess gift when visiting friends and relatives. Since you are both a friend *and* relative . . ."

Taking the extended plate, Mintie led them into the parlor. "Oh, tut, tut, we don't need to make an issue over a few cookies. I'm sure they'll make a nice addition to our tea," Mintie conceded, gracing Lilly with a tentative smile. She directed them toward the settee before fluttering into the kitchen.

"Thank you, Lilly, but you shouldn't have told a falsehood," Addie whispered. She hesitated a moment. "Of course, I should have corrected your falsehood, so I'm as guilty as you. I believe we're both in need of forgiveness—and over something as simple as a plate of cookies!"

"I didn't tell a total falsehood. My mother *did* teach me that it was proper etiquette to take a gift when visiting," Lilly whispered with a smile.

Mintie returned with the teapot and cups. Lucy, the little ten-year-old doffer who assisted as Miss Mintie's part-time servant, followed close behind carrying a tray laden with tiny sandwiches and delicacies. Lucy placed the tray on a small serving cart, then backed against the wall, although she continued to stare at the food with ravenous eyes.

"All of the men except for that Englishman have gone out for the afternoon," Mintie commented in a hushed tone while pouring hot tea into three cups. She handed each of them a small china plate. "Try these sandwiches, Adelaide," Mintie instructed her sister. "Go on. Get out of here, Lucy," she continued, waving at the child as though she were shooing away an insect.

"I believe this would be an excellent opportunity to teach Lucy how to conduct herself among genteel women. My mother insisted it was best to learn proper etiquette at an early age," Lilly put in.

Mintie stared at Lilly, mouth agape. "I don't think a serving girl need know how to conduct herself at tea. What earthly purpose would be served? Lucy is certainly never going to marry into proper society."

"If she knows how tea is to be conducted, it will teach her how to properly serve at those times when you wish to merely enjoy your guests," Lilly countered. "Come here, Lucy. We'd like you to join us for tea. That way you can better serve Miss Beecher's guests in the future." Lilly patted the empty cushion beside her.

The child looked back and forth between the two women and then quickly darted to where Lilly was sitting. The temptation of the food had won out, as Lilly knew it would. "You must pay heed to Miss Beecher's training as you take tea," Lilly instructed, looking toward Mintie for affirmation.

Mintie's spectacles slipped down the bridge of her nose as her head dipped up and down in agreement. "Take a plate and watch," Mintie said to the child.

Once they had filled their plates, Mintie began pouring Lucy's tea into a matching china cup. She turned toward the child, her eyes steely pinpoints. "Conversation at a tea is not to be repeated. That is your second lesson. Do you understand?"

The child's head bobbed up and down in agreement. "Yes, ma'am. I won't hear a thing you ladies say."

Mintie gave an affirming nod before directing her attention back toward Addie and Lilly. She leaned forward with her long nose almost dipping into the teacup that was resting in her hand. "I'm growing more concerned by the minute," she confided in a hoarse whisper. "That Farnsworth fellow has received several letters from Lancashire, and there have been strange men at the front door on three different occasions. I have no doubt he is a spy determined to assist in the downfall of this country."

Lilly stifled a giggle. "I think you're being a bit dramatic, Miss Beecher. I'm sure Mr. Farnsworth is merely becoming acquainted with some of his fellow Englishmen. His visitors are probably men who work at the mills and live on the English Row."

Mintie straightened her shoulders and pursed her lips into a circle. "I suppose that is why they speak in hushed tones and grow silent when I approach?"

"Perhaps they merely want their privacy," Addie suggested.

"I can see you two are cut from the same cloth, neither one of you willing to open your eyes to the—"

"Good afternoon, ladies."

They all looked toward the doorway at the sound of a man's voice. "We're taking tea, Mr. Farnsworth," Mintie declared.

He walked into the room and stood near the settee. "I can see that, Miss Mintie."

Mintie's lips tightened into a straight line. She curled the corner of her linen napkin and then watched as it rolled back into place. Finally she cleared her throat and looked up at the man. "John Farnsworth, one of my boarders," she said, looking toward Addie and Lilly. "Mr. Farnsworth, this is my sister, Miss Adelaide Beecher, and one of her boarders, Miss Lilly Armbruster."

He bowed his head and extended his hand. "It is a pleasure to make your acquaintance, Miss Beecher and Miss Armbruster."

The color heightened in Addie's cheeks. "Would you care to join us, Mr. Farnsworth?" She appeared besotted with the tall stranger. Mintie, however, was momentarily speechless, obviously shocked at her sister's behavior.

Mr. Farnsworth folded his large frame into the chair beside Addie. "I would be delighted," he replied.

Mintie leveled an icy glare at her sister before turning toward Mr. Farnsworth. "You need not feel obligated to accept my sister's invitation, Mr. Farnsworth. I'm sure you have more important things to do this afternoon."

He picked up a teacup and extended it toward Mintie. "Not at all. Tea on a Sunday afternoon is more than I had hoped for."

"More than I had hoped for, also," Mintie mumbled under her breath. She poured his tea and sent Lucy scampering off to the kitchen to set another kettle of water to boil. The child returned to the parlor as a knock sounded at the front door. "See to the door, Lucy. Most likely it's one of Mr. Farnsworth's acquaintances."

Lucy nodded her head and rushed from the room, returning moments later with Matthew Cheever in tow. "Mr. Cheever said he came to call on Mr. Farnsworth. I told him Mr. Farnsworth was taking tea with us, so he could come have tea with us, too," the child proudly announced.

Mintie expelled an extended breath from between pursed lips and crooked her finger. Lucy moved directly in front of her mistress. "Lucy, for some reason I believed that *I* was the hostess of this gathering."

Lucy looked down at the floor, her thick brown hair falling forward and covering her oval face. "You are, ma'am. I'm sorry," she muttered.

Addie strained forward and touched Lucy's arm. "Well, I, for one, am very proud of your behavior, Lucy. You exhibited excellent manners by inviting Mr. Cheever to join us for tea. One must never make a guest feel unwelcome. Isn't that correct, Mintie?" Without waiting for a reply, Addie shifted her gaze toward Matthew. "You have the rare opportunity of joining us for Lucy's etiquette lesson, Mr. Cheever. Do sit down."

Lilly was pleased Addie had rescued the child from Mintie's clutches. However, she wished Addie had stopped short before inviting Matthew to take a seat. There was no way to gracefully escape the group, which was increasing by the minute. Mr. Farnsworth and Addie were now in a discussion. Mintie was busy instructing Lucy how to properly pour Matthew's tea, and Lilly was fidgeting with the pleats of her skirt.

"Lovely day," Matthew ventured.

"Yes, but I must soon return to the boardinghouse. I have several matters that need my attention this afternoon. I must say it was quite a surprise to see you enter the room. Do you often visit your employees at their boardinghouses?" Lilly inquired.

"Not often, but I consider John a friend as well as an employee. I stopped by to offer him an invitation to dinner next Sunday. I've expressed such admiration for John that my parents are both anxious to meet him, Father in particular."

Lilly finished her tea and handed the empty cup to Lucy, whose cheeks now resembled those of a squirrel preparing to store food for the winter. "You like the cookies?" Lilly asked with a warm smile.

"Yes, ma'am," the child mumbled, a few crumbs slipping through her lips.

"I do, too. Which are your favorites?" Lilly inquired.

Mintie watched as Lucy pointed to the cherry-flavored shortbread cookies. "It's impolite to point or to talk with your mouth full," Mintie corrected in a stern tone.

"I don't believe she offended any of us," Lilly commented. "She liked your cookies, Miss Addie. You'll have to give your sister your recipe. I'm sure she'll want to make some soon."

"Those were my favorite, also," John Farnsworth commented. "In fact, I think I'll have another."

"You have as many as you'd like. In fact, I'll leave the plate, and you can have some this evening," Addie replied.

"Only if he promises to share them with Lucy and me," Matthew chimed in, helping himself to another of the buttery cookies. He turned toward Lilly and in a hoarse whisper added, "Unless you'd like to bake a special batch just for me some day soon."

"I don't think so," Lilly whispered in return. Her heart skipped a beat as she met Matthew's gaze.

"You used to like to bake me cookies."

Lucy tugged on Lilly's arm and smiled. "Miss Beecher says it's rude to whisper."

"And she's absolutely correct," Lilly replied. "I really must return to the boardinghouse." The two men jumped to their feet as she stood up. "Thank you for the invitation. It's been most enjoyable, Miss Beecher. Miss Addie, you need not rush home on my account. Please stay and enjoy yourself."

"Why don't Matthew and I escort you ladies home?" John offered.

The flutter of activity appeared more than Mintie could bear. Lilly wasn't sure if Mintie was angry they were leaving or relieved that she would be absolved of continuing Lucy's etiquette training. Either way, she was obviously unhappy.

"Grand idea," Matthew agreed. "I could use a bit of fresh air."

"They live only across the street," Lucy offered. "Maybe you should take a walk into town or out toward the falls if you want fresh air."

Matthew laughed and then leaned down to whisper into Lucy's ear. He stood up and glanced at the other guests. "I know whispering is rude, but I wanted to share a secret with Lucy. Please forgive my impolite behavior."

Lilly gave every plausible excuse in the hope of escaping by herself. She was, however, unsuccessful. By the time she reached the front door, Matthew was clinging to her elbow while John and Addie were deep in conversation, oblivious to everyone except each other. Lucy was behind her, tugging at her other arm.

There was an urgency in the child's appearance. "Miss Lilly, could I talk to you for a moment?"

Lilly separated herself from Mintie and the other guests. "What is it, Lucy? Is something wrong?"

"First, I want to thank you for helping me today. The tea was such fun, even if Miss Beecher will scold me once you've all gone home." She rocked from foot to foot momentarily and with widened eyes looked up toward Lilly. "I know I shouldn't ask, but Mr. Cheever said that if I could convince you to take a walk with him, he would pay me a week's wages. That would be most helpful to my family. We're very poor." Her voice was warbling, and tears threatened to spill over at any moment as she ended her plea.

Lilly stooped down and embraced the child. "You go collect your coins, Lucy. I'll take a walk with Mr. Cheever." Lucy's face immediately transformed. Her wide smile caused her sunken cheeks to become walnut-sized puffs. "Thank you, Miss Lilly, thank you!" the child called over her shoulder as she rushed toward Matthew.

Lilly remained several steps away, observing the exchange between

Matthew and Lucy while feeling angry that he had involved the child in such a scheme. How had a simple afternoon tea turned into this farce?

Matthew approached looking quite pleased. Lilly couldn't help but remember back to a time when the very sight of him had set her heart to racing. Of course, it wasn't exactly beating a funeral dirge at the moment.

"That was hardly called for," Lilly said as he took hold of her arm.

"Would you have walked with me otherwise? Answer honestly."

Lilly looked away, afraid of the way he made her feel. "No, I don't suppose I would have."

"Then it was completely called for," he whispered against her ear.

~ 14 ~

The walk with Matthew wasn't nearly as unbearable as Lilly believed it would be. Addie and John Farnsworth decided to accompany them, and with the two of them carrying on a lively conversation, Lilly and Matthew scarcely had to speak two words.

Still, she was greatly relieved when they turned back toward the boarding-house. Lilly had a long list of reasons already formulated as to why she couldn't linger once they arrived. Seeing Addie was about to invite the men inside, Lilly opened her mouth to excuse herself.

"Well, look who's here," Matthew said before she could speak.

Lilly couldn't believe her eyes. She had finally arrived home, prepared to escape Matthew's company, when Julia and Randolph Cheever pulled their carriage to a halt in front of the boardinghouse.

"What a pleasant surprise!" Julia exclaimed. She was leaning across Randolph's legs, her head poking out of the carriage. "We were going to stop and invite you to join us for a picnic in Belvedere, Lilly. This is going to be especially nice. You can *both* join us. Come along, children; get in the carriage," she ordered.

Lilly stepped back, tugging free of Matthew's grasp on her arm. "I really cannot accept your invitation. I have laundry to complete this afternoon."

Julia gasped. "Have you forgotten it's Sunday, Lilly? Your poor mother would be appalled at the thought of her daughter doing laundry on the Lord's Day."

"Since I work long hours all week, Mrs. Cheever, I have little choice," Lilly replied.

"Nonsense, child. I'll see to that little dab of laundry tomorrow," Addie offered as she and John drew closer to the carriage. "You go and have fun this afternoon."

Matthew grinned and folded his arms. "Now what will you do?" he questioned under his breath.

Lilly wanted to scream at him. Even more, she wanted to wipe the smug grin off his face. But with everyone's attention focused in her direction, she could do neither. "I haven't been home all day, Mrs. Cheever. With church services this morning, tea this afternoon, and a short walk with these gentlemen," she extended her arm in a sweeping gesture, "I truly must beg to be excused."

"I absolutely will not hear of it," Julia insisted. "You're too young to hole up in your room on such a beautiful fall day. Besides, you must eat. You get settled in the carriage this minute, young lady. I'll not take any excuses."

"May I assist you?" Matthew inquired, his grin growing wider.

Lilly ignored his offer. She climbed into the carriage and positioned herself as far into one corner of the seat as possible. Matthew settled in beside her, taking full advantage of the available space.

The carriage had begun on the road out of town when Julia turned and looked over her shoulder. "You look uncomfortable, Lilly. Move over and give her some room, Matthew."

"By all means, do move over, Lilly," Matthew whispered, amusement dancing in his eyes. Before she could protest, Matthew placed his arm around her shoulder and physically pulled her closer. "There. Isn't that better?"

She glanced down at his leg. His knee was leaning heavily against her own. Lilly gave his leg a hefty nudge and forced a smile upon her lips. Matthew's face registered surprise at her action. Good! He need not think she would idly sit by and permit him to make a mockery of her or their previous relationship. For the remainder of the ride, her hands were folded in her lap, her spine rigid and aching by the time they arrived in Belvedere.

"I wanted to surprise you," Julia began as she began to unpack the picnic supper.

"I don't know if I can manage another surprise," Lilly replied. There was more truth than humor in the statement, but obviously Julia found it a charming reply as she giggled at Lilly's remark. "You've always had a way with words, Lilly. It's part of your allure. Isn't it, Matthew?"

Matthew glanced toward his mother, then at Lilly. "That's true, Mother," he said with his brow wrinkled in thought. "However, Lilly has other *strengths* that would amaze you. Why, just today in the carriage, the strength of her "

"What was your surprise, Mrs. Cheever?" Lilly interrupted. "You never told me."

"What? Oh, yes, the surprise. In just a little over an hour," she said while looking at the timepiece pinned to her bodice, "there will be a magic show. A talented magician from Europe is touring the country, and he's performing here. That's why we came to Belvedere for our picnic. We were told the young magician is quite talented. It's said he can pull a coin from your ear—imagine that!"

"Amazing!" Matthew replied in mock surprise. "Actually, truth be told, I was supposed to join Kirk Boott and his family for this very show. Anyway, I'm starving, Mother. Would you like some assistance with the food?"

"Lilly will help me. You men go take a walk. By the time you return, we should be ready."

She shooed the men away and began unpacking embroidered linen napkins, plates, and silverware, along with fried chicken, biscuits, and homemade preserves. Lilly grouped the items together as Julia instructed, the two of them completing the task in quick order.

"You see? Things go much more smoothly when the men aren't here to interrupt," Julia remarked. "Now we have time to relax and visit until they return. You've been on my mind since you visited us last week, Lilly. I know you can't be planning to spend the rest of your life working in the mills. Have you had time to make some solid plans for your future, child?"

Lilly hesitated. "You're right about the mills. I don't plan to work there my entire life, but it's difficult to judge how long I'll need to remain. I buried my dreams the day I buried my father. My future had always included living on our farm in East Chelmsford, being a wife, raising children, and working alongside . . ."

"Matthew," Julia said, completing the sentence. "I can understand that you long to have things as they were, Lilly. I know that it is more comfortable when things remain constant. You must remember, however, that if we don't embrace new adventures in life, we are left behind with nothing but monotony. You would soon bore of such a life, child. There comes a time when we must accept change and make it work for us—move on. Unfortunately, most of the changes you've experienced were beyond your control."

Lilly nodded her head. "Perhaps they were beyond my control, but that doesn't change anything. The future I had hoped for went to the grave with my father."

"Lilly, you need a fresh perspective, new goals for your future. We need to develop a plan." Julia's voice took on a tone of excitement. "I think you need to take one step at a time and focus on one major area. We've established that you don't want to remain in the mills and you do want to marry. I think the first step should be a reevaluation of your relationship with Matthew. He still cares for you—a mother knows these things. And deep down, I believe you still love him."

Her heart hammering, Lilly gave a sigh of relief as Matthew and Randolph reappeared and dropped onto the ground beside them.

"You two appeared to be deep in conversation. What was the topic of interest today? Mrs. Brodmeyer's hat or your new piece of stitchery?" Randolph asked, fondly patting his wife's cheek.

"Neither, Randolph! You men act as though a woman can't have a thought in her head that goes beyond fashion or housekeeping."

Randolph's eyes widened at the retort. "I'm sorry, my dear. It wasn't my intent to offend you. What world event were you discussing? Perhaps the summer launching of the Baltimore and Ohio Railroad. Or maybe that rascal Andrew Jackson's vie for the presidency. Matthew and I would be pleased to converse with you on any such topic."

"We were having a private conversation that doesn't require a male perspective," Julia replied. "But thank you for your apology," she added, handing him a plate.

Lilly glanced at Mr. Cheever from beneath thick brown eyelashes. The poor man appeared totally baffled but filled his plate and began eating without further comment. Matthew, however, continued to bait his mother, obviously enjoying the fact that each of his questions caused her further discomposure.

"Come now, Mother, do tell. I could argue that you and Lilly are being rude, and we all know that proper ladies are never impolite. What about *you*, Lilly? Wouldn't you like to share with Father and me? After all, earlier this very afternoon you taught a little girl about the rules of etiquette."

Julia's cheeks flushed. She stabbed a piece of chicken and flopped it onto Matthew's plate. "*You*, Matthew. I was discussing you and the fact that you're still in love with Lilly. Tell me, son, what would you like to share with the rest of us in regard to that matter?"

His plate dropped to the ground, his discomfort evident. "That was uncalled for, Mother."

Lilly would have laughed out loud had she not been equally embarrassed by the topic. Matthew looked positively mortified.

"No, Matthew, it wasn't," Julia replied in a steady voice. "You would not allow the matter to rest. I answered your question only because you prodded me until I did so. I spoke the truth. Now let's eat our supper. We want to be finished before the show begins."

Throughout their meal, carriages continued arriving from Lowell and the surrounding countryside. Word of the magician and his supernatural abilities had obviously extended well beyond the immediate vicinity. There was an air of excitement as folks strolled about, visiting as they waited outside the old yellow house that had become the favorite spot for visiting entertainment in the surrounding countryside. Julia and Lilly packed the remains of their picnic into the basket and waited with Randolph while Matthew took the basket back to the carriage.

Lilly tried not to think of Matthew or the comments made by his mother, but it was rather like telling someone not to look in the cookie jar. The more she thought of not thinking about Matthew, the more she did think of him.

Julia muttered under her breath and stiffened. Lilly immediately glanced up and saw the object of the older woman's concern. Matthew was striding toward them, accompanied by Kirk Boott and three women.

"Look who I found," Matthew exclaimed. "Mother, Father, Lilly, you know Kirk Boott. I'd like to introduce you to his wife, Anne. And this is Kirk's sister, Neva Locklear, and his niece, Isabelle Locklear. I believe I mentioned having supper with them while I was in Boston." He looked at Lilly as if to ascertain her reaction.

Mr. Cheever extended his hand to Mr. Boott, and the ladies nodded toward each other.

"We've heard the magician is quite talented," Isabelle remarked.

The silence was momentarily deafening. "That's what my parents have said, also," Matthew finally replied.

Isabelle smiled at Lilly. "You are Matthew's sister?"

"No. I'm one of your uncle's hired hands, Miss Locklear, a mill girl. At one time, however, my family's farm adjoined the Cheevers'. That was before the Boston Associates redesigned the landscape and turned East Chelmsford into what is now known as Lowell."

The group stared at her as though she were some lunatic who had escaped from an asylum. Lilly wasn't sure why they appeared shocked at her reply. She would have continued her discourse, but Julia took hold of her wrist in a viselike grip that sent a searing pain up her arm.

Kirk smiled broadly at Julia. "I hope you won't mind, Mrs. Cheever, but I'd like to steal your son away for a while. Isabelle was sorely disappointed when I was unable to locate Matthew before leaving Lowell—he was to have joined us for our outing today. But it appears that fate is with us, Isabelle," he said, now looking at his niece. "We have ample room in our carriage. He can accompany us back to Lowell."

Julia leveled a foreboding stare at her son. "Matthew?"

Matthew avoided making eye contact with his mother. Instead, he looked at his father. "I'm going to join the Bootts and Locklears for the show." He kissed his mother's cheek. Turning away, he added, "Good-bye, Lilly. I'm sure you're pleased to be free of me."

Lilly stared after the group, angry at the longing that invaded her spirit as she watched them leave. Isabelle's laughter floated back where Lilly stood, reminding her that Matthew was no longer a part of her world. He, too, had changed. And not for the better—at least not in her opinion. One minute he acted attentive, almost affectionate, and the next minute he performed in a roguish manner.

The remainder of the day was a haze. The magician appeared; the people cheered and clapped; laughter surrounded her—but Lilly was unaware of it all. She was watching Matthew and Isabelle, unable to focus on anything except the two of them as they whispered and laughed, obviously enjoying each other.

Darkness was beginning to fall and long shadows overtook the roadway as they returned to Lowell. Lilly leaned back against the carriage seat and closed her eyes, anxious to get back to her room. She had planned to spend some time with Nadene today, but there would be little opportunity for much visiting this evening. The thought that she must once again arise before dawn and voluntarily commit herself to a prisonlike existence inside the walls of the Appleton Mill caused her to shudder.

Julia turned sideways in her seat. "I do hope you enjoyed yourself in spite of Matthew's rude behavior. I thought the magician was delightful."

"Now, now," Randolph chided. "It's not as though we had planned for Matthew to join us. He had every right to join Mr. Boott and his family."

The horses slowed as Mr. Cheever directed them down Merrimack Street, then on toward Jackson. He pulled to a stop in front of number 5 and assisted Lilly from the carriage. It was then that she spied three men huddled together. It sounded as though they were having an argument, their voices ringing loud in the crisp autumn air.

She stepped behind the carriage and squinted her eyes to see them in the shadows. The men raised their heads and looked in her direction. Two of them were men she had never seen. She strained to distinguish the features of the third man, the taller one, who had pulled his jacket collar tight about his neck. He looked directly toward her, then hurried off. Lilly had a sudden rush of recognition. It was Miss Addie's escort from earlier that afternoon; it was Miss Mintie's imaginary English spy; it was *John Farnsworth*.

Matthew knew he had angered his mother, and he'd had every intention of stopping at his parents' house upon his return to Lowell. Boott, however, had other plans, insisting there were matters he wished to discuss with Matthew tonight. And so he acquiesced without further argument, accompanying the group back to the Boott mansion. The only bright spot since their return to Lowell had been the fact that Kirk had rejected the ladies' invitation to join them for lemonade. He had insisted there was pressing business that required their attention.

"I trust you found the magic show enjoyable," Kirk said as they entered his office. He poured himself a glass of port and nodded toward another glass. "Care for something a bit stronger than lemonade?"

Matthew shook his head. "No, nothing, thank you. I'm anxious to know what urgent matter you need to discuss before morning."

Kirk seated himself in his leather chair and pulled a fat cigar from the humidor sitting atop his desk. Giving the cigar his undivided attention, he moved it back and forth beneath his nose several times, inhaling the pungent aroma before carefully snipping off the end. "I think we may have the beginning of some problems at the Appleton. I want you to investigate—secretly, of course. A number of incidents have occurred in the spinning room since

Thaddeus Arnold became supervisor. Apparently he believes that an operative has intentionally caused a couple of mishaps within the last few weeks. Personally, I doubt his suspicions, but I have an obligation to investigate."

"Was there any major damage?"

Boott lit the end of his cigar and puffed several times until the ash turned bright red. "No. They were minor mishaps. You know we have frequent accidents."

Matthew leaned forward, resting his arms across his thighs. "I guess I don't understand why Mr. Arnold would even think one of the girls was involved, unless he had some reason for his suspicion. It makes no sense. The girls don't get paid if they miss work. Why would they want to do anything to jeopardize the operation of the spinning room?"

"Exactly! I agree with you, Matthew, but I need to show the Associates I'm on top of things. I wouldn't want it to be said that I'm not checking out information that comes to me. Perform a minimal investigation; talk to a few people. I told Arnold's supervisor I'd get back with them in a few days. If I tell him it's my opinion there's no need for alarm, he'll let it rest, and I can report that the matter has been investigated and has no merit. Fair enough?"

Matthew rose from his chair, "I suppose so. I'll get to it first thing in the morning. However, I don't see how I can be too discreet about the matter. It's going to require talking to some of the people working in the spinning room, isn't it?"

Boott nodded. "Try to find someone you can trust, someone that won't tell the other girls about the investigation. Perhaps Arnold can advise you if there's a girl who can be trusted. I doubt you'll have difficulty. None of them want to lose their position. After all, they've become dependent upon their monthly pay."

Matthew began to move toward to the door. "Was there anything else we needed to discuss?"

Kirk leaned back in his chair and took another draw on his cigar. "There's no need to rush off, Matthew. If nothing else, we can discuss your future with Isabelle."

~ 15 ~

The morning dawned cool and gray, much like Matthew's spirits. He bent his head against the early morning chill and walked toward the Appleton Mill. Lawrence Gault was in the counting room writing in a leather-bound ledger when he entered. Matthew liked the older man; he had a firm handshake, honest eyes, and a quick smile.

"Morning, Mr. Cheever," Lawrence said, pushing away from the desk. "Dreary morning out there, but the sun's shining in here," the older man continued, pointing to his heart.

Matthew smiled. "What's making it shine?"

"Jesus, of course. A man can't have the doldrums too long when he thinks about having a Savior who was willing to die for him. Make sense?"

Matthew nodded. "Couldn't argue that point, Mr. Gault. I was hoping you could help me. I need to speak to Thaddeus Arnold."

"You want me to go get him for you? Be glad to do that."

"No need. Directions will be fine."

Mr. Gault appeared relieved when Matthew didn't take him up on the offer to fetch Thaddeus. Matthew now understood why. The walk across the yard and up the winding stairway would have been difficult for a man of Gault's size and age. Matthew hesitated a moment and took several short breaths before entering the spinning room. The humidity in the mills never ceased to overwhelm him. Kirk had explained that the operatives became accustomed to the heavier air, their lungs adjusting to the moisture after a few weeks. Matthew wasn't sure if Boott's assessment was correct, but it made sense that the body could adjust.

Thaddeus Arnold was near the rear of the room talking with one of the operatives. Matthew moved toward where they stood, the machinery pounding out a vibrating cadence that deadened the sound of his footsteps.

Arnold jumped away from the girl at the touch of Matthew's hand upon his shoulder. The supervisor's face reddened, and he stammered a quick welcome into the deafening noise that permeated the room. Matthew pointed toward the door, and Thaddeus began threading his way toward the entrance as Matthew followed behind. When he looked up, Lilly was staring at him. Damp ringlets clung to her forehead. He smiled, but she didn't acknowledge him. Thaddeus stood anxiously waiting by the door and moved into the stair-well at Matthew's nod. The level of noise diminished only slightly, so Matthew pointed toward the steps.

When they reached the mill yard, Thaddeus quickly turned and looked up at Matthew. "I wasn't doing anything to that girl. She gives me trouble from time to time, and I'm required to reprimand her," he sputtered.

Matthew rubbed his forehead; his head was throbbing. "I'm here to inquire about a couple of accidents. You made some accusations regarding those incidents."

Thaddeus dipped his head up and down several times. "Yes, I'm glad Mr. Boott took my allegations seriously. We've had a number of accidents of late. I have reason to believe one, or perhaps several, of the operatives may be caus-ing these problems."

Now that Mr. Arnold was on the offensive, he appeared more relaxed. Matthew noted that Arnold's stammering had ceased as he made his declara-tions against the girls. Completing his account, Thaddeus squared his shoul-ders, obviously proud of himself.

"Can you give me any reason why it would be beneficial for one of these girls to cause problems with the machinery, Mr. Arnold?"

Thaddeus appeared perplexed by the question.

Matthew took him by the arm and began to walk back toward the stair-well. "You see, Mr. Arnold, it is to the girls' *disadvantage* to have machinery inoperative. They don't get paid unless they are working. That is why I've asked if you can furnish some plausible reason why you think an operative would create such mischief. Otherwise, it would seem that the incidents are purely accidental. There are occasional accidents on all of the floors, both here and at the Merrimack. Unfortunate as it is, people sometimes don't pay atten-tion, and accidents soon follow that inattentiveness. Perhaps there is some problem on your floor, among the girls themselves—or with you?" Matthew ventured.

Thaddeus paled at the remark. "The operatives might have a problem among themselves—I'm not sure," he stammered. "I have no problem with the girls. Well, I am obligated to reprimand them when they're not working up to the requirements—like today when you came into the room," he hastily added. "You may be correct. I may have been borrowing trouble, assuming there was a problem where there is none."

"I can continue to investigate the matter." Matthew left the offer dangling, wondering if Thaddeus would snatch the bone or run off with his tail between his legs.

"You're probably right, Mr. Cheever. I'm new at this position and want to do well. Most likely I've overreacted. I was only trying to look out for the Corporation. I don't want anything to interfere with your profit."

Matthew had guessed correctly. He had suspected Arnold would let the matter drop. He was sure the man was hiding something. Perhaps Lilly knew what it was. "Should you decide that you want me to investigate further, you can tell Mr. Gault to contact me personally. No need to bother Mr. Boott with these matters, Mr. Arnold. I had best not keep you away from your work any longer."

"Thank you, Mr. Cheever. I appreciate your time. I'll do as you said."

Matthew watched as Arnold scampered away, his shoulders stooped over as he rushed back to the stairwell. Something about Thaddeus Arnold bothered him.

～ 16 ～

Prudence twirled about the room in her forest green silk. "I knew you'd change your mind and come. What made you decide? Was it Marmi's description of all the fun or the anticipation of dancing with Kirk Boott?"

Marmi giggled at the remark. "He is quite an excellent dance partner. I had the privilege of two dances with him at the Blowing Out Ball last spring."

Lilly smiled at the girls. She dared not tell them that Thaddeus Arnold had promised he would find a reason for her termination if she didn't attend this evening. Instead she replied, "I think it might be unwise to remain at home and permit you to have all the fun, Prudence. Besides, I don't think Nadene would forgive me if I didn't go along."

Nadene offered a smile. "That's true. I dislike these required functions. They make me uncomfortable, while Pru and Marmi have loads of fun."

"I wager I'll have more fun than Pru," Marmi replied. "She's too picky about her dance partners. Not me. If someone invites me to dance, I'm going out on the floor and having a whirl."

The four of them made their way downstairs, where Miss Addie stood waiting in a sapphire blue creation. Lilly knew the gown had come from the collection of things Addie brought from Boston. Lilly had helped her touch up the gown, refreshing the style with a bit of lace and trim. She'd also taken out the waistline when Addie wasn't looking. Lilly's reward was her choice of gowns from Miss Addie's collection. Of course, the dress had to be completely remade to accommodate Lilly's slender frame, but it was better than having to wear one of her childish, well-worn pieces from the past. Besides, nothing that Lilly owned was worthy of a ball.

"Oh, just look at you girls. I can't decide which one of you is the prettiest," Addie exclaimed as they paraded single file through the hallway for her approval. "The other girls left a few minutes ago, and we must stop for Mintie. Hurry, now—we don't want to be late."

"Just wait until John Farnsworth sees you in that dress. He'll be coming to call every evening," Lilly whispered as they walked out the front door.

Addie blushed. "I've been so excited by the prospect that I've hardly been able to eat. Why, just look, the waist on this gown is much looser."

Lilly smiled and nodded. "Indeed, I was going to comment that you looked quite trim." No sense bursting the woman's bubble of enthusiasm.

"Oh, thank you for helping me with this dress. I don't know what I would have done without you."

"Nor I without you," Lilly commented, gently lifting the edge of her silk skirt for emphasis.

"That burgundy really is your color," Addie replied. "And you've made it over in such a delightful manner. The way you've cut the neckline is modest yet completely youthful. And your waist, why, it's so very tiny, and that black cording only emphasizes it."

Lilly felt her cheeks grow hot. She hadn't worn anything this lovely in a very long time. Memories rushed in of a time when her mother had waived the rules and allowed her to accompany her parents to a party at the Cheevers. Lilly had worn a very grown-up gown of pale pink. Her mother had even helped her to arrange her hair, pinning part of it up and leaving the rest to hang in ringlets around her face and shoulders. Lilly had felt very special that night, and Matthew's reaction to her had left her feeling weak in the knees.

As if reading her mind, Addie whispered, "I'll bet Mr. Cheever won't be able to even look at another woman tonight. You'll simply take his breath away."

Glancing up, Lilly caught sight of Mintie peering out the front window. The moment the group began to walk across the street, the door flew open, and she marched out the door to meet them. "It's obvious you've been absent from polite society much too long," Mintie greeted. "We are going to be late! Apparently you've forgotten that *proper* ladies do not enjoy making a spectacle of themselves. You are supposed to be setting a proper example for your young charges, Adelaide. Tsk, tsk," she chastised through pursed lips while casting a look of disdain in Addie's direction.

"And your gown is once again inappropriate. The style is much too youthful. You're a woman of forty and five and should dress in accordance."

"Speaking of gowns, I thought you had discarded that dress several years ago, sister. Isn't that the frock the Judge described as frumpy?" Addie inquired.

The girls giggled and Mintie gasped, smoothing down the dull brown gown. "For a woman of my years, this dress is most assuredly better than that which you've chosen for yourself."

Lilly could see that Addie hadn't meant to make her sister feel bad. Unfortunately, Miss Mintie just seemed to bring out the worst in people.

"I'm sorry, Mintie. That was a most insensitive remark," Addie said. Mintie failed to accept or reject the apology. Neither did she offer an apology for her own biting remark only minutes earlier.

If Addie noticed, she gave no evidence. Instead, she joined in with Prudence and Marmi's infectious laughter, forgetting the caustic beginning to their evening. Even Mintie began adding to the animated conversation as they approached the Old Stone House on Pawtucket Street.

"The balls are not nearly as grand as what we held in Boston, but they do their best to charm the Lowell society," Mintie stated rather casually.

Lilly found it amusing that Mintie would actually allow herself to be momentarily caught up in the revelry. Lilly had never seen her this way. It made Mintie more accessible—more human.

"I've never gone to a ball in Boston," Marmi commented, "but I simply adore the parties we have. I shall dance all night."

"No doubt you'll need a hefty supply of salts for soaking tired feet," Mintie told Addie. "If you need extra, I might have some to share."

Lilly found Mintie's generosity out of character. Perhaps the party spirit had found its way into the old woman's heart after all.

"Right this way, ladies," Phineas Whiting welcomed as their small group entered the slate stone edifice. He appeared to enjoy nothing more than having his establishment filled with patrons determined to have a good time. He tugged at his graying beard and smiled at the near-capacity crowd. "There's punch if you've a thirst and food if you've a hunger, courtesy of the Associates, of course," he announced, waving his arm in a welcoming gesture, "and music for your entertainment."

"Indeed there is." Someone pressed his hand into the small of Lilly's back. "After searching the room and not seeing you, I was afraid you hadn't taken me at my word," Thaddeus Arnold whispered in her ear. "I believe this is my dance." His fusty warm breath caused her to shiver. His hand clenched around her waist. "Don't refuse me," he hissed from between his yellowed teeth.

Mr. Arnold's fingers dug deeply into the flesh around her waist. "I wouldn't want to deny your wife the privilege of being your partner," Lilly replied, searching the crowd, hoping to see his wife's familiar face. Yet she could not escape his grip. Even worse, John Farnsworth was escorting Miss Addie toward the dance floor, leaving Lilly alone to fend off Arnold's advances. There was no escape as he pulled her forward onto the dance floor and pushed firmly against her. Lilly wished the orchestra was playing anything but a waltz.

Bracing her hand against his left shoulder, Lilly pushed until there was a small space between them. "You need not hold me so tightly. I'm sure your superiors would find such behavior unseemly, especially for a married man."

"You'll learn to enjoy having me close to you," he replied, his eyes now alight with wickedness.

Lilly glared in return. "I don't know how any women could bear to have you close at hand, but hear me well, Mr. Arnold. I will *never* permit you to take advantage of me."

He tightened his grasp and twirled her around. "You may change your mind. There are certain advantages to be gained when you're nice to me, Miss Armbruster." The words slid from his mouth with practiced ease. "You should talk to Mary Caruff. She can tell you the privileges that flow to those who enjoy spending a little extra time in my company."

He had Lilly's attention. She had assumed all of his advances toward the girls were unwelcome. Was she to believe there were girls who were willing to permit his advances in exchange for favors? That concept was even more disturbing than the thought that he would take unfair advantage of an employee.

"Talk to Mary Caruff and Rachel Filmore," he said, apparently observing the confusion etched upon her face. "They'll tell you how, shall we say, *profitable,* their extra time with me has been."

Lilly was incredulous. "Am I to understand that you actually pay Mary and Rachel for their company?"

"I didn't say that I pay them," he said, tugging her closer. His mouth was against her ear. "They grant me certain privileges, and I do the same thing for them. Understand?"

Pulling her head away, she looked into his beady eyes. "You give them special favors at work, is that what you mean?"

He looked at her as though she didn't have sense enough to come in out of the rain. "Of *course* that's what I mean—for those who willingly cooperate. I overlook the fact that they come in late on occasion, and I make sure they have the best machinery. It's good that you are beautiful. If you were required to depend upon your intelligence or wit to figure things out, you'd die a certain death."

Lilly didn't acknowledge his comment. "What about the girls who don't cooperate? What do you do for *them*?"

His eyes glistened and his fingers moved up her back. "If you must know, they have a great deal of difficulty accomplishing their work to meet specifications, and within a few weeks they find themselves out of work. And without their good conduct discharge, they are unable to work in any other mill. Most are required to return home. I'm told one of them was so distraught that she jumped from Pawtucket Falls to her death, although I assured Mr. Boott it was most likely an accident, that the girl surely wouldn't have taken her life over losing her job. Wouldn't you agree?"

"I find it difficult to believe such a vile man as you is able to sleep at night. Do you ever wonder what the elders of the church would think of your behavior? I seem to recall that you are among the leadership at St. Anne's."

His look of surprise was worth every ounce of fear in her heart. It was obvious Thaddeus Arnold was not accustomed to being confronted. Their conversation lapsed at the same time as the music.

"There you are," a voice boomed from behind them. Both Lilly and Thaddeus turned to see John Farnsworth striding toward them. "I've come to claim a dance," he said. "I'm sure you won't object." The Englishman dwarfed

Thaddeus, who was visibly irritated by the intrusion. He finally acquiesced, releasing Lilly's hand and walking toward the door.

Lilly breathed a sigh of relief, hoping that she had seen the last of Thaddeus Arnold for the evening. "I hope you don't mind the intrusion, but Miss Addie said she thought you would enjoy a new partner," Farnsworth said as they began to circle the floor.

"Miss Addie is a very perceptive lady. I am extremely pleased to have you as my partner, Mr. Farnsworth. Have the two of you been enjoying yourselves?"

"Yes, indeed. Miss Addie is excellent company."

Lilly considered the morsels of information she had been fed by Miss Mintie concerning Farnsworth. Surely they weren't enough to consider him a man set upon treason. He was kind and generous, a true gentleman who would be a fine match for Miss Addie. Yet seeing him secreted in the shadows with those men the other night gave her concern. She wanted to encourage him to call upon Miss Addie, yet if there was a question of character . . .

"I've been giving thought to asking Miss Addie if I could call on her. Do you think she would accept an invitation?" John asked, breaking into her thoughts.

"Yes, well—I imagine she would consider such an invitation," Lilly stammered.

John gave a hearty laugh. "You don't sound overly convincing. Perhaps I should rethink my plan."

"No, don't do that—I'm sure she would be very pleased to have you call on her," Lilly quickly replied. She wasn't going to stand in the way of a possible suitor for Miss Addie.

"I thought I saw you with some other men last Sunday night when I was returning from Belvedere," Lilly continued as Mr. Farnsworth twirled her about the floor in a surprisingly agile manner.

Farnsworth gave no sign of recognition. His brows furrowed, as if he were thinking where he might have been that night. "What time?" he asked.

"It was getting dark, around seven-fifteen, perhaps. Our carriage came down Jackson Street. When we approached the corner, I saw three men having a loud discussion. Two of them ran off. I didn't recognize either of them, but the third bore a striking resemblance to you, Mr. Farnsworth."

He appeared to be sifting through her words. "It may have been me. I believe I was out with several other gentlemen on Sunday evening. I can't say that I recall them running off when we parted company, however. Was there some reason you were concerned about my whereabouts?"

Lilly felt the heat rise in her cheeks. "No, not at all. I was merely surprised to see you. I didn't realize you had already developed friendships here in Lowell."

He smiled down at her. "With the number of Englishmen working at the Merrimack, I've had little difficulty becoming acquainted. Thank you for the dance," he replied as the music came to a halt. "I'll trust your advice in regard to Miss Addie and hope she doesn't disappoint me when I seek permission to call."

Lilly quickly surveyed the room, hoping she could slip out the side door without being noticed. There hadn't been any stipulation as to how long she was to remain at the party, merely that she attend. Weaving her way through the crowd, she passed the punch table and was only steps from the door when someone boldly grabbed her by the waist.

"Not planning to run away, are you? We weren't finished with our little talk." Mr. Arnold had pushed her against the stone wall, the cold slate cutting into her shoulders as she backed away from him. "I believe you were commenting that the arrangement shared between several of the girls and me might be of interest to others. I would strongly suggest that you refrain from such remarks." His face was taut, his jaws clenched as he continued to block her movement.

Trembling, Lilly tried to bolster her courage. She twisted her hands together, hoping he wouldn't see how badly they were shaking.

"Is this some new dance where you block your partner's movement, Mr. Arnold?" Matthew asked as he neared where they stood.

Thaddeus quickly dropped his hold and stepped away. "No. We were merely having a discussion about the excellent working conditions in the spinning room. Miss Armbruster is learning how to adapt to her new surroundings."

"I'm sure you don't mind if I interrupt your conversation. Miss Armbruster owes me a dance," Matthew replied, never taking his gaze off of Lilly.

Acting the proper gentleman, Mr. Arnold bowed from the waist and uttered his consent. Lilly avoided looking in his direction, but she could feel his gaze upon her even after Matthew led her onto the dance floor.

"Charming fellow. I didn't realize you cared for his type. And isn't he married?"

"You're not amusing."

"Ah, dear Lilly, you used to think I was quite amusing," he replied, pulling her a bit closer as the orchestra began a waltz. "Remember this song?" he whispered. "Remember how some of the matrons thought us mad to allow waltzing in our gatherings?"

The music, the dance, and his arms all blended together, transporting her back to a time when she was safe and when life made sense. Without thinking of how it might look, she rested her head on his shoulder, desperately wishing her life could return to those happier days. Her fear of Arnold had left her feeling quite weak, and Matthew's supportive embrace renewed her strength.

"It pleases me that you're finally able to show you still have feelings for me, Lilly," Matthew said as he gently pressed her fingers to his lips.

"What? Because I agreed to one waltz you think I'm still in love with you?"

"No, not just the dance—your head on my shoulder, the look in your eyes. I'd have to be blind not to see your devotion, and it pleases me very much."

Mortified, Lilly couldn't believe what he was saying. How dare he assume such utter nonsense? Had she not been cornered by that lecherous Thaddeus Arnold, she wouldn't have even considered dancing with Matthew. "You're completely wrong, Matthew. In fact, you would be astounded if you knew just how loathsome I consider you and the life you've chosen."

Matthew glanced down at her. His gaze was piercing. "Lilly, it's time you stop lying to yourself and to me."

"Really? Is that what you suggest?" She smiled sweetly, lifted her foot, and stomped down on Matthew's foot as hard as she could. "Consider that a token of my love, Matthew," she said as he groaned and lifted his foot slowly.

"*There* you are, Matthew. I have a young lady here who's anxious to dance with you," Kirk Boott said as he and Isabelle walked onto the dance floor. "Good evening, Miss Armbruster," he added.

Lilly nodded at Kirk and Isabelle. "I'm sure Matthew will be delighted to dance with you, Isabelle. He seems to be in fine form tonight. Aren't you, Matthew?" Without waiting for an answer, she rushed from the dance floor.

~ 17 ~

M atthew fussed with his shirt collar, wondering if he would ever feel comfortable when Kirk Boott summoned him. He had no reason to be concerned—at least no reason of which he was aware. Yet the delivery of Kirk's engraved stationery emblazoned with his handwritten scrawl filled Matthew with trepidation. *Come to my office now. Boott.* Minimal phraseology was all that Boott needed to bring any employee running, but most especially one who aspired to become a member of the elite Associates.

Ten minutes later, Matthew knocked on the door of Boott's office. "What kept you?" Boott inquired without looking up from the paper work scattered across his desk. Glancing up, he emitted a loud guffaw. "You needn't look terrified, Matthew. It was my feeble attempt at humor." Kirk pointed toward one of the chairs sitting opposite his desk. "Do be seated, my boy. Can I get you something to drink?"

"No, nothing. How can I be of assistance?"

Kirk leaned back in his chair and propped his lanky legs across the desk. "Isabelle tells me she thoroughly enjoyed spending time with you at the Lighting Up Ball. I believe she was hoping you would extend an invitation for dinner or perhaps the theatre in the near future. Since it's been nearly a month since the ball, I thought I would inquire as to the problem."

Matthew squirmed in the chair, wondering if Isabelle's social calendar was the sole purpose Boott had summoned him. "The distance between Boston and Lowell makes it difficult for me to keep company with your niece and stay abreast of my duties for the Corporation. However, I'm pleased to hear she enjoyed the ball," Matthew hedged.

"Isabelle speculated that you might be interested in the Armbruster girl. I'm certain Isabelle has drawn that conclusion based upon seeing you in Miss Armbruster's company each time she has visited Lowell. I told my niece it was mere happenstance." Kirk's forehead furrowed into deep creases as he lifted his eyebrows and looked at Matthew. "I know you'll be pleased to hear that my sister and Isabelle will be visiting next weekend. I was hoping you could join us for dinner on Saturday evening, shall we say around seven o'clock?"

Matthew longed for the courage to tell Boott he wouldn't be available. Instead, he nodded his agreement. "Was that all you wished to discuss?"

Kirk rose from his chair and moved toward the window looking out on his gardens at the back of the house. "No, no, of course not. There are several matters that need our attention. Did you have an opportunity to investigate the accidents at the Appleton?"

Kirk continued staring out the window with his back toward Matthew. "Yes, and I believe your assessment was correct. After spending some time talking with Mr. Arnold, he agreed that he may have overreacted to the incidents. As you know, he's new to his position and is anxious to make a good impression."

"That's not a bad thing—wanting to impress me. Wouldn't you agree?" Kirk inquired, turning the unwavering gaze of his steel-blue eyes on Matthew.

They both knew there was only one acceptable answer to Kirk's question. Matthew hedged momentarily, not certain where Kirk was headed. "I would agree as long as it doesn't compromise one's personal beliefs," he finally replied.

A wry grin wrapped itself around Kirk's lips. "Not willing to sell your soul for a position with the Associates? Is that what you're telling me, Matthew?"

"Is that what the Associates require?" Matthew questioned in return.

Kirk ran his hand across the stubble of his jaw. "Let us hope not, for I fear you would fail to meet the prerequisites, my boy," he said, his voice laced with a hint of sarcasm. "I've asked Hugh Cummiskey to join us. He should be arriving momentarily. The Associates agree we should begin working out the arrangements we've made with Bishop Fenwick. Cummiskey is our starting point. I've decided to assign this project to you since you were instrumental in presenting the church as a solution to the increasing Irish problem."

Leaning back in his chair, Matthew considered the consequences of Boott's assignment. If the project were a failure and the Irish continued with their infighting, Matthew would be held accountable. He wondered, however, if the project proved successful, who would receive the accolades. A knock sounded at the front door. Moments later a mobcapped servant escorted Hugh Cummiskey into Boott's office.

"Hugh, good to see you. You remember Matthew Cheever, don't you?"

"Afternoon, gentlemen." The burly Irishman nodded at both men as he made his way into the room. Pulling a flattened cap from his head, he ran broad fingers through a mass of disheveled black curls before seating himself beside Matthew.

"I know you're busy with the canal, Hugh, but I think I have some interesting information for you," Kirk began. Over the next hour, he laid out the Associates' decision to bring a priest to Lowell on a somewhat regular basis and commence building a Catholic church. "You don't appear overly pleased," Kirk said as he completed his explanation.

Hugh leaned forward and rested his brawny arms atop the highly polished desk. "Oh, I'm pleased by the idea of having a church for the men and their families, but here's my concern—where are you gonna put it? We're already divided. I fear a church in one camp or the other will only add to the turmoil."

Kirk gave him a knowing smile and nodded. "We suspected the division of the clans could be problematic. Matthew made a suggestion that appears to have some merit with Bishop Fenwick as well as the Associates."

"What's that?" Hugh inquired.

Kirk pointed to Matthew, and Hugh immediately turned his attention toward the younger man.

"If we build the church directly between the camps, it could serve as a point of unity," Matthew explained. "There's a parcel of land the Associates have agreed they will deed to the Catholic diocese for that purpose. The agreement, however, is hinged upon a labor force consisting of your fellow Irishmen. While the land and materials will be furnished at no cost, labor would be the responsibility of the men living in the camps. We're insisting upon your men supplying the labor for several reasons. One, the cost of the project would be prohibitive from the Associates' point of view if they were required to furnish labor; second, working together on a joint project could aid in bringing the Irish community together; and third, your men are skilled laborers, as well as being the ones who will benefit from the structure." Matthew turned toward Boott for affirmation, but Kirk's gaze was riveted on Hugh Cummiskey.

"What do you think, Hugh?" Kirk asked.

"Quite an undertaking for my men. They'd have to do the work on their off hours, and we both know they don't have many of those—leastwise not during daylight or good weather. These men have got families to feed, and whether those mouths are in Lowell or Boston or Ireland, their families look to them for provision. Don't get me wrong—I think the idea of a church is a good one, but how do I ask them to give up their wages and donate time to build a church?"

"*You* don't. We'll designate that privilege to good Bishop Fenwick. I'll make arrangements to have the bishop come and speak a week from Sunday if he's available. I doubt he'll have difficulty convincing the men that it's a privilege rather than a sacrifice to give their time."

Hugh gave a low laugh. "I don't know if I'd go quite that far, but the bishop's influence will go further than mine."

Kirk rose from behind the desk. "I've assigned Matthew to oversee this matter. In fact, I may send him to Boston to talk with the bishop. I'm sure he could find time to make at least one other call while he's in the city." Kirk cast a sidelong glance at Matthew. "What do you think, Matthew? Are you up to a trip to Boston in the next few days? It will give you an opportunity to set Isabelle's concerns to rest."

Matthew was pleased at the prospect of visiting the bishop on his own.

The fact that Kirk considered him capable of conducting a high-level meeting without accompaniment was flattering. *If* it was his ability Kirk truly believed in. Kirk's caveat that he pay Isabelle a visit gave him pause to wonder. "I'll leave in the morning," Matthew agreed.

"Why don't we walk over to the Acre and take a look about," Kirk suggested as he moved around the desk. Matthew and Hugh rose in unison. There was no doubt in either of their minds that if Kirk wanted to visit the Acre, they would visit the Acre.

Cummiskey's Irish brogue filled the air as the three men made their way to the acre or more of land that contained a ramshackle collection of board, tin, and sod cabins and shanties. The pungent smell of cooking cabbage and potatoes mingled with the odor of human bodies permeating the air. Kirk pulled a crisp, neatly folded handkerchief from his pocket and placed it to his nose.

Cummiskey grinned. "Smell of cabbage bother ya?"

Kirk immediately tucked the handkerchief back into his pocket and gave a strained laugh. "Let's say that cabbage is not among my favorite foods. Now, this camp is primarily Corkonians from the southwest of Ireland, and they occupy the original acre. The Connachts, from west-central Ireland, are on the other piece of land, the half-acre site. Is that correct?" he inquired, smoothly changing the topic of conversation.

Matthew was impressed with Boott's knowledge of the camps. Perhaps Kirk hadn't taken time to visit the squatted land in some time, but he had certainly secured enough information to be well versed in a discussion of the area with Cummiskey.

Cummiskey nodded. "Of course, in Ireland the clans are much more divided. Fortunately we've divided into only two factions in Lowell. Which works in your favor, my friend. You've only two clans to pull together instead of hundreds." His dark eyes sparkled with merriment. "It's a grown man's job you'll have attempting to pull these men together."

"Well, I have you and Bishop Fenwick to aid me in that regard," Boott countered, his laughter matching Cummiskey's.

A natural-born builder, Hugh began measuring the area, obviously beginning to picture the edifice and its placement on the piece of land Kirk had shown him. "Are you planning on using slate like at St. Anne's?" Hugh inquired, the sparkle still in his eye.

"If we have a stockpile of slate, we may decide to do that, Hugh. I was planning on a Gothic style, with a tall central tower topped by a gilded cross. Smaller spires surrounding the central tower would be visually pleasing, don't you think, Matthew?"

Matthew had been following along behind Hugh and now came into a circle with the other two men. "Yes, Gothic for a church is quite beautiful," he replied. "You may want to consider . . ."

His words died away as a woman's shouts echoed down the muddy street, causing the three men to look toward a tin-roofed hovel. Matthew strained to see the man who was rushing away from the shanty. Had the fellow not looked so out of place among the filth and poverty, Matthew wouldn't have been intrigued. Squinting against the sun, Matthew stared at the male figure wearing an expensive-looking coat. The man turned, glanced over his shoulder, and headed off down a side street. A shock ran through Matthew. William Thurston!

"You were saying, Matthew?" Kirk inquired, pulling him back to the present.

Matthew rubbed his forehead. "What? Oh yes, I was saying you might want to consider small spires at each corner of the building to give it a sense of balance."

"Yes, I like that idea. What about you, Cummiskey? Think a spired church building, say about forty feet by seventy, would improve the appearance of the Acre?"

"It certainly can't hurt it," Cummiskey replied. "Just having Matthew convince the bishop to get a priest to Lowell on a regular visiting schedule would be helpful."

"I'm sure Matthew will be successful in his visit with the bishop, Hugh. In the meantime, let's not discuss this project among the people. Don't want to get their hopes built up too high and then have something go amiss."

Cummiskey nodded his agreement. "If we're through here, I think it best if I head back to work. Not that my men can't handle the job without me." Once again he filled the air with his rowdy laughter.

The bulky Irishman waved his arm high in the air as he sauntered off toward the canal. Kirk and Matthew waved in return and then moved off in the opposite direction. The two men walked along in silence for a short distance. Finally Matthew could stand it no longer. "That was William Thurston back there."

"Yes, it was," Kirk replied.

"Is that all you have to say? Don't you find it strange that he would be in the Acre after hearing his disparaging remarks at the Appletons' dinner party?"

Kirk shook his head. "Yes, but I also remember William didn't hide the fact that he spends time in the Acre. In fact, I wondered at the time if he wasn't anticipating just such a circumstance as this. He didn't want questions raised if he were to be seen around the Paddy camps."

"Didn't you hear what that woman shouted?"

"There are some things that should be forgotten, Matthew. This is one of them."

Lilly smiled as she entered the kitchen. Addie was bustling about the warm kitchen, her cheeks flushed a bright pink as she placed the last of the supper dishes on a shelf along the wall. A wisp of her graying hair had escaped and was now firmly clinging to her perspiring forehead. She appeared startled when she finally noticed Lilly. "Am I late? I was trying to hurry," she apologized.

"We have ample time. Please don't hurry so. In fact, why don't you go to your room and get your hat. I'll finish up in here. It's not as though I don't know where these pots and pans belong." The older woman hesitated a moment. "Go on," Lilly encouraged. "I wouldn't have offered if I didn't want to help."

"You're a sweetheart, Lilly Armbruster," Addie called over her shoulder as she rushed from the kitchen, leaving Lilly to complete her few remaining chores.

In no time at all, the two of them were sauntering outside in the cool, moonlit evening. Lilly was bone tired, but she had promised Addie she would go shopping with her. Besides, being with Addie was a joy, for her easy laughter and kind ways never failed to touch Lilly's heart and refresh her spirit. This evening, she was sure, would be no different. She would come home feeling more invigorated than when she left.

"Evening, Mrs. Arnold," Addie called out in her ever-cheerful voice. "Are you out enjoying this fine weather? If you're walking into town, you're welcome to join us."

Mrs. Arnold glanced in their direction as they approached where she stood with an empty basket hanging from her arm. "No, I've changed my mind. I'm not going this evening," she said, raising her head a bit as she spoke. Quickly she turned and rushed back into the house.

"Strange woman, that Mrs. Arnold. Looked like her face was dirty," Addie remarked. "And why would she go to the trouble of donning her shawl and basket without going to do her shopping? She's a rather unfriendly woman, although I've tried to be neighborly in the little time I have for visiting."

"It wasn't dirt on her face, Miss Addie. And she went back in the house because she didn't want us to see she's got bruises all over herself. Her husband beats her."

A look of horror spread across Miss Addie's face. "Oh, child, such terrible accusations you're making. Where would you get such a notion?"

As they continued into town, Lilly explained in detail the first night she'd heard the screams from next door. "Nadene and I made a pact. Whenever either one of us hears Mrs. Arnold screaming, we beat on the wall. He knows that we hear him, and he stops. He still hasn't stopped completely, but at least it doesn't happen *every* night anymore."

"Have you told anyone else? Someone in authority that could possibly help the poor woman?"

Lilly's look of disgust was all the answer Addie needed. "To whom would we go, Miss Addie? Who would listen to us? Nadene can't afford to lose her job."

"Nor can you, my dear," Miss Addie replied as the two of them walked into Markham's General Store, which like the other shops in Lowell, extended shopping hours into the evening to accommodate the full schedules of the mill girls.

"Women are the property of the men they marry," Lilly said softly. "Sometimes a woman marries well, and sometimes she doesn't. Beatings come along with those poorer matches."

"My, but you're cynical for one so young."

"Maybe," Lilly replied, "but I speak the truth and you know it. Mrs. Arnold would be at a loss without her husband, and he clearly abuses her."

"Still, it seems there should be someone who would care, doesn't it?"

Nodding her agreement, Lilly led the way as the two women made their way down the center of the store.

"Now, there's a sight to make a man's eyes sparkle."

Lilly and Addie turned to see John Farnsworth standing behind them. "Good evening, ladies. Out for a bit of shopping and fresh air on this lovely evening?"

"Indeed we are, Mr. Farnsworth," Addie replied with an infectious smile. "And what might you be looking for this evening?"

"Nothing in particular. I just felt the urge to walk into town and get a bit of fresh air. Now I know why. It was to escort you two lovely ladies for a slice of cake and a cup of tea over at Clawson's."

"Why don't the two of you go ahead and have dessert," Lilly suggested, but Addie's look of dismay quickly caused her to reconsider. "On second thought, a cup of tea sounds wonderful." If Miss Addie didn't mind returning to town tomorrow to complete her shopping, why should she object to sitting in the quiet of Clawson's Tea and Pastry Shop? Besides, both Addie and Farnsworth wore expressions of delight.

Mrs. Clawson seated them at a small table near the rear of the shop, where Farnsworth regaled them with tales of the English countryside. He had just begun to tell Addie of his father's debilitating illness when Mrs. Clawson delivered three slices of buttery pound cake covered with a rich, smooth lemon sauce. She placed a sturdy glazed teapot in the center of the table and then surrounded it with china cups and saucers. "Enjoy your cake and tea," she encouraged. Smiling, she hastened off as the small bell over the front door chimed.

Farnsworth extended his arm and waved. "Mind if I join you?" Matthew Cheever inquired as he approached their table.

"Sit down, sit down," Farnsworth encouraged amicably. "I'll have Mrs. Clawson deliver another cup. Would you like a slice of cake?"

Matthew seated himself between John and Lilly. "Are you enjoying your cake, Lilly?" he asked.

"It's very good. Thank you," she replied, keeping her tone formal and uninviting.

"On Miss Armbruster's recommendation, I believe I'll have to try some," Matthew replied, giving Lilly a grin. Farnsworth signaled Mrs. Clawson, who quickly brought another serving of cake along with a cup and saucer.

When Lilly wouldn't banter with him, Matthew turned his attention to Farnsworth and attempted to engage him in a business discussion. Lilly gave Matthew a triumphant grin when John appeared uninterested and turned his attention back toward Addie. "I don't think Mr. Farnsworth finds you particularly interesting this evening," Lilly whispered.

"Then perhaps *you'd* be willing to talk to me," he suggested. "Consider it a gesture of goodwill toward Miss Addie."

Lilly took a sip of tea. "As long as I may choose what we talk about," she said, waiting until Matthew nodded his agreement.

"What delightful thing would you like to speak of?" he questioned. Cutting into his cake, Matthew took a bite and smiled. "This is good but not quite as good as the treats you used to serve me."

Lilly stiffened and murmured, "I wonder if you could tell me what the good Boston Associates think of men who beat their wives."

Matthew stared at her in obvious disbelief. He took a long sip of tea then eyed her as if to regard how serious she was about the matter. "This is ridiculous, Lilly. What are you talking about?" His voice held an edge that conveyed she was speaking nonsense.

"Don't take that tone with me, Matthew Cheever. You know me too well to believe I'd lie about such a thing. There is nothing ridiculous about Thaddeus Arnold beating his wife until she's black and blue." She shook her head as hideous images came to mind. "Poor woman. I'm regularly awakened by her screams begging him to stop. Now, if you'll excuse me, I've finished my tea and cake. I believe I'll walk home."

Matthew looked to where John and Addie sat engrossed in their conversation. Turning back to Lilly, he pressed close and whispered, "Surely you realize we'd need proof of such allegations. You can't just make unfounded accusations."

Lilly tolerated his nearness in order to continue her discussion. "I've seen

her bruises, and so has Miss Addie. She avoids all contact with other people—
a prisoner in her own home—no doubt to keep anyone from asking questions.
She's likely suffering unimaginable horrors. I doubt Mr. Arnold is going to
come forward and admit to his despicable behavior." Lilly pulled away from
him and got to her feet.

"Just a moment, Lilly," Addie said. "John and I are leaving, also."

John pushed himself away from the table and then assisted Addie. "I asked
Addie's permission to escort you ladies back home, and she has graciously
agreed," Mr. Farnsworth said.

"I was hoping to have a bit of time to discuss a couple of matters, John,"
Matthew said, rising from his chair. "I'm sure the ladies would excuse you."

John gave Matthew a look of obvious disbelief. "This may come as a surprise to you, Matthew, but I much prefer the company of these ladies to
yours." Miss Addie gave a nervous giggle while Lilly leveled a smug look in
Matthew's direction. "You're welcome to join us, however."

"It appears I'll be required to do so if I'm going to have any time with
you," Matthew conceded as the group walked out the door. "I suppose I can
force myself to remain in Lilly's company a bit longer," he said as he and Lilly
walked ahead of the older couple.

Lilly glared at him. "I imagine you will have to force yourself since it
appears you can't stand to hear the truth about your employees. I'm sure you'd
be much more comfortable with Isabelle and her fawning behavior."

Matthew looked rather surprised. "You're jealous, Lilly. You see, you do
still care," he said in a hoarse whisper.

Lilly felt a momentary rush of embarrassment as his words hit home. She
pushed her feelings aside and kept walking. "This has nothing to do with
Isabelle; it has to do with Mrs. Arnold," Lilly retaliated.

"If it will make you feel better, I promise I'll check into Mr. Arnold's
behavior."

"Will you truly?" She looked back to ascertain his sincerity.

Matthew's expression revealed his concern. "Lilly, you know how I feel
about such matters. I could never abide a man hitting his wife. I promise I'll
check into it."

Lilly nodded. "It's just that she's . . . she's . . . all alone." The words were
as much a reflection of her own heart as they were concern for Mrs. Arnold.
"If we don't come to her aid, who will?"

"I understand, Lilly," Matthew said softly. For a moment their gazes were
fixed on each other.

They continued to walk, but their steps were slowed considerably. Matthew held tightly to her arm and added, "Lilly, why are you jealous of Isabelle?"

For a moment Lilly thought of sharing her heart. She opened her mouth to speak but fell short when Addie called out, the spell broken. She pulled away.

"You appear to be limping, Mr. Cheever. Did you hurt your foot?"

Matthew stopped, allowing the older couple to move alongside them. "As a matter of fact, I did—at the Lighting Up Ball. A clumsy dancer stepped on my foot and bruised it rather badly. But I'm sure it will heal."

"And it's still sore after all this time? That must have been painful. I'm so sorry," Addie replied, a look of genuine concern on her face. "You should try using a cane. It would help take the weight off your injured foot. The Judge used a cane most of the time—gout, you know. He said it helped immensely," she continued in a motherly tone.

"Thank you for your concern, Miss Addie," Matthew said as the older couple moved ahead of them. Pulling Lilly close, Matthew bent down to whisper in her ear. "You can't deny your feelings forever. I know you care about me."

Lilly didn't want to make a scene in Miss Addie's presence, but neither did she want to give Matthew the upper hand. Turning to speak to him, however, she found his lips only inches away from her own. Unnerved by his nearness, she forced herself to speak. "You'd best watch yourself, Matthew Cheever, or that same clumsy dancer may step on your other foot, and I doubt a cane will do you much good then!"

~ 18 ~

Autumn leaves crunched beneath his feet as William Thurston walked down Merrimack Street. Bending his head against a brisk gust of wind, he pulled a watch from his pocket and then quickened his pace. He certainly didn't want Lewis Armbruster standing around the Acre waiting for him. Worse yet, he didn't want Lewis, a much younger man with an insatiable appetite for women, spending time with Kathryn O'Hanrahan. She'd sell her soul for a crust of bread. In William's mind, that was true of all the Irish; they had no morals, no interest in rising above their circumstances. Instead of working to remove themselves from their plight, they banded together and reveled in their misery. Why he couldn't get Boott and the other Associates to see the Irish for what they truly were was beyond him. The Irish, with their dirty ways and constant brawling, were going to eventually ruin all that was good and pure in Lowell.

William spied Lewis coming from the opposite direction down Adams Street and breathed a sigh of relief. "Hello, Lewis," William said as they drew closer together. Lewis nodded in greeting and matched William's stride as the two of them walked through the mud and muck that filled the crooked paths leading into the Acre. Without knocking, William led the way into one of the hovels.

A young woman with auburn curls and a creamy white complexion sat before the waning fire. She was wrapped in a blanket, a young child asleep on her lap. "I don't like meeting in this place," Lewis whispered as Thurston walked deeper inside the room.

William turned, gave him a look of disgust, and pointed toward the only chair in the room. "Sit down. We agreed our meetings needed to be in a place where we wouldn't be seen together, and we have that safety here. Don't we, Kathryn?" The woman nodded her head but said nothing. "Take him and go outside. We won't be long," Thurston ordered.

"The boy isn't feeling well. 'Tis cold and damp outdoors." There was a pleading in her voice as she looked into William's steely eyes.

He despised the way she was always attempting to manipulate him. "Do as I say, Kathryn," he said from between clenched teeth. He glared down at her until she finally lifted the sleeping child into her arms and carried him out of the shack. When she had finally cleared the doorway, William turned to Lewis. "There have been six accidents at the Merrimack and ten at the Appleton in the last month. Why isn't Boott alarmed? Have you been getting word out that the Irish are to blame for these incidents? Because if you have, Lewis, I certainly haven't heard the rumors. What am I paying you for?"

"No need to take your personal problems out on me, Thurston," Lewis replied as he looked toward the doorway. "As for why Boott isn't concerned about the Irish, you'd need to ask him yourself. I'm afraid I don't have access to Boott or any of your other powerful friends, for that matter. I've done what you requested, but you need to remember that the Irish couldn't possibly have caused some of those incidents. The people of Lowell are not stupid. I'm not going to spread rumors that are unbelievable. I've made accusations against the Irish when there was a possibility they could have been involved, but people haven't put much stock in the idea."

In spite of the coolness of the room, William's face had flushed beet red, and the veins in his neck were throbbing. "Why is it that I'm the only person who can see what a menace these people are? You need to explain that the Irish are angry because of their wages, their living conditions . . . Use some imagination, Lewis! Surely you can do that much!"

Lewis looked up and met Thurston's hardened stare. "I've already tried that. To be honest, I believe the Irish may be involved to a certain extent because I certainly haven't been the cause of all the recent accidents. There were two mishaps at the canals, one at the Appleton, and three at the Merrimack that were not my doing. If the Irish didn't cause those particular accidents, there may be others set on the ruination of the mills—unless you have somebody else working for you. Do you, Thurston? Have you hired someone besides me to assist with your accidents?"

"How dare you question me! You're nothing more than a lackey—a henchman paid to do my bidding. Whether I've hired others to assist in my plans is none of your concern. You just follow my instructions."

"I thought we were more than that. I thought we were friends. After all, we spent a fair amount of time at the gaming tables together—shared quite a few suppers together."

William smirked. "You sound like a jealous wife, Lewis. I trust you to carry out my orders; that should be enough. We were companions on equal footing at one point, but that has changed, hasn't it? You've no fortune to your name. You're not even a propertied man anymore."

Defeat registered on Lewis's face, and Thurston pressed the matter to eliminate any further confusion. "I've hired you to do a job. Our business association makes it necessary for you to recognize my authority. I tolerate your calling me by my given name, but I will not abide your questions of how I conduct my business. Do you understand?"

"Yes, I believe I do," Lewis stated rather flatly.

"Good. Now, tell me, when you make accusations against the Irish, what kind of remarks are you hearing in return?"

Lewis's air of superiority had diminished. His gaze was cast downward as he dug the toe of his boot back and forth into the dirt floor. "People believe the Irish are happy with their way of life here in Lowell. My remarks about their living conditions have recently been countered with a rumor that Boott may be assisting the Irish in securing regular visits by a priest, and although I'm loath to believe it, some say the Associates have donated land for a Catholic church. Do you know if that rumor is correct?"

"What? I've no knowledge of such a donation. That's preposterous! The whole idea is to rid Lowell of this Irish vermin. Why would the Associates even consider such nonsense?" William spewed. Surely such insanity was merely fodder for the rumor mill.

Lewis leaned against the slats of the wobbly wooden chair. "I don't know, William. I'm merely telling you what I've heard. Have you attended recent meetings where anything of this nature was discussed? Do any of the Associates hold individual title to property around the Acre, or is the land jointly held by the Corporation?"

"Da," a tiny voice announced. The little boy who had been sleeping on Kathryn's lap toddled into the room, his eyes still matted with sleep. He raised his arms to William, obviously wanting to be picked up. "Da."

"Go out with your mother," William sternly replied to the child. Hadn't he told Kathryn time and again that the child was not to refer to him as his father?

Just then Kathryn came in, obviously frantic to know where the child was. "Sorry, I was talkin' to me sister and he got away." She grabbed the boy up and headed for the door. "It's awfully cold outside."

"You can come in soon. Go on!" he commanded. The child's lip quivered as though he might cry. Kathryn wrapped him in her shawl and quickly left.

"What was it you were asking me, Lewis?" William inquired, his thoughts having been scattered by the child's intrusion.

Lewis gave him a pensive look before replying. "About the donation of land for a church. Do you have any knowledge of such a transaction?" he reiterated.

"No, of course not. There's been no discussion. . . ." He hesitated and turned toward the small, flickering fire. He hadn't attended the last meeting of the Associates. Nathan had asked him to complete some meaningless business in Nashua; he'd been unable to return to Boston in time for the meeting, and he'd given Nathan his proxy.

The Associates had contrived against him—of that he was now certain. It was obvious Boott had won the allegiance of the Corporation. He turned around and faced Lewis. "I spoke in haste, Lewis. At the time of the last meeting, I was in Nashua at Nathan Appleton's request. It appears as if my colleagues may have conducted some business to which I'm not yet privy. We may have to explore another tactic."

"Like what? I don't see what else we can do."

"Cummiskey may be the key. The Irish listen to anything he says. If he's out of the picture, perhaps . . ."

Lewis rose from the chair. "Now, wait a minute, William. I'm not going after Cummiskey. I'd end up with every Irishman in Lowell after my hide. Besides, even if they didn't have Cummiskey, they'd follow another. O'Malley's his second; he'd step in and take over."

"I was thinking more along the lines of buying him off, Lewis, not killing him," William replied, attempting to hold his temper in check. He needed to find some way to play a pivotal role in turning things around. Why was it so easy for the likes of Boott and Cummiskey to gain power and devotees, he wondered. "For enough money, Cummiskey might be willing to exert his power and veto the idea of a Catholic church. That would surely enrage the Irish; they'd think Boott had gone back on his word." He remained silent, his mind racing. "I need time to think this out, Lewis, develop a plan. I've not decided if we should direct our efforts toward Cummiskey or Boott. In the meantime, you continue in your attempts to foster negative feelings toward these heathens."

"Might I ask a personal question?" Lewis tentatively ventured.

William was absently staring into the fire and nodded his head.

"If you dislike the Irish so intensely, why is it you've fathered a child by an Irish woman?"

William wheeled around and pointed a thick, stubby finger in Lewis's face. "Why, you impudent—! That woman, and what I do with her, is none of your business. As for the boy, he's not your concern. Do you understand me?" Lewis's contrite appearance was enough to convince William he'd made his point. "Go on home. And tell the woman and boy to come in as you leave," Thurston said with a dismissive wave of his hand.

Matthew walked into the small office in the counting room of the Appleton. The space had only recently been assigned to him and bore little evidence that he worked here. It was diminutive compared to Boott's office at the Merrimack, but Matthew found it to his liking. He viewed Boott's willingness to assign him to a different mill as a vote of confidence, and he liked the people who worked in the offices of the Appleton, particularly Lawrence Gault.

"I thought I would stop by and see how you're doing here at the Appleton, Matthew. All settled into your new surroundings?" Kirk asked as he strode into the room and seated himself on one of the two straight-backed oak chairs.

Matthew nodded and smiled. "Yes, it's more than adequate. I'm only just getting settled in, but I'm quite comfortable."

Kirk returned his smile. "Good. I'm anxious to hear about your trip to Boston. You did get my message upon your return?"

"Yes. My condolences to Mrs. Boott on the loss of her mother."

"Thank you. We were required to remain in New Hampshire longer than I'd anticipated. But one must allow women their time to grieve. Quite frankly, Mrs. Boott was so distraught I was beginning to think we'd never get back to Lowell. Ah, well, I digress. Now, tell me about your meeting with the good bishop. It went well, I hope."

Matthew knew the time of reckoning had come. Boott smiled and nodded his head, seemingly pleased with Matthew's report. At least until Matthew related that the bishop couldn't possibly visit until November or possibly December.

"What? That means we can't break ground before next spring at the earliest," Boott said, jumping up from his chair. "I thought he was interested in this project!"

Matthew hoped he could have a calming effect upon Boott, but he doubted whether the remainder of his report was going to accomplish such a feat. "He _is_ interested. However, he believes there will need to be a good deal of groundwork done in order to support the church. The bishop tells me that the diocese expects church funding to come from parishioners. If the parishioners are going to support the church, the bishop believes a more affluent Catholic base of middle-class citizens is needed in Lowell."

Boott was pacing back and forth across the small office. "Why didn't he say these things when we first met with him? Does he expect me to find affluent Irishmen who wish to immigrate to Lowell? They don't exist! I thought you said your meeting went well. I'd hate to think what I'd be hearing if you thought it went poorly."

Matthew bowed his head momentarily. The words stung, yet there was more to report. "Bishop Fenwick believes that within the next year or two, the Irish population of Lowell will swell. The increasing numbers will encourage more affluent Irishmen from Boston—shopkeepers and the like—to open businesses in Lowell. In turn, those men will provide a broader income base to support the church," Matthew explained. "Bishop Fenwick believes that as long as the Irish know the Associates have made a commitment to give the land, they won't be unduly averse to waiting a year or two for the church."

Kirk continued to pace back and forth. "And what about his promise for regular visits by a priest?"

Matthew didn't want to answer. He knew Boott's ire would only increase.

"Why don't we take a walk? You're obviously in need of more space than my office affords." When Boott offered no resistance, Matthew rose from his desk and rushed to open the door.

When they had reached the street, Boott looked both directions, then turned to Matthew. "Which way?"

"Toward the Acre."

"Ah—good idea. Let's take a look at the land we're setting aside to give to the diocese. By the way, how was Isabelle? I trust you two enjoyed your time together?"

Matthew gave his mentor a tentative glance. "As it turned out, Isabelle had a previous commitment. By the time I arrived at your sister's home, Isabelle had already departed for dinner. I fear the entire journey could be viewed as a failure."

Kirk slapped Matthew on the back. "Not entirely. At least we know the bishop has talked to his superiors. We know exactly what is required in order to make a final decision. Any problems arise during my journey to New Hampshire?"

"Nothing outside of the usual—only a small accident at the Merrimack. Other than that, operations have been running smoothly. There is, however, a matter I wanted to discuss with you. I'm not sure my timing is the best," he hesitantly replied.

Kirk laughed. "It doesn't sound like anything I'm going to enjoy hearing. You may as well go ahead and give me all the bad news at once. Is production down?"

"No, nothing like that. It's a matter of a more personal nature. There are some concerns regarding Thaddeus Arnold, the super—"

"I know who he is. What kind of concerns? Is he unable to manage the spinning room?"

"There are reports he's abusive to his wife—that he beats her. Some of the operatives who live in the adjoining house have heard them. It seems it's an almost nightly occurrence."

Boott ran a hand across his forehead. "Is there any proof? Has the wife come forward to complain?"

Matthew shook his head. "Mrs. Arnold has been seen bearing bruises, but there's no proof they were caused by her husband, and she hasn't lodged any complaint."

"Ah, Matthew, what goes on in a man's home is his business. Moreover, we need actual proof of such allegations. After all, Thaddeus is an elder in the church, and we wouldn't want to tarnish his reputation based on unfounded remarks. Such talk could be devastating to his future with the company. Perhaps his wife is the type who needs a heavy hand. She may even realize it herself since she doesn't come forward."

"I beg to disagree, Mr. Boott. I don't think a man needs to beat his wife into submission, and I certainly don't believe that any woman wants to be beaten by her husband."

Boott shrugged. "You're young, Matthew, with much to learn. It's the way things are. Women's opinions and ideas don't count; they need to remember their place. It merely takes some women longer than others to learn to accept their station in life."

Matthew walked along silently, wondering how Lilly might respond if she were to hear Boott's comments. He was certain she wouldn't remain silent.

"Well, there's also the matter of keeping your employees awake throughout the night. We can't have the girls so exhausted by the tirades of Arnold and his wife that they can't perform their duties." Matthew figured if Boott wouldn't see the seriousness of the situation for Mrs. Arnold, perhaps he would care about the well-being of his workers.

"I suppose that does bear some consideration," Boott replied. "Say, isn't that Lewis Armbruster up there? I thought he was in Nashua." Kirk waved his arm, indicating a man who had exited the Acre and was walking toward them. "I haven't seen him since he helped us finalize the purchase of his father's farm."

The man looked in their direction as Matthew was about to answer. "If it isn't Lewis, it's his double. I didn't know he was back in Lowell, either. Apparently he didn't want to be seen," Matthew remarked as Lewis turned and rushed off in the opposite direction.

Kirk nodded in agreement. "It appears there are any number of people interested in visiting the Acre nowadays—and most have little desire to be seen there."

~ 19 ~

An insistent rapping on the front door brought Addie to her feet. She had hoped for a half hour of peace and quiet before beginning the evening meal. For a moment she considered ignoring the interruption. Instead, curiosity won out, and she hobbled to the front door, the aching bunion on her right foot slowing her gait.

"For heaven's sake, Adelaide, what took you so long? I could catch my death of cold standing out here waiting for you," Mintie scolded as a cold November breeze whipped its way inside the door Addie opened. Without invitation, Mintie pushed onward toward the parlor. "No tea?" she called out before Addie had managed to limp back to the room.

"No, sister, I didn't take time to make tea. I was hoping to spend a half hour studying the Bible. Unfortunately, I had managed to read only a few verses before your unexpected arrival."

Mintie ran a gloved finger over the decorative teacart sitting near her chair and then pursed her lips in disapproval. "It appears you need to be dusting your furniture rather than relaxing," Mintie replied, waving her finger in the air as though she were checking for wind currents.

Addie lowered herself into a chair and gingerly elevated her foot on a small upholstered stool. "I'm thinking that the Lord would prefer I read His word than worry about a smattering of dust. But if it bothers you immeasurably, you have my permission to dust everything in sight," Addie said with a sweet smile.

Mintie appeared dumbstruck by the remark but recovered quickly. "I didn't come to do your housework. I came to talk," Mintie retorted.

"Then talk, Mintie. You're the one distressed by my housekeeping. I was only making an offer."

Mintie's face screwed into a look of consternation. "You've changed since we moved to Lowell, Adelaide. And not for the better, I fear. However, that's not what I've come to discuss." She leaned forward, folding her body in half. "It's that John Farnsworth. I know you've taken a fancy to him," Mintie said before raising her open palm toward Addie. "Don't try to deny it. You wear your heart on your sleeve. You always have. However, you must nip these feelings in the bud. There's no doubt he's a traitor—a spy. I tried to warn you, but you wouldn't listen. If you have a broken heart, you have no one to blame but yourself," Mintie triumphantly announced.

Addie tucked a wisp of hair under her white mobcap and stared at her sister in disbelief. "I'm beginning to worry about your mental condition, Mintie. You must get over this fixation with traitors and spies—it's not healthy."

Mintie gasped and turned pale. "Adelaide Beecher! It's difficult to believe we were reared in the same family. Now you listen to me. That Farnsworth is up to no good. He leaves at all times of the night, probably off to meet with other spies or visit those adulterous Irish women—or both. And that's not all." She paused as if to ascertain whether she'd be overheard. Casting a glance over her shoulder, Mintie leaned forward. "He receives missives from England—*all the time.*"

Addie giggled. "You do have a flair for the dramatic, Mintie. I always thought *I* was the gifted child when it came to such matters."

Mintie let out a snort and wagged her finger at Addie. "This is not a matter to be taken lightly. There are men who come to the house at all hours—they don't even leave a calling card. Any man worth his salt wouldn't come calling without a card. What does that tell you?"

Without waiting for an answer, she continued. "They're spies! Just like him, intent on keeping their identity a secret. I tell you, the Judge would have sent them packing. If a man isn't refined enough to carry a calling card, he isn't worth receiving. Why, any such caller to the Beecher house would have been out on his ear!"

Addie set her rocker into motion, careful not to disturb her propped foot. "You need to settle yourself, Mintie. You're overwrought for no reason whatsoever. Our circumstances here in Lowell aren't comparable to those in Boston, and you can't expect people to present calling cards. These are working-class people. And so are we! Our days of receiving calling cards are over."

Mintie was shaking her head in disgust. "Good manners don't begin and end with circumstances, Adelaide. Civility is a necessity for all classes of people."

"I agree. Civility and good manners transcend circumstances. But calling cards are not a necessity among—"

"Posh! They're not leaving calling cards because they are spies. Honestly, Adelaide, you remind me of a mule wearing blinders. It's obvious to *most* people that spies don't leave calling cards because it's their *modus operandi.*" She paused and took on an exasperated expression. "You'll remember that term from the Judge—it means how they operate."

"I remember the term well. I simply do not see how it has anything to do with anything."

"They don't want anyone to know who they are or where they've been,"

Mintie argued. "And you need to stay away from that John Farnsworth!"

"John Farnsworth is a fine man who loves it here in Lowell. The men who come to the house are probably some of the Englishmen from work who need special instructions or some such thing."

"You go ahead and make excuses for him, but when he and the British blow this place to smithereens, you'll know I was right. People no doubt hesitated to believe the British would burn the president's home in Washington."

Addie couldn't stifle another chuckle. She knew her laughter served only to anger Mintie further, but her sister's allegations were preposterous.

"That's right, you keep sniggering, but I know there's a plot underway. I heard Farnsworth talking to some of those men about ordering more blasting powder for the canals. They're not pulling the wool over my eyes! They're stockpiling that blasting powder until the British arrive to take back the country, and your John Farnsworth will supply them with ample explosives to complete their treacherous plans."

Addie realized there was no convincing her sister she was wrong, yet she wished she could find some words that would assuage Mintie's concerns. "Can't you see, Mintie, that there is truly a need for additional blasting powder for the new canals that are planned? They're expanding all the time."

"Your naïveté never ceases to amaze me, Adelaide. Can't *you* see they have those strong-backed Irish brutes to dig out the canals? Why would the Corporation spend money on blasting powder when they have those beasts of burden? You mark my words, Adelaide Beecher, you've set yourself up for heartbreak. I would think you'd have learned that the first time when that Charles went off with another woman." Mintie sat back in her chair with a smug smile on her face.

"Charles did not leave me for another woman, and you know it. We agreed to end our courtship when the Judge insisted I could not marry until some eligible bachelor was willing to wed you. We both knew that would not soon occur."

A small gasp escaped Mintie's lips. She jumped up and rushed toward the front door without so much as a good-bye.

"I'm sorry, Mintie. I shouldn't have spoken such cruel words," Addie apologetically called after her sister. "Oh, Father, why did I let my tongue get the best of me yet again?" she wistfully prayed as she rose from the chair. Her peaceful half hour was nothing more than a memory, and dinner preparations awaited her in the kitchen.

By the time the girls began arriving home, Addie had analyzed her conversation with Mintie so many times she was now convinced her older sister's accusations against John might have merit. The longer she tried to persuade herself Mintie's arguments were nonsensical, the more concerned she became. Perhaps John was a traitor. Yet how could she believe such a thing? He spoke of his fondness for Massachusetts and desire to bring his father from England. And he professed to love the Lord—and certainly acted like a God-fearing Christian man. It was all too difficult to sort out right now, for dinner wouldn't serve itself.

"You sit down right now," Lilly ordered. "I'm going to do these dishes, and you sit there and keep me company. Take your shoe off and put your foot up. Then tell me what's wrong."

Addie's eyebrows arched. "What makes you think anything is wrong? Besides my bunion and gout, of course."

"I know you too well, Miss Addie. You snapped at Prudence when she asked for more apple butter, and when Mary Alice said her meat was a bit tough, you were not very pleasant. I've never seen you like this. I insist you tell me what's happened."

Addie looked down at the floor and placed her hands on her cheeks. "It's Mintie. She came over here this afternoon offering proof that John Farnsworth is a spy. And, Lilly, I'm not so sure she's wrong. I've mulled it over for the past several hours, and what she says makes sense."

"Preposterous! Tell me what evidence she's produced." Lilly completed washing the dishes as Addie recounted the afternoon of tragedy wrought by Miss Mintie.

"I don't want to believe ill of anyone, especially not of John."

"Then don't," Lilly said, wiping her hands on a towel before sitting down beside her friend. Taking Addie's hand into her own, Lilly gazed directly into the older woman's eyes. "Now that you've repeated all of Miss Mintie's allegations aloud, don't you see how foolish they are? John Farnsworth has no more interest in overthrowing the country than you or I. Your sister is saying these things because John has begun calling upon you. Mintie doesn't like the idea of you having a suitor. In a word, Miss Addie, your sister is jealous."

"Do you really think that's all it is? I keep remembering that she was suspicious of him when he first arrived."

Lilly giggled. "Only because he had a letter from England, which doesn't prove anything except that he keeps in communication with his father. I think he should be commended for writing home—not treated like a criminal. The only thing Miss Mintie has proved is that she's a jealous snoop. I think what Miss Mintie needs is a suitor of her own, someone to keep her mind and time occupied—and I think I may know just the person!" Lilly smiled to herself even imagining the stiff-necked spinster on the arm of a beau.

Addie placed a hand over her mouth to stifle her laughter. "I don't think Mintie would consider taking a suitor."

"We'll see. I have a very convincing gentleman in mind. Given a chance, I think he may be able to soften her up a bit." Lilly saw a glimmer of hope return to Addie's expression.

"Thank you for your help, Lilly. Speaking of help, I forgot to mention I've gone next door the past several mornings hoping to visit with Mrs. Arnold. She came to the door the first day but didn't let me in. She said she didn't have time to visit. After that, she didn't even answer the door, but I knew she was in there."

Lilly nodded. "I'm sure she's afraid to talk to anyone. That husband of hers has her frightened to death. And Matthew Cheever was proven to be no better." Lilly tried to keep her emotions under control. Frankly, she was just as mixed up over Matthew as Miss Addie was over Mr. Farnsworth.

"He hasn't done one thing to help," she continued. "I'm certain he's afraid the reputation of the wonderful Corporation might be tarnished if word got out that one of their fine supervisors beats his wife. But there must be some way to help her. We'll figure something out—with or without Matthew Cheever."

"Now, now, dear, Matthew is a fine young man. I'm sure he's looking into the matter. Things don't always move as rapidly as we think they should. He's a busy man."

Lilly folded the dish towel and turned toward Addie. "Sometimes we can't depend on busy men, Miss Addie. Sometimes we must take—"

"Lilly, come quick," Prudence insisted as she burst into the kitchen, her face flushed with excitement. She bounced from foot to foot, obviously wanting immediate attention. When Lilly didn't quickly move, Prudence began tugging at her roommate's arm. "Come on—you have a visitor."

"Hurry! It may be Matthew," Addie urged.

Addie's words caused Lilly to halt midstep and pull her arm away from Prudence. "Is it Matthew Cheever?"

Prudence shook her head. "No. I've never seen this man before, and he wouldn't give his name. He said he wanted to surprise you. He's quite handsome and *very* sophisticated—probably from Boston. If you're not interested in him, promise you'll introduce me? Please?" Prudence begged, folding her hands in prayerlike fashion.

"Stop it, Prudence," Lilly replied with a giggle as she followed Prudence toward the parlor. "I don't know any handsome, sophisticated man who would be calling on me. It's probably a mistake." Lilly stopped in the doorway, unable to believe her eyes. Across the room sat an elegantly clad Lewis, surrounded by at least five fawning mill girls.

The moment he spied her in the entrance, he jumped to his feet and motioned her forward. "Don't stand there staring at me as though you've seen a ghost. Come give your big brother a hug, dear Lilly."

Her roommates sat watching the unfolding scene, envy etched upon each of their faces as she walked toward Lewis. She allowed him to embrace her only for the sake of issuing her edict. "I want you to leave here immediately," Lilly whispered in his ear before pushing away from him.

"Why don't we take a short stroll? I've been anxious to see you since my return from Nashua. We have much to talk about," he said, giving her a piercing stare. "Get your cloak, Lilly," he hissed, taking hold of her arm.

"Oh, don't leave us so soon," Prudence cooed. "Lilly hasn't even had an opportunity to make proper introductions."

Lewis bowed and kissed Prudence's hand. "I'll be returning often, dear girl, and I'm sure we'll have the opportunity to become better acquainted. Trust me." With a self-satisfied smile, he tipped his hat at Prudence and grasped Lilly's arm.

Lilly thought Pru might actually swoon. She held her hand to her face with an expression of complete adulation. The other girls were no better. Lilly looked to her brother and had to admit he was quite stylish and well-groomed. No doubt the gaming tables had smiled favorably upon him.

"Until we meet again, ladies," Lewis said, bowing low. He pressed Lilly toward the door, pausing only long enough to pop a top hat onto his head.

"What do you want, Lewis?" Lilly asked as soon as they exited the door. "I'm not going for a stroll. We can talk right here."

"Truly? Your little friends are watching out the window. If we stand here much longer, I'm sure at least one or two of them will be out here to join us."

Lilly pulled her arm away from his grasp and began walking. "What is it you're after, Lewis? Why have you returned to Massachusetts?" A million thoughts raced through her head. If he was here for money, he'd be out of luck. She wasn't about to part with any of her hard-earned wages to support his lifestyle. Christian charity only extended so far.

"I could tell you I was concerned for your welfare, but we both know that isn't true. Tell me, dear sister, how does it feel to be working for the Corporation you hold in such contempt? Do you ever revel in the thought of somehow usurping their power?" He emitted a callous laugh. "No, that would never happen to my little sister, would it? She's the perfect child who never does wrong. Dear Lilly would never consider doing anything unchristian—she doesn't have wicked thoughts."

His words stung her conscience. If he knew how many people had been the victims of her unkind thoughts and deeds in recent months, he would certainly question her Christianity. The idea was frightening. "I'm not perfect, and we both know that, Lewis. I dislike working for the Corporation, but you left me penniless; I had no choice. Quit avoiding my question. It's cold out here. Tell me what it is you want so I can go home and you can go back to wherever it is you came from."

"I'm not going anywhere, Lilly. I plan to be in Lowell for quite some time. As a matter of fact, that's one of the reasons I've come to see you. I understand that most of the mill girls are quite frugal with their money and some of them have accumulated rather large sums. If you're one of those girls, I could use your help. I'm broke and need money, and you are the only family I have."

"I have no intention of helping you, Lewis. I can't believe you have the audacity to come to me for money."

He shrugged. "If you aren't one of those girls who has plenty of money, then introduce me to one. I'm not interested in the ones who are sending their wages back home to their poverty-stricken families. My inheritance is gone, and I can't be wasting time."

Lilly gaped at him, astonished at his request. "I'll do no such thing. I'm not going to assist you in duping any of these girls out of their hard-earned wages. Surely you can find some other more profitable scheme."

"Poor Lilly. You don't understand much, do you? These girls are vulnerable, unscathed little flowers waiting to be plucked. I can move from one to the other, permitting them the pleasure of keeping company with an educated, handsome man as well as assisting them with the proper investment of their wages."

Lilly was aghast at his proposal. "Investment of their wages into your pocket! So this is how you now intend to support yourself?"

"Don't be ridiculous. Those girls don't have enough money to support my needs, but their funds would be a nice addition to my income. You need not concern yourself with my welfare. I've entered into a business venture with a gentleman of considerable means. However, I'm sure your little friends would be thrilled to purchase an expensive gift or two for a handsome beau," he said with a smirk. "I find that for the right amount of affection, propriety is often overlooked."

Lilly turned and briskly headed back toward the boardinghouse. "You sicken me, Lewis. Do you stay awake at night thinking of vile ways to hurt people?" She gave him a look of disgust. "I will not be a part of your schemes."

"As you choose, but I'll succeed with or without your help. It will merely take a bit longer to weed out the girls who are penniless. Incidentally, did I mention the fact that I saw Matthew and Kirk Boott today? Matthew has certainly managed to endear himself to the Corporation, hasn't he?"

She knew Lewis; his words were intended to cause pain. "If you're interested in Matthew's position in the Corporation, you'll need to talk to him."

"I believe I hit a sore spot. I'm so sorry, Lilly. You know I would never want to open old wounds," he said, sarcasm dripping from each word. "Well, here we are, back to your humble dwelling. Tell me, is it true? Do you really sleep four girls to a bed?"

Lilly turned, fixing him with what she hoped was a scathing expression.

"Get away from me, Lewis. Go away and don't ever return. I have no desire to be associated with you or your scheming."

Without saying a word, Lewis leaned around her, opened the door, and made his way inside the house before she could object. Lilly watched in amazement as Lewis boldly strode into the parlor and immediately took command of the group. "Ladies, I wanted to once again tell you what a pleasure it was spending time with you earlier this evening. I will be returning tomorrow evening if any of you happen to be available for a visit." He smiled broadly. "One more thing," he added, "don't believe a thing my sister has to say about me. She's a teeny bit jealous—fearful of losing my attention. In fact, she sometimes tells horrid tales regarding my behavior, hoping to dissuade young ladies from keeping company with me. Don't you let her convince you with those exaggerated stories. We must join forces and conspire against her if I'm to have the pleasure of calling upon you fair maidens." Lewis directed an exaggerated wink at the group, then bowed and bade them good-night. The girls giggled in delight.

Lilly couldn't believe her ears. Her brother had completely outmaneuvered her.

20

Lilly had given Matthew ample time. It was now blatantly obvious the Associates were not going to hold Thaddeus Arnold accountable for his barbaric behavior. Having weighed the merits of the company's indecisiveness, Lilly prayed with fervor and then decided the Corporation must suffer the consequences of God's disapproval—using her, of course, as the instrument of His displeasure. Arnold's behavior was merely the catalyst God was using to move her forward. She was ashamed she had wavered in her earlier beliefs, but it was now abundantly clear she must move forward and bring the Corporation to ruin before further expansion could be completed.

Developing a plan, however, was much more difficult. Quick, decisive action was needed. However, the feat must be destructive enough to bring business to a halt—damaging enough to insure the Associates would rethink their earlier decision to blemish the Massachusetts countryside with brick and mortar factories. Yet her plan must remain safe enough to keep the operatives from harm. She had learned from her earlier plots that stopping one machine, or even several, was not detrimental to the Corporation. Those incidents had merely succeeded in reprisals being meted out to the operatives by Thaddeus Arnold.

"No, I must figure a way to bring production completely to a halt," Lilly murmured as she strolled through the small but growing town. When the plan first began to grow in her mind, she had never figured it would be so difficult to sabotage the Corporation and their mills.

The wind whipped at her thin cloak, causing Lilly to pull it tight. No one would ever suspect that a worthless mill girl could have such an agenda against the Associates, and that was just as Lilly would have it. As God would have it, too. After all, Lilly felt quite confident that her mission had come from the Almighty himself. God had given her the desire to see the land returned to its original beauty—to see the Associates refund the monies and farms they had so greedily consumed. True, it would be difficult at this stage to see the mills destroyed and the land returned to pastures and farms, but Lilly knew that with God all things were possible.

Days passed as she attempted to devise her method. Finally, in the middle of the night an idea wove itself in and out of her sleep-induced haze. When Lilly awakened, the plan was clear.

"You seem a million miles away," Nadene said as the two finished making their bed.

"Hmm?" Lilly heard the words but scarcely registered them.

"Did you have a romantic dream?" Pru teased. "I did, and it was about that brother of yours."

Those words snapped Lilly to attention. "Lewis is bad news. He lives only for himself. Mark my words, you'll rue the day you met him."

Pru danced away toward the door. "He said you'd be like this, but honestly, Lilly, you don't have to worry about losing a brother." She winked and added, "Maybe instead, you'll gain a sister." She didn't wait for Lilly's reply but instead glided out the door as though she were skating on a pond of ice.

"Silly girl," Nadene remarked.

"More than silly. She's truly daft if she thinks Lewis can bring her anything but pain."

Pulling a brush through her crown of curls, Lilly returned to thoughts of her scheme. She made every attempt to find fault with the plan. She found none. Picking up Pru's tortoiseshell mirror, Lilly momentarily stared at her reflection. Her hair, she decided, was acceptable and so was her idea.

Nadene and Lilly rushed down the stairs, grabbed their cloaks from the row of pegs near the entrance, and rushed out the front door toward the Appleton. By the time the breakfast bell rang two hours later, Lilly's anticipation was rising to new heights. Feigning a problem with her machine, she urged Nadene to return home without her. Lagging behind until the room had emptied, Lilly picked up a piece of roving and held it to the flame of a whale-oil lamp hanging on the wall, then quickly threw the burning rope into a cart of roving that stood near the center of the room. Casting a glance over her shoulder as she left the room, Lilly nodded in satisfaction. The roving was beginning to smolder, and random flames were starting to lick along the edge of the cart.

Lilly hurried from the mill yard and down Jackson Street, finding herself out of breath when she finally arrived at the boardinghouse. The familiar smells of fried ham and biscuits greeted her as she pushed open the front door.

"Hurry, Lilly. I filled a plate for you," Nadene called out.

Lilly seated herself and slowly began cutting the piece of ham. Chewing slowly, she broke apart one of the thick biscuits and began to slather it with butter. "Would you pass the jam, please?"

Nadene stared open-mouthed at her friend. "You don't have time for jam. We need to leave in less than a minute, Lilly."

A tiny smile played at the corner of Lilly's lips. "If you insist," she replied, rising from the chair as she continued nibbling at the biscuit. "I think I'll finish this as we walk."

Nadene scurried out of the room and was waiting at the front door, holding Lilly's cloak. They were nearing the mill when they heard men and women screaming. Suddenly the tower bell began ringing. Nadene and Lilly glanced at each other, then began running toward the mill.

"Fire on an upper floor," one of the men yelled.

Nadene seized the man's arm. "Which floor?"

"Third—spinning room," he replied without hesitation.

"N-o-o-o!" Nadene cried as she began running toward the mill.

Lilly stared after her friend in disbelief. "Nadene, where are you going?" she screamed. "Come back here!" Lilly broke into a run. Why was Nadene rushing toward the building? What could she be thinking? Nadene had already made her way through the crowd of operatives who had gathered closer to the mill. Lilly glanced up. Flames were evident through the glass windows. As she grew closer to the building, Lilly saw Nadene arguing with one of the men. He was shaking his head and had grasped her friend's arm. Lilly watched in horror as Nadene broke loose from the man's grip and raced into the stairwell. With wooden legs she moved onward until she reached the man. "Where is she? Why didn't you stop her?" Lilly screamed.

The man looked at her, his face etched in disbelief. "I tried to stop her. I couldn't follow her—I was ordered to stay here and prevent anyone else from entering the building."

"Well, you didn't do your job very well, did you?" Lilly condemned as she attempted to push past him.

He pulled her back. "Maybe not with your friend, but I won't fail again. Now get back," he ordered.

"She'll die. I have to go after her," Lilly argued, pushing at his arm as she attempted to go around him.

He grasped her shoulder and turned her away from the building. "No! Now get back."

"Lilly! What are you doing? Get back from the building."

Lilly turned to see Matthew running in her direction. "Nadene's up there—she's gone to the third floor. I must get her out. Please help me!" Lilly pleaded.

Matthew placed his arms around her. "If you'll move away from the building, I'll see what I can do. Give me your word that you won't attempt to follow me."

"I promise. Just please hurry," she begged, moving away from the entryway.

She watched until Matthew was out of sight. What if he found Nadene . . . dead? What if he couldn't find her at all? "Matthew will find her—he must. Surely the fire hasn't spread enough to cause Nadene immense harm," she murmured. The hollow words did little to calm the growing uneasiness that was seeping into her consciousness.

She strained forward, watching the stairwell. Two men exited the building and issued orders before rushing off toward some unknown destination. Lilly paced back and forth while maintaining a steadfast gaze toward the entryway. Would Matthew never return? Perhaps she should break through the guards and go search for Nadene herself. Head raised high and shoulders straight, Lilly approached the Appleton.

One of the men stood resolutely, with elbows bent as he rested his beefy hands on his hips. His lips tightened into a straight, determined line as she grew closer. "Where do you think you're going?" he asked, moving directly in front of her.

Lilly attempted to ignore the man's question and push her way through. Too soon she found it impossible to break his grasp. Shaking her arm, she gave him a frosty glare. "Turn me loose!"

"Not a chance," he replied. "I was ordered to keep spectators out—you, in particular," he added with a grin.

Lilly stomped her foot. "You turn me loose or you'll answer to Matthew Cheever!"

"Really? Well, he's the one who told me to keep you out of there," the man replied while turning toward the burning building. "Besides, there's Mr. Cheever now."

Lilly swung her head toward the stairwell. Matthew was carrying Nadene's lifeless body in his arms. "Lilly, come quickly," he called out, never breaking his stride.

Lilly pushed past the men and ran at breakneck speed, her cape billowing open in the crisp breeze until she was finally alongside Matthew. "Is she . . ." The words stuck in her throat.

"No, but her breathing is shallow—there was a lot of smoke in the room. She's unconscious and burned in several places. Let's get her back to the boardinghouse. I'm hopeful she'll come around, but I'm afraid she's going to have some terrible scars. Would you carry that?" he asked, nodding toward the Bible lying atop Nadene's soot-covered dress.

Lilly reached up and gathered the book into her hands. "It was her grandmother's Bible. Her mother gave it to Nadene when she moved to Lowell," Lilly explained as she attempted to clean the stained leather cover with her dress. Words of wisdom and insight to the Scriptures were inscribed upon the pages—Nadene's only link with her beloved grandmother. Of course she would walk through fire to retrieve it.

"I had to pry it from her hand. What was it doing in the spinning room, anyway? There are rules against reading at work," Matthew challenged before breaking into a fit of coughing.

Lilly glared in response. "Rules? My friend is dying and you're telling me about rules?"

Matthew glanced down at her. "Don't overstate the situation in order to change the subject, Lilly. Nadene is injured, but she's not going to die. We don't permit reading or other activities at work because we want to prevent you girls from injury. And although her reading didn't cause the fire, the fact that she ran back in the building was based solely upon the fact that she wanted to retrieve her Bible. Had the Bible been at home where it belonged, Nadene would be safe."

"Or if the fire had never started," Lilly murmured.

"The fire was an accident over which we had no control. Fires and textile mills are constant companions. The Bible, however, should not have been there. Nadene *had* control of that situation. If she had followed the rules, this accident could have been prevented. Do you understand what I'm saying?"

Lilly nodded in acknowledgment. She longed to tell him he was the one who didn't understand—that she alone was responsible for Nadene's perilous situation. Yet she remained silent, lacking the courage it would take to speak the truth. Guilt wound around her heart like roving to a spindle.

"I sent one of the men to fetch Dr. Barnard. Try not to worry. The damage is minimal, and we should be back in operation by morning."

He was obviously attempting to cheer her, but his words only made it more difficult for Lilly to bear. Nadene was injured, and she had failed in her mission. *I should have waited until evening to start the fire,* she thought. But having evaluated the prospect of remaining behind after the final bell, Lilly knew such a feat would have been impossible. Thaddeus Arnold was always the last one out of the room each evening, making sure the lamps were snuffed and the room was in proper order for the next morning's work. He would never permit an operative in the spinning room after his own final departure. But at the breakfast and dinner bells, the man wasn't nearly so cautious. Like the rest of them, he was anxious to rush home for his meal. Knowing she must protect the lives of those working in the mills, Lilly had hoped that the half-hour break would permit the fire adequate time to do its damage. She had been wrong.

She touched Matthew's arm as they reached the front door of the boardinghouse. "If there was so little damage to the Appleton, how is it Nadene's condition is so dreadful?" she inquired with her voice trembling.

"From all appearances, her cloak caught on fire, which caused the burns to her hands and arms. Smoke caused the remainder of her health problems. I'm guessing she became disoriented in the haze and couldn't find her way out of the building."

The front door opened. It was obvious Miss Addie had been watching for them, no doubt informed by some of the girls who had run ahead to explain the situation.

"Follow me, Matthew. We'll put her in my bedroom. Dr. Barnard is waiting," Addie instructed as she led the way to her room. "Put her on the bed—

carefully, we don't want to cause her undue pain."

Matthew nodded his agreement before lowering Nadene onto the crisp white sheet. "I'll leave her in your hands, Dr. Barnard. I must get back to the mill and then report to Mr. Boott."

"Absolutely, Matthew. You've done all you can for the girl. Miss Addie and I will see to her care," Dr. Barnard replied.

Lilly could no longer hold her emotions in check. Tears rolled down her cheeks as she viewed Nadene's condition. Along one of Nadene's arms angry red flesh appeared to be blistering, while the other was interspersed with purplish black wounds. Both hands were charred and blistered. The smell was unlike anything Lilly had ever known. She felt her stomach churn and knew she might very well lose the contents of her stomach.

Backing out of the room, Lilly fought the sensation of dizziness that threatened to send her to the floor. *What have I done? Dear God, what have I done?*

Matthew rushed back to the Appleton, relieved when he was met by a calm-looking Hugh Cummiskey. "We've got things here under control, Mr. Cheever," Hugh reported. "The fire is out and once the smoke has cleared, work can begin."

"How much damage?" Matthew inquired.

"None to the machinery or the building itself. A cart of roving is ruined. Other than that, nothing of consequence."

Matthew breathed a sigh of relief. He didn't want to carry a report of extensive damage to his boss. "I'll feel better if I take a look for myself before reporting to Mr. Boott. He may ask if I've seen the damage for myself."

Hugh nodded in agreement. "No need to explain, Mr. Cheever. I understand."

Matthew ascended the stairway and surveyed the room. Cummiskey was correct. There was little damage, and work could certainly resume by morning if not sooner. Already the unpleasant smell of smoke had subsided, and several men were cleaning soot from the machinery and floor. Satisfied there was nothing further needing his attention, he returned to the mill yard, where Cummiskey awaited him.

He gave Cummiskey a slap on the shoulder. "You were right, Hugh. Thank you for your valuable assistance," Matthew said. Turning to the supervisor, he added, "Mr. Arnold, I'll leave it to your discretion to determine when work can commence." He then headed off toward Mr. Boott's home. He disliked being the bearer of bad news, especially when it entailed production at one of the mills. But he doubted whether anyone else had rushed to inform Boott. After all, it wasn't a pleasant task. He sounded the doorknocker, surprised when Boott himself answered the door.

"None of the help is around when you need them," Kirk said as he ushered Matthew into his office. "What brings you here this time of day, Matthew?"

At Kirk's invitation, Matthew seated himself. "I wanted to personally advise you there's been a fire in the spinning room at the Appleton." Kirk jumped up from his chair at the report. "Very little damage. We'll be operational by morning. Perhaps earlier," Matthew quickly added.

"Details—give me details, my boy," Kirk insisted.

Matthew reported what little he could and awaited Kirk's instructions.

"Of course, I'd like to know *how* the fire got started, but I doubt we'll ever gain that piece of information. However, it appears we may need to take further safety precautions. Why don't you and the supervisors meet and discuss future prevention. You can report your ideas to me, and then we can make a final decision on implementation."

Matthew agreed, pleased that their meeting had been brief and Mr. Boott had remained calm. "I'll report back to you by Friday," Matthew said as they walked onto the expansive front porch.

"Friday will be fine. I almost forgot—Isabelle, Neva, and several other relatives are arriving on Friday. I promised them a tour of the Appleton. They find this industrialization process difficult to fathom without actually seeing for themselves. Once they get inside, I'm certain they won't want to remain for long. I told Isabelle I would have you take charge of the tour. I hope you don't mind. There's no hurry, for I think I've convinced Neva to remain in Lowell until after the holidays. And, of course, we'll expect you to join us for dinner Saturday evening."

"Certainly. I'll be pleased to escort them through the mill," Matthew replied. He knew there was no other acceptable answer.

Soon after Matthew had placed Nadene upon the bed, the cool, fresh air from Addie's bedroom window, along with the vinegar Dr. Barnard had placed under her nose, rendered Nadene conscious. With Nadene's awakening, her pain was clearly evident. Lilly couldn't bear to watch the ministrations as Addie and Dr. Barnard separated Nadene's fingers. Her friend's hands resembled two giant spiderwebs by the time Dr. Barnard secured the splints and bandages. Lilly had followed Dr. Barnard's directions and mixed a salve of linseed oil and limewater and then quickly exited the room, offering to complete Addie's household chores.

While Lilly began paring potatoes for the evening meal, Nadene's moans cut through the afternoon silence of the boardinghouse. Lilly began humming, then singing aloud, hoping she could drown out the sounds of her friend's misery, along with her own guilt. When that didn't work, she began to pray—first for Nadene's healing, then for her own forgiveness. She wasn't sure if it was answered prayer or the fact that Dr. Barnard had completed his treatment, but Nadene's moans finally ceased. Although her own feelings of guilt had not completely diminished, Lilly knew she was forgiven for the part she had played in Nadene's injuries. Along with that forgiveness came the awakening realization that her behavior had been for the fulfillment of her own selfish desires rather than at God's direction.

Your sinful behavior is not from God, a small voice seemed to whisper to her consciousness.

"I know, Lord," she whispered. "Look what I've done in the name of righteous justice." She closed her eyes, hoping she wouldn't cry. But she was unsuccessful, and giant tears wet her thick dark lashes before tumbling down her cheeks. *How could I have been so wrong—so blind to the pain I might cause? I thought you'd given me a mission, but I've messed things up so badly.*

"Are you salting the potatoes with those tears?" Addie asked as she placed her arm comfortingly around Lilly's shoulder.

Lilly sniffed and attempted a smile. "How's Nadene?"

"She's resting. Dr. Barnard gave her some paregoric. You better get back over to the mill. If they've started up production, Mr. Arnold will expect you to be there no matter what Nadene's condition. Don't you worry. I'll be able to hear Nadene if she awakens."

"I know you're right, but going back into that mill is the last thing I want to do, Miss Addie."

Once again Addie pulled Lilly into a comforting embrace. "I know, dearie, but there's nothing to fear. I'm sure the fire was just one of those rare occurrences that won't ever happen again. As the Judge used to say, you can't let fear rule your life—you've got to get back up on a horse when it throws you."

Lilly nodded. The lump in her throat prevented a reply. *If Miss Addie knew the cause of the fire, she wouldn't be so quick to offer kind reassurances,* Lilly thought as she walked toward the Appleton. Wrapping her cape tightly against a bracing current of cold air that whipped down the street, Lilly tucked her head down and moved resolutely toward the mill yard. She must find Mr. Arnold and ask if he would permit her to operate Nadene's frames. Locating Thaddeus Arnold was not difficult. He was rushing about the mill yard with his chest swelled out like a banty rooster as he issued orders to the clustered girls and pointed them toward the stairwell.

Hurrying toward the distasteful little man, Lilly called out, "Mr. Arnold! May I have a word with you?"

He peered over the top of his spectacles, his gaze roaming over Lilly's body in a manner that caused her acute discomfort. He beckoned her forward.

Keeping her eyes focused downward, Lilly approached him. It required all the humility she could muster to stand before the pompous little man. "Would you permit me to operate Nadene's frames until she is able to return?"

His lips formed a malevolent grin. "And my consent would be worth *what* to you?"

Lilly could feel the blood pumping, pulsing and coursing its way through her body, pounding upward into her temples. If she didn't hold her temper in check, she knew she would explode at the pompous excuse of a man standing before her. She lifted her head and met his beady-eyed stare. "Why, Mr. Arnold, I was merely hoping to keep production at full rate—hoping to be of some assistance to you in this difficult time. With Sarah gone home for several months and now Nadene unable to tend her frames, I was certain you would be distraught over their vacancies." Her voice was sweet and melodious, the very essence of a spring breeze floating through a brisk November morn. Even she was surprised by the gentleness of her reply.

Mr. Arnold appeared to be overwhelmed by her response. There was a momentary appearance of trust in his gaze. Ever so slightly, she lifted her eyebrows—waiting, anticipating his agreement. His lips turned upward into a smile that revealed his yellowed teeth. "You're a difficult girl to figure out, Miss Armbruster. I never presumed you would be concerned about production in the spinning room. So you're offering to operate Nadene's frames while she's recovering? Just because you want to help me keep production at full rate?"

Lilly's gaze was fixed on his bony fingers as they moved across the growth of stubble along his jaw. "And because I want Nadene to receive her pay. She has her family to support."

A spark of recognition shone in his eyes. "Ah, so it isn't that you want to help *me,* is it, Miss Armbruster? What you really want to do is help your friend remain on the pay ledger, even though she won't be working. Isn't that correct?"

He was on the attack. "Technically, I wish to help you both, Mr. Arnold," she replied, her voice resonating with all of the meekness she could muster.

He folded his arms across his sunken chest. "You realize I can order you to operate Nadene's frames without additional pay. Operation of the machinery is at my discretion. So once again, Miss Armbruster, I would ask this: what is my agreement worth to you?"

Lilly met his lustful gaze with an icy glare. "My silence. At least for the present time."

Thaddeus's mask of confusion was quickly replaced by a scowl of recognition. "I'll permit you to work Nadene's frames, and you may sign the ledger and collect payment on her behalf. If you betray our agreement, you'll suffer dearly. Speak to no one of this arrangement," he added. She remained transfixed, amazed he had so willingly agreed to her request. "Why are you standing there gaping at me? Get back to work!" he hissed before stalking off toward the counting room.

Lilly rushed toward the steps before he could recant his decision. The disgusting odor of smoke filled her nostrils as she moved up the stairs, but the smell was nothing compared to the vile odor of burnt flesh. For as long as she lived, Lilly would never forget that smell.

The spinning frames remained silent while the girls scrubbed soot from the floors and equipment. One of the mechanics had managed to unseal several of the windows, and cold, fresh air was beginning to waft through the room. Lilly inhaled deeply, grabbed a pail of water, and began cleaning Nadene's frames. She didn't know how she could possibly manage four frames, but somehow she would—she must.

Penance was required, and penance would be given.

21

The next morning, work in the spinning room returned to normal. For everyone except Lilly and Nadene, that is. Nadene was now ensconced in Addie's bedroom having her bandages frequently changed, while Lilly was furiously attempting to operate four spinning frames instead of two.

Shortly after lunch, Kirk Boott came on the floor accompanied by several men. When he recognized Lilly, he paused long enough to inquire as to her health and well-being, then briefly introduced her to William Thurston and Nathan Appleton before moving down the line with Mr. Arnold. Lilly thought Boott scrutinized her for a rather long time, given the situation. He seemed as though he wanted to ask her something but instead turned his attention back to his companions. Lilly felt awash in guilt. Surely he didn't have some idea of her responsibility for the fire.

By the time the evening bell rang, announcing the day's end, Lilly was exhausted. For twelve hours she'd moved back and forth among the frames, dampening her fingers before quickly reaching in and mending the broken strands of roving, replacing empty spindles of roving with full ones, and pulling off each of the full spindles of thread to be replaced by an empty spindle. However, it seemed as if she always had the incorrect spindle in her hand at the improper moment.

"Managing to keep up with your frames?" Thaddeus snidely inquired as she brushed past him on her way through the narrow doorway.

"Yes, thank you." She didn't want to smile sweetly, but she did.

His fingers wrapped around her wrist. "If you decide you'd like to make some other arrangements, I'll try to accommodate. You look quite weary," he whispered, releasing the hold on her wrist and then patting her backside.

She slapped at his hand. He winked and gave her a lewd grin that made her shudder as she ran down the winding staircase, out through the mill yard, and down Jackson Street. Pushing open the front door, she pulled off her cape, hung it on the peg, and hurried in to see Nadene. "How are you feeling this evening?" she inquired, her breath coming in short sputters as she leaned against the doorjamb.

Nadene gave her a smile. "Better than you, it would appear," Nadene remarked in a cheerful voice. "You look as though you've had the longest workday of your life. What's wrong?"

Lilly was making excuses about not sleeping well when Prudence pushed open the front door. "Did you hear there's been another accident?" she called out while slamming the door behind her. "This time at No. 2."

Nadene reached out for Prudence as she entered Addie's bedroom, then stopped when the pain refused to allow her fingers to work. "What kind of accident? Was anyone injured?"

"Nope, no one injured, praise be to God," Pru added almost as an after-thought. "Appears work will be at a standstill unless they get things fixed this evening."

"What happened?" Lilly persisted. She couldn't halt the feeling of adula-tion that swept through her. An accident had occurred; no one was injured; and she hadn't been involved. It appeared God was taking care of matters on His own. After Nadene's injury, Lilly had prayed for forgiveness. She had even promised to bow out of the retribution business, telling God she now realized He could handle matters without her intervention. And so He had. This latest accident was affirmation at its finest, she decided.

"There's a jam in the waterwheel, or maybe one of the cogs is broken. I'm not sure. But from what I heard, Mr. Moody is mad as a wet hen. He says the men weren't being careful or some such thing. Anyway, we're not to report for work tomorrow unless they send someone to fetch us," she finished with a smile.

"No work, no pay. Let's hope things are fixed soon," Miss Addie remarked, a twinkle in her eye. "If they keep you off work too long, you'll be forced to make it through the week without buying a new hair ribbon or two."

Lilly then fetched a plate of food and brought it to Nadene. "Can you manage to feed yourself?" she asked, looking at her friend's splayed fingers.

Nadene gave a deep, racking cough. "No, but I'm not hungry. Why don't you sit with me and you can eat it," she said when the coughing finally sub-sided. "Miss Addie fed me earlier."

Lilly plopped down on the small sewing rocker and began forking the food into her mouth. She was ravenous. Although there was little time for manners when eating her breakfast and noonday meals, she usually attempted to eat her evening meal more slowly. However, it seemed impossible to do so this eve-ning.

"Prudence says your brother has been courting her. They've met after din-ner twice this week. She tells me Lewis is quite the gentleman. I think she's smitten with him. I do wish I could find a man who would take an interest in me. That would certainly take care of my worries," Nadene lamented as Lilly took another bite of lamb stew.

"Or add to them," Lilly replied in between bites of ham and green beans. "I wouldn't wish my brother's attentions on anyone. Believe me, he's not the kind of man who treats a woman with any respect. His interest is in money, not Prudence. Money is the only thing that has ever held Lewis's interest. Perhaps I should talk with Prudence."

"Please don't. She'll know I've told you and never forgive me. Lewis told her you would discourage the relationship. In fact, he said you'd accuse him of being after her money."

"And she prefers to believe him? Has he inquired about her funds?"

Nadene giggled. "Yes, but she fibbed to him. She told Lewis her family is quite wealthy but her father thought working in the mills would give her a better appreciation of money."

Lilly sputtered on the piece of biscuit she had shoved in her mouth. "She didn't!"

Nadene nodded her head in affirmation. "Prudence said he appeared to believe her. I did mention that lying was a sin, but Pru merely smiled and said it was an ungentlemanly question that didn't deserve a proper answer."

"It would appear as if Lewis has met his match—at least for the time being. I hope Pru doesn't get hurt. Lewis can be cruel and vindictive, but I'll not betray your confidence," Lilly replied as she rose from the rocking chair.

Nadene struggled to sit up. "Where are you going? I wanted to visit."

Lilly gave her a feeble smile. "I'd like nothing better. However, I promised John Farnsworth I'd accompany him into town. He said he needed some help choosing a birthday present for Miss Addie. Don't breathe a word."

"So Mr. Farnsworth is courting Miss Addie. They'll make a wonderful twosome, don't you think?"

Lilly nodded. "If I get back early, I'll stop in again."

"Oh yes, please do. I'll want to hear what you pick out."

Lilly glanced at the clock in the hallway, ran her fingers along each side of her head, hoping the loose strands were tucked into place, then hurried out the door. John Farnsworth was waiting when she arrived at the corner. "I hope I didn't keep you waiting long," she greeted.

"I just arrived," he said as he came alongside her and they walked toward town. "I hope you have an idea where we might find a gift. Until now, I've only visited the livery stable, the wheelwright, the general store, and Mrs. Clawson's pastry shop. I've not visited any of the other establishments here in Lowell."

Lilly turned and gave him a bright smile. "Prudence tells me that Mr. Whidden and Mr. Childs have both recently received new shipments in their stores, everything from crockery to fabrics and lace. Did you have something particular in mind?"

He gave a hearty laugh. "Well, I certainly *don't* want to purchase any crockery or kettles. That would only serve to remind Miss Addie of her daily chores. I think I'd prefer to give her something a bit more personal, though nothing that would cause eyebrows to rise. I had given consideration to some pretty combs for her hair. She has these few wisps of hair on each side that appear to escape and cause her bother. But perhaps a pretty shawl might be a better choice."

Lilly pictured the short flying strands of hair that Miss Addie was constantly pushing behind her ears. "I think the combs are a wonderful idea, Mr. Farnsworth. But I'm sure she would be delighted with either item." Lilly couldn't contain her enthusiasm. "I believe we could find the combs or a shawl at Mr. Whidden's store; it's located on Gorham Street," she advised as they rounded the corner.

Mintie was glad she had chosen to wear her woolen cape. A cold north wind was attacking the few leaves that remained attached to their trees. Those that had already fallen now rustled beneath her feet as she clipped along at a steady pace toward Mrs. Hirman's house. She didn't want to be late.

"Tardiness is an excuse for laziness"—at least that is what the Judge had always told his daughters. Not that Adelaide had listened to half of what the Judge had dutifully attempted to teach them in their formative years. "I don't know what's gotten into her," Mintie muttered, still upset that Adelaide had refused to attend the formation meeting of the Ladies' Temperance Society. After all, what would Mrs. Hirman and the other good women of Lowell think of her sister's absence? No doubt she would be forced into making excuses for Adelaide. And what would she say? That her sister had little interest in fighting for temperance?

Mintie slowed her pace a bit, allowing herself to remain behind a group of girls who were obviously walking to the shops in town, anxious to spend their earnings. "Just like Adelaide! Off to purchase a piece of silk or lace, not frugal enough to save for a rainy day," she mused, watching as the girls crossed Gorham Street and entered Mr. Whidden's store. She stopped momentarily when she heard a man's familiar voice as a couple left the store. She squinted her eyes and peered across the street. The two were laughing as the man handed a brown-paper-wrapped package to the girl he was with. Mintie's lips screwed into a tight little pucker and her eyes widened. *John Farnsworth and Lilly Armbruster.* She moved behind the trunk of a giant maple tree, even though they would probably not notice her in the dark, unable to tear her gaze away from the sight. Farnsworth extended his arm, and Mintie watched in horror as Lilly leaned in, said something, then looped her arm through John's. She continued staring after them as they sauntered down the street, slowing in front of the shop windows, pointing at one item or another, their laughter echoing through the thin night air.

When they were finally out of sight, Mintie peeled herself away from the tree and stood staring after them as they continued arm in arm down the street. "I wonder what Adelaide will think about this!" she muttered before turning on her heel and proceeding toward Mrs. Hirman's house on John Street.

The turnout for the meeting was greater than anticipated, and Mintie found herself squeezed into a tiny space at the rear of the parlor, where it was difficult both to see and hear what was being said. Her mind continued to wander back to earlier events of the evening. Perhaps it was a good thing Adelaide had chosen to remain home tonight. What if she had been forced to deal with the sight of John and Lilly? Mintie immediately decided she would stop and visit with Adelaide on her way home.

Mrs. Hirman interrupted Mintie's thoughts when introducing Mr. Thorndyke, who promptly passed pamphlets out, enumerating the necessary steps for organizing an effective temperance union. The illustrious speaker, as Mrs. Hirman had described him, proceeded to discuss each step in minute detail. Just when Mintie thought the meeting could go on no longer, Mr. Thorndyke opened the meeting for questions.

Mintie squirmed in her seat until Mrs. Hirman finally announced that refreshments were being served in the dining room. Making her excuses for an early exit, Mintie offered perfunctory thanks, rushed out the door, and headed toward home.

She was on a mission to save her sister from the English scoundrel who was undoubtedly seeking favors from the young Miss Armbruster. Mintie's feet couldn't carry her quickly enough. Adelaide needed to accept the fact that John Farnsworth was a scallywag through and through. And as for Lilly—well, she was obviously intent on finding a way out of the mills, and John Farnsworth was her answer! "That young woman is getting more than she bargained for. Just wait until she discovers John Farnsworth is a traitor. I'd say that Lilly Armbruster and John Farnsworth are quite a match," Mintie muttered as she scurried toward Jackson Street. Yes indeed, the sooner Adelaide knew of this liaison, the better.

An insistent rapping at the front door caused Addie to shift uncomfortably in order to get to her feet.

Lilly scurried from Addie's bedroom calling over her shoulder, "You sit still, Miss Addie. I'll find out who it is."

The knocking continued nonstop, and Addie couldn't imagine what must be wrong. She looked to Nadene and shrugged. "Someone certainly sounds urgent."

Before Nadene could reply they heard Lilly question, "Miss Beecher, is something wrong?"

Mintie's determined voice demanded answers. "Where's my sister?"

Nadene began to cough, causing Addie to reach for a glass of water. "I wish she'd stayed home," Addie whispered as she offered Nadene the drink.

"Is she in there with that girl—the one that was burned?" Mintie again demanded.

Addie sighed and replaced the glass on the stand. "So much for our enjoyable time."

"Yes. We were visiting in the bedroom—keeping Nadene company," Lilly announced as Mintie entered the doorway.

"Adelaide! Come here—we need to talk," Mintie commanded from the doorway.

"Why don't you join us in here? My foot is causing me pain," Addie said, pointing toward the footstool.

Mintie crooked her finger. "Out here now. We need privacy. It's important."

Addie rose from the chair and limped after her sister. "I'll be back shortly," she whispered to Nadene and Lilly.

Mintie turned toward her sister as soon as she had crossed into the kitchen, which was the only room that proved vacant. "You'd better sit down. I have some news—some unpleasant news—about your Englishman."

"John Farnsworth? Oh, Mintie, I don't want to have that 'he's a spy' conversation again. I've listened to all your stories, and I still don't believe John is disloyal to this country." There was a hint of irritation in Addie's voice.

Mintie pointed toward a chair. "Sit down, Adelaide. It's worse than that. You've been betrayed. Not only is that Farnsworth fellow a traitor and a spy, he's a womanizer."

"A *what*? Oh, Mintie, would you please stop this nonsense."

"It's not nonsense. You may recall that the temperance meeting was this evening." Mintie didn't wait for an answer. "I, of course, attended by myself since you elected to stay home. I was walking down Gorham Street minding my own business when something caused me to look over toward Whidden's Mercantile. And who do you think I saw walking out of the store, arm in arm, laughing and talking like two lovebirds?"

Addie gave her sister a blank stare. "I have absolutely no idea, Mintie, but I'm sure you are going to tell me." Why couldn't her sister just leave her to enjoy the evening?

Mintie pursed her lips and pushed her spectacles onto the bridge of her long, narrow nose. "John Farnsworth and," she paused momentarily, "your little boarder, Lilly Armbruster."

Addie was silent.

"Did you hear me, Adelaide? John Farnsworth is courting Lilly Armbruster. I saw them with my own eyes. I'm sure you'd have to admit that Lilly was gone from the house earlier this evening. Well? She left the house, didn't she?"

Addie nodded her head. "She was gone for a short time this evening."

"There you have it. You can't trust anyone. I told you that Farnsworth was up to no good, but did you believe me? And that Armbruster girl, I didn't like her from the day she arrived. But did you listen to me? No. You took her in, treated her well, and now she's turned on you. I'd wager she even knows you've taken a liking to Farnsworth, but that didn't stop her."

Addie placed her hands over her ears. "Stop it, Mintie. I don't want to hear any more of this nonsense. I can't believe Lilly is interested in John Farnsworth."

Mintie gave her a disgusted look before wagging her finger back and forth in front of Addie's face. "You think Lilly wants to remain a mill girl the rest of her life? Farnsworth may not be wealthy, but I've heard he's paid a handsome wage, and the Corporation is building him that fine house. It's enough to turn a girl's head."

"You'll not convince me any of this is true, so you may as well quit trying," Addie declared. "If you'd like to visit about something pleasant, you're welcome to join us in the bedroom. If not, I suggest you return home," Addie announced as she rose from her chair.

"After what I've seen this evening, I have no intention of exchanging pleasantries with Lilly Armbruster. I'll bid you good-night, Adelaide." Head raised high, Mintie marched out the front door without further comment.

As soon as the front door had closed, Addie sat back down, her mind reeling with the accusations she'd just heard from her sister's lips. Could it possibly be true? Lilly was a beautiful girl, capable of turning any man's head. But wouldn't she choose a handsome young man such as Matthew Cheever over a man old enough to be her father? Not that some girls didn't prefer older men, Addie argued with herself. But it was Lilly who had encouraged the relationship with John Farnsworth. Why would she do such a thing if she were interested in him herself? None of this was making any sense. Perhaps the best thing was to confront Lilly.

Addie hobbled down the hallway, surprised that the throbbing sensation had disappeared from her foot. She could hear Lilly's muffled voice and then listened as both girls said a quiet amen.

"Did Miss Mintie leave?" Nadene inquired as Addie entered the room.

Addie nodded and took her seat opposite Lilly. "My foot isn't hurting as much."

Nadene and Lilly smiled at each other. "We've been praying for you," they uttered in unison.

"Thank you. It appears your prayers are being answered," Addie responded. "It's chilly outdoors tonight, isn't it?" she inquired, her gaze focused upon Lilly.

Lilly gave an enthusiastic nod. "Oh yes, the wind is as blustery and cold as a frosty January morning. It took a good five minutes in front of the fire to ward off the chill when I returned home."

Addie picked up her needle and began darning a hole in one of her woolen stockings. "I was surprised you went out on such a cold night. Did you have a meeting to attend?" she asked without looking up from her sewing.

Addie watched from under hooded lids as Lilly fidgeted and then glanced toward Nadene. "No. One of the girls mentioned a new shipment had been delivered to the bookstore. I was anxious to see what new titles had arrived."

"I see. And did any of the other girls go with you?"

"No, none of the other girls."

Addie couldn't look at her young boarder. Obviously Mintie was correct. If there were nothing to hide, Lilly would have merely told the truth and explained why she and John had gone into town. Unfortunately, there appeared to be no other explanation for Lilly's behavior.

That night before blowing out her candle, Lilly took up her Bible. *Oh, Father,* she began to pray, *thank you for the wonderful day. I'm excited to know that you have the ability to control the fate of the mills, without using me to do something dangerous or harmful. Soon the enemy will fall, and I couldn't be happier. Once they see what they're up against, that you stand between them and their fortune, they'll hightail it out of here once and for all. Please, just keep my friends from harm.*

She opened her Bible and found herself staring down at the twenty-fourth chapter of Proverbs. It seemed as good a place as any to read. Her heart fairly soared, and the idea of bolstering herself further with Scripture was pure delight.

Verse ten caught her attention. " 'If thou faint in the day of adversity, thy strength is small.' " Her voice was barely audible as she mouthed the words. Lilly nodded in agreement. The need was great to stand firm when problems arose. She wanted her strength to be very evident.

She continued to scan the verses, hardly giving them much true attention. Her joy over the problems sustained by the mill that day kept drawing her back to thoughts on the matter. It wasn't until Lilly reached the seventeenth verse that she took notice.

"*Rejoice not when thine enemy falleth, and let not thine heart be glad when he stumbleth: Lest the Lord see it, and it displease him, and he turn away his wrath from him.*"

Lilly read the verse over and over again. Rejoice not. It hardly seemed fair that a person was not to take joy in the defeat of her enemies. Lilly thought perhaps she'd misunderstood the meaning. She tried analyzing the verse in a different way, but there didn't seem to be another way to look at it.

She flipped the page to the twenty-fifth chapter. Perhaps Solomon was simply feeling generous that day. Maybe she'd find further proof of her own feelings in the next passages.

Verse twenty-one loomed out at her. *"If thine enemy be hungry, give him bread to eat; and if he be thirsty, give him water to drink."*

She slammed the book shut. Maybe God would prefer she just go to sleep and not worry about it. After all, she wasn't called to cause further harm, so perhaps she could avoid dealing with her enemies completely. She sighed. *But of course I have to deal with them. They're all around me—maybe not here in my room, but the very room I share has been provided by them.*

She snuffed out the candle and snuggled down into the bed. Sometimes God's Word made no sense at all.

～ 22 ～

Matthew approached the front door of the Boott home at seven o'clock sharp with feelings of both equanimity and trepidation. While he wanted to be counted among Boott's confidants, a member of the elite inner circle, he disliked being thrust into the role of Isabelle's suitor. Other than their connection through Kirk Boott and the fact that they were both single, Isabelle and Matthew shared few interests. Perhaps during this visit they would find some common ground, and Matthew would view her in a new light. Thus far he'd seen a selfish, self-indulgent young woman who cared for little except the latest fashions and traveling abroad.

The front door opened, and Kirk greeted him with a genial smile. "Pleased you could make it, Matthew. I believe there's someone in the parlor anxiously awaiting your arrival," he said as he gave him a friendly slap on the shoulder. "Shall we join the others?"

Matthew nodded, though he had a growing distaste for social gatherings of any type. They made him uncomfortable, yet he had learned long ago that dinner parties were a necessary evil in the business world—invented by a woman in order to spend a bit of time with her husband, he had decided.

The parlor was filled with chattering men and women dressed in their finery, each attempting to impress the others with a bit of gossip or talk of the latest social event. Paul Moody was standing near the fireplace, and Matthew began working his way through the crowd toward the man who capably headed up the mechanics of the mills while supervising the operation of the locks and canals.

"Mr. Moody," he called out as he edged a bit closer. Continuing to weave his way through the crowd, he finally reached Moody's side. "Glad to see you. I had hoped to get over and visit with you today but ran short of time. Any progress to report on that broken cog?"

Paul accepted Matthew's proffered hand, giving it a hearty shake. "Good to see you, Matthew. To be honest, I didn't know if I'd be here tonight. In some respects I had hoped for an excuse to stay away. I detest these required dinner parties," he said under his breath. "However, we managed to repair the waterwheel over at No. 2, and the mill is in full operation once again."

"That's great news. The last I had heard, it appeared we'd be nonoperational for at least the full day tomorrow. Any idea what caused the problem?"

Paul rubbed a weatherworn hand across his forehead. "I dislike reporting this, but it appears there's been some foul play."

"What?" Matthew couldn't believe his ears. "You think someone wants the mill shut down?"

"I don't know what the actual intent might have been, but from our investigation it appears someone spent a great deal of time and effort under the darkness of night in order to damage the waterwheel. That cog couldn't have possibly broken under normal conditions."

"It's not that I don't believe your assessment, but the whole concept is difficult to believe. What purpose would it serve?"

Paul shrugged his shoulders and met Matthew's gaze. "Perhaps someone bears a grudge against one of us or harbors jealousy over the return of profits we've begun to realize. And, of course, there are still those anti-Federalists who believe an agrarian society is the salvation of this country. Who knows how far they would go to make a point."

Matthew stared into the fire, his thoughts whirling with the prospect that the Corporation might be dealing with deliberate criminal activity. If that were the case, there would most likely be future attacks. Any stoppage of the mills would mean a shortfall in profits, a dreadful prospect for the Associates. No doubt the Bostonians' anger would initially be directed toward the Lowell management. And once their anger subsided, they would expect a quick and certain solution. It would be best to have the situation in control before any further trouble erupted. But how?

"How are things progressing with the Catholic church? Kirk mentioned Bishop Fenwick was to make a visit by the end of the year. Any word in that regard? It would appear that a church could be a stabilizing factor with the Irish," Paul commented.

Matthew's body snapped to attention. "You think the Irish are involved in this waterwheel incident?"

"Whoa! I didn't say any such thing—the thought hadn't even crossed my mind. I was making an inquiry regarding a totally different topic, Matthew."

"So you *don't* think the Irish are involved?"

Paul grasped Matthew's shoulder and gave him a broad smile. "If I knew who was responsible, I'd have already taken care of matters. I have no more reason to suspect the Irish than anyone else in this town."

Matthew nodded. "I'm sorry. It appears as if I jumped to conclusions, Mr. Moody. To answer your question, Bishop Fenwick has sent word he'd rather wait until spring for his journey to Lowell. It seems he dislikes traveling in cold weather. He did say he would be able to make an announcement to his Catholic believers in Lowell upon his arrival."

"I assume that means the bishop has received approval from higher authority to bless the project?"

"So it would seem," Matthew agreed. "Mr. Boott was pleased by the message although a bit irritated the bishop was delaying his visit to Lowell."

"*There* you are, you naughty boy."

The syrupy words pulled Matthew's attention away from Moody. He turned, his face now warm from the heat of the blazing fire. Isabelle stood beside him in a pale blue gown, the square neckline and sleeves embroidered with a shimmering gold thread, and her lips formed into a tiny pout. The voluminous sleeves, so popular of late, were held out by some manner, causing it to be almost impossible to stand very close to Isabelle from the side.

"Isabelle! What a lovely gown." Trite, but he could think of nothing else to say at the moment. It broke with etiquette that she should seek out a man who was not a relative. It also went against the rules that she should interrupt two men who were in the middle of a conversation.

"I couldn't believe my ears when Uncle Kirk told me you had arrived nearly half an hour ago. Just why haven't you been able to locate me during that expanse of time?" She gave him a coquettish smile and fluttered her long brown lashes.

"You'd best come up with an excellent reply, my young friend, or I dare say you'll pay dearly," Paul remarked as he slapped Matthew on the shoulder and walked off toward the center of the room.

"You'll have to admit the room is extremely crowded, Isabelle. I spied Mr. Moody, and there was a matter I needed to discuss with him. Please accept my apologies," he dutifully requested.

She gave him a sidelong glance and once again puckered her lips. Her brow creased into what Matthew assumed was intended to be a thoughtful pose. "I don't suppose I have any choice but to forgive you. However, there will be no talk of business while you're with me this evening," she cautioned. "You didn't mention my hair. Do you like it fashioned this way?"

Matthew nodded. "It's lovely, very becoming." For the life of him, he couldn't remember how she had worn her hair the last time he'd seen her, but he'd told the truth. It was a becoming style, even if he couldn't be considered an authority on such matters.

"You look quite stunning in that frock coat," Isabelle gushed. "That shade of brown is quite perfect, and the fawn color trousers are absolutely the height of fashion. I'm pleased to see that you take such care with your appearance."

Matthew tried not to appear amused, but the conversation seemed absolutely ludicrous. "I'm afraid I cannot take overdue credit for my attire. I simply grabbed the first available coat."

"Oh, Matthew, you're such a tease. Now come along," Isabelle ordered, taking his arm as she pulled him into the line of guests that was beginning to form. "Aunt Anne has seated us together, but I'm sure you expected she would."

"Of course," he replied as they found their places at the table. "I would have been shocked by any other arrangement. Your uncle Kirk tells me you're interested in taking a tour of the mills during your visit," he continued as he helped her into her chair. Conversation with Isabelle was difficult. She didn't want him to discuss his work, and he didn't want to hear about the latest fashions or the social activities in Boston.

"Every year since my father's death, his sister has come from England to visit. She's the one who wants to view the operation of the mills here in Lowell. I think Uncle Kirk has failed to convince her that working conditions are dissimilar to those in English textile mills. Mother, of course, insisted that I accompany them. She thinks it will prove to be an excellent educational experience." There was an evident note of disdain in her final remark. Obviously Isabelle was certain there was nothing to be learned anywhere but in Boston or abroad.

"I must agree with your mother. I think you will learn a great deal. At a minimum, it should make you thankful you're not required to work in order to support yourself."

Her head tipped upward and her back stiffened. "What a preposterous comment. The thought of such a concept is ludicrous, and I certainly don't need to visit a mill in order to realize that such a fate is not a part of my future." That said, she turned and directed a question to Jasmine Appleton, who was seated at her right hand.

"I'm sure there are others who have believed exactly the same thing," Matthew softly replied. She didn't hear him. He didn't care. His thoughts were upon Lilly and the long days she now labored in the mills. Certainly she had never entertained the slightest notion that she would be working twelve hours a day at a spinning frame.

A smile formed on his lips. Lilly not only managed under such circumstances, she actually seemed to thrive. He'd never known her to look more beautiful. He thought back on his mother's remark at breakfast several days ago.

"Lilly won't remain single for long, Matthew," she had told him. *"You must come to your senses and establish yourself in her life. You must give her a reason to believe you still care."*

But what of her giving me a reason to believe she cares? Matthew mused. Although he was quite confident Lilly cared more for him than she let on. The crux of the matter was that he wanted her back in his life. He wanted to rescue her from her life at the mills and see her happy again. That didn't seem like too much to ask for—but apparently it was. Lilly wanted no part of him. He represented the mills every bit as much as Kirk Boott did. No doubt Lilly hated them both.

The sound of the morning bell disrupted Lilly's dream. She had been running through the orchard with Matthew waiting in the distance, beckoning her toward him. The continual clanging of the bell was a wretched affirmation the apple-filled orchard had only been a dream; reality was this small, cold room on Jackson Street. Her body longed for additional sleep, but she knew such an idea was no more than a dream—an unfulfilled wish for something that would not occur. She threw back the heavy quilt and was assaulted by the frigid morning air. The November chill had formed an icy crust on the two small bedroom windows, and her breath was creating tiny vapor puffs with each exhale. With a shiver, she longed for the warmth of her family's hearth.

"You'd better hurry, Lilly. Nadene told me you were going to change her bandages before leaving for work this morning," Marmi mumbled through the faded brown dress she was pulling over her head.

The words caused Lilly's feet to hit the floor. She quickly dressed and rushed downstairs, anxious to keep her promise to assist with Nadene's care. Miss Addie had barely acknowledged Lilly's offer to assist with the nursing duties when she had presented the idea. In fact, Miss Addie had been very quiet, almost aloof, since Mintie's departure and the brief interrogation as to Lilly's whereabouts a few nights earlier.

"Good morning," Lilly greeted as she skidded to a halt inside the downstairs bedroom. Her gaze was immediately drawn toward the dirty bandages lying on the table beside Nadene's bed. "I came down to help with your dressings. Has Miss Addie already changed them?"

Nadene nodded and coughed. "I told her you would be here to do it, but she said she didn't need your help. She's not acting like herself. It appears something is bothering her, but when I asked, she said she was fine."

Lilly gathered the dirty bandages and tucked them under her arm. "I was late. I should have been here on time. I'll wash out the bandages and get them into some boiling water before I leave. I'll stop in for a minute when I return for breakfast," she promised, rushing from the room.

Addie was in the kitchen, already setting bread to rise and making preparations for the morning meal. She was silent until Lilly filled a small basin with water and began to scrub the bandages. "Leave those dressings and go on to work. I can manage just fine without your help."

The words sliced through the air like shards of sleet on a winter day. "Are you upset with me, Miss Addie? Have I done something?" Lilly timidly inquired.

"I guess you know better than I whether you've done something improper," Addie replied, keeping her back turned toward Lilly.

Lilly attempted to still the tremor that was rising in her throat. "I don't think I've done anything, but if I have, would you please accept my apology? You've appeared angry with me of late, and the last thing I would ever want to do is hurt you, Miss Addie."

"Is that so? Well, if you don't think you've done anything wrong, then I suppose you have nothing to apologize for—or to worry about for that matter. Final bell's ringing. You best get down the street before they close the gate," Addie replied without a glance in Lilly's direction.

Tears welled in Lilly's eyes as she rushed from the room. The other girls were already gone. She grasped her cape and ran out the door, still tugging the woolen fabric around her body as she raced toward the mill. She scooted into the mill yard as Mr. Gault was closing the gate. "Best hurry, young lady," he called, giving her a broad smile.

Lilly gave him a quick wave as she continued onward. One or two other girls joined her in a sprint toward the stairwell. By the time she reached her floor, Mr. Arnold was perched on his stool waiting to command the machinery into operation. Lilly wound her way down one of the aisles and came to a halt behind her machines just as he lowered his arm, signaling work to begin. Lilly pulled the lever on the four spinning frames and attempted to catch her breath. She glanced toward Mr. Arnold; he was watching her every move.

When the breakfast bell finally rang, Lilly quickly pulled the handles on her frames and scurried toward the door. "See that you're back on time, Miss Armbruster. Let's don't forget I'm doing you a favor permitting you to operate those extra machines," Mr. Arnold stated as she passed him.

She didn't have the energy to argue. "Yes, sir," she replied. The smirk that immediately crossed his lips annoyed her, but Thaddeus Arnold was forgotten by the time she entered the boardinghouse again. Quickly filling a plate with food, she made her way to the bedroom. "I've brought you some breakfast," she informed Nadene.

Nadene gave her a bright smile. "Sit down and eat it yourself. Miss Addie brought me my breakfast before you got here, but I'd love your company."

Lilly attempted to hide her disappointment. It was becoming obvious that Miss Addie wasn't going to accept her offer of assistance. Lowering herself into a chair positioned near the bed, she took a bite of ham. "I think Miss Addie is angry with me, but I'm not sure why. Has she said anything to you?" Lilly asked.

Nadene gave her a thoughtful look. "She hasn't said anything, but I can try to find out if you like. She *has* been unusually quiet."

Lilly swallowed a mouthful of food and wiped the corners of her mouth. "I've already asked her. She didn't give me a straight answer, but I honestly can't think of anything I've done to upset her."

"Try not to worry, and I'll see if I can get her to talk to me while she's doing her mending this afternoon," Nadene said. "Are you having a good morning?" A cough wracked her frail frame.

Lilly grimaced as Nadene's breathing came in ragged gasps. Had her lungs been further damaged by the fire? "I'm not sure there's much else that can go wrong today. I'd better take my plate to the kitchen and get back to work. I don't dare rush in at the last moment again. Please rest easy," she said, turning back to her friend. "You must get well."

Matthew pulled the carriage to a halt and then assisted Isabelle and her mother and aunt toward the front gate of the Appleton Mill. "Here we are," he announced as they neared No. 2. "It's a bit noisy inside," he absently warned the women, his thoughts wandering back to the sight of William Thurston and Lewis Armbruster entering one of the newer hostelries known as the Wareham House as he had passed down Merrimack Street only minutes earlier. Seeing Lewis and William deep in conversation caused Matthew to recall the day he and Kirk had observed both of them slinking about the Acre. Those two men were cut from the same cloth—both self-serving, angry tyrants willing to hurt anyone who might get in their way. He wondered why they might be keeping company.

Isabelle tugged at Matthew's arm, a look of disgust crossing her face. "It's beginning to snow. Are we going to stand out here in the cold, or are you intending to take us inside?"

Matthew started to attention. "My apologies, ladies. This way, please," he said as he led them to the front gate and rang the bell. Mr. Gault came outside and gave them a hearty wave. "Good afternoon, Mr. Gault. I plan to take the ladies through No. 2. I thought we would stop here for a moment before getting started."

"Pleased to have you," he said as he opened the gate and led the group across the yard and into the building. "In this building we have girls who trim, fold, and prepare the cloth for shipment," he explained, pointing across the room. "We also have an office where we maintain the time cards, pay records, and accounts of the Corporation," he advised as he led the group into the counting room.

Isabelle glanced about the room. "Why do you keep the employees locked in here?" she inquired, nodding toward the gate they'd entered.

"The bells ring announcing the time schedule of the mills—when to rise, when to arrive, when to leave for meals, when to return from meals. The gates are closed once the final bells ring. If an employee is late, it's noted on the pay and attendance records," he replied. "Surely you've heard the bells ringing since your arrival in Lowell."

Isabelle nodded. "A person would have to be totally deaf not to hear those annoying bells ringing all the time," Isabelle replied, looping her hand through the crook in Matthew's arm and stepping closer.

Matthew glanced at her fingers that were grasping his arm in a possessive grip. "Thanks for your assistance, Mr. Gault. I think we'll go over and let the ladies have a look at the carding machines. Shall we, ladies?" he asked while leading the three women out the door. "The Corporation has what we refer to as a bale-to-bolt operation. The cotton arrives in bales, then it's opened, picked, and then cleaned on the machinery over on that side of the room. And these machines," he hollered above the noise, "are the carding machines—very dangerous. These machines comb and strain the cotton fibers into slivers."

Isabelle tugged on his arm. Matthew knew she wanted to leave, but Neva and Mrs. Danbury appeared to have an interest in the operation, asking questions as they slowly moved about the room. Matthew leaned down to Isabelle's ear and said, "Go and wait by the stairs. We'll be out shortly."

When they finally joined Isabelle, she was pacing back and forth in the tiny stairwell. "I'm freezing out here."

"I doubt that, dear," Neva replied. "The stairway is enclosed."

Isabelle stomped her foot. "Well, it may be enclosed, but it's not heated, and my feet feel as though they turned into icicles."

"Would you like to remain in the counting room until we've finished?" Matthew offered.

Neva moved forward and took hold of her daughter's arm. "I don't think an hour of discomfort will do you any harm, Isabelle. Come along," she said while giving Isabelle a gentle push toward the steps.

Matthew led them onward until they stood in front of the door to the third floor. "We have drawing and spinning machines in separate areas on this floor. As you can already hear, it's very noisy. There are drawing machines, where the long slivers from the carding machine are stretched until the ropes are about two inches thick. Those fragile ropes go to the roving machine, where they are drawn out and lengthened still further and given a slight twist, although the fiber is still very weak and breaks easily at this point," he explained, looking among the three women as he spoke. "Let's go in and have a look," he said before pulling open the door and escorting them inside.

Isabelle immediately thrust a finger in each ear. Matthew grimaced while watching her attempt to zigzag through the aisle of machinery, her elbows flapping in midair. Reaching from behind, he grasped her arms and pulled them down. "You need to keep your arms down, or your clothing may get caught in the machinery," he said while leaning over her shoulder and speaking into her ear.

It seemed the afternoon would never end. Lilly turned off one of the frames, bent over, and removed a row of thread-laden spindles, placing them into a box that one of the young bobbin girls was awaiting. Lilly gave the child a quick smile and began refilling her frame with empty spindles. Her back aching, she finished the chore and stood up, poised to slap the lever into action. Her raised arm, however, stopped in midair. Matthew was a few feet away, leaning toward Isabelle and whispering into her ear. Lilly watched a demure smile play at the corner of Isabelle's perfectly shaped lips as she glanced over her shoulder toward Matthew. An unexpected knot formed in Lilly's stomach as she viewed the two of them—Matthew, Kirk Boott's favored protégé, arm-in-arm with Isabelle Locklear, Boott's very available niece. Why was the sight of them almost more than Lilly could bear? After all, she no longer cared one whit about Matthew Cheever. She attempted to turn her gaze, but the sight of them held her captive until she realized Matthew was returning her stare. He smiled and began moving toward her with Isabelle following quickly behind. *Exactly what she didn't want!*

"Lilly!" Matthew mouthed her name.

She nodded while reaching into one of the frames to fasten a broken thread. He moved to her side and yelled above the din, "We're touring the mill. Could we observe you working at your machines?"

Shrugging her shoulders, Lilly pointed toward Thaddeus Arnold. She wanted to scream at him to take his lady friends away from this place—away from her. Instead, with Mr. Arnold's permission, they gathered around, watching each movement as Lilly tended the frames, their finery a stark reminder of her disheveled hair and shabby dress. Thankfully, they attempted to ask few questions. The older women appeared entranced at the sight of the machinery; Lilly felt entranced with Matthew.

Lilly breathed a sigh of relief when the group finally exited the floor. Matthew had touched her arm and mouthed his thanks before escorting them toward the door. Lilly had continued working, ignoring his overture—angry he had singled her out as an example to his *respectable* friends. The final bell rang, and she hit the four levers and hurried toward the door. Her head throbbed, her arms and legs ached, and Lilly longed for peace and quiet. But there was no place of solitude in the boardinghouse. Perhaps Miss Addie would be happier this evening. The strain of Miss Addie's cool behavior toward her these past few days had taken its toll. A hint of misery seeped into her step; she missed the older woman and her cheery camaraderie.

~ 23 ~

Kirk kissed the cheek his sister offered as the driver completed loading trunks onto the awaiting coach in front of his home. "I really would prefer you wait until after the Christmas holiday for your return to Boston, Neva. You did promise you'd stay with us at least six weeks," Kirk said while eyeing his niece, who had already seated herself inside the carriage.

Neva held Kirk's hand momentarily. "I know, and we truly appreciate your hospitality, but under the circumstances . . ."

Kirk nodded his understanding while assisting Neva into the coach. "I'll be in Boston after the first of the year. I'll call on you at that time, but please send word immediately if you should need anything before then."

"You know I will, and please don't worry. Isabelle will be fine once she's back in Boston. There will be a flurry of parties for her to attend. You and Anne have a wonderful holiday."

Kirk motioned to the driver, who immediately flicked the reins and set the horses into motion. Neva waved a gloved hand as they pulled away from the house. Watching until the coach was out of sight, Kirk placed his beaver hat firmly upon his head and headed off toward the Appleton. It was cold, but he decided the brisk air would do him good. Wondering how much of the information Isabelle had related was truth and how much was exaggerated rhetoric due to a deflated ego, he determined a visit with Matthew should set the record straight.

Stomping the mud from his boots before opening the door, Kirk entered the counting room of the Appleton. The ever-watchful Mr. Gault had seen him coming and rushed out to have the gate open for his arrival. *Good man, Gault,* he thought. *Wonder if Matthew's considered him for a promotion.*

"Ah, there you are, Matthew. I was hoping you'd be in here," Kirk said as he entered Matthew's small office and seated himself in the one available chair for guests.

Matthew glanced up from his desk. "What brings you out in this cold, damp weather? Is there a problem at one of the mills?"

"No, nothing so dreadful. Our Boston visitors left a short time ago, and I thought you and I might discuss what happened between you and Isabelle. I don't mean to appear obtuse, but I'm not sure if she was completely forthright with me. Would you consider telling me exactly what occurred? She seemed positively adamant about returning to Boston immediately."

Matthew rubbed his forehead and met Kirk's gaze. "We had a disagreement after she toured the mill. She told me she would never consider living in a small city such as Lowell and that she finds the whole concept of the mills disgusting. She was planning to have you arrange work for me in Boston, and when I told her I had no desire to leave Lowell, she became angry, saying I was attempting to manipulate her. Quite frankly, I think she believed our relationship had developed to a much more serious level than I had yet considered, sir."

Kirk rose from his chair and walked to the window. He stood with his back toward Matthew. "I suspected as much, although I will tell you that I'm disappointed. I had hoped you and Isabelle would find a common ground, but I know she's a determined, self-centered young woman. She led me to believe that you had, well, how shall I say it? Treated her with less than proper respect."

Matthew could feel his heart begin to race. "What? I did no such thing, and I'm shocked that Isabelle would stoop to such tactics. Granted, she was angry when I told her I had no intention of making my home in Boston or of an imminent marriage, but I thought we parted with a mutual understanding that we weren't compatible. She even spoke of a man in Boston who had recently proposed to her," Matthew explained. "I hope you believe that I would never do anything to compromise any woman. It's not who I am nor what I believe in."

Kirk turned around and faced Matthew. "I suspected Isabelle hoped you would be the recipient of my wrath. Isabelle doesn't take rejection easily."

The subject of Isabelle was soon discarded for talk of production and expansion, with Kirk spending the greater share of the afternoon in Matthew's office. By the time Kirk started toward home, he knew hiring Matthew had been an excellent decision. There was no doubt the Associates needed Matthew more than Isabelle did. And besides, they would appreciate him more.

Rather than sit with the other girls, Lilly prepared a plate of food and carried it into Addie's bedroom. "Have you eaten?" she asked Nadene, who was propped up in bed reading a book.

"Yes. And I've talked to Miss Addie, too. I know why she's upset with you."

Lilly moved to the edge of her chair. "Why?"

"It seems that Miss Mintie was on her way to a meeting the night you and John Farnsworth met to shop for Miss Addie's birthday present."

"What difference does *that* make?"

Nadene gave her a look of exasperation. "I'm going to tell you, if you'll give me a minute. Miss Mintie saw you two together, and she couldn't wait to tell Miss Addie. Mintie has convinced her sister that Mr. Farnsworth is romantically interested in you and that you've betrayed her by alienating Mr. Farnsworth's affections."

"Oh my! How could Miss Addie believe such nonsense? Mr. Farnsworth is old enough to be my father."

Nadene scooched up a little farther and leaned against her pillow. "I know, but I think Miss Mintie has succeeded in winning her over. Why don't you go and talk to her after supper when she's alone in the kitchen?"

Lilly agreed that a private discussion with Miss Addie would be best. "Will you pray with me?" she asked Nadene. "I want to be able to tell Miss Addie the truth without ruining her birthday surprise, but most of all I want to restore our friendship. I can't do that unless she trusts me. I fear I won't find the right words."

"Let's pray that God will give you the perfect words to set things right. I'm certain God wants your relationship restored, too."

Lilly gave her friend a smile. "Thank you, Nadene. I think you're right— the words do need to come from the Lord."

An hour later, bolstered by the time she and Nadene had spent in prayer, Lilly walked into the kitchen and offered to help with the supper dishes.

"I would think you have other things of more importance, perhaps a gentleman caller to go shopping with in town," Miss Addie replied as she picked up a worn dish towel and began drying a plate.

"We need to talk about gentlemen callers, Miss Addie. Nadene told me what you believe—about John Farnsworth and me—and none of it is true."

Miss Addie wheeled around and glowered. "You expect me to believe my sister *didn't* see you in town with John Farnsworth? Mintie is many things, but a liar isn't one of them."

Lilly wanted to pull back her words. After all that prayer, she'd still said the wrong thing. "I misspoke. The part about there being any romantic involvement is totally false. We were in town together. I was assisting him with a purchase—for a friend. We stopped in several shops and then came back home." Lilly paused before continuing. "Miss Addie, John Farnsworth is old enough to be my father. Surely you don't think I could have feelings for him. He's a kind and generous man—a wonderful suitor for you. But certainly not for me. And even if Mr. Farnsworth were a man who captivated my interest, I would never seek his affections when I know that you find him . . ."

"The most wonderful man on earth?" Addie concluded, a blush rising to her cheeks.

Lilly smiled. "Exactly! Miss Addie, I would never intentionally do anything to hurt you or destroy our friendship. I love you," Lilly said, the words fighting their way around the lump that had risen in her throat.

"Come here, child," Addie said, beckoning Lilly into a warm embrace. "I've missed you, too, more than you can imagine. I must tell you that Mintie's words were very convincing. I had hoped that young Matthew Cheever would come calling and assuage my fears. When that didn't occur, I thought you were probably meeting John on the sly so I wouldn't suspect."

As if on cue, Prudence rushed into the kitchen. "You have a caller in the parlor, Lilly—a gentleman," she announced with a broad grin.

"Not John Farnsworth?" Addie inquired, then quickly placed a hand over her mouth. "I'm merely jesting, Lilly."

"No, much younger and much more handsome," Prudence replied. "Guess!"

"I certainly hope it isn't my brother," Lilly replied. "Lewis is the *last* person I want to deal with this evening."

Prudence crossed her arms and gave Lilly a scowl. "Well, personally, I'd love to see Lewis, but I've not seen him for several days. It's Matthew Cheever."

"Speak of the devil," Lilly muttered. "Please tell Matthew I'm busy this evening," she said to Prudence, then turned to pick up the dish towel. Miss Addie was staring at her with a question in her eyes. If Addie's suspicions about John Farnsworth and Lilly were going to be laid to rest, Lilly knew she must see Matthew. "Pay me no mind, Prudence. I'll be into the parlor momentarily. I'm tired and didn't want Matthew to see me looking so disheveled, but I doubt he'll even notice."

"Don't keep him waiting, or one of the other girls will soon have his attention," Prudence warned as she left the kitchen.

Lilly forced her lips into a bright smile and tucked a loose curl behind one ear. "You see, Miss Addie? Matthew has been quite busy. Mr. Boott has had relatives in town, and Matthew has been required to spend his evening hours at the Boott residence. Otherwise, I'm sure he would have been here."

"I do apologize, dear. I allowed my mind to conjure up all sorts of wild ideas. Do forgive me," she asked, placing her plump arm around Lilly's waist.

"Of course you're forgiven."

"You need to give your cheeks a pinch. You need a little more color," Addie instructed as Lilly walked out of the room.

Matthew was standing in the doorway, holding her cape. "I thought we could walk into town," he said as she neared him.

"Do you have Isabelle's permission?" she asked, immediately scolding herself once the words were out. She sounded like a jealous lover worried about competition for her beau.

Matthew grinned as he held out her cape and escorted her out the door.

"You have nothing to fear from Isabelle. Isabelle and I have nothing in common; we're totally unsuited."

Lilly stopped in her tracks. "Is there some reason you came calling upon me tonight, or were you merely hoping to heap more misery on what has been a wretched week?"

He pulled her hand into his arm and tugged her along toward town. "Wretched because I came to the mill with Isabelle? Because if that's the case, I've come to set your mind at ease," he said with a smile.

She moved onward, intrigued by his statement. "How so?"

"Isabelle has returned to Boston to find a man she considers more suitable. She wants to live among her privileged friends in Boston, and of course I have no interest in living anywhere but Lowell. When I made it clear we were not of like minds, she insisted on immediately returning to Boston."

The moonlight shone upon Matthew's finely chiseled profile. As he turned and smiled, Lilly's heart began to melt—his gaze warm upon her icy heart. Quickly she turned away, forcing herself to remember the pain he had caused in the past. Matthew Cheever would not hurt her again. "And you think that because Isabelle has rushed off to Boston, you'll begin calling on me. After all, I should fall at your feet in thankfulness for the privilege. Is that correct?"

Matthew stared at her in obvious disbelief. "What has gotten into you, Lilly? You sound angry and bitter."

"Perhaps because I *am* angry and bitter. And it's you that's helped to turn me into what I am, Matthew," she fired, her hands curled into fists.

Matthew looked down at her. "Take charge of your own life, Lilly. I'm not the cause of your happiness or your sadness. You're the girl who once told me your joy was in the Lord. Is it not still so? Because you've fallen upon hard times, have you forgotten where true happiness lies?"

She knew he was right, but that only served to increase her anger. "How dare you talk to me about bitterness or happiness, Matthew. You've experienced nothing but prosperity and good times. Come and talk to me when you've had to suffer losses, and we'll see where *your* joy lies," she spat.

"I'm sorry," he offered in a voice that suggested true sympathy. "I know your losses have been great. Perhaps we should change the subject to something more neutral," he suggested as they sat down in the Wareham restaurant.

"Coffee, tea, hot cider?" said the young man who stood poised to wait upon them.

"Tea," Lilly replied.

"I'll have tea, also," Matthew said, then turned back toward Lilly. Before he could speak, however, several other patrons entered the room, their voices loud and excited.

"The mills are truly giving life to this community," an older man said to the group. "I would have been in the poorhouse by now, but the mills brought prosperity to my business."

"You don't have to sell me on it, Benjamin," another man said. "I couldn't be more delighted. I was ready to take a loss on the farm and move south with my sister. I watched my father die trying to work the land, and I wasn't going to follow suit."

The words hit Lilly hard. She'd never heard any of the locals, with exception to the Cheevers, sing the praises of the mills. How could they be so delighted to see the land torn up and scarred with huge brick monstrosities?

"Without this industrialization, my boy would have had to leave the area to find work. He was certainly no farmer and no storekeeper," the first man continued. "I know at first I was against the mills, but in the past five years they've definitely convinced me. I don't know when I've enjoyed a better life."

Lilly looked up to find Matthew watching her. He knew she'd overheard the conversation. It was hard not to as the men had taken the table next to theirs. Without taking his gaze from her face, Matthew reached out and took hold of her hand.

"I'm not the devil, and neither is Kirk Boott."

Lilly swallowed hard. Matthew's touch was doing things to her that she'd just as soon ignore. But she couldn't. She tried to fight it, but the memories came rushing back. Memories of his tender touch, his sweet, soft words, his gentleness.

Matthew's voice was low, almost husky, as he added, "When you look at the overall scheme of things, more people have prospered from this than suffered."

Lilly pushed aside the memories and replaced them with anger, for it was her only defense. "So my suffering and that of my family's is unimportant because more people have prospered than endured what we have?"

"The mills didn't rob you. Lewis did," Matthew said matter-of-factly. "Sooner or later, you're going to have to understand that."

"Lewis may have squandered the money given him by the Associates, but he would never have had the money to begin with if it hadn't been for their greediness to buy up all the land."

"Lilly, be fair."

She pulled her hand away. "Like the Corporation has been fair to me—to my father?"

"Your family received more than most," Matthew countered. "Your father didn't have to sell, but it was prosperous to do so."

"Lewis connived him into doing it."

"Lewis didn't want to be a farmer. Your father knew that—knew, too, that he was getting too old to run the place alone."

"He had me!" Lilly exclaimed, her voice raising an octave.

Matthew shook his head. "No, Lilly, he thought you belonged to me."

Lilly felt the age-old tightness in her chest. The misery of the past few years and the bitterness that had taken root in her heart caused her no end of pain. She lowered her gaze to the table, fighting the urge to cry. It would do no good. It couldn't take back the years of sorrow.

The waiter came with their tea, but Lilly could hardly drink it. She wanted to return home, to hide away in her bed and never get up again. She wanted to forget about bells and roving and loud machines that she seemed to hear long after they'd been turned off.

"I didn't ask you out to fight with you, Lilly." Matthew's words were soft and soothing. "I want to find a way to get beyond your anger with me."

The men at the table beside her were laughing and discussing plans for the holidays. One man confided that the extra money his business had made would allow him to take his wife to see her mother in New York. Lilly felt ill.

"Your tea is getting cold," Matthew offered after several minutes had passed in silence.

Still Lilly said nothing. As her emotions tumbled over each other, she tried desperately to think of a way to dismiss herself from the table without creating a scene.

Matthew picked up the conversation again as if nothing had ever happened. "Speaking of your brother, I've seen Lewis several times over the past few weeks. I didn't realize he was back in Lowell. The last I knew he was in Nashua. What brings him back?"

Thinking of Lewis was the trick she needed to steep herself in protective anger. Looking up, she met Matthew's gaze. "I have no idea. Lewis and his whereabouts aren't a topic I care to discuss," she said in what she hoped was her most dismissive tone.

Matthew reached across the table and took hold of her hand once again. "Lilly, this is important. I'm concerned that Lewis may be involved in some unsavory activity. I'm concerned that he and a man named William Thurston are up to no good. I want you to be honest with me," he said, his voice sounding urgent.

"You're hurting me," Lilly said, pulling from his grasp. She pushed back her chair and stood up. Everyone turned to look, but Lilly didn't care. "If you want to know, I suggest you invite Lewis to join you for tea," she said as the waiter came to check on them, "because I certainly don't want the tea—or your company." Pulling her cloak around her shoulders, Lilly turned to leave. "Please don't follow me, Matthew."

Although Lilly truly expected him to come running after her as she stormed down the block, it appeared he had taken her words to heart. She glanced over her shoulder one last time. Matthew was nowhere to be seen.

Her thoughts turned to Lewis. *What is he up to?* she wondered. And what of that Thurston man? She remembered the name from when Kirk Boott had brought him and Nathan Appleton to the mill. Lilly knew nothing about William Thurston, but if there were underhanded deeds to be done, she had no doubt Lewis was involved.

Against Lilly's wishes, he had occasionally called upon Prudence and probably several other girls who lived in different boardinghouses. Most likely he was garnering as much attention and money from the girls as his charm would permit. The thought of her brother preying upon girls who spent long, tedious hours in the mills sickened her.

Slowing her pace, Lilly tilted her head ever so slightly and listened. Footsteps. Perhaps Matthew was following her. In spite of her anger, she smiled and slowed her stride. A hand reached out to take hold of her, the arm coming around her shoulder.

"What are you doing out alone on this cold night?"

Lilly turned and looked up. Instead of Matthew, however, she looked into her brother's face. "Lewis. How strange that you should suddenly appear."

"Not so strange. I'm coming to call on your dear friend, Prudence. She promised to have a special gift for me this evening," he said. "You do need to purchase something a little warmer than this cloak for winter, Lilly. And in case you haven't noticed, it's really quite shabby. They've been receiving new shipments of some very fine clothing in town."

"I don't have money for a new cloak, so there's no need for me to go shopping. Obviously you have both time and money, Lewis. How is it that you can afford that new beaver hat?"

"Ah, not just the hat, but all of my clothing—even the boots and an expensive engraved pocket watch," he replied. "Your little friends are most generous. Pru, Mary, and even little Franny make marvelous companions. So sweet and so giving. I'm going to have to redirect them soon, however. They truly enjoy buying me gifts, but now that my wardrobe is complete, I'd rather have their money."

"Young ladies shouldn't be buying articles of clothing for a man to whom they aren't related. Nothing so personal should ever pass between you and those girls."

"Ah, but they adore me."

Lilly's teeth were clenched so tightly that her jaw began to hurt. "You have no conscience, Lewis." She wanted to hurt him, just as he was hurting the girls who worked in the mills—just as he had hurt her for years. "By the way, Lewis, exactly what *is* your relationship with William Thurston?"

He grabbed her arm, his fingers digging into her flesh. "How do you know about William Thurston?" His face was etched in both anger and fear.

Lilly met his gaze and pulled loose of his grasp. "So you *have* formed some kind of alliance with Mr. Thurston. You're planning something terrible, aren't you, Lewis?" she asked as they reached the boardinghouse.

He pushed her against the cold, hard bricks of the house and pinned her there, his hands on either side of her shoulders. "I want to know who has been making inquiries. How have you come by this information, Lilly? I trust you remember how cruel I can be when you're not cooperative," he threatened.

"I'm not a little girl anymore, Lewis. You no longer frighten me, and I'll not tell you what I know. Suffice it to say that you have been seen in Thurston's company, and people are wondering about such a liaison. Perhaps you and Thurston should consider setting aside any plans you might have—unless they be for good," she said, ducking under his arm and hurrying inside.

Lilly leaned against the front door and listened to the sound of her brother's footsteps as he walked away from the house. Prudence would have no gentleman caller this night.

～ 24 ～

Matthew and Kirk pulled on their gloves and mounted their horses, one a bay gelding, the other a chestnut mare. "I want to ride out toward the falls," Kirk said as the horses began to trot away from the livery. Matthew nodded as both men urged their horses into a gallop and moved toward the outskirts of town. It was an unseasonably warm December Sunday, perfect for a ride in the country and talk of the Associates' expansion projects.

"The funding has been arranged for additional mills," Kirk said as they neared Pawtucket Falls. "We're going to begin work on another canal this spring, as soon as the ground has thawed sufficiently. Which means additional work for Hugh and his Irishmen. There's certainly been no lack of work for them when the weather cooperates. I worry about problems through the winter, though. Idle hands can breed problems. Speaking of which, you know how disappointed I was with the bishop's decision to delay his visit."

Matthew moved his horse ahead of Boott's, leading the way through a thick stand of leafless trees. "I understand, but we can't move forward with building a church during the dead of winter, either. There are plans to send a priest for Christmas mass. That should help."

Shots rang out in the distance, and Matthew tightened the hold on his reins. "Someone hunting for dinner, I suspect," he said, glancing over his shoulder and then shifting in his saddle to gain a better view.

Boott fought to control his gelding, but the horse reared and dumped Kirk off the back. After hitting the ground, Boott didn't so much as try to get out of the way of the stomping horse.

"Whoa there, boy," Matthew called out to the horse in a reassuring tone. Turning his own horse, Matthew approached slowly, not wanting to startle Boott's horse, and grabbed the reins. Another shot echoed in the distance, followed by the sound of pounding hooves. Somebody was hunting, but not for dinner. Matthew jumped down from his horse, holding fast to both sets of reins. Trying to take shelter among the trees, he looked off into the distance, hoping to catch a glimpse of someone, wanting to make sense of what was happening. He looked to where Boott lay on the ground. There was no movement, no sign of life. "Mr. Boott, can you hear me?" he called.

There was no answer. Crawling closer, Matthew could see that there was blood along Boott's temple. Apparently he'd hit his head when the horse had thrown him. Another cursory glance revealed a telltale reddish stain on Kirk's pant leg. He'd been shot! Matthew had to get Kirk to a doctor. Struggling under Boott's weight, he lifted the man into his arms and then hoisted him onto the horse. Then Matthew held the older man in the saddle while mounting up behind him. He pulled his own horse along by the reins. Every muscle in his body was stretched taut, anxiously awaiting the next shot, expecting to feel his flesh torn open by the searing pain of a lead ball. He urged the horse onward, praying they would be safe.

The ride into town seemed endless, the heaviness of Kirk's body constantly shifting to and fro. The horse was unaccustomed to carrying two riders and was now pulling against the reins. The horse's skittishness and the blood that now stained Kirk's breeches and coat caused Matthew to wonder if they would arrive before his boss was dead.

A short time later, he dismounted in front of Dr. Fontaine's office and carefully pulled Kirk off the horse. "Give me a hand," he called to a group of Irishmen ambling down the street. "Mr. Boott's been shot."

Once Kirk was in the office, Dr. Fontaine took charge. He insisted Matthew immediately inform Mrs. Boott of Kirk's condition. "And don't bring her back here to the office. I don't need to perform surgery with a weepy wife looking over my shoulder," he warned. No doubt Mrs. Boott would be distraught, and Matthew had no idea how to handle such a situation. He thought of Lilly but immediately rejected that thought. A mill girl calling upon Anne Boott, relating ill-fated news of her husband? *Never.* But then he thought of his mother. It would be only a short distance farther to stop by home and ask that she accompany him.

Julia Cheever was delighted Matthew had sought her council and assistance, and once they arrived at the Boott residence, she quickly shooed him away, insisting that he could be of little help. "We'll prepare things here at the house. You go back to Dr. Fontaine's office and make yourself available to transport Mr. Boott home once his wounds are tended," Julia instructed.

Matthew wasn't sure Dr. Fontaine would be sending Kirk home any too quickly. In fact, he wasn't sure if Kirk was still alive—but he wasn't about to inform the two women of his fears.

A beaming Addie sat surrounded by all of her young boarders as well as Mintie and John Farnsworth. "What a perfect birthday this has been," she said.

"And it's not over yet," Prudence said, placing a forkful of birthday cake in her mouth. "We're pleased your birthday is on Sunday; that way we can celebrate all afternoon, can't we?"

There was a declaration of agreement among the girls. Mintie, however, appeared a bit nonplussed at the amount of attention being showered upon her sister. "The Judge didn't approve of birthday parties," Mintie commented unpleasantly.

"But he always bought us a special gift for our birthday," Addie replied. "It was Mother who disliked birthdays."

John drew a bit closer to where Addie sat. "Speaking of presents," he said, holding out a package, "I hope you'll accept this along with my very best wishes for your special day."

Addie gave him a smile. "Why, John, you shouldn't have bought me anything."

Mintie's lips shriveled up tighter than a prune. She crossed her arms across her bosom and glared in Addie's direction. "You're right—he *shouldn't* have purchased a gift. It's inappropriate."

However, her comment went unheeded. The girls gathered around, watching as Addie's plump fingers untied the brown cord and peeled away the paper. Nestled inside the wrapping were two tortoiseshell combs.

"They're beautiful, John," she said, her cheeks flushed as she held out the combs for the girls to see.

"I can't take all the credit for choosing them," he said. "Lilly accompanied me into town a couple weeks ago and assisted with my choice."

A spark of recognition shone in Addie's eyes. "She went with you one evening after dinner, didn't she? Probably the night of the temperance meeting," Addie said, turning her gaze toward Mintie.

"I don't know about the temperance meeting, but we did go after dinner," John replied. "We managed to keep our secret from you, however. I swore Lilly to secrecy, and she was true to her word."

Addie met Lilly's gaze. "She certainly was. I never suspected she had gone with you to purchase a birthday gift. *You* would never have suspected such a thing, either, would you, Mintie?" Addie inquired, turning toward her sister.

Mintie glowered and shifted in her chair. "You're not going to accept those combs, are you? What would the Judge think of a man purchasing such a gift for you? It's improper, that's what it is," Mintie retorted, adjusting her shawl more tightly around her neck.

"I *am* going to accept them, Mintie. And quite happily, I might add. As for the Judge, I don't know what he would say, and quite frankly, I don't care."

Mintie's eyebrows arched high on her forehead, and her mouth opened to form a large oval. A loud knocking at the front door interrupted whatever retort may have been upon her lips.

Lawrence Gault entered the room, his gentle composure visibly shaken. "John, come quick. I've received word that Kirk Boott and Matthew Cheever were riding near Pawtucket Falls, and they've been shot. They're at Dr.

Fontaine's office. I was told it might have been an ambush."

John quickly donned his coat and hat. "Someone intentionally shot Mr. Boott and Matthew? Why would anyone do such a thing?"

Lilly hurried along behind the two men, her hand at her throat. "Wait, Mr. Farnsworth, I want to accompany you," she called after him. He turned and gave her a questioning look. "I've known Matthew since we were children."

He nodded. "Come along, then," he said, taking hold of her arm.

Lilly felt her heart begin to race. What if Matthew were dead? The very thought brought her more pain than she could have imagined. He couldn't be dead. He just couldn't be.

Her feelings didn't so much surprise her as worry her. She did still have feelings for Matthew Cheever. Feelings that went far beyond that of merely caring for his well-being. She hoped neither man would die from such an attack but felt honest grief at the thought of Matthew being wounded.

They arrived at Dr. Fontaine's office in record time, the three of them breathing heavily when they finally entered the doctor's office. Lilly's eyes widened at the sight of Matthew pacing about the doctor's front door. He wasn't hurt. She didn't know whether to hug him or scream at him for worrying her.

John quickly extended his hand toward Matthew. "We heard you'd been shot. I'm pleased to see that we received a false report. What about Mr. Boott? Was he injured?"

Matthew gave them a grim look. "I'm afraid that report is true. Dr. Fontaine is with him. He was shot while we were out riding. His horse reared, and Boott fell and hit his head. He didn't regain consciousness. It appeared serious, but I'm not an authority on such things. Mrs. Boott is expecting me to transport him home once the doctor has finished with him."

"I could use some assistance in here," Dr. Fontaine called out from the other room.

Lilly watched as the men exchanged glances. Matthew seemed to pale at the request. "I'll go," John replied. "Lawrence, why don't you get word to the other Associates. They'll want to know."

"I could do that," Matthew offered.

John furrowed his brow and gave a negative nod. "Mrs. Boott will be expecting to hear from you. It's best you remain here."

The moment both men were out of earshot, Lilly turned on her heel and faced Matthew. "You don't even bear a scratch," she remarked with relief.

"I didn't know you cared so much," Matthew said, his voice bearing a hint of amusement.

Lilly's anger flared to mask her embarrassment. She hadn't known that little fact, either, but she wasn't about to let Matthew believe she cared.

"Were you hoping for sympathy? Is that why I received a message you'd been shot? Do you realize how frightening it is to hear such a report?"

Matthew gave her a smile. "I didn't send out *any* report, Lilly, but if I had realized it would bring you running to me, I might have done so. Your appearance serves to prove what I've already told you."

She glared in his direction and folded .her arms. "And what might that be?"

"That you're still in love with me."

"I am *not* in love with you. Right at this moment, I don't even like you," she sputtered. "The fact that you would flatter yourself with such a notion is . . . is . . ."

"Marvelous? Enchanting? Wonderful? We're meant to be together, Lilly. You know it and so do I," he said, reaching out to draw her into his arms.

"I suggest you stop right there, Matthew Cheever, or the story going about town that you've sustained an injury *will* be true," Lilly said, pulling out of his grasp. Confusion made reasonable thought impossible. *I'm not in love. I'm not.*

Lilly hurried from the house and walked back to the boardinghouse, angry that she'd once again given Matthew reason to believe she still cared for him. Even if she did.

But I don't, she told herself, desperate to push aside any doubt. *I reacted that way only because we've known each other forever. I don't care for him. I could never . . . love . . . him.*

Such a possibility was out of the question, for she could never align herself with a man who was intent on forcing industrialization upon the farmlands of New England. It seemed as though no matter how much she prayed about her life and the miserable takeover by the Associates, God was continually confronting and challenging her to accept the changes. She didn't want to, yet within her heart she knew she must.

After all, others had. Some people were quite happy with the change, as she'd heard that night at tea. Some people were thriving, excited, joyous even at the prosperity that had come their way. The girls she lived with were grateful for the opportunity to come in from their farms and poorer country life. They thrived on earning money for themselves and while some sent home most of their pay, others were living quite nicely, dining out and buying new clothes.

Lilly looked down the street, seeing the mills in the distance. The mills had given this community new life. Lowell wasn't her beloved farm community. Instead the simple country maiden had grown into a sassy, citified woman of the world. And to Lilly's sorrow, it appeared people were beginning to accept—even embrace—the change.

"Things will never be the same," she murmured.

"All things change in time—some for the good, some for the bad. But change they

will." The words had been spoken to Lilly by her mother. She sighed. "Oh, Mama, things have changed, and I don't know how to change with them. It hurts so much to know you're gone—that Father and the farm are gone." Wiping a tear from her eye, Lilly bolstered her courage and approached the boardinghouse. *I have to be strong,* she told herself. But inside, she found little strength to draw on.

Prudence and Marmi hastened into the hallway upon her return. "How badly are they injured? Is Matthew . . ." Marmi hesitantly inquired.

"Matthew is fine. He wasn't injured. Mr. Boott was shot, but the wound wasn't fatal. The doctor was operating when I left." Lilly pulled off her bonnet and set it aside.

"That's certainly good news," a familiar voice commented.

Lilly turned. "What are *you* doing here, Lewis? Did you have anything to do with this?" she whispered as she pretended to draw him into an affectionate embrace.

"Dear sister. Why would I be involved in such an incident? How can you think such a thing of your brother?" he whispered in return.

"Quite easily," Lilly responded as she moved away from him and turned toward Prudence. "Don't give him any of your money, Prudence. He's been calling on at least two other girls who have been buying him gifts, also. If you don't believe me, I'll give you their names, and you can verify what I'm saying. Lewis is a cad who will do nothing but hurt you. It pains me to tell you this, Pru. If you continue keeping company with him, he'll take every cent you have, and then you'll never hear from him again. Please heed my words," she begged her friend before leaving the hallway and making her way upstairs.

That night, Lilly again tried to find solace in her Bible reading. A troubling thought flittered through her mind. *If I'm going to rejoice in Kirk Boott's downfall, I would have to rejoice in the possibility of Matthew's, as well.* The thought of him bloodied and dying actually brought tears to her eyes.

I don't want anything bad to happen to Matthew. Whether or not there exists hope for us to remain friends, I don't want him hurt. But the destruction of the mill and all that he's worked for would hurt him, she thought.

Fearfully, like a child about to be reprimanded, she opened the Bible. She flipped through the pages, heading for the back of the book. There was no way she wanted to get stuck in Proverbs again.

Colossians seemed a safe distance away, so she focused her attention on the third chapter. The second and third verses went straight to her heart.

"Set your affection on things above, not on things on the earth. For ye are dead, and your life is hid with Christ in God."

God, Lilly prayed, *I don't fully know what this verse means. In some ways, I've placed my affection on the earth—on the way things used to be. I'm mourning the past, the loss of my loved ones, the hope of things remaining the same. I want to understand your Word, but it seems every time I open it, I'm just that much more confused. Please help me.*

Shortly after breakfast the next morning, a knock sounded at the front door. Addie knew it was Mintie coming to further chastise her about the combs she'd accepted from John Farnsworth. For a moment she considered not answering the door, but experience had taught her Mintie would persist. "I don't have time to sit and visit, Mintie," Addie said as she pulled open the door.

"What kind of greeting is that? Living in this hamlet has caused you to lose all sense of proper etiquette," Mintie chided after pushing her way through the door and stomping snow off her feet. "It's difficult to believe it could snow through the night after that beautiful day we had yesterday."

"I'm surprised you'd be out in such weather," Addie replied as she headed off toward the kitchen.

"Where are you going? I don't want to sit out in the kitchen," Mintie said.

Addie glanced over her shoulder. "I told you I was busy. I'm paring apples, and I can't do that in the parlor." She heard Mintie's *hurrump* and sigh of exasperation but chose to ignore both.

"I have news," Mintie said, seating herself in one of the straight-backed wooden chairs.

Addie didn't comment.

"Did you hear me? I have news," Mintie repeated.

"I heard you. And I have no doubt you're going to tell me every word of it."

It was obvious Mintie chose to ignore her sister's sarcasm. "I sent Lucy to pick up a few supplies this morning. There's word about town that the Irish are responsible for shooting Kirk Boott. Folks are saying the Irish are upset over their living conditions in the Paddy camps. I think that's a bunch of nonsense. The Irish have always appeared to enjoy living in squalor."

"And I'm sure you'd be an authority on what the Irish enjoy," Addie muttered.

"Speak up! I couldn't hear you," Mintie admonished.

"Nothing, Mintie, I didn't say a thing."

Mintie nodded and moved her chair closer to the fire. "I'll tell you what I think. I'm convinced it's the English. They're trying to find a way to stop the production of cloth here in New England. They fear a decline of our imports from them."

"Goodness, Mintie, the Tariff of Abominations has already dealt imports a heavy blow. The English goods are taxed very high and . . ."

"Exactly my point. The English have reason to hate us and to put an end to our mills. I know you don't want to hear this, Adelaide, but there is no doubt in my mind that John Farnsworth is at the very root of this. In fact, I believe he hired someone to kill Kirk Boott and made his appearance at your birthday party in order to cover his involvement in the deed. He is a covert, traitorous man, sent here to aid in the ruination of this country."

Addie gasped in disbelief. "I cannot believe you would say such things about a fine man like John Farnsworth. When you arrived, I thought you had come to berate me for accepting his gift. Now I find you've come to accuse him of attempted murder and treason against this country. Since you're intent upon defaming John Farnsworth, I must ask you to leave this house. I'll not tolerate such talk, Mintie."

Mintie jumped up, her chair toppling to the floor. "You would choose that British spy over your own flesh and blood? I can't believe what has happened to you, Adelaide Beecher. No doubt the Judge is rolling over in his grave at this very moment," she harangued while darting toward the front door.

"Mintie," Addie said, following her. "I want to say something, and I want you to hear me out."

The older woman turned, her face fixed in a pinched expression. "Go ahead, you could hardly shock me further."

Addie drew a deep breath and let it out slowly. "I don't understand why you feel you must hurt me. For as long as I remember, you've seemed to go out of your way to cause me pain. You berate me at every turn, never offering a single word of kindness or praise. You disdain my choices in clothes and friends, and you bring up hurtful things from the past to emphasize my shortcomings." Tears filled Addie's eyes. "I don't understand how you can hate me so much."

Mintie's expression fell. She appeared to be genuinely stunned by Addie's words. "I . . . You can't believe that I hate you."

"Then why do you do these things? Are you afraid I'll embarrass you? If John happened to be a spy, and I had made a terrible mistake in caring for him, it would be my mistake—not yours. Don't you see? Your fearfulness of the English and your bitterness over whatever it is you hold against me is tearing apart any affection we might have between us. I am your sister, Mintie, flesh and blood just as you said. Yet I've seen you treat stray dogs better than you do me." Tears streamed down Addie's cheeks, much to her dismay. She didn't want Mintie to think her weak, but her pain was so deep there was no way to contain her emotions.

"Please go now," she told Mintie and opened the door for her. "I want to be alone."

25

L illy slipped into her gown of layered yellow muslin and shivered. It was hardly warm enough for the winter, but her choices were few, and this was one of the last of her gowns acceptable to wear to Sunday services.

While doing up the buttons, she silently chastised herself for agreeing to accompany Miss Addie to St. Anne's for Sunday services. The ritual at the Episcopal church made her uncomfortable, for she hadn't attended often enough to learn the order of service. She much preferred attending the Methodist church with Nadene, where she knew exactly what to expect. But Miss Addie had asked if she would attend St. Anne's with her during the Advent season. The older woman said it would be her Christmas gift from Lilly since she disliked attending services alone. Lilly had hastened to point out that Mr. Farnsworth and Miss Mintie both attended St. Anne's, but Miss Addie had quickly retorted that it was Lilly's presence she desired.

Addie was waiting at the foot of the stairs in her fur-trimmed coat, a relic of the prosperous days when she, Mintie, and the Judge had resided among Boston society. "You look lovely," she greeted as Lilly descended the staircase, "except for that frown you're wearing."

Lilly smiled at the remark. "It's not a frown; I was merely deep in thought."

Peeking from beneath her matching fur-trimmed bonnet, Addie gave a bemused look. "Then you must be thinking *terrible* thoughts."

"I was contemplating the fact that I don't want to see Matthew Cheever. And Matthew attends St. Anne's," Lilly remarked as they left the house. She fussed with the ribbons of a bonnet she'd borrowed from Miss Addie, hoping the woman would just let the matter drop.

"Your feelings for him run deep."

"No, they don't," Lilly said in protest. "It's just that our past makes me uncomfortable."

Addie smiled. "Not near as much as your future."

"Don't say that. I don't have a future with Matthew."

"Say what you will, my dear. I won't nag at you to be honest with me, but I think sooner or later you'll have to be honest with yourself. Have you prayed about it—asked God what He desires for your life?"

Lilly refused to even contemplate her friend's question, confusion washing over her. First Julia Cheever had worked to put Lilly back in Matthew's life. Then Matthew himself, in that smug, self-confident way of his, had made certain Lilly knew he still considered a future for them. And now Miss Addie. It was just too much.

"Oh, here comes John," Addie whispered.

At that moment, the older woman reminded Lilly of a blushing young girl excited at the sight of her first beau. Lilly felt a twinge of envy. She remembered feeling that way.

John pointed toward the western horizon. "Looks like snow clouds over there. Perhaps you'd like to join me for a sleigh ride one day soon, Addie." It was more a comment than a question.

Lilly glanced toward the older woman, curious how she might react to John's offer. The fact that God had blessed Addie with a modicum of joy in the midst of a humdrum daily life gave Lilly hope. Hope for herself and all the other girls that they, too, might find some respite from the monotony of the mills.

"A sleigh ride would be lovely, John. Perhaps Lilly and Matthew could join us."

Lilly couldn't believe her ears. She jabbed an elbow in Miss Addie's direction but missed the mark. "I don't want to go on a sleigh ride with Matthew," she hissed in Addie's direction.

Addie turned and gave Lilly a gentle smile. "Of *course* you do, dear. You just haven't accepted the fact that you and Matthew still care for each other," she answered sweetly.

Lilly would have rendered a protest, but it was no use. The church bells would drown out anything she might say. Besides, it was obvious her denial would fall upon deaf ears. She remained silent as the three of them approached the gray slate church building. The vestibule was filled with churchgoers not yet ready to enter the sanctuary. Lilly nervously glanced about, but Matthew was nowhere to be seen. She breathed a sigh of relief.

"Are you ready to go in and be seated?" Addie inquired. "John is going to sit in our pew. Mintie will have a fit," she said with a nervous giggle.

"I'll go in last. That way Miss Mintie will be seated next to me," Lilly replied, knowing that Mintie's attendance would dramatically diminish Addie's ability to enjoy John's presence.

"Thank you, Lilly," Addie said as John held open one of the heavy wooden doors leading into the sanctuary.

A firm grasp on Lilly's shoulder caused her to stop and turn. A smiling Randolph Cheever met her gaze. "What a pleasant surprise. Look who's here, Julia," he said as he turned toward his wife.

Julia Cheever was in her Sunday finery, her drawn bonnet of navy blue silk impeccably matching her empire dress. "Lilly! I didn't realize you'd begun attending St. Anne's. I insist you come and sit in our pew."

"Thank you for the invitation, but I'm attending with Miss Addie. I fear it would hurt Miss Addie's feelings if I were to sit with you," Lilly explained.

Julia nodded in obvious understanding. "I'll not argue. I certainly wouldn't want anyone to think I would encourage bad manners. However, I doubt you can find an excuse to turn down a dinner invitation. We're going to take you home with us after church, aren't we, Randolph?" There was a note of triumph in her voice.

There had to be some way Lilly could offer her regrets and escape dinner at the Cheever residence. Matthew hadn't yet made an appearance, but there was no doubt he would attend Sunday dinner at his parents' home. "My friend Nadene sustained severe burns at work several weeks ago, and I really must return home to help tend her bandages and keep her company," Lilly replied. She had spoken the truth—she did want to visit Nadene, and sometimes she helped change her bandages.

Mintie Beecher scurried into the vestibule and then stopped momentarily to clear the fog from her glasses. Lilly tensed at the sight of the older woman, thankful Mr. Cheever was now urging his wife forward. "Services are going to begin," he said.

Julia stepped alongside him. "We'll discuss this after church," she promised.

Pretending she didn't hear, Lilly made her way down the aisle and opened the small door that permitted entry into the pew. Scooting in close beside Miss Addie, she folded her hands and waited. The swishing sound of Miss Mintie's dress was drawing nearer. The pew door clicked. Lilly flinched but kept her gaze focused upon the floor.

Mintie sat down and gave Lilly a poke with her needle-sharp elbow. "What is everybody doing in our pew?" she inquired in an irritated whisper.

Lilly sat still, her head bowed. "Worshiping God. And I'm certain that He's glad you've joined us," she whispered in return. She forced herself to swallow hard as a giggle bubbled up and threatened to spill out.

"You be careful with your sass, young lady," Mintie warned as she leaned forward in an obvious attempt to gain Addie's attention. Fortunately for Addie, she had chosen a bonnet that successfully kept Mintie out of view.

Once again the pointy elbow stabbed into Lilly's side. "Tell Adelaide to look this way. I want to tell her something," Mintie ordered in an authoritative whisper.

Lilly placed a finger to her lips, hushing Miss Mintie as if she were a small child. "Miss Addie is praying," she replied, then bowed her own head. She could feel Mintie's unyielding gaze throughout the remainder of the service. The moment the organ sounded the last chords of the final hymn, John and Addie quickly exited out the opposite pew door.

Lilly attempted to follow them, but Mintie's fingers dug into her arm. "I wanted to sit next to my sister. You should have stepped out and permitted me entry beside her. You should be sitting in your own pew or with one of the other girls. Do you pay pew rent here?"

"No, I don't."

"Then you should go where you pay your own pew rent and let me sit where I pay mine," Mintie snarled.

Lilly looked deep into the older woman's eyes. There was no doubt she was irate, yet behind the angry facade there was something else. Fear? Isolation? "I'm sorry you're unhappy, Miss Beecher. I know you miss your sister. Perhaps if you would reconsider your feelings toward John Farnsworth, the two of you could set things aright. I'm sure it would please Miss Addie as much as it would you."

There was a faint softening of Mintie's frown as she peered down her nose at Lilly. "The impertinence of youth."

"Who, me? Or were you meaning Miss Addie?" Lilly questioned.

"Never mind," Mintie said, stiffening. For a moment her expression seemed quite sad, and Lilly actually felt sorry for the older woman.

They said nothing further, and Lilly stood silently watching as Mintie marched out of the church with her shoulders squared, head high, and back straight as an arrow. No doubt she let anger and irritation be her companions—it kept people from getting too close. Close enough to hurt you. Lilly had learned this very well for herself.

In a flash, she saw herself growing old—old as Mintie Beecher. Just as old and just as lonely and cantankerous. *Do you really want that for yourself?* a voice seemed to question. *Do you really want to lose your chance at real happiness?* Lilly shook the penetrating thoughts away.

The aisles were crowded but Lilly could see Julia Cheever wending her way through the congestion, heading directly toward her. She felt a twinge of guilt as she left the pew and pushed her way through to catch up with Addie and John.

Moments later a horse halted a short distance ahead of where the three were walking, and Randolph Cheever jumped down. "Lilly! We want you to join us for dinner. Let me help you into the carriage."

She could hardly turn and run. Smiling, she permitted him to assist her, thankful that Matthew was not present.

Matthew unlocked the front gate to the Appleton and went directly to his office. He would be glad when Kirk was finally able to return to work. Not that he had any aversion to the additional responsibility. In fact, he found it flattering that Kirk now relied upon him even more. But when Kirk was present there seemed to be an air of authority that permeated the mills. Of course, Mrs. Boott was disinclined to have her husband return for at least another six weeks, saying he could comfortably work from his office at home. Matthew doubted his boss would stay away that long!

He wasn't sure if it was the unsettling silence of the mill on a Sunday or the fact that he was meeting William Thurston and Lewis Armbruster for a secret discussion that was causing his anxiety. He read through several ledgers Mr. Gault had placed on his desk Saturday afternoon and reviewed the paper work Kirk had given him. He was finishing his notes when the gate bell rang. He startled to attention.

The two men stood waiting, talking in quiet tones, Thurston wringing his leather-gloved hands as Matthew approached. "Gentlemen. Come in," Matthew said while holding open the gate.

Matthew couldn't shake his feeling of uneasiness as they walked in silence to his office. He now wished he had insisted on waiting until Monday morning. "I'm expected somewhere within the hour, so perhaps we should get to our business. Tell me, what's so important that we need to meet in secret on a Sunday afternoon?" Matthew asked, looking back and forth between the two men.

Armbruster turned toward Thurston, who was obviously the delegated spokesman. "Lewis and I have become privy to some information. We've weighed the merits of coming forward and with whom we should discuss this matter. After a great deal of thought, we determined you were the best choice."

Matthew leaned back in his chair and met the man's gaze. "And why am I the best choice?"

Thurston leaned forward, arms resting upon his thighs. "You live here in Lowell, you work closely with Kirk and, I dare say, you have almost a father-son relationship with him. I know how devastated you've surely been over his harrowing experience—the thought that he could have been killed! Well, it's more than I even care to think about! I'm certain we would all be extraordinarily delighted to mete out punishment to the culprit who shot him."

Matthew listened intently, careful to hide his excitement at the prospect of finally discovering who had ambushed Boott. "Do I understand that you're prepared to give me the name of the person responsible for Mr. Boott's injury?"

Thurston shifted in his chair. "We have information."

Matthew attempted to hide his irritation. "What does that mean? Either you know who's responsible or you don't."

"We know who's responsible, but we don't have a name. We know it's a young Irishman."

Matthew stared at the duo in disbelief. "Well, *that* certainly narrows it down."

"Sarcasm doesn't suit you," Lewis retorted. "And, quite frankly, telling you it was a young Irishman certainly *does* narrow the possible suspects."

William held his hand up and silenced Lewis. "If you'll permit me to continue, I will more fully explain. There is an informant, also an Irishman. I need not tell you what a tenuous situation it would place him in if word leaked out regarding his willingness to cooperate in the investigation. He wants assurance his name will not be involved in any way. And, of course, he would expect a reward for the risk he would be taking."

Matthew stood and began pacing in front of the window along the south wall of his small office. "So this unnamed informant doesn't want anyone but you and Lewis to know his identity. Does he have any proof to substantiate his accusations?"

"He has a piece of cloth that was torn from the coat of the person he says committed the act; the cloth was found out in the woods near where Boott was shot. My informant also told me that once he names the person, you could check with Hugh Cummiskey about the culprit. It appears this fellow and Boott had an argument, and Cummiskey witnessed their disagreement."

Returning to his chair, Matthew sat down. His head hurt. He rubbed the back of his neck and then met William's piercing gaze. "It sounds convincing, but I want names before I talk to Mr. Boott. Your man will have to wait upon any possible reward until we're certain the name he gives you is the actual offender. I'm certain you realize the ramifications if these accusations are correct," Matthew said, once again rubbing his neck.

Thurston nodded. "I've said it before and I'll say it again. The Irish are a blight on this community. They're an unruly, uneducated bunch of rabble-rousers who are spreading like the plague throughout the town. Their tempers often lead them to take matters into their own hands. If this incident with Boott doesn't prove my point, I don't know what it's going to take to convince the rest of you."

"I'm not sure everyone shares your views on the Irish, William. In any case, I'll need to have *all* the evidence—names, the piece of fabric, exact location where your man retrieved the cloth, and any other information he's got that will substantiate his accusations against this as yet unnamed Irishman. Once I have that information, I'll go to Mr. Boott. Tell your man that he'll have to furnish the name of the culprit and his proof before we'll move forward and investigate his claim. No reward until we're certain his information is correct. Get back with me after you've talked with him."

"Investigate? I've already done that for you. You're expecting a lot from this man, and yet you're doing nothing to show your good faith," Thurston argued.

Matthew shrugged. "Any reward would come from Mr. Boott. Surely you can convince your informant that he's dealing with a man who will do right by him."

William rose from his chair and moved toward the door. "He was hoping for a speedy resolution. As you can understand, he wants to leave Lowell as soon as possible. He'll need money."

"I understand. As soon as you fulfill my requests, I'll go directly to Boott. You have my word. We both know he is a generous man and one who is willing to make a quick decision. If he's convinced by the evidence, I'm sure a reward will be immediately forthcoming."

William nudged Lewis on the shoulder. "Come on, Lewis. I want to get this resolved. I should be back with you in the morning, Matthew. You'll be here at your office?"

Matthew nodded and then walked out with the two men and unlocked the gate. "Until tomorrow."

A blast of cold air whipped down the street, and Matthew bent his head against the chill. He watched the twosome walk off in the direction of the Paddy camp. He wanted to discuss Thurston's proposal with Boott, but he would wait. Perhaps William would be unable to secure the information and wouldn't return. He walked back to his office and retrieved his coat and hat. Why would anyone choose Lewis Armbruster or William Thurston as confidants to carry an offer? Especially an Irishman!

Matthew glanced at the clock atop the tower in the center of the mill yard. He was famished. If he hurried, perhaps he could make it home before all the food was cleared from his mother's table.

The Cheever home had been modestly decorated for the Christmas holidays. Evergreen boughs trimmed with red ribbons lined the banister and fireplace, making the place quite festive. Lilly thought it homey and very beautiful. She thought of her childhood and the special way her parents used to make her feel on Christmas morning.

Not that they didn't make me feel special throughout the year, she chided. But Christmas was always special. They had wonderful times of singing and laughing. They would share gifts, most handmade but all very precious, and they would dine on wonderful delicacies. Lilly had almost forgotten how wonderful it had all been. The last five years with her father had been meager and less than festive. In part because of the impending realization that soon the farm would be lost to them forever. And partly because that's the way Lilly chose it to be.

For a moment she felt overcome with guilt. She could have made it far more special for her father. His last years shouldn't have been spent dealing with someone so steeped in anger and hatred as Lilly had been.

"I hope you've saved room for dessert," Julia Cheever told Lilly.

Lilly silently chastised herself for having attempted to avoid Mr. and Mrs. Cheever's dinner invitation. The food was delicious, and the quietude of three people around the table was refreshing. She had almost forgotten the pleasure a family meal afforded.

"We have cherry pie," Julia said. "Matthew's favorite. It's a shame he isn't here to enjoy it."

Lilly withheld any comment regarding Matthew. "Let me help you remove the dishes," she offered while pushing back her chair.

The two women cleared the table while Randolph enjoyed a cup of coffee and awaited his dessert. They were preparing to cut the pie when the front door opened and the sound of stomping feet could be heard in the hallway. "It's me, Mother. Have I missed dinner?"

Matthew! She had relaxed too soon. At least dinner was over, and she could make her excuses for an early return to the boardinghouse. After all, she had told the Cheevers she wanted to spend time with Nadene.

"Would you mind fixing Matthew a plate while I cut the pie, Lilly?" Julia asked.

How could she refuse? "Certainly," she replied as she started to heap a plate with food.

Julia beamed. "There! I told you that you'd be surprised, didn't I?" she chortled at Matthew as Lilly entered the dining room.

Matthew gave Lilly a broad smile. "Why, thank you. I can't remember when I've been served by a lovelier hostess," he said as she set his plate before him.

Lilly didn't fail to note that, in her absence, Julia had seated Matthew directly beside her at the table, where a piece of pie now awaited her return. She pulled her chair out and moved it as far away from Matthew as possible without appearing overly obvious. "I must leave shortly," Lilly said as she forked a piece of the flaky pastry toward her mouth.

Julia jerked to attention. "Nonsense! I'll hear nothing of you leaving so soon."

"Nor I," Matthew agreed. "We have several things to discuss," he quickly added.

"In that case, your father and I will retire to the parlor and give you two a bit of privacy while you finish eating, Matthew. Come along, Randolph," she ordered, turning her attention toward her husband, who was shoveling his last bite of pie into his mouth while nodding his head.

Lilly glanced back and forth between the couple, wishing she could jump up and rush into the other room with them. She didn't want to be alone with

Matthew, for it would serve no purpose. Their conversations always culminated in harsh words and disagreement. She finished her pie and prepared for the worst.

"It's good to see you, Lilly. I've been wanting to talk with you ever since our last . . ." he hesitated for a moment.

"Disagreement?" she asked, finishing his sentence.

He gave a comfortable laugh and nodded his head. "I hope we'll do a little better."

"We always fight. Even when I don't plan to, you say something that brings out the worst in me."

"Like when I questioned you about Lewis?" Matthew asked softly. "I apologize for that. I know he's hurt you greatly. Still, I would like to know what brought him back here."

While his questioning at the restaurant had seemed forceful and imperious, his simple retiring statement had the opposite effect. She found herself now wanting to share her own concerns regarding Lewis. "Then it may be best to discuss Lewis first. You wondered why he's in Lowell, and the only answer I can give is that he generally comes home when he has no money and nowhere else to go. I do know he's short on funds. All of his inheritance has been gambled away, and as usual, he's looking for some way to support himself that doesn't require work on his part."

Matthew finished eating and pushed his plate toward the center of the table. "Did he actually tell you his money is gone, or is that supposition based upon his return home?"

"He asked me for money when he arrived, saying his inheritance was gone. I don't doubt his word, especially since he told me he planned to begin escorting some of the mill girls. He assumed they would be easy prey. Obviously he was right. I know he's been accepting gifts and money from several different girls."

Matthew smacked his palm on the table. "Despicable behavior. How could he do such a thing?"

"He appears to have no conscience. He did mention some time back that he had entered into an alliance with a man of means. When we were last together you mentioned he was keeping company with William Thurston. I saw Lewis that very night and asked about his relationship with Mr. Thurston."

Matthew leaned forward and met her gaze. "What did he have to say?"

Lilly thought for a moment. She wasn't sure she wanted to take Matthew into her confidence. And yet Lewis had threatened her—surely she should tell someone. "He appeared extremely upset that anyone knew of the liaison, though I'm not certain why, and he wanted to know who had made inquiry regarding their association."

"And what did you tell him?"

Lilly gave him a thoughtful look. "I told him if there was an evil plan afoot he should set it aside. He firmly asserted I should stay out of his business."

"So he may be working for Thurston, but we know he's being at least partially supported by his lady friends."

"Oh yes. He appears to accept gifts regularly from the girls. I've attempted to convince the girls he's a scoundrel. They don't believe me, but once he's taken their money and run off, it's *me* they'll be angry with," she lamented.

He stood up from the table and then assisted Lilly with her chair. "Unfortunately that's probably true, but if you've warned them, I don't know what else you can do. Why don't we move into the parlor? It's much more comfortable."

Randolph was reading, and Julia was embroidering on a piece of linen that she immediately placed in her sewing basket. "I gave Cook the rest of the day off. I'm just going to go to the kitchen and clean up. And your father is going to help me. Aren't you, Randolph?" Julia added quickly.

Randolph glanced up from his book with a puzzled look on his face. "I'm not certain. If you're merely arranging for the children to be alone, Julia, I think I would prefer to take my book and sit in the dining room."

"Randolph!" Julia chided as her husband followed along behind her, chuckling.

Matthew settled onto the settee and patted the cushion beside him. "Please sit down," he said, glancing up at Lilly. "I have something else I want to ask you," he said as she settled beside him and then turned, giving him her full attention. "About your appearance at Dr. Fontaine's office," he began.

Lilly could feel herself stiffen. He was going to confront her again. "I don't think there's anything to discuss."

"I want to thank you for your concern. My behavior was arrogant and unseemly. I hope you'll forgive me. Instead of acknowledging your act of friendship, I made assumptions that were obviously incorrect and made you uncomfortable. Can you forgive me?"

Lilly relaxed into the settee's padded cushion. She didn't know how or why Matthew had changed his opinion. "I forgive you," she murmured, feeling a trembling start somewhere deep inside her.

"Lilly, we've known each other too long to play games with one another. I know your heart is wounded from the things that have transpired. Things you believe me responsible for. I'm sorry for any part I've had in hurting you."

She looked into his eyes. Instantly she realized the mistake. She looked away just as quickly, but Matthew took hold of her chin and drew her back to face him. "Please believe me. I know your feelings for me have changed, but I would like very much for us to be friends."

Friends.

The word stuck in Lilly's mind. Why was he saying this now? Perhaps another woman had gained his attention; perhaps he finally believed she no longer loved him. For whatever reason, the word felt empty and void of any real meaning.

26

Thurston arrived at the Appleton shortly after eight o'clock the next morning. "I thought I'd get an early start, before Mr. Cheever is caught up in the day's work," William told Lawrence Gault, who was escorting him in through the gate.

Lawrence gave a hearty laugh. "If you're going to get an early start around here, you'd best be here by five-thirty," Gault replied with a grin. "We've already gone home for breakfast and returned."

"Mr. Thurston to see you," Lawrence announced as William brushed past him and walked into Matthew's office.

"Morning, Matthew," William said, closing the door. "I have what you've requested with one exception."

Matthew looked up from his desk.

"The informant prefers to remain anonymous, but he's given me the information and the piece of cloth. He's directed me to continue as his liaison. I hope you will find that arrangement satisfactory."

Matthew shrugged. "It's not up to me to decide, Mr. Thurston. I'll take Mr. Boott whatever information and evidence you give me. He can evaluate it and make a determination."

"Johnny O'Malley's the one who shot Kirk. Here's the piece of cloth that was torn from his coat."

Matthew took the piece of fabric as William explained exactly where O'Malley had been situated when the shots were fired and offered to ride with Matthew to the very spot. "Excellent idea. That way there can be no confusion."

"Exactly," Thurston agreed, leading the way.

They mounted and rode in silence.

"Over there," Thurston said, pointing toward a wooded area. "My informant said he found the piece of cloth over in those trees."

"You're sure?" Matthew inquired while riding up alongside William's horse.

Thurston nodded. "Absolutely."

Matthew rode into the wooded area with Thurston following close behind. "So O'Malley was on his horse in this grove of pines, and the informant found that scrap from his coat somewhere right in here?"

William sat astride his horse and held his arms as if aiming a musket toward the clearing. "That's right," Thurston replied. "And O'Malley shot Kirk right over there. That *is* where Kirk went down, isn't it?"

"Yes, exactly," Matthew replied. "Don't think there's anything else for us to see out here. I'll go directly to Boott's house and talk to him."

They returned in silence.

William gave Matthew a satisfied nod as they rode down Merrimack Street. "I'm staying at the Wareham House. You'll get word to me?"

"Yes," Matthew replied as he tugged on the reins and directed his horse toward the Boott residence. He was glad to be free of William's company. Merely being with the man made him uncomfortable and filled Matthew with a hundred questions.

Anne Boott led Matthew into Kirk's office. "He won't stay in bed. I doubt his leg will ever properly heal," she reported.

"Nonsense! My leg is healing just fine. What brings you here this morning, Matthew?"

"A few developments concerning that wound to your leg, sir."

"I want to speak with you, Miss Armbruster," Thaddeus Arnold said, grasping her arm as the other girls exited the building.

Lilly's heart began to pound in her chest as the last of the girls rushed out the door. She wanted to rush along with them.

"I've been permitting you to operate Nadene's frames, and she's been receiving full pay," he said, his fingers now relaxing their grasp and slowly moving up her arm. "Any word from the doctor when she'll be returning to work?"

Lilly flinched away. "He says she won't be able to return until February or possibly March. Her hands were badly burned. The doctor doesn't want her to return until he's certain she can operate the machinery without causing herself further harm." Lilly didn't bother to add that the doctor had serious doubts of Nadene being able to return at all—and not entirely because of the fire. Nadene's lungs were badly damaged by consumption. Truth be told, she probably wasn't going to recover.

"I've decided I need additional *encouragement* if you're to collect Nadene's pay."

"I told you I would remain silent about your behavior with the other girls here at the mill, and I've done so—I'll do no more."

"And I've decided that without someone to substantiate your silly accusations, no one will believe you," he said, grabbing her around the waist and pulling her close.

"Let go of me," Lilly screamed, twisting loose of his hold. "I'll never agree to what you're asking." She raced from the room and didn't stop running until she was inside the boardinghouse.

That night Thaddeus Arnold beat his wife. Lilly knocked on the wall with her shoe, but he didn't stop. She covered her ears as the screams continued. It was obvious. He wanted her to hear.

"I'll meet you around the corner from your house tomorrow evening at eight o'clock," Lilly whispered to Thaddeus Arnold as she left work the next day.

He smiled an evil, yellow-toothed smile. "Why not just stay here after work?"

"There would be questions at home," she quickly replied. "I change Nadene's bandages after work, and I have plans for this evening." She hurried out the door and down the steps before he could say anything further. Her gaze was drawn toward the flickering light in Matthew's office.

Matthew!

Perhaps he could help her out of this dilemma she had just created for herself. *But he didn't help when you first told him of Mr. Arnold's behavior,* a small voice whispered into her thoughts. She shoved the negative thought to the back of her mind. Matthew said he wanted to put the past behind them—that he wanted to be friends. Perhaps he would feel this was one way he could prove his friendship. After glancing back toward the stairwell and assuring herself Arnold was nowhere to be seen, Lilly hurried into the counting room.

Mr. Gault was donning his overcoat as she entered the room. "Is Matthew—I mean, Mr. Cheever—in his office?" she gasped while attempting to catch her breath.

He smiled and nodded. "I'm sure he won't mind if you go in," Mr. Gault stated. "Have a nice evening."

"Thank you, and you do the same," Lilly said with a wave. She quickly tucked several loose strands of hair behind her ear. "I hope I'm not disturbing you," she said in a timid voice, "but I've come to ask for your help."

Matthew rose from his chair and walked toward her, his handsome features enhanced by the flickering oil lamp. He offered her a seat and then listened to what she told him. His face revealed emotion from time to time, but he didn't interrupt.

"Will you help?" Lilly inquired as she finished telling him of the plan she had devised to finally bring an end to Mr. Arnold's abuse of his wife and his molestation of the girls in the spinning room.

Matthew gave her a slow smile. "Yes, I'll speak to the elders. But let's keep the particulars between the two of us. No need for others to know what is happening. And I hope for my own sake that you never plot against me, Miss Armbruster."

Lilly gave him a hint of a smile. "Then perhaps you should be very careful how you conduct yourself."

"I'll do my best to keep in your good graces," he replied. "May I walk you home?"

"I don't want to take a chance of being seen by Mr. Arnold," she replied. "But thank you," she quickly added, beaming him a bright smile.

The following day, Lilly's apprehension steadily increased. By the end of the workday, an unrelenting queasiness had developed in the pit of her stomach. She shut down her frames and moved a little more slowly than usual to assure she would be the last of girls leaving the floor. "I think it would be safer to meet farther away from the boardinghouse. I'll meet you across the street from St. Anne's. Eight o'clock." She didn't give Arnold an opportunity to reply.

Hurrying home, she attempted to remain calm as she ate dinner and waited. With Mr. Arnold living next door, she decided it would be best if she left the house early. She certainly didn't want to chance an encounter with him before reaching St. Anne's. Fortunately, Matthew was waiting near the church, his carriage one of several lining the street. "You'll be warmer in the carriage," he said, helping her inside.

She didn't argue. "Are the elders going to meet us?"

"They're waiting in the church vestibule. Mr. Sachs is watching for my signal."

"Here comes Mr. Arnold," Lilly said in a hushed whisper. She slipped out of the carriage, and Matthew quickly signaled toward the church doors.

Lilly moved from behind the horses and held up her arm, waving it back and forth. Arnold looked in her direction and headed across the street. He stepped close to her and placed his gloved hand on her arm.

"Thaddeus! So pleased you could make our meeting on such short notice," Elder Sachs greeted as he, Elder Jones, and Matthew stood waiting inside the iron fence that surrounded the churchyard. "Come in," he said, holding open the gate.

"What is going on?" Thaddeus asked under his breath.

Lilly quickly moved away from Mr. Arnold and through the gate, keeping herself distanced from him as they entered the building. His confusion and discomfort were obvious as they sat down in a small room off the foyer.

"We understand you've been good enough to continue paying wages to

Nadene Eckhoff so long as Lilly is able to operate her looms at an adequate output. First, we want to tell you we're proud that an elder of this church has acted in such a charitable manner," Elder Sachs stated, his chest puffing out ever so slightly.

Thaddeus gave Matthew a sidelong glance. "Thank you," he mumbled.

"I'm sure you'll be pleased to know that Mr. Cheever has agreed that this arrangement may continue throughout Nadene's recuperation from her injuries. We thank you for that generosity, Mr. Cheever, as I'm sure Thaddeus may have had some concerns about the company's attitude about such an agreement. Wouldn't that be true, Thaddeus?"

Thaddeus's head bobbed up and down, his gaze never leaving the mosaic inset beneath his feet.

Elder Sachs laced his bony fingers together atop the wooden table. "We're attempting to help all of the girls working in the mill, and Lilly has mentioned several girls on your floor who might need some guidance and counseling, particularly regarding how to handle themselves in difficult situations. We were thinking of having a symposium. Of course, it wouldn't be for just the mill girls," he said.

Lilly straightened in her chair. "Perhaps your wife would like to attend, Mr. Arnold."

He met her stare. "She doesn't enjoy socializing in large groups," he replied.

"If she's reticent to attend, I'm sure the elders would be happy to call at your home and encourage her," Lilly replied in a firm voice.

"Absolutely. We would be delighted. And now that we're discussing your wife, I don't believe I've seen her in church for some time. Has she been ill?" Elder Sachs inquired.

"I believe she has, hasn't she, Mr. Arnold? But I'm certain she's on the road to a *complete* recovery. Isn't that correct?" Lilly tilted her head and gave Thaddeus a bright smile.

His thin lips were set in a tight line. "Yes. She should be well enough to attend church by next week."

Lilly realized Arnold was giving his wife enough time to recuperate from the latest beating. But granting him this one concession would be a small price to pay for Mrs. Arnold's future safety. "And I'm sure Mrs. Arnold would enjoy meeting with the ladies for Bible study. Miss Addie tells me a group of them remain for a quilting bee in the afternoons. I'll tell Miss Addie to visit with your wife about attending."

Elder Jones slapped his knee. "Absolutely. My wife attends, as well. She comes home, prepares lunch, and then returns for an afternoon of sewing. Mrs. Jones always has a wonderful time. I'll tell her to make a special effort to invite Mrs. Arnold."

"How grand!" Lilly said.

"I'm glad we've had this meeting," Elder Sachs replied. "I want to do what I can to ensure living in Lowell is a positive experience for these young farm girls. I believe the elders of this church have a duty to them. Their parents have entrusted them to our community, and we must honor their confidence that no harm will come to any of them. Don't you agree, Thaddeus?"

The room was cool, yet a small line of perspiration beaded across Arnold's upper lip. His voice trembled slightly as he said, "Yes, of course. If that's all, gentlemen?" There was a note of hopefulness that they were through for the evening. He leaned forward and rose from his chair.

"I believe so," Elder Jones said, glancing about the table. The meeting quickly adjourned, and Thaddeus made a hasty retreat back in the direction from which he had arrived.

"Did our meeting accomplish everything you had hoped for?" Elder Sachs asked Matthew as they walked from the church.

Matthew nodded and shook hands with both of the men. "I believe everything has been satisfactorily resolved. And I appreciate the trust you've exhibited in me."

Once the men had departed and Matthew assisted her into the carriage, Lilly turned and faced him. "You didn't tell them about his behavior with the girls, did you?"

"No. I merely explained my fear that the behavior of some men in the community toward the girls could become a problem. I told the elders I thought it would be beneficial for them to meet with one or two key supervisors who are members of St. Anne's and reinforce the church's position. It's more likely that the Arnolds' marriage will heal if there isn't gossip about town regarding his immoral behavior."

Lilly furrowed her brow and gave him a pensive look. "I'm surprised you thought about such a thing."

"We humans tend to worry about what other people think about us. In fact, I think half the time folks make decisions based solely upon what *others* may think and the other half based upon their own selfish desires. It's too bad we don't worry more about God's perception of our behaviors and His desires instead. After all, that's the true test, isn't it?"

She was startled by the acuity of his observation, convicted by his words.

Lilly didn't permit herself to look in Mr. Arnold's direction as she entered the spinning room the next morning. He made his way up and down the aisles several times, much as he always did. She watched from beneath hooded lids, not wanting him to notice as she observed his movements. This morning his hands remained to himself; there were no unseemly touches or pats, no leaning over and whispering into an ear—only the necessary supervision of an overseer checking production. She relaxed a bit, the tedium of the work calming her roiling emotions. It appeared as if last night's meeting produced the desired effect.

The breakfast bell tolled in the distance, and Lilly slapped the loom handles, the metal foursome shuttering into silence as the buzzing bobbins ceased their whirling. Thaddeus stood in the aisle blocking her departure. She remained frozen in place, unable to speak.

He sneered at her. "My wife would like to attend the symposium. Would you ask Miss Beecher if she would be so kind as to pass along the particulars to Mrs. Arnold once they become available?"

Lilly bobbed her head up and down. "Yes—yes," she stammered. "I'm sure Miss Addie will be most pleased to meet your wife."

He stepped aside, careful there was ample room for Lilly to pass by. She continued staring at him as she inched her way around him, waiting, expecting, certain he would reach out and grasp her.

He didn't. Instead he said, "This isn't over, Miss Armbruster, but I know how to mind my business and bide my time. You'll pay for this."

She chilled and looked into his face. "If you don't cooperate . . ."

"I never said a word about not cooperating. Like I said, I know how to bide my time." He walked away at that, leaving Lilly shaken. Perhaps she'd only made matters worse.

Matthew met Lilly halfway up the stairs. "Are you all right? I was waiting in the mill yard. When I didn't see you come out, I was concerned." He grabbed her by the hand. "Come on, I'll walk you over to the boardinghouse."

"Everything's . . . well . . . Mr. Arnold confronted me a few minutes ago, and I must admit my faith wavered."

"He confronted you?" Matthew pulled her to a halt.

"He blocked my exit in order to make a request."

"What?" Matthew's indignation was obvious.

"He asked if I would have Miss Addie call upon his wife regarding the time and date of the symposium."

Matthew exhaled and loosened his grip on her arm. "That shows cooperation."

Lilly nodded. "Yes, but he also said this wasn't over. That he knows how to mind his business and bide his time."

"You've wounded his pride, Lilly. It's going to take him time to deal with that. Men don't handle wounded pride very well. I know that firsthand."

She looked up at him, her breath catching in her throat. "I know about wounded pride, as well."

"Time heals all wounds," Matthew replied, his loving gaze upon her.

Lilly struggled with her emotions. Putting on a smile she didn't feel, she said, "Could we move along now? Breakfast will be over before I reach home, and I'm fairly famished."

He laughed as the two of them broke into a run. "I wouldn't want to be accused of causing you to miss a meal, Miss Armbruster."

27

Christmas morning dawned bright and clear with a fresh covering of snow to make everything look pristine and white. Lilly awakened, not to the sound of the work bell but rather to the sound of merriment. The other girls were giggling and preparing for the day. Some were making short trips home. Others, whose families lived too far for a day's journey, were making plans to celebrate together.

Lilly had been invited to join the Cheevers for Christmas dinner, but her heart wasn't really in it. She thought of this being the first Christmas without her beloved father, and depression washed over her in waves. It had been so hard to lose her mother, but at least there had been the comfort of her father's love. Now there was no one.

"Come on, sleepyhead," Pru teased. "Miss Addie has promised a gay Christmas Day. I'll see you downstairs." She hurried from the room, leaving Lilly alone.

"I'm coming," Lilly murmured, throwing back the covers. The chill of the room nearly made her change her mind and pull the covers tight again. Nevertheless, Lilly forced herself to get up. Sitting on the edge of the bed, she yawned and stretched.

Draped over her trunk was a beautiful gauze-over-satin gown, compliments of Julia Cheever. The woman had arrived the night before with her husband, laden with packages. Christmas gifts for Lilly.

Lilly had tried to refuse them, for after all, she had no gift for the Cheevers. Julia would hear nothing of it. She'd had these gifts specially made, and they would suit no one else. Besides, she told Lilly, it would simply break her heart if Lilly were to refuse.

Hurrying through her morning rituals, Lilly took up the new petticoat and added its warmth to her freezing frame. She'd heard that many women were actually taking to wearing more than one petticoat in order to make their skirts stand full. Lilly thought it rather nonsensical, but she had to admit the material warmed her quite nicely. Two petticoats would probably be even better.

Pulling on the gown of white trimmed in pink, Lilly struggled to do up the buttons before tying the pink waist sash. She would be the height of fashion today, there was no denying that. The gown even boasted the popular puffed gigot sleeves, although Lilly gratefully noted they weren't nearly as full as some she'd seen.

The gown fell to several inches above the floor, trimmed in three rows of pale pink ruffles. No woman in Boston, not even Boott's niece, Isabelle, could boast being more fashionable or up-to-date than Lilly Armbruster.

Taking up the accompanying new bonnet and gloves, Lilly made her way downstairs.

"Oh, your gown is the most beautiful I've ever seen," gushed Marmi. "I wish I were your size—I would beg to borrow it."

Lilly laughed. "And I would let you, of course."

Miss Addie appeared and nodded enthusiastically. "Oh yes. Yes, it's perfect. How positively delightful. Mrs. Cheever has impeccable taste."

Lilly smiled and nodded. "I cannot complain about her taste or the fashion. I do wish she'd saved her money, however. I have nothing to give in return."

Addie leaned in close enough for only Lilly to hear. "It would make quite the gift if you were to marry their son."

Lilly stepped away and waggled her finger. "Miss Addie, you would do well to plan your own wedding."

The girls fussed over Lilly's gown, marveling at the bonnet and expressing their desire to have one made just like it. Even Nadene thought the gown to be most incredible, although she wasn't feeling all that well. Her cough had kept her awake for a good portion of the night, and her burns were still far from healed.

After a delicious breakfast that included a dense cake filled with dried fruits and nuts, which Miss Addie had labored over the day before, Lilly made her excuses and went to take up her cloak. The shabby thing seemed an inappropriate covering while wearing such a rich gown, but Lilly had no choice. She couldn't afford to be wasteful with her money, and the old cloak was still serviceable.

Tying her bonnet securely, Lilly made her way outside. Thankfully, the snow had been shoveled from the walkway. The town was nearly silent, almost as if it were napping. The mills were quiet, and everyone was tucked safely in their homes to celebrate the birth of Jesus.

Lilly walked slowly, considering her mission. She had not gone back to her father's grave since the day of his funeral. For some reason, it seemed very important to go there today. She opened the iron gate to the small cemetery and slipped inside. Making her way through the rows of headstones, she came to the one bearing the name ARMBRUSTER.

This was the final earthly resting place of her parents. Bending down, Lilly pushed the snow from the top of the stone, then stepped back. "I miss you both," she whispered. "It just doesn't feel like Christmas without you." She paused, feeling rather silly for talking to the headstone. She knew her parents were in heaven, but somehow being here made her feel closer to them.

"I don't know what to do," she continued. "I thought I knew what was right. I had a purpose, and that purpose was to cause as much grief for the Associates and their horrible mills as I could, but now it's different. What little I did do ended up hurting Nadene, and she was already so fragile and sickly. I've only made it worse.

"I know many people here feel just as I do—they hate the mills and the fact that the beauty of the land has been forever spoiled. They feel just as duped as we did. But there are others who see the change as good. The Cheevers have accepted this change and have thrived. Matthew seems very happy." She sighed and shivered against the cold.

"I don't know what to do anymore. I feel lost and confused. I'm so uncertain of the future and what direction to take."

"Seek the Lord in all things. He will guide your steps." She could almost hear her mother's words.

"I haven't been very good about seeking Him or His will for my life. I've been too preoccupied with what I wanted and how I thought it was what God wanted, as well. After all, even though I discontinued my attacks against the mill, the mishaps continued. It surely must have been the hand of God." Yet even as she spoke the words, Lilly wasn't sure she believed them.

"I want to do whatever you want, Lord. I just need some direction." Looking heavenward to the crystal blue skies, Lilly sought her answers. "What is it you want for me? What am I to do?"

"You'll get a stiff neck that way."

Lilly startled as she looked in the direction of the voice. Mintie Beecher stood on the other side of the iron gate.

"Merry Christmas, Miss Beecher," Lilly said, leaving her parents' graves.

"What were you craning your neck to see, child?" The old woman seemed so small snuggled down in her heavy wool coat and bonnet.

Lilly smiled. "The face of God. I thought maybe I could hear Him better if I could see Him. Soul-searching comes in all forms."

The woman's face wrinkled as she pursed her lips in consideration. "Stuff and nonsense, child. It's cold out here, and you'll catch your death in such a thin cloak."

"Why are you out here, Miss Beecher?"

"That's really none of your concern," she snapped.

Lilly shrugged. "I was just being sociable. I meant nothing by it." She thought of the sour woman and how hard it had been for her to deal with her sister's romantic situation.

Mintie softened her expression. "I'm just taking a walk. Nothing more."

"I understand," Lilly said softly. She came through the gate and closed it behind her ever so gently. "I suppose I must get back to the house. Will you be joining us? I know Miss Addie extended you an invitation."

"I'm considering it," Mintie replied, then her voice took on a strained sound. "Although with that John Farnsworth present, she'll hardly notice whether I'm there or not. She doesn't listen to me when he's around."

"Maybe you have your own soul searching to do," Lilly replied gently. "Good day, Miss Beecher. I truly hope you can make it."

Mintie watched the young girl walk away. Her footprints in the snow seemed so small, yet there was a wealth of strength in Lilly Armbruster. There was a great deal of strength in Adelaide, as well. Mintie's shoulders slumped forward, something she never allowed to happen. She felt a sense of defeat wash over her.

Mintie had prided herself on being strong all of her life. She had taken charge of the household upon their mother's death, not even allowing herself time to mourn. Tears that had never been allowed to fall then now gathered in her weary eyes.

"You would not be so proud if you saw me now, Mother," she whispered. She pulled her spectacles from her face and wiped her tears with her gloved fingers. "I am harsh and unfeeling. In my attempt to help direct Adelaide, I have hurt her with my envy and fears."

Lilly Armbruster had spoken of soul-searching, and the words had hit Mintie harder than she wanted to admit, for that had been her very intent upon taking her walk this morning. She needed wisdom and a renewal of strength in order to deal with what most certainly would come. Adelaide would have no reason to put aside this suitor. The Judge would not be around to send this beau away as he had the others.

"And when she marries, I shall be alone," Mintie mourned softly.

You are never alone, my child. I am with you always.

Mintie startled. The words sounded almost audible. Replacing her spectacles, she looked behind her and then across the small cemetery. There was no one. The words had come from no human source.

Then without concern for how it might look or what others might say about her, Mintie very slowly raised her face to the sky. The brilliance of the day hurt her eyes, yet she refused to look away. "Perhaps there's something to this," she murmured. "Perhaps I've not taken the trouble to listen for the truth. Maybe I've sought the wrong companion all along."

Lilly knew the Cheevers would call for her at exactly noon. It gave her time to enjoy the festivities of the boardinghouse and still be able to stand ready when the carriage arrived.

To her surprise, Matthew was the one who called for her. He smiled and greeted them all with great holiday spirit. "Merry Christmas!" he declared as he stomped his boots at the door.

"Merry Christmas, Mr. Cheever," Addie said, coming forward. "Won't you join us for some wassail?"

"I'm afraid not. My mother is expecting us." He turned to Lilly. "Are you ready?"

She nodded, feeling rather weak in the knees. He was so handsome in his long black coat and top hat. "I just need to get my cloak."

He took the piece from her as she pulled it from the peg. "Is this all you have?"

Lilly stiffened. In anger she snapped, "I know it's not very fashionable, but—"

He put his finger to her lips. "Shhh. Remember the day. I wasn't disdaining the fashion but rather the thinness of the material. You'll freeze out there in this."

She calmed her spirit. "I'll be just fine. I walked out to the cemetery this morning and hardly felt the chill." It was a stretch of the truth, but in all honesty her feet suffered more than her body on that walk.

Shrugging, Matthew put the cloak around her shoulders and waited until she'd retrieved her bonnet and secured it atop her head. "Come along. Mother has a feast fit for a king—or in this case, a queen." He smiled in his charming way, and Lilly found her voice completely gone—along with her breath.

He handed her up into the carriage, then climbed aboard and pulled heavy blankets around them both. "Don't scoot clear across to the other side. It's too cold, and your cloak is much too light. We will share our warmth together, and that way you won't catch your death."

"I hadn't planned to catch my death," Lilly said rather snidely. She truly relished the warmth Matthew offered her, but she hesitated to say so for fear of what he might think. Nevertheless, she did as he suggested and moved closer.

The day had gotten much colder than it had been that morning, and now the skies were overcast and threatened snow again. As the wind shifted, Lilly couldn't help but snuggle even closer to Matthew.

"You'd do well to buy yourself a new coat," Matthew said as he snapped the reins. The matched bays strained against their harness and easily pulled the carriage on its way.

Lilly felt a flare of temper but held it in check and decided to tease

Matthew instead. "But then I'd have no excuse to sit close to you on carriage rides."

He looked at her for a long moment, his gaze warming her to the bone. His voice came out low and husky. "You never need an excuse to sit close to me, Lilly."

That night as Lilly settled into her bed, a hundred memories from the day danced through her head. But none came so easily as her time with Matthew in the carriage. Her heart stirred, and the ache that radiated from that stirring robbed her of any real comfort. She had hoped to remain disentangled—keeping her heart completely safe from harm. But that wasn't the case. And for the life of her, Lilly had no idea how to make it all right again.

"I can't love you, Matthew," she whispered into her pillow. "I simply can't."

28

M atthew didn't report back to Thurston as arranged. Instead, heeding Boott's advice, he had waited for the man to reemerge. Surprisingly, it had taken a week for Thurston to appear at the Appleton. He'd pushed his way past Mr. Gault and walked into Matthew's office unannounced, his fury evident.

"I specifically remember you saying you would get back with me after you talked to Kirk," William snarled.

Matthew looked up from his paper work. "Good morning, Mr. Thurston. Care to have a seat? I assumed you had returned to Boston for Christmas with your family. I trust you had a joyous holiday."

Thurston crossed the office in two long strides and fell into one of the chairs while maintaining a glowering scowl upon his face. "I didn't come here to discuss Christmas, I came for a reply from Boott."

Matthew looked up from his ledger. "He isn't interested," he said simply.

"What do you mean Boott isn't interested?" Thurston yelled. "I've given him the name of the man who shot him, along with tangible proof to substantiate Mr. O'Malley's guilt, and you tell me Kirk Boot isn't interested? I should have gotten the reward money before I gave you the name. That's it, isn't it? He doesn't want to pay for the information," Thurston growled.

Matthew folded his arms and met Thurston's glare. "You know better than that, Mr. Thurston. That's not Mr. Boott's style. He doesn't plan to use the information. If he intended to make use of it, he would reward your informant."

"This makes no sense," Thurston retorted through clenched teeth.

Matthew shrugged. "I suggest you let it go, Mr. Thurston."

Lewis pulled his pocket watch out of his waistcoat several times as he paced back and forth in the foyer of the Wareham House. Thurston was not in his room, nor was there any evidence of him in the restaurant. He was sure Thurston had said to meet him at nine-thirty. He sat down at a table near the window and facing the door—he preferred a good vantage point. The image of a ragged-looking Irish boy, his coal black hair bobbing up and down, reflected on the sun-streaked window of the hotel before the child actually entered the establishment.

A startled look crossed the manager's face before he moved into action, loping around the desk and meeting the child midlobby. He was obviously unsettled by the child's appearance. Rightfully so, Lewis thought. The last thing patrons wanted to encounter at the finest hotel and eating establishment in town was a reminder of the Irish clans.

The manager grasped the child by his ear, practically lifting him out of his rundown, shabby boots. "What are you doing in here?" he fumed at the boy.

He held up a dingy-appearing missive. "I've a message for Mr. William Thurston."

The manager glanced toward the child's hand. "He's already checked out of the hotel, but that man in there is waiting on him," he said as he waved in Lewis's direction.

"May I help?" Lewis inquired as he approached the man and boy.

The manager gave Lewis a beseeching look. "This lad has a message for Mr. Thurston. May he leave it with you?"

Lewis extended his hand. "You may feel confident that I will deliver your message to Mr. Thurston. You may tell the writer that you delivered the dispatch to Lewis Armbruster on Mr. Thurston's behalf."

The child handed over the letter and waited, his dark pleading eyes and tattered clothes providing evidence of what was expected. Lewis handed the child a coin, then watched as the boy raced out of the hotel and back toward the Paddy camp.

"Ragged little beggars," the manager snarled under his breath. "Thank you for your assistance," he hastily added, giving Lewis a weary smile.

Lewis returned to his table and placed the correspondence beside his cup of coffee. The writing was crude, apparently scrawled in haste. He wondered who would be delivering mail to Thurston at the hotel. The thought of opening the seal crossed his mind. That idea was quickly followed by the thought of Thurston's possible retribution should he discover such an indiscretion.

Lewis was holding the missive between two fingers, snapping it up and down on the table, when Thurston entered the restaurant and seated himself. Annoyance was etched on the man's face, and Lewis issued a sigh of relief, thankful he hadn't opened the letter.

"Stop that incessant clicking," he ordered.

The letter dropped from between Lewis's fingers and floated onto the table. With his index finger, he pushed the missive toward Thurston. "This was delivered shortly before your arrival."

William eyed the letter and then shoved it into his pocket. Lewis hoped his disappointment wasn't evident. "An Irish lad brought it," he added, hoping to pique his interest.

Thurston showed little curiosity in the added information or the letter. He rubbed the back of his neck and stared out the restaurant window. "I've just returned from a meeting with Matthew Cheever—regarding O'Malley's involvement in the shooting."

Lewis straightened in his chair. Perhaps this was going to be a profitable day after all. "I hope the reward was generous."

William slammed his fist on the table. The surrounding patrons glanced in their direction but quickly averted their attention when met by William's glowering stare. "He had the audacity to report that Boott was not interested in any of the evidence I presented—not my willingness to testify that it was O'Malley, not the piece of fabric that proves he was in the grove of pines, *none* of it. I even told him I could produce the weapon, but he said Boott didn't want to hear any more allegations against O'Malley."

Lewis was dumbfounded by the revelation. "Why? I can't imagine that Kirk Boott doesn't want to avenge the person who harmed him."

"Cheever wouldn't give me a direct answer. He merely said to 'let it go.' I attempted to discover whether they had received any other reliable information regarding the shooting, but Cheever said he wasn't free to discuss the matter. It's another example of Boott pandering to the Irish. Even if he knows it was O'Malley, he doesn't want to risk admitting he's wrong about those papists. The man's a fool! There's a meeting of the Associates at the end of the week. I doubt whether Kirk will be able to attend, but *I* will certainly be present." William stood, shoved a hand in his pocket, and pulled out the crumpled letter. His eyes now focused on the scrawled writing, and recognition registered in his face. Dropping back into his chair, he ripped open the message.

Lewis watched intently as Thurston read the letter. His jaw appeared to lock, and a slight tic developed in his right eye, culminating in an uncontrollable wink. Thurston rubbed the eye. It continued to flutter. "Do you have any idea what this is?" he asked from between clenched teeth.

"No," Lewis replied. He certainly *wanted* to know. He also knew better than to put voice to his desire.

"Kathryn," he said, brandishing the letter through the air as though it were a double-edged sword. "She's making threats."

Lewis sat silently waiting, hoping for more.

Thurston didn't fail him. "Kathryn has written that if I don't support her on a regular basis, she's going to tell my wife about the child."

Lewis restrained the gasp rising in his throat. Instead, he took a gulp of air and gave William his undivided attention.

Thurston's eyes narrowed as he met Lewis's gaze. "This is going to require your assistance, Lewis. As always, you'll be well paid."

There was an ominous tone to Thurston's voice that commanded Lewis's attention. "I'll do what I can to help. Within reason, of course."

Thurston emitted a dark laugh. "You have no choice, Lewis. You'll do whatever I require—within reason or not." He hesitated, staring out the window at some indeterminate object. "Kathryn and the child are of no consequence to me—they're disposable. My wife, on the other hand, is not. I was accepted into Boston society through my marriage to Margaret. It was her family name that garnered the attention of the Boston Associates and their invitation to join with them and invest in Lowell. I've invested too much time and effort into my success. I'll not permit that Irish tramp to threaten me for the rest of my life. And that's what she would do, continue to make more and more demands upon me until eventually I refused to pay. Then what? After years of handing her money, she'd still go to my wife and ruin my life." He shook his head. "No. I'll not have it. She and the child must both be done away with."

This time it was impossible for Lewis to restrain a gasp. Undeniable horror washed over him. For all his lack of morals and disregard for other people, he'd never had to resort to killing. The very thought made him positively ill.

He didn't want to kill a woman. He couldn't! "You would have me kill the mother of your child?"

"*And* the child," William hastened to add.

Lewis attempted to hide his revulsion. "I'm sorry, Mr. Thurston, but I can't do what you're asking—not a woman and child. I've been responsible for my share of underhandedness, but this goes beyond that. This is well beyond what I'm willing to do for money."

Thurston reached across the table and grabbed Lewis by the wrist. "Don't you tell me what you can't do, Lewis," he hissed. "You *will* kill them. Both of them. And it will be done when and how I tell you. Do you understand me? I have too much information on you, Armbruster. You have no choice in this matter."

Lewis jerked his arm out of William's grasp. "There must be some other way to handle the situation besides killing them," he said in a hoarse whisper.

William's eyes clouded as he spoke, his mind obviously racing to develop some sinister strategy. "It won't be difficult. I'll formulate a plan that can't go awry. Something simple yet effective."

Lewis stood. "I don't like it."

"I didn't ask you to like it. And don't attempt to leave town without my permission, Lewis. I wouldn't want to reveal to Kirk Boott that I was mistaken and that you are truly the person who shot him."

Lewis leaned down across the table and stared into Thurston's eyes. "There's no one who will believe you. You've already pointed the finger at O'Malley."

"You really don't know me very well, do you, Lewis? Do you think me so foolish that I wouldn't have a plan if you decided to betray me? I told you before that I have other contacts who perform assignments for me. One of them was at the scene of the shooting, Lewis. He watched you shoot Kirk Boott; he's willing to testify whenever I say the word. The horse you rode that day? It belonged to another contact. He'll testify to the fact that you borrowed his horse, rode out of town in time to accomplish the deed, and returned his horse in a lather shortly after the shooting was reported. Why, he can even state with authority that you came from the direction of Pawtucket Falls. Combine that testimony with the fact that Boott doesn't believe O'Malley shot him, and any judge would convict you."

Lewis winced. "I'll tell that you were the one who plotted and hired me," Lewis feebly countered.

"*You* have no one who can tie me to the incident, Lewis, nor do you have the funds to buy testimony or silence. In other words, you have no reliable contacts. Now sit down. I believe I've already developed a simple plan."

William wet his lips and leaned across the table, speaking in hushed tones. Lewis listened, his stomach churning as he stared at the puffy lips spewing forth his ruthless plot. "If you follow my instructions, you'll have no difficulty," Thurston said as he finished speaking and leaned back in the chair.

Lewis lowered his head, his chin nearly resting upon his chest. "Is there nothing I can say that would cause you to reconsider?"

"Nothing." William said, pressing payment into Lewis's hand. "Half now and half when the deed is accomplished."

Lewis hated himself for accepting the money. He walked down the street with his mind reeling. Shooting Boott had been one thing—he had shot merely to injure. Killing an innocent woman, not to mention the child, was an entirely different matter. He needed time to think. More than that, he needed something to drink. Bowing his head against the cold, Lewis turned and set off toward Nichol's Tavern, anxious for a tankard of ale.

The remainder of the afternoon was a blur. People came and went while Lewis remained at a corner table attempting to blot out the memory of a dark-haired toddler and his strong-willed Irish mother. By nightfall the ale had done its work—the faces of Kathryn and the little boy were but a fuzzy blur. What he must do, however, had not completely vanished from his mind.

Lewis glanced toward the doorway. A boisterous group of Englishmen entered and seated themselves at a nearby table. Their camaraderie captured his attention as they joked and laughed together. He watched as they were served bowls of steaming fish chowder and hunks of hearty rye bread, and in his inebriated state, he found himself longing for friendship. Only one of the men looked familiar. Lewis recognized John Farnsworth, who was now pushing aside his bowl and unfurling papers on the table.

Lewis's natural curiosity about the business of others caused him to straighten in his chair and strain to catch a glimpse of what the four men were so intently reviewing. It appeared to be a drawing or diagram, but the picture was hazy, his vision impaired. One of the men spoke of the recent mishaps at the Merrimack and Appleton mills. "These latest mishaps were obviously intentional. Any fool could have seen they weren't accidents but purposefully caused."

"Are you saying they lacked a level of professional talent?" another man said with a laugh.

Intoxicated or not, Lewis's interest was immediately piqued by the comment, and he wondered if John Farnsworth and his English cohorts were numbered among William Thurston's hirelings. He wanted to see what it was these men were studying so intently. Pushing aside his schooner of ale, Lewis leaned heavily on the table and then stumbled from his chair toward the men.

"Hullo, Farnsworth," he slurred, leaning down until he was practically nose-to-nose with Farnsworth. His arm smacked against the papers strewn across the table, sending several fluttering to the floor. Lewis grabbed at one of the pages and swept it upward until it was well within his view. It appeared to be detailed drawings of the power system at the Appleton mills.

"I'll take that," Farnsworth said, pulling the crumpled drawing from Lewis's grasp and handing it to one of the other men. "Appears you may have had one tankard too many, Mr. Armbruster."

"Or not quite enough," Lewis replied, his voice garbled as he staggered out of the tavern, wondering why Farnsworth and his friends were so absorbed in drawings of an already operational power system.

Lewis continued onward, his thoughts shifting from the fine-lined drawing of waterwheels and pulleys to the friendship and harmony exhibited by Farnsworth and the other men. He needed someone in whom to confide, someone who could help him make sense of his unruly life. *Lilly!* Without warning, her name flashed into his mind. Surely she could help him.

His hand balled into a tight fist, Lewis pounded on the door of number 5 Jackson Street. It was nearly ten o'clock, quite late for someone to be calling at the boardinghouse, but he didn't care. He pounded again. The door opened just a crack, and Miss Addie peeked through the narrow opening. Pressing his face near the gap in the doorway, Lewis said, "It's Lewis Armbruster. I must see my sister." The heavy odor of spirits wafted through the night air as he spoke.

Miss Addie sniffed several times, her nose in the air like a bloodhound following its scent. "There's no doubt where you've spent your evening," the older woman admonished. "The girls have retired for the night, but if you care to wait outside, I'll go and see if Lilly is asleep. I won't permit you entry in your condition."

"I'll wait," Lewis said, sliding down onto the front step. "I saw your friend, Farnsworth, at Nichol's," he added.

"John? At Nichol's? Was he by himself?" Addie asked before quickly placing an open palm over her mouth.

Lewis gave her a lopsided grin. The woman was obviously embarrassed by the inquiry. "He was with three other men, all of them engrossed in drawings of the waterwheels and power supply at the Appleton mills. No need to worry, Miss Beecher," he said with as much reassurance as he could muster in his drunken condition. The door closed and he leaned his head against the hard, cold wood. He doubted his sister would appear, but he closed his eyes and waited.

He was unsure how long he had been there when the door jerked open. Lewis fell backward, his upper body sprawling across the threshold. "Good evening, Lilly," he said, staring upward.

"What brings you here at this time of night, Lewis?"

Lewis managed to pull himself into an upright position and meet his sister's gaze. "I need to talk to someone who can help me understand why I've made so many wrong choices in my life." He hesitated a moment. "I thought of you, Lilly. You're the only one who truly knows me. I need help," he whispered.

Lilly glanced toward Miss Addie, who nodded her head. "You may come in, Lewis, but we can talk for only a short time. Boardinghouse rules state I am to be in bed by ten o'clock."

Lewis turned to Miss Addie. She beckoned him in. "I'll wait in my room with the door open, Lilly. No more than ten minutes," she cautioned.

Lilly nodded and then led Lewis into the parlor. "We haven't much time, Lewis. What choices were you alluding to? The boardinghouse girls, your gambling, your drinking, selling the farm . . ."

"You've kept quite a list, haven't you? It would take more time than either of us has to address even those items," Lewis said as he leaned forward on his chair. "And they're not even what I came to discuss. I should leave."

Lilly grasped his arm. "Wait, Lewis. I'm sorry; I know I've been harsh. Tell me why you've come. I'll do my best to help."

He looked at her oddly, wondering why she was so compassionate when he'd been nothing but mean-spirited toward her. Perhaps it was all that religious nonsense she adhered to. Perhaps he looked as bad as he felt. Either way, it didn't matter.

"I've become involved in some matters that are terrible, unforgivable—matters so heinous I dare not speak of them."

"Lewis, you must confide in me if I'm to be of any assistance. *Please!* Tell me what you've done."

Now that the influence of his ale was beginning to wear off, Lewis realized that coming here had been a mistake. What could he do? Tell his sister he was William Thurston's henchman, hired to murder a helpless woman and child? The thought of making such a statement to his sister was ludicrous. Besides, how could Lilly help?

"There's nothing you can do, Lilly, and telling you could place your life in danger. Forget that I ever came here. I don't want to cause you further trouble."

Lilly gently touched his face. "I could pray for you, Lewis. In that regard, I fear I have failed you."

There was an overpowering sadness in his sister's voice that caused Lewis to regret the very essence of who he was and what he had become. "I doubt it will help, Lilly, but I'll not reject your offer of prayer."

Lilly stared at Lewis as he left the room. There was little doubt something sinister was occurring. She knew she must intercede for her brother, pray for his protection and strength to overcome whatever evil had permeated his life. The thought surprised her, yet the urgency to pray was unmistakable—unwavering, overwhelming. A palpable fear for Lewis's eternal salvation consumed her every thought. Falling to her knees, Lilly translated her fear into supplication as she lovingly whispered her words into the ear of God.

29

A rapping at the front door brought Addie scurrying from the kitchen. "Mintie!" She hesitated momentarily. "I'm surprised to see you."

There were dark circles under Mintie's eyes, and her face was etched in a weariness that gave proof to sleepless nights. "May I come in?" she haltingly asked.

"So long as you understand that I remain steadfast in my admonition regarding John Farnsworth."

Mintie nodded and stepped inside the door. Removing her woolen coat and bonnet, she turned toward her sister. "I've missed your companionship, Adelaide."

Addie gave her sister a guarded smile, still somewhat fearful of Mintie's motivation. "Would you like a cup of tea?"

"Yes, that would be most welcome. I can come into the kitchen if you're busy with meal preparations."

Addie's eyebrows danced upward. Her sister was certainly compliant this morning. "That would be most helpful. I was in the midst of peeling turnips. I'm preparing lamb stew for the noonday meal."

"I'll be glad to finish paring the turnips if it will help," Mintie offered as she followed along behind.

Addie's mouth fell open at the suggestion. Mintie offering to assist her? Something was amiss, but for the life of her, she couldn't figure out what Mintie wanted. Handing her sister an apron and a knife, Addie began chopping hunks of carrot and dropping them into a kettle. "Was there something in particular you wanted to discuss?" she ventured.

Mintie nodded, her eyes cast downward as she continued to peel the vegetables. "I've been giving thought to Mr. Farnsworth and his possible predisposition of loyalty to the Crown ever since you told me I was unwelcome in your home."

Addie gave her sister a sidelong glance but didn't interrupt. Instead she silently waited, permitting her sister an opportunity to complete her explanation.

Mintie cleared her throat and continued. "I'll admit I may have jumped to some unwarranted conclusions. However, there were things—still are, for that matter—that give me cause to wonder about Mr. Farnsworth. There's no denying the items I've seen in his room or the men who come to the house—without calling cards," she hastened to add.

"I've spent a good deal of time pondering this situation and seeking the best way to mend our relationship. I don't want an outsider to come between us, Adelaide. After all, we're blood, and we shouldn't permit anyone to cause a breach in our family."

Addie wiped her hands on her stained apron and met her sister's gaze. "Does this mean you no longer suspect he is a traitor?"

Before Mintie had opportunity to reply, Addie's boarders came clattering into the house with their shrill voices filling the air. "Miss Addie, Miss Addie, there's been another accident at the mills," Lilly called, her voice muffled until it finally reached the kitchen.

"Come join me, Lilly," Addie called in return, anxious to hear the details. "What happened?" she asked as Lilly entered the room.

"It's terrible, Miss Addie. Something was jammed in the waterwheel. Several men were attempting to get it loose. When they finally succeeded and the wheel began turning, one of the men lost his footing and dropped into the rushing water below. He was crushed by the wheel," she said in a hushed voice. "The man has a wife and three children. We were told to return home until someone sends for us. Mr. Arnold said it wouldn't be until after lunch for certain and perhaps not until tomorrow."

Lilly's words pierced Addie's heart, each utterance a tiny dart of suspicion. The clattering of Mintie's knife upon the floor caused Addie to startle and whirl around.

"John Farnsworth had diagrams of the Appleton Mill in his room. I saw drawings—large, intricate drawings of the waterwheel and machinery. They were atop his trunk," Mintie hastily added, placing her open palm against her chest. "And to think that only moments ago I was prepared to retract my accusations against John Farnsworth. What folly! I trust you'll now heed my advice and keep your distance from that traitorous man who nearly destroyed our family ties."

Addie stared down at the knife lying on the floor. Her throat constricted. She could not speak, but her mind was racing back to the sight of Lewis Armbruster standing at her front door several nights ago. What was it Lewis had said? *"I saw Farnsworth at Nichol's. He was with three other men, all of them engrossed in drawings of the waterwheels and power supply at the Appleton mills."* Why would John have been discussing those diagrams at Nichol's Tavern? Most likely the men who were with him were some of those secretive gentlemen who came calling upon him at Mintie's boardinghouse. A sensation of nausea swept over her. Could the man she had grown to care for be a party to this frightful incident? Surely not. And yet she was filled with apprehension—and questions.

"Did you hear me, Adelaide? Promise me you'll stay away from that treacherous man."

Addie gave her sister a dazed stare. "After listening to any explanation he cares to offer, I'll make my decision. Condemning Mr. Farnsworth without giving him an opportunity to defend himself is contrary to my beliefs, Mintie. I wouldn't want others to treat me in such a manner."

Mintie momentarily perched on the edge of her chair and then rose, her back straight and her neck reaching toward the heavens, as she gave her sister a look of haughty disdain. "You were always a willful child, and it appears you've not changed an iota. What is it going to take for you to realize you are a wretched judge of character?"

"I know I'm a failure in your eyes, Mintie. You consider me no more than an undisciplined child. But you're wrong. I'm a grown woman with my own opinions. The difference between us is that while I tend to see the best in people and situations, you tend to see the worst. You consider that tendency to be a flaw in my character; I consider it a blessing."

Mintie tied her bonnet ribbons into a snug bow beneath her sharp chin. "Once again you're choosing that traitorous Englishman over your own flesh and blood."

Addie watched her sister flee from the house.

Lewis pulled his gold pocket watch from his waistcoat, gently rubbing his thumb over the engraved initials before snapping open the case. Nine o'clock. Tucking the watch back in place, he quickened his step. He noticed a woman and a group of boys on a nearby corner eyeing him suspiciously and cast his gaze downward, hoping the shadows of evening would prevent them from observing his face. He didn't want anyone to remember he'd been to the Acre, especially on this night.

Pulling up the collar of an old tattered coat furnished by William Thurston, Lewis wondered how he had stooped to this level. It was better not to think, he decided. After all, thinking wouldn't change anything, and by now, he was in too deep to dig his way out. Thurston held all of the trump cards.

When Lewis had objected to an early evening arrival at Kathryn's house, William assured him the woman and child would be asleep. With a malevolent grin, Thurston explained that it was Kathryn's practice to sleep in the early evening in order to keep him company during his late-night arrivals. He hoped Thurston knew what he was talking about! Lewis walked the litter-strewn street, seeking the abhorrent hovel Kathryn called home. He listened outside, and hearing nothing, he entered quietly, spying the woman asleep on a crude cot pulled close to the waning fire. The child was slumbering in the crook of her arm. Shadows danced across the room as he silently edged closer and lifted a pillow. He stared down at Kathryn's creamy complexion, her features relaxed in sleep. Paralyzed, he gazed at her unbridled beauty for a moment before gaining a sense of courage and then pressed the pillow tight against her mouth and nose. The shabby covers fell to the floor as she briefly struggled before her body suddenly turned limp. He removed the pillow from her face and stood transfixed, unable to look away from her youthful appearance.

The boy cried out in his sleep, startling Lewis, who had been standing there as if in a trance. The child's waiflike body was restlessly seeking warmth against his mother's already chilling form. The boy couldn't be much over a year old. Lewis shivered. His fingers continued to clutch the pillow, yet he could not muster courage enough to bring it down upon the child's face. A piece of firewood dropped in the hearth. The crackling embers glowed, illuminating a purplish mushroom-shaped birthmark on the boy's arm. Grabbing one of the tattered blankets, Lewis threw it over the child. "If the boy is lucky, someone will find him by morning," he muttered as he rushed out of the room and down the street.

The streets were quiet, with only an occasional passerby to avoid as he hurried toward the Wareham House. He would report to Thurston and hopefully receive the balance of his blood money before morning. For a time he had given thought to refusing the money, thinking that would somehow assuage his guilt. But if Thurston was true to his word, the sum should be large enough to pay his passage to South America and a new beginning. How he longed for a new beginning. Lewis walked past the front desk and up the steps to Thurston's room. He rapped lightly on the door.

William was bare-chested, his shirt dangling from one finger. "I'm preparing to go out. I hope you're bringing me good news," he said as he moved away from the door and stood by the fireplace, his exposed back toward Lewis.

Lewis stared at Thurston's unclothed torso and immediately knew why Thurston had feared Kathryn's threat. William and the child carried the same birthmark on their arms.

"It went as planned. They're both dead," he said, struggling to keep his voice impassive.

William's lips curled into a cruel grin. "Excellent! I still find it difficult to believe that Kathryn had the audacity to think she could hold me hostage to her threats. You know, Lewis, if I didn't already have plans, we'd go and celebrate," he said, quickly changing moods.

Thurston's disdain for the woman who had given birth to his child amazed even Lewis. It was becoming increasingly obvious that Thurston's cruelty knew no bounds. He thought of the little boy, and a tinge of fear crept into his consciousness. "I was considering a trip to South America," he cautiously remarked.

"What? You're joking, of course," William said with a laugh. "We have work to complete right here. Besides, there's no one waiting for you in South America—or is there?" he questioned, making an obscene gesture.

"I merely thought it might be best to keep a low profile. England doesn't appeal to me, and I certainly don't want to move into the western wilderness of this country." Lewis watched as Thurston carefully affixed his cravat. "You mentioned unfinished business. Perhaps it would be best to use someone else since I've been deeply involved in several of your other ventures."

William gave a wicked laugh. "Your involvement is exactly what makes you the perfect person to continue assisting me, Lewis. I won't have you leaving the country. Besides, once I've managed to oust Boott and gain the helm here in Lowell, you'll be my right-hand man. You can't do that from South America. Sit down," he said, pointing to a chair. "I have another half hour before I must leave. I'm sure you've come to collect your money."

Lewis nodded. "I assume you've heard of the difficulty with the waterwheel over at the Appleton?" he ventured.

"You're wanting to know if I'm involved in that disastrous event? Word about town has it that there could be any number of suspects. I'm certainly not among the numbered few being discussed, but I have a feeling there's ample evidence to assure that our Mr. O'Malley is involved in this crime, along with several of his Irish comrades. I do believe that once O'Malley is found responsible for the assault on Boott and the incident at the Appleton, the Associates will be convinced of Boott's incompetence as a leader. Of course, the death of Kathryn and the child will further demonstrate the incivility of the Irish. All things considered, it appears as if matters aren't boding well for the savages. If events don't move in the direction I'm planning, I'll have another assignment for you in the near future," Thurston said as he smiled back at his own image in the mirror.

Lewis felt his heart begin to palpitate rapidly. He didn't want another assignment. All he wanted was to disassociate from this web of horror in which he was now trapped. He watched as William began counting out his money.

"Give up the idea of South America, Lewis. At least for now," Thurston said as he turned and pointed toward the gold lying on the table. "Attempting to remove yourself from my plans could prove—shall we say—fatal? I have eyes and ears everywhere, even along the docks, should you attempt to depart the country against my wishes. Men who enjoy trading information for a few coins. Make no mistake about me, Lewis. If I was unwilling to tolerate Kathryn's demands, I'll not tolerate yours. Do I make myself clear?"

Lewis nodded. "Abundantly," he said. "However, I wasn't attempting to make demands, but I have no desire to run these mills or live in Lowell. My genuine desire is to live in a larger city. Perhaps we could strike an agreement that I'll complete one last assignment for you—then we'll forget we ever knew each other?"

William gave him a thoughtful look. "You have my word."

Lewis gave a nod of affirmation as they shook hands. "I believe I'll go and have an ale before calling it a night. Enjoy your engagement," he called over his shoulder.

Inhaling a deep breath of the cold night air, Lewis knew it was going to take more than one ale for him to forget Kathryn O'Hanrahan and her child. For several hours he sat at Nichol's Tavern, quickly downing one tankard after another, while a conscience he had never before known gnawed at him, prohibiting him from shaking a vision of the woman and child from his mind. Finally weary of attempting to blot out the squalid event, Lewis threw a coin on the table and left. He began walking and then suddenly turned back toward the Acre. He couldn't seem to stop himself; he had to know if someone had rescued the child.

Growing closer, he could hear an increasing commotion as he neared the house. A wagon rumbled by and came to a halt in front of Kathryn's shanty. Moving closer, he stood watching from across the narrow street as a woman pulled herself up into the wagon and then held out her arms toward a child. Permitting the ale to give him false courage, Lewis stepped out in front of the wagon as it began to turn.

"Watch yer step!" the woman cried out, pulling her team of horses to an abrupt halt.

Lewis tipped his hat. "Sorry. I was wondering about all the turmoil and didn't realize you were going to make such a sharp turn. Do you know what's going on over there?" he asked, hoping the woman would take a moment to reply.

Wiping tears from her face with the dirty hem of her dress, she met his gaze. "Me sister's died in her sleep, leavin' this poor child without a ma or pa to love him."

"Truly, died in her sleep, eh?" Lewis said hoping that no one ever suspected the death to be anything else.

"Where are you rushing off to with the child? Must you not see to a proper burial for his mother?" Lewis inquired.

The woman pulled the child close. "I must see to the child's safety. Ya can't be havin' a babe in the midst of death. For sure it'll be causin' a curse upon him. Once I care for the boy, then I'll bury me sister."

Lewis stood watching until the wagon rolled out of the Acre before making his way home to fight the demons who visited him in his sleep that night. The woman had no way of knowing it was too late. The boy already had a curse upon him.

"This had better be important," Nathan Appleton muttered to Tracy Jackson as they waited for the remainder of their colleagues to arrive. "Making a trip to Lowell in the dead of winter is not my idea of pleasure."

"Nor mine," Jackson agreed. "However, William sent word it was urgent, and although the man tends to exaggerate at times, we can't ignore his warning, especially with Kirk still recuperating."

"Yes, I understand. I think I'll acquiesce and let you take control of tonight's meeting, Tracy. Since Thurston contacted you directly, it just seems more appropriate."

The remainder of the men finally arrived and one by one filed into the offices at the Merrimack. When the sound of scraping chairs and murmuring voices had finally quieted, Tracy stood. "Good evening, gentlemen. I thank you for your cooperation and willingness to travel to Lowell for this meeting. Hopefully, we will find resolution to several issues that have been brought to my attention by one of our members, William Thurston." Tracy watched as William's chest visibly swelled when the men turned in his direction and acknowledged him. Clearing his throat, Tracy continued. "Rather than attempt to explain the issues, I think it would be most expedient to read William's missive, which I received earlier this week."

The men listened attentively as Tracy read the allegations, all of which pointed toward Kirk Boott's inability to properly handle the ongoing problems within the community and, in particular, his disinclination to tackle the Irish problem and bring the papists to heel. Murmurs once again filled the room until Tracy finally tapped on the desk in order to regain control of the meeting.

William rose from his chair. "If you have no objection, Tracy, I would be most willing to entertain any questions. But first let me reiterate that I feel Boott has been useless with his sweet talk and promises of a church for the papists. I believe we must make an example of the culprit who committed the shooting. Once that has been done, I believe we must impose severe restrictions and curfews on the Irish. If we force them to use identification passes, cease permitting them to settle in the Paddy camps, and cut their wages, we can keep them from further infiltrating the town. I believe we should hire Americans, even if it requires higher wages and a decrease in our profit. Now, any questions?"

Paul Moody lifted his cigar in the air. "I have one. Is Kirk not attending because he wasn't invited or because he's unable to be here due to his injury? It seems he should have the opportunity to answer these allegations."

"I have presented all of my evidence to Mr. Boott; he is well aware of the involvement of the Irish in all of these incidents. And I would think you, of all people, Mr. Moody, would want these Irish thugs punished. It was one of your most valuable employees who died at the Appleton."

Paul glowered at Thurston. "I don't need you to tell me I've lost a valued employee, William. There's nobody who wants the guilty party punished more than I do. However, when punishment is meted out, I want it to be upon the guilty person."

"You sound like Boott. How much more evidence do you want? It's obviously the Irish, and in fact, I've given you the name of the man who shot Boott and participated in the incident at the Appleton. I've reason to believe he and his cohorts have been involved in all of the mishaps that have been occurring at the mills. This Irish faction needs to be brought under control."

All heads turned at the sound of a closing door and shuffling feet entering the building. "I am deeply touched, William, that you are so doggedly pursuing the criminal who attacked me," Kirk Boott said as he limped into the room. He removed his beaver hat and placed it in Tracy's extended hand. "Thank you, Tracy," he said before continuing. "William is correct. He did send me what he purported was evidence that would convict Johnny O'Malley of shooting me. As some of you know, Johnny is a fine Irish man who is closely associated with Hugh Cummiskey. He carries a great deal of influence among his countrymen. In fact, he's been vital in securing additional workers from Boston when we needed them for new canal construction."

The men nodded in agreement, all of them having seen the detailed reports Kirk had submitted to the Associates as their projects in Lowell progressed.

"For that very reason, I found William's allegation against Johnny disquieting. After he left, Matthew Cheever and I thoroughly dissected the so-called evidence produced by William. It is all a lie. Had Johnny been located where William purports, it would have been impossible to shoot my right leg."

William jumped to his feet. "Perhaps I misunderstood the exact location, but you can't deny the piece of fabric from O'Malley's coat."

Kirk's resolve was obvious as he pointed his cane toward William. "O'Malley tells me that coat came up missing several days before the shooting, and—"

"And you believe that?" William yelled. "Surely you men can see what I've been saying all along. He's not fit to run this operation."

"Sit down, William," Tracy ordered from between clenched teeth. "You'll have an opportunity to speak when Kirk has finished. Continue, Kirk," Tracy said.

Kirk nodded. "As I was saying, the piece of cloth was found in the clump of trees where William alleges the shooter was located. If he's now changing his mind about where the assassin was hiding, the piece of fabric is of no consequence, is it, William?"

William's face had turned bright red. "Possibly not, but that doesn't nullify the information regarding the incident at the Appleton. I told you I have men who will testify that O'Malley's responsible for the death of Simeon Jones."

"And I have evidence that Johnny O'Malley wasn't even in town on the date of the accident," Kirk rebutted. "Evidence that wasn't bought and paid for."

"What are you saying? That I concocted this whole thing? That's absurd and you know it, Kirk. You put your evidence before these men, and I'll do the same. We'll see what's been bought and paid for," William challenged.

"Gentlemen, gentlemen," Tracy called out, "let's call a halt to this inappropriate behavior right now. We're all gathered here to resolve this matter. Let's do it in a civilized manner. William, you may present whatever evidence you have to prove your allegations that Kirk is unfit to continue as manager for the Corporation. Kirk, you may then defend your position."

The group recessed while the two men sent for various witnesses to substantiate their allegations. It was growing late when Tracy finally called for a vote. "What say you, gentlemen? Let me have a show of hands. All those in favor of retaining Mr. Boott as manager of the Corporation? Those opposed?" Tracy nodded. "It appears you're the only member opposed to Kirk's retention, William."

The group sat in stunned silence as William pointed his finger at the group. "You've not heard the last of this. You've made a grievous error."

30

Lilly watched as Miss Addie glanced across the street toward her sister's boardinghouse. She wondered if the two sisters would ever resolve their differences. The waterwheel incident at the Appleton was still fresh when Mintie's sharp tongue had lashed out against John Farnsworth. Unwilling to abide Mintie's harsh attitude any longer, John had rebuked her for a lack of civility. Offended by his reproach, Mintie had unleashed her wrath upon him before finally accusing him of being a traitor. John had immediately packed his trunk and taken up residence at the Wareham House.

Had it not been for Lilly's intervention, Matthew, now in charge of the boardinghouse keepers, would have immediately fired Miss Mintie as the keeper at number 7 Jackson Street. And had it not been for Miss Addie, Lilly would have bid Miss Mintie a fond farewell. But Addie's despair over the situation had been heartwrenching. "It's her upbringing that makes her act in such a manner," she'd argued on her sister's behalf. "If she loses her position, she's likely to end up in a poorhouse, what with the Corporation unwilling to give her a reference," Addie had wept. "I can't bear to see her brought to ruin."

When Lilly could listen to no more, she had gone and spoken to John, telling him of Addie's anguish. John, in turn, had spoken to Matthew. And Matthew had told Mintie that had it not been for the kindness of John Farnsworth, she would have been sent packing.

In the weeks that followed, very little was seen of Miss Mintie. She remained tucked away in her house, caring for her boarders but doing little else. It appeared, however, that she hadn't entirely given up her snooping. On occasion, she could still be seen peeking out from behind the heavy draperies at the front window.

"You've been very quiet of late, Miss Addie. What's wrong?" Lilly questioned as she walked alongside the older woman while they headed toward town.

"I've been worried about Mintie. She's not socializing at all. I hear she hasn't attended her temperance meetings, and she hasn't been at the sewing bees at the church. In fact, she appears to be sending Lucy to do most of her shopping nowadays. I fear she's becoming a recluse. I'm hoping that once spring arrives, she'll venture out a bit."

Lilly patted Miss Addie's hand. "I fear it may take more than a bit of warm weather to thaw Miss Mintie's heart."

"Most likely, you're correct. She's a proud woman, but deep down, she's a good person, Lilly. I know that may be difficult for others to believe, but it's her spirit that's wounded. She feels unloved and unlovable."

Lilly listened, her mind churning for some way she might encourage her friend. "I'll try to come up with an idea to get her out of the house," she promised, wondering how she could possibly make a chink in Miss Mintie's armor.

"I believed the letter I wrote explaining John's loyalty to this country, as well as the Corporation, would soften her. I even invited her to tea, but she didn't respond," Addie lamented.

"I must admit—I had my own concerns about Mr. Farnsworth at one time," Lilly sheepishly admitted.

Addie gave her an astonished look. "Really? What made *you* question John?"

Lilly smiled. "One night when Matthew's father was escorting me home, I saw John and several men huddled together in a seemingly clandestine meeting; they appeared to be arguing. When Mr. Cheever and I came into view, they rushed off. After listening to Miss Mintie's accusations that Mr. Farnsworth was an English spy, I wondered if she was correct."

Addie shifted her shopping basket to her left arm and smiled. "And what changed your mind?"

"Some time later, when Matthew and I were together, he mentioned Farnsworth and his loyalty to the Associates. I mentioned the meeting and my concerns. He laughed, telling me it was quite the opposite."

Addie leaned in a bit closer, obviously intent on not missing a word.

"He explained that Mr. Farnsworth was unjustly fired from his position in England because the mill owners thought he had been bribed to help Mr. Lowell sneak plans for the looms out of England."

"Did Matthew tell you that John escorted Mr. Lowell through the English mills? It was because of those tours that they accused him of commiserating with Mr. Lowell."

"Their treatment of Mr. Farnsworth was reprehensible!" Lilly declared. "Matthew said that Mr. Farnsworth was so angered by his employer's shoddy behavior that he decided he would come to the United States and help make the mills in New England better than those in the old country. Before he left, he formed an alliance with several of his friends who were being treated poorly. Mr. Farnsworth agreed to pay their passage if, upon their arrival, they brought him additional information concerning the machinery and operation of the mills where they worked in England. They arranged their meetings prior to the men being employed by the Corporation so no one would know of their association with Mr. Farnsworth."

Addie nodded. "That's what John explained to me, also. John feared there might be retribution against the men's families if any word leaked out they knew him. He didn't want the men who were assisting him to face accusations of being spies. So instead of working against American industrialization, John and all of those men were *aiding* the industrialization in New England. I clearly explained those facts to Mintie when I wrote her, but obviously she has chosen to disregard the truth."

"I imagine she's embarrassed, especially since Mr. Farnsworth has proven to be a strong ally rather than a traitor. And since Miss Mintie's so proud, it's easier to seclude herself than face possible ridicule by others."

They continued walking, stopping for a moment to glance in a window along the way. "I can understand Mintie's hesitation to place herself in a position of public ridicule, but I'm her sister. It's almost as if she's unwilling to face the fact that she is wrong."

Lilly thought about Addie's words. "Admitting you're wrong is difficult. I've wrestled with that issue myself. Perhaps we need to concentrate our prayers upon Miss Mintie. What do you think? If we can't soften her, perhaps the Lord will."

A glimmer shone in Miss Addie's eyes. "Is that what helped change your attitude toward the mills?"

"A lot of prayer and several long talks with Matthew Cheever," Lilly replied. "Even if Matthew and I never restore our relationship, he managed to show me that industrialization is a necessity. We can't remain reliant upon England if we're to be a free country. I continue to dislike the fact that East Chelmsford was the chosen spot, but I now accept that the mills are something I can't change. I'm still praying about forgiveness toward those who wronged me. I believe I've come a long way in that regard, but when a day or two passes and I haven't prayed about forgiveness, that same resentment creeps back into my mind. I think it will be an ongoing project for me."

The women entered Whidden's, stopping for a moment to examine a display of newly arrived lace. "Every one of us is an ongoing project that needs God's forgiveness. You've matured in your faith right before my eyes, Lilly. If we can pray Mintie into that degree of maturity, perhaps we can mend our family ties. As for your relationship with Matthew, I believe you two are well on the way to restoration."

Lilly ran her fingers across a shimmering piece of pale blue fabric. "I haven't seen much of Matthew lately. It seems he is always busy with Corporation business and when he is finally available, I'm too tired or have made other plans."

"That fabric would be a good choice for you—perhaps a new gown for the Blowing Out Ball," Addie absently commented. "With Nadene starting back to work on Monday, I'm certain you'll have more energy. I'm pleased she's healed so well. I do admire your loyalty to Nadene."

"It was the least I could do," Lilly murmured, the compliment a reminder of the role she had played in Nadene's injuries. She was certain God had forgiven her willful behavior. Forgiving herself, however, was proving more difficult. "I hope returning to work won't prove too strenuous for Nadene. I know her burns have healed, but her cough seems to be getting worse. Have you noticed?"

"Occasionally she seems to have difficulty breathing deeply, but the last few weeks she has seemed stronger. Besides, she's anxious to get back to work."

The sound of pounding horse hooves, rumbling carriages, and loud voices sent Mrs. Whidden scurrying to the front of the store. "Wonder what's going on out there?" she asked her husband.

Moments later, the bell above the door sounded, followed by laughter and chattering as several patrons entered the shop. Lilly glanced toward the shoppers and felt her knees buckle. She grasped the edge of the display case and steadied herself as she watched Matthew escort Isabelle Locklear into the store.

"This stop wouldn't be necessary if Mother had permitted me ample time to prepare for the journey," Isabelle cooed to Matthew. "I know you didn't want to stop, but I simply refuse to go any farther knowing I've forgotten my hairbrush," she continued. "You are sure a dear to indulge me."

Lilly continued staring at the couple as Matthew patted Isabelle's hand. "We musn't take too long. Bishop Fenwick is waiting in his carriage. He's anxious to get settled."

"I promise I'll hurry," she replied, demurely peeking up from beneath the brim of her silk bonnet.

Lilly wanted to run from the store, but she would have to pass directly in front of Matthew to do so. If she could shrink behind one of the counters, perhaps she could remain undetected until Isabelle and Matthew completed their purchases. She began edging toward a tall display, then stopped and turned toward Miss Addie, who was now overcome by a fit of coughing. Matthew immediately looked in their direction. He appeared startled as he met Lilly's unwavering gaze.

Moving forward, Matthew patted Addie on the back for a moment. "I'll be right back," he said to Isabelle. "Let me get you a cup of water," he offered.

Addie ceased her coughing and gave Lilly a smug grin while Matthew rushed toward the rear of the store. "You were going to hide. But I wanted to be certain he saw you."

Lilly gave the older woman an astonished look. "Why? So I would be further embarrassed?"

"Of course not," Addie chided. "But knowing how you react, I was certain you would avoid Matthew. He wouldn't have an opportunity to explain why he's with that woman, and this whole matter would remain unresolved. There's probably a very good explanation for all of this."

"That's Isabelle Locklear, Miss Addie. Kirk Boott's niece. The one Boott wants Matthew to marry. Matthew told me they had parted company, but it appears he wasn't as forthcoming as I had believed."

Addie gave a gentle cough as Matthew approached. "Don't jump to conclusions," she whispered to Lilly before turning her attention toward Matthew. "I think I'm better, but thank you for your assistance. I believe I will drink that water," she said, taking the cup.

"We need to talk," Matthew whispered to Lilly while extending his hand to receive the emptied cup from Miss Addie. "I'll stop by tomorrow evening."

Lilly opened her mouth to refuse, but Matthew walked away without giving her an opportunity to protest.

Matthew slowed his stride to match Bishop Fenwick's as he escorted the rotund cleric up the steps of the Boott residence the next morning.

"I trust you slept well, Bishop," Boott greeted. "I understand the rooms at the Wareham House are quite comfortable."

"The accommodations were satisfactory," he replied. "I'm not sure the weather is going to cooperate for an outdoor Mass. Have you made any alternate plans?"

Boott nodded as he led the visitors into the dining room. The bishop offered a blessing over the breakfast before Boott continued. "I discussed the matter with Hugh Cummiskey and suggested we could make arrangements to hold the services at St. Anne's if the weather was uncooperative. However, Hugh didn't think the Irish Catholics would attend services at St. Anne's. He had some of his men construct a lean-to that will give you some protection. He said they are willing to withstand the elements."

The bishop furrowed his brows. "There's apparently more antagonism than I anticipated. However, I don't want to make anyone uncomfortable. It's been quite some time since a priest has been here to conduct services. There wasn't even a priest available for Christmas mass. So if my people want to meet outdoors, we'll meet outdoors."

"Do you plan to announce the new building after the services?" Kirk ventured.

The bishop slathered a layer of butter onto his biscuit. "So long as we have time to review all of the documents in order to transfer the property prior to departing for the Acre," he replied, licking his finger.

Kirk pushed away from the table. "I had no idea you wanted to complete the legalities this morning, Your Eminence. Matthew and I will finalize the papers for your signature while you finish your breakfast."

The Bishop smiled broadly and nodded his agreement.

"How dare he corner me like this!" Boott exclaimed as he closed the door to his office.

"Apparently he wants assurance everything will be completed to his satisfaction before making the announcement," Matthew remarked.

Boott gave him a look of annoyance. "Obviously! However, I find his tactics heavy-handed *and* insulting. He's determined to secure that extra piece of land. I had hoped I'd have time to convince him otherwise."

Matthew shuffled through the papers and began arranging them in piles for proper signature. "It would appear the bishop has outmaneuvered you this time."

"I've no choice but to sign over the property. I've already told Hugh the announcement would be made this morning. Bishop Fenwick has missed his true calling; he has far too much business acumen for a man of the cloth!"

<hr>

Thurston opened the door to his room at the Wareham House. "What took you so long? I told you to be here after lunch," he growled.

Lewis pushed past him and entered the room without responding. He was weary of Thurston and his schemes. Worse yet, he was sick of being forced to appear at Thurston's beck and call.

"Have you been drinking, Lewis?"

Lewis flopped into one of the two chairs in the room. "Why do you ask?"

"Your insolent behavior speaks volumes. I won't tolerate drunkenness. You talk too much when you've been imbibing."

Lewis gave a feeble salute. "Yes, sir."

Thurston gave him a look of disgust. "Listen carefully, Lewis. I've brought you here because I've completed my plans to dethrone Kirk Boott. This is serious business, and I need your complete attention."

Lewis grunted and shifted in the chair. "I haven't had *that* much to drink. What is it you're scheming?"

"A fire at the Merrimack," he replied, rubbing his hands in obvious delight. "It will, of course, be your handiwork, but I am going to convince the Associates otherwise."

Lewis gave an ungentlemanly snort. "When are you *ever* going to give up on this nonsense, Thurston? The Associates will never place their trust in anyone but Boott. Can't you see that he's the man they want running their business interests? Why don't you just accept the fact that you're not going to be the manager, go back to Boston, and let me get on with my life," Lewis blustered, his ale giving him artificial confidence.

William jumped up from his chair. His face was red, and the veins along his neck had swelled into a pulsating protuberance. "Don't you begin to tell me what I should or shouldn't do. The fact is, you want to get on with your life and out of your obligation to me. The Associates *will* embrace me as their new leader if you do as you're told. Remember, Lewis, I can be your ruination if you attempt to cross me."

Lewis sighed and settled back in the chair. He knew he had no choice. "So when am I to set this fire?"

Thurston's lips coiled into a satisfied grin. "I think it would be best if we both left town for a period of time before the next 'accident' occurs. I'll send word when the time is right. You can come back to town on the pretense of visiting your sister. Don't forget we've made an agreement, Lewis. I expect to know where you are at all times."

Lewis stood and nodded. "Will you be sending instructions or am I left to my own devices?"

"I'll send specific instructions. You do your best to follow them," William replied in a threatening tone.

There was nothing left to say. Lewis exited the room and walked down the narrow hallway of the Wareham House. He didn't stop walking until he reached the corner table of Nichol's Tavern, where he ordered a bottle of whiskey. Filling his glass with the amber liquid, Lewis quickly downed the contents and poured another. He wanted to forget, and if he couldn't forget, he would at least numb himself of feeling.

Mintie peeked from behind the draperies that covered the parlor windows. She longed to once again have Addie's companionship, yet she could not walk across the street and beg her sister's forgiveness—pride blocked her path. Instead, she pulled Addie's letter from the walnut desk that had once been the Judge's prize possession and sat down in the parlor. Adjusting her glasses, she continued her ritual of reading the letter, just as she had every day since its arrival.

She was now certain the contents were true, that John Farnsworth was not a traitor. Perhaps she had known it all along. But the fear of Addie becoming interested in a man and possibly taking a husband—well, it was more than she could bear to think about. How could their bond remain the same if Addie should marry?

The front door opened, and Lucy bounded in with a smile. "Morning, Miss Beecher. You reading your sister's letter again?"

Mintie quickly folded the letter and tucked it into the desk. "I was merely looking over some of my old correspondence."

"Why don't you write her a letter?"

Mintie gazed over her wire-rimmed spectacles. "And why do you think I should write Adelaide a letter?"

The child shrugged. "Because you like the one she sent you so much. You're reading it most every day when I come in," she replied before skipping off to the kitchen.

Mintie stared after the child. "Perhaps that's exactly what I'll do!"

By the time Lucy had finished the breakfast dishes, Mintie had a penned a well-thought-out note of apology to her sister. "Lucy! I have an errand," she called.

The child came scampering and screeched to a halt in front of Mintie. "How many times must I—oh, never mind. Take this note across the street to Miss Beecher. Tell her you would be happy to wait for her reply."

Filled with a mixture of fear and excitement, Mintie watched out the window for what seemed an eternity. Finally the door opened. Addie stood in the doorway for a moment, then raised her hand and waved before sending Lucy on her way. A smile spread across Mintie's lips as she pulled the drape back a bit farther and waved in return.

"Miss Beecher says she would love to come to tea this afternoon," Lucy said as she entered the front door. "Do you want me to begin dusting upstairs?" the child asked before heading up the stairway. "Miss Beecher?" Lucy turned toward her mistress. "How come you're crying?"

"It's nothing, Lucy. Sometimes folks cry when they're happy. You go ahead and start the dusting. I'll be up shortly."

31

Prudence nearly danced into the upstairs bedroom, a mischievous smile lighting her face. "There's someone here to see you, Lilly."

"Who is it? I'm preparing to leave for town."

Prudence giggled. "He said not to tell you."

Lilly squeezed past Prudence, out the bedroom door, and started down the stairs. She stopped midstep. Matthew was standing at the foot of the stairway, smiling up at her.

Hat in hand, he bowed from the waist. "I've come to offer my explanation."

Lilly arched her eyebrows at his remark. "You owe me none. You are free to keep company with Isabelle Locklear or any other woman you so desire. It's none of my concern," Lilly replied as she took her cape from one of the wooden pegs in the hallway. "Besides, I'm on my way to town. I wasn't planning on entertaining a guest."

"That's fine. I'll walk along with you since I'm expected at the Boott residence by eight o'clock."

"Well, I certainly wouldn't want to be the cause of your tardiness. Isabelle might not prove forgiving if you're late," Lilly replied as she tied her bonnet and walked out the front door.

Matthew laughed as he hurried down the walk to catch up with her. "There you go again, letting your jealousy get the best of you."

Lilly skidded to a halt. "What? How dare you, Matthew Cheever! You walk about town with Isabelle Locklear on your arm, you bow and scrape to her every whim and smile as she flutters her eyes, all after disavowing any romantic interest in her. What you hear is not jealousy; it's anger!"

Matthew followed Lilly into the milliner's shop and waited until she had finished. "Well, I think you'll find there's no reason for anger or jealousy," he said with a grin as they left the store. "Mr. Boott asked that I escort Bishop Fenwick from Boston to Lowell. I didn't know Isabelle was planning on making the journey. When I arrived in Boston to fetch the good bishop, he advised me that Isabelle would be accompanying us. Mrs. Locklear has been ill. She recently admitted herself to a sanatorium and insisted Isabelle come to Lowell. If it makes you feel any better, Isabelle is no happier to be in Lowell than you are to have her here."

"I don't give a whipstitch where she is," Lilly protested.

Matthew's boisterous laughter caused Lilly to glare in his direction. "Good! Well, since we've settled that matter and I'm absolved of any wrongdoing, I want to know if you'd do me the honor of attending the Blowing Out Ball with me?"

Lilly stared at him in disbelief. How had he moved from one topic to another so smoothly? Her every inclination was to tell him yes. Instead, she said, "We'll see what happens with you and Isabelle in the next couple weeks."

"I'll take that as a yes," Matthew said, leaning down to place a kiss on her cheek. "I must be off to meet with Mr. Boott," he said, hurrying off before she could wage an objection to his reply or the kiss.

Staggering from the tavern, Lewis zigzagged his way down Merrimack Street until he neared Jackson. He had watched Matthew kiss his sister's cheek and then hurry away. "Lilly! Wait, I want to talk to you." He attempted to steady his gait while hastening toward his sister.

She stood waiting with a look of expectation etched upon her face. "Lewis, you look terrible. You've been drinking," she said, her voice filled with disappointment.

He guiltily nodded his head. "Do you have a few minutes you could spare, Lilly? I need to talk."

Shifting her parcel, she took hold of her brother's arm. "We dare not go to the boardinghouse with you in this condition. We can walk back to the Wareham for a cup of coffee."

He quickly took a step backward. "Not the Wareham. I don't want to go there," he replied. "The Old Stone House—would you go there?"

Lilly grasped his arm. "I suppose, since I'm with an escort, but we must sit in the eating establishment, not the pub," she replied as they hurried back down Merrimack Street. "Can you tell me what's wrong, Lewis? You're trembling."

Lewis glanced over his shoulder at the sound of footsteps behind them. "I'd rather wait. I don't want to take the risk of being overheard."

A short time later, Lewis located a table situated away from the crowd. He was certain Thurston expected him to leave town immediately, and he didn't want to be seen.

Lilly leaned her head close and took Lewis's hand. "Tell me what has happened."

Holding his throbbing head, Lewis momentarily pondered his decision to burden Lilly with his problems. She couldn't help extract him from this dilemma. Yet he needed a confidant and quickly squelched his noble thoughts of keeping Lilly out of harm's way. "My life is in quite a mess. I've made a lot of wrong choices, all of them selfish and unscrupulous."

"I've made my share of mistakes also; we all have. And I know that in the past you've chosen to turn your back on God and even denounced His existence. But it's not too late to turn your life around. Repentance is difficult, pushing aside all that pride and asking God's forgiveness. But the benefits are overwhelming: you're a totally new person in the eyes of God. Clean! Won't you consider asking God's forgiveness, Lewis?"

The sincerity of her words touched him, and he gave her a gentle smile. "You don't understand the gravity of my sins, Lilly. There isn't enough soap in all of Massachusetts to wash me clean." He patted her arm. "You can't understand the seriousness of my involvement. I'm in a precarious position that forces me to do the evil bidding of another man. I've been hired to set fire to the Merrimack," he blurted.

There was stunned silence. Lilly stared at him in obvious disbelief. "No, Lewis, you can't. Please tell me why. What could possibly—"

Holding up his hand, Lewis shook his head back and forth. "I've already said too much, Lilly. You must forget what I've told you. Promise me that you'll say nothing to anyone."

"Only if you'll promise you won't be party to such a thing. Please, Lewis, promise me. You don't want to be involved in anything else that will cause you more guilt and shame," she pleaded.

Lewis gave her a feeble smile, knowing what he must do. It had been a complete error of judgment to come here. "I promise, Lilly. In fact, I'm going to escort you home, and then I'm going to leave town. I may even head for the wild western frontier. What do you think of that? Do you think I could survive out among those savages we've read about?"

Lilly grasped his hand. "Oh yes, Lewis. That's a wonderful idea. You must leave town immediately. I promise, I'll not breathe a word. But why not consider heading south? Life is gentler and slower in the south, I'm told. I can better picture you as a southern gentleman than an Indian fighter," she said with a grin. "We'd better be leaving, or I'll find myself locked out of the boardinghouse. Will you at least give careful thought to seeking God?"

Lewis gave her a reassuring smile. "We'll see." It was a small concession, the least he could do—he'd been the cause of enough pain in her life.

Lilly tiptoed up the steps to her bedroom, thankful to find her roommates asleep. The girls would have questioned her late arrival, and she didn't want to mention that she had been with Lewis—especially to Prudence, who still believed Lewis would one day be her husband. She settled into the warmth of the bed, but sleep wouldn't come.

It seemed strange not to have Nadene with her. Even though Nadene had planned to go back to work Monday, the doctor had insisted on sending the girl home. Addie had broken the news to the girls.

"The doctor believes Nadene's time is very limited. The consumption has only grown worse, and he feels she is in no shape to return to work." Addie had talked to them for some time, tears streaming from her eyes, as well as from the eyes of the girls who had come to care so deeply for Nadene.

Now Nadene was home, and the loss to Lilly was acute. How difficult it had been to share a bed with a total stranger, yet now how equally odd to be without her. Lilly pushed aside her emotions and tried not to think of Nadene. She prayed for her friend, hoping that the doctor might be wrong—knowing that most likely he was right.

Her thoughts then fell upon the conversation with Lewis, wrestling with the idea that perhaps this fire at the Merrimack would be God's punishment, the answer to all of her once-earnest prayers for the destruction of the Boston Associates. She silently chided herself, remembering the harm that had come to Nadene through the fire at the Appleton. Besides, the Boston Associates wouldn't be the only ones harmed by a fire at the Merrimack.

In one way or another, a major fire at the Merrimack would bring ruination to almost every resident of Lowell, and she didn't want that. After all, if enough tragedy did befall the Associates, Miss Addie might well be out of a job, and Lilly could even find herself out of a home. An idea of what she would do beyond her employment with the mills had never really materialized in her thoughts.

Months ago, I would have been happy at the thought of such destruction, she thought. But that was before, when her heart had been hard and her focus hadn't been God so much as revenge. And hadn't she already resolved those issues and asked forgiveness? Why was she permitting herself to dwell on these thoughts?

Slipping from her bed, Lilly dropped to her knees, seized by an overwhelming sorrow for her brother. She prayed for his protection and ultimate happiness. She prayed he would find a safe haven and loyal Christian friends, that he would seek God's forgiveness, and that God would direct his path toward righteousness.

She crawled back into bed, amazed by her feelings for Lewis. In spite of their past and all of his transgressions, she loved him. Perhaps God would send that same healing power to her brother.

32

March blew in like a lion, but despite blustery beginnings, the month gradually began to show signs of spring. The night of the Blowing Out Ball had finally arrived, and Lilly actually found herself a mix of emotions. Worry for Lewis reigned uppermost in her mind, but thoughts of Matthew had affixed themselves to her heart.

"Let me see how you look!"

At Miss Addie's request, Lilly twirled about in her pale blue lace-trimmed gown.

"I told you that shade of blue was just right for your complexion when we first saw the fabric at Whidden's," Miss Addie remarked with a twinkle in her eye. "And I was correct. Would you consider helping an old woman with her dress?"

Lilly smiled and gave Addie a hug. "I would consider helping a *very dear friend* with her dress," she said, following Addie into her bedroom.

Addie carefully plunged her arm into the sleeve of her dress. "Matthew has certainly been a frequent visitor lately. And how many times have you been to dinner at his parents' home recently? Seems things are getting serious between you two. Is there anything you want to tell me?"

Lilly ceased buttoning Addie's dress. "No, there is nothing to tell you. Matthew and I are merely friends, just like you and me. And what of you and John Farnsworth? He's been coming to call on you frequently. Do *you* have something to share with me?" Lilly asked with a giggle.

Addie placed a hand on each side of her waist in an attempt to make the buttoning easier. "We have talked about the future—about sharing it— together," she stammered.

"Really? Oh, Miss Addie, that's wonderful. When? Why didn't you tell me?"

"Don't get so excited. I said we've *talked* about the future. We haven't made any decisions, although John has asked me to help him decorate his house once it's finished. They've begun work on it again since the weather has warmed up a bit. He thinks it will be completed by June. We ordered the fabric for the draperies last week."

"Oh, Miss Addie, how exciting. I can't think of anyone who deserves a good husband more than you. And you'll be a perfect wife for Mr. Farnsworth. Addie Farnsworth—that has a nice sound to it. Have you told Miss Mintie?"

Addie shook her head. "Now that we've finally mended our differences, I don't want to do anything to upset her. Until John and I have actually decided we're going to share our future together, it's best I don't say anything to Mintie. Having worked so diligently to heal our relationship, I'm sure you understand how fragile it is. Mintie's made great strides in accepting my relationship with John, but we need more time. And if you hadn't come up with the idea of finding a beau for Mintie, I'm not sure she would have attended the ball this evening."

Lilly nodded as she arranged the layers of Addie's skirt. "Who would have ever thought Miss Mintie and Lawrence Gault would find anything in common? Yet he seems to have a wonderful, calming effect upon her, don't you think? I'm so fond of Mr. Gault, I almost felt guilty when I suggested he call upon your sister," she said with a giggle.

"I must admit that I would never have dreamed such a sweet man would give Mintie a second glance, but he appears to enjoy her company, and she's like a different person since he's come into her life," Addie said as she handed a string of pearls to Lilly.

"I attempted to convince Mintie to purchase a new gown for the ball, but she wouldn't budge. Stitching a row of new lace around the neckline of her frock was the most I could manage," Addie added with a giggle.

"Not that old brown dress?"

Addie gave an exaggerated nod of agreement, and the two women burst into gales of laughter. "She certainly can't be accused of attempting to turn Mr. Gault's head with her wardrobe."

"That's true. You, on the other hand, are going to turn everyone's head in this lovely gown. And your string of pearls and earbobs are perfect accents."

Addie blushed at the compliment. "Thank you, dear, but the only person I want to please is John. I can hardly wait—we're going to have such a gay time this evening. I can just feel it in my bones. Now, please make sure my sash is straight in back."

Lilly examined the mauve-colored gown to ensure there were no flaws. The full gigot sleeves were quite complimentary on Miss Addie. Lilly straightened the sash and then picked a piece of lint from the shoulder.

"Everything is perfect," she announced.

Prudence and Marmi descended the staircase and gathered in the dining room along with the other girls, all of them admiring one another's gowns, offering to loan a piece of jewelry or pair of gloves to complete an ensemble. The laughter and chattering charged the room with an air of excitement.

"I do wish Nadene could have been here with us," Lilly said sadly.

Addie gently touched Lilly's hand. "I wish she could be here, too, but we must trust that God has it all under control. Nadene would not wish us to be sad tonight. Let us go and share good company in her honor."

Lilly nodded. "She'd like that, I'm sure. Afterwards, why don't we all write her a letter and tell her every detail."

"That's a marvelous idea," Addie agreed.

A knock at the front door sent one of the girls rushing to the hallway. "It's too early for Mr. Farnsworth or Matthew," Lilly commented as she tucked a curl into place.

"Lilly, you have a caller. It's Lewis," Marmi said as she neared the dining room.

"Lewis?" She rushed past Marmi, down the hallway and into Lewis's extended arms. "It's good to see you. You look wonderful," she said, leaning back to look into his face. "What brings you back to Lowell? Not a problem, I hope?"

Lewis gave her an enormous smile. "Everything is fine. I wanted to see my sister, but it appears I've chosen the wrong night to come calling," he convincingly replied. "Is there a party tonight?"

"The Blowing Out Ball. You can attend. It will be great fun. Please say you'll come," Lilly begged. She was surprised at the sincerity of her emotions, but she truly wanted Lewis to attend. God had done a work in her heart— there could be no doubt.

"No, I don't want to interfere with your evening of fun. You go on, and I'll see you tomorrow."

After several minutes of pleading, with Lilly insisting it would only make this joyful occasion more memorable, Lewis finally agreed to attend the ball. After giving Lilly his promise to meet her at the Old Stone House, he departed in order to secure a room at the Wareham for the night.

Lilly sat beside Matthew in the carriage, her voice filled with excitement as she told him of Lewis's surprise arrival. "Isn't this perfect?" Lilly asked, clapping her hands together. "Lewis appears to have put his past behind him. I'm so anxious to hear what he's been doing since he left Lowell."

Matthew's face creased with concern. "Please don't be disappointed if you're unhappy with what he tells you. I want you to have a wonderful time this evening."

Lilly nodded her agreement then smiled as she glanced across the carriage toward John Farnsworth and Addie sitting opposite them. It was obvious Mr. Farnsworth was enchanted with Addie's devoted attention, the two of them talking softly as the horses clopped down the street. Catching Lilly watching them, John beamed a smile.

"I nearly forgot to tell you. I received a missive from England. It seems I'm to have company."

"Is your father finally going to join you?" Lilly questioned.

"Not just yet. No, this is from my nephew. My sister's boy, God rest her soul." John's expression sobered. "Sherman Manning, my brother-in-law, passed on a few months back. I didn't know until Taylor sent me this letter. Anyway, Taylor desires a new life in America. His siblings are safely established with his grandmother in London, and he asked to join me here, perhaps to work at the mills."

"We're always in need of another good man," Matthew remarked.

John nodded. "I hoped you'd feel that way. He should be here by the first of May."

"When he arrives and you've gotten him settled in, send him to see me," Matthew replied.

"Oh, look, there's Mintie with Mr. Gault," Addie announced as they stepped out of the carriage. "Mintie!" she called out, waving a gloved hand in the air.

Mintie waved in return, giving them a bright smile. "Good evening," she pleasantly greeted as the foursome approached. "Perhaps we can find a table and sit together," she ventured as they walked in and joined the frivolity.

Matthew took hold of Lilly and led her toward the dance floor. "I believe Lilly and I will begin with a dance. You go ahead and find a place to sit, and we'll join you shortly." The candles and oil lamps cast an enchanting glow throughout the rooms as they whirled about in time with the music.

"There's Lewis," Lilly reported, twisting in Matthew's arms and nearly tripping over his feet as she attempted to keep her brother in sight. He glanced in her direction, and she excitedly waved in return. "He's coming this way."

Lewis tapped Matthew's shoulder. "Would you mind if I cut in, Matthew? I promise to return her quickly."

Matthew smiled as he released Lilly to her brother. "I don't think I have a choice," he said with a laugh. "She's been tripping over my feet since you arrived. I think she was afraid you would dance with someone else first."

"That's not so. Lewis may dance with anyone he wishes," Lilly protested.

Matthew slapped Lewis on the back. "It's good to see you, Lewis. I hope we'll have time to visit a little later."

"Thanks, Matthew," Lewis replied as he grasped Lilly's hand and began to move across the dance floor.

Lilly gave her brother a winsome smile. "You look wonderful, Lewis. I want to hear everything. Tell me where you've been and what you've been doing, because whatever it is seems to agree with you."

"Thank you for the kind words, Lilly. I took your sisterly advice and went south, although not very far," he said with a laugh. "I've been in Philadelphia working with some men who are developing a new import and export business." Lewis glanced about the dance floor and then back toward his sister. "You are by far the most beautiful young lady in attendance this evening, Lilly—but you always *were* a pretty girl."

Lilly felt an overwhelming affection for her brother. "Why, Lewis? Why have we had so many years of ugliness between us? Why did you . . . hate me?"

He frowned and turned her effortlessly. "I wish I could take back those years—I truly do. Upon reflection, I can only say that my actions were born out of jealousy and fear."

"Jealousy and fear of what?" she questioned, watching him intently, as though she might ascertain the answer from his expression.

"I was jealous of you and fearful that our parents would no longer have any use for me after you came along. You were so lovely, like a little doll. People were always commenting on it. I felt misplaced. I'd had Mother and Father's undivided attention, and suddenly I had to share."

"But I adored you," Lilly said, shaking her head. "I used to plead with Mother to tell me why you were mad at me. I wanted so much for us to be close."

An expression of pain crossed Lewis's face. "I suppose it's too late for that now."

Lilly squeezed his hand. "Of course it's not too late. We've already grown closer just in the past few months. Remember when you showed up here in Lowell? I wanted nothing to do with you. The past, and all that stood between us, was too much to contend with. You were planning to use the girls for your greater gain. . . ."

"Which I did and am now deeply ashamed."

"What made the difference, Lewis?"

He made a halting step but quickly recovered. "Coming face to face with who I am and what I'm capable of doing made me realize just how far I'd sunk. I can't change the past, Lilly, and I'm certain there is no future—not for someone like me."

"But . . ."

He shook his head. "Let's forget such sad things and enjoy the music. I'll soon be returning to Philadelphia, and I desire to enjoy a pleasant moment with you before I go."

They continued dancing through several musical arrangements, Lewis seeming to enjoy Lilly's company. He spoke of his excitement over his new business venture and beginning his life anew while Lilly listened attentively, thrilled by his report.

Returning her to the table where Matthew sat, he said, "I think I should dance with Prudence. I believe I owe her an explanation of my disappearance," Lewis told Lilly. "You need not fear. I don't plan to woo her, merely tell her I've moved to Philadelphia."

Lilly gave Lewis an endearing smile, watching as he walked toward the table where Pru and several other girls were seated.

"If he weren't your brother, I believe I would be overwrought with jealousy," Matthew softly remarked as he and Lilly approached a table laden with punch bowls and silver trays filled with tiny sandwiches and cookies. "Your face is fairly aglow with love."

Lilly took a sip of her punch. "There's been such a wonderful change in Lewis. It appears he's finally become the man God intended him to be. I can't believe the change."

"I must admit he appears to be happy and content. And from the cut of his suit, I'd say his new business opportunity has already proved financially successful." Matthew glanced about and said, "Don't look now, but Thaddeus Arnold and his wife are walking in this direction."

Lilly stiffened. "He's never made good on his threat that things weren't yet resolved." She continued to drink her punch, even as she watched the man from across the room.

"I'm telling you, Lilly, his threats were probably nothing more than manly pride. Men don't like to have their plans altered—especially by women."

"Well, he does appear to treat all of the girls on our floor with dignity and is evenhanded in his decisions. *And* I can now sleep at night without fear of hearing his wife crying out in pain during the night."

Matthew held up the punch ladle and raised his eyebrows. "More?" he inquired.

Lilly nodded and held out her cup. "Good evening, Miss Armbruster and Mr. Cheever," Mrs. Arnold greeted as she came alongside them. "Mr. Arnold stopped to talk with one of the men. I thought I would have a cup of punch," she explained. "And I wanted to thank you," she whispered to Lilly.

Lilly snapped to attention at the word of thanks. "For what?" she cautiously questioned.

"Well, I'm not sure I rightly know the truth of it, but I know you had something to do with the change in Mr. Arnold." She smiled and lifted the cup of punch. "Sometimes he still loses his temper, but he's never laid a hand on me since the day he came home ranting and raving something about you and the church."

Mrs. Arnold's face revealed how the years of worry and harsh treatment had taken their toll. Lilly patted her arm. "I cannot take credit for anything. I'm just glad to have your company in church and at our ladies' social gatherings. Your quilting puts them all to shame."

Mrs. Arnold blushed. "Oh . . . I . . . well, thank you."

Thaddeus Arnold arrived at that moment. He looked at Matthew and nodded before fixing his gaze on Lilly. Lilly shivered, recognizing his dislike of her.

"Miss Armbruster. Mr. Cheever. Good to see you both." He looked to his wife. "If you two will excuse us, I intend to dance with my wife."

Lilly watched the smiling woman put down her cup. She took hold of her husband's arm with a cautiousness born out of experience. Lilly wondered if the woman would ever have a truly peaceful life.

Matthew finished his plate of sandwiches and held out his hand to Lilly. "I believe this dance is mine."

Lilly pushed aside her thoughts of Mrs. Arnold and nodded. Allowing Matthew to lead her onto the dance floor, Lilly relished the gaiety of the moment. "This is one of the happiest days of my life. I see the work God has done in my heart, and I can only thank Him. And Lewis! Would you believe that before he left Lowell, he told me he was going to set fire to the Merrimack? And now he's—"

"What?" Matthew interrupted, stopping midstep. "Lewis threatened to set fire to one of the mills, and you didn't tell me? Why would you withhold such vital information, Lilly?"

"Could we continue dancing before we cause a spectacle?"

Matthew jerked into motion. "Well?" he insistently questioned as he began to maneuver her through the crowd of dancers.

"Lewis told me he had become entangled with a disreputable scoundrel who threatened to ruin him if he didn't set the fire. He believed he had no options, but after we talked, he decided he would leave Lowell and begin his life anew somewhere else. When he left town that night, I saw no reason to tell anyone. Lewis wouldn't tell me any of the particulars or the name of anyone else involved. He feared I would come to harm if I knew too many details. Besides, the threat to the mills and the possible destruction of human life were gone. To taint Lewis's name when he'd actually done nothing would have been unfair."

"I suppose you're right. Still, I wish you had confided in me," Matthew replied as the music stopped. He took hold of Lilly and led her toward their table. "So what brings him back to Lowell? Can the threat have passed so quickly?"

Lilly gave him a look of consternation. "He said he was anxious to see me. I believe he wanted to show me he was doing well and had begun making changes in his life. How silly of me! I should have realized he was putting himself in harm's way and immediately sent him on his way. Instead, I all but forced him to come to the ball and make a public appearance."

Matthew gently pressed his thumb along a crease in Lilly's brow. "It's a beautiful night and a lovely party. We shouldn't be discussing anything more distressing than the fact that the punch is overly sweet. Forget my thoughtless prying," Matthew said, giving her a tender smile. "Why don't we step outside for a moment and get some air?"

Lilly nodded her head in agreement, anxious to push the unpleasant thoughts into the recesses of her mind. Lewis had returned a changed man, and nothing else mattered right now.

They stepped outside, and Lilly shivered from the chill of the night air but said nothing. She wanted very much to sort through her feelings for Matthew and to better understand his for her. Still, it was hard to speak her mind. She was enjoying a tender balance of emotions and actions on both her part and Matthew's. She had come a long way in learning to control her temper and had come to realize that Matthew's choices had not been as unwisely made as she had originally believed. With that thought in mind, she turned to face Matthew.

"I want to apologize," she said.

"For what?"

"I've treated you poorly these last few years. I've blamed you for the inevitable changes on the land. I pushed you away in my bitterness."

"I never wanted to see you hurt, Lilly. I never realized what my choices would mean to you," Matthew replied softly. "Given the fact I intended to marry you, I should have discussed the entire matter more thoroughly with you."

Lilly felt warmed by his words and looked away. She didn't know if she could bear to talk about what she'd lost with Matthew. She shivered again and rubbed her arms.

"Come on, let's get you back inside," Matthew said, reaching out to take hold of Lilly. "We've had enough confessing and apologizing for one evening."

Lilly smiled and nodded. "Besides, we might have people talking if we stay out here too long."

Matthew chuckled. "Let them talk. Better yet, maybe we should give them something to talk about."

~ 33 ~

The swirl of colorful dancers blended with the lively music. They were dancing a reel, swaying in and out of the aligned ranks, when Lilly and Matthew
came back to the room. Addie and John seemed to be enjoying themselves
immensely, which to Lilly was no surprise. What was surprising, however, was
the fact that Miss Mintie and Lawrence Gault were among the dancing couples. Furthermore, Miss Mintie was actually laughing out loud. Lilly couldn't
help but smile and motion to Matthew.

"It's amazing what the right man can do in the life of a lonely woman."

"I've heard that to be very true," Matthew said, leaning close to her ear.
"And likewise, the right woman can completely fill the heart of a lonely man."

Lilly met his gaze, his lips only inches from hers. She wanted very much
for Matthew to kiss her—for him to be the right man who would forever
change her loneliness. Moving a fraction of an inch closer, she prayed he might
understand.

"Fire! Fire! The Merrimack!" A chilling silence momentarily quieted the
frivolity of the ball. Then suddenly chair legs began scraping across the wooden
floors as the men jumped to their feet and rushed from the room.

Lilly pulled away, looking frantically around the room. "Where's Lewis?"

Matthew took a moment to survey the crowd. "I don't see him, Lilly. I
must get over to the Merrimack."

"Do be careful," she urged, watching as Matthew hurried off with John
Farnsworth and a limping Kirk Boott, who followed behind.

Lilly grasped Addie's arm, hoping her friend would provide a steadying
influence. "I must find Lewis."

"I'm sure he's gone with the other men to help put out the fire. There
doesn't appear to be a man left in the room. Even Mr. Whiting's gone to help,"
she soothingly replied.

Once again scanning the room, Lilly took Addie's hand and moved away
from their table. "Let's find Prudence. Lewis was going off to dance with her
about an hour ago. I didn't see him after that."

Addie pointed toward the door. "There she is—with Marmi."

Stretching up to wave, Lilly called out and quickly crossed the room. "Pru,
where's Lewis? Have you seen him?" she asked, silently praying that Prudence

would say he had been with her all evening.

Prudence shrugged her shoulders. "I don't know, Lilly. We only danced one dance. He apologized for treating me boorishly last winter. He also told me he had moved to Philadelphia and said he wasn't going to be in Lowell for long. I accepted his apology, and we parted after the dance. After that, I'm not sure where he went."

"Shouldn't we go over to the fire? Perhaps there's something we can do to help," Lilly suggested while silently praying that Lewis's reappearance in Lowell and the fire were merely a coincidence.

"I don't know that we can be of much assistance, but at least we can see how much damage has been done," Addie replied.

Clustered together, they scurried off toward the Merrimack with Mintie and Addie leading the way. Smoke filled their nostrils as they hastened down French Street. Mintie slowed her pace as soot showered down from the glowing sky. Several small explosions filled the air as windows shattered and leaping flames engorged with fresh air soared toward the heavens. Fire illuminated the mill yard as the harried men frantically worked to extinguish the blaze. As they approached, several men could be seen leaning over a moaning figure.

Pointing a finger toward the groaning form, Prudence turned toward Lilly, her face etched in horror. "Lilly, look—someone's been burned!"

Lilly felt a deep sense of dread. As she pushed closer, edging through the congregated men, she feared the worst. Although he was burned almost beyond recognition, Lilly knew it was the body of her brother. She fell to her knees beside Lewis, tears in her eyes. His breathing was shallow and irregular as he lay unconscious on the cold ground.

"Oh, Lewis, no," Lilly moaned.

The quiet murmur of conversation was interrupted by William Thurston's determined voice rising above the crowd. "I, for one, can attest to what happened here tonight. I was out for an evening stroll as I am wont to do on evenings when I need to clear my head and think," he pontificated.

"Has anyone sent for a doctor?" Lilly shouted toward the men that encircled her brother's body.

"Yes, yes, of course," William Thurston replied, obviously irritated by the interruption. Loudly clearing his throat, he regained the attention of the crowd. "As I was saying, I was out for my evening stroll when I came upon Lewis wrestling with several Irishmen—apparently the ones who had set fire to the building. It appeared Lewis was unable to apprehend the culprits. As I quickened my pace and drew closer, I saw Lewis rushing forward, attempting to douse the blaze. It was then his clothing caught fire, leaving him in this tragic condition."

Lewis groaned, his eyes fluttered open, and he began mumbling, beckoning Lilly closer, but someone held her back.

Lilly looked up to see William Thurston's intense expression. He gripped her shoulders to keep her from drawing closer to Lewis and dropped to one knee. "Don't talk, Lewis. You need to save your strength," he said, the words a hushed command. He looked to Lilly, saying, "It's for the best."

"Mr. Boott wants to talk to you, Mr. Thurston. He heard you were privy to some information regarding the fire," a soot-covered worker called out.

Thurston hesitated. "Don't say anything, Lewis," he ordered. "Do you hear me? Nothing!" He stood and straightened his coat before strutting off to meet with Kirk Boott.

Lilly looked after the man momentarily before turning her attention back to her brother. "Lewis, can you hear me?" Lilly whispered. "Please don't die," she begged, choking back her tears.

Her brother's eyes opened a mere slit. He moved his mouth, but she couldn't hear him. She bent her ear to his lips. "I . . . did . . . the best I could." His words were interrupted with weak coughing spasms. "I . . . set . . . the fire at night . . . so no one . . . would be injured," he rasped in a barely audible tone. Lilly raised up and looked at him in disbelief. Surely he couldn't have said what she thought he said.

"Step aside. Let me get to him," Dr. Barnard said, moving toward Lewis's side. He stooped down beside Lewis and performed a cursory examination before requesting the aid of several men. "We need to get him to my office. Quickly!"

William Thurston came rushing back as the men moved Lewis onto a board. "What are you doing?" he hollered as they hoisted Lewis into the air.

Lilly remained close to Lewis's side, certain that her brother's life was hanging in the balance. "Taking him to Dr. Barnard's office for treatment," Lilly replied.

Thurston hastened to Lilly's side. "I can't let you do this alone. Lewis has been a loyal friend, and I want to be with him until the . . . well, uh . . . until he regains consciousness," he stammered.

"Don't you think they need you here, helping put out the fire?" Lilly inquired. "I can stay with my brother."

Thurston remained close by her side. "No, I won't hear of it. I won't desert a friend in his time of need. Besides, you shouldn't be alone right now, either, Miss Armbruster."

"Lilly!" Matthew called out. "I'll join you at the doctor's office as soon as possible." Lilly turned and waved.

"No need, Cheever, I'll accompany her," Thurston replied.

Lilly wished Matthew would call Thurston back to fight the fire. She didn't like William Thurston, and she certainly didn't want him accompanying her to the doctor's office.

Once they reached Dr. Barnard's office, he instructed the two to wait outside. "My wife will assist me. If I need further help, I'll call you."

The two of them waited. Nothing Lilly said could persuade Thurston to leave. Finally she ceased her attempts and began to pray for her brother. She wanted Lewis to live, but if that wasn't to be, she at least wanted one last opportunity to talk with him. There were questions that needed to be answered before her brother left this world.

Lilly startled when Dr. Barnard entered the room. "I wish I had better news to bring you. Unfortunately, I think Lewis is going to slip from his state of unconsciousness into death very soon."

Thurston jumped up from his chair. "You're certain he won't regain consciousness?"

The doctor solemnly wagged his head back and forth. "It doesn't appear likely," Dr. Barnard replied and then turned toward Lilly. "I'm so sorry. Even if I had arrived sooner, there would be nothing I could have done. His burns are too severe."

Thurston had donned his coat and top hat and stood with his gloved hand covering the front doorknob. "I'm sure you'd like to say your good-byes in private, Miss Armbruster," Thurston said quickly before departing.

"You can come back and sit with him if you'd like," Dr. Barnard offered.

Lilly followed the doctor and took a chair beside the bed. The smell of burnt flesh again reminded her of her own misdeeds. She desperately wished she'd never succumbed to her need for revenge. Although Nadene had recovered physically from her burns, Lilly knew the pain and misery suffered could never be wiped away.

She wanted to soothe her brother but realized there was nothing she could do that would make him more comfortable. So she bowed her head and began to pray, silently at first and then softly out loud, asking God to ease her brother's pain.

"Lilly, is that you?" Lewis's voice was a mere whisper.

"Lewis . . . oh yes, Lewis, it's me."

He groaned as he turned his head toward her. His voice was low and gravelly. "You were always a good sister, Lilly. I don't know how you tolerated my treatment of you. . . . I was a terrible brother, and I've been a terrible man." He gasped for air, making an awful wheezing sound, chilling Lilly to the bone.

"Shh, Lewis, don't be so hard on yourself. It was my belief in God that enabled me to endure. However, I must admit it wasn't always easy." She smiled and gently touched his singed hair. "Sometimes you certainly put my faith to the test, but God was true to His word and sustained me. Lewis, I need to know—have you accepted Christ? Have you invited Him into your heart as your Savior? Have you repented of your sins and asked God's forgiveness? All you need do is ask," she fervently explained.

"You don't know . . . the depth of my sin. I couldn't ask to be . . . forgiven of the heinous crimes I've committed. Jesus won't forgive me, even if I asked," he replied, his voice fading.

"Lewis," Lilly urgently whispered. "Lewis, can you hear me? Lewis!" She leaned over his face until she felt his shallow breath upon her cheek. He had slipped back into unconsciousness, but he was still alive. She sat down, covering her face with her hands, and wept. *Please, Lord, let him live until he realizes there's no sin you won't forgive,* she silently prayed.

She didn't know how long she had been praying when Lewis once again moaned her name. Bending near, she whispered in his ear. "Lewis, just ask God's forgiveness."

"Irish woman, she's dead . . ." he muttered.

"Lewis, you need to ask Jesus to forgive you," she sighed.

"Baby still alive . . ."

Lilly couldn't believe the words. "Lewis, what are you saying? Do you have a child? A baby? Where's the child, Lewis?"

"Yes, baby . . . a boy. Alive. Paddy camp. He has a mushroom birthmark . . . on his arm," he replied, wheezing for breath.

There was no doubt Lewis was growing weaker by the moment, yet she hadn't confirmed if he had asked God's forgiveness. Desperation rose from deep within her. "Lewis, do you understand that God will forgive *any* sin— you have but to ask. Do you understand?"

"Yes, Lilly, I understand," he whispered.

"Have you accepted Christ into your heart, Lewis?" she urgently questioned. "Lewis, please answer me."

Lewis exhaled, emitting a soft gurgling noise before his head turned against the pillow.

He was dead—without telling her if he had accepted God's grace, without saying if he'd asked for forgiveness. She grasped his charred hand, her tears flowing freely as she mourned her brother's passing.

Someone touched her shoulder. "Lilly, how can I help?" Matthew gently asked.

She jumped up and fell into his arms. "Oh, Matthew, he's gone. Lewis is dead. He died before telling me if he had accepted Christ," she said through her tears.

Pulling her close, Matthew held her for several moments, then led her from the room. "There's nothing more you can do here, Lilly. Let me take you home. Look, I've brought your wrap. Miss Addie thought you might need it." Gently, he helped Lilly on with her cloak and directed her toward the door.

Lilly turned around. "I should tell Dr. Barnard I'm leaving," she murmured.

"I talked with him when I came in. He knew I was going to escort you home."

The smoky air filled Lilly's nostrils. "The fire, Matthew? Were you able to save the mill?"

"We won't be able to evaluate the actual damage until daylight, but the fire is out. Most of the damage was to the printworks. Mr. Boott and Farnsworth and I will assess the damages first thing in the morning," Matthew explained. "It doesn't appear we'll be shut down for more than a week or so."

Lilly sighed. "I hope it won't be too long. The girls can't afford to pay their room and board when they're not receiving wages."

"I'm certain the Corporation will make arrangements to protect the girls," he said.

The two of them walked in silence until they neared the boardinghouse. "Matthew, I believe Lewis has a son," Lilly blurted.

Matthew stopped and gave her a look of surprise. "What would give you such an outlandish idea?"

"He mentioned a baby on his deathbed—a boy. I don't think a man lies while on his deathbed, do you?"

"No, I don't suppose a man would have much reason to tell falsehoods on his deathbed, but what did he actually say?"

Lilly gave him a thoughtful look. "He said the mother was dead. It's a boy. I don't know how old he is, but he has a birthmark, a mushroom-shaped birthmark on his arm," she recounted.

"Anything else?"

"He said the child is in the Paddy camps. I assume the mother was Irish."

Matthew rubbed his jaw and gave her a thoughtful look. "I do recall several occasions when I saw Lewis around the Acre. I wondered why he was there. Perhaps he did have more reason to be there than I imagined, but he never mentioned anything to me. You should remember, however, that his words might have been the delirious ramblings of a dying man. Please promise me you'll not worry any further. I plan to spend a good deal of time in the Acre over the next few days, and if I find any evidence of a child, I'll tell you."

"Oh, Matthew, would you? Thank you so much," Lilly replied, giving him a weary smile. "But why are you planning to spend time in the Acre?"

"Didn't you hear William Thurston say he had observed Lewis fighting with some Irishmen who were supposed to have started the fire? I need to investigate his allegations."

Lilly thoughtfully considered his reply. "I don't think you'll find anyone to substantiate Thurston's claims. Lewis admitted he started the fire," Lilly said, her voice barely audible.

Matthew held her by the shoulders. "Lewis *told* you he started the fire?"

"Yes. He said he set the fire at night so none of the workers would be injured. Somehow he felt it was the one noble thing he could do if he was going to set the fire," she said, beginning to weep. "Oh, Matthew, I'm truly alone in the world now. My entire family is gone. Even though Lewis and I weren't close, he was my brother. And just as he was beginning to turn his life around, he's snatched away. When my father died, I didn't think the void could be any greater. Now I know I was wrong. I have no one."

Matthew pulled her into his arms, and Lilly relished the comfort of his embrace. It felt so right to be with him. Perhaps he would speak words of reassurance, even love.

"Everything's going to be fine, Lilly."

Lilly looked into his eyes. She had once loved this man and had pushed him away in anger. Her own pain had made it impossible to continue their relationship. Now her pain made her desire that relationship more than anything.

Matthew gently touched her cheek. "You needn't feel alone. God is always with you, and besides that, you have Addie—and the girls here at the house are your friends. And you know how much my family cares for you."

Lilly felt a wave of disappointment. Stepping back, she wiped her eyes. "Thank you for helping me tonight. It was good of you to see me home from the doctor's. Good night, Matthew."

She walked up the stairs, remembering Matthew's words and wondering why he had failed to include himself among those who cared about her. When he had asked to escort her to the Blowing Out Ball, she was certain he had romantic feelings for her. Better still, she finally felt that she might be ready to accept her own feelings for Matthew, maybe even open her heart to him. Obviously she had once again misinterpreted his intentions.

~ 34 ~

Matthew bounded up the front steps of his parents' home, still wondering if he had done the right thing. He had wanted to declare his feelings for Lilly the night before, but it seemed inappropriate to avow his love when she was grieving her brother's death and the loss of all familial bonds. Holding back was the hardest thing he'd ever endured—short of losing Lilly in the first place.

Julia Cheever rounded the corner of the parlor as Matthew entered the front door. "What a wonderful surprise, Matthew. You're just in time for breakfast," she greeted, her hair perfectly coiffed and her pale green dress setting off the color in her eyes. She embraced her son, kissing him lightly on his cheek as he bent obediently to receive her greeting.

"Do you miss living on the farm, Mother?" Matthew inquired as they walked to the dining room.

She turned and gave him a puzzled look. "Why are you asking about the farm?"

"I suppose because life seemed much more simple back then."

Julia patted his hand. "That's because you were a child, Matthew. Life has complexities in varying degrees throughout the years; where you live is of little importance. It's *how* you handle the difficulty that really counts. How we deal with life's problems gives evidence to our love and compassion as well as our relationship with God. Don't you think?" she asked. "Good morning, Randolph," she said as her husband entered the room.

Randolph pulled out a chair and seated himself at the table. "Good morning, my dear. Matthew, this is a pleasant surprise. To what do we owe this unexpected visit?"

"We were just discussing the complexities of life," Julia replied.

Randolph gave her a hearty laugh. "That's a rather profound subject for so early in the morning, isn't it? Is that truly why you came over here this morning, son?"

Matthew gave his father a grin as he helped himself to a piece of ham. "Not exactly. I came to tell you that Lewis Armbruster died last night—from the injuries he sustained in the fire at the Merrimack."

"Oh, Matthew, how sad. When your father returned home last night, he told me Lewis had been injured. I didn't realize it was so serious."

Matthew nodded. "Lilly is distraught. With Lewis gone, she has no family. Added to that is the fact that Lilly wasn't sure where Lewis stood before the Lord prior to his death. She's feeling an overwhelming sense of loss."

"And well she would, Matthew. I can't believe you took her back to that boardinghouse. Why didn't you bring her here to be with family?" Julia chided.

Matthew stared at his mother momentarily. "Because we are *not* Lilly's family, Mother," he said in a patronizing tone.

"Exactly!" Julia replied, giving Matthew a stern look while pointing a serving ladle in his direction. "When are you going to set aside your foolish pride and make Lilly your wife?"

"My foolish pride? It's Lilly who's filled with pride and won't admit that she's in love with me!"

"Well, of course not. She did that once and what did it reap? You went off to school and came back filled with pride and arrogance, telling her that life on a farm was a foolish dream. Then you prance about town with that uppity Boston socialite who's related to Kirk Boott holding on to your arm. And you expect Lilly to declare her love to you while you sit back and wait? Such foolishness, Matthew!"

Matthew looked toward his father, hoping for some assistance. It was obvious none would be forthcoming. Instead, while propping his chin in one hand, his father grinned and remained silent. Turning toward his mother, Matthew took a sip of coffee. "I wanted to tell Lilly of my feelings last night, but it didn't seem the appropriate time. After all, Mother, she had just lost her brother."

Julia stirred a spoonful of sugar into her cup of tea. "You always find one excuse or another to wiggle out of tying the knot," Julia scolded.

"I don't think a funeral would make a very romantic setting for a proposal," Matthew countered. "And what about the proprieties? Why, proper society would surely be of the opinion that Lilly remain out of social settings for at least six months."

"Oh, bother with proper society," Julia replied. "Sometimes love must overrule society."

Julia continued stirring and gave Matthew a stern look. "You know, Matthew, there are some distinct differences between men and women. Obviously, you don't know how women think and what makes them happy. I, on the other hand, know that a bit of good fortune is exactly what Lilly needs. I'm sure she's bereft. I can't think of anything that would cheer her more than . . ." Julia hesitated and met Matthew's gaze. "Did you say *proposal*?"

Matthew nodded and continued eating his breakfast.

"So you *are* going to ask Lilly to marry you?"

Matthew gave her a winsome smile. "Yes, Mother, if she'll have me."

Julia appeared to digest the affirmation before bounding from her chair and embracing Matthew.

Matthew pulled back. "But I intend to give her time to think this through. I don't want her to marry me simply because she's feeling her loss over Lewis. I want her to marry me because she loves me."

"Of course she loves you, darling boy," Julia said, hugging him close again. "Who wouldn't love you?"

Lilly wandered through the early June blanket of grass that covered the cemetery until she stood before the small granite stones that marked her parents' graves. Only a few scattered blades of grass could be found on the freshly turned earth that marked Lewis's final resting-place. Lilly picked up a clump of the dirt and sifted it through her fingers, watching the fine soil drop onto the grave. She would save enough money to purchase a proper marker for Lewis, she decided.

Why had God taken him? she wondered. Hadn't the death of her parents been enough without the loss of her only other relative? And Nadene's death only days after Lewis's death had been equally devastating. Lilly had wept bitter tears when the letter had come from Nadene's mother. It had simply stated Nadene had succumbed to death, no longer able to fight the debilitating illness that had caused her cough and weakness through her final years.

For a time Lilly had avoided everyone. The pain of her loss threatened to eat her alive, and dealing with her ragged emotions consumed her time. Work had become nothing more than routine, but at least it filled her days. Nothing, however, had filled the lingering void in her heart. She prayed for God to fill the emptiness, and yet she continued to yearn for something more, something that seemed unobtainable: family.

The birds chirping overhead as they built their nests served as another reminder of her isolation. "Why, Lord?" Lilly murmured. "Just when Lewis was beginning to change his ways, when we could have resolved our problems and drawn closer—why did you take him then, Lord? Why did you leave me all alone?"

Gazing heavenward, Lewis's dying words came to mind. Something about a child, a boy, in the Paddy camp, he had said. "I *do* have family," she announced to the sky. "I have a nephew—and somehow I will find him!"

"I know you think me rude, but you'll enjoy the day if you only get out and give it a try," Miss Addie stated as she fairly pushed Lilly ahead of her.

"You sound just like Matthew. This morning after church, he said that I needed to get out and enjoy myself, that I had been mourning far too long."

Addie nodded in agreement. "That young man has a good head on his shoulders. You listen to him," Addie clucked. "He's been more than patient in waiting for you."

"Lewis has only been dead three months, Miss Addie. I'd hardly say I've been in mourning too long," Lilly contradicted. "Besides, what do you mean Matthew's been patient in waiting for me?"

Addie began fussing with the bow on Lilly's dress, pulling it first in one direction and then another. "You're a young woman, Lilly, and I think mourning three months for a brother who spent his entire life tormenting you is sufficient. I know, I know," she said, holding up her hand, "you and Lewis had begun to reconcile your differences, and he was changing his ways. I commend him for his repentant behavior, Lilly. The fact remains, however, that moping around here with your chin on your chest every day is not going to bring your brother back, and it certainly doesn't help you. Now go out and have a little fun," she said, giving the bow one final twist.

Lilly reached down and embraced Addie in a hug. "Thank you."

"You are most welcome," Miss Addie replied, opening the front door. "I believe your young lady is ready," Addie said to Matthew with a sweeping gesture.

"Matthew!" Lilly gasped.

Matthew held out his arm to Lilly. "Our carriage awaits," he said with great formality, which caused all three of them to laugh. "It's good to hear you laugh again, Lilly," Matthew said as he helped her up into the carriage. "There's a place not far from Pawtucket Falls where I thought we could picnic."

"That's private property, Matthew. Are you planning to trespass?"

He gave her a smile. "I think we'll be safe," he replied as he urged the horses onward. "I've been concerned about you, Lilly. You've been so withdrawn since Lewis's death."

She nodded. "I realize that's true, Matthew. I've been feeling so alone, floundering for some sense of identity. I know it may sound feeble, but I've been dwelling on the fact that I'm the only Armbruster left. Then the other day I went to the cemetery and was praying, wondering why God had permitted Lewis to die, questioning why I had to be completely alone, without family. It all seemed too unfair. I didn't want to be alone."

Matthew pulled the carriage to a halt. "Good! I'm glad to hear you don't want to be alone, because that's what I want to discuss with you," Matthew replied as he helped her down and retrieved the picnic basket.

"Really? Well, let me tell you what God revealed to me the other day," she said, her words gushing forth. "I'm not alone. I have a nephew, Lewis's child. I want to find him, Matthew. I know you asked a few questions at the Acre shortly after Lewis died, but you didn't *really* look for the child. I want to find the boy. He's an Armbruster. Will you help me find him?"

Matthew placed a cloth on the ground and began to spread out their picnic luncheon. "Sit down," he said, patting the blanket and waiting until she seated herself. "I would be willing to help you find the child if you would agree to help me in return," he said. "Is that something you think you could agree to?"

Lilly gave him a quizzical look. "I can't imagine how I could possibly help you with anything, but I promise to do my very best."

Matthew nodded and slowly pulled a small box from the inside pocket of his coat. He carefully arched his hand over the box, and although Lilly tried her best, she was unable to peek around his fingers.

Matthew gave her a solemn look. "Now, remember what you've promised," he said with finality.

Lilly was beginning to question the propriety of her decision. Surely Matthew wouldn't ask her to do anything inappropriate, would he? "I remember," she meekly answered.

Matthew handed the box to Lilly. Nestled inside was a beautiful sapphire ring. "This ring once belonged to my grandmother," he said.

"It's beautiful," Lilly replied, handing it back to him.

He smiled. "I'm pleased you like it, because my grandmother gave me the ring so that I could one day give it to my wife, Lilly."

It took a moment before she understood the full impact of what Matthew was saying. She gazed at him in disbelief. "Are you—do you—I mean . . ." she stammered.

"Yes, Lilly, I'm asking you to marry me. I want you to become my wife."

Tears streamed down Lilly's cheeks. Matthew wanted her to be his wife. She was going to belong to someone—have a family.

Matthew softly brushed away her tears. "I know I can't make up for all you've lost, but I'm determined that together we can create an even better life. It won't replace your old family, and that's not what I want to do. You need to keep your memories. But I want to make you happy. I want to build new memories with you, Lilly. I want you to be my wife." He paused and gave her a look so full of love and longing that Lilly thought her heart would burst. "I love you, Lilly. I've never stopped loving you."

"Oh, and I love you, Matthew. I did you wrong by blaming you for everything that happened here in Lowell. I wanted so much for life . . . for us, to go on as it had always been. It was safe and I was happy."

"I want to make you happy again. Will you marry me?" He paused and gave her a roguish grin. "Don't forget your promise that you'd do anything I asked."

Wiping away a stray tear, Lilly permitted Matthew to slip the ring on her finger. "It would make me very proud to be your wife, Matthew," she said, gazing down at the ring. Tears of joy spilled over and trickled down her cheeks. "Yes, yes, I'll marry you," she said, lifting her lips to accept his kiss.

"I'm not sure how I'm going to hide my ring," Lilly said, gazing down at the sparkling stone as they arrived at the boardinghouse.

Matthew gave her a look of surprise as he pulled the horses to a halt. "Why would you want to do that?"

Lilly took hold of Matthew's hand as he helped her out of the buggy. "I thought you would want your parents to know our plans first—before I told Miss Addie or any of the girls here at the boardinghouse."

Matthew pulled her into an embrace. "My mother won't care who knows first, so long as I've asked you to marry me and you've accepted," he said, leaning down and kissing her lightly on the lips. He pulled away and added, "She's been quite enthusiastic about this for some time." He kissed her a little longer this time, then pulled away again to say, "I must say, I'm getting quite enthusiastic about the idea myself." This time he kissed her quite soundly.

Lilly giggled and melted into his arms, the warmth of Matthew's lips against her own and his strong arms surrounding her enchanting. But then she remembered herself and quickly pulled away. "Miss Mintie is probably hiding behind her curtains watching every move we make," Lilly whispered. "And I have no desire to be the talk of the town."

Matthew tilted his head back and laughed, an enthusiastic, resonant chuckle. "Well, I hope Mintie Beecher gets her eyes full!" he said as he pulled Lilly close for another sweet, lingering kiss.

~ 35 ~

Didn't I tell you you'd be married before a year was out?" Addie teased as she helped to adjust Lilly's wedding veil.

"Yes, you did, but it's actually been a few days beyond a year," Lilly replied.

Addie laughed. Standing on tiptoe she checked the top of the veil. "Well, I'll not begrudge you a few days over. The important thing is that you're marrying your true love." She stepped back and shook her head. "And aren't you the picture of perfection?"

Lilly gazed at her reflection in the mirror and could scarcely believe the image she found there. "I look so . . . so . . ."

"Beautiful!" Addie declared.

Lilly studied the gown as she turned first one direction and then the other. The layered muslin rippled gently. She liked the way the pleated bodice had been trimmed with white satin ribbon. "I'm just amazed at the workmanship of this gown. Mrs. Cheever arranged to have it created for me, and I simply can't imagine what it must have cost her."

"That's unimportant," Addie told her. "She knows the worth of the woman inside the gown. That will always be much more important." She smiled and put one more pin in Lilly's upswept hair. "There, now that should hold."

Miss Addie had given her the lace piece that acted as her veil. "This lace is exquisite. Oh, Miss Addie, I'm so happy I could cry."

"Well, they say if you don't cry on your wedding day, you'll cry for the rest of the marriage. But I'm not of a mind to believe it. I'd refrain from crying," Addie admonished. "You don't want to go to your bridegroom with puffy red eyes."

"I can't believe I'm actually marrying Matthew. It seems like a long-forgotten dream, and now it's coming true," Lilly declared, turning to Addie. "You've been such a dear friend throughout this ordeal. I'm so blessed to have your friendship. I hope you know you'll be welcomed in our home anytime."

"Oh, my dear, I'm the one who has been blessed. You taught me to cook and made my boardinghouse one of the most sought after in all of Lowell. I'll have no trouble filling your vacancy, but I'll miss your company more than I can say."

"Then we'll have to make certain we share tea at least once—no, two times a week," Lilly declared. "No matter what, we mustn't lose touch or let time separate us."

"Agreed," Addie said as though making an earnest pledge.

With Addie and John to stand with them, Matthew and Lilly were joined in marriage in a quiet ceremony at St. Anne's. Lilly listened to the solemn tones of the minister and felt Matthew's reassuring touch. With her friends from the mills present to witness their vows, Lilly felt quite blessed and loved. She knew her parents would have smiled upon the union and felt confident in the knowledge that she was doing the right thing.

A noise from the congregation brought Lilly out of her reflective thoughts. She glanced over her shoulder to find Julia Cheever sobbing into a lace-edged handkerchief. Had she not known better, Lilly would have fretted that the woman was unhappy. Matthew's father smiled reassuringly at Lilly and put his arm around his wife in a loving manner. Lilly smiled and returned her attention to the man at her side. If he were half as compassionate as his father, then Lilly knew he would be a prize.

The minister issued a series of commands regarding marriage, prayed a long, intense prayer over the union, then pronounced them man and wife. In a matter of moments the ceremony was over and she was Mrs. Matthew Cheever.

Matthew kissed her soundly but didn't linger. He winked at her as they pulled away. He whispered, "I'll make up for that later."

Lilly felt her cheeks flush. In the months that had passed since her acceptance of Matthew's proposal, she had known some very long, lingering kisses. Matthew wouldn't be obliged to make up for anything, but Lilly rather hoped he would try.

The congregation hurried from the church and arranged themselves to greet the couple. Lilly watched as Lawrence Gault guided Miss Mintie from the sanctuary. The woman was actually wearing a gown of powder blue with black trim. The color alone took years from Miss Mintie's face and frame, but her smile accomplished even more. And Lilly couldn't be sure, but she thought perhaps Miss Mintie had added little wispy bangs to fall upon her forehead. She giggled at the thought of how decadent Miss Mintie must have felt in doing such a thing. Lilly strained to get a better glimpse, but the bonnet Miss Mintie wore was rather wide brimmed.

"Are you ready?" Matthew questioned, pulling Lilly possessively to his side.

"Absolutely."

They moved down the aisle of the church and out the door.

"Here they are!"

A rain of rice came down upon them as Matthew and Lilly moved toward their awaiting carriage. "I'll soon have us away from here," Matthew said, taking up the reins.

Lilly waved behind her. "Don't forget, they're all coming to the boarding-house for the reception. We have to be there for that."

"Says who?" he questioned as he gave the reins a flick of his wrist. The horses, a matched pair of black geldings that were a gift from his father, stepped into motion.

"Matthew, they'll be expecting us. We can hardly just drive about Lowell hoping they'll not notice we're missing," Lilly said, laughing.

The day had turned out to be quite beautiful, with just a hint of fall crispness to the air. Lilly knew that soon the leaves on the trees would change and the countryside would be a riot of color. She had come full circle. Only a year ago, as Miss Addie had pointed out, she had been bitter and angry, ready to do harm to those who supported the mills.

The only explanation was that God had changed her heart. She had not come willingly into His submission—not at first. She remembered her anger and cringed inwardly. Such hatred could never have been used to serve a God of love and justice.

Lilly had been so deep in thought that she didn't realize Matthew had stopped the carriage. She looked up to find him watching her, one brow raised ever so slightly as if to try to read her mind.

"You looked almost sad," he said softly. "You aren't regretting your decision already, are you?"

Lilly smiled and shook her head. "No. I could never regret you."

"You did at one time. I remember feeling quite overwhelmed by the regret and anger you hurled my way."

"I know and I'm sorry."

He pulled her into his arms. "I know that, silly. I know, too, that your heart has changed. You're not the same woman you were a year ago. I like the soft, sweet creature who has come to take her place."

He lowered his mouth to hers, his lips warm and tender. Lilly felt her breath catch in her throat as he tilted her head to better meet his kiss. His touch did strange things to her, and Lilly marveled at the sensation that spread out from her stomach and seemed to warm her entire body.

"I'm so happy you're finally mine," he murmured as he pulled away ever so slightly. He kissed her nose and cheeks, then recaptured her lips.

Lilly melted against him, completely forgetting where they were. The rest of the world no longer existed. It was just the two of them together—alone.

Abruptly, Matthew pulled away and tugged down his top hat. "I think we'd better get to the boardinghouse now, or I might be inclined to forget it altogether."

"Oh, Matthew. You are such a tease."

He looked at her with a gaze that revealed there was little teasing in his words. Lilly found herself caught up for a moment, then licked her lips and nodded. "Yes, we'd better go now."

Matthew turned the horses and directed them toward town. "I hope you know I'm very serious about doing whatever is necessary to find Lewis's son. I'm only sorry we haven't already accomplished the deed. There simply isn't much in the way of evidence to lead us."

Lilly felt tears come to her eyes. "Thank you so much for caring about the boy. I know it won't prove easy to locate him, or we'd have already found him."

"But we will find him. You mark my words. And when we find him, we'll raise him as our own son."

"Perhaps one day we'll have our own son, as well." She felt her cheeks warm at the thought of bearing Matthew a child.

Matthew looked at her and laughed. "Indeed, Mrs. Cheever. In fact, I'd like at least a dozen."

Lilly's mouth dropped open. Matthew roared with laughter and pulled her close.

"I didn't mean we had to have them all at once. One a year will be just fine."

Lilly picked up easily on his playful spirit. "Just for that, maybe I'll only give you daughters."

Matthew looked at her for a moment, then shrugged casually. "As long as they're as beautiful and smart as their mother, I suppose I can bear it. Although when they're of an age to court, I'll be hard-pressed to let them out of the house. I think we should make a rule that our daughters will not be allowed to take a suitor until they're . . . umm . . . say, thirty years of age."

"I'm sure they'll have something to say about that," Lilly replied. "Besides, I'm just twenty-one, and look at the plans you have for me."

Matthew nodded. "Exactly my point." He grinned wickedly. "I know exactly what I have planned for you, Mrs. Cheever."

Lilly grew flushed again and buried her head against Matthew's shoulder. What a wonderful, marvelous wedding day. What a loving and perfect spouse. She couldn't ask for anything more. She stood in awe of the grace and mercy God had extended to her and relished the blessings that had come in the place of what she truly deserved.

As they rounded the corner and headed toward Jackson Street, Lilly smiled. She had once dreaded the very sight of the mills. Now they didn't hold such a threat against her. The past was laid to rest, sleeping neatly in a bed of what might have been. The future, however, rose up before them, and like a weaver to the loom, they would yet choose to make the patterns of what would be. But no matter what might come, Lilly knew with great confidence that God would guide those choices—not toward a road of revenge and destruction but rather to a path that would lead them into hope and love. A path that would draw them closer to Him and to each other.

A
FRAGILE
DESIGN

~❧ 1 ❧~

Arabella Newberry raced through the woods, the fallen leaves crunching beneath her feet and the echo of her footsteps beating the message *Hur-ry, Hur-ry, Hur-ry*. Darting through the timbers, she hastened by a grove of rock maples and onward toward the sheltering heavy-needled pines. Her breath came hard as she edged her agile body between two of the prickly green trees, the needles now poking her arms as they punctured her gray woolen cloak. She forced herself to breathe more easily, then leaned forward and listened. All was quiet, save the occasional chattering of a squirrel or the scampering feet of a frightened rabbit.

Without warning, a hand clamped around her arm and pulled her from the bristly nest. A sick feeling churned in her belly as she twisted to free her arm.

"You're late, Bella!" Jesse Harwood stood beside her, his cloudy gray eyes filled with recrimination.

She expelled a ragged breath. "Only a few minutes. I couldn't manage to get away from Sister Mercy. She asked me to assist her with one of the children."

Jesse's look softened and he released her arm. "I'm sorry. I was beginning to fear you weren't coming. I think I've worked out a plan for us."

Wisps of straight blond hair had escaped from under her palm-leaf bonnet. She automatically reached to tuck them out of view before giving Jesse a tentative smile. "I'm listening, but we must hurry before I'm missed."

"We'll leave tomorrow night, after the others have gone to sleep. We can meet right here and make our way toward Concord under cover of darkness. If we can't find your relatives in Concord, we'll continue on to Lowell. Pack only as much as you'll be able to comfortably carry, and I'll do the same. Be sure to bring some food."

"What if I awaken one of the Sisters as I'm preparing to leave?"

Jesse's eyes flashed with concern for a moment. "Say you're ill and can't sleep—that you don't want to bother the rest of the Sisters and you're going to make some tea and sit up for a while."

Bella shook her head back and forth. "But that would be a lie, Jesse. I can't lie to one of the Sisters."

Jesse gave a quiet chuckle. "We lie to the Sisters and Brothers every day when we fail to tell them of our love for each other."

Her brow furrowed at his reply. "Jesse, I'm not sure what I feel is the kind of love that need be confessed to the Society. If we merely love each other as brother and sister, we've done nothing wrong."

Jesse took her hand and looked deep into her eyes. "The love I feel for you is one that requires confession, Bella. And I hope the love you feel for me is much different from what you feel for Brother Ernest or Brother Justice— or any of the other brothers, for that matter."

"You know I care for you more than the other brothers, Jesse. But we have little knowledge upon which to base the love between man and woman. I feel no guilt in not confessing our friendship, but I would feel guilt if I openly lied to one of the Sisters."

Smiling, Jesse continued to hold her hand. "You'll soon realize that what you feel for me is love—the love that binds husband and wife together for a lifetime. If you're concerned about lying to the Sisters, I suppose we'd best pray that they remain sound asleep." He looked out into the quiet. "We should return soon or someone will miss us. You go first, and I'll follow in just a bit. Until tomorrow night," he said, pulling her hand to his lips and placing a kiss upon her palm.

Bella's face grew warm at Jesse's boldness. She quickly withdrew her hand and rushed back down the path. Slowing as she reached the children's dormitory, Bella removed her cape and attempted to casually walk toward the east door, which led to the side that was occupied by the young girls. Opening the door as quietly as possible, Bella made her way into the large room where the children were napping.

Daughtie Winfield glanced toward Bella as she slipped into the room. "Was I missed?" Bella inquired as she brushed a stray wisp of blond hair under her cap.

"No, but I was fearful for a short time. Sister Minerva walked with me until we reached the entrance of the dormitory. Fortunately Eldress Phoebe summoned her away before she had opportunity to inquire of your whereabouts. Did you meet Jesse?"

Bella nodded as she lifted one of the toddlers to her lap. "We're leaving tomorrow night, so this will be our last opportunity to visit, Daughtie. I transfer to the kitchen tomorrow. I'm sorry we'll not be together on my final day, but if we must be apart, I'm pleased I'll have some time with Sister Mercy before my departure."

Daughtie began to wring her hands, a nervous habit that brought constant remonstration from the older Sisters. "Are you sure you won't reconsider, Bella? Do you understand that you are leaving the safety of the Family? Won't you miss your Shaker Brothers and Sisters?"

"I'll miss you, Daughtie—and Sister Mercy and the children, of course."

"And your father?" Daughtie ventured.

"My father? You forget, Daughtie. Among the Shakers, I have no earthly father. Besides, Brother Franklin wishes his life to be separated from mine. How can I miss something I haven't had since my father—excuse me, Brother Franklin—convinced my mother four years ago to join the United Society of Believers in Christ's Second Appearing?"

"He cares for you, Bella. It's the rules of the Society that forbid him to show his affections," Daughtie insisted.

Bella stared out the window. The naked trees surrounding the house were forming small buds, awaiting the touch of a springtime sun before finally bursting into fragrant blooms. Like the trees, Bella waited. She, too, needed warmth before she could fully blossom, the warmth of knowing she was loved by another. The child on her lap snuggled closer. Bella turned and looked at Daughtie. "If my father cares for me, why did he push me away when I went to him seeking comfort after my mother's death? What kind of father does such a thing to his child? I don't believe the Shakers have correctly interpreted God's plan for our lives, and I can't remain among people that force parents to separate and withhold love from their own children."

"But your parents knew the rules when they signed the covenant—and so did you, Bella," Daughtie added hesitantly.

"I signed because I knew not doing so would cause a further breach between my father and me. Besides, Daughtie, what was I to do? What choices did I have at such a young age? But now I do have a choice, and I choose the world over the Shakers. You can come with us, Daughtie. I know that Jesse wouldn't mind, and you have no reason to stay here." Bella lifted the sleeping child and placed her in bed. She turned toward her friend with a surge of excitement. Why hadn't she thought of inviting Daughtie before this moment? "Say that you'll come, Daughtie," Bella pleaded.

Daughtie's mouth went slack as she gazed at Bella, who had now returned to the rocking chair. "You're running off to marry Jesse. Where do I fit into that arrangement?"

"I'm not running off to marry Jesse. I'm not even sure what love for a man is supposed to feel like. I'm leaving this place with Jesse because he knows the way to Concord and Lowell. It will be safer traveling with Jesse, and he's determined to leave the Society. I've not pledged my love or my hand to Jesse. The world has so much to offer, Daughtie. I know you've been here among the Believers since you were a tiny child, but there's more to life than this protected existence. Don't you ever long to know more about the lives of the people who come here on Sundays to observe our worship service? Don't you want to see what lies beyond this acreage?"

Daughtie was thoughtful for several minutes, obviously weighing her friend's words. "I can't say that I haven't felt a tinge of envy since you first told me that you were planning to leave."

Bella clapped her hands together and leaned forward in her chair, hoping to draw her friend into their scheme. "There's no need to be frightened. You know the Believers will welcome you back if you decide against the world."

Daughtie nodded. "Yes, but I'd certainly never be considered faithful enough to become an Eldress if I left and then later returned."

"Is becoming an Eldress what you aspire to, Daughtie? For if that is your heart's desire, I'll say no more. But if you're merely using the hope of achieving religious rank as an excuse because you fear any change in your life, then I'd say, 'Be brave, dear friend.' The three of us will learn how to survive in this new life. There's much I remember from my early years living in the world. And Jesse knows much more about the outside world than I do. With his weekly visits into town to sell and barter goods with Brother Justice, he knows how to talk and act among the world's people. He assures me we'll be able to work and support ourselves. Will you at least consider going? You have until tomorrow night."

Daughtie gave Bella a timid smile but said nothing.

"Why don't we both agree to pray about the decision to leave and see what happens tomorrow night? Would you agree to do that, Daughtie?"

Her friend gave Bella an enthusiastic nod. "Yes, Bella. And if I believe that God is leading me to leave, I'll accompany you and Jesse."

Slumber came in short spurts throughout the night, and when the first bell rang at four-thirty the next morning, Bella was already awake. She sat up and swung her legs around until her feet touched the pine floorboards. After waiting for Sister Mercy to finish, she padded across the floor and took her turn at the washstand. The familiar waking sounds of muffled voices and quiet footsteps could be heard next door and across the hall as members of the Society prepared for the day. Bella dried her face and hands, then exchanged her loose cotton nightwear for a plain blue cotton and worsted gown. She fastened the dress and then with long, even strokes, brushed her long ash-blond hair before deftly twisting it into a knot and tucking it under her white starched cap. After carefully fastening a kerchief across the bodice of her dress, Bella pulled back the bedcovers, neatly folded them over the foot of her bed, and went about her other chores until her sheets were properly aired.

"You appear tired this morning," Sister Mercy commented as she patted Bella's shoulder. "Didn't you sleep well?"

Bella gave the older woman a smile. "I'm fine, Sister Mercy. And I'm looking forward to helping you with the pies later today."

"And I'm looking forward to your company, also," Sister Mercy replied while pouring additional oil into one of the lamps. "We're low on oil. Would you kindly remind me to ask the Deaconesses for more?"

Bella nodded her agreement as she quickly ran a cloth over the windowsills and built-in drawers. The second bell rang, and the Brothers could be heard leaving their rooms and walking down the steps as they headed off toward the barn. Without a word, Bella, Daughtie, and two other Sisters moved across the hall to clean the rooms of the Brethren before returning to complete their mending.

Absently retrieving a sock from the willow basket by her chair, Bella pushed her needle in and out, darning over the spot until the hole finally disappeared. She glanced over at Daughtie and wondered if her friend had made a decision. This would be the last morning Bella would sit in these familiar surroundings mending socks and stitching initials onto clothing—of that, she was certain.

The breakfast bell sounded, breaking Bella's reverie and the early morning silence. She moved along with the rest of the Sisters as they joined the Brethren in the hallway and made their way down the separate stairways. The two groups converged in the rectangular dining hall that was now filled with long trestle tables laden with heaping platters of sausage, biscuits, and eggs, and gravy boats filled to the brim. They filled their plates and ate in silence, then rose to leave.

"Any decision yet?" Bella questioned in a hushed tone.

Daughtie shook her head. "I'm still praying, but I do need to talk to you."

Bella smiled broadly and gave her friend's hand a quick squeeze. "I'll see if Sister Mercy will permit me to come to the children's dormitory after we've set the pies to bake. Be thinking about what you want to take with you."

Daughtie pulled Bella closer. "I haven't yet agreed that I'm going."

"I know, but it's best to be prepared in case you do decide to come along. I must hurry to the kitchen. Sister Mercy is expecting me. Keep praying, Daughtie, and I'll see you later this morning."

Bella rushed down the path between the laundry and syrup shop, skidding to a halt as she entered the kitchen.

Sister Mercy gave her an apple-cheeked smile. "You best not let Eldress Phoebe see you running about with your cap askew."

Bella grinned as she adjusted her cap, then grabbed a knife and began paring apples while Sister Mercy mixed enough dough for thirty pies. "I have a favor to beg of you, Sister Mercy," Bella said.

The rotund sister chuckled while setting her rolling pin to the stiff pie dough. "And what good deed might you need of me?"

Bella continued peeling. "I need a few minutes to talk with Daughtie.

Could I take a few minutes later this morning to visit her at the children's dormitory?"

Sister Mercy wiped her flour-covered hands on the large white apron that protected her woolen dress. "I think I can accommodate that request," she replied with a smile. "You can go see her before the dinner bell rings."

"Thank you," she said to the Sister as she whispered more words of thanks upward.

The pile of apples in the barrel seemed unending. Bella continued to work in silence, attempting to pray as her knife skimmed across the apples, peeling away the red and gold covering to reveal the white fleshy fruit. Each of her supplications was quickly interrupted by thoughts of her father and Jesse, which were occasionally interspersed with a warm recollection of her mother. Jesse seemed so sure of himself and their plan to leave. She didn't doubt the decision to leave; however, she did doubt that she would have the feelings of love for Jesse that he so desired. With love comes trust, and trusting was a dangerous thing. Her mother had blindly trusted her father, and he had ended their marriage by joining the Society against her mother's wishes. Bella was certain her mother had died of a broken heart. And she didn't plan to follow in her mother's footsteps.

"You can go visit Daughtie," Sister Mercy said, releasing Bella from the kitchen. "Be sure you're back here in fifteen minutes, or you'll be late to dinner and I'll have Eldress Phoebe looking to me for answers regarding your whereabouts," she cautioned.

"I'll be on time," Bella promised as she hurried out the door. With her heart pounding, she breathlessly hurried down the path and entered the dormitory. "I have only a few minutes, Daughtie. What do you need to talk about?"

Without waiting for an answer, Bella plopped down in a rocking chair and beckoned one of the children closer. Mary Beth, a chubby two-year-old, waddled across the room and buried her face deep in Bella's skirt. Bella reached down and lifted the plump toddler onto her lap. Giving Mary Beth's cheek a fleeting kiss, Bella quickly turned her attention to the little girl's neck, nuzzling until Mary Beth laughed in delight. The high-pitched laughter brought several other children running, each one obviously eager to become a part of the frivolity. Bella held Mary Beth close to her chest as she leaned down to tickle the fair-haired Genevieve and dark-eyed Martha. "I shall dearly miss these children," Bella lamented. "Save Sister Mercy, most of the Sisters expect them to act like miniature adults. I pray once we are gone they will appoint several young replacements to take our positions with the children. They don't need any more dour faces peering down upon them."

"Who would they appoint? You know there are only a few other girls our age, Bella, and they already take their turns with the children. With the rotation of work among the Sisters, our leaving assures the children additional hours with pinched-faced sisters who would much rather spend their time mending and weaving than chasing after these children. Perhaps we should remain—for the children's sake," Daughtie ventured.

Bella lightly rested her chin atop Mary Beth's head, the child's downy soft hair tickling Bella's face. "You know how much I love the children, Daughtie. And I already know that once I'm gone I shall long to cuddle them in my arms. However, should I remain in this place, I would evolve into one of those pinched-faced sisters we've been speaking of. More importantly, it would be dishonest for me to indoctrinate these children with beliefs I do not embrace and accept as true."

Daughtie's lips curved into a tiny smile. "I know, but if I can convince you to stay, I won't be forced to make a decision. I suppose I'm merely attempting to make life easier on myself."

Bella shifted Mary Beth's weight on her lap. Daughtie's comment brought Bella's thoughts back to her earlier question. "I didn't give you a chance to answer me when I first arrived. What is it you need to discuss with me?"

Daughtie hesitated momentarily. "I was thinking, Bella. Why don't we just tell the Family that we've chosen to leave the Society? It makes more sense—we'd be given funds to cover our journey, and one of the Brothers would take us to board a coach. We could pack our belongings and leave in an honorable fashion rather than sneaking off like thieves in the—"

"I can't do that," Bella interrupted. "I know what you say is true, but the Ministry would bring Brother Franklin to talk to me. If they knew I was planning to leave, they'd suddenly believe it permissible to use my birth father to try to dissuade me. I will not argue my decision with him. Besides, if they knew Jesse was going, they'd accuse us of wrongdoing. And, Daughtie, I pledge to you that there has been nothing inappropriate between us. Besides, the Ministry would not believe us—they'd shame us and encourage us to confess and repent before the Believers. I'll not take their money, and I'll not confess or repent to something I've not done. Please, Daughtie, don't base your decision upon my willingness to seek approval from the Ministry."

Daughtie seated herself on one of the straight-backed wooden chairs and stared at her friend. "I understand, but you must admit it makes more sense to leave with money."

"You're right. It would be easier to have their help, but I'm unwilling to pay the price they'd demand for a few coins and a ride to the stagecoach. It's almost dinnertime, and I promised Sister Mercy I wouldn't be late. We can talk more on the way to meeting tonight," Bella promised as she leaned down and gave her friend a quick hug. She ought not take the time, but she knew she might never see these children again. Kneeling down, she held her arms wide and pulled each child into a warm embrace before leaving the room.

A tear trickled down her cheek as Bella glanced toward the Sisters' Weaving Shop. She exited the dormitory and hurried back toward the Dwelling House. Rounding a turn in the path, she looked up toward the bell, hoping it wouldn't sound until she had safely returned to the kitchen. If detected, it was certain one of the Sisters would question why she was outdoors rather than baking pies. Worse yet, she didn't want to cause a problem for Sister Mercy, whose judgment in permitting such a visit between the young Sisters would be closely scrutinized by the Ministry.

"Just in time!" Sister Mercy exclaimed as the bell began to toll.

Bella met the older Sister's smiling gaze, a keen sense of melancholy suddenly assaulting her senses. The time when she would flee Canterbury was quickly approaching. The thought of never again seeing Sister Mercy, coupled with her good-byes to the tiny children she had helped care for over the past several years, was more distressing than she had imagined.

"Something is bothering you, child. I can always tell when you're troubled. You know you can talk to me, don't you? I love you like you're my own. Many's the time Eldress Phoebe has accused me of caring too much about you."

Bella struggled to hold back her tears. "And what did you tell Eldress Phoebe when she made her accusations?"

"Same thing I'd tell her right here and now if she were to ask me again: It's impossible to love or care too much for a child. We all need as much love as we can get," Sister Mercy proclaimed, her cheeks dimpling as she gave a wide smile.

"That's certainly true. You're a wise woman, Sister Mercy. Had it not been for your love, prayers, and consolation, I don't know how I would have survived those terrible weeks after my mother died. You know you'll always be very special to me, don't you?" Bella asked, unable to hold her tears in check.

Sister Mercy pulled Bella into a warm embrace and lovingly patted her back as if she were a small child. "There, there," she comforted. "Tell me what's caused you such misery. If you'll only let me, surely I can help."

Knowing she must deceive dear Sister Mercy caused Bella further sorrow, yet she could not confide in the woman. Bella knew Sister Mercy would never break a confidence. It was for that very reason Bella would not take the older woman into her confidence. The Elders would surely question Sister Mercy once they discovered Bella's disappearance. The older woman's allegiance to Bella would become grounds for chastisement by the Elders, and poor Sister Mercy's loyalty to a wayward Sister would certainly become the subject of a sermon. Bella could not abide being the cause of such embarrassment for the woman she loved so dearly.

"It's nothing, Sister Mercy. Merely a bout of melancholy," Bella finally replied.

Sister Mercy hesitated a moment. "If you're certain there's nothing I can do, then we'd best hurry along. If we're late, Eldress Phoebe will expect a confession for our tardiness. But just remember, Bella, I'm always here should you need me, and you are always in my prayers."

Bella swallowed the lump that had risen in her throat and nodded. "Yes, I'll remember. I could never forget anything about you, Sister Mercy."

The older woman gave her a strange look, almost as though she realized something was amiss, but before Sister Mercy could question her further, Bella gave the older woman a bright smile and said, "We've made it just in time. Eldress Phoebe will have nothing to complain of this noonday."

～ 2 ～

Shh!" Bella's warning hissed through the night air as she turned to face Daughtie. There was a slight chill to the moonlit evening, and Bella pulled her cloak more tightly around her shoulders before readjusting her satchel. She waved her friend onward toward the stand of pines—toward Jesse and their new life among the outsiders.

"Can we talk now?" Daughtie whispered. "I don't think anyone can hear us this far from the Dwelling House."

Bella glanced around the area. "Jesse!" she called. "Are you here?"

They waited in silence. "I don't think he's here," Daughtie offered. "What time was he supposed to meet us?"

"We didn't set a specific time. There was no way to guarantee when the others would be asleep. Apparently the Brothers don't go to sleep as early as the Sisters," Bella replied. "He'll be here soon."

Slowly, minute by minute, the night wore on. "I don't think he's coming, Bella. Let's go back. If we're careful, we can return to the Dwelling House and be back in bed before anyone misses us."

"No! I'm not going back. If Jesse doesn't arrive shortly, we'll go on without him."

A look of fear crossed Daughtie's face. "We can't go without Jesse to lead us. What are you thinking, Bella?"

"It seems I'm always surrounded by men who convince me to trust them and then disappoint me—first my father and now Jesse. But that doesn't change my decision to leave. We merely need to follow the road south until we reach Concord. I copied my aunt's address from my father's journal. I don't know if she still lives in Concord, but we can at least attempt to locate her. I'm sure she'd give us shelter." She reached out and grasped Daughtie's hand. "I want you to go with me, but if you must return, I'll not hold it against you, dear friend. I know you're frightened."

"No. I'll not leave you here to go on alone, Bella, but I believe that returning to the Family is the prudent thing to do. We could return and find out what's happened to Jesse. There's nothing to prevent us from leaving tomorrow or next week, is there?" Daughtie asked, her question filled with the same hope that sparkled from her eyes in the moonlit night.

The hood of Bella's cape fell back as she vigorously shook her head back and forth. "We're ready now. Either Jesse has decided he's not going or he's already left for Concord, thinking we weren't coming. Perhaps he expected us earlier than we arrived and, like us, decided it was best to go on alone."

Daughtie was silent for a moment. "If you're sure we can find Concord, I suppose we'd best be on our way. The longer we wait, the greater the possibility of being discovered."

Bella nodded and took the lead, hoping she could remember all that Jesse had told her regarding the route they would follow. "As soon as we find the road to Concord, we'll rest for the night. Jesse mentioned highwaymen can sometimes be lurking about, waiting for unsuspecting travelers," she advised.

She carefully chose each turn of the path until they finally reached the main road that would lead them to Concord. "I'm certain this is the road we'll need to follow come morning," she told Daughtie. Pointing toward a stand of pines, she smiled broadly and grabbed Daughtie's hand. "There's a place over there where we'll be out of sight and sheltered for the remainder of the night."

The heat of the sun as it rose into the eastern sky began to warm their bodies as the girls arose the next morning. Nestled among the small clump of trees, Bella discovered a fallen log and pulled it in front of two maples. "There! I've formed two chairs for us, Daughtie. We can sit on the log and lean against the trees and rest our backs," she said, offering the loaf of rye bread and a wedge of yellow cheese to her friend.

Daughtie tore a piece of bread from the loaf. "Nothing ever tasted so good. I'm famished."

Bella nodded as she stuffed a piece of bread into her mouth. "If we keep a steady pace, I think we can reach Concord in three or four hours and then get directions to Lowell."

"Lowell? I thought we were going to stay with your relatives in Concord."

Bella nodded her head in rhythm with her chewing and then swallowed hard. "I've been thinking about that. I doubt we'll find them. Jesse and I had planned to go on to Lowell if we didn't locate my aunt and uncle."

Daughtie's eyebrows raised in obvious concern. "I certainly think we should try to find them, Bella. Isn't it a long way to Lowell? Do you know anyone there who can help us?"

Bella gave her friend a smile that she hoped was reassuring. "No, I don't know anyone in Lowell, but it's not so far that we can't make it with proper directions."

"Then why not stay in Concord? At least for a short time?"

Bella quickly packed the leftover bread and cheese into her satchel and stood up. "Do you remember the Family discussing the new textile mills in Lowell? There's work for girls our age. You may recall Mary Wiseman that wintered with us at the Village last year."

Daughtie's brows furrowed. "I vaguely remember her, but we never talked. Wasn't she the girl who got in trouble for talking during meals on several occasions?"

Bella nodded in agreement. "Yes, that's Mary. She never did learn to remain silent at the proper times. Anyway, she told me they pay good wages in the mills. We'll be able to support ourselves, but in Concord we'd be fortunate if we found employment as housekeepers or teachers. Lowell is our best choice, Daughtie."

"Unless we find your relatives," Daughtie added.

Leaving their makeshift dining room, the girls walked back toward the road. "Even if we find them, we'll have to find work, and I doubt we'll find anything in Concord that will pay the wages Mary received in Lowell."

"If life was so good in Lowell, why did Mary find it necessary to live off the Shakers all winter? She should have had ample money to support herself if she was receiving those fine wages you speak of."

Bella nodded at her friend. "Yes, one would think so, but Mary spent her money on every new fashion and whimsy her heart desired. She spent her money as quickly as she made it. Then, when she was least prepared for losing her employment, she became ill. With no money and unable to work, she made her way to the Family. The Ministry realized she was a bread-and-butter Shaker and would remain only until she was once again able to make her way in the world. Mary never did indicate any desire to become a Believer."

"I just think it might be safer to at least try and find your aunt."

Bella could hear the worry in Daughtie's tone. "If it makes you feel better, we'll do exactly that. It couldn't hurt to rest up and have a good meal."

The sound of approaching horses could be heard in the distance. Bella grabbed Daughtie's hand, pulling her behind a stand of forsythia bushes. "Keep down!" Bella warned.

Daughtie crouched beside Bella until the last rider had passed. "Why are we hiding?" she asked as they stood.

"The Brethren may be looking for us," Bella replied, surprised by her friend's question.

"They won't come after us—you left a letter for your father saying you were leaving. And you know the Believers have no respect for those who run off in the night. They've probably bid us a 'fare thee well and good riddance.' "

"I suppose you're right, but I'd rather err on the side of caution. Besides, you never know what kind of highway bandit or scoundrel might be on the road."

Daughtie giggled. "Well, a bandit would be sorely disappointed if he sought to enrich himself with our meager belongings."

Bella joined in her laughter, trudging onward, the dust clinging to their cloaks and shoes. Three and a half hours later they rounded a bend in the road. "Look, Daughtie! We've finally reached Concord," Bella exclaimed, pointing to the south.

"And none too soon. My shoes are pinching. I'm sure I'll have blisters come morning."

The girls moved with renewed vigor, the thought of a warm meal and soft bed beckoning them onward.

Bella pulled the folded scrap of paper containing her aunt's address from the inner pocket of her cloak. "We'll stop and ask someone directions."

A kind middle-aged woman directed them to the corner of Franklin and Ridge Streets, telling the girls to remain on Franklin until they reached the fourth house from the corner.

"There it is," Bella announced. "Let's see if my aunt and uncle are living here," she said, walking up the wooden steps to the small front porch. Bella knocked on the weatherworn door.

A large woman with a strange accent opened the door. "They live up there," she said while pointing to the stairs. "Room three. Go on," she encouraged, waving her hand toward the stairway.

Bella led the way up the dark stairway. The odor of strange-smelling foods, mixed with the stench of unwashed bodies, caused Bella to immediately long for a breath of fresh air. Instead, she held a kerchief to her nose as she knocked on the door of room three.

The gaunt stoop-shouldered woman who came to the door appeared much older than her years. "Ida Landon?" Bella questioned, not sure that the woman standing before her was truly her mother's sister.

The woman nodded.

"It's me, Bella, your sister Polly's daughter."

A look of recognition crossed the woman's face as she opened her arms and pulled Bella into an embrace. "You're all grown up," she said, placing a kiss on Bella's cheek. "Let me take a look at you." She moved an arm's length backward and smiled, nodding her approval. "From the look of those clothes, I'd say your parents are still among the Shakers."

Bella nodded and said, "This is my friend Daughtie."

"Hello, Daughtie. Goodness, where are my manners? You girls come in and let me take your cloaks."

The room was small and sparsely appointed yet somehow appeared cluttered. The walls were sorely in need of whitewash, and the wood floors lacked care. A tiny potted plant sat drooping on the windowsill, a testament of those who lived within. Bella scanned the room, seeking a place for Daughtie and her to sit down. Ida appeared to follow her gaze and hastened to remove drying clothes from the two straight-backed wooden chairs.

"Sit here," she offered, gathering the laundry into a bundle and placing it on a narrow cot. "I'd make some tea, but I'm fresh out," she apologized.

Bella reached into her satchel and withdrew a small cloth bag. "We can use this, Aunt Ida," she offered. "I brought tea with me for just such an occasion as this."

A tentative smile appeared on Ida's lips. "Thank you, dear. You're as sweet as your mother. I want to hear all about her. How is she faring among the Shakers? I never thought she'd stay there. Polly was the one who always wanted a family with lots of children. Guess folks change, though," she remarked, setting a pot to boil in the tiny corner that served as a kitchen. Seating herself on the cot, she leaned back against the bundle of laundry and rubbed her hands together. "Now! Tell me everything."

Bella hesitated a moment. "I'm not sure how to tell you this. I don't suppose there's any way to soften what I have to say, Aunt Ida, but Mother died of consumption not long after we arrived at Canterbury. I was certain that Father had written."

Ida was silent for several moments. "He may have written, but we left this place for nearly two years. Arthur was sure he could do better in the South. He had a strong inclination to live where it was warm. Unfortunately, we didn't make it any farther than Pennsylvania. He decided if he was going to be poor and cold, he had a greater fondness for New Hampshire than Pennsylvania. We returned the following year and made our way back to this same place. Just our luck that it was still unrented."

Bella looked around, unconvinced that landing back here was a stroke of luck.

"Times have been hard, but Arthur says it's only a matter of time before he finds a better paying job." Her voice was filled with a sorrow that belied the upward curve of her lips.

"I'm sure things will take a turn for the better," Bella encouraged.

Ida jumped up from the cot and took the few steps to her makeshift kitchen. "Just listen to me! Here you've made a long journey with sad news and I'm heaping my problems upon you the minute you walk in the door. Let me pour you girls some tea."

"We'll be leaving as soon as we finish our tea, Aunt Ida," Bella said as she took the chipped cup her aunt offered. "We've a long ways to go."

"And where are you off to?"

"Daughtie and I have decided we'll go to Lowell. We plan to seek employment in the mills," Bella replied, giving her friend a sidelong glance.

"I've heard tell there's good wages being paid down there. But you girls had best spend the night with me. Arthur's gone to Boston on a delivery with his employer. We can make do, just the three of us."

"That certainly makes more sense than sleeping along the roadside," Daughtie whispered as Ida returned to pour herself a cup of tea.

"I suppose we could stay, Aunt Ida," Bella said. "If you're sure it won't be an inconvenience," she quickly added.

Ida beamed. "It will be fun. Just the three of us—we can visit, and you can tell me all about life in the settlement. I'm surprised Franklin gave you permission to leave the Shakers. It's out of character for him to be so agreeable."

"I didn't seek his permission. Daughtie and I ran away."

"Oh my!" Ida placed a hand on each cheek and stared wide-eyed at the two girls.

3

An early spring storm refused to let up, and Bella and Daughtie soon found their shoes weighed down with the muck and mire of the roadway and their woolen cloaks heavy with rainwater. Bella grabbed Daughtie's hand and pulled, hoping they could avoid the splattering mud from a passing coach. But her feet wouldn't take hold in the slippery mud, and they both were showered with flying sludge before the coach finally came to a halt a short distance down the road.

"Would you want a ride? I've space available," the driver called down from his perch.

"Yes!" Daughtie shouted.

Bella stepped in front of her friend. "We've no money to pay."

"I wasn't expecting any—ride or walk, it's up to you."

There was no stopping Daughtie. She had opened the carriage door and climbed inside before Bella could reply. "It appears we'll take your offer."

"Good enough. Get in. I need to keep moving."

Bella seated herself beside Daughtie and pushed back the hood of her cloak. "Hello," she said to the other passengers.

Two girls who appeared to be near her age stared back. "Hello," one of them ventured.

The greeting was tentative, and Bella was careful to keep her muddy shoes and wet clothing away from the clean, dry passengers. "I'm Arabella Newberry—everyone calls me Bella. This is my friend Daughtie Winfield. We were caught in the storm."

"That much is obvious," one of the girls said.

"No need to be rude, Sally. I'm Ruth Wilson and this is Sally Nelson. We're going to Lowell—to work in the mills," she added. "I'm from Maine. My family has a small farm where we raise sheep, and Sally's home is in Vermont. Where are you and Daughtie going?"

"From their appearance, they've lost their way. You're Shakers, aren't you?" Sally questioned with a tone of condemnation.

"We've left the Society. We're going to Lowell, also," Bella replied with as much decorum as her drenched appearance would permit.

"Do you suppose the driver will permit us to ride all the way to Lowell?"

Daughtie asked, obviously pleased to be out of the rain.

"I wouldn't know why not. So long as you sign a paper saying you're seeking work in the mills, he'll provide you a seat in the coach and pay for your room and board when we stop for the night."

"Really?" both girls cried in unison. Bella couldn't believe their good fortune. She hesitated for a moment. "But why would he do such a thing?"

Sally gave her a look of disdain. "It's his job. He travels throughout all of New England seeking farm girls who are willing to sign on for work at the mills. The Corporation pays the cost of transporting us to Lowell."

"I see," Bella replied. This sudden blessing seemed like affirmation from God that she'd done the right thing.

Sally looked down and made a purposeful show of pulling her feet away from Bella's shoes. "Let's hope it's soon. I'd like to arrive in Lowell without mud on my shoes."

When they stopped at the inn later that afternoon, both Daughtie and Bella were chilled, and the breeze did little to warm them as they descended the coach. At least it had ceased raining.

"You two willing to sign on to work in Lowell?" the driver called out as he handed Ruth her bandbox and Sally her leather satchel.

Bella and Daughtie nodded.

"Good! Only need to locate three or four more girls and we can return to Lowell. Grab your belongings, and I'll arrange for a room with the innkeeper."

"That means four of us will be sharing a room instead of two," Sally muttered.

"Don't mind her. She didn't want to leave home, but her folks forced her to come along. That pride is all a show. Her parents stand to lose their farm if she doesn't go to work and send her earnings home," Ruth confided.

"And what of you? Why are you going to Lowell?" Daughtie inquired.

Ruth smiled. "I'm going to send most of my money home for my brother's education. He wants to attend college."

"But what of your education, Ruth? Once your brother has finished college and found a position, will he then pay for your schooling?" Bella inquired.

Ruth giggled. "Why on earth would he do such a thing?" she asked as she grabbed her bandbox and entered the inn. It was obvious she didn't expect an answer.

Bella hastened to reach Ruth's side. "Because you're worthy of an education, also. Men and women are of equal value."

Both Sally and Ruth stared at Bella as though she'd gone mad. Sally wagged her head back and forth, then said, "I don't know where you ever got such a notion, but you'd best readjust your thinking if you plan to live in the real world. Short of finishing school, there's really very little available for women. And if you're of a lower class, there's no need to even consider finishing school." Her words were spoken with a harsh tone that suggested Sally had a bit of history with this topic. "Come on, follow me." Several coarse-looking men leered in their direction as the girls wended their way through the inn and up a narrow stairway to one of the rooms above the dining area.

The room was small, dirty, and they suspected even lice-infested, but the girls were weary. Daughtie and Bella quickly removed their clothing and began spreading the garments out to dry.

"As soon as you've changed, come downstairs and we'll have supper. Once we have something warm in our stomach, we'll be so sleepy that we won't notice how awful the room is," Ruth said.

Although the food wasn't flavorful or appetizing, it was hot. By the time they made their way back upstairs, all four girls were longing for sleep. The men in the dining room below, however, were still drinking their ale, with their drunken voices growing louder as they continued to imbibe.

"I miss the quiet of home," Daughtie said. "I fear we've made a mistake, Bella."

Ruth patted Daughtie's shoulder. "Don't make a decision just yet. Lowell is a wonderful place to live. The boardinghouses are clean and the food is good. You'll soon find that working in the mills provides girls with a good opportunity to be independent."

"So you've lived in Lowell?" Bella inquired.

Ruth nodded. "Yes. I worked there for three months last year but had to return home to care for my ailing mother and help out at home. My prayers were answered and she's better now, so I'm off to the mills again and hoping I'll not have difficulty being rehired."

"Why would you have difficulty being hired? The coachman said they needed workers, didn't he?" Bella questioned.

"They do need workers, but each girl is required to sign a contract before commencing work. Among other things, the contract says you agree to stay one year in your position. If you don't give proper notice and gain approval before leaving, they place a mark beside your name and then share that information with the other agents so that none of them will hire you. You're blackballed as a bad employee," Ruth explained.

Daughtie shook her head back and forth. "No wonder you're fearful."

"It's not as bad as it sounds. Most of the time the agents are so much in need of girls that they don't care if you've left without approval. They're pleased to have an experienced worker return. I witnessed them taking back several of the girls who had left without warning, so I'm hopeful for my situation. At least my supervisor knew the condition of my departure. He knew it wasn't for some nonsensical matter. Besides, the coachman said they've opened another mill since my departure, so I'm fairly certain we'll all find employment."

"Tell us about the boardinghouses," Daughtie entreated. "I hope it's not a room such as this that we'll be living in."

Ruth smiled. "You'll be crowded. Two or three girls to a bed and not much storage room, that's for certain. But you'll not spend much time in your bedroom, anyway. We're awakened early and off to work by five o'clock in the morning. We return to the boardinghouse two hours later for a half-hour breakfast, then back to work until noon when we have three quarters of an hour for dinner. Supper is waiting when we return home at seven o'clock in the evening, and we have free time until ten o'clock. That's curfew, and if you're not back in the boardinghouse by then, the keeper will lock you out. The rules are all set out in your contract, so you'll know what's expected before you agree to work for the Corporation."

Daughtie appeared overwhelmed by the concept. "Free time to do as you please every evening? You're not required to attend Union Meeting?"

"They don't have Union Meeting, Daughtie," Bella whispered.

Sally sniggered. "No, we don't have Union Meetings, but I'm told the contract requires church attendance. But from what I've heard about the Shakers, I doubt you'll find a place to attend that will suit your fancy."

Bella held her temper in check. "I don't know what you've heard about the Shakers or their worship, Sally, but I hope we'll be able to find believers among the world's people who are more open-minded than you appear to be."

Sally glared across the room at Bella. "The world's people? Is that what we are, the world's people? Well, you're one of us now, Bella, so you'll have to adjust to *our* life. And believe me, you'd best spend your first pay on some clothes! I'm told many of the mill girls dress as well as society ladies do. You'll be outcasts in those clothes. You can't begin to imagine how the world's people clothe themselves."

"We know how they dress, Sally. There were some of the world's people at our settlement every Sunday to watch us worship. Some of the most prominent people from all over the country—even Europe—have been there. The finery will come as no surprise."

Ruth moved closer to Bella. "Why did they come to watch you worship—if you don't mind my asking?"

"We dance during our worship. I assume they find it entertaining or amusing. Perhaps both. They come to satisfy their curiosity about a people they don't understand. Unfortunately, they leave with little more wisdom than they arrive with, but they go back into the world and tell others, who come to see for themselves."

Sally swung around on the bed. "Dance? I thought Shaker men and women were forbidden such familiarity. Then you and Daughtie should be well prepared for the dances in Lowell."

"Our dances are not the type of which you speak. They are a part of worship, and the men and women don't touch in the manner of the world's dances," Bella replied.

Voices of bellowing liquored men sounded loudly through the floorboards and were followed by what sounded like crashing furniture and then the frightening roar of a gun being discharged. The girls squealed and huddled together on the bed.

A knock sounded at their door. "You girls all right?" the coach driver called from the other side of the door.

"Yes, but what's happening down there?" Ruth timidly inquired.

"Just a bit of an argument between a couple of men. I think things should quiet down now. You girls get to sleep. We've an early start in the morning."

"Yes, sir," Ruth replied.

Bella blew out the candle and burrowed under the covers. "Everything is going to be just fine, Daughtie," she whispered, hoping the words she spoke were true.

4

After eight days of crisscrossing New Hampshire, Vermont, and Rhode Island, the horses lumbered up a small rise pulling the damsel-filled carriage as their heavy hooves churned the dusty roadway.

"There's Lowell," the driver called. He snapped the reins, urging the horses onward.

Bella sighed as she shifted her weight to her right hip. "Finally!"

Daughtie nodded her agreement. "I seem to remember the driver saying he was going to seek only two more girls."

Ruth wiggled in her seat. "I think he wanted us to be as uncomfortable as he was."

"If that was his intention, he certainly succeeded," Sally snarled. "But I think he's greedy. The more girls he delivers, the more money he makes."

Priscilla, the newest passenger to board the coach, scooted forward on the seat, her gaze riveted on Sally. "How do you know that?" she asked in an awe-filled voice.

Sally looked down her nose at the girl. "It's an obvious conclusion."

Bella watched as Priscilla shriveled back in her seat. "Don't be upset by Sally's manner," she whispered. "She treats all of us with the same disdain."

"Look, Bella," Daughtie said. "Those brick buildings must be the mills."

Sally leveled a look of contempt toward Daughtie. "You and Priscilla should become fast friends. You seem to be endowed with the same level of intelligence," she remarked as the coach came to a halt in front of the Appleton Mill.

The driver pulled open the door. "Here we are, ladies. I'll escort you inside. As soon as Mr. Gault assigns you to your boardinghouses, I'll deliver your baggage."

The girls dutifully followed behind as the driver pulled a rope hanging over the iron gate. A bell rang and a portly gentleman strode toward them. "Morning, Luther," he greeted.

"Mornin', Mr. Gault. Got a surprise for you. Eight girls when you was only expectin' four or five—all good workers."

"And how would you know?" Sally asked, directing her annoyance at the driver as they squeezed into Mr. Gault's small office.

Mr. Gault took a draw on his pipe. "And how are you able to make such an assertion, sir?" he asked the driver, exhaling a puff of smoke that circled and then floated upward.

The coach driver shuffled his feet and gave a sheepish grin. "Well, I guess I don't know for a fact that they're good workers, but they all signed the paper saying they wanted to come work for the Corporation," he replied, waving the documents in the air.

Mr. Gault nodded, took the paper work, placed it on his desk, and quickly surveyed the girls. "Any of you girls related or friends that want to live in the same boardinghouse?" he asked while looking at Bella and Daughtie.

"We'd like to be together," Bella replied, taking Daughtie's hand.

"I'd like to be with them, also," Ruth added quickly.

"Why?" Bella asked, surprised at the request.

Ruth shrugged her shoulders. "I enjoy your company, and I don't know anyone else," she replied simply.

"You can deliver the luggage of these three girls to Adelaide Beecher's boardinghouse here on Jackson Street," Mr. Gault told the driver. "The other five girls will go to Hannah Desmond's boardinghouse. They'll be assigned to the Lowell Mill."

The driver began to leave, then hesitated as he neared where Bella stood. He motioned to Mr. Gault. "I was wondering if I could maybe get paid today," he stammered.

Bella attempted to pretend she couldn't hear the conversation, for the driver's embarrassment was obvious.

"Payday's the same for everybody, Luther, you know that. Last Friday of the month. You'll need to line up out in the mill yard with everybody else," Mr. Gault quietly replied. He drew closer to the driver and lowered his voice to a whisper. "If you'll come back later, I can personally advance you a few dollars."

Luther's cheeks flushed a rosy red. "Thank you, Mr. Gault. You're a kind man." Squaring his shoulders, the driver made his way to the door. "Your bags will be waiting at your boardinghouses, ladies. I wish you well." He tipped his hat and quickly departed.

"Ladies, I apologize for my inability to offer seating to each of you, but I will attempt to be brief. Each of you signed this document," he said, raising the documents the driver had given him into the air. "However, there is an actual contract that must be signed prior to commencing employment with the Corporation. Until a full-time agent is hired at the Lowell Mill, I'm hiring for both the Appleton and the Lowell. You girls assigned to the Lowell will, most likely, have no further contact with me. The three of you," he continued while looking at Bella, Daughtie, and Ruth, "will see me from time to time in the mill yard or here in the offices. You will certainly see me on payday," he said with a smile as he handed each girl one of the contracts.

"You can all read?"

"Yes," they replied in unison.

"Excellent! Please read the contract. If you agree to the terms, you will sign here." He pointed to the blank line at the bottom of the page.

There was something about this room that reminded Bella of the Trustees' Office at Canterbury, where the world's people signed their contracts to enter the Society. It wasn't the quietude or formality of the setting, for certainly this place was far from serene. And Mr. Gault's manner, although forthright, held none of the austerity of the Elders as they had questioned novitiates. Perhaps, she decided, it was the solemnity of contracting her life to others, which was a concept she found particularly disquieting.

The girls took but a few moments to peruse the paper work. Bella watched each one sit at Mr. Gault's desk and pen her name and was surprised when no questions were asked.

When her turn arrived, Bella seated herself, folded her hands, and looked up at Mr. Gault. "I have questions."

"Certainly," he replied, smiling down at her.

"How much will I be paid?"

"Three dollars and twenty-five cents per week. You receive your pay every Friday."

"Room and board?"

Mr. Gault smiled. "One dollar and twenty-five cents is your share. The balance is paid by the Corporation."

"And our hours of work?"

Mr. Gault carefully explained that the first and final bells tolled at differing times throughout the year, the workday beginning earlier in the summer and later in the winter.

Bella listened and then mentally tabulated what Mr. Gault had told her. "And so we work approximately seventy-three hours per week?"

The older man nodded, a look of admiration crossing his face. "I believe that would be correct. Any other questions?"

"I'm satisfied," Bella said before dipping the pen into ink and carefully signing her name.

"Should I sign?" Daughtie whispered to her friend before dutifully seating herself.

Bella nodded and handed the pen to Daughtie.

"Now that you've all signed your contracts, I have but a few comments before sending you off to your boardinghouses. I need to advise you of your choice to begin work in the morning or take the day to rest. If you decide you need a day to recover from your journey, you will owe room and board for the day. You are not paid for any day you do not work. However, you will not be charged for your room and board for the remainder of today."

"How very charitable," Sally retorted.

Mr. Gault glanced in her direction. "You have a quick tongue, Miss Nelson. You would do well to remember that it is best to think before you speak. I believe you'll find that piece of advice particularly helpful with your overseer in the mill."

Turning his attention back to the girls assigned to Hannah Desmond's boardinghouse, Mr. Gault offered instructions for locating the boardinghouse as well as where they should report the next morning. He escorted the five girls to the door and then returned to the remaining three.

"Any of you girls have previous experience in the mills?" he asked, seating himself behind the desk.

"No, sir," Bella and Daughtie replied.

Ruth hesitated a moment before replying. "I do."

"Thank you for your honesty, Miss Wilson. I saw your name in my book. It has a black mark beside it, so I am assuming you left before your contract was completed?"

"Yes," she replied, her voice barely a whisper.

"The circumstances were beyond her control. Her mother was ill, and she was forced to return home to help her family. Surely you're not going to hold that against her. I'm sure her overseer would vouch that she was a good worker. Weren't you, Ruth?" Bella questioned.

Mr. Gault grinned and leaned back in his chair. "I appreciate the argument on behalf of your friend, Miss Newberry. However, I'm sure that she can speak for herself. Miss Wilson?"

"What Bella said is true. My family needed me and I was required to leave. I worked at the Merrimack in the spinning room and was tending twenty-eight spindles when I was forced to return home. I truly want to work in the mills, and I don't take my contract lightly. But my family is of great importance to me, also."

Mr. Gault looked down at the page, seeming to consider the black mark beside Ruth's name, then snapped the book shut. "Again, thank you for your honesty, Miss Wilson. You three girls will be working here at the Appleton operating the weaving looms. You may report directly to your overseer, Mr. Kingman, in the morning. For now, you may present yourselves to Miss Addie at number 5 Jackson Street, which is across the street and down the road a short distance. I'll escort you out and open the gate. I'm sure that Miss Wilson can find her way to number 5."

"Yes, of course," Ruth replied as the trio followed Mr. Gault out the door.

The girls patiently waited as Mr. Gault unlocked the gate and pulled back on the metal bars. "Good day, ladies. I wish you well as you begin your new positions."

The clanking of the iron gates could be heard in the distance as the trio walked across the street, with Bella and Daughtie attempting to gather in the details of their new surroundings.

The rows of sturdy brick boardinghouses lay before them, an occasional flower box sporting a few green sprouts, evidence that summer's blooms would soon arrive. A mobcapped boardinghouse keeper was busy hanging clothes at one house while at another, the keeper was diligently sweeping her entryway. The scene unfolding before them gave the appearance of warmth and welcome whereas the gated fortress to their rear cast a shadow of detachment and apprehension.

"The mills remind me of prisons that Brother Jerome used to speak of," Daughtie commented, taking one last peek over her shoulder.

Ruth giggled. "Only because of the gate. They close it five minutes after last bell so that anyone who is late must pass through the counting room. The agent and overseers won't abide tardiness."

Bella looped her arm through Ruth's and gave her a warm smile. "The Society believed in punctuality, also. I was pleased that Mr. Gault rewarded your honesty and rehired you, Ruth."

A tinge of pink colored Ruth's cheeks as she nodded in agreement. "Unfortunately, I wavered for a moment, but I'm glad I gained enough courage to tell the truth. I was fearful Mr. Gault would send me home."

"Here we are—number 5," Bella said, pointing to the stenciled address.

A giant white apron covered a matronly woman's ample figure as she pulled open the front door and gave the girls a beaming smile. "I've been expecting you. Come in, come in! I am Miss Addie, the keeper of this house," she welcomed. "I bribed the coach driver with a piece of apple pie, and he carried your baggage upstairs. And believe me, until you've climbed those stairs, you won't appreciate his deed," she informed them with a giggle.

She led the trio into a large room and settled herself on the tapestry-covered settee. "Let's get acquainted," she offered, patting the cushion beside her. "I'll show you the rest of the house if there's time before the others arrive for dinner."

Bella liked the woman's unrestrained laughter and pleasant countenance. She had an easy way about her. Though Miss Addie's questions were sometimes prodding, they somehow seemed unobtrusive, for her manner was gentle, and when the conversation became gloomy, she would pepper the discussion with an amusing anecdote to lighten the mood. It was obvious she was attempting to set them at ease—so dissimilar to the welcome that had been extended to Bella's family when they first arrived at the Shaker community.

That meeting was one she would not soon forget. Inside the Trustees' Office they had been greeted with prying eyes and pursed lips, and by the end of their meeting, the Elders had leveled looks of displeasure and disgust. Bella wasn't sure exactly what had caused their displeasure during that interview. In fact, four years later, she still wasn't certain. Her parents had been honest in their declarations to the Family, had severed all ties to the world, had willingly surrendered their meager belongings, and against her mother's wishes, had relinquished their parental rights to Bella. Miss Addie's acceptance today was as welcome as a cool drink on a hot summer day.

"Would you prefer to see the rest of the house or have your tea first?" Miss Addie inquired.

The girls quickly agreed they would take the tour first and the tea later if time permitted.

The older woman chuckled. "I knew that's what you would choose," she said as she stood up and led them to the stairway. They ascended at Miss Addie's slow pace, finally reaching the top floor. "One step short of heaven, that's how I feel when I finally arrive in this room," Miss Addie said, the words bursting forth in short puffs as she made her way around the girls' baggage.

The three girls glanced around the room, Bella taking note of the personal belongings atop a small chest and clothing strewn about. "It would appear this room is already occupied, Miss Addie."

Addie carefully lowered herself onto one of the two beds and began rubbing her knees. "It's only partially occupied—at least until today. You girls will room with the other three girls already assigned to this room. Three in each bed. You share the chests and what other bit of space you can find available."

"I told you the room would be crowded," Ruth said. "But we won't spend much time up here."

"It looks like someone needs to spend some time up here," Bella replied, retrieving an embroidered glove and satin-bordered sash from the floor and placing them on one of the beds. "It's obvious your boarders aren't particularly interested in tidiness."

"They're up early and busy until bedtime. I fear tidiness isn't their top priority. They'd rather spend their free time at a lecture or visit in the parlor. Not that I blame them, of course."

"You launder the bedding, and we wash our own clothing. Isn't that correct?" Ruth asked.

Addie nodded. "Right as rain," she said with a smile. "I clean the downstairs, but you girls are responsible for your rooms. Some are neat and clean while others are rather . . . shall we say, unkempt?"

After one bump on her head, Bella moved about the room more carefully, examining what little space wasn't occupied. "And there are no other rooms available?"

Addie shook her head. "You're taller than most of the girls, and I know these sloping walls and low ceiling will be difficult, but this is the best I can offer for now. You will have an opportunity to move downstairs when a space becomes available; however, you'll have to wait your turn. First ones here have priority in choosing if they want to move to another room. Since this is pretty much the worst of it, they almost always want to move," she said while checking the timepiece pinned to her dress. "Goodness, look at the time! The girls will soon be home. You get settled; I'll go down to the kitchen."

Bella met Daughtie's look of alarm with a waning smile. "We can make this better. We'll put pegs on the wall to hold our clothes, and if we move those chests over here," she said, pointing across the room, "it will provide additional space. This bed can be moved against the wall."

Ruth bobbed her head in agreement. "We had ten girls in the room at my former boardinghouse."

Bella glanced at Daughtie. A tear trickled down her friend's cheek. "We're going to be fine, Daughtie. I promise."

Now Bella prayed that God would provide her with the capability to keep that promise.

~ 5 ~

Clad in a dove-gray cutaway and matching cravat, Kirk Boott stood in the foyer of his large frame home awaiting the arrival of his guests, members of the Boston Associates and the key employees of the corporate operation in Lowell.

Matthew Cheever placed his hat and gloves upon a receiving table as was the routine, then turned to greet his employer. "Good day to you, sir." Matthew knew that as far as Boott was concerned, it would be the very best of days.

These semiannual meetings were a source of pleasure to Kirk. He enjoyed receiving the accolades bestowed upon him by the members of the Corporation. The bursts of applause that occasionally interrupted his reports of progress at these meetings were almost as important to Kirk as the tidy sum he was paid to oversee the paternalistic community created with the Associates' money. As general agent for the Corporation, Kirk continued to receive the complete support of the Associates—except for one or two recalcitrant men who harbored ill will toward him.

Kirk grasped Matthew Cheever's hand. "Glad you arrived early, Matthew. I'm depending on you to assist me during this meeting. I'll remain at the door. You see to their comfort once they enter the sitting room."

Matthew knew exactly what was expected. Matthew would see to the comfort of Kirk's guests, ensuring that their glasses were full, their cigars were lit, and adequate seating was available. Kirk was careful that his servants couldn't overhear business conversations, and it was a foredrawn conclusion that women would not be in attendance. Matthew didn't mind. As the evening progressed, the other men would realize Kirk had also begun to rely upon him for loftier responsibilities.

Taking his position in the large sitting room adjacent to Boott's office, Matthew offered a welcoming hand and glass of port to the gentlemen as, one by one, they began filling the room.

Paul Moody entered the room and made his way to where Matthew stood. He gave Matthew's shoulder a friendly squeeze. "Helping the boss keep his guests happy?"

Matthew nodded as he filled several goblets with the expensive port Kirk enjoyed serving. "If you'd care to help, you can deliver these to William Thurston and Nathan Appleton."

Paul laughed and drew a weatherworn hand across his balding pate. "I'll be happy to deliver Nathan's glass. William is another matter. I have no use for that man. I fear he is a double-minded sort who has only his own best interests at heart."

"He's not one of my favorite people, either, but you can always count on him to be present at the meetings."

Paul nodded. "Exactly! He wants to cause Kirk as much grief as possible. Given any opportunity, he'll be up to his same old tricks this evening."

Matthew picked up the glasses and gave Paul a grin. "Let's hope Boott can hold him at bay. Otherwise we'll be here until the wee hours of the night, and I don't think that would please either of our wives."

"How is Mrs. Cheever? My wife reports there's to be an addition to your family."

"It seems there are no secrets in Lowell. She is doing very well, thank you. Needless to say, we are delighted with the news."

Paul took one of the goblets. "I'll take this to Nathan. No need to worry about your news. It's safe with me—and I'll tell my wife that she's to keep her lips sealed until you and Mrs. Cheever have an opportunity to spread the word."

Matthew strode toward the other side of the room, wondering how Evangeline Moody knew that Lilly was with child. He offered the glass of port to William Thurston, who stood staring out the sitting room window. "With all those buds on the trees, it appears we're going to have an early spring," Matthew said.

William startled at the words, appearing embarrassed as he turned around. "I was deep in thought. I didn't realize anyone was close at hand."

"Quite all right," Matthew replied. He waited only until William accepted the glass before turning away. He didn't want to be drawn into a conversation with a man he didn't trust—especially this one.

John Farnsworth, the Englishman in charge of the print works operation at the Merrimack, grasped Matthew's hand as he turned. "Good to see you, Matthew. It appears you've got things well in hand for tonight's meeting."

William Thurston glanced over his shoulder, his features contorted into a sneer. "If a mobcap and frilly apron are all that are required to have things well in hand, I'd say that Kirk's lackey is certainly prepared."

Matthew's jaw clenched and he could feel the blood rising to his cheeks. Farnsworth gave a slight nod of his head as he took hold of Matthew's elbow. "I believe there's a more intelligent level of conversation across the room," John said, tugging at Matthew's arm. "Ignore him. He isn't worth your time or trouble, and nobody here values his opinion. That's why he's been standing by himself since his arrival," John said in a hushed voice.

"I know," Matthew replied. "But he's so puffed up—full of conceit. I'd like to take him down a peg or two."

John laughed. "That's your youth speaking, my boy. There are more effective ways to deal with the likes of William Thurston."

"Such as?"

John gave him a sly grin. "Pray for him. Let God deal with William Thurston. Men such as William want to be the center of attention. He's insecure and angry. A fist won't change his heart—only God can do that."

"You're right, of course, but I'm not certain I want God's grace to shine down upon that man," Matthew replied. "Perhaps you should pray for me, John."

John slapped Matthew on the back. "I'll be praying for the both of you. How's that?"

"Gentlemen, I believe everyone is here. Shall we get started?" Kirk inquired as he strode into the room. There was no doubt Kirk Boott was in command. "We have several matters upon which to report, and then I'll be glad to entertain any questions or new ideas."

The account grew lengthy as Boott reported on the Merrimack, Hamilton, Appleton, and Lowell Mills, carefully explaining the profits and expenditures of each mill. "Of course, the Lowell Mill hasn't been in production long enough to show a profit, but I believe it will do so more rapidly than any of our other mills. I believe Nathan's strong encouragement to expand into rug production was another stroke of genius. Our fine friend and associate Tracy Jackson has given me several contacts for overseas buyers, and orders within the country are burgeoning."

"Hear, hear!" a few men called out, while others applauded loudly.

Matthew watched as Kirk basked in the adulation for a moment or two before continuing. "I'm certain you are all interested in hearing about our latest projects. I believe Matthew Cheever can give you a more detailed report on those ventures," he said while motioning Matthew to his side. "As many of you know, I'm relying on Matthew more and more as we continue to expand."

This was Matthew's first opportunity to speak before the assembled group, and he didn't want to embarrass himself or Boott. Thanking Kirk, he took his place and told the men that projections were on target for the Middlesex Mill to begin production in the fall. There were murmurs of approval from the group.

"During your tour earlier today, I'm certain you noted that even with a particularly harsh winter, Hugh Cummiskey and his Irishmen have continued to make excellent progress on digging and laying stone for the new canals required to power the Suffolk and Tremont Mills. Those two mills remain on schedule to open in 1832. As our capable agent-in-residence, Mr. Boott, has pointed out, there is great demand for our products both overseas and here at home, particularly in the South. Not only for rugs but many of our other goods, as well. We plan to expand the production of our lightweight Negro cloth for our southern states as well as warmer climates overseas. The demand has been beyond our highest expectations," Matthew acknowledged. "Although the weather sometimes causes us to become innovative in order to continue work on these new buildings and canals during the winter, I think you will all agree that we have prevailed and excellent progress is evident."

Once again, resounding applause filled the room. Somewhat embarrassed by the ovation, Matthew nodded and took his seat. Kirk stood and moved forward, basking in the continuing applause.

At length the room grew silent, and Kirk continued. "We've had a profitable six months, gentlemen, and I trust the next six months will prove even more to your liking. Your vision for expansion has given birth to a thriving community," Kirk complimented. "Questions or comments?"

Tracy Jackson raised his lit cigar into the air. "You didn't mention the Catholic church. I'm sure we'd all like to know how that's progressing, Kirk."

Boott nodded his head. "Hugh Cummiskey tells me the final work should be completed by summer's end. He's looking for an accomplished stonemason before finalizing the interior work. We're planning to invite Bishop Fenwick to come from Boston the last Sunday in August to preside over the first Mass."

"Just what we need—more Irish," William Thurston called out from the far end of the room. "They're swarming into Lowell faster than flies settle on manure, and Boott encourages them. He spends as much time trying to make Cummiskey happy as he does all the rest of us combined."

An uncomfortable silence hung in the air for several long minutes before Tracy spoke. "I hear tell there's been discussion around town in regard to the schools, Kirk. Apparently there are those who think a better education should be offered. . . ."

Kirk held up his hand. "I've heard the talk, but I understand the murmuring comes from only a small faction of townsfolk. I doubt there's anything of consequence to concern us."

"Any issues that impact the community will in turn impact the Associates. We don't want to be caught unprepared. Matters such as this bear watching," Tracy warned.

Taking a sip of the expensive burgundy liquid in his glass, Kirk leaned against his carved walnut desk before speaking. "Rest assured, Tracy, that the best interests of the Associates are always foremost in my mind. I will personally keep abreast of this matter and give you my word that you will be well informed on this and all other matters of consequence."

"Good enough! I can't ask for any more than that. We all know you're a man of your word."

Matthew sighed a breath of relief. The exchange between Tracy Jackson and Kirk had ended amicably. Kirk had spoken in a quiet, even tone, maintaining his deportment and composure, though Kirk's mounting anger at Jackson's comments had been obvious to Matthew. Perhaps the others had not noticed.

"I, for one, would like to get back to the problem of the Irish. If, as Mr. Boott purports, the Associates are always foremost in his mind, why has nothing been done to control their growth in this town?" William Thurston grumbled from the rear.

Nathan Appleton turned in his chair and faced Thurston. "I don't think anyone else in this room shares your intense passion to rid Lowell of the Irish, William. The remainder of us seem to be in accord. We realize that these men fill a need. They work hard, and they're willing to perform the necessary manual labor that no one else is willing to undertake—at least none that we're aware of. We are also keenly aware that the married Irishmen desire to live together with their families. I can't fault a man for wanting his family nearby, although you seem to spend a great deal of time away from yours, William. By all appearances, you spend more time in Lowell than in Boston, which I am hard pressed to understand. Aside from pursuing problems with the Irish population, what is it you do here in Lowell?"

A chorus of laughter filled the room as a crimson-faced Thurston glowered. "Mark my words—one day you're going to regret that you didn't take this problem seriously. One day you'll come to me, hat in hand, apologizing for your shortsightedness." The venom-filled words echoed down the hallway as Thurston made a hasty departure out of the house, the front door slamming with a resounding thud.

Matthew had no idea what might be going through Boott's mind, but his own thoughts suggested that Thurston was a man to be watched. As Nathan Appleton noted, no one was really all that sure what Thurston did in Lowell. His many visits were apparently given to some purpose—but what?

~ 6 ~

Daughtie pulled an initial-embroidered handkerchief from her pocket and dabbed it to her eyes. "I don't think I'm ever going to become accustomed to the world's ways," she lamented. "You know I'm not one to complain, Bella, but these people move so rapidly. Everything is measured by speed, both at work and at home. I feel like a pig being slopped when I rush to the table for a meal; there's no time for manners or even the slightest civility. Why, just this morning Margaret was so intent on forking the last serving of bacon that she reached across me, her elbow striking my cheek. Even worse, she didn't take a moment to apologize! And the noise—at work it's all the machines, and when we come home, everyone talks at once. There's no peace, no time to reflect or meditate. Tell me—is this how you remember the world? Because if it is, I can't imagine why you wanted to return."

Bella squirmed on her chair and gave Daughtie a pensive look. "Life here in Lowell is very different from what I experienced with my family. But I was living on a small farm, not in the city. Living here is unusual for everyone, not just us. Each girl who comes here must go through an adjustment."

Daughtie's chin drooped and rested on her chest. "I don't think I can adjust to this life," she whispered. "I don't like it here, Bella."

Bella's mind was racing. She didn't want Daughtie returning to the Shakers, for although she liked Ruth and the other girls, they didn't understand her—not like Daughtie. She lowered her voice to avoid being overheard. "Give yourself more time. It's too soon to make a decision. Only yesterday the supervisor said that you and I were already the best weavers on the floor. Didn't his words of praise make you feel good? And I was thinking that we could take some Scripture verses and tack them to our looms. I know the supervisor sometimes frowns upon reading material, but many of the girls have pages tacked to their machines. We can memorize Scripture while we work. It will make the time pass more quickly, don't you think? And we'll spend more time alone. We can go upstairs in the evening when no one else is there and talk quietly." The words spilled out, tumbling over one another in a panicked staccato.

"Please don't be angry with me, Bella. I'll stay a while longer, but I wanted you to know that I'm giving thought to returning to the Society," Daughtie hesitantly replied. "But I do like your idea about the Scripture verses. We can copy some verses tonight and begin memorizing tomorrow." She gave Bella a wistful smile.

"That's the spirit. In time, we might both find Lowell to be exactly what we're looking for."

"But what about Jesse?"

Daughtie's question caused Bella to sober. "What about him?"

"Don't you wonder what happened to him? I mean, you were to leave the Society together. Don't you want to know why he didn't appear—where he might be today?"

"I don't really think about him, at least not much. Like I told you before, Daughtie, I wasn't in love with Jesse. He thought he was in love with me, but if he couldn't even follow through on our plans and leave the village with me, then why should I give his kind of love a second thought?"

A persistent knock sounded at the front door. "Would you see who's at the door, Bella?" Miss Addie called from the kitchen.

"Yes, ma'am," Bella answered. "I'll be right back," she promised Daughtie as she rose from her chair.

Obviously the three girls sitting in the parlor with their gentlemen callers couldn't excuse themselves long enough to answer the door, Bella decided. A prick of irritation assailed her as she glanced at the giggling girls, all too self-involved to be bothered.

Turning the knob, she gave the door a tug. "Yes?" she inquired a bit more curtly than planned.

"Well, good evening to you, too. Apparently I've come at a bad time?"

Bella felt the heat rising in her cheeks. A young man of about twenty years stood before her. A mass of straight hair fell forward over his eyes as he removed his felt hat. Raking his fingers through the blond strands, he gave her a roguish grin.

"Were you going to invite me in? Or do you prefer standing in the doorway?" he quickly added.

Jumping back, Bella nearly lost her balance as she made way for the handsome gentleman caller. "I apologize for my rude behavior, sir. May I be of assistance?" she inquired formally, closing the door once he had entered the hallway.

"Why, yes, thank you," the man replied, bowing deeply from the waist in mock formality as he once again thrust his tousled hair off his brow. "Taylor Manning to speak with Miss Addie, if you please. And you are?"

"Bella—Arabella Newberry of New Hampshire. I'll tell Miss Addie that you've come to call. She's in the kitchen," she replied, turning to make her way down the hallway.

"Good. I'll just follow along behind," he replied. "Miss Addie won't mind if I call on her in the kitchen."

Bella could feel his towering presence matching her steps as he followed her through the parlor, past a wide-eyed Daughtie sitting at the dining table, and into the kitchen. "Mr. Taylor Manning to see you, Miss Addie," she announced as they entered the warm kitchen.

Miss Addie twirled around to face them with damp gray curls clinging to her forehead. "Taylor! What a surprise. It's early—I wasn't expecting your uncle just yet."

"That's why I've come. Uncle John asked that I advise you of the fact that he's going to be detained. We have a meeting of the Mechanics Association this evening—"

"Come in the parlor, Taylor. I don't entertain guests in the kitchen," Addie interrupted as she pulled off her apron and tucked a few stray strands of hair into place.

Taylor hesitated. "I've come merely to deliver Uncle John's message," he insisted.

"Tut, tut, I'll hear none of that. Come along—you, too, Bella," she clucked. "Come along, Daughtie," she said, grasping her by the arm as they reached the dining room. Daughtie took her place behind Miss Addie, the three of them resembling a brood of chicks following a proud mother hen. "Make room, ladies and gentlemen," Miss Addie commanded the girls and their guests already assembled in the parlor. "Daughtie and Bella, this is Mr. Taylor Manning. He's John Farnsworth's nephew and because he has an artistic flair, he's been hired on to work on the fabric designs." She looked at each of the young women and then offered, "Taylor, this is Miss Daughtie Winfield and Miss Bella Newberry." The girls curtsied and Taylor bowed.

Taking a seat, Addie nodded for her three followers to sit down. Folding her hands, she rested them in her ample lap and smiled at Taylor.

"As I said, I've come to advise you that Uncle John has been detained. There's a meeting of the Mechanics Association," he said, pulling out his pocket watch and glancing at the time, "for which I certainly don't want to be late. Uncle John has agreed to assist a group of us who will be scheduling some lectures in the near future."

Margaret and Harriet ignored their visitors and immediately turned their full attention to Taylor, both of them obviously besotted with his confident behavior and strapping good looks. Bella found their behavior annoying.

"The other men must value your opinion greatly if you're assisting with such important matters," Harriet fawned in a syrup-sweet tone.

Margaret nodded. "You must be very worthy of their trust." She batted her lashes and lowered her head in a coy manner. Bella had to admit this was not something she'd had to deal with in the Society. She had to smile at the very thought of Sister Mercy lowering her head and simpering for one of the Brethren.

Taylor squared his shoulders and nodded. "Why, thank you," he replied, tucking away his watch. "These lectures are of enormous value to the men. They aid us in keeping abreast of current topics of importance. There's absolutely no way of evaluating how much good these lectures and the library are accomplishing for the men, but I must say that I'm proud to be a part of this noble venture."

"These lectures you speak of—are they only for the men, or may we attend also?" Bella asked as she perched on the edge of her chair. She'd opened her mouth almost before she'd given herself a chance for thought.

The room grew silent. All of them, save Daughtie and Miss Addie, stared at her as though she'd spoken a foreign language.

"The lectures and library are both sponsored and funded by the Mechanics Association, which is comprised of skilled tradesmen."

Well, I'm committed to this now, Bella reasoned. *I might as well continue.* "The women working in the mills are certainly skilled workers." She tried to keep her voice soft and nonthreatening. "I'm certain many of them would be pleased to spend a small portion of their earnings in exchange for a membership that would permit them to enjoy the valuable services you've so aptly described."

Taylor shifted in his seat and cleared his throat. "You do understand, Miss Newberry, that there is a vast difference between a skilled tradesman and someone who merely passes a shuttle back and forth through a loom, don't you?"

Struggling to keep her temper in check, Bella clenched her hands together in a white-knuckled clasp. Gone was her attempt to keep her voice decidedly calm. "Where I come from, Mr. Manning, women are treated as equals, given the same opportunity to expand their minds as men, and encouraged to explore all the abilities God has given them. Am I to understand that the men of your Mechanics Association find that an unacceptable ideology?"

Taylor rose from his chair and paced back and forth on the floral-designed wool carpet. "I believe you're twisting my words, Miss Newberry. However, we do not have female members, nor do they utilize our library nor attend the lectures."

"Aha!" Bella retorted, now matching him step for step as he continued pacing. "But you obviously believe women are inferior since you disallow them the use of your facilities and attendance at your lectures. I'd venture to say that if women were permitted to assist with these lectures and the library, you would see an improvement."

Taylor raised a finger and pointed it toward Bella. "So you're saying that women are more enlightened than men, Miss Newberry? What makes you the better in this disagreement? You argue on behalf of women while I argue on behalf of men."

Bella pushed his finger away and stood facing him, hands on hips. "No. I do not argue solely on behalf of women, Mr. Manning. I argue on behalf of both men and women. I believe that opportunities should be available in equal measure."

Taylor gave a husky chuckle. "I hail from England, Miss Newberry, where such a concept would be viewed with disdain. Where in New Hampshire were you taught such principles?"

"Canterbury, where I lived among the United Society of Believers, who not only taught the principle of equality but also lived it."

"Based upon its name and your attire, I assume this society is a religious sect of some nature. I do wonder, though, if you hold their beliefs in such high esteem, how is it that you've come to Lowell, miss?"

The group turned its attention toward Bella, obviously anxious to hear her reply. She hesitated a moment and looked at Taylor. His eyes were sparkling with anticipation; a mischievous grin played at the corners of his lips.

"Both my attire and my reasons for leaving, sir, are personal matters that I'll not discuss with a stranger," she curtly replied.

The group applauded her remark. "Well done!" hollered one of the young men. Soon the others were cheering along with him. When they had quieted, the same young man who had spoken out smiled at Taylor. "I believe she's bested you, Mr. Manning."

Taylor nodded to the group. "Perhaps she has. We'll see how she fares the next time we meet. Please know, Miss Newberry," he said, turning to face her, "that I truly desire to remain and discuss this matter further. However, I must depart or I'll be late to my meeting. In the meantime, you might consider forming a sewing circle. I'm sure you and the other young ladies would find that enjoyable—and I promise I won't attempt to join."

Bella gave him a demure smile. "We would certainly welcome you, Mr. Manning, and perhaps one day you'll be inclined to extend an invitation to me to attend your meeting."

He shook his head at her remark and strode toward the front door with Miss Addie following closely at his heels. "Once the meeting is over, Uncle John will be calling on you, Miss Addie."

Miss Addie extended her thanks and then rejoined the others. "I believe young Mr. Manning was somewhat befuddled by you, Bella."

With Taylor Manning gone, everyone's gaze remained fixed on Bella. She immediately regretted her sharp tongue and quick response. "That wasn't my intent, Miss Addie."

"Well, you certainly managed to gain his attention, which is more than the rest of us have been able to do," Margaret offered, her beau scowling at the remark. "Why don't we walk into town?" she questioned her gentleman caller, obviously realizing her blunder.

Addie, Bella, and Daughtie remained in the parlor while the other girls and their gentleman callers retrieved their wraps and made a hasty departure to view the latest shipment of goods to arrive in the shops and, perhaps, stop for tea and cake.

"While I have reason to regret the hasty manner in which I responded, I do not regret making a stand for the women of this town. I hope your Mr. Farnsworth is a freer-thinking man than his nephew," Bella remarked.

Addie giggled. "I'm not sure that he is. Of course, I'm not sure you'll find too many men in New England who believe women are their equals. However, I must admit that young Taylor has much to learn in his dealings with people."

"I don't believe I've ever seen a gentleman so proud of himself—and for so little. He seems to think that his mere membership in an association gives him reason for puffery. And did you notice the way he was watching Harriet and Margaret? The moment he saw them swooning, he became even more obnoxious."

"'Tis true the boy's a bit of a rascal, and he's certainly aware that his roguish good looks attract the women," Addie replied. "According to his uncle John, that handsome face and muscular build have gotten him into difficulties in the past."

This was getting interesting. Bella leaned forward, giving Miss Addie her full attention. "What sort of difficulties?"

Addie looked about the room as though she expected an intruder might be lurking in one of the corners. "It seems that young Taylor became involved with the daughter of a wealthy aristocrat. Of course, Taylor comes from a fine family, but certainly not from the same level of society as this young woman."

Bella furrowed her brows in concentration. She wasn't sure she understood the import of Miss Addie's words. "And that creates a problem?"

"Yes, my dear. Crossing social barriers is frowned upon in England—even more than it is in America," she explained. "In fact, the girl's father told Taylor that if he saw him anywhere near his daughter again, he wouldn't bother with an honorable challenge to a duel. Rather, he said he would shoot Taylor where he stood. You must understand, the girl was engaged to be married and the banns had already been read. A duel seemed very much in order to maintain the girl's honor."

Bella gasped and then quickly covered her mouth with one hand. "It's difficult to believe that a member of the aristocracy would exhibit such unrestrained anger," she replied. "Of course, it isn't difficult to believe Mr. Manning would find himself in such a predicament! He is obviously a man who prides himself on getting ahead by using his appearance and contrived charm."

"My! Those are harsh words, Bella. John is hoping that with a firm hand, his influence, and continuing prayer, his nephew will begin to see the error of his ways and perhaps even seek the Lord. Personally, I doubt there are many young men that possess Taylor's rugged good looks who wouldn't use them to advantage," Addie exclaimed.

Bella gazed out the window. "There may be some," she replied.

Jesse had never attempted to influence anyone with his appearance, and although Jesse and Taylor looked nothing alike, Jesse was handsome in his own right. In all their conversations he had been honest and forthright—at least she thought he had. She wanted to believe Jesse had spoken the truth when he had told her of his desire to leave Canterbury. Daughtie's previous questions now haunted her. Why hadn't Jesse appeared or somehow sent word to her by now?

"I find that men are difficult to trust. Their willingness to commit themselves seems lacking," Bella absently commented.

Addie patted Bella's hand. "Now, why would you say such a thing, dear? Has some young beau broken your heart?"

"The Shakers are a celibate society. I've never had a beau, although my friend Jesse Harwood had planned to leave Canterbury along with Daughtie and me. He never appeared."

"And based on that one incident you believe all men are untrustworthy?"

Bella hesitated for a moment. "No. That incident only served to confirm my beliefs. It's my father who demonstrated the inability of men to honor their commitments," she replied in a soft voice.

Daughtie placed her arm around Bella's shoulders. "Bella's parents came to the Shaker village when they were in financial difficulty. Her father decided they should become members of the Society, but her mother was against joining. She wanted to go back to their home near Concord after their first winter with the Believers."

Bella nodded. "But my mother finally gave in to my father's wishes and signed the papers. The three of us lived separately—Father in the Brothers' Order and Mother in the Sisters' Order. I was in the Children's Order until I was fourteen, when I signed my papers and went into the Sisters' Order. By then my mother was very ill and only the physician and the nursing sister were permitted to see her. And so our separation continued. When she died a short time later, I was told that shedding tears was inappropriate behavior. My father offered no comfort nor did he appear saddened at her death. When I asked my father how he could choose to stay with the Believers rather than live in the world with his family, he said the Believers' way was easier."

Miss Addie gasped. "Easier?"

"Yes. It wasn't his deep level of religious belief that caused him to remain but the fact that he enjoyed the lack of responsibility living among the

Believers afforded him. He didn't like the commitment of being responsible for a family."

"Dear me. No wonder you've come to such a conclusion. But you must remember, child, that you've judged all mankind upon one man's actions," Addie countered.

A lump rose in Bella's throat. "Two, if you count Jesse."

Taylor glanced over his shoulder toward number 5 Jackson Street as he hurried off toward his meeting. The spirited girl from New Hampshire was provoking his thoughts. A pretty young woman—at least she would be if she'd wear some proper apparel and fix her hair in a more becoming style, he decided. He'd never met a girl quite like her. She certainly wasn't afraid to speak her mind. Even when he'd flashed his sapphire blue eyes at her, she'd continued on with her arguments as though she conversed with astonishingly handsome Englishmen every day of her life.

"Amazing!" he murmured, shaking his head as he entered the meeting room.

"What's amazing?" John Farnsworth inquired. "That you're over half an hour late?"

Taylor pulled out his watch and clicked open the gold case. Eight o'clock. He shook his head in wonderment. "Is the meeting over already?" he asked while glancing about the room. There were only a few men gathered reading books.

John nodded. "It didn't take long to decide we needed to acquire more information before scheduling any lectures. None of us was knowledgeable about available speakers, and I didn't think you'd had time enough to gather a list. I suggested that each of us secure a few names and topics and meet again in two weeks. I hope you don't mind; I saw no need to continue waiting for you, and I prefer to spend my evening with Addie," he said, clutching his felt top hat in one hand and walking toward the door.

Taylor turned and matched stride with his uncle. "So you're going to Miss Addie's now?"

John stopped and leveled a look of concern at his nephew. "Yes. Isn't that what I said a few moments ago? Are you sick, boy?" he asked and then continued walking.

"No. I was wondering if you'd mind if I joined you."

"You want to accompany me while I call on Miss Addie? Now I know you're sick."

"I don't exactly want to accompany you while you're visiting. I merely want an excuse for reappearing at the boardinghouse."

"What for, pray tell?"

Taylor gave his uncle a sheepish grin. "When I stopped to give Miss Addie your message, I became engaged in conversation with a young lady who is now boarding there. We didn't have time to complete our conversation, and I thought—"

"I should have known this had something to do with another conquest," John replied, shaking his head.

"It's not what you think, Uncle. Conquest, yes—but in an intellectual capacity."

Clasping an earlobe between his thumb and index finger, John tugged on the lobe several times in rapid succession. "Excuse me? Did I hear you correctly? You want to conquer a young lady on an intellectual level? Forgive me if I have difficulty believing such an avowal."

"This girl is different, Uncle John. She's from New Hampshire. Belonged to some sort of religious sect—the United Society of Believers or some such thing. I admit she's an attractive enough girl, but it's her philosophy that intrigues me," Taylor explained.

John laughed. "I see. And just what is this intriguing philosophy?"

"She believes in equality, that men and women are equal. Actually, it was a discussion regarding the Mechanics Association that detained me. She was of the opinion that women should be entitled to use the library and attend the lectures of the association."

John arched his eyebrows. "That is quite a philosophy. And how did you defend your position, Taylor?"

Taylor glanced down. "Instead of defending my position, I turned the tables on her by asking why she had left her religious group and come to Lowell if, in fact, she preferred their way of life."

"Not an impressive argument on your part," John declared.

Taylor agreed. "That's why I want to return. Perhaps I can give Miss Newberry a worthy reply."

"In that case, I suppose I couldn't possibly turn down your request," John said as he knocked on the front door of the boardinghouse.

Taylor straightened his coat. Since he was a small boy he'd been used to girls falling at his feet. He'd never met a woman he couldn't intrigue and entice with a wink or a smile. Miss Newberry promised to be something of a challenge, and that idea alone was much too exciting to pass up in his otherwise dull world. Memories of his mother's warnings against arrogance and pride filtered through a hazy veil, but he quickly ignored them. Miss Bella Newberry had rather asked for this attention, and Taylor was only too happy to comply.

The door opened and Bella stood at the threshold with a look of surprise etched upon her face. "Mr. Manning! What brings you back again so soon?"

B ella lay still, not wanting to awaken Daughtie or Ruth before the first bell. Surely the customary clanging would soon begin. She'd wakened several hours earlier and had been unable to once again fall asleep. Her body now ached, protesting the hours she'd remained stiff and motionless, longing to stretch the cramped muscles and throbbing joints into another position. She yearned for the sound of the reverberating toll she normally detested.

"Not yet," Ruth groaned, pulling the covers over her head at the sound of the first bell. "I don't want to get up."

"You'd best hurry or Daughtie will be tugging off the covers to air them out while you're still abed," Bella warned.

Bella was already at the pitcher and washbasin, glad to be up yet aware that she would be exhausted by day's end. However, she wouldn't complain to Daughtie, no matter how tired she was or difficult the day might be, for Daughtie would use such talk as yet another reason they should return to the Society of Believers. Although Bella understood her friend's discomfort with these new surroundings, she was of the opinion they both needed more time in which to make their final decisions regarding the world and its ways.

"You dressed quickly," Daughtie commented as she pulled back the covers on the bed to air.

"I can't find my shoes," Harriet whined from across the room. "Does any-one see my shoes?" She held a candle at arm's length as she scoured the room.

Daughtie shook her head. "If you'd put your belongings in their proper place when you disrobe, you'd have no difficulty finding them in the morning."

"I don't need a lecture, Daughtie; I need my shoes," Harriet replied, her candle illuminating the cross look etched upon her face.

Shrugging her shoulders, Daughtie sat on Ruth's trunk and brushed her hair. "You ought not expect our help. If we give you assistance, we're merely encouraging you to continue in your slothful habits."

"What did you call me?" Harriet shrieked.

Bella stepped forward and took Harriet's arm. "Your shoes—they're over by the window," Bella said, pointing across the room.

Harriet pulled her arm from Bella's grasp and, after one last glare at Daughtie, went to retrieve her shoes.

"You could be less critical," Bella whispered as she handed Daughtie a comb.

Daughtie gave her a look of consternation. "This room is too small for Harriet and Margaret to throw their things about. I'm used to orderliness and so are you. Why are you taking her side?"

Bella pulled the sheet taut, tucked it under the mattress, then pulled up the covers. "I'm not taking her side. I'm merely trying to keep peace. I agree that the disarray makes it difficult, but harsh words among us will make this room seem much smaller than it already is. Perhaps kind words and deeds will go further with Harriet than criticism."

"I'll try, Bella, but she is lazy."

Bella grinned. "Come on. We have time for prayer and a bit of Scripture reading before the second bell. Let's go downstairs and give the others space to finish getting ready for work."

By the time Bella and Daughtie completed their Bible reading and uttered a brief prayer, the other girls came racing down the steps, their thumping shoes and volubility drowning out the clang of the second bell.

"I wish we could eat breakfast before going off to work," Daughtie complained as they joined the group of girls hurrying out the front door.

Bella hooked arms with her friend. "We did our mending and cleaned the Brothers' rooms before eating breakfast in Canterbury."

"Performing routine daily chores isn't the same as going off to work in a mill before having a bite to eat."

"True, but leaving the mill for breakfast gives us a break and an opportunity to get out in the fresh air," Bella countered.

"And shovel down our meal without the time to properly chew or digest the food," Daughtie shot back.

Bella grinned and gave her friend's arm a squeeze. "It is obvious nothing I say is going to cheer you or change your mind, so I'll permit you the last word on this topic."

Daughtie laughed. "I'm sorry. I sound like Sister Eunice—never willing to cease my arguing."

"You haven't quite reached Sister Eunice's level, but promise you won't make that a goal," Bella said, joining in Daughtie's laughter.

"I'm pleased to see you two so cheerful this morning," the overseer greeted as they entered the room. "We have several girls out sick, and I'll need each of you to tend an extra loom."

"So much for memorizing Scripture today," Daughtie whispered as she patted her pocket.

"But, Mr. Kingman, we've only just learned to manage one of those metal beasts. Surely you don't expect us to capably tend two," Bella replied.

"You'll do fine. Besides, I have no choice. Too many of the operatives are either ill or leaving without proper notice."

Bella gave Daughtie a waning smile as they walked toward their looms. "We can paste them up today. That way they'll be ready and waiting for us tomorrow." At the moment it was as much encouragement as she could offer.

"If we can find time to do even that," Daughtie replied. "I find it appalling they expect us to take over another loom. It's obvious all they care about is quantity. They care little about the quality of their products or the well-being of their workers."

Bella nodded. She couldn't argue with what she knew was truth. These mills were a moneymaking proposition for the owners, who were interested in a handsome profit above all else. On the other hand, the Shakers placed incomparable workmanship above all else. Reconciling the opposing concepts was not possible.

"We'll just have to do the best we can," she replied as they took their places at the looms and awaited the bell's pealing before setting their looms into motion.

Taking up the brass-tipped hollowed-out piece of wood, Bella filled it with a long thread-laden wood bobbin. Lifting the shuttle to her mouth, she sucked in, pulling the bobbin thread through the small hole near the tip of the shuttle and then set the prepared shuttle in the metal box at one end of the race before moving to the next machine and picking up the second. As she sucked the thread through the eye of the second shuttle, the bell tolled and the weaving room clamored to life.

Bella slapped the handle of her machine and watched momentarily as the shuttle carrying the weft thread flew across the race between the shed of warp threads. The reed swung forward, beating against the weft, evenly tightening the latest addition of thread against the already-woven cloth. The beam crashed up and down, raising and dropping the heddles into position as the shuttle, flying in and out of the shuttle box, continued journeying back and forth at breakneck speed. The floor reverberated as she moved back and forth between the machines, repeating her routine: replacing empty bobbins with full ones, tying a weaver's knot when an errant thread snagged, always mindful to watch that the finished cloth was uniformly winding onto the take-up.

Glancing across the room, she took a moment to watch Daughtie moving back and forth between her two assigned machines. Her friend appeared miserable, with her face screwed into a look of anxiety as she stopped the second machine to insert a filled shuttle. A tight fist of remorse formed in Bella's stomach. She shouldn't have encouraged Daughtie to come with her. It had been a selfish act. If Daughtie decided she wanted to go home, Bella determined she would accompany her back to Canterbury. But she would not remain in New Hampshire herself—of that she was certain. Once Daughtie was safely delivered, she would return to Lowell and this new life by herself.

Adjusting to the world's ways would take perseverance, but Bella was willing to accept the hurried meals, the crowded boardinghouse, the deafening noise of the mills, and the lack of privacy in exchange for the freedom to explore her beliefs and make decisions based upon those new discoveries.

Daughtie, however, was not one who questioned anything. Whatever the Society taught, Daughtie believed. But their early lives had been differently formed, Bella reasoned. While Daughtie had spent her entire life among the Brothers and Sisters, steeped in the teachings of Sister Ann and the United Society of Believers, Bella had spent her early years within the nurturing nest of her parents, who had encouraged her inquiring personality. At least until they moved to Canterbury. But unlike her father and Daughtie, Bella and her mother had never completely embraced life among the Believers.

Time moved slowly until the ringing tower bell announced the breakfast break. The machines groaned to a halt, the whirring leather belts ceased turning, and the roomful of operatives raced between the rows of machines toward the stairway.

"Are you able to keep up with both looms?" Bella asked as they joined the throng of workers scurrying into the mill yard.

"I suppose I'm doing well enough, although this day can't end soon enough for me," Daughtie replied. "I only hope those sick girls are well come morning."

Bella nodded her head. "I agree, but it's been easier than I anticipated. I even pasted up the Scriptures on my loom. Did you have an opportunity to place yours?"

Daughtie gave her a frown. "I feel fortunate I was able to stop the looms when I saw an uneven weft row or snag, but I fear I may have missed some imperfections in the cloth. I surely hope not, but I did my best. My verses are still tucked in my pocket."

Reaching to embrace her friend in a quick hug, Bella said, "I know you did your very best."

"It comes easier for you, Bella. I'm not making excuses for myself, but you move among those hideous monsters without fear. When the power comes on and the looms heave to life, I fear that the trembling floors will drop from beneath my feet. The whole room seems synchronized to the incessant rumbling of the looms," Daughtie replied soulfully.

"It will get easier," Bella promised as they entered the boardinghouse.

"I hope so," Daughtie replied as they hung their cloaks near the door.

Bella and Daughtie joined the other girls in the dining room and were soon filling their plates with breakfast fare, passing bowls of oatmeal and boiled potatoes seasoned with chunks of bacon with one hand while forking food into their mouths with the other. There was little time for the formalities of courteous dining. The girls had not yet completed their meal when the tower bell pealed out its warning signal. Chairs scraped, silverware clanked, and napkins were tossed toward the table, a few missing the mark and tumbling to the floor as the operatives jumped up and hastened off to the mill.

Bella remained near Daughtie as they returned to work, hoping somehow the closeness would provide encouragement to her friend. "We can spend the whole evening together," Bella offered as they neared their looms.

Daughtie smiled and squeezed Bella's hand. "That would be nice—if we're not too weary to remain awake by day's end."

The routine resumed in earnest at the clanging of the bell. As the hours began to pass, Bella was able to read the Scripture verses tacked to her loom. She glanced about the room while attempting to memorize the words, enjoying the challenge. Bella smiled at Clara, the young doffer who came running to gather her box of empty bobbins. The child was no more than ten, with hazel eyes and long chestnut brown hair. As Bella nodded, the girl opened her hand to reveal a beautiful glass marble for Bella's inspection.

"It's beautiful," Bella mouthed to the child.

Clara smiled her obvious appreciation for the compliment while pushing the cart of empty bobbins away from Bella's looms. She continued down the narrow aisle, her small stature permitting her to move through the machinery with apparent ease.

Returning her gaze to the Scripture, Bella was beginning to repeat the words aloud when the young doffer dropped to the floor and began crawling through the machines. Bella saw the marble rolling across the floor with Clara in pursuit.

"Nooo!" Bella screamed, her voice drowned out by the perpetual thump and bang of the surrounding machines. She felt as though her shoes were fastened to the floor, her body moving in sluggish, laborious motion as she struggled to reach the young child whose screams now matched her own.

Clara, anxious to reclaim her marble, had reached through the gears of Annie Williams' loom. Before Bella could reach her, the girl's fingers were snapping like brittle twigs. Annie stood frozen, her machine continuing its inhumane torture, the child unable to remove her hand. Shoving Annie aside, Bella grasped the handle and slapped it to the off position. The loom groaned to a stop, yet Clara's screams were unrelenting as Mr. Kingman made his way toward them.

"What are you doing away from your looms, Miss Newberry?" he hollered, his baritone voice resonating above all other noise in the room.

Bella pointed toward the child. "She's injured—her hand . . ."

The overseer scooped up Clara. "Back to work," he commanded before carrying the limp child out of the room.

Bella spun around and retreated to her looms, gazing toward Daughtie as she made her return. Daughtie stared back—a wide-eyed vacant look, as though her mind was unable to process what she had just witnessed.

~ 8 ~

Lilly Cheever straightened the folds of her lavender silk carriage dress as the horse-drawn buggy came to a halt in front of Addie Beecher's boarding-house. Her frock wasn't of the latest fashion, but when topped with the double-pointed cashmere-lined pelerine, she could pass the scrutiny of Lowell's fashion-conscious society women. Adjusting her large leghorn hat, she tightened the matching lavender ribbons before stepping down from her coach.

"You may return for me at four o'clock," she instructed the driver, who nodded and tipped his hat.

Lilly walked up the wide step to number 5 Jackson Street. Eighteen months ago, she would have burst through the door without knocking. But that was when she was one of the operatives at the Appleton who boarded with Miss Addie. Nowadays, she was Miss Addie's visitor, so she raised her gloved hand and firmly knocked at the door of what was once her home.

The sound of Miss Addie bustling toward the door could be heard even before it opened. "Lilly! Do come in, dear," the rosy-faced keeper greeted. Her lips were turned up in a welcoming smile that caused dimples to form in each of her plump cheeks. "I just prepared our tea," she said, leading Lilly into the parlor. "I didn't want to waste a minute of our visiting time out in the kitchen," she explained with a giggle.

Lilly seated herself beside Miss Addie on the familiar overstuffed settee and watched as Addie filled two delicate china cups with the hot brew. "It's been too long since we've gotten together for a visit," Lilly commented as she took the cup Miss Addie offered. "I must admit, however, that it is still difficult for me to think of myself as other than one of your girls," she observed. "In fact, I still awaken with a start at the sound of the bells and think it's time to get ready for work."

Addie chuckled and patted Lilly's hands. "You'll always be one of my girls, Lilly. How could you not be? Were it not for all of your help teaching me to cook and manage this house, the Corporation would have dismissed me long ago."

"You were a capable student. Besides, you would have learned on your own had I not appeared on your doorstep."

"Eventually. But I doubt any of the girls would have remained in the house long enough to find out. I'm just thankful you came knocking. God was certainly looking out for me that day."

Lilly took a sip of her tea. "Now, tell me, what's been going on with you and John Farnsworth? I've been expecting a wedding invitation."

"I don't think a wedding is in the offing right now, Lilly. I care deeply for John and I believe he feels the same, but we've encountered an obstacle upon which we disagree. Until we're able to reach a resolution that's suitable to both of us, I doubt you'll hear any wedding bells."

Lilly furrowed her brow. "Please don't think me forward, Miss Addie, but dare I inquire as to the nature of your obstacle?"

Addie nodded. "Of course, dear. You know the Corporation built that fine house for John?" she asked.

Lilly nodded. "It appears to be a lovely home."

"John is very fond of it. But I am very fond of this boardinghouse and my girls. I want him to move in here when we marry. He wants me to give up the boardinghouse and move into his big house. Accordingly, we reached an impasse. Now that his nephew has arrived from England and moved into the house with him, John seems content to keep our arrangement as it is. There's been little discussion of marriage since young Taylor's arrival."

Lilly gave her friend a thoughtful look. "I'm guessing your decision may have been based on more than leaving the boardinghouse."

Addie glanced toward the floor. "Whatever do you mean?"

"I would guess you're concerned about Miss Mintie and how she might react if you married John and moved into his fine house. You don't want to hurt your sister. Am I correct?"

A slight blush colored Miss Addie's full cheeks. "I know I'm entitled to a happy married life with John, but I won't deny that I worry about Mintie's reaction should I wed. I believe she's beginning to soften a bit—her occasional outings with Lawrence Gault have helped, but he appears unlikely to make a commitment at this time. Mintie tells me his mother is ailing and he feels the weight of responsibility for her care. Even though his mother doesn't live in Lowell, Mr. Gault travels home frequently and provides for all of her financial care."

"Mintie's problems aside, Addie, it's time you thought of your own future. I realize doing so seems selfish to someone of your sweet nature, but John is a fine man who wants only the best for you. I'm sure he doesn't want to see you laboring in this boardinghouse every day, waiting on all these girls when he is perfectly capable of providing a fine home for you. You haven't always lived like this. You were once a part of Boston's upper society. Now, I realize Lowell is a far cry from that, but think of the good you might do. You could have teas for the girls. You could open your home for lectures and such.

Besides, what would become of that fine home the Corporation built for him?"

"Speaking of houses, how are you and Matthew enjoying your new home?"

It was obvious Miss Addie was moving the topic of conversation away from her dilemma with John, but Lilly pretended not to notice as she took a bite of her tart.

"This is delicious," she complimented. "Perhaps you'll share the recipe."

Addie grinned. "Now, who would have thought the day would arrive when I could share a recipe with you?"

"Well, it doesn't surprise me a bit!" Lilly exclaimed.

"Thank you, dear. Now, please, do tell me about your new home."

Lilly gave Addie a mischievous grin. "I don't think I will."

Addie's face reflected astonishment at the reply. "What? Whyever not?"

"Because I want you to come and see it for yourself. I'm extending an invitation to tea for a week from Sunday if you're available. I decided upon Sunday afternoon because I'd like you to invite any of your girls to come along who might enjoy the outing."

"Oh, Lilly, that would be such fun. How kind you are to include the girls. But you may end up with quite a houseful when they discover they'll get to see your fine new home."

Lilly smiled at her friend's excitement. "I've not been gone from this boardinghouse so long that I don't fondly remember those special outings that made the routine of working in the mills more bearable."

"Especially the ones with Matthew?" Addie teased.

"Yes, especially those," Lilly agreed, returning Addie's smile. "It will be fun meeting—"

A knock sounded at the front door, interrupting Lilly's remark.

Addie rose and walked toward the hallway. "I can't imagine who would come calling at this time of day," she remarked before pulling open the door.

"Are you entertaining this afternoon?" The words were more of an accusation than a question.

Lilly immediately recognized the voice. Mintie Beecher. Most likely she had spied the carriage when Lilly arrived. From all appearances, life hadn't changed much in the past year and a half. Miss Mintie was still peeking out at the world from behind her drapery-covered windows in the boardinghouse across the street and was still inserting herself in Addie's affairs whenever she pleased. She believed it not only her right but her duty as elder sister to see that Addie lived above reproach.

Mintie swooped into the parlor and peered over the top of her wire-rimmed spectacles while conducting a survey of the room. "Just as I thought," she condemned. "I'm not invited when you have special guests come to visit."

Miss Addie's face screwed into a tight knot at the reprimand, and Lilly immediately came to her friend's rescue. "Please direct your anger at me, Miss Beecher. I haven't seen Miss Addie for some time and requested a private visit. However, we'd be pleased to have you join us," Lilly responded graciously.

Mintie appeared somewhat mollified as she settled onto one of the straight-backed chairs and primly folded her hands. "I see. Well, since you insist, I suppose I could stay for a short visit." Her pinch-faced expression never altered. Mintie Beecher appeared as though perpetually guilty of sucking on sour lemons.

Lilly arched her eyebrows at the reply but said nothing.

"I'll go and get another teacup," Addie said as she bustled off toward the kitchen.

"Has Adelaide told you about her newest boarders?" Mintie inquired with a note of expectancy in her voice.

Lilly shook her head before taking a sip of tea.

"They're Shakers," Mintie continued. "You know, the ones who dance during worship services—heathens, if you ask me. Whoever heard of such a thing?"

Lilly couldn't resist. "I believe David danced before the Lord, Miss Beecher."

The birdlike woman pursed her lips. "That's Old Testament."

Lilly waited a moment, thinking the woman surely had more to say. "And?"

"And nothing. History. David and his antics are history. You don't hear tell of the disciples dancing in the New Testament, do you?"

Lilly stared at her, open-mouthed.

"I rest my case!"

"What case?" Addie inquired as she entered the room. "Shall I pour your tea?"

Lilly turned toward Miss Addie. "Your sister was explaining to me that the disciples didn't dance," Lilly said with a grin.

Addie began giggling and nearly spilled the tea. "You're discussing dancing disciples?" she sputtered.

"They didn't dance," Mintie angrily replied. "And the disciples are not a topic of amusement, Adelaide. What we're truly discussing are the heathen practices of those Shaker girls."

Addie gave her sister a disgusted look. "They are not heathens, Mintie. They belonged to the United Society of Believers and left that life behind when they came to Lowell. They attend church every Sunday, which is more than I can say for some of the girls who lie abed pretending to be ill until after church services. Bella and Daughtie are fine young ladies attempting to adjust to a very new way of life. They need our support, not our criticism."

Lilly nodded her agreement. "Adjusting to the mills and living in a board-inghouse is difficult, even when you don't have faith issues involved. I imagine those girls are struggling on a daily basis to adapt to this new life."

"Oh, pshaw! It's not as though their life in that Shaker community was so different. The men and women live separately—no marriage allowed—and the women live together in big rooms, just like the boardinghouses. They're required to work, and I doubt the transition has been any more difficult for them than for any of the other girls."

"You seem to be quite the authority, Miss Beecher. Where did you gather your information, if I might ask?" Lilly inquired.

"Mrs. Goodnow. She visited that Shaker village up near Canterbury. She said it's the devil's workshop for certain. Those people dancing and whirling about and calling it worship of the Lord. It may be worship, but I assure you it's not of the Lord!" Mintie smugly retorted.

"With all the information you've gathered, I'd think that instead of reviling the girls for having once belonged to that community, you would be encouraging others to help them adjust to this new life," Lilly replied. "Of course, I believe people sometimes unwittingly exaggerate their stories, don't you?"

"Indeed, I do," Addie agreed. "I've spent several evenings visiting with Bella. She's an enchanting young lady who is seeking to find the truth by studying God's Word. Some of the Shaker beliefs are in conflict with what she learned before her family joined the community, and that's one of the many reasons she chose to leave Canterbury. We should remember that most of the young people in the Shaker communities had no choice in their placement. And there's something to be said for a group of people who are willing to assist others when they find themselves in desperate circumstances."

Mintie glanced heavenward before giving her sister an intolerant scowl. "Honestly, Adelaide! Must you always argue with me? I'm sure Reverend Edson would be pleased to confirm everything I've said about the Shakers and their strange habits."

"Really? I've always considered Reverend Edson more of a visionary, a man devoted to seeking innovative ways to win souls to the Lord as opposed to condemning souls who are seeking the truth," Lilly interjected.

Mintie sputtered and turned her attention toward Lilly. "Of course you would take Adelaide's side in the matter."

"I'm not taking sides, Miss Beecher. I am merely stating my opinion," Lilly calmly replied. She had yet to know a visit with Mintie that didn't turn into an argument. Mintie Beecher would brook no opinion that differed from her own.

Mintie placed her cup on the tea tray and announced that she was going home. She was slow in making her departure, most likely hoping that Addie or Lilly would beg her to remain. However, both remained silent, and Lilly watched as Addie firmly escorted her sister to the door.

"She's angry," Addie announced as she returned to the parlor. "But she'll come around in a few days. She always does."

Lilly nodded. "She doesn't appear to have softened so much that one would notice. And I'm quite certain we won't have to worry about her dancing in church," Lilly said before bursting into giggles.

Miss Addie soon joined in, the two women settling down momentarily before once again launching into gales of laughter. Tears streamed down their cheeks before they finally regained their composure.

"Dear me!" Miss Addie exclaimed as she blotted her eyes. "I don't know when I've laughed so hard. I must admit I'm a little ashamed I could find such enjoyment in my sister's displeasure."

"I suppose it isn't very charitable of us," Lilly agreed, "but you must admit that she was set on an argument when she first came in the house. She always is. If she sees something going on without her involvement, she's hard pressed not to thrust herself into the middle of it no matter what."

Addie nodded. "You're right. She's always been that way. I'd think she would tire of the routine, but I remember her being this way even from our younger days. But let's not spend the rest of our afternoon discussing Mintie. I want to hear more about you. I've wanted to ask about your progress finding Lewis's child. Has there been any success?"

At the mention of her brother's name, a lump began to form in Lilly's throat. "No. Matthew has failed me in regard to the little boy," she whispered. "I fear he's satisfied himself the child cannot be found. He conducted a hasty search shortly after Lewis's death. Locating nothing and unable to find any leads, he seemed content with the idea that the child never existed."

"Perhaps he's right," Addie replied quietly. "You didn't have much information to go on, my dear."

Lilly snapped to attention, prepared to defend her position. "I doubt he would have made such a declaration from his deathbed if the child didn't exist. He even spoke of a birthmark."

"I don't mean to offend you, child, but I've heard tell of dying people who sometimes become delusional and babble on incoherently before they finally die," Addie offered. "In fact, you'll remember I told you about my father— the Judge—doing just that."

"Your father's circumstances were entirely different, Miss Addie. He lingered in his illness for a period of time. However, Lewis knew his burns would soon render him dead. He wanted to do the right thing. I believe Lewis told me of the boy's existence because he wanted the child to have proper care."

Addie nodded. "But you may have to accept the fact that even if the boy does exist, you may not find him. Knowing about a little boy with a birthmark doesn't mean that you have a great deal of information."

"I also know that the mother was Irish, so there's little doubt that someone in the Acre knows something about the boy. However, Matthew tells me the Irish are slow to cooperate, especially about personal matters such as children born out of wedlock," Lilly related. "It seems that if Matthew really wanted to find the boy, he would talk to some of the men working for the Corporation. Surely one of them would trust him enough to do a bit of investigating."

"I'm not so sure," Addie replied. "The Irish have learned they have to stick together and look out for their own."

Lilly sighed. "You're probably right. I just don't want to accept the fact that I have no family left in this world."

Addie's mouth dropped open. "Child! You have a husband. He's your family. And what of Matthew's parents? You couldn't ask for finer relatives."

Lilly held up her hand to stave off the onslaught of Addie's words. "Yes, and I love all of them very much. But they're not blood relatives, Miss Addie. I've watched both my parents die, and then just as Lewis and I were beginning to mend the problems of our childhood and build a relationship, he, too, died."

Addie took Lilly's hand in her own. "It's difficult to understand the way of things, Lilly, but if you are meant to have this boy, God will direct you to him. If He doesn't, you must learn to accept the fact that you are not the person intended to rear the boy. Otherwise, you'll become bitter and contentious. And heaven knows I can't deal with another Mintie," she added in an obvious attempt to lighten the mood.

Lilly smiled, deciding it was time to share her secret. "I promise I'll not become bitter—I doubt I'll have much opportunity for such things. You see, I've just discovered Matthew and I are going to have a child of our own."

Addie clapped her hands in delight. "So you will have a blood relative, after all," she responded. "Isn't God gracious? He's giving you your heart's desire, Lilly."

Lilly's eyebrows molded into thinly knit strips as she stared at the older woman. The ticking of the mantel clock resonated in the background, with each click of the tinny pendulum proclaiming the passing moments as she considered Addie's words.

"To be honest, I hadn't thought of this new life in those terms, Miss Addie. It's true that the child will be my blood relative. Yet the fact that Matthew and I are going to have a child doesn't lessen my desire to locate Lewis's boy. I'm sure it will sound strange to you, but Lewis's child gives me a connection to the past, while this child is my connection to the future. One does not supplant my need for the other. I don't want to sound ungrateful, for I realize our marriage has been blessed by God's goodness. However, my prayers remain steadfast: I want to find Lewis's child."

Addie nodded and gave Lilly a cautious smile. "I didn't mean to imply this babe would be a replacement, dear girl. But do remember that living in the past can sometimes thwart a healthy future, not to mention the present. I wouldn't want that happening to you."

"Nor would I," Lilly agreed.

Bella slipped into her blue worsted gown, the normal attire for Sunday meeting among the United Society of Believers. Not that she was attending church among the Shakers—far from it. This Sunday she was attending St. Anne's Episcopal Church with Miss Addie, analyzing yet another array of beliefs. She and Daughtie had listened to the Methodists, Baptists, and Unitarians. Now the Episcopalians would have an opportunity to divulge the tenets of their faith, at least to Bella. Daughtie refused to observe another form of worship, certain she would only become more confused. So while Bella and Addie prepared to attend St. Anne's, Ruth and Daughtie set off for services at the Methodist church. Bella feared her friend's refusal to further explore the churches in Lowell was a harbinger of what would lie ahead. Bella worried Daughtie would soon announce her plans to depart Lowell.

Descending the steps, Bella walked through the parlor and then into the kitchen, where Miss Addie was busily packing items into a large basket. "I thought perhaps you had left without me," Bella remarked.

Miss Addie gave her a wide grin. "Not a chance! I wanted to get our lunch packed because immediately after church services today we'll be attending the annual church picnic. I wanted to surprise you."

"Well, you've certainly managed to do that," Bella replied. "I've never attended a church picnic. What are the rules for such a thing?"

Addie giggled, her fleshy pink cheeks jiggling ever so slightly. "The only rule is to have fun," she announced. "And I plan to see that we both follow that rule."

"Are you going to carry that heavy basket to church? Surely we don't need all that food for just you and me," Bella protested.

"No need to worry about the basket. John Farnsworth is calling for us in his carriage. And I've packed enough food for four, not two," Addie sheepishly explained.

"Four?"

"Yes. Taylor Manning will be joining us."

Bella sat down on the small wooden stool. The sound of the front door opening and closing, along with the voices of chattering girls moving about the house, filtered into the room and interrupted her thoughts. Bella could enumerate a long list of objections to spending the day with Taylor Manning. Miss Addie was an understanding woman, but she might be offended to hear that the thought of spending a day with Taylor Manning and his outlandish ideas about women was probably more than Bella could bear.

"Goodness, that certainly comes as a surprise. I was thinking that perhaps it would be better if I joined you for church next week, when there are no special activities," Bella ventured.

"Nonsense! The picnic is wonderful fun. That's why I specifically requested you visit this Sunday. And don't you concern yourself about young Taylor. John will see that he's on his best behavior."

A knock sounded at the front door, and Addie scurried off to answer it before Bella could offer any further protest. It appeared there was to be no escape. Bella stewed silently for a moment before standing up and straightening her skirts. Grasping the heavy basket by its handle, she swung it around, nearly knocking Taylor to the floor as he entered the room.

"My leg!" he hollered, grabbing one leg by the shin while hopping around on the other.

Bella dropped the basket to the floor. "I'm so sorry," she apologized hurriedly. "Sit down and let me take a look at it," she ordered while pointing toward the stool.

"No thanks—you've done quite enough already," Taylor replied as he rubbed the bruised leg. "Uncle John and Miss Addie are waiting for us in the carriage. I was sent to fetch you and that confounded basket," he said, grabbing it from her hand.

"Mr. Manning! Please don't use foul language in my presence," Bella ordered.

Taylor stared open-mouthed at her. "What are you talking about?"

"If you think I'll repeat your words, rest assured that I will not."

Taylor's brow wrinkled into deep creases, which caused him to appear years older. "Confounded? Is that the word? *Confounded?*"

His words punctuated the air like a needle piercing cloth. She glared at him. "Stop using that word—now!" she commanded.

Taylor shook his head. "It's going to be a long day," he muttered.

Bella stopped in her tracks. "I share your sentiments. Spending a day in your company is not my idea of pleasure, either," she rebutted before marching off.

"Don't worry about me and my injured leg. I'll be fine carrying this heavy basket," he called, his voice laced with sarcasm as she walked out the front door, leaving him in the wake of her anger.

Addie smiled down from the carriage. "Oh, good, I was beginning to wonder where you were. Now, where is Taylor?" she asked, looking expectantly toward the door.

"He'll be along. He's nursing his injured leg."

"Oh, my! He's injured? John, you'd better go and see to him," Addie fluttered.

"No need, Miss Addie. Here he comes now," Bella said as Taylor limped slowly toward them.

John jumped down from the carriage and assisted Taylor with the picnic basket. "What happened to your leg? You run into something?"

"You might say that," Taylor replied. "Miss Newberry swung that basket into my shin."

Bella gasped at Taylor's explanation while Addie twisted around on the seat, a look of astonished surprise etched on her plump face.

"Bella!" the older woman exclaimed in horror.

"It was an accident, Miss Addie. He came into the room unexpectedly just as I was lifting the basket off the table. As I turned, the basket swung around, tapping him on the leg. Then he began cursing, and when I requested that he refrain from such ill-bred language, he used the word several more times. And that is the truth of what happened," Bella explained. Then she leaned forward and whispered to Miss Addie, "He's acting like a big baby. The basket barely touched his leg."

With John's assistance, Taylor heaved himself into the carriage, making a great show of his pain and leaning heavily against Bella as he adjusted his leg.

"Get off of me!" Bella commanded, pushing him away with all her might.

Once again Miss Addie twisted around in her seat as Taylor gave Bella a dejected look. "I am terribly sorry, Miss Newberry. I wasn't attempting to be offensive, but I'm in pain and needed to straighten my leg."

"Give him a little more room so he can make himself more comfortable, Bella," Addie instructed before turning back toward the front of the carriage.

Taylor gave her a smug grin and then winked. Winked!

"You are no gentleman, sir," Bella hissed. "It's good that we're on our way to church."

"And why is that?"

"Because you're certainly in need of help from the Almighty!"

Taylor gave a hearty laugh. "I doubt you'll find me any more proper after the church sermon than before," he responded jovially.

Bella tapped Miss Addie on the shoulder. "You see? He's laughing and feeling much better already," she said with a look of satisfaction on her face as she leaned back against the leather-upholstered seat.

Taylor leaned close, his hair sweeping down across one eye. "You're out of your element, Bella. I'm more practiced than you are at this type of behavior. They may listen to your words, but they won't believe my leg is healed until I've convinced them."

She stiffened and looked away in an attempt to push down the boiling anger that was welling up inside. If she spoke, her words would spew out the anger she felt for this man. Rather than speak, she shifted her body toward the buggy door and directed her gaze at the passing scenery.

"Don't be angry with me, dear Bella," Taylor whispered, his breath on her neck causing her to shiver. "I want to be friends. Give me just a little smile," he pleaded. Still leaning close, he ran his finger along her cheek.

Unable to restrain herself any longer, Bella slapped his hand away from her face. "Keep your hands to yourself!" she hissed through clenched teeth as the carriage came to a halt.

Bella noted Taylor's obvious lack of pain as he stepped out of the carriage and offered her his hand. "May I assist you?"

"Oh no, I don't need any help. You take care of yourself. I wouldn't want you to hurt that leg."

Miss Addie gave her a sweet smile. "That was very kind of you, dear."

"Obviously Miss Addie didn't notice the sarcasm dripping from your reply," Taylor commented as they sauntered toward the gray-slate church building.

"Nor your lack of discomfort when you jumped out of the carriage," Bella replied. She chastised herself for speaking to him. Silence! That was the key to ridding herself of Taylor Manning. Somehow his words forced a rebuttal from her lips. If nothing else, surely all those years in the Shaker community had taught her restraint. She merely needed to put that teaching into practice.

Bella caught her breath as they entered the sanctuary of St. Anne's. The midmorning sun was glowing through huge stained-glass windows, casting a rainbow of colors across the rows of walnut pews. Midway down the aisle, Miss Addie stopped beside a pew. John unlatched a small door permitting them entrance to their seats.

"Why are there doors on the pews?" Bella whispered to Miss Addie.

"The sermons are boring, and the doors prevent our escape," Taylor said with a snicker.

Bella ignored his reply and waited for a response from Miss Addie. "In the winter, the church is difficult to heat. It's so large," she said, glancing toward the high ceiling, "and the heat all rises upward. In order to keep everyone a bit warmer, heating bricks or warming pans are placed on the floor inside each pew. The doors help keep the heat in," she explained. "However, I must add that there are probably others who share young Taylor's view," she said, giving him an agreeable smile. "Oh, here's Mintie," she exclaimed. "Do unlatch the door, Taylor."

"Good morning, all," Mintie greeted, squeezing herself into the seat alongside Taylor. Pushing against Taylor's chest with her parasol, she bent forward in an effort to gain her sister's attention. "Will you be attending the picnic, Adelaide?"

"Yes, we're all attending. And you?"

Mintie peered over the top of her glasses and pursed her lips. Before she could reply, her attention was drawn toward the girls entering the pew in front of them. Once again making use of her parasol, she tapped one of the girls on the shoulder. "You girls need to go to one of the pews near the rear of the church. That pew belongs to the Behren family."

Bella watched as the girls, their cheeks flushed with embarrassment, vacated the pew and hastened toward the rear of the church while the finely dressed citizens of Lowell strolled down the aisle, stopping to visit with one another as they moved toward their seats. Chattering and laughter had been evident in all the churches Bella had visited thus far. Worship in the churches of Lowell was unusual—so different from Canterbury, where the women and men formed separate rows and marched in through their individual doors of the Meeting House, with men on one side and women on the other, quietly taking their seats on opposing sides. What would Sister Mercy think if she could see Bella sitting beside a gentleman during church services? Well, perhaps not a gentleman, but a man, she decided.

Taylor leaned toward her. "You might want to take note of the fashions these women are wearing and give thought to wearing dresses that are a little more—" he hesitated a moment—"becoming?"

Bella held her tongue and remained silent. *How dare he comment on my apparel,* she thought. Obviously her Sunday Shaker dress didn't meet the standards of the world, but it was all she owned, and it was neat, clean, and freshly pressed.

"No need to clench up like that," he said. "Feel free to say whatever it is you're thinking."

Bella remained silent and kept her gaze turned forward, giving full attention to the services that had now begun. She wanted to impartially evaluate each church she attended. Otherwise, how could she decide where she belonged? Besides, it shouldn't be so difficult to find a church that followed the Bible's teachings. And yet, if that were true, why were there so many divergent beliefs? The Shakers had added Mother Ann's teachings to those of the Bible, and each of the Protestant churches appeared to have something that set it apart from the others, like the way they baptized or took communion. And the Catholics had their own way of interpreting things, too. It was, she decided, not such an easy matter to determine where one belonged.

"You're frowning," Taylor whispered an hour later as the benediction was given. "It doesn't become you."

"Shh!" Miss Mintie hissed with an index finger placed over her pursed lips.

"I was only—"

Before Taylor could complete his reply, Miss Mintie jabbed a sharp elbow into his side. "Quiet!" she commanded.

Bella arched her eyebrows and gave Taylor a warning look. Obviously Miss Mintie was a force to be reckoned with; she was not about to put up with Mr. Manning's tomfoolery.

Taylor waited until Reverend Edson left the pulpit and had walked to the rear of the church before asking, "Do I now have your permission to speak, Miss Beecher?"

"Don't be foolish, Mr. Manning. The church service is over; of course you can speak. You understood exactly what I meant when I told you to be quiet. I will not tolerate rude behavior." She lifted her closed parasol and tapped the pointed end into his chest. "And you, Mr. Manning, were being rude."

Bella leaned around Taylor and smiled demurely at Miss Mintie. "Will you be joining us for lunch, Miss Beecher?"

Mintie shook her head. "I didn't pack a lunch, but perhaps I'll return for some of the afternoon activities."

Taking her cue from Taylor's apparent look of relief, Bella sprung into action. "We would love to have you join us. Miss Addie has packed enough food to feed a small army. Haven't you, Miss Adelaide?" Bella inquired while tugging on Addie's sleeve.

"Haven't I what?" Addie asked, turning away from her conversation with John and several other parishioners.

"Prepared ample food—so Miss Beecher may join us."

Addie nodded. "Well, of course, sister. You are more than welcome. To be honest, I anticipated you would join us."

Mintie appeared to be giving the matter grave consideration before giving her reply. "Well, I suppose I might as well stay."

Addie nodded, Bella grinned, and Taylor's expression wilted.

They gathered momentarily outside the church before the men rushed off to fetch the picnic basket. "Don't forget to limp," Bella cautioned Taylor as she walked off with Mintie and Addie to seek a shade-covered site for their blanket.

Bella managed to seat herself between Mintie and Addie until they'd finished their lunch, but soon thereafter John suggested he and Addie take a stroll. Immediately Taylor moved to Bella's side, a lopsided grin spread across his face as he made himself comfortable.

"Gather up those dishes and hand them here," Mintie ordered Taylor as she began packing the leftovers into the wicker basket. "You can lie around in the sunshine after we're done."

Taylor grimaced as he dutifully followed Miss Mintie's commands and helped pack, fold, and organize everything to the older woman's satisfaction. "Have we finished?"

"You do have a smart tongue, young man. It's obvious we're finished—

there's nothing more to put in the basket, is there?"

Taylor gave her a sheepish grin. "No, ma'am."

Mintie brushed some imaginary crumbs from the folds of her skirt and then directed her attention toward Bella. "I'm pleased we have this time together, Bella. I've been wanting to ask you about those Shakers up in Canterbury," she began. "I've heard all kinds of stories about them."

"Really? Like what?" Bella inquired.

"That they dance and twirl around in church and sometimes even commence to shouting and running during worship. I also heard," she continued, "that the women and men can't even talk to each other. Is that true?"

"There's dancing during church, and occasionally someone becomes filled with the Spirit and whirls, but the dancing isn't like the world's dances. Our dancing is a form of worship offered to God. I don't know who told you the men and women can't
speak to each other, but that isn't so. The men and women converse, but a man and woman are not permitted to go off alone and keep company," she explained.

Mintie nodded. "So how does that work?"

"Yes," Taylor chimed in. "How does that work?"

"We converse during Union Meetings about topics of interest. For instance, if I found a piece of literature particularly interesting and one of the gentlemen was also fascinated by the same writing, we would sit opposite each other in Union Meeting and discuss the merits of that piece of work."

"But didn't those conversations cause men and women with similar interests to become attracted to one another?" Taylor inquired.

"The conversations were never intimate, and if the elders feared any impropriety might arise, they would have another person join you."

"And did that ever happen?" Taylor asked, moving closer.

"Yes, frequently," Bella replied honestly.

Taylor appeared taken aback. "To you?"

Bella laughed and then felt a blush begin to rise in her cheeks. "Only once."

Suddenly Miss Mintie became interested. "Aha! So that's why you left. You have a beau," she announced smugly.

"No, it wasn't like that," Bella defended. "Jesse is my friend—just like Daughtie. We had made plans to leave Canterbury because we didn't believe the teachings of Mother Ann—at least that's why I left. However, I fear Daughtie came along because of my influence rather than her own convictions."

"And this Jesse, why did he leave?" Mintie inquired.

Taylor drew closer, his gaze unwavering as she answered.

"I'm not certain he left," she quietly replied. "He didn't appear as planned, so Daughtie and I left on our own. You see, we were a little late arriving at the meeting place we'd decided upon, and I don't know if he decided to go on without us or if he arrived after us and left on his own. Or perhaps when we didn't arrive, he remained behind."

"Or never appeared at all! Just like a man—leaving you to fend for yourself," Mintie retorted.

Bella glanced up at Miss Mintie. The older woman's words echoed Bella's thoughts, but she hadn't wanted to give voice to them. Jesse had failed her, just as her father had in the past.

"Well, it's not as though he had pledged his love," Taylor replied, obviously feeling a need to defend the man.

"Yes he had. He said he loved me and wanted to be married," Bella blurted out without thinking. She wanted to snatch back the words the moment they were spoken. Miss Mintie was giving her a pitying look while Taylor appeared self-satisfied—pleased that he had successfully elicited such revealing information.

He reached over and patted Bella's hand. "Don't spend another minute concerning yourself with this Jesse fellow. I always have time for a beautiful woman," he said while running his fingers through the hair that had fallen across his forehead.

Bella felt herself become rigid at his words. He was going to use this to his advantage if she didn't soon turn things around. "Miss Beecher, did you know that the Shakers believe in the complete equality of men and women?" she inquired.

"You don't say! Now, that's a belief I could probably take hold of," she said. "Tell me more," she encouraged, giving Bella her rapt attention.

She quickly determined that she wouldn't explain the basis for the equality. Instead, Bella decided she would explain the benefits of equality. After all, Miss Mintie might look askance once she realized such equality was based upon the Shaker's belief that Mother Ann represented the second embodiment of Christ's spirit. The first, of course, had been Jesus, but this second embodiment in a woman now made both sexes equal—at least that's what Mother Ann proclaimed. It was only one of several proclamations Bella couldn't bring herself to accept. But just because she didn't accept Mother Ann's deity didn't mean Bella didn't believe in the equality of men and women.

"The men and women share equally in all things. There is nothing granted to a man over a woman—or a woman over a man. The Shakers have both male and female Elders; they share work equally. They are educated equally. If a woman is more skilled in caring for the ill or keeping ledgers, she is permitted to do so. Women may discuss matters of social concern on equal footing with men and are encouraged to make their views known. The men don't go off into a drawing room and discuss matters of import while the women are relegated to gossip and stitchery in the parlor."

"Now, that makes good common sense. Women are every bit as bright as men. Personally, I believe they fear we are more intelligent, and that is why they send us off to another room. Now the Judge, my deceased father," she explained, "tended to be more like your Shakers—at least in that respect. Well, only where I was concerned. He never included Adelaide in discussions regarding the business of the day because, quite frankly, she wasn't interested. But I was. The Judge and I would talk well into the evening hours. He coveted my thoughts and opinions regarding matters of substance. Men like the Judge are few and far between," Mintie soulfully replied. "My, how I miss that man," she added softly.

"I believe in equality for women," Taylor interjected.

Both women turned to stare at him, Bella giving him a look of disbelief. "Did you say you believe in equality?" she asked.

He puffed his chest. "Yes, absolutely."

"Why, that's marvelous news, Taylor. Then I assume you'll be permitting the young ladies of Lowell access to the Mechanics Association library and lectures. Isn't that wonderful, Miss Beecher?"

Taylor turned ashen while Bella smiled and reveled in the moment.

~ 10 ~

Liam Donohue planted his work-worn hands on his hips and gave a satisfied nod. He'd been working in the home of James Paul Green, known as J. P. to his close associates. And although Liam wasn't considered such an associate, Mr. Green had specifically sought him out to carve and lay the intricate stonework he desired around each of the five fireplaces in his fancy Boston home. Unfortunately, the work had been both tedious and worrisome. Liam had split, shaped, and sculpted the granite, fieldstone, limestone, flagstone, shale, and slate into a combination of sizes, shapes, and textures, all with an eye toward enhancing the imported Italian tiles that had been individually carved as the focal point of each fireplace. Liam had been handsomely paid for the work, but most of the funds had already been sent to Ireland to care for his aging parents as well as several brothers and sisters who still remained at home.

A satisfied smile graced Mr. Green's lips as he surveyed the fireplace in the library that doubled as his office. "You've done a fine job, Liam. I don't believe an Englishman could have performed better stonework."

Liam held his tongue, though it was difficult. Personally, he doubted whether Mr. Green could have found anyone to perform better stonework, much less an Englishman.

"If you're in need of a recommendation, please use my name," he said while extending his hand.

Liam gripped Mr. Green's soft, fleshy hand in a muscular handshake. "I'll be thankin' ya for yar kind offer. I'll not be in Boston long, 'owever. I've been offered a position in Lowell, and I'll be leavin' once I've finished cleanin' up here," he said in a thick Irish brogue.

Rubbing his jawline, J. P. leaned against the walnut mantel in a swaggering fashion. "So it's Lowell you're off to. I have many connections there, also. Nathan Appleton, one of the founders of the Boston Associates, is my partner in the shipping business. We export almost all of the textiles produced in Lowell," he said. "Surely you're not going to waste your talents building mills?"

"No. At least not for the present. Hugh Cummiskey contacted me regardin' the Catholic church bein' constructed in Lowell. He's hired me to complete the decorative stonework at the church. After that job's completed, I'm not sure what I'll be doin'. But certain I am the good Lord will provide."

Green gave him a derisive laugh. "After you've seen the living conditions of your fellow countrymen in Lowell, I'd wager you'll be looking to your own talents for provision. I don't think God's spending much time providing for the Irish," he callously remarked before continuing. "Appears you'll be finished before noon. I'm expected at a meeting in a few minutes. You can let yourself out."

Liam nodded, glancing over his shoulder as Green exited the house. He might need Mr. Green's recommendation one day. Otherwise he would have told Mr. J. P. Green what he thought of arrogant, uncaring men who grew fat and stodgy while others starved.

Leaning down to gather his tools, Liam began placing them in his case and then sat down in front of the fireplace to clean a small trowel. He scraped at the tool, his glance shifting toward the hearth. A bundle of papers was lying in the grate alongside several pieces of wood. Reaching in, he pulled out one of the pages and gave it a cursory glance. It had writing on only one side.

Did J. P. Green not realize that the other side of the paper could be used for writing letters, drawing plans, or compiling lists? He glanced toward the hallway, wishing Mr. Green hadn't left. If Liam took the paper, it would be put to good use and save him hard-earned coins. Surely Mr. Green wouldn't consider it stealing. After all, if he left it in the fireplace, the papers would be destroyed.

Folding the pages, Liam packed them into his satchel, left the house, and made his way to the Beacon House, where he would board a stagecoach for Lowell. He'd considered going by boat, using the canals that wound their way into Lowell, but he didn't want to wait until morning.

He pulled a thick-crusted chunk of bread from a loaf he'd purchased earlier that morning and sat in front of the hostelry.

Within half an hour, the coach came rumbling into town at breakneck speed. The driver yanked back on the reins, which caused the wide-eyed horses to dig their hooves into the dusty roadway and bring the coach to a jarring halt. The carriage continued to sway on its leather straps for several minutes, the driver appearing to take great pleasure in the jostling he'd caused his passengers.

Spitting a stream of tobacco juice, the driver jumped down from atop the carriage. "All out that's getting out," he hollered, pulling open the door.

Several frazzled, travel-worn passengers disembarked from the coach as the driver tossed their baggage onto the street. "You that's riding with me, get on in there. I ain't got time to waste. I'm on a schedule," the driver barked.

Liam and two other men boarded the coach, all of them seated along one end of the coach facing two women on the opposing side. He was grateful the center seat remained empty, permitting them a bit more space for their legs.

"Schedule? Not so as anybody would notice," one of the women called back. "The only time you hurry is to delight yourself in throwing us around inside this torture chamber."

The driver chortled and slapped his leg. "Surely you don't think I'd do such a thing as that, ma'am," he said, his coarse laughter continuing as he climbed up to his perch.

"That man is a maniac," the woman said to no one in particular as the driver flicked the reins and the coach lumbered out of town.

"He seems to have settled down a bit," one of the men commented as they made their way through the outskirts of Boston.

A wry smile crossed the woman's lips. "Just wait. He takes great delight in urging the horses into a full gallop when we're on a deep-rutted road or crossing a rickety bridge. And don't bother asking to get out and walk across the bridges—he ignores our pleas," she warned.

Regrettably, the woman's words proved accurate. By the time the stage rolled into Lowell, Liam had bounced off the side of the coach, as had everyone near him. His body was bruised, and his head ached. He'd lost count of how many times his head had thumped the top of the carriage. At least those huge leghorn hats provided the women's heads with a bit of protection.

He stepped down from the coach, thankful he had to travel no farther and sorry for those who would remain and go beyond Lowell. The woman was right—the driver was a maniac. He enjoyed every minute of discomfort the passengers had endured. Liam picked up his case of tools, which the driver had tossed to the ground. He'd kept his satchel with him in the coach and now slung it across his shoulder as he glanced in all directions.

"That way," the driver snapped as he pointed northwest.

Liam gave him a look of surprise.

"You're going to the Acre, ain't ya?"

Liam nodded.

"Well, it's thataway. You'll know when you've arrived," he declared before throwing the remaining luggage onto the ground.

"Thank you," Liam replied and headed off.

Lowell certainly wasn't as large as Boston, but it was a likeable town, he decided, passing the shops that lined Merrimack Street. It appeared to be a place where a man could settle down and be happy. He walked onward, not sure how he was to know when he'd arrived at the Acre, but he was enjoying the sights while remaining mindful to watch for his destination. He passed the mills, impressed with the brick facades and grandeur of the buildings with their many windows and small flower gardens. Soon the well-kept street ended, and a few rods from the canals, Liam was confronted with a hodge-podge of shanties built of slabs and rough boards that varied in height from about six to nine feet high. Stacked flour barrels or lime casks sat on the roofs, obviously topping out the fireplaces inside the shacks. Chinked-out holes served as windows, while makeshift doors hung open, with pigs and chickens roaming freely from the muddy streets into the shanties. Liam shuddered at the sight. The Acre.

"I'm lookin' for Hugh Cummiskey," he told a raggedly clothed boy sitting outside one of the hovels.

"Over at the church," the boy replied, running his hand across the dirt smudge on his face and then pointing toward the church.

Liam nodded and thanked the boy before heading off to the church. Mercifully, the church was as Cummiskey had described, an edifice worthy of a skilled stonemason. At least something in this part of town wasn't an eyesore. Liam approached a group of men preparing to leave for the night. "Can ya be tellin' me where I might find Hugh Cummiskey?"

One of the men stopped directly in front of Liam. "Who wants to know?"

"Liam Donohue, stonemason from Boston."

The man nodded. "He's inside. Go on in."

Liam voiced his thanks and entered the building. No doubt it was going to be a beautiful church once completed. Nothing comparable to the great churches of Ireland, but a fine structure nonetheless.

"Are you looking for work?" a man asked, walking up behind Liam.

Liam turned. "I think I've found it," he replied. "I'm Liam Donohue, stonemason from Boston, lookin' for Hugh Cummiskey," he once again explained.

"Well, you've found him," Hugh replied, holding out a beefy hand. "So you're Liam Donohue. I pictured you to be a bigger man," he said in a light, almost nonexistent brogue. Apparently the man had worked to rid himself of sounding too Irish.

"Go on with yarself. I'm big enough to get the job done, and besides, I'm not thinkin' ya've got much size on me," Liam retorted with a quick grin.

Hugh laughed and slapped him on the shoulder. "Well, then, I don't imagine your stature is of any consequence. What do you think of our church?"

Liam took another glance about the building. "It appears to be the only structure o' consequence in all of this part of town. I'm understandin' this is called the Acre?"

Hugh nodded. "That it is, or the Paddy camp, or New Dublin, or any number of derogatory names the Yanks could think of since we first arrived to build this place. We came to build the mills and canals—all of the heavy manual work. Some refer to us as lords of the spade. No matter—I suppose that's what we are. The Associates have continued their expansion in Lowell, which has been good for us. Their expansion provides us with jobs. 'Course, more and more of our countrymen have arrived from Ireland looking for work. But now the Yanks are beginning to raise a ruckus. They don't want any more Irish settling in Lowell."

"Aye. The good folks of Boston aren't overly welcomin', either, although I expected wee better living conditions here."

Hugh shook his head back and forth. "We're on the same small acre of land me and my men camped on when we first arrived here. The Yanks won't let us expand any farther if they can avoid it. Trouble is, we don't help matters much. There's still the fightin' among the clans, which the Yanks use against us. Fact is, the Corporation donated the land for this church in the hope it would bring the clans together. I'm hoping it will help."

"Seems that sometimes we hurt ourselves even more than the outsiders do," Liam noted.

"That's true. Come on now and let me show you what I've got in mind for this stonework. I'd be pleased if you could do some carving for us, but we'll have to see what that will cost. I fear your talent is beyond our purse."

Liam smiled. "We'll see. I'm sure we can work somethin' out. My dear old mother back in Ireland would never forgive me if I rejected work for the church."

The two men talked for several hours, well into the evening. Liam's excitement over the stone designs in the new church had surpassed the gnawing of his stomach, but now it would not be silenced. "It's getting late, Hugh. I've not found a place to live, nor have I eaten since I departed from Boston early today."

Hugh nodded. "I've kept you much too long. Come along with me. You can spend the night at my house, and tomorrow morning we'll find a sleeping space for you to rent."

Cummiskey's home far surpassed anything else in the Acre, yet it was little more than a hovel. The meal, however, was another matter. Not only was Hugh's wife cheerful, but she could cook a meal that would give his own mother strong competition. Both the meal and clean bed provided a welcome sanctuary for which Liam was thankful.

Early the next morning, Liam's safe haven disappeared like a mist. The pealing of the tower bell startled him awake hours before any of the roosters wandering the Acre had been given an opportunity to announce dawn's arrival.

"I'll take you to meet Noreen Gallagher," Hugh said as they finished their five o'clock breakfast. "My wife tells me Noreen may have a sleeping space for rent."

Liam glanced about the candlelit room. "Will she be awake at this time of the day?"

Hugh's laughter filled the small room. "She'll be up. The bells that wakened you this morning do the same for all the other residents of this town. It's not just those working inside the mills whose lives are governed by the sound of the bells. Noreen's no exception. The people living with her either work for the Corporation or are looking to get hired. Either way, she'll have them up and out of her house as soon as humanly possible."

Liam wasn't certain that calling upon someone at this time of day was entirely suitable, but he placed his reliance in Hugh. After profusely thanking Mrs. Cummiskey for her kindness, he gathered up his belongings and followed Hugh out the door and into the muddy street that fronted the hovel. They followed the crooked road until it became no more than a path winding its way among the maze of shacks. Hugh stopped short and pounded on the door of one of the shanties. A wiry woman with matted reddish-brown hair cracked open the dilapidated piece of wood that served as a front door She blinked against the darkness, obviously unable to make out the faces of her visitors.

"It's Hugh Cummiskey, Noreen. I've brought you a new tenant."

The woman stepped aside, permitting them entry. "Mr. Cummiskey! Come in, come in."

She bent from the waist while gesturing her arm in a sweeping motion that crossed her body, obviously pretending royalty had arrived on her doorstep. Liam smiled. Perhaps she wasn't pretending. Conceivably Mr. Cummiskey was viewed as royalty among the residents of the Paddy camp.

The smell of fetid bodies mingled with the odor of a mangy dog, two chickens, and an indistinguishable scent that curled upward from an iron pot hanging over the fire. The stench nearly caused Liam to retch. Filthy pallets lined the floor where the dirty bodies had lain only a short time earlier. The group now sat huddled near the fire, spooning the foul-smelling concoction that bubbled over the fire into makeshift bowls.

"Mr. Donohue's in need of a sleeping space, and my wife said you had one available. That true?" Hugh inquired.

The woman narrowed her eyes into thin slits and looked Liam up and down. She appeared to evaluate his every feature. "Have ya money to pay?" she asked, her gaze darting toward his bags.

Liam nodded. "Could I talk to you alone for a moment, Mr. Cummiskey?" Liam inquired.

Noreen gave Liam a disgruntled look but moved to the fire when Hugh waved her away. "Is there a problem, Liam?"

He didn't want to appear ungrateful—or offensive. He hesitated a moment and then cleared his throat. "Might there be another place, uh, a hotel, or . . ."

Cummiskey shook his head. "You've the luck of the Irish with you to find this," he replied. "As for a hotel—we've no such luxury in the Acre, and ya'd not be welcome at the Wareham. Yanks only, ya know." His brogue seemed a bit more pronounced.

"I see. Well, then, I suppose I'll stay here, but if you or your missus should 'ear of anything better, would ya keep me in mind?"

Hugh nodded his head. "That I'll do, my boy, that I'll do," he said before waving Noreen back to where they stood.

"I'll vouch for Mr. Donohue. He'll be working with me over at the church, so you've no need to worry about being paid regular. See that he gets a decent place to sleep—and you might try cooking something of substance for your tenants," he suggested with a glance toward the fireplace. "I'm sure you could find yourself a few potatoes to toss in with that water you boil every day."

Noreen dug the toe of her shoe into the dirt floor as a splash of red tinged her cheeks. Liam wasn't sure if the woman's embarrassment was due to the poor treatment of her tenants or the fact that Hugh Cummiskey had noted her neglect. Probably the latter, he surmised.

"We're heading off to work at the church, but Mr. Donohue will be back this evening. I trust he'll find enough food to fill his belly, Noreen."

"If 'e pays me before you leave, 'e will," Noreen countered.

The woman watched closely as Liam reached into his satchel and then handed her two dollars, which, from the gleam in her eyes, was more than she'd received in many a day.

"Where'd ya work before comin' to this place?" she asked while rubbing the coins in her hand.

"Boston."

Hugh gave Liam a reassuring pat on the back. "Mr. Donohue's a stonemason—very talented. God's blessed us yet again by sending him to work for us."

The woman kept her gaze fixed on Liam's satchel. "Indeed, a blessin'," she agreed, reaching out toward the shoulder strap of Liam's bag. "Ya can leave yar belongings here. I'll see to them while ya're at work."

Liam turned, stepping out of her grasp. "No, I'll keep my belongings with me," he replied before joining Hugh outside the shanty.

Hugh gave him a hearty laugh as they walked back down the muddy path. "I know Noreen's place isn't particularly appealing, but I doubt you'll spend much time there. Most of the single men spend their evenings at the pub."

Liam's thoughts wandered back to the boardinghouse where he'd roomed in the Irish part of Boston. It hadn't been palatial by any means, but the house had been neat and clean, and the food had been wholesome and plentiful. Liam wasn't one to spend his time sitting in pubs, but there was no doubt he would soon begin. A reasonable alternative to Noreen's shack would be a necessity.

"Once you've begun your work at the church, I'll head off for the canal. We're running a few days behind, and I need to push the blokes a bit," Hugh said as they moved toward the church.

"Perhaps you need to hire some extra help," Liam suggested.

Hugh gave a growling snort and pushed back his flat woolen cap. A mop of black curly hair fell across his forehead. "The Yanks are already up in arms about the number of Irish living and working in Lowell. There are about five hundred of us now. The Yanks want us to perform their labor and disappear like a vapor until we're needed for some other grueling manual labor. Instead, they must face the fact that the Irish are here to stay. They don't like that idea, and they surely want no more of us coming here."

"So that's why ya instructed me to say me work was temporary?"

"Exactly," Hugh replied. "But as I told you, I'm certain I can keep you busy should you decide you want to remain in Lowell. Personally, I'm anxious to have skilled artisans stay among us."

"Ya don't think ya'd be happier somewhere else? A place where ya'd feel more welcome?" Liam inquired.

"Hah! And where would that be, Liam? Surely you don't think there's a city out there anxious to see the Irish arrive? Lowell's not a bad place for the Irish—better than most. I've made my place here and you can, too, if you like. Keep yourself clean, work hard, stay away from the liquor, and try to stay out of the Yanks' way."

Liam felt an overwhelming sadness envelop him. "What I'd be likin' is for all of us to 'ave the same advantages as the Yanks born in this country without anyone carin' for whether we were born in Ireland—or any other country, for that matter. I'd like a bit of equality for all of us."

"Well, I doubt you'll find that here or anywhere else, my friend. We're a step above the slaves down South, but the Yanks will make sure we don't move much higher. It seems as if we get one matter of dissension solved between us and another arises."

"Like what?" Liam inquired.

"As I told you earlier, the Yanks feel we're taking jobs away from them, even though a few years ago they wouldn't consider dirtying their hands with this kind of work. When there's a fire anywhere but the Acre, the fire company shows up to fight the blaze. But they don't come here—they'd prefer the whole Acre burn to the ground. I suppose the most recent agitation with the Yanks is due to the Irish girls that have come up missing. No one seems to care. We can't even get the police to talk to the families. I tried—even went and talked to the police myself—but they don't appear to care," Hugh explained.

Liam stopped outside the church and turned toward Hugh. "How long have these girls been missin'? Would they be knowin' each other? Were they all separate incidents?"

"Do you double as a policeman?" Hugh inquired with a chuckle.

"No, but this is a frightenin' matter."

"That it is. All the girls have been of marrying age, but none involved with a fellow; all of them were pretty. The girls knew each other—we all know each other in the Acre. Each one disappeared at a different time and from a different place," Hugh explained. "I fear the Yanks' lack of concern will soon cause some of our men to retaliate against them."

Liam shook his head. "Not against their womenfolk?"

"Let's hope not. I've been talkin' my heart out to them. Violence returned for violence serves none of us well," Hugh replied.

~ 11 ~

Bella gathered with twelve other girls in the parlor of Miss Addie's board-inghouse, a stack of books on her lap. She gave the group a tentative smile, uncertain whether the others shared her passion for this idea.

"How long will we be?" Jennie asked. "Lucy and I are going to Mr. Whidden's store; a new shipment of lace arrived this morning," she added, already wiggling in her seat.

"I suppose it depends on how interested we are in expanding our minds," Bella replied more curtly than she'd intended.

Jennie appeared offended. "You needn't attempt to make me feel guilty because I want to purchase a piece of lace, Bella."

"I'm sorry, Jennie. You and Lucy, and any of the rest of you," she said as she looked about the room, "may leave whenever you choose. The purpose of this gathering was to determine if there's enough interest for us to form a literary circle. I have a few books Miss Addie has donated for our use until we can perhaps purchase some others."

Lucy straightened in her chair while furrowing her brow. "I thought you convinced Taylor Manning we should be admitted to the Mechanics Association library. I'd rather use their books."

"I'm not sure Mr. Manning was able to secure agreement from the membership. And even if he does, it would be laudable if we had some books and offered to donate them to their library, don't you think?" Bella asked.

"Perhaps," Lucy replied with little conviction in her voice.

"I don't have money to spend on books. My family needs every cent I can send," Hannah dolefully responded.

Bella smiled at the girl. "I realize that for you and several others who must send all of your money home, purchasing books is out of the question. But others of us, the ones who have additional funds to purchase a piece of jewelry or lace, might want to think about using the money for a book instead."

Hannah raised her hand, and Bella nodded toward her. "If we don't help purchase books, will we still be permitted to read them and join in with your group?"

"That would certainly be my desire, Hannah. There are many good things we could accomplish as a group—not just for ourselves but for others, as well."

Jennie gave her an apprehensive look. "Like what?"

"Tutoring lessons for the girls who have difficulty reading, and perhaps classes or topical discussions of foreign languages, literature, or current events. I even hoped we might secure enough funds to host our own speakers from time to time—a poet, perhaps. If we can elicit enough interest, we could charge an admission fee to help defray costs of the speaker, and if we could host the event at St. Anne's or one of the other churches, it might be successful," Bella enthusiastically offered. "We could start out with a lending library among the girls in all of the mills, not just the Appleton."

"I think it's a wonderful idea," Ruth agreed.

Addie pulled off her apron as she entered the room. "Yes, it is. And you girls should use every opportunity available to expand your education. After all, an education is something no one can ever take away from you."

Bella smiled as a murmur of excitement began filling the parlor. "Perhaps our first step would be to schedule a meeting inviting all of the girls."

Miss Addie nodded. "If you girls make invitations, I'll deliver them to each of the boardinghouses and ask the keepers to post them for their girls."

"That would be wonderful," Bella replied. "We could work on the invitations tomorrow evening. Oh, but where can we meet? Do you think St. Anne's would give us permission to meet there?" she asked, turning toward Addie.

"I'll go and talk with Reverend Edson tomorrow, and although I'm certain there will be no problem using the church, I think he'll want to know exactly what day and time you plan to meet. Perhaps you should give me several dates in case there's a conflict," Addie suggested.

"If there's nothing else," Jennie said, "Lucy and I want to leave for town."

"I told you earlier, you're free to leave whenever you want," Bella said, unable to hide her irritation. "No one is forcing you to expand your mind, Jennie."

"There's no need to scorn me," Jennie replied as a knock sounded at the front door. Turning on her heel, Jennie marched into the hallway and pulled open the front door.

Bella glanced toward the open door just as John Farnsworth and Taylor Manning entered. "Good evening, everyone," John greeted the group of ladies in the parlor. "I hope we're not disturbing anything," he said, giving Addie a questioning look.

Before Addie could answer, Jennie sidled up to Taylor. "I understand the Mechanics Association has refused permission for us to use their library. Rather selfish, I'd say."

"To be quite frank, I haven't made a proposal to the association regarding your use of the library just yet."

"You haven't?" Bella asked, walking closer.

Jennie gave Bella a triumphant grin. "Oh my, Bella! It appears as if Mr. Manning didn't take your request seriously." She turned toward Taylor. "Now you've gone and done it."

Taylor appeared totally confused. "Done what?" he asked.

"I believe you may have offended our literary organizer. I doubt whether Bella will want to keep company with the likes of you, Mr. Manning. However," she said resting a hand on his arm, "I wouldn't be affronted if you would care to call upon me." She gave him a beguiling smile before flashing Bella a fleeting glance of victory. "Would you care to accompany Lucy and me into town?"

John moved forward, breaking Jennie's grasp on Taylor's arm. "I'm afraid Taylor is with me this evening," he replied on behalf of his nephew.

"That's a shame," Jennie responded, fluttering her eyelashes.

"Or perhaps a blessing," John muttered as he and Miss Addie moved into the parlor. "I didn't realize you were otherwise occupied this evening," John apologetically remarked.

Bella followed behind Taylor as he made his way along with John and Miss Addie. She wanted to find out why he hadn't bothered to talk to the Mechanics Association on her behalf.

Addie patted his arm. "There's no need to concern yourself, John. After all, I knew you were coming to visit this evening. I think the girls have completed their business, and they'll be scattering into town or up to their rooms. We can go into the dining room if you prefer."

"No, no, I enjoy the young people."

Addie gave him a bright smile. "I'm pleased Taylor came along. Perhaps he and Bella will have time to visit about the association's library. The girls are planning a meeting to form a literary group." She glanced over her shoulder and smiled.

"Did I hear my name?" Taylor asked as he took the seat beside Miss Addie.

Addie nodded and beckoned him closer. "Indeed you did. I was just telling your uncle that some of the girls are hoping to form a literary group. Bella was under the assumption the men had voted against the girls using their library."

Taylor shook his head. "Well, it sounds as though Bella is taking my advice and starting her own little reading circle. Besides, I never told Bella any such thing."

Bella seethed. "No, but you made it clear you didn't like the idea. I knew you wouldn't promote the concept of nonmembers using your library, and I was correct. You didn't even present it for a vote, did you?" she challenged.

Taylor grew wide-eyed as Bella marched toward him and then stopped directly in front of his chair. She was on the attack, and it was obvious Taylor was surprised at the confrontation.

"Well, did you?" she reiterated, her voice rising a decibel.

Taylor stood up and faced off, toe-to-toe with Bella. She didn't retreat. Instead, she looked upward into his eyes and leveled an accusatory stare. He looked down, his hair falling forward over one eye, which gave him a mischievous appearance.

He winked the other eye, gave her a playful grin, and in a velvet-smooth voice replied, "No, dear Bella, I didn't. But if you'd care to have a seat here beside me, I'd be happy to explain my egregious behavior."

"You find this enjoyable, don't you, Mr. Manning? Withholding something of value to others obviously makes you feel powerful. It's rather sad that your insecurity causes you to stoop to such a level," she retaliated.

"Wh—wh—what?" he stammered. Clearly shaken by her comment, Taylor lowered himself into a nearby chair. "You think I'm insecure?"

"Among other things," Bella said, plopping down on the settee while enjoying his obvious bafflement. "Why else are you afraid to permit women in your library?"

"It's not my library," he countered.

"Exactly!" she retaliated, pointing her finger. "So why don't you permit the membership to make the decision rather than withholding it on your own? Why didn't you present our request?"

John leaned forward and gave his nephew a hard stare. "Yes, Taylor, I'd be interested in your response to her question, also."

Taylor shifted in his chair like a caged animal seeking escape. "Well, I thought it could wait until our next meeting. We had a full agenda and several other committee meetings afterward. I have every intention of bringing it before the membership next week."

John shook his head back and forth. "I don't think that was your decision to make. You should have brought the request before the group and let them determine whether to act upon it or wait until the following meeting, Taylor. The Mechanics Association grants all members equal rights in the decision-making process."

Addie pulled a lace handkerchief from her sleeve and dabbed at her brow as she glanced back and forth between John and Taylor. Clearly, John's stern lecture to his nephew was causing her discomfort. "Perhaps Bella and I should prepare some tea," she suggested.

"Tea would be nice," Taylor replied, a grateful smile crossing his lips.

John nodded. "Yes, that would be fine."

Addie rose from the settee and waited a moment. "Bella?"

"What?" Bella unwillingly turned her gaze away from the unfolding scene between John and Taylor and gave Addie a questioning look. "Oh, you want me to help in the kitchen?" She remained seated and turned back toward Taylor, hoping Miss Addie would permit her to remain behind.

"Bella!"

No further words were necessary. Bella stood up and dutifully followed Miss Addie out of the room. Truth be known, she longed to remain in the parlor and hear John Farnsworth continue lecturing his nephew. Perhaps if she lagged behind just a little, she could catch a few more words. But it was not to be. Her ability to overhear the conversation was snuffed out by the clattering of dishes in the kitchen.

"Eavesdropping is unbecoming, my dear, and I believe young Taylor has already suffered enough embarrassment," Addie chastened.

Bella whirled around. "He brought this upon himself, Miss Addie. Surely you don't condone his behavior," Bella challenged.

Addie busied herself arranging a plate of biscuits. "I think Taylor used poor judgment. Clearly he was wrong. However, his uncle is taking him to task for his actions. I take no pleasure in observing his comeuppance."

A blush stained Bella's cheeks. "Unfortunately, I do, Miss Addie—my imperfection revealing itself. Sister Eunice enjoyed telling me my flawed character rose up as regularly as cream floating to the top of the milk." She frowned and thought maybe there was no hope for her character. She tried to be of a more generous nature—tried to offer forgiveness, knowing there would certainly be times when she needed it.

Miss Addie lovingly hugged Bella. "Oh, dear me. It doesn't sound as though Sister Eunice was a very charitable woman. You're a sweet girl, Bella, with many, many fine attributes. Any parent would be proud to have a fine daughter such as you. Why, you're bright and industrious and generally very kindhearted," she said with a bright smile.

A tear trickled down Bella's face and fell upon her bodice, the wetness creating a black splotch on the gray fabric.

"What is it, Bella? Why are you crying?" Addie's voice was filled with distress as she pulled Bella into another embrace. "I truly believe Taylor acted improperly, too," she said, obviously searching for a clue to the girl's tears.

"It's not Taylor," Bella sniffed, searching for her handkerchief. "It's what you said about any parent being proud to have me as a daughter," she continued in a warbly voice. "My father didn't feel that way about me. He chose life among the Shakers rather than living with his wife and daughter." The pain of her thoughts caused Bella to realize the source of so much bitterness. Her father had walked away from her as though she were nothing more than a spare dog.

"Oh, Bella," Addie lamented as she pulled the girl into a tighter embrace. "Sometimes we're not meant to understand—at least not at the time a particular happenstance occurs. Perhaps one day you and your father can discuss his decision and you'll have a clearer understanding of his motives. I know it's painful to feel rejected by your father. But you must remember that our heavenly Father is the only one who is perfect. We humans are flawed. Unfortunately, we tend to hurt those people we love the most. Possibly because we think they'll continue to love us in spite of our behavior, though I'm not sure that's always true," she added.

Bella leaned back and stared into Miss Addie's clear blue eyes. "Did your father love you?"

A faraway look clouded the older woman's eyes. "The Judge? Yes, he loved me—in his own way."

"What does that mean, 'in his own way'?" Bella asked.

Miss Addie removed the boiling water from the fire before she spoke. "He loved Mintie and me differently, but he loved us both. Equally, I believe. Mintie and I have very different personalities, so beyond his affectionate peck on the cheek each evening, the Judge exhibited his love uniquely to each of us. He would sit and discuss business matters with Mintie. He realized that doing so exhibited the fact that he valued Mintie's opinions; it expressed his love for her. With me, he would comment on my pretty dresses or ask me to accompany him to social events. He knew I enjoyed being in the company of others. He expressed his love for me by acting as my escort. However, he didn't tell us he loved us, and I truly wish he had. I'm not even sure whether he enjoyed those discussions with Mintie or attending dinner parties with me. But the time he spent with each of us was an expression of his love. And whether you choose to believe it or not, Bella, I'm certain your father loves you in his own way."

"I find it hard to believe my father loves me, Miss Addie, but I thank you for your kind words. I suppose we'd best get this tea into the parlor or Taylor and Mr. Farnsworth will think we've deserted them," Bella said, tucking her linen handkerchief into the pocket of her dress. "Of course, Taylor is most likely hoping I won't return," she added with a nervous giggle.

Addie chuckled. "I doubt that. I think Taylor has taken an interest in you," Addie remarked as she bustled off with one of the trays. "Bring the other tray, please," she said, walking out of the kitchen.

Bella stood staring after her. Taylor interested in her? Preposterous! The only person Taylor Manning cared about was himself.

Long after his evening with Bella and Miss Addie had concluded, Taylor Manning continued to think of their gathering. Bella saw nothing wrong in speaking her opinion. He liked that in some ways but in others he found it annoying. She was certainly unlike any other young woman he'd had a chance to know. Usually all he had to do was smile or throw a girl a wink and she was his. Bella was clearly not going to be that easily conquered. Perhaps that was why Taylor found her all the more intriguing.

All of his life he'd known he had the charm and looks to captivate the girls. He'd used it to his advantage over and over. His mother's warnings aside, Taylor simply didn't see that it caused that much harm. Of course, there was that whole matter back in England. What a jolly time that had been.

But even as Taylor considered the women of his past, it was Bella's face that came to mind. She wasn't going to be easily swayed. He smiled. *Maybe not,* he reasoned, *but the game will be only that much more challenging. Winning Bella—bringing her to a place where she's captive to my charm—will give me something to do.* He snuffed out the candle beside his bed and smiled again. "Ah, Miss Newberry, if you only knew the plans I have for you."

~ 12 ~

Liam hunkered down in a corner of Noreen's shanty. He longed for the peace and privacy the quiet room in Boston had afforded him. Noreen's place was filled with a constant din that she seemed to enjoy. If the room began to grow quiet, she would break the silence with her yammering until she stirred the others into a frenzy of noise and activity. Worse yet, he didn't trust the woman. Her frizzy auburn hair spiraled upward in wiry coils while her green-eyed gaze flitted about the room like the beacon in a lighthouse searching for trouble. It was obvious nothing in the house escaped her scrutiny. Moreover, she'd been obsessed with his belongings since the day he arrived, constantly encouraging him to leave them behind when he left for work in the morning.

His eyelids were growing heavy and he'd just begun to doze off when Noreen edged to his side and dropped to the floor. The odor of her body mixed with the smell of the cheap liquor she'd obviously been drinking all afternoon. The smell was dreadful. Liam leaned aside, hoping to avoid the stench. "And what would ya be wantin', Noreen?" he muttered.

"Just lookin' for some friendly conversation, Liam. I get lonely stayin' in the 'ouse all day with nothing but my cookin' and cleanin' to keep me occupied."

Liam emitted a loud guffaw. "For sure ya must be keepin' yourself occupied with something other than cookin' or cleanin', woman. This place is filthy, and the food isn't fit to slop hogs."

"Now ya've gone and insulted me again. Why is that? For sure I'm just wantin' a little company. Used to be I could go and visit with me sister, Kathryn. Did I tell ya she died?" The words were slurred yet laced with an edge of melancholy.

"Several times," Liam replied.

She ignored his comment. "I loved Kathryn and the wee babe—little Cullan. Kathryn let me name him, did I tell ya that?" She didn't wait for an answer before continuing with her recitation. "Cullan was a sweet one, always smilin' and cooin'. He'd just begun to talk when Kathryn died. How I wish I coulda kept him. But I promised Kathryn that if anythin' ever happened to 'er, I'd see the boy was protected," she said, her voice trailing off.

Liam knew he'd regret asking, but his curiosity got the best of him. "What of the boy's father? Couldn't he care for 'im?"

Noreen turned a hate-filled stare in his direction. "Cullan's father is a well-to-do Yank. The child was born out o' wedlock. You can be bettin' yar life that the Yank would prefer the child 'ad never been born. I took Cullan away from Lowell because I feared for him."

Liam straightened a bit. "Ya think the Yank would have done the child harm?"

Noreen shrugged. "Who knows? But certain I am 'e worried his wife would find out about Kathryn and the child. He didn't want his powerful friends to be findin' out, either. It woulda been an embarrassment for 'im, now, wouldn't it? I told Kathryn he was takin' advantage of her, but she wouldn't listen. Ha! Tweren't nothin' lovable about that man," she spat.

"So you knew 'im?" Liam asked.

"I wasn't never formally introduced, but Kathryn told me his name, and I know how 'e treated her. He never worried about her welfare or the child's, for that matter. All he worried about was a warm bed where 'e could be takin' his pleasures. I couldn't have kept the child safe here in the Acre if the Yank had decided to do 'im harm. And I'd rather go the rest of my life without seeing Cullan than have harm come to him at his father's hand."

"If I was in your shoes, I'd be watchin' me tongue. Those are mighty strong accusations to be makin' against a Yank," Liam warned.

"I ain't worried. The Yanks don't care what some Irishwoman has to be sayin' about them. Besides, I'm speakin' the truth. The Yanks take advantage at every turn, treat us worse than animals, they do. Them highfalutin' Boston Associates never give one thought to the livin' conditions in the Acre. The only time thar thinkin' about us is when there's some canal to be dug out or stone to be hauled. It's not fair," she said, her eyes bleary from the ale.

"You'd best be gettin' some sleep, Noreen," Liam said.

He watched as Noreen moved off to the area she referred to as her room, which was merely a small space cordoned off by a blanket hanging across a piece of rope. Most likely everything she'd said was true. Distaste for the Irish was prevalent everywhere, not just in Lowell. Yet he wondered about Noreen and how she reconciled the mistreatment she doled out to her kinsmen. Did she not believe it grievous to furnish only putrid gruel and lice-infested bedding to her fellow Irishmen in exchange for their hard-earned coins? She constantly derided the Yanks for their misbehavior while nosing about to steal from one of her Irish boarders. She wasn't, Liam decided, much different from the Yanks whom she abhorred. Her behavior only confirmed what he already knew: he must locate another place to live, but until then, he needed a place to store his belongings. Leaving his satchel unattended in Noreen's shack was an invitation to disaster.

The next morning Liam bypassed the gruel bubbling in Noreen's fireplace. He decided he'd rather pay for a decent meal at the pub.

"You can leave your satchel here while ya're at work," Noreen said while grabbing at the sleeve of his jacket. "I'll watch after it for ya." She gave him a crooked smile and held out her hand. She recited the same litany each time he prepared to leave.

Liam pulled away. "I'll be takin' it with me," he said without meeting her gaze. Noreen's actions only served to confirm what Liam already knew—given any opportunity, Noreen would steal him blind.

It was a short distance from Noreen's hovel to the church; that was the only positive thing Liam could say about boarding with her. As usual, he was the first of the small crew to arrive at the church, even after stopping at the pub for breakfast. After lighting one of the whale-oil lamps inside the front door, he found a candle, held it to the flame of the lamp, and then located an opening in the foundation permitting entry into a crawl space under the church. The space was higher than he could have hoped, which allowed him easy movement on his hands and knees. Pulling a chisel from his coat pocket, Liam began to carefully loosen the mortar surrounding an interior stone. He dug until his fingers could finally grasp a tight hold on the piece of granite that abutted the outer wall of the foundation. Methodically, he wiggled the stone back and forth until he felt it release and then slid it forward, finally placing it on the dirt floor.

He placed the candle close at hand, removed a few belongings from the satchel, and carefully counted the money. He placed enough for a few meals in his jacket pocket and returned the remainder of the money to the satchel, along with some letters from home and a few personal items from Ireland.

The sheaf of papers he'd retrieved from J. P. Green's fireplace lay scattered before him. Liam gathered the pages, glancing from time to time at the long rows of figures—some sort of business accounts, he decided. He ruffled through the papers, hoping to find at least one sheet that was clean on both sides. Two weeks had passed since he'd written home, and his parents would be concerned if they didn't hear from him soon. He knew his parents well. Each letter would be bandied about the village for all to know that the Dono-hues' dutiful son was writing home and thriving in America. Permitting his parents a scrap of prominence among their neighbors was the least he could do for them, but he dare not waste any more time. Grabbing several sheets, he shoved them into the box with his tools and then returned the remainder of the pages to his bag. Wedging the satchel into the existing hole, Liam pushed the piece of granite back into place. The stone didn't fit tightly, but at least his satchel was out of Noreen's grasp.

Several men were arriving to work as Liam made his way back to the entryway of the church. "Did ya fall on yar way in to work, Liam?" one of the men asked while looking at Liam's trousers.

Liam glanced down and brushed off the dirt. "No, for sure I was doin' a few chores before startin' work," he replied.

"Ain't ya the industrious one," Thomas O'Malley commented with a boisterous laugh before heading off with several other men to work on the roof.

Liam gave him a broad smile in return. "Will ya be goin' to the pub for dinner, Thomas?"

"Sure! I'll be needin' a glass of ale come noon. If ya want to join me and some o' the boys, just meet us out front when the noon bell sounds."

"Aye, I'll do that," Liam replied, waving a hand before walking into the sanctuary to begin carving on a large block of limestone.

The morning hours passed quickly for Liam. The creativity of stonemasonry excited him, especially when he was given a bit of freedom. Unlike J. P. Green, who had insisted there be no deviation from his prepared sketches, Hugh Cummiskey had given Liam free rein in designing the stonework. It was a level of trust that Liam had never before experienced, and he was determined to excel.

When the noonday bell sounded, Liam's stomach was growling with hunger. Removing the coins from his toolbox, he placed them in his jacket pocket before joining the group of men in front of the church.

They made their way to the bar and found Michael Neil standing behind his makeshift bar, obviously awaiting the crowd. "Ales all around?" he asked as the group entered the doorway.

The men gave their hearty approval to his question and soon were downing their mugs. Mrs. Neil appeared with crockery bowls filled with fish chowder and placed a bowl in front of each man. A young boy followed behind carrying loaves of soda bread. Liam tore off a chunk of the bread, dipping it into the creamy chowder before stuffing it into his mouth. It was the best food he'd eaten since leaving Boston.

"So what do you think of our church, Liam?" one of the men called from the end of the table. Beckoning to Mrs. Neil, he pointed toward his empty bowl. She refilled it and moved on to the next man. Liam wiped the back of his hand across his mouth and swallowed hard. "It's goin' to be a beauty, and I'm goin' to do my best to make sure o' that," he shouted back as he held up his mug of ale in salute. "It's a well-built church of good outward design. Any town would be proud to 'ave it in their midst."

"For once I think the Yanks are doin' right by us," O'Malley agreed.

Liam nodded. "I've looked that buildin' over, and it's a fine piece of architecture. Looks a bit out o' place among all the shanties, but you can be sure it'll stand the test of time. It's good and tight—secure! You could hide a king's ransom in that buildin' and it would be safe and sound."

"Probably a lot safer than those banks the Yanks are sayin' we should use.

I can tell you that the Yanks and their fancy banks won't ever see a coin outta my pocket," O'Malley replied.

A middle-aged Irishman sitting at the bar turned and lifted his glass in the air. "If any of us had the good sense God gave the Irish, we'd hide our money and maybe even some rifles in the church. With the help of the good Lord, we could come together and overtake the Yanks and their fancy banks. I'm not about to mix any o' my money with the Yanks'. They'd steal us blind for sure. And there ain't a man here who doesn't believe we could run those mills better than the Yanks, but they ain't never gonna give us the chance. Only way we'll ever get outta the Acre is to take the town by force," he said in a slurred voice that seemed to quell the anger flashing in his eyes.

All gazes were fixed on the man as the barkeep snapped his fingers. "Settle yarself, Robert," he warned while glancing nervously about the room.

"I know there's them that don't belong in this pub that sit around snooping," the man slurred, turning to look toward a table in the corner. "That fancy pants from Boston comes to the Acre and noses about our business. I wonder how it would set if some of us went to the bar in the Wareham House and hid out in a corner listenin' to them Associates discuss their business. And ya don't suppose they'd mind if we were to take up with their women, do ya? After all, we've got the likes of 'im and his friends doin' just that," he continued while pointing toward the well-dressed man.

Liam leaned toward O'Malley. "Who is that Yank over there, and why's 'e in this place?"

"His name is William Thurston, and Robert's speakin' the truth. Thurston is one of the Boston Associates and he spends far too much time in the Acre. He had him an Irishwoman for quite a while, but then she died. . . ."

"Not Noreen Gallagher's sister?" Liam asked.

"Yeah, that's exactly who she was—Noreen's sister, Kathryn. Some folks say she had a baby by Thurston, but I'm not certain. She was married to a fellow named O'Hanrahan, but I don't know what ever happened to 'im. Might have been his whelp. Who knows? Come to think of it, I don't know what happened to the child. Seems as though I recall it was only Kathryn that died."

Liam hunched forward and glanced over his shoulder. The fellow known as Thurston seemed oblivious to the comments circulating the room. He continued drinking his ale, acting as though his presence among the Irish was desired and welcome. "Noreen says the child is alive, but for some reason she feared for 'is life—thought perhaps the child would come to some harm at his father's hand. Anyway, she took him away."

"Did she now? Seems as though Noreen has taken you into her confidence, Liam. Best watch yarself, or she'll be settin' her cap for ya," O'Malley said with a loud guffaw.

Liam shook his head in disbelief. "Noreen's enough to make any man want to remain single. There's nothing comely about her, not her appearance or her words—and worst of all, she can't even cook."

O'Malley gave Liam a sly look. "So cooking's where your heart is? In that case, why don't you come to my place for supper? I've got a sister I'd like you to meet. She prepares a tasty pot of stew."

Liam slapped O'Malley on the shoulder. "What I'm truly looking for is a decent place to room and board. Nothing would please me more than to move out o' Noreen's place. Can you help me find a place to live?"

O'Malley shook his head. "Don't know of anything offhand, but if my sister took a likin' to ya and you two was to marry, you could live with her. She's got two rooms in the back of our place."

"I think I'll turn you down on that offer—at least for the time being. I'll be sure and let you know if I change my mind."

"Suit yourself, but she ain't half bad to look at neither," O'Malley urged as the group pushed away from the table.

Before Liam rose to leave he turned for one final glance over his shoulder. William Thurston met his stare, and a chill rushed down Liam's spine. Even at a distance the man emanated evil.

William Thurston stared after the group of men as they walked out of the pub and then lifted his empty mug into the air. "Another!" he shouted when the barkeep glanced in his direction. He pulled an engraved silver watch from his pocket, clicked open the case, and stared at the time.

"Here you are, Mr. Thurston," Mr. Neil said, placing a full mug of ale on the table. "Anythin' else? Something to eat, perhaps?"

"No, not now," he replied without looking up. His thoughts weren't on food. Instead, he was mulling over the ramblings of the drunken man the barkeep had referred to as Robert, wondering how much of what he'd said was fact and how much was fiction.

A short time later two shabby men approached William's table, interrupting his thoughts. "Sorry we're late. I thought you said we would meet at the Wareham. We been waiting outside of there for half an hour," Jake Wilson said.

"I told him you said we was meeting here at the pub, but he wouldn't listen," Rafe Walton rebutted.

Thurston gave them a look of disgust. "Why would I ever consider meeting you two at a place like the Wareham? Do you ever use your brain to think, Jake?" he sneered. "Sit down," he commanded. "Bring them each an ale," he shouted to the barkeep.

"Thanks, Mr. Thurston. I'm mighty thirsty," Jake said.

"Your thirst is the last thing I'm concerned with, Jake," William said as he turned his attention toward Rafe. "You heard anything about money or rifles being stockpiled in that Catholic church that's being built down the street?"

"Where'd you ever get such an idea?" Rafe fired back.

Thurston noted Rafe's startled countenance. "Why are you answering my question with one of your own?"

Rafe shrugged. "I was surprised, that's all. I don't know anything about rifles or money."

Thurston leveled a cold stare across the table. "You'd best not be lying to me, Rafe. If the Irish have a plan underway, I want to know about it, do you understand me?"

"Plan for what? I don't know what you're talkin' about, Mr. Thurston."

Thurston smirked and pointed his finger. "I'll remember we've had this conversation. If I find you're being less than honest with me, you'll have the devil to pay. I want to know if there's anything going on in the Acre. Do I make myself clear? And that goes for you, too, Jake," he added, turning toward the other man.

Rafe nodded. "I'm being straight with you, Mr. Thurston."

Jake took a long drink and then wiped the mustache of foam from his upper lip. "I ain't got no idea what's goin' on down here in the Acre. He's the one who spends his time with the Micks."

"Watch your mouth, Jake," Rafe scowled.

"Be quiet, both of you! I didn't come down here to listen to you two exchange barbs. Just find out what's going on."

~ 13 ~

Matthew and Kirk disembarked the *Governor Sullivan,* one of the finest packet boats traversing the Middlesex Canal, at Charlestown, where a stage was waiting to transport them into Boston. "This was a pleasant journey, Matthew. Traveling the canal brought back fond memories. When we lived in Boston, Anne and I used to traverse the canal to Horn's Pond for picnics during the summer months. We should make time to do that again this summer," Kirk mused. "You and Lilly would enjoy a weekend at Horn's. They've made it into quite a tourist attraction."

Matthew smiled at the thought. "Perhaps I'll arrange a surprise for her. Lilly loves surprises—and picnics," he added.

Kirk glanced at his pocket watch. "Three o'clock. We made good time. I want to get settled at the hotel and rest my leg. The aching is constant."

"I'm sorry to hear that, Kirk. Fortunately, you'll have ample time to rest. We're not meeting Nathan and J. P. for dinner until seven o'clock."

Kirk slipped the engraved watch into his pocket. "We're dining at the hotel?"

Matthew shook his head. "No. J. P. wanted us to dine at his home. He's just completed renovations . . ."

"And wants to show off," Kirk said, completing the sentence.

Matthew laughed as he seated himself beside Kirk in the stagecoach. "Exactly! He's quite proud."

"That's an understatement. The man borders on pompous, though I'm not certain why—he's not overly bright, not overly handsome, and is certainly far from being overly wealthy," Kirk remarked.

They rumbled off toward the hotel, the coach now filled with jostling passengers who, after a leisurely passage down the Middlesex Canal, were anxious to join the hustle and bustle of Boston's city life. The women were chattering among themselves, exchanging information about the location of shops and the best places to find the latest fashions. Kirk looked at Matthew, rolled his eyes heavenward, and tightened his lips into a thin line. Matthew grinned and settled back on the uncomfortable seat, glad they would have only a short ride in the coach.

After stops at two other hotels, the coach came to a jerking halt in front of the Brackman Hotel on Beacon Street. The driver was unfastening their luggage when Kirk stepped down. "Don't throw that case to the ground!" Kirk shouted at the driver, who was now holding Kirk's bag in midair above his head.

The driver obediently lowered the bag and handed it down to Kirk. "And don't toss that one, either," Kirk ordered while pointing toward Matthew's case.

"Yes, sir," the driver sheepishly replied.

Matthew laughed as they walked into the foyer of the hotel. "Apparently you carry a good deal of authority in Boston, too."

"No, I just surprised him," Kirk replied as he signed the register. "Is Nathan meeting us here this evening or going directly to J. P.'s?"

"He's going to bring his carriage to the hotel so that we can travel together," Matthew replied.

Kirk took his room key from the clerk and turned toward Matthew. "Good. And we meet with Bishop Fenwick in the morning?"

"No, not until tomorrow afternoon at three o'clock—for tea," Matthew added.

Kirk flashed a sardonic grin. "Ah, yes, I forgot the bishop likes to sleep late."

Matthew wasn't privy to the bishop's sleeping habits but somehow felt as though he'd erred in scheduling the afternoon appointment. "I didn't think you'd mind. We'll be required to remain in Boston an extra day no matter what time we meet."

"I don't mind, Matthew. You're correct, it makes little difference what time we meet. We'll have the morning free in the event Nathan or J. P. needs additional time with us. I'll see you out here in the lobby a little before seven."

Matthew nodded and watched as Kirk moved down the hallway and began to climb the circular staircase. He was limping, favoring his right leg, which was a sure indication Kirk's pain was greater than he'd mentioned earlier. Matthew understood his necessity for rest. Besides, he could use this time to review some of the paper work for expansion of the shipping company. Several months had passed since Nathan originally proposed the matter, and the Associates were now ready to expand their overseas market.

The ledger of figures and calculations was mind-boggling. Matthew studied page after page, quickly becoming envious of Kirk's ability to decipher and then remember facts and figures after one presentation. Several times he dozed off, his head falling forward onto his chest and awakening him with a start. Finally he gave up and permitted himself the luxury of a short nap.

By the time Matthew left his room, he was refreshed and ready for the meeting. Nathan and Kirk were waiting in the foyer as he approached.

"Right on time," Kirk said. "You have all the paper work?"

Matthew patted the leather case. "Right here."

Nathan's carriage was much more comfortable than the stage, and Matthew relaxed on the leather-upholstered seat. "Is it quite a distance to Mr. Green's residence?"

"No, not far. His home is in the Beacon Hill district. It would be more to my liking if we met at the hotel, but J. P. is so anxious to entertain in his home, I couldn't dissuade him," Nathan explained.

"As I told Matthew earlier, the man's pride is unfounded; but I find that's generally the way of things. The man who has the least reason to boast usually crows the loudest."

Nathan nodded. "True, Kirk, but if this shipping venture grows as I believe it will, J. P. stands to become quite wealthy."

"But not as wealthy as you, Nathan," Kirk responded with a wide grin.

"Well, no. But formation of the shipping venture is my idea, and I began the company. With the help of the other Associates," he added quickly.

"And since J. P. doesn't have earnings from the mills—only the shipping company itself—he can't begin to compete with your wealth and stature," Kirk replied.

Nathan gave an embarrassed laugh. "What stature? I'm a businessman with humble beginnings."

"No need to be modest, Nathan. There's nothing wrong with wealth—you've accumulated yours honestly. And worked hard for it, I might add."

"Not nearly as hard as you've worked in Lowell, Kirk. I don't know what we'd have done without you to manage the business," Nathan responded. "Goodness knows, none of us wanted to live in Lowell. I believe that my wife would have deserted me had I even expressed the vaguest interest in leaving Boston."

"If the two of us continue bragging upon each other, perhaps J. P. will realize how he sounds and keep quiet," Kirk remarked as the coach rolled to a halt in front of the Green mansion.

"He's a bit pompous, but he means well," Nathan said. "Don't spend the entire evening taking him to task."

Kirk disembarked the carriage and gave Nathan a slap on the back. "Only as a personal favor to you, Nathan."

The house went beyond Matthew's idea of good taste. It was opulent—every nook and cranny was crowded with ornately carved furniture, the windows were draped in the most expensive velvets, and inlaid marble floors surrounded carpets of the finest weave. No cost had been spared in building the house, but it was such a mismatch of styles and designs that nothing looked quite right.

"It is a genuine pleasure to host such illustrious visitors in my humble home," J. P. said as he led the men into his library. "May I offer you something to drink? A glass of port or sherry?"

"Port is fine," Nathan replied, seating himself on the tapestry-covered couch in front of a huge fireplace. "Fine craftsmanship," he said, pointing toward the stonework.

J. P. nodded in agreement. "The best I've ever seen—an Irishman, if you can believe that! He came highly recommended, but I didn't let him take a chisel to any of the stones until I'd seen some of his work. Much of this stone is imported from Italy, and I didn't want it ruined by some Mick," he added. "You might look him up if you have need of some masonry, Kirk—said he was going to Lowell."

"Lowell? He'll not find folks willing to spend their hard-earned money on fancy work such as this," Kirk replied as he waved his arm toward the fireplace.

"He said he was going to do the stonework at some new Catholic church being built in Lowell. Surely you're knowledgeable about something as important as a new church, aren't you?"

Matthew looked toward Kirk, whose face had tightened, a slight twitch evident along his jawline. It was obvious J. P.'s remark had not endeared him to Kirk.

"I'm aware of everything of consequence that occurs in Lowell. And that includes the Catholic church. In fact, we're meeting with Bishop Fenwick tomorrow to finalize plans for the dedication," Kirk replied from between clenched teeth. "By the way, what's this stonemason's name?"

J. P.'s chest puffed out at the question. "Donohue. Liam Donohue. He's expensive but worth every cent, and you'll have your wife's undying devotion—believe me."

Kirk laughed. "I merely wanted his name; I'm not planning on hiring him," Kirk said as a servant approached, held a whispered conversation with J. P., and scurried back out of the room.

"I apologize for the interruption, gentlemen. Life has been in a bit of an upheaval of late. Someone entered the house and managed to break into my safe. I had hoped the matter would be resolved before our meeting, but it appears the police have had little success. It has been most trying."

"I can imagine, but thank goodness for banks. At least we no longer keep vast amounts of wealth in our homes," Nathan replied.

J. P. gave a feeble smile. "Yes, banks are a wonderful institution, but it is imperative I recover the contents of my safe. My future depends upon it. I kept important records in that safe."

Kirk shook his head. "No need to be dramatic, J. P. Life will go on even if you don't recover those few stolen belongings. I'm sure you can duplicate any lost documents."

"Of course, you're right," J. P. replied, although his nervous countenance belied his words. "Let's have supper," he said, leading the men into the dining room.

Kirk motioned Matthew to drop back a few paces. "When we return to Lowell, I want you to find out if Hugh has hired that Irishman—Donohue. If so, I want to know what he's paying him. I didn't authorize hiring any new employees, especially Irishmen. We've got enough problems brewing between the Yanks and Irish as it is."

Matthew nodded. "I'll see to it."

"J. P. has certainly worked himself into a frenzy over a small robbery, wouldn't you say? It makes no sense that a man who can afford to spend this kind of money," Kirk said as he looked about the house, "would be so upset over the contents of a small house safe."

"He did say there were important documents," Matthew whispered as they sat down at the table.

"What idiot would keep important papers in his personal safe unless he had duplicates stored elsewhere?"

Matthew shrugged. Having never been faced with such a problem, he hadn't given the matter much thought, although what Kirk said made sense. There should be duplicates of important papers. After all, the Corporation maintained duplicate signed copies of its important documents.

From the twenty-foot-high ceiling of the formal dining room, not one, but two crystal chandeliers offered candlelight on the elaborately decorated table. And the meal was much like the house—overindulgent, with their host remaining preoccupied throughout supper. Kirk and Nathan discussed politics, both of them excited over the possibilities of new tariff laws.

"The Tariff of Abominations will soon be a thing of the past," Kirk announced. "The legislators who so stupidly voted in those legal means by which to pick our pockets will soon have to reckon with President Jackson's ideas for improvement."

"I suppose Calhoun will be his biggest opponent," Nathan said, sipping his wine. "The man has been a thorn in his side since taking the vice-presidency."

"He was a thorn in his side prior to that," Kirk said, laughing, "as Adams' vice-president. The Tariff of 1828 was not pleasing to the poor man. I thought for certain he might very well have South Carolina seceding before the year was out."

"He still threatens it," Matthew threw in. "I heard of quite an incident over a birthday party for Thomas Jefferson. It seems President Jackson gave the toast, 'Our Federal Union—it must be preserved!' and Vice-President Calhoun came back with, 'The Union—next to our liberty, the most dear!' According to the report, the men are worse enemies now than when they began their administration."

"To be sure," Kirk said, nodding. "I share a rather casual acquaintance with Calhoun. It wouldn't surprise me to see the man resign his position and return to South Carolina."

"Resign the vice-presidency?" Nathan questioned. "That would be sheer lunacy."

Kirk smiled and pushed his plate away. "No, sheer lunacy is having those two under the same roof for any purpose—much less the running of the country." The men enjoyed a good laugh over this.

"So, Nathan, I understand the Corporation has given you the nod to expand into some new markets," Kirk commented as the men finished their meal and retired to the library. J. P.'s butler followed the men into the room, poured drinks for all, and offered cigars. Matthew had no interest in either refreshment and settled back into the plush wing-backed chair. The supple cushioning and upholstery seemed to embrace Matthew. He'd have to look into purchasing some of these chairs for his own home.

Nathan took a cigar from the humidor and clipped the end. "There's ample interest in the carpets being produced at the Lowell Mill, and we can't seem to keep up with the demand for Negro cloth. I'd like to expand markets for our calicos, finer linens, and cotton to the southern states. The demand is certainly strong in all of the larger cities of the South for those fabrics. I've also received several missives from a New Orleans businessman who wants to purchase carpets—probably more than we can produce in the next year."

J. P. came to attention. He waved his butler away and questioned, "New Orleans?"

"Yes. He wants to distribute carpets throughout the South as well as overseas. By my calculations, the Corporation would make more money shipping directly to him for further distribution. That may not always hold true, but for now we can make more money sending to only one destination."

"I like the idea of New Orleans. I'd be pleased to go and meet with the distributor you're considering," J. P. offered excitedly.

Nathan glanced at Kirk then back toward J. P. "I'll keep your offer in mind. A trip to New Orleans may be necessary to finalize the agreement," Nathan replied as he blew a puff of blue gray cigar smoke into the air.

Matthew glanced toward J. P. The man had appeared to be daydreaming as they had discussed shipping fabrics to the South—at least until Nathan mentioned New Orleans. It was at that point J. P. had come to life, his behavior becoming quite animated. It was obvious the mention of New Orleans and the overseas markets excited him more than anything else they'd discussed all evening. Matthew couldn't help but wonder why. After all, the profits from the other markets would be much greater than those for the carpets. It was, he decided, an interesting conundrum.

Bella and Daughtie stood among the throng of girls gathered in the hallway. Miss Addie clapped her hands several times, resembling a schoolteacher summoning an unruly class to attention. "Now, remember that I expect each of you to be on your best behavior. This is an excellent opportunity to utilize the manners you're forced to push aside during weekday meals. I know that you can have a good time and still make me proud of your conduct."

Janet Stodemire was standing on the steps. "I've changed my mind. I'm not going," she called out.

"I sent a formal response on behalf of all those who signed up to attend Lilly's tea. Did you sign the sheet?"

"Yes, ma'am, but a friend who works over at the Lowell Mill saw me in church this morning. She invited me to spend the afternoon with her. We're going on a picnic with two boys," she proudly announced.

"No, Janet, you're not going on a picnic. You have a prior engagement, and you will attend with the rest of us. If there is time for your picnic after the tea, then you may go," Addie staunchly replied.

Janet's eyes flashed with anger. "You can't force me to go."

Bella gasped. "You ought not speak to an elder in such a fashion," she said without thinking.

"Stay out of this, Bella. We all know you and Daughtie are the perfect little Shakers or Quakers or whatever you call yourselves. This is none of your business."

Bella glanced at Janet and then toward Miss Addie. "You're right; it isn't. I apologize for interfering."

"Thank you for your apology, Bella," Miss Addie replied before tilting her gaze upward to meet Janet's stare. "Come along, Janet," she said firmly. "Otherwise, I'll be forced to write a letter to your supervisor that I'm requesting your removal from my house for failure to abide by the rules."

Janet clenched her fists and glared at Miss Addie. "Where does it say I must attend a tea at Lilly Cheever's home?"

"The contract you signed says that you will conduct yourself in a proper ladylike manner. The rules also say that I am the judge of acceptable behavior. Now please get your cape and let's be on our way. I don't intend to be late."

It was a beautiful early summer day as the girls walked down Jackson Street, two by two, with an excited buzz filling the air as they passed the row of boardinghouses. It wasn't often the mill girls were invited to visit one of the fine homes in Lowell. Several of Miss Addie's girls had known Lilly before she married Matthew Cheever, when she had been a resident of Miss Addie's boardinghouse while they all worked at the Appleton. Now they dreamed about the same fairy-tale marriage occurring in their own lives.

Bella thought them rather silly. It wasn't a matter of not wanting to ever marry; it was the way the girls seemed to put such stock in marrying someone well-to-do. Whatever happened to marrying for love? Marrying a man whom you love, no matter his station, made you glad to be alive. Bella wanted that kind of marriage.

She ignored the chatter of her friends and thought instead of Jesse. She wouldn't have had that kind of marriage with him. He was sweet and gentle-natured, but he would never be the kind of man Bella needed. Bella needed a man who could stand his ground with her—who wouldn't be overrun by her temper or opinionated manner.

Not that I don't need desperately to alter those areas, she thought. *I need a man who won't be afraid of my mind or the fact that I enjoy learning and expanding my knowledge. I don't need someone of high status or lofty ambitions, but I do need a man who can provide for his family.*

Bella's breath caught in her throat as they arrived at the Cheever home. It was a large frame house with a wide porch wrapping around the front and side, unlike anything Bella had previously seen. Willow chairs sat on the porch, beckoning visitors to sit awhile and smell the early summer blooms that lined the stone walkway and surrounded the outline of the covered porch. Rose-bushes with their buds revealing a hint of pink were strategically planted in a small garden on the east side of the house, and the afternoon breeze was heavy with the smell of fragrant honeysuckle blossoms.

"It's difficult to imagine living in a place such as this," Bella whispered to Daughtie.

Daughtie nodded her head. "It's as big as the house all the Sisters and Brothers lived in. Don't you love the porch? It's a shame the Society thought porches too worldly."

Bella smiled. "It's not so much the porch, Daughtie, it's the ornamentation a porch provides that causes the Believers to fault them. The Brothers and Sisters would be aghast at the ornate carving on the front door," she said. "But I find it beautiful."

"Ohhh, and look at the columns. They look like the drawings from the Roman Empire in our history book. Don't you think?"

"Yes, that's probably where they got the idea. Sister Minerva said every generation copies from the preceding generations—that nothing is original," Bella replied.

"Well, I find that statement difficult to believe. There are new inventions every day. Aren't those monstrous machines we use at the mills a new idea? I don't think any of that machinery was in use several generations ago," Daughtie replied.

"Perhaps you're correct, Daughtie. It would be nice to think of Sister Minerva being wrong at least once in her lifetime, wouldn't it?"

Bella and Daughtie giggled in unison as they walked into the foyer, where Miss Addie stood alongside Lilly to introduce each guest as she passed by.

"And these are my two newest friends and boarders," Miss Addie told Lilly. "This," she said, patting Daughtie's shoulder, "is Miss Daughtie Winfield. And this," she continued while taking Bella's hand, "is Miss Arabella Newberry— we call her Bella. Both the girls have come from the Shaker community outside of Concord."

"Oh yes, I've heard tell of it. In Canterbury, isn't it?" Lilly inquired.

"Yes, that's correct," Bella answered.

Lilly gave them an inviting smile. "I'm eager to visit with you. Please be sure to save a few moments so that we may chat."

"Why does she want to talk to us?" Daughtie inquired as the girls worked their way into the parlor and then moved onward into the adjoining music room.

"She was merely being courteous, Daughtie. You needn't be so suspicious of everyone. Oh, look at this piano. Isn't it beautiful?"

Lilly approached and stood to one side. "Do you play?"

Bella nodded and turned. "My mother was quite accomplished. She taught me when I was very young, but I haven't played for years."

"You're welcome to entertain us," Lilly offered.

"No. It's been too long, and playing the piano reminds me of my mother. She died several years ago," Bella explained. Sometimes it seemed as if her mother had died only yesterday—the pain was so tangible.

Lilly took her hand. "I understand."

Daughtie drifted off with Miss Addie and the other girls as they took their places visiting in the various rooms. Because of this, Bella felt free to question Lilly Cheever. "Your mother is deceased, also?"

"Yes," Lilly replied. "Come sit down and let's visit. Miss Addie tells me you've become one of her favorite people, and she's an excellent judge of character."

Bella followed Lilly to one of the settees across the room and sat down. The cushioning made Bella feel as though she were sitting on a cloud. "Your home is beautiful," Bella complimented while gazing about the room. Gold-framed oil paintings decorated the wall opposite her. The paintings were of a variety of pastoral settings. The only exception was the large oil over the fire-place. This painting was a most becoming memorial to Lilly Cheever's wedding day. Bella couldn't imagine what it might be like to sit and pose for such a thing. Pulling her thoughts back to Lilly's questioning gaze, she added, "I particularly like the porch."

Lilly smiled and nodded. "Matthew said large porches belong in the South, but I envision lots of children playing out there, even on rainy days. Wouldn't that be delightful fun?"

Bella laughed. "Yes, I suppose it would. Miss Addie is quite proud that you once lived with her. She tells all of us how you saved her position with the Corporation by teaching her how to cook. I'm sure you know that you have her undying devotion."

Lilly blushed at the praise. "Miss Addie gives me far too much credit for her success. I am pleased, however, that her boardinghouse is considered one of the finest in Lowell. It's obvious she enjoys her work—perhaps too much."

"How can it be harmful to enjoy your work?"

"Sometimes she tends to put you girls ahead of her personal life," Lilly hedged.

Bella gave a knowing look. "You mean with Mr. Farnsworth, don't you?"

"He's a fine man. I think she should marry him, move into his home, and begin a joyous life with him. Unfortunately, she thinks if they marry, he should move into the boardinghouse, where she would continue with her boarding-house duties. I doubt whether he'll come around to her way of thinking. But I fear she'll lose him to another if she doesn't change her mind," Lilly explained, shaking her head. "I'm not sure why I'm telling you this except I can tell you've come to care for Miss Addie, as I did. Perhaps we can conspire to convince her to reconsider."

"I would think Mr. Farnsworth would be delighted to move into the boardinghouse if for no other reason than to rid himself of his nephew," Bella confided. The memory of her encounters with Taylor Manning caused Bella to twist her hands together.

"Taylor Manning? You don't find him amusing?" Lilly inquired.

"Frankly, I find him rather pompous and lacking in manners."

Lilly didn't immediately respond. Instead, she gave Bella a curious smile. "You would agree that he's very handsome, wouldn't you?"

"I would agree that Taylor Manning believes himself very handsome. To me, however, his appearance is completely diminished by his boorish behav-ior," Bella countered. "Someone is attempting to gain your attention," she said, glancing toward the doorway.

"If you'll excuse me, I believe the servants are ready to serve tea. We'll visit again," Lilly said, rising from the settee.

Bella watched as Lilly swept away in a gown of amber and cream. The dress was most magnificent, with a scalloped flounce along the skirt's edge and ruching tucked with piping along the bodice. Bella looked down at her own gown of gray homespun. The simplicity was a sharp contrast to Lilly's gown. Bella glanced around the room and realized that her gown was quite plain compared to everyone else's, save Daughtie's. Taylor had chided her for not dressing more fashionably, and seeing the beautiful dresses of the other girls made Bella almost wish she could comply. *But if I make a new dress now,* she reasoned, *Taylor Manning will think I'm doing it merely to impress him.* She stiffened at the thought. There would be no new gown.

The time passed quickly as the servants poured tea and offered scrumptious egg and watercress sandwiches accompanied by fancy breads and jelly-filled pastries. Tea was followed by a tour of the house for those who were interested. Bella couldn't decide what she found the most intriguing, the beauty of the home or the fact that only two people lived alone in this large house.

The girls clustered together in small groups, one discussing the new millinery shop opened by a widow from Boston who was abreast of the latest fashion news from England, while another group discussed several men who had recently arrived in town. Bella and Daughtie stood on the fringes of one group, where one of the girls whispered that Lilly was expecting a baby. The remark was followed with oohs and aahs from around the circle.

"What ever happened to her brother's child?" someone asked.

"They never found him, but I understand Lilly hasn't given up hope. She believes the boy is still alive somewhere, but don't you think it's doubtful they would find him now? How long has it been?"

"A couple years, I think," another girl replied.

Bella was intrigued by the conversation and sat down beside Marmi, one of the girls who had known Lilly prior to her marriage. "What happened to Mrs. Cheever's brother?" Bella asked.

"He died in a fire at the mill. Some say he set the fire, while others say he was helping to put it out. Either way, he died shortly afterward. While on his deathbed, he supposedly told Lilly he had fathered a child. . . ."

"By an Irishwoman," another girl added in a hushed voice.

Marmi shook her head. "It doesn't matter to Lilly if the mother's Irish. She wants to find the boy. Some thought Lilly might never have a child of her own. I'm truly pleased to hear her news. Perhaps it will ease her pain in case they never find her nephew."

Several more girls joined them, and the talk soon shifted to clothing and jewelry, one of them mentioning the recent shipments of lace and gloves that had arrived in Lowell earlier in the week. Bored with their conversation, Bella excused herself and sauntered into the parlor. Finding an unoccupied chair near a large window overlooking the flower garden along the west side of the house, Bella seated herself. A stoop-shouldered man busied himself pruning bushes and packing fresh dirt around several plants, and as she watched him work, her thoughts drifted back to her earlier conversation with Lilly Cheever. It was clear Lilly had suffered her share of sadness. To lose her mother and brother was difficult enough, but then to know there was a child—one that couldn't be found—would be a tragedy. It was good, Bella decided, that Lilly had a fine husband and would soon have a child of her own to love. She stood to gain a better view of the gardener as he began planting a bush.

"I'd like to think you find me as intriguing as you find the gardener."

Bella whirled around and found herself face-to-face with Taylor Manning.

"What are you doing here?" She forced herself not to notice the sparkle of his sapphire blue eyes.

He gave her a wide grin. "I'd like to tell you that I knew you would be here and I couldn't stay away. But that wouldn't be the truth, and I know with all the religion that's surrounded your life, you might take a dim view of my lying to you. Actually, I've come to fetch Mr. Cheever. He told me I could wait in here while he informs Mrs. Cheever he must take his leave; there's a bit of difficulty that needs his attention. By the way, I'm pleased to see you've taken the time to fancy yourself up a bit."

Bella stared at him in disbelief. "Taken the time to fancy myself up?"

"That trim," he said, pointing his finger toward the lace that now surrounded the cuffs and neckline of her dress. "You fancied your dress a little. Of course, another color would be better. In fact, a whole new dress would be best, but at least you made an effort."

Her mouth dropped open and formed a small oval. "Do you spend all of your free time practicing rude behavior, or is your appalling conduct a natural happenstance, Mr. Manning?"

Taylor appeared completely baffled by her remark. "What do you mean? I paid you a compliment."

"No, you insulted me," she retaliated.

"Then I apologize. I was attempting to point out that those Shaker dresses don't enhance your beauty." He crossed his arms and gave her a proud grin.

Bella glanced heavenward. "Shaker dresses, as you call them, are specifically designed to detract from a woman's . . ."

Taylor laughed. "Shape? Size? Form? Figure? Beauty?"

Bella could feel the heat rising in her cheeks. "All of those," she huffed, quickly turning to walk away.

Taylor stepped forward and blocked her path. "Don't rush off after pointing out that my manners need improvement. The least you can do is remain and lend your assistance."

"There isn't sufficient time in my day to correct your manners, sir."

A wide grin spread across Taylor's face. "Then perhaps we'll need to schedule several sessions. I'll make myself available at your convenience."

Had she not been so angry, the expectant look on his face would have caused her to laugh. "Either I have a problem speaking or you have a problem understanding. Your manners are reprehensible. I am not available to instruct you in proper etiquette."

"Well, then," he replied, obviously unruffled, "I suggest you accompany me to the lyceum. I understand there's to be a talk on phrenology. The speaker is personally acquainted and has studied with J. G. Spurzheim while in Europe."

Bella hesitated. The Brothers and Sisters at Canterbury had discussed the possible benefits of phrenology in Union Meeting on several occasions. The topic was controversial yet one that had captured the interest of the forward-thinking Shakers—one that Bella found unbelievable but intriguing.

Taylor shifted his weight to one foot and casually leaned against the thick oak woodwork surrounding the doorway. "You don't know what phrenology is and you don't want to ask me, do you?"

His smug tone annoyed Bella. "Do *you*?" she inquired.

"Well, no, but Uncle John said that J. G. Spurzheim is quite renowned in Scotland and England."

"Phrenologists teach that the human skull takes its shape from the brain. Therefore, by reading the skull an individual can be evaluated for psychological aptitudes and tendencies," Bella articulated.

"What?"

Matthew and Lilly laughed at Taylor as they approached. "By all appearances, I would guess that Bella has completely confounded you, Taylor," Lilly observed.

"Perhaps just a bit," he admitted. "I invited her to attend the phrenology lecture with me."

"Oh yes, I can hardly wait. We're planning to attend. Perhaps we could all go together," Lilly suggested.

Taylor gave her a satisfied grin. "Why, that would be wonderful. Wouldn't it, Bella?"

She knew what Taylor was up to. But it wouldn't work. "Quite frankly, I would enjoy attending the lyceum. However, Mr. Manning has insulted me numerous times since his arrival this afternoon, and I find his company abhorrent."

Matthew's eyebrows arched. "Well, in that case . . ."

"I'm sure Taylor would be on his best behavior, Bella. And the lecture is sure to be a fine one. Why don't you rethink your decision?" Lilly interrupted. "In fact, if it will make your decision easier, you can pretend that Taylor isn't even along—except for the ticket, of course. I understand that the program is sold out," she added.

"He's already insulted my attire. I'm sure my dowdy appearance would prove an embarrassment," Bella explained.

Matthew cleared his throat and grinned at his wife. "I hate to interrupt before you've reached a resolution to this quandary. However, Taylor came here to fetch me. Seems there may be some difficulty brewing with the Irish, and neither Kirk nor Paul can be found."

Lilly gave Matthew a frown. "On a Sunday afternoon? What kind of difficulty, Matthew?"

"There are rumors spreading that the Irish have begun stockpiling weapons in the foundation of the new church. I want to put a stop to it before trouble begins," Matthew replied.

"That's preposterous. Why on earth would the Irish want to accumulate weapons?"

"I doubt that there's any truth to the rumors."

Lilly's mouth was agape. "But what if . . ."

Matthew patted her shoulder. "Nothing to concern yourself with, my dear. I'm certain that at most it's only a small group of troublemakers, but the Corporation does need to halt any rumors. I'll see what I can do," he said. "While I'm gone, why don't you ladies make a decision regarding attending the lyceum? Taylor and I will be pleased to accommodate your choice. Won't we, Taylor?" he asked while moving toward the front door.

Taylor didn't appear pleased with the pronouncement but he was obviously unwilling to argue Matthew's position. "Yes, sir," he replied. "Will you . . ."

"Whatever the decision, I promise I'll get word to you," Matthew said, while pushing Taylor onward.

Lilly giggled as they walked out the door. "That young man is enchanted with you, Bella. And I believe you're quite smitten with him, also," she said, linking arms with Bella. Before Bella could protest, Lilly pulled her toward a corner of the foyer. "Proper attire isn't a problem. I have several dresses that would fit you handsomely," Lilly offered. "I would be honored if you would permit me to give you one. I don't know if you've heard, but I'm going to be a mother. My waist has thickened, and most of my dresses no longer fit."

"But they'll fit you again—after the child," Bella replied.

"I promise I'll give you one that will soon be out of fashion. Would that make the gift more acceptable?"

"I didn't mean to imply that I find your offer unacceptable," Bella apologized. "However, it's a thorny issue, changing my attire to suit Taylor Manning's request—although I very much want to attend the lyceum," she confided in a whisper.

"Do you find wearing worldly clothing goes against your religious tenets, Bella? Because if you believe you must continue to wear your Shaker dresses, I would never encourage you to disobey your beliefs. But if it's merely that you don't want Taylor to win an argument . . ."

Bella blushed and turned away. "I've never believed that it was necessary to wear drab clothing in order to love God. As you can see, I've already added some lace to this dress," she replied, then hesitated. "And although Taylor is prideful, he's probably no worse than most men."

Lilly grasped Bella's hand, her face etched with concern. "What's hardened your heart toward men at such an early age, Bella?"

"In the case of Taylor Manning, I find him arrogant and entirely self-absorbed. He believes himself to be the finest thing in shoe leather. He has an attitude of pride regarding his looks, and I can tell by the way he acts that he's used to getting his own way with the ladies."

"But Taylor Manning isn't the one who started this feeling toward men, is he?"

Bella gave Lilly a wistful smile as her thoughts wandered down a dark path of memories. "There have been two men in my life. My father and Jesse Harwood—and even though they both avowed their love, neither chose me over life among the Shakers. I trusted both of them; they both disappointed me. I've finally concluded that the pain meted out by men is more than my heart can withstand."

Lilly pulled her close. "Sit down here," she said, leading her to a small divan. "Not all men are the same, Bella. I've experienced pain at the hands of men I've loved, but there are good men, men who will love and cherish you. As I labored with my own pain, my heart was quickened to pray for those who caused the pain. It was difficult, but there is a balm of healing that comes with prayer for wrongdoers. Perhaps if you could begin praying for your father and Jesse, it would help. Tell me about them—your father and Jesse."

Bella felt as though she'd met a kindred spirit. The chattering girls and tea party formed a hazy milieu while she poured out her heart to Lilly, first explaining the pain of rejection at her father's hand, then her mother's death, and then Jesse's unexplained nonappearance the night she and Daughtie left Canterbury.

"So you love Jesse and wanted to become his wife. Now I understand why you find Taylor's advances offensive," Lilly said.

"No, I don't want to marry anyone. I'm not sure what that kind of love is—between a man and woman, I mean. Jesse said he loved me, but I knew my love for him wasn't the same. He insisted we should be married, and I thought perhaps he was right, although I confess I was fearful of the arrangement. My mother loved my father, and he deserted her love for the Shakers. What if Jesse decided he wanted to return to Canterbury after we were married? I was frightened, but I wanted to leave the Family."

"But not because of Jesse?"

Bella shook her head back and forth. "I find fault with some of their important beliefs; they go against what the Bible says—at least I think they do," she replied.

"I see," Lilly replied. "Then you actually left the Shakers in order to exercise your religious freedom."

"Exactly," Bella replied, gracing her hostess with a grateful smile.

"Good! Then you can wear my dress and attend the lyceum without compromising your beliefs," Lilly triumphantly replied. "You remain behind with Miss Addie after the others leave this afternoon, and we'll decide upon a dress. In fact, it appears as if several of my guests are preparing to leave. I'd best resume my hostess duties. Promise you'll stay," Lilly urged.

Bella nodded her agreement. She hoped her decision would prove judicious.

Taylor mulled over the conversation he'd had with Bella and couldn't begin to imagine how he'd insulted her. Yes, he'd been forward and open with his statements, but he didn't believe it served him very well to veil his thoughts. Still, she had been upset with him. As if reading his thoughts, Matthew interrupted with a question.

"You didn't really insult that poor young woman, did you?"

Taylor shrugged. "I didn't think so, but apparently she found my words offensive. Bella is a true mystery to me."

"That's why you've come to like her so much more than the other girls, correct?"

"I never said I liked her more than anyone," Taylor replied defensively. "I've no need to choose one woman over another. I tend to spread myself among the ladies," he said, grinning.

Matthew frowned. "That's hardly the kind of attitude I would brag about. Your heart seems not to care at all for the misery you cause, yet you seem considerate enough with some. I suppose you find the attention rewarding at this stage of your life, but let me assure you, Taylor, the love of a good and godly woman cannot compare to the adoration of hundreds of addlepated ninnies. Find a woman of character—godly character—and you'll have found something of great value."

The words stung Taylor's pride. Surely Matthew Cheever believed in more than inward beauty. After all, the man was married to a beautiful woman, had an opulent home, and dressed impeccably in the best of fashions. Taylor smiled to himself. Matthew was probably just speaking in such a manner because his wife had suggested it. He nodded to himself and felt the weight of his concern lift. That's all it was. Lilly Cheever had probably instructed her husband to chide Taylor for his brusque and open manner with Bella. It was surely nothing more than that.

~ 15 ~

William Thurston relentlessly plodded down one of the mucky paths toward Michael Neil's pub in the Acre. It wasn't his need for liquor forcing his portly body into the rapid pace; rather, it was the overheard conversation from a nearby table the evening before while he had dined at the Wareham House. He'd briefly considered going to the Acre last night, but going after dark was risky for a Yank. He decided his visit could wait until today. If luck was on his side, several of his lackeys would be in the pub downing ale.

He pressed onward, keeping his head bowed against a warm breeze, the stench of the litter-filled streets assaulting his senses. Relief washed over him when he finally reached the pub and recognized the faces of two men sitting in a darkened corner. Weaving his way among several tables, Thurston motioned at the barkeep to deliver ale to the corner table and then seated himself.

He leaned across the table toward the two men in an intimate fashion. "I understand there was a bit of a ruckus down here yesterday."

One of the men nodded. "How'd you find out?"

"I keep telling you boys I've got eyes and ears everywhere. When something happens, I hear about it. Remember that." He wasn't about to tell them he'd been eavesdropping in the hotel restaurant. Besides, whether real or perceived, the veiled threats gave him a feeling of power. "Now, tell me what occurred. I'm anxious for all the details."

Rafe took a swig of his ale, set his tankard down with a thud, and leaned in toward Thurston. "I've been doing like you said, snooping about for any word of an uprising or hidden weapons," he reported.

"Or money," Thurston added.

"There've been a few stories circulating, but most of the talk seems to be among the Yanks. The tales appear to have died down, right, Jake?"

Jake nodded. "Word I'm hearing is there's a handful of Yanks convinced the Irish are planning an uprising. They believe there are guns and money hidden away in the church. There are plenty of Yanks wanting the Irish run outta town, saying they can't find work because of the Irish. Like Rafe said, there doesn't seem to be much talk in the Acre, and if there are any rifles or money stored in the church, it's the best-kept secret in the Paddy camp. But it don't take a whole lot up here," Jake said while pointing to his head, "to figure out the Irish ain't got enough money to live on, let alone use it to buy rifles to stash away in that church."

"As though you have a lot up here," Thurston sneered, pointing to his own head. "The Catholic Church has lots of money, you fool. Don't you think the church would finance a rebellion if it was in its best interest?"

"I think you're takin' this whole story out of proportion," Rafe said. "Things have already begun to quiet down; they always do. The Irish will stay down here in the Acre except for work, and the Yanks will stay in their part of town."

Thurston glared at Rafe. He sounded just like Kirk Boott, thinking the Irish belonged in Lowell. Well, he didn't want things to settle down. The Irish were a blight on this idyllic community, and Thurston had been prophesying problems to the Boston Associates for three years. The Associates wouldn't listen—none of them. They always sided with Kirk Boott, believing his rhetoric that the Irish were necessary—that locals didn't want to perform manual labor. Well, it appeared the good people of New England were changing their attitude about the interlopers, and he was going to do everything in his power to prove the Irish were the problem he'd predicted. He'd see this town free of the lowlifes if it was the last thing he did.

"The two of you listen to me. Rafe, I want you out here in the Acre talking to your Irish friends. You tell them you have it from a reliable source that the Yanks are preparing to expel them from the Acre. Tell them the Yanks want their jobs and are willing to fight for them." Turning his attention toward Jake, he said, "Spread word around Lowell that the Irish are storing up arms with an eye toward a takeover of the mills."

Both men stared at Thurston in disbelief. Rafe spoke first. "When I'm asked about my reliable source, whose name should I use? Yours?"

Jake appeared to draw courage from Rafe's question. "I don't care if there is some murmuring around town about money and guns in the church. Nobody is going to believe that the Irish are storing up weapons in an attempt to take over the mills. That's the craziest thing I ever heard. Nobody in their right mind would believe they'd try such a thing. How many Irishmen are there? Only three hundred—maybe five hundred if we count the women and children? And you want me to tell people they're gonna attempt a takeover?"

"The Yanks'll think he's daft," Rafe agreed.

"No they won't—they'll want to believe the story, and the gossip will feed upon itself as it spreads. I expect you both to do as you're told—why do you think I pay you? And if you want to chart your own course, there's always an alternative. If you no longer want to work for me, you say the word. I've had others leave my employ."

"I didn't say I wouldn't do what you asked, but I know I'll be questioned about my source," Rafe replied.

"Tell them you heard it from Hugh Cummiskey," Thurston responded.

Rafe's eyes grew wide at Thurston's response. "Cummiskey? I can't use his name, Mr. Thurston."

"Why? You fear him more than you fear me? If you don't want to use Cummiskey's name, you figure out whose name to use. Once word begins to spread, it shouldn't take long before the fires of hostility spread," Thurston said. He leaned back, took a long drink, and gave them a satisfied smile. "Yes, fear and whispered accusations should do the trick. You boys pass the word among your cronies; tell them to feel free to share the information," he emphasized. "And don't forget that I hear rumors the same as everyone else. If I haven't heard the gossip around town, I'll assume you're not doing your job."

Jake nervously pulled at the two-day stubble growing on his chin. "You said earlier you've had others leave your employ, Mr. Thurston. What if I decide that's what I wanna do?"

Thurston leveled a wicked smile in Jake's direction. "You might want to rethink that decision. No one who has quit working for me is alive."

"You mean . . . Are you saying . . . Did you . . ." Jake stammered.

An evil gleam shone in Thurston's eyes. "Draw your own conclusions," he replied.

"Well, I was merely asking—I plan to remain in your employ just as long as you want me," Jake replied, keeping his gaze focused on the tankard of ale before him.

"In that case, I'll leave you men to your work," Thurston said, hoisting his ample body from the chair. "I'll be in touch." He made his way to the door and donned his hat. Squaring his shoulders, he walked out the front door, knowing the two men were watching his every move, hating him. He smiled.

16

D aughtie had openly expressed her dismay when Bella confided her plan to attend the phrenology lecture with Taylor. This evening it was obvious that Daughtie was even more apprehensive as Bella twirled about in Lilly Cheever's rose-colored silk gown.

"You look like a bird prepared to take flight," Daughtie said while flapping her arms up and down. "I think the dressmaker should have taken some of the fabric out of those enormous sleeves and used it in the bodice to give the gown a modicum of modesty."

Bella ran a finger along the folds and cords decorating the double collars that served to widen the shoulders of the dress. "You believe the dress immodest?"

Daughtie appeared taken aback by the question. "Perhaps just a bit."

An embroidered muslin overlay topped the double collars. Bella tugged at the muslin and bunched it over her neckline. "Is this better?" she asked with a giggle. "Look at the shoes Lilly gave me—and they fit ever so well," she added while holding up the shoes of thin woolen cloth with a pleated frill at the top. "They lace down the back. Isn't that clever?"

Daughtie sat on the bed watching Bella's every move. "The shoes are quite clever," she replied. She quietly cleared her throat and then hesitated a moment. "I . . . um . . . fear you're straying from your beliefs." A note of recrimination hung in the air.

Bella ceased tying one of the shoes and gave Daughtie a thoughtful look. "Which beliefs that were truly my own have I disavowed, Daughtie? Years ago, before my parents joined the Believers, I saw my mother and other godly, chaste women wear fashionable clothes; their religious convictions weren't compromised. And although the Shakers don't attend lyceums, they are quick to gather the world's latest intelligence and discuss it among themselves. I'm merely gaining my information firsthand," Bella replied. Somehow the words sounded defensive, which wasn't her intent. Still, she didn't want Daughtie thinking her wayward.

Daughtie glanced at the floor and then gave Bella a sheepish grin. "You're right, Bella. Perhaps I'm feeling a tinge of jealousy because I'll be sitting home while you attend the lecture. Please accept my apology for acting the spoiled child."

"There's no need to apologize. We'll attend the next lecture together—I'd much prefer your company to the pomposity of Taylor Manning. Had we known in advance, we could have purchased our own tickets like most of the other girls. Ruth told me this is the first lecture that has sold out so quickly," Bella replied. "I'll be careful to remember every word of the speech and share it with you the minute I get home."

Daughtie gave her a delighted smile. "Promise?"

"Promise!" Bella said, pulling her friend into a quick hug before picking up her hairbrush.

"Let me," Daughtie said as she reached for the brush. "I think I can fashion your hair in the looped braids that appear popular with the society ladies," she said, parting Bella's hair down the center.

A short time later, Bella gazed into the oval mirror. "It looks lovely, Daughtie," Bella said, touching the tightly formed braids her friend had woven with ivory ribbon and looped on each side. She turned and gave Daughtie a hug. "Thank you, dear friend."

"You look quite beautiful," Daughtie said. "Keeping Taylor Manning at a distance may prove difficult this evening."

Bella shook her head. "I'll stay close to Mrs. Cheever," she said, hastening toward the door as one of the girls called up the stairs that her escort had arrived.

Taylor stood at the bottom of the stairway, tugging at the sable-brown claw-hammer jacket that topped a frilled white shirt and silk vest. Giving Bella a smile, he leaned down in a courtly bow, causing his hair to fall forward over one eye. "You look lovely, Miss Newberry," he said, his voice barely a whisper as he straightened.

"Thank you, Mr. Manning. I trust that Mr. and Mrs. Cheever are in the carriage?"

He appeared momentarily confused by her question. "Oh yes," he finally replied. "My uncle and Miss Addie left a short time ago. They've promised to save us seats should the lecture hall become overly crowded before our arrival," he added as they walked out the door.

Bella took his extended hand and stepped up into the carriage. Scooting into the far corner, she gathered the fullness of her dress across the seat. There was barely enough space for Taylor to squeeze in and be seated near the opposite door.

Lilly Cheever turned and looked over her shoulder. "I can hardly contain my excitement. Matthew was unusually late coming home, and I feared we would be late," Lilly said, grasping her husband's arm in an affectionate squeeze.

"We have more than sufficient time, my dear. You fret overly."

She gave him a winsome smile before turning back toward Bella and

Taylor. "You two make quite a handsome couple," she complimented.

"Thank you, Mrs. Cheever. I was thinking much the same thing," Taylor replied.

Bella gave him a sidelong glance. "We're not really a couple, but I thank you for the kind words."

Taylor leaned his head back and chuckled. "I don't think she wants to be associated with me, Mrs. Cheever. I believe Bella finds me crass and arrogant; the only reason she's willing to be seen in my company is because of her interest in the lecture."

Bella wasn't certain if what she was feeling was embarrassment or anger—perhaps a combination of both, she decided. "As I recall, my acceptance of your invitation was forthright, Mr. Manning. You're aware I'm not interested in your companionship."

"There you have it, Mrs. Cheever. If there was ever any doubt of Bella's undying devotion, we know that it's not directed at me," Taylor said as the carriage came to a halt in front of the lecture hall.

Bella carefully positioned herself beside Lilly as they entered the lyceum. "There's Miss Addie and Mr. Farnsworth. They're waving us forward to join them. It appears Miss Mintie is with them," Bella added as she and Lilly made their way down the aisle with Taylor and Matthew following behind.

"We've saved you chairs," John said, stepping into the aisle.

When the group finally juggled into their seats, Mintie was seated to Bella's left and Addie to her right. Taylor was sandwiched between John and Matthew. Bella gave a self-satisfied grin as Taylor leaned forward to verify her whereabouts.

Mintie glanced over the top of her spectacles and clucked her tongue. "You'll have a spasm in your neck if you remain in that position much longer, Mr. Manning. Sit up!" the older woman commanded, straightening her own spine as she gave the order. She nodded in obvious satisfaction as Taylor wedged himself back between the two other men. "I'm pleased you're sitting beside me," Mintie said, patting Bella's hand. "Tell me, do you Shakers practice any of these skull readings?"

Bella smiled, trying to repress a giggle. She tried to imagine Sister Evangeline or one of the Brothers trying to read the bumps on one of the other Believers' heads. "No, at least not in Canterbury, although we've read about it—and discussed it at length. It's very interesting, don't you think?"

Mintie's eyebrows curved into two half moons. "Yes, although I find it a bit disconcerting to think someone can evaluate you through touching your head."

"It's my understanding that there are employers in England and Scotland who demand a character reference from a phrenologist before they hire a prospective employee," Bella said.

Mintie lifted a hand to her head as if to ward off any stranger's hand that might be moving in her direction. "What ever would make them do such a thing?" she asked with a note of incredulity in her voice.

"Supposedly, they want to ensure a person is honest and hardworking," Bella replied.

"Well, I certainly hope the Corporation doesn't take up those strange practices," she said. "Did you hear that, Adelaide? The next thing you know, we'll have someone running his fingers through our hair before he'll hire us," she said as she reached across Bella and clutched at her sister's arm.

"Rest easy, Miss Mintie. I doubt the Corporation will agree to pay a phrenologist any time in the near future," John Farnsworth commented.

Had Bella not recognized the genuine concern etched upon Miss Mintie's face, she would have giggled at the older woman's shocked appearance. "They're ready to begin," Bella whispered as two men walked onto the stage at the front of the room.

After an impressive introduction, Lucius Applebaum stepped to the podium and began his oration. It was only after he'd talked for ninety minutes that he scanned the audience and said, "May I have a volunteer who is willing to have a skull reading join me on the stage?"

Taylor immediately stood up and began waving toward the speaker.

"Wonderful! We have a willing participant," Mr. Applebaum told the audience as Taylor made his way toward the front of the room.

Bella was surprised yet privately pleased Taylor had volunteered. She was curious to see exactly how the reading was performed. In fact, she would have gone forward herself had she not been certain a female volunteer would be considered inappropriate. She watched and listened carefully as Mr. Applebaum explained that the bumps on Taylor's skull told of his honesty, veneration of God, and intelligence—completely confounding Bella. After diligently listening to the presentation, Bella had been growing convinced the readings might be quite scientific. Now, however, her convictions were dashed. To hear Mr. Applebaum assign such noble characteristics to Taylor Manning was preposterous. Taylor didn't revere or worship God! And he wasn't brimming with intellect—of that she was certain!

The lecture concluded and Taylor made his way back toward them as his companions began making their way into the aisle.

"So," Taylor said, meeting Bella's gaze, "wasn't that marvelous? It was as if he knew me through and through. Like he'd reached inside my soul and pulled out all the wonderful bits for the world to see."

"It was very much like he pulled something out, but I wouldn't call it wonderful bits," Bella muttered.

Taylor took hold of her elbow as several people jostled past them. Leaning over he whispered, "The entire lecture hall knows how wonderful I am. Why do you continue to deny it?"

Bella stopped in midstep and looked into Taylor's blue eyes. "You may be the most intelligent, marvelous specimen of humankind," Bella said. "But if you are, no one knows it better than you do, and that, Mr. Manning, I find most unattractive."

She made her way out without giving Taylor a second glance. Would that she could put him from her mind as easily as she put him from her sight.

"Do tell us what it was like, having Mr. Applebaum perform the reading," Lilly insisted as they began the carriage ride home.

"The procedure was extremely enlightening. I expected it might be rather painful—that he would push and prod without consideration," Taylor began. "However, he was quite gentle, merely circulating his fingers upon the skull in a relaxing manner. I fairly enjoyed the whole thing. Would you like me to demonstrate, Bella?" he inquired, giving her a grin.

Bella scooted farther into the corner. "Absolutely not!" she exclaimed.

"I'm sure she'd give me permission were it not for her fancy hairdo," Taylor said, causing Matthew and Lilly to laugh.

"I'm not certain I agree with your analysis of her decision, Taylor, but I must say that I admired your willingness to go up on that stage this evening. Did you ever consider the possibility that Mr. Applebaum might have given the audience a report that would have embarrassed you?" Matthew inquired.

Taylor shook his head and laughed. "How could that ever happen when he had such an excellent subject?"

Lilly and Matthew joined in the laughter, but Bella merely gave him a thoughtful glance. It was obvious Taylor held himself in high esteem—a quality she didn't find endearing.

"Shall we wait for you?" Matthew asked Taylor when they arrived at the boardinghouse.

"No need," Taylor quickly replied. "I don't want to detain you. Thank you for permitting us to accompany you this evening."

With a sweet smile, Bella expressed her genuine thanks before descending the carriage.

"I hope to see you again very soon, Bella," Lilly replied. "And don't be too harsh with Taylor," she added in a whisper. "I think he means well."

Bella nodded and gave Lilly a faint smile as she walked alongside Taylor to the front door. Once inside, she turned toward the parlor and began to unfasten her cape. Yet her hand remained suspended in midair, her mouth agape as she stared at Jesse Harwood sitting beside Daughtie on the velvet-covered settee.

"Jesse." His name spilled from Bella's lips with an ease that belied the wave of nausea sweeping over her. Her knees began to tremble and dizziness washed over her in waves. Jesse, dressed in his dark blue Shaker surtout and straw hat, moved toward her.

"Bella," he greeted warmly, taking long strides across the room. Lightly grasping her shoulders, he held her at arm's length, his gaze traveling up and down the length of her body before finally looking into her eyes. "You are even more beautiful than I remember. And the color of that dress is perfect on you," he said, pulling her into an embrace.

The rasping sound of Taylor clearing his throat startled Bella. Pushing away from Jesse, she moved to his side and glanced toward Taylor. "Jesse, I would like to introduce you to Taylor Manning. He furnished me with a ticket to the phrenology lecture at the lyceum this evening."

"And escorted her," Taylor added, giving Bella a sidelong glance before extending his hand toward Jesse. "Bella has mentioned you," he said while pumping Jesse's hand up and down.

Jesse beamed a smile in Bella's direction. "That's good to hear."

"You're the one who pledged your love and then left her in the woods to fend for herself, aren't you?" Taylor inquired.

Bella wanted to stomp on Taylor's foot. How dare he interfere? Poor Jesse looked as though he'd taken a strong fist in his midsection.

"You told him that I left you to fend for yourself?" Jesse gave her a baffled look.

"You didn't appear. Daughtie and I finally left Canterbury, certain you weren't coming. Isn't that right, Daughtie?" Bella asked, hoping Daughtie would affirm her reply. However, Daughtie had apparently fled the room unnoticed, as the settee was now unoccupied.

Jesse's forehead creased into deep lines. "You believe I would willingly abandon you?"

"What else was I to believe? Daughtie and I waited. You didn't arrive. Now you suddenly appear and rebuke me for saying you broke your promise."

"It wasn't intentional. I couldn't leave that night without . . ." He hesitated and glanced at Taylor and then back at Bella. "Could we possibly have this conversation alone—without him?" Jesse asked as he pointed a thumb in Taylor's direction.

Bella moved toward the door. "Taylor, I'll see you out," she said, turning the doorknob.

"I'm not anxious to leave. It's still early," he said, remaining in place.

"It would please me if you would exhibit your fine English manners and leave Jesse and me to discuss this matter in private. Thank you for permitting me the opportunity to attend the lecture," she said while holding the door ajar.

Taylor turned to face her, leaned down close to her ear, and said, "I'll bid you good-night if you promise to see me again in the very near future, dear Bella."

"I won't bargain with you, Mr. Manning," she whispered firmly.

Taylor smiled. "That's fine. I'll be happy to remain here with the two of you," he said, beginning to push the door closed.

Bella seethed inwardly as she pulled back on the door. "Very well. I'll agree—just leave."

Taylor nodded. "Good! I feared we were going to ruin Miss Addie's door by shoving it back and forth," he said, emitting a chuckle. "Nice to meet you, Jesse," he said, tossing a mock salute in Jesse's direction. "And you," he said, turning back toward Bella, "I'll be calling on you soon," he said loudly enough for Jesse to hear.

He was out the door before Bella could object to his boorish behavior. Had Jesse not been watching and waiting, she would have chased him down the street and insisted upon an apology! Instead, she took a deep breath, exhaled slowly, and closed the door with a resounding thud before smiling at Jesse.

"Shall we sit in the parlor?" she inquired in what she hoped was her calmest voice.

Jesse followed close at her heels and seated himself beside her. Bella folded her hands, placed them in her lap, and gave him her full attention. "Well? I'm awaiting your explanation."

"I was prepared to meet you. My belongings were packed; I was certain the other Brothers were asleep. But I was wrong. I rose from my bed and went down the stairs. However, when I went to the barn where I had stored my belongings and some food, I couldn't find them. I searched for what seemed an eternity, knowing I was late to meet you. When I finally realized someone must have found my satchel, I hurried from the barn and ran headlong into Brother Ernest. He grabbed me by the ear and pulled me back into the barn, demanding I explain my conduct. I told him I was leaving, that I could no longer adhere to the beliefs of the Society. He asked why I was sneaking off like a thief in the night when I could have gone before the Elders and told them of my decision. He wondered why I would choose to leave the Society without at least a modicum of dignity and enough money for a few meals and a room. I fumbled for words, knowing anything I said would make no sense to them."

Bella sat transfixed as she listened to Jesse's words. "So what did you tell him?"

"I decided I could either tell him I was planning to run off with you, which would have immediately explained why I didn't go before the Elders, or tell him I decided to sneak off because I lacked the courage to face the Elders. However, I knew I would be caught in my lie if they discovered you missing the next morning. So I told him the truth."

"That we were leaving together?"

Jesse nodded his head.

"Well, then, I'm even more pleased I didn't remain behind. Just think what might have happened if I had returned to my room—the wrath of the Elders would have poured down upon us," Bella observed.

He gave her a tentative smile. "It did pour down—upon me. Until I finally took a firm stand and told them I was leaving."

Bella ran a finger down a deep fold in the rose-colored dress, her gaze fixed upon the painting of the New England countryside hanging on the far wall. "My father—" she haltingly began—"did he appear concerned or distraught that I was gone?"

"He said he would be praying for your swift return to the Society, adding that you'd surely lost control of your senses. He was angry that you'd broken your vows," Jesse replied in a plaintive tone. "Of course, his words of recrimination were directed toward me. He said it was my behavior that rekindled your desire to live in the world and gave you the courage to make such a foolhardy decision."

Bella shook her head in anger. "How can he call himself a good Shaker when he speaks falsely? He knows that I never adjusted to life among the Shakers and my desire to leave the Society always remained firm. Had you been the catalyst for my departure, I wouldn't have left without you. I think it should have been obvious to all of them that you were not to blame."

"I'm not sure who or what they believe. I departed two days after you and Daughtie, before their meetings and discussions had ended. I'm sure they knew I was coming to find you. Sister Mercy requested I give you her love and best wishes. I agreed to do so, not realizing so much time would pass before we would reunite. Most likely, they all believe we are married by now," he said, taking her hand.

Bella lifted her hand from his and wriggled into the far corner of the settee. "Where have you been for all this time, Jesse?"

He appeared taken aback by her question. "In Concord. That's what we planned," he replied. "I attempted to locate your relatives, but I didn't know where to begin looking."

Bella nodded. "I should have given you the address," she agreed.

"Or at least a last name. All you ever told me was that your Aunt Ida and Uncle Arthur lived in Concord. Of course, I thought we would be traveling together, so I never asked. When I arrived in Concord, I wasn't sure what to do. Thinking you might still be there, I didn't want to leave, yet I worried you might not be there. My decision was difficult. However, the innkeeper mentioned a local cooper was in need of an assistant. When the cooper hired me, I decided it was providence that I remain and look for you. What if I had headed off for Lowell while you were waiting for me in Concord? Besides, I didn't think you and Daughtie would venture to Lowell on your own. I wanted to believe you were anxiously awaiting me, ready to become my wife."

She intentionally ignored his statement regarding marriage. "Then what made you finally come looking for me in Lowell?"

"As the days passed, I began asking customers if they knew anyone named Arthur or Ida. Each time someone gave me a name, I would search for the person. Eventually, a man who knew your uncle came into the shop. He gave me the address of your aunt and uncle. Your aunt told me you and Daughtie had been there but that you had left for Lowell the day after you arrived in Concord. I can't tell you how devastated I was when I heard that piece of news," he said in a saddened tone.

"You found my aunt in good health?" she inquired, wanting to keep the conversation neutral.

"Yes, she's fine. In fact, she told me she had recently received letters from you and that you were doing well. I asked her if she would give me your address. At first she was reluctant, but your uncle convinced her I meant no harm. I've rented a small place for us to live—not far from my work. Your aunt is delighted we'll be living in Concord. She asked that we wait and marry in Concord so she and your uncle may attend the wedding."

It was difficult to ignore the hopefulness that punctuated his words. "I'm sorry, Jesse, but I won't be moving to Concord. I don't plan to marry you," she replied in a soft yet firm voice.

Jesse wiped beads of perspiration from his forehead. "My late arrival has permitted you to pledge your love to that other fellow, hasn't it? The minute Daughtie told me you had gone to the lyceum with another man, I knew my fate was sealed—that I had lost you to another. He's pledged his love, hasn't he?"

Bella stifled a giggle. The very thought of Taylor Manning pledging his love to anyone other than himself was wishful thinking. "You're overreacting, Jesse. First of all, you can't lose something you never possessed. I never promised to marry you. We agreed only to leave Canterbury together. You mistakenly assumed my decision to leave was based upon a betrothal pledge. And secondly, I am not planning to marry anyone," she staunchly replied.

"You need not attempt to protect my feelings, Bella. I saw the way he was looking at you. And whether you wish to admit to your feelings or not, I saw you return his look of affection," Jesse said with his tone growing louder and more accusatory.

Bella stiffened her back, her chin jutting forward ever so slightly. "Jesse Harwood! How dare you sit in my presence making false allegations! You're treating me no better than a tribunal of Shakers would. My decision to remain in Lowell has nothing to do with you or Taylor Manning. It has to do with me! I want an opportunity to make decisions for myself, to seek the truth of God's Word for my life, to heal from wounds, both old and new. Ultimately I hope to discover where I belong."

"And am I the cause of some of those wounds you speak of?" he asked.

She nodded her head. "Yes. Although after listening to your explanation, it does appear I judged you too harshly."

Jesse's face brightened. "Then if I remain in Lowell and find work, would you give me permission to call upon you? I know we are destined to marry, Bella."

His voice was filled with excitement, making Bella's reply even more difficult. "I cannot tell you where to live, Jesse; that is your decision. But I don't believe we are destined to marry. Since I've never experienced the kind of love I believe God intends between marriage partners, I don't even know that marriage will be a part of my future," Bella said. "You have been a dear friend, but I only agreed to leave the village with you because I was desperate to go."

He stood and gave her a waning smile. "It's obvious you have no desire for me to make my home in Lowell," he said mournfully. "Perhaps it's best I return to Concord. At least I have a job and there are a few people who have befriended me. May I at least write to you?"

"Of course. I would be pleased to correspond with you," she replied.

Jesse nodded. "It's getting late. I had best bid you good-night. I'll leave for Concord in the morning. I'm staying at the Wareham Hotel—in case you should change your mind."

She escorted him to the door and watched as he dejectedly walked down the darkened street. He stopped and glanced over his shoulder for a brief moment before continuing onward.

"I pray I've made the right decision," Bella murmured into the quietude of the night.

Later that night, after the other girls in the room were sleeping soundly, Bella lit a single candle and took up her Bible. Sleep would not come, and she felt as though the weight of the world were on her shoulders. *Maybe I've done the wrong thing. Maybe I should have gone with Jesse. I don't love him, but maybe that isn't a part of the plan God has for me.*

She opened the book to the forty-first chapter of Isaiah. *Oh, Lord,* she prayed, *just show me the truth of what I need to know. I so desire to have answers to my questions. I'm afraid that maybe I'm making all the wrong choices. I'm afraid that I've done myself more harm than good.*

She looked down at the page and her gaze fell upon the tenth verse. *"Fear thou not; for I am with thee: be not dismayed; for I am thy God: I will strengthen thee; yea, I will help thee; yea, I will uphold thee with the right hand of my righteousness."*

Peace slipped in past the barricades she'd erected around her heart. "I don't want to be afraid," she whispered, her breath touching the flame of the candle and blowing it out. The darkness engulfed her at once. Bella thought of lighting the candle again, but instead she eased back against the pillow, still clutching her Bible close.

"Lord, I won't fear. I'll trust you, and you will strengthen me as you've promised."

17

A steady stream of girls filed into St. Anne's Episcopal Church. Bella was surprised how their numbers steadily increased each time they gathered. "It's going to be our best turnout ever," Bella whispered to Ruth, who had become her strongest ally in forming the study groups and classes. Even Daughtie had worked alongside the others, distributing notices, encouraging the attendance of the mill girls, and quietly lending her support wherever needed.

Today Daughtie was seated in the front row, and Bella beamed a smile in her friend's direction. She truly hoped Daughtie would remain in Lowell, yet somewhere deep within she feared her friend's heart still remained in Canterbury. But for now, she knew Daughtie was doing what she had promised—she was giving this new life a chance before making her final decision.

Bella stepped to the platform and gave the crowd a welcoming smile. "I am pleased to see so many of you in attendance. It gladdens my heart to know that women are willing to come together and search for ways to educate and better themselves. I applaud your commitment," she said. "Together we are making great strides, and I want to report to you what has been accomplished thus far."

A smattering of applause began and then erupted into a loud ovation. When the room had sufficiently quieted, Bella thanked the group and continued. "We have successfully begun four study groups and have retained qualified teachers for each of them. Mr. Hazen, who has traveled extensively in France and Italy, even making his home in France for a period of time, is teaching two French classes. A waiting list is being compiled for the next sessions, so if you are interested, I suggest you give your name to Ruth Wilson. Ruth, why don't you stand so everyone knows who you are," she said, turning and motioning her friend to rise to her feet.

The group's attention was quickly divided between Ruth and the rear doorway, where a group of men had entered the room and were now seating themselves in the back rows. Bella ignored the intrusion and calmly continued with her speech.

"Ruth will take your name after the meeting today if you are interested in any classes. Thank you, Ruth," she said as Ruth took her seat. "We also have a group studying literature. I understand that each girl enrolled in that class will write an essay dealing with the literary work being studied. We have explored the possibility of printing those essays for all to read, as I feel certain they will be enlightening compositions. Mr. Leatherman has agreed to print them, charging only his cost to us. And for those of you who may not know it, Mr. Leatherman has printed all of our pamphlets at cost, and our fliers have been free. I would ask that if you have any printing needs, you support his business. He has been most benevolent to our cause.

"Now, back to our class schedule. Our final class is for those girls who, for various reasons, did not receive the basic level of schooling before moving away from home. This class teaches reading, penmanship, biology, arithmetic— I won't enumerate further, but the class offers all of these studies. It is tailored to each student's needs. So if you should find yourself lacking in only one or two areas, you could study only those particular topics. As I said earlier, all of these classes are full, but because you have shown there is a need and desire for education among women, we are seeking additional teachers in order to expand. We also welcome your ideas for new classes."

Ruth stepped forward and whispered in Bella's ear. "Oh, yes. Ruth has reminded me that next Tuesday evening Mr. Clark will begin violin lessons for interested pupils. There are three openings available in that class."

A girl near the front raised her hand, and Bella nodded in her direction. "Is the cost for all of the classes the same?"

"No, some are less than others. However, if the teacher requires specific study materials, you must agree to purchase those before the class begins. Some of the girls who have already purchased books for the current classes have agreed to loan those to the next group of students."

A round of applause and murmuring among the audience followed this remark.

"The sharing of class books caused me to wonder how many of you own books that you might be willing to loan for other girls to read. In fact, even more than educational classes, it was the sharing of reading materials that originated the formation of this group. As some of you know, I had hoped—"

A shuffling of feet and scraping of chairs near the back of the room caused Bella, along with most of the audience, to shift her gaze toward the commotion. The men who had earlier entered the auditorium now stood, one of them with his hand high in the air.

"Yes, what is it?" Bella inquired of the man and at the same time noticed that Taylor Manning was standing next to him.

"We're members of the Mechanics Association, and as you may know, our organization has a library."

Bella nodded. "I'm aware of your library, sir. In fact, I sought permission for women to use your library some time ago."

"So I understand. Well, it appears we men don't move with the same swiftness as the good women of Lowell. However, we have finally discussed your request at length, and upon Mr. Taylor Manning's recommendation, we have agreed to extend library privileges to your membership, Miss Newberry."

A roar of applause filled the auditorium while Bella met Taylor's gaze. He seemed rather proud of himself, smiling in his self-confident manner. What was he up to? she wondered. Why hadn't Taylor made the offer? And was there some reason they had come before the group rather than notifying her beforehand? Perhaps Taylor thought the girls would be overwhelmed with gratitude and accept the proposal without question. And from the enthusiastic response of the crowd, it appeared as if they would do so. She, however, wanted more information.

Bella patiently waited until the clapping subsided. "Thank you for your generous offer, sir. Are you prepared to discuss this matter at greater length for our group? If so, why don't you join me on the platform," she invited.

"Come on, Taylor," the man who had first spoken directed, pulling Taylor along by the arm until they were beside Bella on the stage.

"Why don't you introduce yourselves," Bella encouraged.

Taylor gave her a sheepish look. "This here's Taylor Manning," the other man said while pointing a thumb in Taylor's direction, "and I'm Oliver Franks. We're officers of the Mechanics Association," he proudly announced.

"Thank you, Mr. Franks. Will there be any cost for the use of your library materials?" Bella inquired with a sweet smile.

Mr. Franks shifted his position on the stage, moving behind Taylor. "Mr. Manning can share the details with you," he said as he bobbed his head around Taylor's shoulder.

Taylor cleared his throat. "Mr. Franks is correct that we have agreed to permit use of the library. However, because there is an expense connected with the operation of the library, we would expect you to pay the same yearly dues as the men. Of course, the dues need not be paid in one sum; they can be paid in a weekly or monthly sum—whatever best suits the particular needs of each patron."

Taylor's answer was followed by shuffling feet and murmurs as the women turned to discuss the matter with each other.

"Ladies! Ladies!" Bella called out. "May I have your attention, please. If there are questions, please raise your hand and Mr. Manning or Mr. Franks," she said, looking first at one man and then the other, "will answer. I would like to begin by asking if these dues will afford us all of the same privileges granted to the men."

Taylor appeared momentarily puzzled by the question, glancing first at Oliver Franks and then back at Bella. "Exactly what privileges are you referring to, Miss Newberry?"

"Well," she began, "I was thinking we should have somebody on the committee that makes book selections as well as a representative on the committee that makes selections for the lyceum speakers—if those are different groups," she said, gracing him with a bright smile.

Her request brought excited agreement from the ladies in the audience.

Taylor pulled at his collar. "Those decisions are made by the officers and then reported to the members for their discussion and vote, which has been more of a formality as the men have never requested any changes," he replied. "With these rules in place, I don't see how a woman could become a part of that decision-making group, do you?"

His tone made it obvious he thought his question was rhetorical, but Bella met the inquiry head on. "I think we could overcome that obstacle with little difficulty," she countered.

"Wh-wh-what?" he stammered. "A woman can't be an officer of the Mechanics Association."

"No, but you could form committees to make these choices instead of using your board. That way, some of the committee members could be women," she suggested.

His mouth dropped open in surprise. "Some? You want more than one representative on the committees if they're established?"

"Naturally," she calmly replied. "If we pay equal dues, we should have equal representation."

"She has a point," Mr. Franks quietly remarked.

Taylor gave Oliver a stunned look. "Whose side are you on?" he whispered back.

Bella listened to the exchange with satisfaction. "He's right—I do have a valid argument. And I'm sure you wouldn't disagree that women should have equality. Additionally, there are some of your members who might be pleased to turn over the duty of selecting books and speakers. It would free their time for other more important work of the Association," she submitted.

Together with the women in the audience, most of the men were murmuring and nodding their agreement. Taylor appeared surprised at their immediate willingness to succumb to Bella's persuasive words and sweet smile. She had won them over with little effort.

"But the men pay the rent, and they've paid for the books that are already in the library," he argued. "They must maintain primary control of this Association they've established. It is rightfully theirs."

Bella acknowledged a young woman in the audience who had raised her hand. "I think Mr. Manning is correct. The men should maintain control of their Association, but I believe the concept of creating committees with one or two representatives from our group would be acceptable. Perhaps we should vote on such a proposal."

Taylor quickly stepped forward. "If you want to vote on a proposal, I can't stop you, but I don't have the authority to accept or reject your suggestion. I'll agree to take your request before the Association and report back."

A show of hands verified the girls were in agreement. They requested Taylor take their proposal before the Association and report back the following week. Bella would have preferred to push for additional women on the committees, but this was a start. They could move toward further representation in the future. All things considered, she was pleased Taylor and his group of men had attended this evening, although she wasn't so sure Taylor himself was pleased with the outcome. The meeting concluded, and Bella began to gather the pamphlets and fliers, tucking them into a small case. The sound of approaching footsteps caused her to look up.

"I was hoping to escort you home. There's a personal matter I'd like to discuss with you," Taylor said.

Bella hesitated, not sure she wanted to spend time alone with Taylor. She wasn't certain he truly believed women should be involved in the Association's decision-making process, and she didn't want to argue the matter with him privately. After all, he had agreed to take the proposal before the Association.

"I walked over with Daughtie and Ruth," she replied.

"I know. I told them I was going to escort you home. They've already departed," he replied. "And before you become angry, let me assure you that this isn't a ploy. Miss Addie is going to need your support over the next few weeks, perhaps longer."

His words captured Bella's attention. She reached out and grasped his arm with a sense of urgency. "Has something happened to Miss Addie? She was fine when I left the house this evening."

Taylor enveloped her hand in his own. "I didn't mean to alarm you; Miss Addie is in good health. This is more—" he hesitated, obviously searching for an explanation—"a matter of the heart. Yes, I think that would best describe the situation."

Bella was intrigued. Accepting Taylor's proffered arm, she accompanied him through the arched doors of the gray-slate church. Why would Miss Addie suffer from a matter of the heart? She and John Farnsworth were deeply committed to each other. Thoughts of their relationship caused her to stop midstep.

"Has John Farnsworth taken up with another woman?" Her words sliced through the air.

Taylor's mouth dropped open; he gaped at her in obvious disbelief. "What a terrible accusation! Do you think all men are unable to honor their word?"

Bella thought for a moment before answering. "My limited observation has shown me that it depends on the commitment and the person to whom it is made. I find men fall short in keeping their word when it is given to a woman."

"Really? Well, my uncle John is not one of those men. He's not a cad or philanderer. He cares very much for Miss Addie. He would never intentionally hurt her," Taylor defended as they moved onward.

"If this has nothing to do with your Uncle John, why would she be troubled?"

"You're twisting my words, Bella. You do that all the time—you win people to your point of view by manipulating words."

Once again Bella tugged him to a halt. "I do not manipulate words, but I'm not afraid to speak the truth. Why don't you just tell me about the situation with Miss Addie and then we won't be required to argue about my choice of words," she fumed.

"I didn't tell you outright because I wanted to spend some time alone with you. I knew you wouldn't permit me to escort you home if I merely blurted out what I had to say."

She glanced up and gave him an embarrassed grin. "You're right. I would have refused your invitation."

He gave a quick nod of his head. "My uncle must leave in the morning. He was called to Kirk Boott's office and told he is needed to journey to the southern United States for the Corporation."

Bella's eyebrows furrowed at his reply. "Why would the Corporation send your uncle John?"

"Mr. Boott was to make the journey, but his health has failed him during the past week and he's unable to travel. He requested Mr. Cheever take his place. However, Mr. Cheever didn't want to make the trip unless he could wait until after the birth of his child. When Mr. Boott said the journey must be made as soon as possible, Mr. Cheever suggested Uncle John."

"Surely a short journey to the South won't be overly upsetting to Miss Addie," Bella determined.

"I didn't say short journey. He may be there for some period of time."

"But why?"

"Uncle John didn't tell me the details, but he did remark upon the fact that his skills of diplomacy would be needed. He'll be meeting with plantation owners regarding cotton production and prices. Mr. Boott has been consulting with him for hours."

"Wouldn't you think there's someone equally as qualified as your uncle?" she questioned. For Miss Addie's sake, Bella didn't want the Corporation sending Mr. Farnsworth.

"I'm certain there are more qualified men, but apparently none of them will agree to make the trip. Uncle John doesn't have much choice in the matter. In fact, Mr. Boott is now convinced Uncle John will perform magnificently. Those are Mr. Boott's words, not mine."

"Poor Miss Addie. She will miss him ever so much."

Taylor nodded his agreement. "Miss Addie won't have much time to become accustomed to the thought of Uncle John's departure; he leaves in the morning."

"I'll do all I can to help Miss Addie while Mr. Farnsworth is away. Perhaps she would like to become involved as a representative on one of the committees."

Taylor chuckled. "Your mind never stops working, does it? You're always looking for an advantage."

"I was merely suggesting one way to keep Miss Addie busy," she demurely replied.

"Well, just keep in mind that the membership must approve this plan of yours before anyone's time will be filled choosing reading material," he jibed.

"And speakers," she quickly added.

"Yes, Bella," he said as they neared the boardinghouse, "speakers, too. That's Uncle John's carriage."

"At least they've had some time alone with all of the girls attending the meeting this evening," Bella commented as the front window revealed the silhouette of John and Addie.

The older couple had walked to the carriage by the time Bella and Taylor approached the front door.

"Ah, Taylor, you can drive me home," John said, affectionately slapping his nephew on the back.

The tear stains on Miss Addie's face were evident as she embraced John one last time. "Please take care of yourself. I want you to come home safe and sound," she cautioned in a choked voice.

"I'll be safe and sound and back here before you even know I've gone. Promise you'll give serious thought to our discussion."

Addie nodded her head. "You know I will," she said as the men drove away.

Bella gently touched Miss Addie's shoulder and drew near. "It's obvious he cares deeply for you, Miss Addie. Mr. Farnsworth seems a fine man. There's no doubt he'll be back as quickly as his business will permit."

Addie nodded and then gave Bella a look of surprise. "How did you know John was going away?"

"Taylor. He was concerned about you. I hope you don't feel he betrayed a confidence by telling me."

"No, it's quite all right. Everyone will know by this time tomorrow. Word travels fast in this small community. I had best tell Mintie first thing in the morning. If she hears from someone else, there will be no end to her bruised feelings."

Bella nodded. "Let's just take care of today, Miss Addie. Tomorrow will take care of itself—that's what Sister Mercy used to tell me. She said there were enough worries in one day without borrowing from the next."

Addie chuckled. "Perhaps Sister Mercy was right."

"Why don't we have a nice cup of tea?" Bella suggested while leading Miss Addie toward the kitchen. "I'm positive Mr. Farnsworth will make every effort to return quickly."

Addie made a valiant effort to smile. "I certainly hope so, my dear. I fear I'm going to miss him dreadfully."

Taylor stoked the fire in the stove and sat down to consider his evening. With John now gone to bed in order to accommodate his early morning travel, Taylor felt rather alone and found the memories of his past rushing in like a cold December wind. He remembered his home in London, the scent of rain in the air, the sounds of the merchants and their customers. He thought from time to time of the pleasures he'd stolen—a kiss here or there, a quiet moment under the stars. He'd thought such diversions were all he'd ever want, but listening to his uncle speak of Miss Addie Beecher tonight, Taylor was no longer all that certain of his choices. John had stirred something deep inside Taylor that he had thought dead and buried.

"There's something to be said for a good woman," John had told him on the way home. "A woman who will faithfully await your return, no matter where you go or how long it will take. Just the idea of knowing someone is home, anticipating your arrival, well . . . it makes living worthwhile."

Taylor knew his mother and father had shared that kind of love. When his mother died it had nearly destroyed his father. He mourned her to his dying day—never quite being whole again. Never quite enjoying life as he had before her death. For that very reason, Taylor had difficulty in taking any kind of commitment seriously. He never wanted to duplicate the pain his father felt. It was easier to toy with women, to play the games they initiated. Games of pursuit—games to land a husband who would take care of them.

Taylor had played the game better than most. Maybe too well. Now he wasn't at all sure where the amusements left off and real life stepped in. A woman like Bella wasn't interested in playing the coquette, and because of this Taylor didn't know quite how to handle her. She wasn't easily swayed by his appearance or manners. Enticements that had worked on other girls simply eluded Bella Newberry. Taylor told himself it didn't matter, but deep down inside, it did.

He'd relied upon his good looks and quick wit all his life. They were his bargaining tools—even with men. He had a boyish charm and roguish nature that he could use at will, no matter the situation. Of course, it hadn't helped him with the matter of his last affair of the heart. That girl's father had not been interested in being charmed out of his anger. But that was all behind Taylor now.

"I've spent my adult life—short though it may be—avoiding the possible pain found in the commitment of genuine affection. And now John makes me remember the love of my parents, and I find myself confused. Have I only deluded myself?" he murmured. What more was there? Where was he to find solace and happiness?

"Taylor, my darling boy," his mother had once said, *"God did not put you on this earth with a fine face and solid mind in order to see you do the devil's work. He put you here for His will and glory. Find out what His will is and you will bring Him glory. And neither, I assure you, will have anything at all to do with your outward appearance. It will have everything to do with the quality of your heart."*

Taylor felt more haunted by his mother's words here in America than he'd ever been in England. She'd been worried about him even as she slipped from this world. Burying his face in his hands, Taylor longed for peace of mind and heart.

My inability to deal openly with others has also hindered my ability to deal with God. The phrenologist said I was a man who respected God, but I seldom give Him the time of day, Taylor admitted to himself. *I've turned into that horrible man my mother warned me about, and I have no idea how to turn back.*

Looking up with a sigh, Taylor knew he'd find no answers that night. No, the things that troubled him deep in his soul would take time and effort . . . and most likely more commitment than he'd ever invested. Taylor, however, wasn't at all sure he had it in himself to give.

18

I 've been offered a position as a drawing-in girl," Bella told Daughtie as the two of them hastened off toward the mill, the early morning still shrouded in darkness.

The tower bell clanged, warning them the gate would soon be closing. Several girls rushed past, while another group was clustered close behind. "That would mean more money, wouldn't it? Are you going to accept the position?"

Bella detected a hint of fear in Daughtie's question. "If you'll be happier if I remain nearby, I won't accept. The money isn't that important to me, Daughtie."

Daughtie shook her head back and forth. "No. Asking you to remain a weaver wouldn't be fair. You should accept the position. I hear that it's much quieter," she said, a note of longing in her voice.

"Would you be interested in the position?" Bella asked.

"It wasn't offered to me. I'm sure they feel you're better qualified."

"But we both know that I'm not. You would do a much better job; you have more patience, and you don't mind working independently. When I decline the position, I could recommend you."

They hurried through the mill yard and began their ascent up the spiraling stairwell. "I don't want you to refuse on my account. But if you should decide you're not interested, you could mention my name," Daughtie added quickly.

Bella gave her a smile. "It will be my pleasure, although I will miss you. But I fear that your Bible memorization will far surpass mine if you take the drawing-in position."

Daughtie giggled. "Then perhaps I will be forced to tutor you each evening."

"You go on to your looms. I'll stop and talk to Mr. Kingman," Bella said as they walked through the door of the weaving room.

Bella breathed a sigh of relief. Mr. Kingman wasn't occupied repairing one of the looms or busy with his paper work. He was a stern man, and the girls quickly learned he hated interruptions. "Mr. Kingman? May I speak with you?"

He turned and nodded. "Have you made a decision about the drawing-in position?" he curtly inquired.

Bella nodded. "I realize it pays more money, but I'd prefer to stay here in the weaving room—at least for now. But if I may be so bold, I would suggest you offer the position to Daughtie. I mentioned there was an opening, and I know she's interested. To be honest, Mr. Kingman, she would be much better at the position. She's much more patient and prefers more solitary work. You know how quickly she's learned her looms. She can even—"

"Bella," Mr. Kingman interrupted, "I'm aware of Daughtie's workmanship. I agree she would be a good choice. If you're not interested, she may have the position. Tell her to report to me. She can begin today. Now get to your looms."

"Thank you, Mr. Kingman," Bella enthusiastically said as she clasped her hands together. She rushed down the aisle, careful to keep her skirts away from the machines that had already clattered into motion. When she finally gained Daughtie's attention, Bella motioned her friend toward Mr. Kingman.

Daughtie nodded, slapped her looms to a halt, and hurried off. Bella was going to miss seeing her friend smile from across the aisle, but perhaps this new position would help Daughtie determine whether she should remain in Lowell or return to the Society. Already Daughtie had agreed that a portion of the Shaker beliefs were inconsistent with the Bible, yet Bella knew her friend was still drawn to the familiar environment in Canterbury. Perhaps God would speak to Daughtie's heart.

Daughtie had been gone for only a short time when Mr. Kingman appeared. He had a young girl with long chestnut hair and a rather sallow complexion in tow. He motioned for Bella to shut down her looms and pulled the girl forward. "Bella, this is Virginia Dane. You'll train her on the looms; she's been on the spinning floor working for Thaddeus Arnold. He recommended her for this position."

The girl appeared frightened. Bella offered a broad smile and took Virginia's hand. "Come stand by me at my looms and watch. I won't start you on your own loom until—"

"She can begin on her own looms this afternoon. You can move back and forth across the aisle and help," Mr. Kingman interrupted. "I don't want both of Daughtie's looms sitting idle any longer than necessary. Idle looms don't make money."

Bella didn't argue. She disagreed with Mr. Kingman, but she disagreed with many decisions regarding the operation of the Appleton. Nobody cared what she thought; after all, she was only an operative, easily replaced by another girl looking for work. Besides, the men who owned these mills touted themselves as forward-thinking simply because they employed women, when such an avowal was simply untrue. Bella had quickly realized the Associates hired women merely to benefit themselves and their profits. However, she believed these jobs would ultimately lead to a measure of equality for women.

There was no doubt the Shakers were far advanced on the issue of equality.

When the breakfast bell finally rang, Bella pointed to the loom handle and motioned Virginia to stop the machine. "When we return from breakfast, I'll have you try your hand at the loom," Bella said, pulling the handle of the other machine.

Virginia's eyes grew large, and the smidgen of color in her sallow complexion drained from sight. The girl scurried along in Bella's footsteps until they reached the bottom of the stairs. Virginia's hands were shaking in spite of the warm morning sun.

"I don't think I can ever learn that," she said as she pointed up the stairwell.

"Of course you can, Virginia. If the rest of us can learn to manage those beastly machines, you can, too," Bella said, forcing a note of cheer into her voice. "You're going to do just fine, and in a couple of weeks, you'll wonder why you were ever concerned."

Virginia wagged her head back and forth. "I don't think so. I wish I could go back to spinning," she lamented.

Bella gazed into the girl's frightened eyes. "Why did you move to weaving, Virginia? The money?"

The girl continued to walk alongside Bella. "My family can certainly use the money, but Mr. Arnold gave me no choice. He said Mr. Kingman had requested a recommendation to fill a vacant position."

"Then you must have been a very good spinner; otherwise, Mr. Arnold wouldn't have recommended you. It appears as if Mr. Arnold believes you're bright enough to learn a new job, and he's giving you the opportunity to make additional money," Bella encouraged.

Virginia gave her a feeble smile. "No, that's not why. He wanted to hire another girl for the spinning room. She's quite lovely—long flaxen hair and sparkling blue eyes. Mr. Arnold likes pretty girls, and I'm not pretty," she said in a flat voice.

Bella startled at Virginia's comment. She had heard rumors about Mr. Arnold and his behavior—stories of abusive behavior toward his wife and aggressive behavior toward the operatives. But that had been a couple of years ago. The Arnolds now had a baby girl. Surely Mr. Arnold wasn't returning to his former way of life. Perhaps Virginia misunderstood his intentions.

Unsure how she should react, Bella gave Virginia an encouraging hug. "You'll be fine, Virginia. All you need is a little practice and a dose of confidence. I'll do my best to help you gain both."

Virginia tilted her head to the side as though it would help her digest the information. "Then I'll try very hard, and perhaps I will learn," she agreed.

They had reached the edge of the mill yard when Daughtie raced up behind them. "Well, did you miss me?" she asked with a grin.

"Of course I missed you," Bella replied. "This is Virginia Dane," she said, turning toward the new girl. "She's going to work your looms."

"Hello, Virginia," Daughtie said.

"Hello," Virginia replied. "I go in this direction," she said, pointing toward a distant row of boardinghouses.

"I'll see you after breakfast," Bella said, watching as Virginia departed.

"She's a frightened little mouse," Daughtie commented.

"Yes, very frightened," Bella agreed. "Come on—the bells will be ringing us back to work before we've had our breakfast," she said, urging Daughtie into the house.

After gobbling down her breakfast, Bella darted into the kitchen to check on Miss Addie before returning to work. Spying the older woman coming in the back door, Bella rushed toward her. "How are you today, Miss Addie?"

The older woman patted Bella's shoulder. "You need not fret about me, dear. I'm doing fine. Come visit with me tonight."

"There's the bell—I'll talk to you this evening," Bella promised as she rushed back into the dining room, through the parlor, into the hallway, and out the door. She quickly moved alongside Daughtie. "Did the morning go well for you, Daughtie?"

Daughtie nodded as they walked down the street at a brisk pace. "I think I'm going to be much happier, but it will take time to become proficient. It is quieter, and for that I am grateful. I'll give you all the details tonight," she promised.

Bella was pleased by Daughtie's enthusiasm. Perhaps they could visit with Miss Addie together this evening. Daughtie's new position could prove an interesting topic to keep Miss Addie's thoughts on something other than John Farnsworth's absence, Bella decided.

Virginia, appearing even more fraught than she had a half hour earlier, stood beside Bella's looms, awaiting her instructions. "Did you have a good breakfast?" Bella inquired, hoping to relieve the girl's anxiety.

"It was fine. I promise I'll do my best, but I don't remember anything you showed me, and I've been gone only a half hour." The words tumbled from her lips as though she might forget them if she spoke slowly.

Patiently, Bella once again instructed Virginia, methodically moving her through the weaving process, step by step, until the girl appeared to gain confidence. Two hours later, Bella motioned to Virginia to take charge of one loom. Standing close at hand, Bella supervised the girl's every move. Her first attempt at threading the shuttle proved difficult, but she persevered, finally succeeding. Bella applauded her success, hoping the praise would bolster Virginia's confidence. Unfortunately, she appeared to grow more distraught each time a thread broke or a snag appeared in the cloth, her forehead lined with deep creases.

"You're performing as well as any of the new hires," Bella shouted.

"I find that difficult to believe," Virginia shouted in return.

Bella hadn't expected Virginia would believe her appraisal. The girl lacked self-confidence, and Bella wouldn't change the girl's level of assurance by speaking a few kind words. By midafternoon Mr. Kingman insisted on moving Virginia across the aisle. Bella didn't argue, but for the remainder of the day she moved back and forth across the walkway, assisting Virginia while continuing to monitor her own machines, thankful it would soon be quitting time.

Bella was tending her own looms when Virginia stopped her machine to insert a full bobbin. Bella watched as Virginia sucked a bobbin thread through her shuttle and placed it in the race box before pulling the handle of her machine, sending it into action. Without warning, the shuttle jumped out of the race and flew through the air.

A piercing scream sliced through the humid atmosphere of the room. Bella turned in the direction of the deafening cry. Irene Duncan was on her knees as rivulets of blood cascaded down the side of her head and face. Virginia's shuttle lay beside Irene.

"You! Bring some clean rags for her head," Mr. Kingman hollered as he rushed to Irene's side. "The rest of you get back to work. You're serving no good purpose standing around gawking." He grabbed the shuttle from the floor. "Whom does this belong to?" he called out while holding the piece of wood and brass aloft.

"It's mine," Virginia replied, her voice cracking with emotion. She retrieved the shuttle and dashed back down the row, her face as white as hoarfrost on a November morn. Not one of the other girls moved toward their looms.

Instead, Bella walked to where Virginia stood and drew her close. She wanted to ease the girl's obvious horror. "I'm sure Irene's going to be fine. This isn't the first time a flying shuttle has hit an operative, and I'm sure it won't be the last."

"That's for certain," another girl said as the other operatives murmured their agreement.

"Until they let us operate these machines at a safe speed, one where we can ensure quality and safety, there are going to be injuries," Bella replied, raising her voice in order to be heard above the clanging tower bell. "It seems the owners care little about anything but a quick profit."

"That's likely true, Bella, but we're here because we need the money, and I don't think the Boston Associates are much interested in what a bunch of girls think," another operative responded as they made their way out the door and began descending the winding staircase.

Bella nodded. She knew that come tomorrow morning, the machines would run at the same rapid pace as they had today. Yet the Associates' unwillingness to make changes didn't mean the men were right. In fact, Bella was certain they were wrong—dead wrong.

Daughtie rushed to meet Bella at the bottom of the steps. "Who was that Mr. Kingman carried down the stairs?"

"Irene Duncan," Virginia lamented. "She's my first victim."

Daughtie grinned at Bella. "I think you're overstating just a bit. I mean, it's not as though you set out to intentionally harm her, Virginia. Accidents occur frequently in the Appleton—I'm sure you've had your share on the spinning floor, haven't you?"

"Well, yes, but I didn't cause any of those."

"Had Irene's shuttle jumped out of the race and hit you, would you think she had planned to harm you?" Bella asked.

"Of course not," Virginia replied.

"Well, then, why would you decide Irene, or anyone else, would consider you some sort of villain? Stop condemning yourself for the accident. Instead, offer your apologies and then do something to show your concern for Irene's welfare. If she's unable to immediately return to work, seek out girls who are willing to operate her looms so that she doesn't lose her pay, offer to perform her errands, or offer to wash the clothing she was wearing at the time of the accident. She'll be grateful, and it will ease your feelings of guilt and helplessness," Bella suggested.

Virginia stared at her wide-eyed. "You're very wise, Bella. I'll go to her boardinghouse right now."

"Perhaps you ought to eat supper first and then go visiting," Bella offered.

"I'll do that, and I'll see you tomorrow morning at first bell," she added, rushing off toward her own boardinghouse.

Daughtie linked arms with Bella. "You *are* very wise, Bella. You gave her good counsel. The Sisters would be proud."

"It's the Lord I'm trying to please, Daughtie, not the Sisters at Canterbury."

"I know, I know, and I'm sure He's pleased, also," Daughtie said. "Come along. I'm hungry and I can't wait to tell you about my day."

When supper was over and the dishes washed, Miss Addie made her way back into the dining room, where Bella and Daughtie sat visiting. She carried a tray with a teapot and three cups. "I thought we could have a cup of tea while we visit," she suggested. "Would you like to join me in my sitting room?"

"Yes," the girls agreed in unison.

Miss Addie poured and served each of the girls, then stirred a bit of cream and sugar into her own cup before leaning back in her chair. "I hear you have a new position in the dressing room, Daughtie. I would enjoy hearing what you do. I've visited the mill on only one occasion and only got as far as the counting room. It's difficult for me to imagine what your workday must be like."

"My workday has gotten much better, thanks to Bella. She was offered the position first but turned it down. I think she would have accepted had it not been for me," Daughtie said to Miss Addie in a conspiratorial tone.

Addie winked at Daughtie and then gave Bella a warm smile. "I'm sure Bella would be willing to give up almost anything to make certain you're happy, Daughtie."

"Enough! Enough!" Bella protested. "Tell us about your day."

"As you're well aware, Bella, where I now work is much quieter than the weaving or spinning floors, and it's airier, too. Of course, there are fewer girls on the floor, which helps, also. Today was Nancy Everhardt's last day. They told her she was to train me for the full day. Can you imagine? She was very patient and kind."

"And I'm sure you were an exceptional student," Miss Addie interjected.

Daughtie smiled at the compliment. "The dressers with their frames are on one side of the room to ensure the yarn is properly sized and dried before being wound onto the take-up beam, which is a job I don't think I would enjoy. But once they have the warp threads on the beam, the beam is moved to the drawing-in girl. One by one, the warp threads are drawn through the harness and reed with a long metal hook before the beam is delivered to the girls in the weaving room."

Addie appeared surprised. "You pull each thread by hand? I thought everything was done by machine."

Daughtie's face shone with a bright smile. "Praise be, they've not yet developed a machine to perform this task, Miss Addie."

Bella considered Daughtie's explanation. "So if I understand correctly, you sit on a stool or chair all day long, using a metal hook to pull the individual threads through the weaver's beam?"

"That's right," Daughtie said in a pleased voice.

"Then I'm glad you have the job. I think after one day, my back would ache from leaning and reaching through to pull the threads," Bella said.

"No, Bella. It's much better than standing at those noisy, monstrous looms that threaten injury at every turn. The drawing room has no flying shuttles such as you experienced on your floor today."

"What's this? Another accident? Was anyone injured?" Miss Addie inquired, her eyes filled with concern.

"Irene Duncan. I don't think you know her," Bella replied. "This morning I was training Daughtie's replacement, Virginia Dane." Bella continued with the story, explaining the unfolding events to Miss Addie.

"These injuries concern me. Some time ago I discussed them with John, but he says they are a common occurrence when man and machine join forces. And what of Irene? Were her injuries serious?"

"She was terribly stunned by the blow, and her head was bleeding. Mr. Kingman took her to the doctor. I'm not certain if she'll be well enough to return tomorrow, but I don't expect to see her. But what of your day, Miss Addie? I hope it was peaceful."

Addie poured another cup of tea. "Yes, it was a good day. I accomplished a great deal. I went into town—oh yes, and that reminds me, I saw a notice posted by Reverend Edson concerning the graded school system he's proposing. There's to be a meeting of the residents of Lowell concerning the proposal. Word about town is that Kirk Boott is strongly opposed to Reverend Edson's plan and will be at the meeting to argue against the concept."

Bella's eyes sparkled with excitement. "We need to discuss this at our next meeting with the literary group. Having most of the girls attend the meeting could give the proposal a boost. I, for one, hope Kirk Boott doesn't win this argument. Education is one of the necessities of a civilized society, and as citizens of Lowell, we need to support the best possible form of schooling—for both the boys and girls."

Miss Addie listened attentively while nodding her agreement. "You make valid arguments, Bella, and I'm sure your comments would sway those who attend the meeting. Your eloquence is a testament to your excellent education."

Bella gave her hostess a sheepish grin. "I've been pontificating again, haven't I?"

Daughtie giggled. "That was Sister Phoebe's favorite way to end a debate; she'd accuse Bella of pontificating and call a halt to further discussion," Daughtie explained. "But the Society did provide us with superior schooling, didn't it, Bella?"

"Yes, I'll give you no argument on that issue. Fortunately for us, they value education for both men and women. They know it is through education a person can live a better life."

Miss Addie gave her a thoughtful glance. "I'm sure I didn't appreciate the education that was offered to me nearly as much as you girls do. And I certainly didn't learn as much! But I believe the true path to a better life is achieved through drawing closer to God."

Bella pondered the remark a moment before responding. "Let's see," she began, her index finger pushing a dimple into her chin. "Is education or the pursuit of God the true path to a better life? That would be quite a topic for debate," she concluded.

"I'm not so sure. Perhaps the topic is better suited for personal reflection and prayer than public debate," Addie responded.

"I believe you're right, Miss Addie," Bella replied, glancing toward the mantel clock above the fireplace. "The hour is growing late—it's almost ten o'clock. I suppose we'd best go upstairs and prepare for bed," Bella said as she stifled a yawn.

"Oh, I've nearly forgotten to tell you about Clara," Daughtie said, suddenly sounding very excited.

"The little doffer whose fingers were broken in the machinery?" Addie questioned.

"Yes. Her mother works just down the aisle from me. She said that Clara has recovered nicely. She may have a crooked index finger, but she seems to be able to use her hand without any trouble."

"That's wonderful news!" Bella declared. "I've wondered what became of her. No one ever likes to mention the accidents or even the recoveries."

"Well, hopefully there will be no more accidents for a while," Addie said as she gathered the teacups, placing them back on the tray. "I've enjoyed our time together," she added, picking up the tea tray and following the girls toward the door.

Bella stopped and glanced over her shoulder. "Have you seen Mrs. Arnold lately, Miss Addie?"

Addie beamed. "Why, yes, I saw her just this morning. She was outdoors with the baby, and what a darling child she is—smiles at everything and has lots of wispy dark hair."

"Did Mrs. Arnold appear content?"

"She appeared quite happy. Why do you ask?"

"Oh, nothing . . . just curious," Bella replied. "Sleep well, Miss Addie," she said with a wave of her hand.

"And you girls do the same," she replied.

The bed that evening seemed lumpy and the gentle snores of the sleeping girls louder than usual. The stale air hung heavy with an insufferable dampness, and Bella could not sleep. She tossed and turned, but sleep would not come. Miss Addie's words flitted through her mind. Were her good works not considered a means of drawing closer to God? Did she place too little emphasis on her relationship with Him? But wasn't helping others meet their full potential a godly thing to do? After all, relationships required hard work and commitment, and she had tried that with her father. She had longed for him to love her, but her efforts had been met with his rejection. If her flesh-and-blood father wasn't interested in her presence, how could Almighty God desire a relationship with her?

Her eyes fluttered closed. She lay silent, drifting to sleep when a still voice whispered to her heart, *If you will but seek me, I will be your constant companion. I loved you enough to die for you—I will not turn away.*

~ 19 ~

Hugh Cummiskey hailed greetings to several Irishmen, his bass voice resonating throughout the interior walls that now formed the outer shell of
the Catholic church. The boisterous sound caused Liam to turn from his work
and sit back on his haunches. He squinted against the filtering sunlight in an
effort to identify the man at Hugh's side.

"There you are, my boy," Hugh shouted. "I've brought someone to meet
you. This here's Mr. Matthew Cheever, Kirk Boott's second-in-command," he
continued while pointing a thumb toward Matthew. "Seems Mr. Cheever and
Mr. Boott saw a bit of your handiwork when they last visited Boston."

Liam turned his gaze toward Matthew and swiped one hand on his jacket
before reaching out to shake Matthew's extended hand. "For sure? And where
was that?"

Matthew grasped Liam's hand in a firm shake. "At the home of J. P. Green.
He spoke highly of you," Matthew replied. "But had he not said a word, your
craftsmanship would have spoken for itself. In fact, I'm amazed that someone
with your talent was willing to leave Boston. I'm sure there's more than
enough work to keep you busy among the wealthy Beacon Hill residents."

Liam wiped off his trowel and gave the men his full attention. "Ya're probably correct, but who could be turnin' down the likes of Hugh Cummiskey
and the opportunity to live in the Acre?" he asked, giving Hugh a wink.

"Ah, so you've noticed the Acre isn't languishing in luxury, have you?"
Matthew asked with a chuckle.

Liam gave an appreciative grin. "I like a man who can meet a barb head-
on, Mr. Cheever."

"Then I'd say we ought to get along famously. And if all it took was
Hugh's coaxing to bring you to Lowell, I think we've underestimated his abilities."

"In that case, I'll be glad to see your appreciation when I go through the
pay line on Friday," Hugh replied. "To be honest, I don't think it was me that
brought Liam to Lowell; I think it was the church."

"So you're a man of faith. I'd say this is a perfect place to use your talents
for the Lord. I applaud your willingness to make such a sacrifice," Matthew
replied.

Liam shook his head back and forth. "My intentions are not so lofty as servin' the Lord. Truth is, I don't consider meself a man of God. I've never quite figured out the whole concept o' religion. For as long as I can remember, my mother filled our house with shrines that were a confusing mixture of elves, fairies, and saints. Each morning she'd scurry off to church as if the devil himself was sweepin' her out the door, but when problems arose, she expected no more from God than she did from the elves and fairies. I found it all very bewilderin'—still do. Trouble is, I wrote a letter home tellin' me mother about this church and Hugh's offer. She immediately wrote back sayin' she'd had a divine word from either God or an elf—I'm not sure which—that her life was in danger unless I came to Lowell."

Hugh clapped a beefy hand against his thigh. "Good for your ma. We'll be counting it as God's intervention since we're erecting this church for His glory and not the elves'," he said.

"Ah, she's not foolin' me. It wasn't intervention by God or the elves; it was because she wanted to do a bit of motherly braggin'. She'll be goin' about the village tellin' everyone that I'm buildin' a church for the Irish immigrants in America, and the women will all be in awe until someone else has somethin' better to make a fuss about," Liam replied.

"But that's what mothers are for, my boy," Hugh put in. "They keep us on the straight and narrow one way or another. I'll use any advantage offered if it means I get a skilled craftsman like you working on this church building."

Matthew glanced back and forth between the two men, a look of confusion etched upon his face. "Who is paying your wages, Liam? The Corporation donated the land, but Hugh agreed to provide the necessary labor from among the Irishmen living in the Acre."

Puzzled, Liam didn't know how to respond. Certainly he had discussed his wages with Hugh prior to accepting the job, agreeing to an hourly wage that was somewhat lower than the sum he normally charged. Inquiring where the money would come from had never entered his mind. He looked toward Hugh for an answer.

Hugh flipped his broad hand as though he were shooing a fly. "Don't worry yourself over Liam's pay. It's taken care of," he said, quickly turning his attention toward Liam. "I've a bit of good news for you, Liam. I've found you a new place to live. You'll soon be able to bid Noreen a fond farewell," Hugh said, smoothly turning the conversation away from Liam's pay.

Liam gave Hugh a broad smile. "You've made me a happy man, Hugh Cummiskey! When can I be movin' in?"

"You're not even going to ask the location or cost?"

"No! I trust that whatever ya've found will be an improvement."

"You can move in tomorrow. I think you'll find your new home and the food a bit more to your liking. But remember that nothing in the Acre will compare to your room in Boston."

"All I want is edible food and a bed that's free of lice. As I told ya, my accommodations in Boston were meager but clean."

Hugh nodded. "Then I think you should be happy."

Matthew ran an appreciative hand over a portion of the intricate stonework. "This design is truly outstanding, Liam," he complimented before turning back toward Hugh. "Could we return to our earlier discussion, Hugh? I need to report to the Associates within the week regarding the progress on the church. We're attempting to schedule the dedication service. Mr. Boott and I visited with Bishop Fenwick when we traveled to Boston, and the three of us began making preparations for the dedication. Bishop Fenwick is available the first week in September. Does that seem a good date for you, Hugh? And what about you, Liam? Will your work be completed by then?"

"I'll be meetin' my finish date—never missed one yet," Liam replied.

Hugh nodded. "September sounds fine to me. The building should be completed by then."

"Good! And since I know the diocese is furnishing funds for any of the materials you haven't been able to wangle out of Mr. Boott, I'm going to go ahead and report that they're also paying Liam's wages. We both know that J. P. will make Liam's craftsmanship a topic of discussion; the subject of wages is bound to arise. I want to answer truthfully, Hugh, but if you'll not give me a direct answer I'll take your silence as an affirmative reply."

Hugh gave a hearty laugh. "I thought we left the matter of Liam's wages in the dust, but it appears as if Mr. Boott has trained you well, Matthew. You may report that Liam's wages are being paid by the diocese—but please do so only should the topic arise. I'm certain that if some of those tightfisted Associates find out the diocese agreed to pay Liam's wages, they'll think the church should have paid for the land instead of asking the Corporation to donate it."

Matthew smiled and nodded. "I'd say you're likely correct about that assumption. You have my word. I won't volunteer the information unless asked—except to Mr. Boott, of course."

Hugh grinned. "Of course. And if you'd like to complete your inspection, we can move along and Liam can get back to his work."

Matthew offered his hand to Liam. "A pleasure meeting you. I hope we'll have an opportunity to visit in the future. Especially about those religious issues you mentioned."

"We'll see, Mr. Cheever—I'm not one to get into discussions dealin' with religion. Seems that even those folks who are usually even-tempered get themselves all heated up when they start talkin' religion."

Matthew nodded. "You're right about that, Liam. Perhaps I should have phrased my invitation a little differently. Instead of talking about religion or religious issues, why don't we get together and talk about God—not how folks choose to worship or what church they attend, but how a man goes about seeking and building a bond with his Maker."

Liam hesitated, mulling over Matthew's suggestion—a bizarre concept, indeed. Yet his pulse quickened at the notion of mankind being drawn into some sort of personal connection with Almighty God. "Ya've captured my interest with yar words, Mr. Cheever, but I doubt we'll be frequentin' many of the same places," Liam replied, giving Matthew a broad grin.

"Who knows? Some barriers are more easily overcome than we think," Matthew replied as he turned and began following Hugh.

Liam filled his trowel with mortar and began spreading it between two smooth pieces of Italian stone. A wry smile creased his face. The thought of Matthew Cheever wanting to discuss God with him was reason for more than a grin—it was a laugh-out-loud event. Why would a Yank, especially an important one, want to talk to a lowly Irishman about anything except his ability to lay stone? It made no sense. Why, if they were ever seen together, the good people of Lowell would certainly wonder about such a liaison. The barriers between Irish and Yanks in Lowell would not be so easily overcome. Certainly Liam and Matthew could meet in the Acre and discuss God, but barriers would remain intact. The Yanks would stay in their part of town, and the Irish would stay in the Acre.

Carefully smoothing the mortar, Liam continued filling the crevices between each stone. Attempting to push Matthew Cheever's words from his mind, he studied the stones piled before him and concentrated on his choices before picking up a beautifully formed stone. He rubbed his thumb across the intricate pattern of the rock, mesmerized by the beauty created in a simple stone that had been pulled from the ground. Why was he thinking about the creation of a rock? He'd never had such thoughts before. And then another question came to mind—when Matthew spoke of a barrier, was he talking about the difficulty between the Irish and the Yanks or the break between man and God? And who had caused this break by declaring God unapproachable? Was it man or God? Surely it must have been God, because the concept of God desiring to associate himself with a lowly Irishman was almost as improbable as Matthew Cheever ever reappearing to discuss the multitude of questions exploding in Liam's mind.

The bell tower clanged in the distance, hushing Liam's thoughts as the workday came to an end. Packing up his tools, he placed them in the wooden box and then headed off, stopping to visit with several fellow workers. Turning at a fork in the narrow, dusty path, Liam remembered Hugh's news of another living arrangement. Anxious though he was to depart from Noreen's squalid house, he dreaded telling her of his plan to move. He decided her degree of sobriety would control the level of tongue-lashing hurled in his direction.

Dinner at the pub seemed a better option, he decided as he turned back in the direction from which he'd come. If he waited long enough, Noreen would be passed out in a drunken stupor when he returned home, and if he arose early enough the next morning, he could avoid her entirely. His rent was paid for three more days; he wasn't about to ask for a refund. Instead, he would leave her a note stating he had terminated his tenancy. Liam was seeking the path of least resistance, and a simple letter of explanation prudently placed on Noreen's kitchen table appeared to be his answer.

The pub was nearing a capacity crowd when Liam arrived. Several men who regularly worked at the church called out to him. Waiting until his eyes adjusted to the semidarkness of the room, he wove his way through the groups of drinking, joking workmen who were enjoying a tankard along with the company of one another before returning home for the night. Squeezing between two men who worked at the church, he seated himself and soon joined in the laughter and conversation, now certain that he'd made the correct decision. The camaraderie in the pub far surpassed being harangued by Noreen Gallagher.

The men surrounding the table were prodding each other to buy another ale when shouts at the rear of the pub captured their attention. Liam and several others leaned back from the table and looked toward the back of the room, where the talk continued to grow louder and more heated.

"You mark my words—if you don't go after those uppity townsfolk first, they'll be storming and ransacking that church you're building," a man yelled.

Liam squinted his eyes until an obviously drunk William Thurston came into focus. The Yank was spouting his opinion for all to hear.

"I know you think I don't know what I'm talking about, but the Yanks aren't going to tolerate losing jobs to the likes of you," Thurston yelled, waving an arm about the room. "They know you're planning to take over the town and steal their mills, thinking you'll have a ready-made place to bring in more and more of your kinfolk from Ireland. Do you really think they're so stupid they don't know what you're up to? They'll be down here in the Acre stealing both your money and rifles out of that church building before you have a chance to finish building up your arsenal of weapons. If you're smart, you'll take what weapons you've got and make the first move. Take them by surprise!" he yelled, the words a slurred, shrieking command. He was obviously hoping to provoke the crowd into action. Instead, he passed out and fell to the floor.

The men turned back to their conversation, ignoring the Yank in his fancy suit except to occasionally step over him as they made their way back and forth to the bar.

"You think there's anythin' to what he was saying about the Yanks stormin' the church?" Liam asked.

One of the men took a long swig of ale and then leaned across the table, his dark eyes sparkling in the candlelight. "Why? Are you scared of gettin' a bit o' blood on yar hands?" he asked before emitting a rancorous guffaw.

Liam met his stare. "I never fight when a disagreement can be settled another way," Liam replied. "Just wonderin' if and when you thought this battle might occur."

"Don' know if it ever will. Then again, might happen before mornin'. Can't tell what them Yanks is thinkin'. And that one," he said, nodding his head toward Thurston, "nothin' he says or does can be trusted. I wish he'd stay outta the Acre and mingle with 'is own kind."

"I ain't heard nothin' about the Yanks comin' this direction to take over the church, and I sure ain't heard nothin' about the Irish taking over the town. Not that it wouldn't be a pleasant enough thing to see 'appen. Right, Mc-Gruder?" another asked, poking an elbow into his friend's side.

"Right ya are on that one," McGruder replied. "But I ain't got time for this all-important conversation ya're having—got to get home to my missus afore she throws my stew to the dogs," he said, rising from the table.

"I best be getting home, too," another man agreed until soon all of the men except Liam had risen and left the tavern.

It was much too early to head back to Noreen's—she'd still be awake. He moved to a corner and sat by himself, thinking about William Thurston's remarks. The man had been drunk when he'd begun his ranting, but given Noreen's comments about William Thurston, perhaps the only time he spoke the truth was when he'd had one too many. What if the Yanks were planning to storm the church? His belongings were stored there. As soon as he left Noreen's in the morning, he'd go to the church and remove his satchel. He couldn't take a chance on losing the money he'd worked so hard to save. If he was going to bring his parents from Ireland, he needed those coins. Perhaps he could leave his satchel at his new lodging without concern of theft. He would make that determination once he moved into the house.

Remaining in the corner for the balance of the evening, Liam ate a bowl of fish chowder and then borrowed pen and ink from the barkeep, who was willing to oblige. He penned a short note to Noreen, choosing his words carefully, thanking her for making space available when he desperately needed a place to live. Asking her to please keep the balance of his rent as well as the extra dollar beside his note, he went on to explain he'd been successful in finding a private room to rent. The Acre, after all, was small; he didn't want to make enemies.

Before the bell pealed the next morning, Liam left the shanty, his money and handwritten note awaiting either Noreen's delight or wrath, depending upon her mood when she awakened. A dog barked in the distance as he tripped on some unknown object and then stepped on something that squished underfoot. The cloudy moonless night withheld its light and caused Liam to slow his step. It seemed he'd taken forever to walk the short distance to the church. He found the stub of candle and a short time later, satchel in hand, sat down to await Hugh Cummiskey's arrival.

Liam spotted Hugh's outline in the semidarkness as the sturdily built Irishman approached, his arm extended in a wave. "Appears you're anxious to go and meet Mrs. Flynn," he said. "How long have you been waiting?"

"An hour or so," Liam replied.

Hugh gave a loud guffaw, breaking the quietness of the morning. "Noreen send ya packing when she found out you were moving?"

"No. I didn't get home until after she was asleep last night. I left a note on the table this mornin'. She was still asleep when I left," he added.

Hugh slapped him on the back as he continued to laugh. "You're scared of that feisty little Irishwoman, aren't ya?"

Liam gave Hugh a sheepish grin. "For sure, I didn't see any need to be upsettin' her and everyone else last night. Figured the letter and an extra coin or two would be the easiest—"

"Escape?" Hugh interrupted. "It's all right, my boy. I understand. Noreen's a handful and that's a fact. 'Course, she can't read," he said, once again bursting into boisterous laughter.

Liam stopped in his tracks, staring at Hugh. "She can't read?"

"I doubt it—but rest assured she'll find someone who can decipher your note before day's end."

They walked a bit farther before Hugh pointed toward a small shanty.

Liam's hopes plummeted as he looked at the shack. "This one?" he asked, unable to hide his despair.

Hugh gave Liam a grin as he knocked on the door. "Trust me, Liam."

A cheerful dumpling of a woman greeted them at the door. "Good mornin', Mr. Cummiskey. And you must be Mr. Donohue," she said, giving Liam a wide smile that plumped her cheeks into two rosy orbs. "Come in, come in," she offered, stepping aside to clear the entrance.

They stepped inside the hovel and then followed Mrs. Flynn into a large room that obviously served as the main living area in the house. "Liam, this is Mrs. Flynn," Hugh said.

Liam nodded, his gaze flashing about the room. "Pleased to meet you. Mr. Cummiskey tells me ya've an opening for a boarder."

"Is that what he told ya, now?" she questioned, turning a merry smile in Hugh's direction. "He stretched the truth just a wee bit, Mr. Donohue. Truth is, I've never rented space in my house to anyone, but after a pitcher of ale, Hugh convinced the mister he was missing out on a good opportunity."

Liam's cheeks heated with embarrassment. The woman didn't appear upset over his arrival, yet it sounded as though Hugh and her husband had forced her into taking him in as a boarder. He didn't want to be an intruder in this kind woman's home, but once inside, he knew he couldn't return to Noreen's. Mrs. Flynn's home was neat and clean; this was a place where he could be comfortable.

"Now look what you've done. You've gone and embarrassed him," Hugh said, returning Mrs. Flynn's smile. "You'd best be tellin' him the whole truth, or he'll be headin' back to Noreen's."

Mrs. Flynn folded her chunky arms beneath an ample bosom. "Go on with ya! We both know better than that! Given the choice, nobody in his right mind would live with Noreen Gallagher. Ya're more than welcome in our home, Mr. Donohue. The mister asked me if I'd be interested in makin' a bit of extra change for meself by taking in a boarder. Ya'd best know from the outset that you won't have much space. I hung a curtain to give you a bit o' privacy," she said, showing him where he would sleep. "You can use this chest for yar belongings. 'Course ya can spend as much time as ya like out here with the mister and me of an evenin'," she continued. "Ya can be payin' me the same amount as ya were payin' Noreen," she added.

A sense of relief washed over Liam. "Ya have a new boarder, Mrs. Flynn—a happy one, I might be addin'."

"Good. I do washin' on Mondays. Ya can leave yar dirty clothes on the floor by yar bed."

Liam looked at her in stunned silence. "Ya'll be doin' my washin'?"

"Of course. Ya get three meals a day, laundry, and cleaning," she replied. "Don't want ya smellin' up the house," she said with a chuckle.

He could barely contain himself as he thanked her. Reaching into his pocket, he pulled out enough money to pay her twice what he'd given Noreen. "Here's for my first week," he said, shoving the coins into her hand.

She looked down at the money and then shook her head back and forth. "That's enough for more than two weeks. Mr. Cummiskey told me what Noreen charges," she said, taking several coins and holding them out to him.

"I want to pay ya more, Mrs. Flynn. Noreen provided me only one meal a day, her house was filthy, and she didn't wash my laundry. Ya're offerin' much more."

Liam watched as she glanced toward Hugh. He nodded for her to accept. "Thank you, Mr. Donohue, but if ya find yarself fallin' on hard times, ya let me know and we'll go back to the lower amount."

"Now that we've got things settled, we'd best be gettin' to work," Hugh said.

"Ya can put yar belongings on the bed and unpack them this evenin'," Mrs. Flynn offered.

Liam nodded. He was certain his money and belongings would be safe in this woman's care.

"Thank ya for yar efforts," Liam said as he and Hugh walked toward the church.

"You're welcome, my boy. I didn't want you rushin' off to some fancy job in Boston because you were forced to live at a place like Noreen's. Just remember—you owe me now. You can't be leavin' until your work at the church is completed."

"I'll be around at least that long. Ya've got my word," Liam said as he stopped in front of the church and momentarily watched as Hugh strode off.

Both the noonday and evening meals exceeded Liam's expectations. The food was hearty, well prepared, and served with a dose of pleasant conversation. Mrs. Flynn and her husband proved to be a good match. Both had a cheerful attitude and enjoyed good discussion, and they were quick to involve him in their repartee.

Liam rose from one of the wooden chairs that formed the sitting area of the large room. "If ya'll excuse me, I'd best unpack my belongings before bedtime."

"Ya don't need to ask our permission to move about the place," Mr. Flynn replied as he tapped his pipe on the hearth. "This is yar home, too."

"Thank you, Mr. Flynn," Liam replied before moving off to the cordoned area that was now his room.

Everything was exactly as he'd left it. The satchel, his small trunk of clothing—nothing had been touched. He ruffled through the trunk, moving his clothes, except for his heavy winter clothing, into the small chest the Flynns had provided.

Sitting on the edge of the bed, Liam opened the satchel that had remained hidden in the church until this morning. Digging into the bag, he pulled out the sheaf of papers he'd retrieved from J. P. Green's fireplace and tossed them behind him on the bed as he dug deeper, his fingers tightening around a small leather bag and pulling it into sight. Untying the cord, he carefully counted the money and then returned it to the sack, refastened the tie, and with a satisfied smile, tucked it into the bottom of his trunk.

Gathering the loose papers, he began stacking them together. Seeing row after row of figures penned on the sheets of paper, Liam ceased stacking the sheets and spread them out on the bed, reviewing the entries and becoming more and more fascinated as he looked at the numbers. He was no mathematician, but he'd had his share of education both in school and under the tutelage of a stonemason in Ireland. The old man had insisted a business could be successful only if you maintained proper ledgers.

For the next two hours Liam sat on the bed, matching the pages of the export business of J. P. Green and Nathan Appleton, unable to understand exactly what lay before him. He juggled a few more pages and then stared intently at the papers, suddenly realizing he was looking at a system of book-keeping that revealed thousands of dollars being siphoned out of the company owned by Appleton and Green. It appeared J. P. Green was systematically transferring funds into his own company and falsifying the books of Appleton & Green Exports. Liam's hands trembled as he stacked the sheets. No wonder Green had thrown the papers in the fireplace. He folded all of the papers except a small stack of pages that still were unclear. Dates were listed in each row, followed by a last name, first initial, and amount of money. The entries made no sense, but he didn't want to uncover any more surprises. No doubt his knowledge of the siphoned funds could put his life in jeopardy; discovering further incriminating information would only serve to tighten the noose around his neck.

～ 20 ～

William Thurston selected a small table in a far corner of the Brackman Hotel on Beacon Street. He'd arrived in Boston last evening and hoped to be on the *Governor Sullivan* early the next morning, heading back to Lowell. This journey to Boston did not need to be lengthy, and he was pleased there was no need to linger. The social circle to which his wife and her wealthy parents belonged had already departed Boston for the summer. Of course, he'd have to make at least one appearance at The Haven this summer; after all, they must keep up appearances. His wife's family name provided him with access to Boston's high-powered elite, and he saved her from being called an old maid. The arrangement was unspoken but understood. It suited both of them.

He took a sip of coffee while perusing an old copy of the newspaper he'd picked up in the lobby and waited. He glanced at his pocket watch a short time later, neatly folded the paper, and kept his gaze fixed on the entrance, hoping to conclude his business as early as possible.

"More coffee, sir?" a waiter inquired.

"What? Oh, yes," he replied.

"I'd like one also," J. P. Green said as he walked up behind the waiter.

Thurston breathed a sigh of relief. He was beginning to wonder if Green had forgotten their engagement.

"Sorry for the delay, William. Hope I haven't kept you waiting too long," Green said as he seated himself opposite William. "Did you have a pleasant trip? Lovely weather for making the journey by boat."

Thurston stirred a dollop of cream into his coffee. "Pleasant enough. I found several gentlemen willing to rid themselves of their money at the gaming table."

Green laughed at the remark and then downed his coffee. He set the cup down hard before bending forward and placing his folded arms atop the table. "We've got a bit of a problem, William, and you're the one who will need to correct it," he said.

A knot formed in William's belly. Green hadn't mentioned any problem in his letter—he'd merely written to say that they needed to meet and go over future plans. "You know me, J. P., I'm always willing to work with you. I didn't know I'd done anything that required altering. How can I help?" he asked, feigning cheerfulness.

"I hope I didn't give the wrong impression by my remark. It's not so much that you've done anything wrong, William. I suppose it's more a matter of change . . . yes, that's it. Things are changing, and I need your help if we're to be successful."

The tension in William's face relaxed slightly. "What kind of changes?" he inquired tentatively.

"Good ones—at least financially good. For both of us," he added, wagging his finger to and fro. He moved closer and cupped his hand along one side of his mouth. "We've opened several new markets. One, in particular, excites me. The expansion is going to be greater than either of us ever imagined. So much so that I doubt we'll be able to meet the demand," he said, now leaning back with a look of defeat replacing his earlier excitement.

"Wait—don't give up before you've even told me the details," Thurston said, his excitement building. "Where are these new markets?"

"Some additional overseas markets, particularly India, have captured Nathan's interest, but we've begun additional shipments to the South, specifically New Orleans, and that is the market that most interests me," J. P. answered.

Thurston's eyes grew wide. "New Orleans?" He rubbed his fingers along his jaw. "Oh, how I love that city—the decadence is a joy to behold. I've not found a better place to wallow in sin," he said, thinking of his last visit to the city and the mulatto girl who'd been his constant companion for five satisfying days.

"I agree. And that's what makes it such a wide-open market for us—but only if we can provide quality merchandise." He leaned in close once again. "If we're going to succeed and corner the market, I need the highest obtainable quality. Better than what you've provided in the past."

Thurston was shocked at his comment. "Higher quality? Surely you jest. I've given you nothing but the best. I can't believe there's any better to be had in New Orleans—or anywhere else for that matter."

"Don't play games with me, William, or I'll find someone else who's willing to supply what I want. It's not as though you don't have access. But if you're averse to the risk that might be involved . . ."

"Might be involved? You don't realize what you're asking, J. P.," he replied.

Green pushed away from the table and began to stand up.

"Sit down! I didn't say it was impossible or that I wasn't interested. I said there's a great risk involved. Sit down," Thurston repeated. "Please," he added, waiting until J. P. was once again seated before continuing. "You understand that what you're asking for is going to create an uproar in Lowell—this will go beyond Kirk Boott—and the citizens will expect a higher level of participation from the Corporation. They'll expect involvement by at least some of the Associates."

J. P. nodded. "You act as though you're not one of the Associates, William. That's the beauty of this whole thing. You spend more time in Lowell than all the rest of the Associates combined. You can volunteer to lend your assistance on behalf of the Associates, permitting them the freedom to continue their lives without interruption, yet giving an appearance of concern and support. What better way to remain operational while thwarting the investigative process? It's a beautiful concept," he gleefully determined.

William was silent for a moment. "And the funds? This plan increases my risk dramatically. I'm certain you've already considered that I will need additional money."

"Ah, William, there are some matters where I know I can always depend upon you . . . and the desire for more money is one of them."

"That's entirely unfair, J. P.! I'll need men that I can trust implicitly, and such men don't come cheap. I don't want to have someone turn on me for a few dollars. Besides, your level of involvement doesn't change at all while mine increases substantially. The only people who know you're involved in this scheme are the man you've hired to negotiate with the ships' captains and me. Otherwise, you're in the clear."

"And who's told you that I don't negotiate with the ships' captains myself?" Green inquired with a curious grin.

William met J. P.'s gaze. "I don't need anyone to tell me. I know you're too smart to involve yourself with talkative seamen."

J. P. nodded. "I'll take that as a compliment, William. And I know you're too smart to take a greater risk without additional payment. I'll pay you half again what you've been receiving on each delivery. Do we have an agreement?"

Thurston nodded. "How soon will you want to begin shipping the higher quality?"

J. P. gave him a cunning smile. "We can begin immediately, but I'll bow to your expertise as to the amount of time needed to make arrangements in Lowell. And if you foresee a problem with storage in Lowell, I have ample space available in Boston. Send word of the time and mode of transportation, and I'll have men available to assist with the transfer."

"I'll begin making arrangements upon my return to Lowell," William replied.

21

Bella paced back and forth between the parlor and hallway, her shoes clicking on the wooden floor with each step.

"Do sit down, Bella," Daughtie urged.

"You're going to wear out your shoes with all that pacing," Ruth added.

Bella ignored the request and moved into the hallway. "I do wish Miss Addie would hurry. I'm sure the meeting will be crowded, and I want to get a good seat."

"She can't see you out here, so continuing to clomp back and forth is not going to hurry her along. I'm sure she's moving as quickly as possible. After all, she did have to clean up after supper," Daughtie retorted.

Bella stalked into the parlor and plopped down beside Ruth, her eyes flashing with anger. "Are you happy?" She folded her arms and leveled a steely gaze in Daughtie's direction.

Daughtie tilted her head and gave Bella a playful smile. "You needn't attempt to intimidate me, Arabella Newberry. I've known you far too long for such antics. Save it for the meeting."

Bella bit her lower lip. She didn't want to smile; instead she needed to gather courage from her anger in order to speak eloquently should the need arise this evening. And she was certain a strong argument would be needed for education to blossom in Lowell. Yet the issue wasn't so much education as it was money—and reforming the present school system would take money—something near and dear to the hearts of those in opposition.

Miss Addie's door burst open, and she bustled into the room while still tying her bonnet. "I'm sorry to keep you waiting, girls. Shall we go?"

"I just hope we can find a seat," Bella mumbled as they moved off toward St. Anne's Episcopal Church.

Addie gave Bella a reassuring pat on the arm. "I asked Mintie to save our pew for us. We'll be close to the front."

"Your pew was probably taken by the time Miss Mintie arrived. She had dinner chores to perform after supper, didn't she?" Bella countered.

Addie nodded. "Yes, but she's employed Lucy's younger sister to help out now and again. She paid her to do the dishes tonight."

"Still . . ." Bella permitted the word to hang in the air as a silent accusation.

"Besides, if there's anyone sitting in our pew, you know Mintie will shoo them out—with her parasol, if necessary."

"I suppose you're right on that account! She's quite adept with a parasol," Bella agreed, remembering how the older woman had wielded her umbrella against Taylor Manning in that very church pew.

They hurried along, arriving at the church doors only minutes before the meeting was to begin. Mintie was standing guard over the pew, waving them forward with a dark green parasol as they entered the rear of the church.

Addie shook her head back and forth and motioned for Mintie to sit down. "I suppose she thinks I've forgotten where we sit every Sunday. For someone who's worried about what other people think, she's certainly making a spectacle of herself waving that parasol in the air," Addie said to nobody in particular.

"That's true, but you'll notice nobody is going anywhere near her with that pointed instrument flailing in all directions."

Nodding in agreement, Addie worked her way down the aisle, clearing a path for the three girls.

"Finally!" Mintie greeted. "I thought you would never arrive. Saving these seats was no small task. Everybody wants to be near the front," she announced in an explosive burst.

"I was certain you'd be up to the feat," Addie replied as she seated herself. "Come on, girls, sit down," she instructed, patting the space beside her.

The three girls plunked down as instructed, Bella taking the seat closest to the aisle. After all, she might need immediate access to the aisle if she wanted to step forward and voice her opinion. Of course, if the discussion went well, she might not speak at all. That concept seemed improbable, yet she acknowledged the possibility.

Bella quickly surveyed the church. Matthew and Lilly Cheever were two rows in front of them, along with several other prominent-looking men with their fashionable wives in tow. The pews were full, and an overflow crowd was gathering at the rear of the church when a shadow fell across the pew and Bella looked upward.

"May I?" Taylor Manning inquired, looking over her head toward Miss Addie.

"Taylor! Do join us," she invited. "Scoot down, girls—we've plenty of room for one more."

Bella held fast to her position as the other girls began sliding down the pew. She wasn't relinquishing her aisle seat to anyone. "Why don't you sit next to Miss Addie? I'm sure she'd enjoy your company," Bella said loudly enough for the older woman to hear.

"Oh yes, do sit here," Addie said as she pushed closer to Ruth, making a space between Mintie and herself.

Taylor arched his eyebrows and then gave Bella a defiant grin. "Perhaps it would be easier if I went around to the other side. Or, better yet, since the meeting is about to begin, why don't you move down, Bella, and I'll take the aisle. That way I won't disturb quite as many people."

"How thoughtful! You are a dear boy," Addie replied, giving him a winsome smile.

"Bella?"

Taking great effort to move her legs and tuck her skirt closer around her body, Bella looked toward the empty space to her left. "I prefer to remain near the aisle," she said. "You can sit there." She nodded toward the vacant seat. "Or you can go around and sit by Miss Addie, whichever you prefer."

"You win," he said while wedging himself between Daughtie and Bella. "At least this time," he added with a grin.

Bella frowned before placing a finger in front of her pursed lips. "Shhh! The meeting is about to begin."

"If we could come to order, I'd like to present the recommendation of the school board," Reverend Edson said. "Once I've finished, I'll open the floor for discussion, but I would request you wait until you've been acknowledged before speaking. Otherwise, we'll have chaos and nothing will be accomplished.

"The board members have spent countless hours studying the problems of our current district school system and the possible resolutions in order to provide a better education for—"

"The children of Lowell are already receiving a decent education," a booming voice declared. All eyes shifted to the rear of the sanctuary, where an impeccably dressed Kirk Boott was making his way down the aisle. "I'm sorry to interrupt your little speech, Theodore. Oh, excuse me. I should be addressing you more formally since this is a public meeting. Do you prefer reverend or doctor, Theodore?"

"I really don't have a preference. In fact, Theodore will be fine. As soon as you've been seated, I'll continue."

"That's Kirk Boott?" Bella whispered to Taylor.

"Yes. Making quite an entrance, isn't he?"

Bella nodded and watched while Mr. Boott casually sauntered down the aisle, obviously enjoying the attention his entrance was eliciting. When he finally took a seat beside Matthew and Lilly Cheever, Reverend Edson continued.

"As I was saying, the board has considered the present school system, and we are of the opinion that the district system served the residents well prior to the expansion and incorporation of Lowell. Now, however, we believe our children would be best educated if we changed to a graded system. There are certainly more than enough children in the community right now to sustain the graded system, and with each passing year we'll have additional students to educate. The board believes two new schools would adequately provide for a transfer to the new educational system."

There was an eruption of applause throughout the room.

Boott rose to his feet. He didn't request permission to speak. Rather, he immediately took control, motioning the crowd to silence. "You can applaud the recommendation, but new schools are not going to be erected in Lowell. Everyone in this room is expecting the Corporation to pay for these schools. Well, the Corporation has paid for everything else in this town, and it is not going to pay for two more schools. Our investment in this community is going to be conducted in an economically sound manner. In order to accomplish financial stability, debts must be paid rather than incurred. I know that concept may be difficult for some of you to understand, but trust me when I say that you'll need to find some other method to finance these schools."

"The Corporation got our land dirt cheap, thanks to you. It won't hurt them to make up the difference by building a couple of schools," someone called out from the back of the room.

A man sitting several rows behind Bella shouted, "If the cost of the schools is paid by taxes, the Corporation will have no choice but to pay its fair share."

Reverend Edson rapped a wooden gavel on the podium and began calling for order. "Please—stand and be recognized before speaking. We need to conduct this meeting in an orderly fashion."

Once again Kirk Boott stood and turned toward the crowd without being recognized. "It would behoove all of you to vote against this measure," he said. "You're all in line for your pay every week. Remember where your loyalty belongs. If the Corporation fails, you'll all be without jobs. It would be folly to impose further burdens upon the Corporation."

Bella rose to her feet and waved an arm in the air, waiting to speak until recognized by the moderator. "You," Reverend Edson said, pointing in Bella's direction.

Bella cleared her throat and met Mr. Boott's indifferent gaze. "Fear and intimidation are a poor substitute for a worthwhile defense, sir. The children of this community deserve an education that will one day help them achieve their full potential. It is education that will aid them in contributing to the future growth and expansion of Lowell. Surely your Corporation is willing to invest in the further development of what it has already begun."

By the time she finished speaking, Mr. Boott's apathetic stare had evolved into a condescending sneer. "I realize this will be difficult for your female mind to understand, Miss. . . ?" He waited.

"Newberry. Arabella Newberry," she replied through clenched teeth.

"Yes. Well, Miss Newberry, let me explain a thing or two. This community is an experiment. Never before has such a concept been attempted, and we have yet to determine the success or failure of Lowell. Quite frankly, in only a few years a traveler may find nothing but a heap of ruins where Lowell now stands," Kirk solemnly stated.

"And if a traveler should examine the relics of this town in a few years and find no trace of a schoolhouse," Bella responded, "he would immediately know what led to its demise. Education is the backbone of a solid society. Educate the children and your town will stand firm, your Corporation will be strong, and your coffers will be filled with the gold you so earnestly seek."

Applause and hoots of laughter filled the room as Kirk leaned down and talked to Matthew Cheever and then whispered something to Theodore Edson. Moments later Matthew stood alongside Mr. Boott.

"Unfortunately, I have a previous engagement I must attend. In my absence, Matthew Cheever will speak on behalf of the Corporation. I trust that before this matter comes to a vote, you will all give considerable weight to my words." That said, Boott stalked down the aisle and out of the building.

The crowd quickly turned its attention back to Reverend Edson. "Thank you for your fine remarks, Miss Newberry. And for waiting to be recognized before speaking," he added. "Other comments?" he asked, looking about the assembly and then pointing to a woman on the other side of the aisle.

"I appreciate what Miss Newberry said. It's clear from hearing her talk that she's had good schooling. I'd like to be sure the girls here in Lowell receive as much education as the boys. It appears that the schoolmaster spends more time and effort with the boys and discounts the need for education for our girls. I'm told that lately he's discouraged the girls' attendance by telling them they don't need schooling once they're able to read a bit and sign their names."

A man jumped up two rows behind her. "That's because the Corporation is counting the number of pupils. They've begun keeping records in an attempt to prove there's no need for more schools."

Matthew raised his hand and waited to be acknowledged before replying. "That, sir, is a false statement. It is true that the Corporation has recently taken a head count at the schools. However, we have performed such a count every year in order to track growth, not for the reasons that you allege. We also track the number of residents living in the community. There's nothing secret about our actions."

Bella rose from her seat. "But it's those very numbers that identify the needs of a community. A town of three hundred has fewer children than a town of ten thousand, hence the need for fewer schools, particularly schools of the graded system. However, a town with only ten Catholic residents does not need a Catholic church in which to worship. A town with a growing Irish population that is primarily Catholic needs a church. The same holds true for fire and police protection—the larger the community, the greater the need. So whether it be directly or indirectly, I believe your figures do contribute to the decisions made for the citizens of this community, Mr. Cheever."

Matthew hesitated. "What you've said is partially true. However, the Corporation did not coerce the schoolmaster into making such statements. I'm a staunch advocate of education, but the Corporation does not believe Lowell needs two more schools."

"Of course not. The Lowell school system doesn't affect the lives of the wealthy. You send your children off to fancy private schools without regard to what's available for ours."

"Now, just a minute. I grew up and attended a district school in East Chelmsford, and my education served me well. I consider my fundamental education to be as fine as that of any of the others attending Harvard University," Matthew replied.

"We were a small farm community back then," Lilly Cheever rebutted.

Bella glanced first toward Matthew and then toward Lilly, unable to believe her ears. Lilly had contradicted her husband's opinion in a public forum. Surely she would apologize and shrink quietly into the background.

Instead, Lilly continued with her lecture. "I have no intention of sending my children off to boarding school to ensure that they receive a quality education. We have an obligation to provide our children with a superior education right here in their own community."

Matthew didn't respond to his wife's remarks. Instead, Reverend Edson, with wisdom and kindness, came to Matthew's rescue. "It's getting rather late. Perhaps we should put the matter to a vote."

"Are you certain you wouldn't prefer to wait? Perhaps hold another meeting?" Matthew suggested.

The crowd immediately began murmuring, voicing their disagreement. "We want to vote now," several men hollered.

Matthew Cheever and Reverend Edson exchanged a look and then spoke privately for a moment. Bella leaned forward, listening.

"I think these folks prefer to vote now," Reverend Edson replied.

Matthew shrugged his shoulders. "I fear you're taking quite a risk, Reverend."

Reverend Edson nodded. "Perhaps. But it's the proper thing to do."

22

M atthew insisted Lilly remain seated in the pew until the crowd dispersed. He said he wanted to visit further with Reverend Edson, but she suspected he didn't want to subject himself to any further questioning by the townsfolk. She sat quietly while the two talked and the sanctuary emptied.

Finally, Lilly rose. "Matthew, there is absolutely nobody left in this church except Reverend Edson and the two of us," she said, moving toward where the men stood. "I'm exhausted. May we please leave?"

"Yes, of course, my dear," he said. "Thank you for your time, Reverend Edson."

"Of course, Matthew. Anytime you want to visit further, please stop by," Reverend Edson replied, escorting them to the front door of the church. "Good night," he called out from the doorway when they finally reached their carriage.

"After the way you acted tonight, I'm surprised that Reverend Edson is still speaking to you," Lilly commented as Matthew assisted her into their carriage.

"He's a man of the cloth: he's supposed to forgive. Besides, he knows I wasn't attacking him personally. I was merely doing my job."

Matthew walked around the carriage, hoisted himself up, and dropped onto the seat. He flicked the reins and set the horses into motion as a refreshing breeze began to stir the air. Shimmering stars illuminated the distant sky, and a hazy full moon hung overhead. Although it was a beautiful evening for a carriage ride, Lilly found it impossible to savor their surroundings.

"I find it repugnant that you're taking sides with the Corporation on this issue. Surely you don't truly believe what Mr. Boott said this evening."

"Lilly, I think the new schools and the graded system would be best for Lowell, but I will not go against the Corporation on this. I would lose my job, and we can't afford for that to happen, especially with a baby on the way."

"How can you believe one thing and argue for another? Don't you find such behavior immoral?"

"Immoral? We're not talking about depraved conduct, Lilly. I'm doing my job."

"You're living a lie," she replied.

"What would you have me do, Lilly?"

Lilly leveled a look of exasperation in his direction. "What I want is for you to admit you've acted improperly. The fact is, Matthew, making me feel better is not the issue. You're the one compromising your standards and beliefs. You've shown Mr. Boott that you're willing to do whatever is necessary to protect your job and the Corporation."

Matthew's eyes blazed with anger. "That's completely unfair, Lilly. The people at that meeting knew I was speaking on behalf of the Corporation. Kirk told them I was doing just that prior to his departure. I'm not living a lie, but you are speaking in anger. I suggest we move on to another topic. I don't want to argue with you, Lilly."

"What did you and Reverend Edson discuss?" she asked.

"His future at St. Anne's," Matthew answered simply.

Stunned by Matthew's reply, Lilly remained silent, waiting to revisit the subject until they were preparing for bed.

"What did you mean earlier when you mentioned Reverend Edson's future at St. Anne's?"

"It seems that Kirk told him that if he went against the Corporation and continued fighting for the graded system and new schools, there would be no further monetary assistance for the church."

"From the Corporation, you mean?" Lilly inquired.

"From the Corporation or from Kirk personally. He's threatened to leave the church and withdraw his substantial weekly gifts as well as donations by the Corporation. It could prove devastating to the future of the church."

Lilly stared at Matthew, a look of skepticism etched on her face. "Reverend Edson was Mr. Boott's personal selection as rector of St. Anne's. He brought Reverend Edson to Lowell," she argued. "Why, the church is named after Anne Boott," Lilly continued weakly.

"I know, I know," Matthew replied. "None of it makes any sense, but Kirk is determined to prove his power will withstand this school movement. I think he almost views it as a personal affront that the town would oppose his point of view."

Lilly unfastened her hair, letting it fall around her shoulders. "We can't afford for him to win, Matthew. I want our children living at home with us—not off in some boarding school growing up without our love and the comfort of their own home. And what of Lewis's son? When we find him, he's going to need all the love and comfort of a family, too. Sending him off would be devastating. You've got to find some way to convince Mr. Boott he's wrong on this issue."

"I think the vote this evening has already proven that he's wrong—at least in the eyes of the community. I doubt whether he'll find any way he can stave off the new schools now that the vote has passed, and I don't intend to take up the banner of convincing him he should gracefully accept the decision."

Lilly turned and faced Matthew. "You could assist in making this matter go more smoothly if you truly embraced the idea."

"Don't start . . ."

Lilly's eyes widened as loud knocking sounded at the front door. "Who can that be at this hour?"

Matthew quickly donned his trousers and rushed down the steps while Lilly stood in the bedroom doorway. She heard Matthew open the door and then heard another man's voice. Sitting on the edge of the bed, she repetitively pulled a silver hairbrush through her long, thick mane until she finally grew weary and slipped under the bedcovers.

"I almost fell asleep," she said when Matthew finally returned. "Who was that?"

"Mr. Cummiskey," he replied, removing his trousers. "Problems in the Paddy camp. Another girl has disappeared, and the Irish are up in arms."

Lilly bolted upright in the bed. "Not another one," she said in a choked whisper.

"How stupid of me! I shouldn't have said anything. I don't want you upsetting yourself, Lilly."

"Then tell me what has been occurring," she insisted.

He sat down on the bed and took her hand. "At first we thought perhaps the girls had run off with their beaux or just run away from home. However, it appears that's not the case. At least the families say none of the girls had reason to run off and none of them had a steady fellow. Hugh has given the police a great deal of information regarding each of the girls, but it seems that the police aren't doing much. Folks in the Paddy camp think the police don't care because the girls are Irish."

"Do you think that's true?" Lilly asked.

"Possibly. If the girls were Yankees, I imagine the matter would receive more attention. Most townsfolk haven't given the disappearances much thought, although the mill girls appear concerned. I think they worry such a thing could happen to one of them."

"Oh, Matthew. How terrible!" She clutched the coverlet into her fist and drew the knotted fabric to her chest. "I know how my heart aches with longing to be united with Lewis's son. The girls' parents must be suffering intolerable anguish. Surely there's some way to help them," she pleaded.

He pulled her into an embrace, stroking her hair. "I've promised Hugh that I'll do all in my power to help. I'm going to talk to the police tomorrow, but I want you to promise that you'll not overly worry yourself."

She tilted her head back and looked into his eyes. "I promise, Matthew. And while you're with the police, would you talk to them about Lewis's boy again? See if there's anything to report?"

"Yes, dear, I'll inquire. Now I want you to get some sleep."

Slumber came, followed by dreams—visions of a little boy, a miniature Lewis, lost in a dark abyss, stretching a tiny hand toward hers. She grasped her hand around the pudgy fist, pulling, pulling, until she awakened—exhausted and aching. Aching for Lewis's child but beginning to lose hope that he would be found.

23

A sharp rapping sounded at the front door, interrupting Addie and Bella's conversation.

"Sit still, Miss Addie, I'll go. It's probably another suitor come to call on one of the girls," Bella said, rising from the settee. "I think Daughtie should be joining us soon. She wanted to finish her laundry first," Bella continued, glancing over her shoulder as she moved toward the front door. There were several girls gathered around the dining room table, and four more were entertaining young men in the parlor. The quietude of Miss Addie's rooms was a pleasant reprieve from the deafening noise of the weaving room and the chattering of the girls and their beaux.

Bella's smile disappeared when she opened the door. "Taylor! Were you expected this evening?"

"No, but I thought perhaps I'd find you at home," he said, still standing on the step. "May I come in?"

Bella hesitated for a moment, then moved aside. "I suppose, but I can't be long. I'm visiting with Miss Addie in her parlor."

"Oh, good. I was hoping to see Miss Addie. Shall I join the two of you?" He didn't wait for an answer. Instead he moved toward Miss Addie's living quarters.

Bella stood staring after him as he waited just inside the parlor door.

"Taylor, do come in. What a pleasant surprise," Addie greeted. "What brings you calling this evening—and what's happened to Bella?"

Bella walked to the doorway. "I'm right here, Miss Addie."

Miss Addie patted the settee cushion. "Come sit down. I thought you'd deserted me."

Taylor was leaning against the mantel, oozing charm as he smiled down at Miss Addie.

"Why don't I leave the two of you to visit? I'm sure you'd both enjoy an opportunity for some private conversation," Bella suggested.

Taylor immediately moved away from the fireplace. "I think our conversation would be much livelier if you remained. Don't you agree, Miss Addie?"

"Of course. We have nothing to say that you can't hear. Now come sit down," Addie insisted.

"Have you heard from Uncle John?" Taylor inquired as Bella seated herself.

"I received a short letter yesterday. He said the journey was tiring and he had hoped for a few days' rest before beginning his meetings, but that wasn't the case. He fears his meetings thus far haven't gone as well as he had hoped. I got the impression he's very tired and hasn't had much time to himself. I'm concerned about his health," Addie replied.

Bella moved closer and took Miss Addie's hand in her own. "Perhaps the best thing we could do right now is pray for Mr. Farnsworth."

Taylor jumped up from his chair as though he'd been jabbed by Miss Mintie's pointed parasol. "I'm not much on praying. I'll wait in the other room until you've finished," he said, attempting to make a hasty retreat.

"Sit down, Taylor," Miss Addie instructed. "Bella and I will pray after we've concluded our visit." The words were spoken in a chiding tone, followed by an unmistakable frown leveled in Bella's direction.

Why was Miss Addie upset with her? After all, she was offering to help. Taylor was the one ready to flee from the room without praying for his own uncle. Dismayed, Bella watched Taylor seat himself on the brocade-covered chair close to the door—obviously preparing to bolt and run should Bella once again mention prayer or God. She now wished she had insisted upon leaving when Taylor first arrived. Instead, she was trapped in this room, feeling very much the fool.

Bella's gaze was fixed upon her folded hands, half listening as Miss Addie and Taylor discussed Mr. Farnsworth's whereabouts and the contents of his recent letter.

"I was wondering if you'd be interested in a carriage ride tomorrow."

"Bella?"

Miss Addie's voice drifted through her hazy thoughts, drawing her gaze upward. "Yes, ma'am?"

Miss Addie's forehead was creased into thin ridges, her eyebrows arched in an upsurge of expectation. "Were you going to answer Taylor?"

Befuddled, she glanced back and forth between Taylor and Miss Addie. "I'm sorry. Answer what? Apparently I wasn't listening," she apologized.

"Perhaps you should repeat your question, Taylor," Miss Addie prompted.

"I was wondering if you would like to accompany me on a carriage ride tomorrow," he said.

"After church?" She glanced toward Miss Addie. "I suppose if Miss Addie would like me to accompany her on an outing with you, I'd be willing to come along," she replied.

Now they were both giving her a dumbfounded look. "I believe Taylor was inviting you, Bella," Miss Addie replied.

"Oh! I don't think . . ." she stammered. "Unless you'd care to join us, Miss

Addie, I don't believe it would be appropriate for me to accompany Mr. Manning on a carriage ride without a chaperone."

Addie gave her a look of surprise. "All of the girls go on unaccompanied outings—especially during the daytime hours. And it's not as though Taylor were a stranger."

"Exactly right, Miss Addie. Why, in the near future, Miss Addie and I will likely be related. At least I'm sure that's Uncle John's desire," he said, giving her a charming smile.

Miss Addie's cheeks immediately tinged pink at the comment. "I think a carriage ride would be a wonderful escape from your daily routine, Bella."

Bella didn't want to encourage Taylor Manning's attention. In fact, she preferred to avoid his company completely, but from all appearances, Miss Addie was of a different mindset—and Bella didn't want to argue.

"We can leave immediately after church services. That way I can be home in ample time to complete some unfinished tasks," Bella replied as she glanced toward Miss Addie for a sign of approval.

Bella sighed in relief as the older woman nodded and smiled her affirmation.

"I was thinking later in the day would be more suitable. I have some business for the Mechanics Association and had already made plans to meet with several other members tomorrow afternoon," Taylor replied.

"I have an idea," Miss Addie said, her face glowing with excitement. "Why don't you pack a light picnic supper, Bella. A picnic near the falls, or some other lovely spot you locate while on your ride, would be restful, and it will be much cooler in the evening."

Taylor appeared to be delighted with the idea, his head bobbing up and down in agreement. "Yes, and that would permit you time to complete your tasks before we leave for our carriage ride."

"Right!" Miss Addie agreed. "It's much more relaxing to have your work completed beforehand."

Bella felt as though she were being sucked into a swirling black whirlpool. She could barely breathe, and there was no doubt she had lost control of this conversation.

"I'll be here at five thirty," Taylor said without waiting for further discussion. "Now, if you ladies will excuse me, I must be on my way as it's getting rather late."

Bella remained in her chair while Miss Addie rose to escort Taylor to the door. The older woman's words floated back into the room as she reminded Taylor to speak to Matthew Cheever and told him she looked forward to seeing him in church the next morning. Before bidding him good-night, Miss Addie promised to find some delightful morsels to place in their picnic basket the next day.

Miss Addie returned to the room, giving Bella a comforting pat on the shoulder as she walked by. "You and Taylor will have a fine time tomorrow. You do need a bit of relaxation, you know." The words hung in midair—expectantly, longingly, anxiously—awaiting Bella's confirmation.

But Bella wasn't interested in discussing her need for relaxation. She wanted an explanation of Miss Addie's earlier behavior and she wanted it now. Pushing any doubts aside, she charged forward with her interrogation. "Why did you appear offended when I offered to pray for Mr. Farnsworth?" she quizzed, more anger in her tone than she'd intended.

Miss Addie appeared to shrink back at her words. "It's obvious I've hurt your feelings. I'm sorry," she apologized. "Truth is, I've been earnestly praying for Taylor and his relationship—"

"Then why wouldn't you allow me to pray?" Bella interrupted.

"Permit me to finish, dear," Miss Addie calmly replied. "I truly appreciated your offer to pray for John. When we've finished talking, I want to do just that—and I hope you'll join me," she said with a sweet smile. "However, it appeared Taylor was extremely uncomfortable with your suggestion. I've found that forced participation in almost anything can have an adverse effect. Taylor struggles against God—at least that's what John has told me. Had we continued, I fear we would have appeared sanctimonious. Now, I may be wrong," she concluded.

"No. You're absolutely correct, Miss Addie," Bella replied. "In all honesty, I wanted him to feel uncomfortable. I'm terribly ashamed of myself," she admitted.

"It wasn't my intent to cause you discomfort, Bella, but since you've broached the topic, remember that if Taylor is to be won to the Lord, we need to set an example. Once he sees how wonderful life can be when you have a close relationship with God, he'll begin asking questions. But if you won't spend time with Taylor, it's going to be difficult for you to guide him in the proper direction," Miss Addie instructed.

"Me?" Bella wasn't sure she wanted to guide Taylor Manning anywhere, but Miss Addie's plea was heartfelt. "Even though I don't want to go with him tomorrow, I'll do my best," she told the older woman, not wanting to disappoint her.

"Thank you, dear. I think Taylor will be much more apt to listen and learn from someone closer to his own age," Miss Addie said, leaning back in her chair with a sigh. "You know, Taylor is a very lonely young man. The past troubles him. He lost his mother when he was only seventeen. John tells me that he suffered greatly, eventually turning to John for encouragement when his father became more and more lost in his grief."

Bella thought of her mother's grief when her father forced the lifestyle of the Shakers upon them. Her mother's sorrow at being separated from her husband had killed her as sure as anything. As if reading her mind, Miss Addie continued.

"Losing his father was equally difficult. But Taylor felt his father really died the day he lost his wife."

"I saw my mother's own will to live diminish as my father became more and more devoted to the Shakers," Bella admitted.

"Taylor may come across as rather . . ." Miss Addie paused, as if thinking for a word.

"Crass, rude, bossy?" Bella offered.

Addie smiled. "I was thinking more along the lines of independent. He tries very hard not to need anyone, John says. I think the loss of John during these days, however, has impacted Taylor more than he'd like to admit. Since coming to America over a year ago, Taylor has had John to keep him company. I hope you'll do whatever you can to ease his loneliness—for my sake. He seems to genuinely like you, and I think that if you'd allow yourself the luxury, you might very well find him pleasurable company."

"But I'm not looking for pleasurable company, Miss Addie. I've no interest in acting like those girls who are only here to seek out a husband."

"Then what are you seeking, my dear?"

Addie's question pierced Bella's heart. *What am I seeking?* She gave the question some thought for several minutes. The ticking of the clock reminded her that the hour was growing late. "I don't know," she finally whispered. "I suppose I desire to know God better—to better understand His word. I would like to make a comfortable life for myself, and I know for sure it won't always include working at the mill." She met Addie's concerned expression. Feeling the weight of the topic, Bella shrugged it off and gave a light laugh. "I'll accompany Taylor if it makes you happy, Miss Addie."

"I think it would be a very charitable thing—a good thing to do. Just don't tell Taylor you've set him up as a charity case. He would be most grieved. Besides, as I said, I think you very well may be able to reach Taylor for God in a way that might have eluded the rest of us."

"And it will give me an opportunity to further persuade him he needs women on the selection committee of the Mechanics Association," Bella said, giving the older woman a satisfied grin.

That night, Bella took up her Bible. The last thing in the world she wanted to do was join Taylor for an outing and bear him a Christian witness in her kindness and gentle spirit.

"I feel neither kind nor gentle," she murmured, hoping Daughtie, who also was reading her Bible, wouldn't be disturbed.

She glanced up momentarily, seeing the other girls in the room content to chatter about their day. Ruth was draping still-damp stockings over the end of their bed while one of the newer girls, Elaine, shared an animated tale of her life in New York City.

Bella tried to ignore them all and put her mind to reading the Bible. The seventh chapter of Romans led her to a most convicting verse. *"For I know that in me (that is, in my flesh,) dwelleth no good thing: for to will is present with me; but how to perform that which is good I find not. For the good that I would I do not: but the evil which I would not, that I do."*

The good that I should do would be to extend kindness to Taylor, she told herself. *But he's so very smug and self-serving. He irritates me with his manner—or rather his lack of good manners. He isn't very nice, and he speaks whatever he pleases without giving thought to how the other person might feel.*

A voice spoke to her heart. *But you do the same thing.*

The painful truth settled over her. Bella had used her quick wit and ability to speak eloquently to hold many people at arm's length—but surely no one suffered from this as much as Taylor Manning. She swallowed hard. Her own pride was an equal match to his.

She snapped the Bible shut with such vehemence that Daughtie and Ruth immediately looked to her as if to question the problem. Bella smiled. "I didn't realize it was getting so late."

She put the Bible aside and quickly scooted down into the bed and pulled the covers high.

"Good night, ladies," she called out as cheerily as possible while tears trickled down her cheeks and dampened her pillow.

24

Bella, Ruth, and Daughtie walked in the front door of number 5 after returning from church on Sunday. Miss Addie crooked her finger and beckoned Bella into her parlor. "Come see me for a minute, Bella," she requested.

The older woman was carefully removing a decorative pearl stickpin from her hat. "Taylor was quite disappointed because you weren't at the Episcopal church this morning," she reported.

"Was he? I'm surprised to hear he was in attendance." Bella tilted her head slightly to the side and gave Miss Addie a thoughtful look. "I was just thinking—this would be the first Sunday he's been in church since Mr. Farnsworth's departure, wouldn't it?"

Miss Addie appeared amused by the question. "I'm not certain. It appears you've been maintaining a closer watch on his attendance than I. In any event, I would have enjoyed your company this morning."

"Had Daughtie and I not promised Ruth we would attend the Methodist services, you know I would have gone with you, Miss Addie."

"I know, my dear. Now don't let me hold you back from your chores. I want you to be ready for an enjoyable carriage ride, and you needn't worry about the food. Since I suggested the picnic, I'll pack a nice basket for the two of you." She beamed.

Bella returned the smile. "That's kind of you, Miss Addie, but I don't want you to go to any bother. In fact, some bread and a bit of cheese will be plenty."

Miss Addie pursed her lips and made a soft clucking sound. "On with you. Take care of your mending or letter writing or whatever it is you must accomplish this afternoon," she said, shooing Bella from the room. "I'll tend to the food."

Bella slowly climbed the stairs. As the temperature grew warmer with each step, she became thankful that she wasn't on the top floor of the house any longer, where the rooms remained intolerably warm all night during the summer months.

Daughtie was busy writing a letter while Ruth was mending the hem of her skirt when Bella entered the bedroom. "Another letter to Sister Mercy?" Bella asked.

Daughtie glanced over her shoulder and gave Bella an apologetic look as she nodded her head. "I miss her so much."

Her friend's words rekindled Bella's guilt. She doubted that Daughtie was any more comfortable in Lowell than she'd been the week they arrived. "You need not apologize," Bella replied, giving her friend a hug. "I miss her, too. And the children—how I miss each of them."

"Do you remember when we found the bird's nest and little Minnette stuffed tiny pieces of strawberries down the fledglings' throats until they were so full they nearly burst?" Daughtie asked with a giggle.

"And how Eldress Phoebe reduced the poor child to tears by telling her she'd most likely killed the baby birds?" Bella continued.

Daughtie nodded. "Had it not been for Sister Mercy taking Minnette out to see those birds were still alive the next day, I don't think Minnette would have recovered from Eldress Phoebe's tart words. What would she have said had she known of the days we pulled off our shoes and stockings and waded in the creek?"

"I doubt she could have withstood the shock," Bella replied.

"I wonder if anyone else has left the Society since our departure. I do wish I could see some of them again," Daughtie reflected aloud. "Minnette was such a sweet little girl. And the two tiny boys who were always clamoring for you, Bella, toddling about in their oversized butternut breeches and little shirts."

A pang of sadness stabbed at her heart. "Yes. How they missed their mothers. I'm sure they still do." She paused, then wanting to forget the little boys who cried for their mothers, said, "I'd best get busy or I'll not be done with my laundry by the time Taylor arrives."

"So you're going?" Daughtie asked.

"Yes. Miss Addie would be very upset if I backed out now," she explained.

Daughtie gave her a sidelong glance. "I think you want to go. You're beginning to have feelings for him, aren't you?"

Bella attempted to squelch her rising sense of exasperation. "I've already explained this to you, Daughtie. Miss Addie is hopeful Taylor will open his heart to God. She's hoping I can help point him in the right direction."

"The only thing open in Taylor Manning's heart is fulfillment of his own desire," Ruth said with a blush.

"Amen to that," Daughtie replied. "Bella, I fear you're leaving yourself at risk to his scheming ways."

"I'm not afraid of Taylor. Besides, this will be a good opportunity to further plead our case for representation on the selection committee. I plan to find out just how much he's accomplished in scheduling a vote by the Association."

"As you wish, but I doubt he'll remain on that subject for long," Ruth countered.

"I believe I'll go downstairs and begin my laundry. Please don't follow me—I can see you two are in agreement on this issue and I'm rushing off to escape your scolding," she said, giving them a giggle as she walked out the door.

By the time Bella had completed her laundry and mending and had written a letter to Aunt Ida in Concord, there was little time to prepare for her outing with Taylor. Dashing upstairs, she quickly rearranged her hair, slipped out of her gray-striped Shaker work dress, and donned a yellow organdy with embroidered crewel work, one of the gowns Lilly Cheever had given her. A quick glance in the mirror caused her to stop and straighten the lace at one sleeve before rushing downstairs and off toward the kitchen.

Miss Addie gave her a bright smile while tucking a linen cloth atop a basket that appeared to contain more than ample supplies for two people. "I hope the size of that basket indicates that you plan to join us," Bella said with a grin.

"Young men have large appetites. Mintie tells me that no matter how much food she prepares for the men in her boardinghouse, they empty the bowls and ask for more. Besides, I'm sure Taylor hasn't been eating well since John's departure," Addie replied. "Their housekeeper has been ill and still hasn't returned to her duties."

Bella shook her head back and forth. "I doubt whether Taylor Manning will starve. Although I don't think he'd attempt any cooking on his own, I'm certain he'd solicit dinner invitations in order to keep his stomach filled."

"Now, now," Miss Addie clucked.

Bella had just opened her mouth to answer when a knock sounded at the front door. Miss Addie bustled past her, obviously excited to welcome Taylor. Bella lifted the hefty basket, the wooden handle cutting into the fleshy padding of her fingers. She edged down the hallway with the cumbersome container shifting at her side.

Taylor moved toward her and in one fluid motion took the basket from her hand. "Let me help you. You must be anxious to be off," he said, giving her a broad smile.

Bella decided his smile bordered on a smirk. Most likely he truly believed she was fervently anticipating his company. "I'm in no hurry. Did you want to come into the parlor and visit with Miss Addie for a while?" she inquired in her sweetest voice.

He fidgeted for a moment, obviously uncertain how to answer without offending Miss Addie. Bella, on the other hand, was enjoying his discomfort.

"You children be on your way," Miss Addie said, shooing them toward the door and saving Taylor from further uneasiness.

Moving with unusual celerity, Taylor whisked Bella to the carriage, loaded the picnic basket, and climbed up beside her. "My! Suddenly it appears you're in a hurry—or is that my imagination?" Bella inquired with a demure smile as he flicked the reins.

"You did that on purpose!" he accused.

She swallowed hard and sucked in on her cheeks to keep from laughing. "Did what?" she innocently asked.

"You know exactly what I'm talking about," he countered.

Her eyes grew wide as she gave him a questioning look and feigned innocence.

"You intentionally suggested we visit with Miss Addie in the parlor before leaving the house in order to make me uncomfortable," he alleged.

"And you, sir, did the same to me. I returned no more than you gave," she said, giving him a winsome smile.

"I suppose you're right about that," he said, giving her a hearty laugh. "I'm not accustomed to ladies who . . ." He hesitated for a moment, appearing befuddled.

"Ladies who don't care if they keep company with you?"

His eyes darkened as he met her gaze. "You care—you just won't admit it," he replied.

Bella shook her head. "I'll not argue with you. It's obvious you need to feed your ego with such nonsense. Where are we going for our picnic?" she asked, abruptly changing topics.

"I had planned on stopping near Pawtucket Falls, but then Matthew Cheever mentioned a spot that's a bit farther away. He says the view is worth the extra time it takes to get there. Of course, I can't think of a lovelier view than the one I'm gazing upon at this moment."

Bella turned in the opposite direction, her gaze fixed upon the passing countryside. Her cheeks surely resembled two bright red apples. He would enjoy knowing that he'd caused her embarrassment.

"You have no response to my compliment?" he asked.

"No. We both know such talk is inappropriate."

"I spoke the truth. Surely that's not improper."

"What was the topic of Reverend Edson's sermon this morning?" she inquired.

"Let's see—how do I summarize an hour of preaching in one sentence? It is best to perform acts that are in the best interest of the body of Christ, even though such acts may be detrimental to you as an individual. God will honor your obedience. That was two sentences, wasn't it? See there? It took him an hour to say what I told you in less than a minute."

Bella turned in her seat and faced him. "It sounds as though Reverend

Edson's sermon was directed at the people who oppose the school issue," she replied. "Was Mr. Boott present?"

"Indeed he was—at least for a portion of the sermon. However, after the topic became evident, he and his wife got up and walked out of the church."

"No! Surely they wouldn't act in such an offensive manner. Miss Addie didn't say a word about this. Are you making up this story to entertain me?"

Taylor laughed as he pulled the horses to a stop. "This is beyond my story-telling ability. Obviously Kirk Boott doesn't care what other people think. On the other hand, his wife doesn't appear to share his views; she appeared extremely uncomfortable as they left the church," he said as he assisted her out of the buggy.

Bella spread one of Miss Addie's quilts on the nearby bed of grass, then gazed about her. "Mr. Cheever is right. This is a beautiful spot."

"I'll tell him you approve," Taylor replied as he placed the basket between them. "Are you hungry, or would you prefer to take a short stroll?"

"Perhaps we should eat first and take our walk afterward," she suggested as she began unpacking the basket of food. "And you enjoyed the sermon?" she asked.

Taylor gave her a look of confusion. "You do change issues rapidly. I'm going to have to stay on my toes if I'm going to keep up with you," he said with a grin. "I suppose the sermon was as interesting as most. Personally, I don't see the need to talk so long in order to say something people already know."

"Obviously the words bear repeating since people don't live by them," she replied. "And I'm certain Reverend Edson used the additional time to detail his thoughts and point the congregation toward the Scripture he used as the basis for his sermon."

"That's exactly what he did, but please don't ask me to quote the Scripture. I listened to enough of that when I was growing up," he replied absently.

Bella placed a piece of Miss Addie's baked chicken on a plate and handed it to Taylor. "You learned to quote Scripture as a little boy?"

"Um," he said, nodding his head affirmatively as he stuffed a piece of chicken into his mouth and licked a finger. "That's right."

She was amazed at the revelation. A young Taylor Manning committing Scripture to memory was quite difficult to envision. "How did you make the transition from a child reared in a godly home to someone who, who . . ."

"Are you at a loss for words, Bella? Let me help you. Perhaps you were going to say someone who enjoys life? Or someone who enjoys the company of ladies?"

"Or someone who enjoys life by keeping company with nearly married ladies," she snapped. She slapped a hand across her mouth the moment the words slipped off her tongue.

"You seem to know a great deal about my past. I find it charming that you know of my past indiscretions yet you permitted me to call upon you and agreed to accompany me on a picnic to this secluded place," he said while moving closer.

"Stop right there, Mr. Manning," she commanded. "I don't find your actions humorous."

He leaned back against a large maple tree and gave her a wide grin. "Anything else you've been told about me that you'd like to share?"

"No, but I wondered when the Mechanics Association was going to vote on our request to have representatives on the selection committee."

His forehead furrowed in deep creases. "There you go changing subjects again," he said. "But because I'm such a gentleman, I'll answer your question anyway. We'll be voting on that issue soon."

"It seems as if it's taking quite a while for the matter to come to a vote," she said, slicing a piece of cheese.

He picked up an apple and tossed it into the air, caught it, and then pitched it upward again. "These things take time. We presented the proposal at our last meeting, but because of machinery problems at the Merrimack, there were very few members in attendance. It seemed unwise to move forward."

"Until you had enough men there to vote it down?" she asked.

He raised a brow. "That's not what I said. In fact, I've decided having additional representatives would be a good idea, and I think many of the men are in agreement," he replied in a gentle tone before giving her a tender smile.

His words surprised her and she returned his smile. "Thank you, Taylor." She thought of her convictions from the night before. Here she had such grand plans to be all gentleness and kindness, and she'd really done nothing but antagonize Taylor since they'd come out together. Her thoughts were quickly shattered, however.

Before she realized what was happening, Taylor had gathered her into his arms, his lips capturing her mouth. She momentarily struggled against him and then succumbed to the warmth of his embrace.

Moving back ever so slightly, he waited until her eyes fluttered open and then gave a soft chuckle as he cupped her face in his hand. "I knew you'd fall prey to my charms. Even a straightlaced little Shaker girl can't resist me."

His words and actions ignited her anger. Without further thought, Bella drew back her arm and, with all the force she could muster, slapped his face. She gave a self-satisfied nod as red welts began to form along his cheek. Attempting to jump to her feet, Bella dropped back to her knees as Taylor's fingers grasped her wrist.

"Turn me loose," she commanded, wresting her arm from his hold and moving out of his reach.

"Bella! Come back! It'll be dark before long," he called out.

She hurried, relieved to find the narrow road before darkness began to fall. Rushing off had been foolish, yet she wasn't going to abide Taylor's boorish behavior. Gray clouds were moving in overhead, bringing darkness sooner than usual. Without benefit of illumination, she tripped along the rutted path. Twice she twisted her ankle before deciding the grassy area alongside the road might provide more stability.

Soon she could hear Taylor's slowly approaching carriage. Obviously he was looking for her, hoping to rectify the situation he had so callously created. He certainly wouldn't want Miss Addie to find out he hadn't changed a jot since moving to Lowell. Secreting herself among a stand of trees, she pulled her skirts close and peeked around the trunk of a towering elm, watching for his approach. Let him worry. He needed to suffer the consequences of his ill-mannered behavior, she decided.

"Bella!" he called out.

Permitting herself only the shallowest of breaths, Bella flattened herself against the tree and waited until the buggy passed. She remained sculpted in place until the clopping sound of the horses grew faint to her ear. Suddenly she realized how very alone she was.

"You're being silly, Bella," she told herself. "You spent the whole night in the woods before traveling from the Shaker's village to Concord. You are no more at peril here than you were there." The words bolstered her courage. "And look what you've done. You've put that pompous ninny in his place once and for all. God would surely never have expected you to compromise yourself all in hope of sharing the Gospel."

She took only a moment to bask in the delight of having outwitted Taylor before departing her hiding place. The hoot of an owl startled her into movement. Perhaps she should have kept the buggy in sight, she thought as she attempted to remain close to the path. The bushes up the road appeared to rustle. Was it the wind? Her palms grew wet, her breath coming in short, shallow spurts. Her instincts told her to run, yet her feet remained firmly planted. She couldn't make them take flight. There was a sticky dryness in her mouth, a tackiness akin to a sturdily woven spider's web. And in the midst of this fear, why was she remembering the stirrings of Taylor's embrace, the warmth of his kiss? She pushed the unseemly thoughts from her mind, feeling cheap. She'd been nothing more than one of his conquests.

Finally able to force one foot forward, she slowly moved along the path, though she was still unable to allay her increasing terror. *If there is anyone out there, it's Taylor attempting to assure himself I'm going to make it back to town,* she decided. *He's probably still hoping to convince me to remain silent about his behavior. Or possibly he thinks he can frighten me and I'll rush to his carriage. He would certainly enjoy playing the hero!*

Shadowy branches stretched in eerie patterns across the road as a breeze once again whispered through the trees. "I know you're out there, Taylor," she uttered in a trembling voice, realizing her newfound courage had already deserted her.

She was making a futile attempt to pray when her thoughts went careening off in another direction. What about those Irish girls who'd been reported missing? Only last week she'd heard of another one. Most likely those girls had been out alone—just like her. The thought sent a chill coursing down her spine, and her heart began pounding.

Bolting as though she'd been shot from a cannon, Bella heeded her innermost warning. She ran as though the devil himself were on her heels, hysteria nearly overtaking her as she arrived at the edge of town and finally the boardinghouse. She stood on the front step, grasping the door handle while hoping she could avoid prying eyes.

"Thank you, Lord, for getting me home safely," she whispered, trying hard to bring her breathing under control. "Help me now so that I don't have to answer any of Miss Addie's questions."

She opened the door, looking hesitantly into the house. No one was nearby. If she hurried, she might enter and be up the steps before anyone noticed. Drawing a deep breath, she gathered her skirts in one hand and widened the door's opening with the other. *I won't let them see me as the fool,* she told herself. *Let Taylor Manning explain this one.*

~ 25 ~

Taylor knew he would have to find out if Bella had made it back to the boardinghouse safely, but he didn't want to arouse unnecessary suspicion. It had been too late to go the night before. Besides, he knew if he showed up without Bella and she was still out there somewhere on foot, he'd never hear the end of it from Miss Addie.

Why had Bella become so annoyed? Surely she could see how giving in to her feelings for him was better than living a lie. His hope had been to push her into accepting that she felt something for him other than disdain. He'd hoped to convince her . . . convince her of what? He wasn't at all sure. He had to admit there was that prideful side of him that was more than a little bit delighted to have felt her grow yielding in his arms. But there were other feelings that he didn't understand. He felt guilty for having pushed himself on her—guilty for toying with her emotions. But why? Why did he suddenly feel so vulnerable? Taylor decided he would return Miss Addie's picnic basket and see what Bella had told her, since he had a bit of time on his hands before the mills would let out for the day. If Bella had told Miss Addie all that had happened, he was certain to get an earful, but at least the girls wouldn't be around to hear it, as well. And if she had said nothing, then he might get out of this situation without much more than a slap to the face.

With basket in hand, he knocked on the boardinghouse door. Miss Addie opened the door and for a moment looked at him as though he'd grown wings. "Taylor! What brings you here? You haven't had bad news from John, have you?"

He breathed a sigh of relief and held up the picnic basket. "I brought this back. We forgot to return it last night."

"Oh, do come in and have a cup of tea. I have a bit of time, and you can tell me all about your outing with Bella. I'm afraid she must have been very tired when she came home for she went right to bed without a word."

Taylor followed, after allowing her to take the basket. "Now, you sit here in the parlor," she told Taylor. "I'll just take this to the kitchen and bring back some tea and cookies."

Within a few minutes she was as good as her word. Taylor sat uncomfortably on the edge of the settee, still uncertain as to what he might say about the night before. He certainly couldn't lie to Miss Addie.

She smiled and handed him a cup of tea. "Would you care for sugar or lemon? Cream?"

He shook his head. "This is just fine."

"I'm glad you came by. I haven't had any word from John and sometimes I miss him so much. Seeing you is almost as good as having him here."

Taylor took a long drink and tried to think how he might voice his concern about Bella without arousing her suspicions. "So was . . . ah . . . Bella overly tired today?"

Miss Addie laughed. "She didn't appear so. She came home for breakfast and dinner with the other girls but said very little. Did you have a pleasant time together?"

"Not exactly," he said, refusing to tell her the truth. "You know things have never been right between us. She's hated me since she first laid eyes on me." *She especially hates me now,* he thought.

"I don't believe she hates you, Taylor, so much as she dislikes your pride and self-assured nature. You must understand—you two are very much alike. You pride yourselves in needing no one . . . God included."

"Now, Miss Addie, that might be true for me, but Bella is a very godly young woman. She's always praying and talking of her faith and of what God wants for mankind."

"Yes, but she has trouble, just as you do, in believing God can be relied upon and truly trusted. You both need to come to an understanding that there is something more than religious notions when it comes to putting your faith in God."

In the silence that followed, Taylor grew most uncomfortable. He finished his tea and got to his feet. "I should go. I know you'll need to see to supper soon."

Addie followed him to the door but never tried to stop him. "Taylor, your Uncle John and I care a great deal about what happens to you. Please understand that you might put the topic of God off for a good long time, but you'll never be able to put off God himself. He'll always find a way to reach you."

Taylor nodded, saying nothing more. He took up his hat and hurried down the street. What he'd hoped would be a journey to ease his mind and comfort him had only made matters worse.

Ruth rushed in the front door, her face flushed with excitement as she skidded to a halt in the parlor. "Good news, Bella," she announced. "I saw one of the men who attended our meeting at the church. He said the Mechanics Association voted last night, and the vote was in favor of female representation on the selection committee!" she screeched while jumping up and down.

"Are we forgetting how proper young ladies behave?" Miss Mintie inquired as she poked her head out from Miss Addie's private parlor.

"I'm sorry," Ruth apologized. "It won't happen again."

Miss Mintie gave a satisfied nod and disappeared.

"Where did she come from?" Ruth whispered with a giggle.

Daughtie pointed toward Miss Addie's parlor. "She's been visiting with Miss Addie for the last hour."

"Poor Miss Addie," Ruth lamented before quickly changing back to her news. "Are you surprised? Or had Taylor already told you?" she excitedly inquired while dropping onto the chair across from Bella.

"I'm very surprised, Ruth. I knew the men were meeting, but I hadn't heard the results," Bella replied. She forced herself to smile. "This is going to provide the girls with an excellent opportunity."

"The girls? You make it sound as though you're not one of us," Ruth said, giving her a quizzical look.

"Of course I'm one of you. I just don't plan to serve on the committee."

Ruth nodded, seemingly unconvinced. "I see."

"We'll need to arrange a meeting for our own election. I'm sure many of the girls would like to participate," Bella said.

Ruth appeared to contemplate her words before speaking. "I'm surprised Taylor didn't come to the house immediately after the voting was concluded."

"I'm sure he was aware someone would get word to me," Bella hedged.

Ruth leaned forward, propped one elbow on her knee, and rested her chin on her palm. "Yes, but you two are . . ."

"Are what?" Bella snapped.

"Friends?" Ruth ventured.

"Taylor Manning doesn't know the meaning of the word *friend*."

"I see," Ruth replied, standing up. "I'm not certain how many of the girls have heard anything. I'm going to Mrs. Desmond's boardinghouse to visit Sally and the other girls. I promised I'd let them know if I heard the results. When do you think we'll have our meeting, Bella? I'm sure I'll be asked."

"Next Tuesday evening?"

Ruth nodded. "That should give us plenty of time to get word to all of the girls," she said, tying on her bonnet. "Maybe Sally or one of the girls will want to go with me to some of the other boardinghouses. We could stop just long enough to tell one of the girls in each house the outcome of the vote and that we'll be meeting next Tuesday. She could then tell the others in her house."

"That's an excellent idea, Ruth," Bella replied.

Obviously pleased with the compliment, Ruth graced them with a broad smile and waved good-bye.

"I believe I'll go upstairs, Daughtie. I've a letter to write," she said.

"To Jesse?"

Bella nodded. She'd received Jesse's letter five days ago; he deserved a reply.

"You never did tell me what he wrote. Is he happy in Concord? Does he still want to marry you? Or has he decided to return to the Society?"

Detecting the wistful longing in her last question, Bella took Daughtie's hand. "You still want to return, don't you?"

"Not so much as before. I'm beginning to adjust. But if you tell me you're going off to Concord to marry Jesse, then I'll return to Canterbury," she said. "I wouldn't want to live in Lowell if you weren't here."

"Well, you need not worry. I'll not be going off to marry Jesse. It seems he's quite happy in Concord. In fact, he's going to become a partner in the cooperage where he's working."

Daughtie folded her hands and stared wide-eyed at Bella. "My! He's done quite well for himself. Of course, the Brothers always said Jesse was an excellent craftsman, and it appears he's put his woodworking skills to good use."

"He's marrying the cooper's granddaughter," Bella replied flatly.

"What? You're jesting, right?"

"No, it's true. He said that after receiving my last letter, he determined he should move forward with his life—without me."

Daughtie gave her a frown. "What did you say in your last letter?"

"The same thing I told him when he was in Lowell: that I didn't see any more than friendship in our future. And I told him that if he was in love with the cooper's granddaughter, he should ask for her hand."

Daughtie appeared aghast. "Bella! You didn't."

"Yes, that's exactly what I told him. I have no hold on Jesse's future. If he's found love with another, he should marry her," Bella replied.

"Then why must you write? What remains to be said?" Daughtie inquired.

"He told me he would wait to propose until he had my final word on the matter. I must not keep him waiting any longer. It's unfair."

Daughtie was wringing her hands. "Are you certain you want to completely dismiss him from your life?"

Bella glanced toward Daughtie's hands. "I thought you'd broken that habit," she said, touching Daughtie's hands. "I can either dismiss Jesse from my life or marry him. Those are my choices. I certainly can't marry him, so I'll write and tell him I wish him happiness in his marriage to the cooper's granddaughter." Bella stood and walked toward the stairs. "Are you staying down here for a while?"

Daughtie nodded. "Miss Addie's asked me to assist her in making some needle cases once Miss Mintie leaves."

"Needle cases?"

"Yes, Miss Addie saw mine and thought it quite lovely. I told her the needle cases were one of the items that the Sisters made and sold in Canterbury. She thought they would make nice gifts for the ladies in her sewing circle."

"Yes, they will. How very thoughtful of you to help her, Daughtie. I believe I may retire after I finish my letter, so I'll bid you good-night."

"Good night, Bella," Daughtie replied.

Bella climbed the stairs slowly, weighed down by her thoughts of Jesse and Taylor and all that had happened to her since leaving the Shakers. She went to her room, grateful to find it empty. Sitting on the edge of the bed, she reached for her writing paper.

"I don't love Jesse as a wife should love a husband," she whispered. "This is the right thing to do. If I had feelings for him like I have for . . ."

She pushed the thought aside. "No!" She jumped up from the bed. "I won't have feelings for Taylor. I won't give in and be just one more of his conquered ninnies. The man I give my heart to will love me in return. Just me. He won't be given to toying and teasing women. He won't be heartless and rude."

She straightened her shoulders and drew on all of her reserved strength. "He won't be Taylor Manning."

Bella found it impossible to discern whether she was awake or dreaming, certain she'd heard a woman's screams followed by thumping and slapping noises. She scooted up into a sitting position. Leaning against the wall, Bella strained to listen for further unfamiliar sounds. All was quiet.

Then there it was again, a thump against the wall and the sound of a woman crying. The muffled words of a man's angry voice seeped through the walls. He was commanding the woman's silence. Was Mr. Arnold abusing his wife? Bella could think of no other explanation. After all, the Arnolds' place and Miss Addie's boardinghouse shared a common wall. Bella shuddered as she remembered Virginia's comment the day she'd arrived in the weaving room—Mr. Arnold likes pretty girls, she'd said. And then there were the stories from a year or two ago, allegations that Mr. Arnold had abused his wife. Although unconfirmed, rumor was that Lilly Cheever had played a part in rectifying the situation. Bella decided she wasn't going to wait until Mrs. Arnold suffered an irreparable injury before bringing the matter to someone's attention. Besides, if Mr. Arnold was returning to his abusive behavior, he might injure their little daughter. Perhaps Lilly Cheever would be willing to intervene once again.

Too anxious to sleep, Bella hoped Daughtie and Ruth would forgive her for awakening them. She reached down to arouse the girls but found only Daughtie in the bed.

"Ruth's probably gone out back to the privy," Bella murmured. Quickly deciding she would meet Ruth downstairs, Bella quietly padded across the room and down the steps.

A short time later Bella returned to the bedroom, the earlier concern for Mrs. Arnold swept from her mind.

Bella grasped Daughtie's arm and jostled the limp appendage. "Daughtie, wake up!" Bella whispered as loudly as she dared. Daughtie's deep breathing continued. Leaning closer to Daughtie's ear, she again whispered her friend's name.

"What?" Daughtie croaked, attempting to turn away. "I didn't hear the bell."

"The bell didn't ring," Bella whispered. "Ruth isn't in bed." She faltered momentarily. "Did she return home before you came upstairs this evening?"

Daughtie rubbed at her eyes while scooting her body upward. "I don't remember seeing her. She's probably gone out back to relieve herself."

"No!" Bella replied while wagging her head back and forth. "That's why I'm awake. I was just now outside; she's not downstairs and she's not in bed."

"Do you think we should awaken Miss Addie? I don't want to get Ruth in trouble for staying out beyond curfew, but she's never been late before. If she's in trouble . . ." Daughtie's whispered words trailed off into the darkened room.

"She's beyond merely being late, Daughtie. It's probably near time to get up, and you know Ruth isn't one to break the rules. Besides, there's no earthly reason for her to remain out all night."

"Perhaps she has a secret gentleman friend," Daughtie offered.

"I seriously doubt Ruth could keep from telling us if she had a beau. And even if she did, Ruth wouldn't likely break the rules. Besides, her plan was to visit the boardinghouses and advise the girls we'd be having an election, but she couldn't go to any of the houses after ten o'clock."

Daughtie pulled her knees to her chest and wrapped her arms around them. "I know! Maybe she realized she wouldn't make it home before curfew and stayed at one of the other houses."

"Maybe, but I think Ruth would just come home, explain the circumstances to Miss Addie, and take her punishment," Bella replied in a hushed voice.

"You're probably right, but I don't know what else could have happened to her."

"I fear something terrible."

"What could happen?" Daughtie asked in a raspy whisper.

"She could have disappeared—like those Irish girls we've heard about."

"Oh, Bella, don't be histrionic. Those girls disappeared from the Acre. There's never been a problem anywhere else in Lowell. Besides, I heard the girls disappeared in order to hide the fact that they had shamed their parents."

"Daughtie! What a vicious story. Who told you such a thing?"

Daughtie shrugged her shoulders. "Some of the girls in the folding room. I don't know their names, but they said all the Irish girls have loose morals."

"That's as preposterous a statement as saying all the Yankee girls have perfect morals."

"There's no need to become angry, Bella. I'm merely telling you what I've heard. She's probably fast asleep somewhere while you're keeping me awake," Daughtie replied as she plumped her pillow and then lay down.

"Go back to sleep. I'm going downstairs," Bella replied. "I think I hear Miss Addie. It must be near time for first bell."

"Oh no," Daughtie moaned as Bella exited the room and bounded down the steps at breakneck speed. She skidded to a stop only inches before colliding with Miss Addie, who, properly ensconced in a lightweight green-striped wrapper, was making her way toward the kitchen.

Miss Addie gave her a wide-eyed stare, her hand tightly clasped over her heart. "You nearly frightened the life out of me!" the older woman scolded. "I'm on my way out back," she explained. "And you?"

"What time is it?" Bella quizzed.

"Too early to be up scampering about. I think it's close to three o'clock."

"May I wait until you come back inside? I need to talk to you."

"If it can't wait until morning," Miss Addie replied in a tone that suggested she, too, would prefer sleep rather than conversation.

"No, it can't wait," Bella replied, following Miss Addie through the kitchen. When she reached the back door Miss Addie turned to face Bella. "You need not follow me to the privy, Bella. I promise I'll return."

"I'll light a fire," Bella remarked.

Miss Addie's face sagged at the offer. "So this is going to be a long conversation?"

"I'm not certain," Bella replied tentatively. "I thought you might like a cup of tea."

"Not nearly as much as I'd like another hour of sleep," the older woman replied with a feeble smile. She patted Bella's cheek. "Don't look so forlorn. I'll be right back."

Bella nodded. She didn't know if she should start a fire or not but finally decided she'd wait. Perhaps Miss Addie would go directly back to bed after hearing her concerns. If so, there certainly wouldn't be time to lay a fire, much less heat water for tea.

The back door opened and Miss Addie bustled back into the kitchen, obviously more awake than when she'd left moments earlier. "Now, then, what did you need to talk about?" she inquired, pulling a chair away from the small worktable and seating herself.

"Ruth," Bella replied. "She's not in bed."

Miss Addie gave her a look of concern. "She didn't come home tonight?"

"I don't know. I went to bed before the others. Daughtie said she didn't see her come home this evening. I noticed she wasn't in bed when I got up a little while ago. Now I'm worried. She was making stops at boardinghouses last evening to tell them we'd soon be having a meeting to elect delegates for the Mechanics Association committee. I fear some harm may have come to her."

Miss Addie patted her hand. "Let's not panic just yet. She may be sleeping in one of the other rooms. She may have even decided to remain at Mrs. Desmond's for the night. I know you girls do that from time to time," she said with a grin.

"That's true," Bella acquiesced. "I suppose it would be best to wait until morning and see if she appears."

Miss Addie nodded. "There's only an hour until first bell, and we won't resolve much in that short time," she said, giving Bella a comforting smile. "I'm going to return to my room and rest until then. I suggest that you do the same. You're going to be weary." Miss Addie walked her to the foot of the stairs. "Off with you now. Try to get a little sleep," she instructed.

"I will," Bella hesitantly replied, though she would have preferred to remain in Miss Addie's company. Instead, she trod up the stairs and walked to the bedroom, though her steps were heavy and halting. For a moment she remained in the doorway of the bedroom, her gaze lingering on Ruth's unoccupied section of the bed.

One look at Miss Addie's face dashed Bella's expectations. "Nothing?"

"No," Miss Addie woefully reported. "I enlisted Mintie and Mrs. Desmond, and we spent the entire afternoon going to all the boardinghouses. Many of the keepers reported Ruth visited at their houses last night, but she didn't remain very long at any one place. Mrs. Desmond told me that Sally Nelson went along with her but grew weary after an hour and returned home. Sally reported that Ruth appeared determined to continue calling at the boardinghouses until curfew."

"Did Sally say what direction Ruth was headed when they parted company?"

"It seems Ruth called upon the houses on the east side of the street on her way to Mrs. Desmond's house and was calling upon houses on the west side of the street on her return. Of course, she may have gone off onto the side streets along the way. I doubt whether there's any way to track exactly where she was at a specific time. Folks don't tend to remember those little details," Addie replied. "I think we should report Ruth's disappearance to the police. I do wish John were here. He'd know what to do. Did you speak to Ruth's supervisor regarding her absence?"

"He was more angry than concerned, saying his production was already off this week. He said Ruth's absence would only make matters worse for him and unless she had a very good excuse, he'd make certain that she would never be hired again. I told him Ruth was responsible and needed her job, but he wouldn't listen. He thinks she's run off with a man," Bella replied.

Janet Stodemire glanced toward the ceiling and arched her eyebrows. "You're the only one who thinks she's met with foul play, Bella. The rest of us are more realistic. She was very interested in that salesman, but I'm sure you didn't notice," Janet remarked.

Bella's jaw tightened as Janet spoke. "And you don't even know if the salesman was in Lowell yesterday," she argued from between clenched teeth. "I'm willing to appear foolish in order to learn what's happened to Ruth."

"Now, girls, bickering won't solve anything. We need to be unified if we're going to help Ruth," Addie cautioned.

"You're right; I'm sorry," Bella replied.

"It's still early. Why don't we go and pay a visit at the Cheever home? I'm certain Lilly would be pleased to see us, and if Matthew isn't home, she can relate our concerns to him. I think someone from the Corporation should be informed of our apprehension."

Bella jumped up from her chair. "I'll get my cape." She moved swiftly and retrieved her wrap from one of the pegs near the door. Tossing the shawl around her shoulders, she then turned back toward the parlor. "Aren't you coming?"

Miss Addie nodded. "Yes, but I'm not planning on running a foot race," she replied with a grin. "We should be back by nine o'clock," she told the girls who were gathered in the parlor visiting.

Although it was difficult, Bella was forced to slow her stride in order to accommodate Miss Addie. She wanted to run at full tilt rather than promenade down Merrimack Street at a snail's pace. Somehow she needed to expend some physical energy in order to feel as if she were actually doing something to help Ruth. But she knew Miss Addie could walk no faster, and she couldn't rush off, leaving the older woman behind. It seemed an eternity had passed by the time they reached the front door of the Cheever home.

"Miss Addie—and Bella! What a wonderful surprise," Lilly greeted as she opened the front door. "Do come in," she offered, stepping aside to permit them entry. "Let me take your capes," she said. "Matthew, come see who's here to pay a visit," she called out.

Matthew strode into the foyer with a smile curving his lips. "This is an unexpected pleasure," he said, leading them into the parlor.

Addie gave him a bright smile as she followed along. "I hope we're not taking you away from anything important."

"Not at all. I had just completed plans for the dedication ceremony for the Catholic church. I'm hoping it will be a momentous occasion for the Irish folks."

"With you in charge, I'm sure it will be grand. I didn't realize work on the church had been finished," Addie said.

"Sit down, sit down," Matthew offered. "Construction of the church is still in progress, but the only date the bishop is available is the first Sunday in September. So completed or not, we'll have it dedicated on that date."

Lilly placed a hand on her husband's shoulder. "Now, Matthew, no more talk of work. Ladies, make yourselves comfortable, and I'll get us some tea."

"No, we don't need tea, Lilly. Please sit down and relax."

Lilly gave Matthew a winsome smile. "You sound like my husband. He says I'm not happy unless I'm fluttering about."

"She doesn't listen well," he answered, returning her smile before turning toward Addie. "To what do we owe this unexpected visit?"

Addie wriggled forward just a bit. "Actually, it concerns one of my girls,

Ruth Wilson. She attended the tea you hosted. Ruth is fair skinned, her hair a rather mousy brown, and she has—what color are her eyes, Bella?" Addie asked.

Bella furrowed her brow, anxious to give an accurate description. "Gray— yes, cloudy gray. She's rather thin, not very big at all, and her teeth protrude just a bit," Bella explained, looking at Lilly rather than Matthew.

"I remember her. She was quite taken with my garden."

Bella straightened in her chair and bobbed her head up and down. "Yes! That's her. She loved your flowers."

"Well, what about her?" Matthew was obviously ready for the discussion to move forward.

"She's disappeared," Bella proclaimed. "Without a trace."

"What? One of the mill girls has truly disappeared?" he questioned loudly as he stood and began pacing.

"We *think* she's disappeared," Miss Addie said, her voice calm and steady as she revealed the facts of Ruth's departure the evening before and their subsequent efforts to find her.

"So she did have a gentleman caller?" Matthew asked.

"Not last night," Bella quickly replied. "I don't believe he was in Lowell yesterday. At least nobody remembers having seen him since last week. He wasn't due back until the end of the month."

Matthew glanced toward Lilly and then at Bella. "I doubt she would have confided her plans to run away, and I'm sure her suitor would keep himself secreted in order to keep from arousing suspicion."

"I know Ruth, and she didn't run off with a man. Something terrible has happened to her. Why won't anyone help?" Bella lashed out in frustration. "Now I understand how the Irish people must feel when no one will help find their missing girls."

Matthew came to attention at her words. "You think your friend has been kidnapped?" He appeared to think the idea incredible.

"Yes, I do," Bella replied. "She vanished, just like the other girls. She visited a number of boardinghouses last night. Why would she have even bothered to do such a thing if she planned to run off?"

"You have a point," Matthew agreed. "Have you gone to the police, Miss Addie?"

Addie tugged at the lace border of her handkerchief. "No. I wasn't sure what I should do," she said. "Do you want me to go and talk to them?"

"No, I'll go and talk to them. If they want further information, they can stop by the house and talk to you. Bella, did you happen to notice if any of her belongings are missing?"

"All of her belongings are in the room. Nothing has been disturbed," she replied with certainty. "If she'd been running off to marry some salesman, she surely would have taken her clothes and other belongings. Why, she just bought a new pair of gloves," Bella added as though that should sum up the speculation and assure them Ruth had been taken against her will.

"I don't want to be an alarmist, Matthew, but if Ruth has actually been kidnapped, it's not safe for any of us to be out and about at night," Lilly said.

"If you can manage to encourage the girls to travel in groups without causing undue alarm, it would be wise," Matthew said to Miss Addie. "You might want to pass that instruction on to the other keepers, as well."

Bella wasn't certain if Mr. Cheever's words brought a sense of satisfaction or dread. Perhaps it was a strange mixture of both, for a tight knot had now formed in her stomach, and her mouth was curiously dry as she attempted to speak. "So you do think Ruth was abducted."

Matthew gave a one-shouldered shrug and raised his eyebrows. "I'm not certain. But it makes sense to take simple precautions, don't you think?"

"Yes," the three women replied in unison.

"I do believe we should return home," Addie said, obviously taking her cue from Matthew, who was fidgeting with his pocket watch.

"I was just planning to leave, myself. Permit me to take you in the carriage," Matthew insisted as he leaned down to place a kiss on his wife's cheek.

They journeyed in silence, each of them wrapped in disquieting thoughts, until the carriage drew to a halt in front of the boardinghouse. "I plan to stop by the police station on my way home," Matthew assured Miss Addie as he held out a hand to assist her.

"Thank you, Matthew."

"Should any news of Ruth surface, please let me know. I'll do the same," Matthew said before bidding them good-night.

"Any news?" Daughtie inquired as they stepped inside the house.

"No, I'm afraid not. Mr. Cheever is going to talk with the police, though. Perhaps they'll agree to help," Miss Addie replied. "Bella, I'd like to visit with you a moment in my parlor before you retire for the night."

Bella followed Miss Addie and seated herself. "What is it, Miss Addie?"

"I'm probably acting like a foolish old woman, but all this talk of the missing girls has caused me additional worry about John. He said he wasn't feeling well in his last missive, and it's been longer than I expected between letters. I know he's probably fine and my concerns are likely unnecessary," she confided.

Bella took Miss Addie's hand. She wanted to comfort her, yet she respected the older woman too much to spout platitudes. "How may I help?"

"I'm going to pen a note to Taylor and ask if he's heard from John. I was hoping you would deliver it for me," she said. "Of course, you mustn't go alone—but I want your companions to be discreet."

Bella swallowed hard before answering. "I'm sure there are any number of girls who would be pleased to deliver your note to Taylor. Why don't I ask one of them?"

Miss Addie wagged her head back and forth. "No. I don't want all the girls chattering about my personal business. I know you wouldn't breach my confidence. I can't be sure about the other girls. I'm worried, Bella. Won't you do this small thing for me?"

Bella's lips formed a tight line. "You know I would do almost anything for you, Miss Addie. However, I must refuse this request. I can't deliver your note." Her shoulders drooped. She couldn't meet Miss Addie's gaze.

"Something has happened between the two of you, hasn't it?" Miss Addie asked, placing the palm of her hand under Bella's chin and lifting her head until their eyes met.

"Yes." Her voice was a hoarse whisper.

"Tell me, child."

"You remember we went on a picnic?"

"Yes, of course," Miss Addie replied, her eyes filled with concern.

"Taylor's behavior was less than gentlemanly. He kissed me and then laughed, saying I'd fallen prey to his charms. I was so angered by his behavior that I ran from him and walked home alone, and I haven't seen him since. If I go and deliver your note, he's sure to think it's merely a ploy so that I can see him."

Miss Addie's face had gone ashen. She appeared horror-struck by the revelation. "I do believe that young man needs to be taken down a peg or two. Don't you give the delivery of my note another thought! I believe I'll pay our young Mr. Manning a visit tomorrow evening."

~ 27 ~

William Thurston hunkered down in a rickety chair near the rear of Neil's Pub. His gaze remained fixed on the door as he hoisted a tankard aloft. The barkeep nodded and sent a buxom waitress in his direction. The woman leaned forward in order to reveal a bit more of her bosom and gave Thurston an exaggerated wink. She shoved a full tankard in front of him. "See anything else you'd like?"

"No. Get out of the way. I can't see the door."

She leveled a steely glare at him before walking away. He knew she was intentionally obstructing his view of the entrance as she undulated her hips in suggestive movements and sauntered back to the bar. William Thurston knew her type. She wanted him to lose his temper and create a scene, some sort of confrontation that would make her the center of attention. But he wouldn't give her the satisfaction. Instead, he took a drink of his ale and silently seethed.

Jake Wilson and Rafe Walton walked into the pub a few minutes later. They stopped and picked up their drinks before joining William at his table. Jake had already downed half of the dark, stout ale before seating himself.

Rafe pulled a chair away from the table and seated himself. "Your message sounded urgent."

Thurston kept his gaze fixed on Rafe as he leaned forward and rested his arms on the pockmarked wooden table. "Is everything arranged?"

Rafe nodded. "Just as you instructed. Is there a problem?"

"No. I merely wanted affirmation. Let's go over the plan one last time," Thurston insisted. "I worry about him," he continued while pointing his extended thumb toward Jake.

"No need. He'll do as he's told. Come this evening, the Yanks'll be storming the church, all of 'em hoping to walk away with gold lining their pockets or at the very least enough dead Irishmen to assure themselves jobs."

Thurston rubbed his hands together. "This is going to be delightful. If this ruckus doesn't make the Associates take a long, hard look at Kirk Boott and his inability to manage the Irish, nothing will," he said before emitting a malicious laugh. He glanced to his left, where an old Irishman sat staring out the dingy window and nursing a half-empty mug of ale. "Lowell will be better off without the likes of him," Thurston said as he pointed to the old man.

Pushing away from the table, Rafe looked at William. "Are we through?"

"As far as I'm concerned, we're through," Thurston replied. He stood up and edged his way between the tables, the other two men following close behind. Thurston turned toward the two men once they were outside the pub. "I expect you to be merciless. Destroy that church if you must! Do you understand me?"

"Yeah. Now quit your worrying. Everything will go as planned," Rafe replied.

Thurston nodded, turned, and walked off. "It better," he muttered when he was out of earshot.

Liam cleaned and packed his tools into his old wooden toolbox. He'd worked later than usual, but there was no reason to hurry. The Flynns were in Boston for a funeral and wouldn't return until tomorrow. He decided to eat supper at the pub, drink a mug of ale or two, and have a quiet evening at home. He examined the stones he'd laid in the form of a cross only a short time ago and gave a quick nod of satisfaction. The pattern had turned out better than he'd expected.

Ominous-appearing clouds were rolling in, darkening the early evening sky as Liam walked out of the church. For a moment he thought his eyes were deceiving him. An old man was perched atop a pile of granite stacked alongside the church. Liam lifted his arm and hollered, "Good evenin' to ya. How are ya on this fine night?"

The old man hoisted a gnarly walking stick into the air and brandished it about. "Good as can be expected, better'n most," he replied, giving Liam a toothless grin. "Best be gettin' away from that church," he warned.

"And why would that be?" Liam inquired, walking toward the hunched-over figure.

"It's not gonna be safe in there much longer," he replied simply.

Liam flashed him a smile. "I think it's probably safer inside the church than atop that pile o' stone."

The old man shook his head back and forth, wisps of white hair forming a billowy cloud above his head. "There's gonna be a battle happenin' any time now."

No doubt the old man was feebleminded. Yet something forced Liam to continue talking. "What kind of battle?"

" 'Tween the Yanks and us," he replied. "Irish are better at fightin', so it shouldn't take long to finish them off," he cackled in a gleeful voice. "And I'm gonna have the best view."

Liam drew closer. "How'd you come by this piece of information?"

"Some fancy-pants Yank and a couple of his lackeys talking down at the tavern earlier today. Said the Yanks was gonna storm the church and steal the rifles and gold this evenin'."

A shockwave coursed down Liam's spine. He bounded up the pile of rocks and stood towering over the ancient Irishman. "Have you told anyone else about this?"

The old man cowered at Liam's approach. "I told the barkeep once the Yanks left the pub. He spread the word among the rest of his customers. Did I do wrong?"

"No, ya did just fine. Did the men talk as though they were comin' to defend the church?"

"They talked like they was gonna defend the church with every man and boy who could hold a weapon—said they'd be here afore the Yanks arrived. They're gonna hide and surprise 'em," he said in a hushed voice. "Fer all I know, some of 'em may already be hiding in there," he said, pointing his stick toward the church. "I told the barkeep those Yanks might just be talkin' big— might not even show up, but he said we should be prepared."

Liam feared the story was true. After all, it hadn't been so long ago that he'd heard similar talk in the tavern. He glanced over his shoulder at the impressive stone edifice. Only yesterday he'd helped mortar two stained-glass windows into place—gorgeous works of art from a Boston benefactor. The thought of those windows being pelted by stones or bullets struck horror in Liam's creative soul.

He would not stand by and do nothing. "A battle will not serve the Irish well. 'Tis our church and homes that will be pummeled. I'm going to find someone with a voice of reason. Perhaps we can halt this madness before anyone is injured. It would be best to keep the fight away from the church. Tell our men to stand firm at the old stone bridge. They must stop the Yanks before they come into the Acre. With a bit o' luck, I'll be back before the Yanks," Liam told the old man.

"Ya'll need more than the luck of the Irish, me boy. I'll say a quick prayer for ya," the old man replied. He shoved a thin, knobbed hand into the depths of his pants pocket and pulled out a string of wooden beads. The strand dangled from his finger momentarily before the old man took hold of one bead and automatically began his rhythmic litany.

Liam quickly descended the heap of rocks and hurried off toward town. By the time he reached the edge of the Acre, he had only one thought in mind: he must locate Matthew Cheever. Although it was well past the last bell, he would go to the mill first. He hoped Matthew was working late, for it would take five additional minutes to reach Matthew's home. As he neared Jackson Street, he glanced in both directions. There were small clusters of men gathering, moving toward each other as if to join forces. Liam's breath was coming hard; he gasped, inhaling as much fresh air as his strained lungs would permit without slowing his pace.

The iron gate to the Appleton was tightly closed. Liam reached up and pulled the dangling rope hanging from the gate bell. He clanged it hard and waited, his face pressed against the cool metal gate, willing Matthew to appear. Again he clanged the bell, long and hard. He continued yanking the rope, determined to stir Matthew to attention if he was nearby.

"What's going on?" Matthew shouted as he rounded the corner of the countinghouse and hurried toward the gate. "Liam?"

"Aye. There's a problem, Mr. Cheever! Hurry!" Matthew shoved a key into the gate and pulled open the cumbersome barrier. "Ya've got to come with me," Liam commanded, grasping Matthew's arm. "There's an uprisin' between the Yanks and Irish. I fear it will already have begun by the time we reach the Acre."

Matthew's forehead furrowed into deep creases, causing his eyebrows to settle into parallel strips of concern. "Settle yourself, Liam, and tell me exactly what has happened."

"I'll explain while we walk," Liam insisted. "There's no time to waste." Unwilling to stand idle, he continued tugging on Matthew's arm, pulling him along as he explained the old man's warning. "Should Mr. Boott be informed?"

Matthew shook his head back and forth. "He's in Boston," he explained. "And you think the battle is imminent?"

"I've never seen groups of men gatherin' together with their weapons in Lowell until today," Liam replied. "I fear they'll destroy the church, or worse yet, there will be deaths and injury on both sides."

"You believe your people are ready to fight?"

"I don't know. I'm hopeful Hugh is aware of what's happenin' and has called for level-headedness among the Irish. I left word that if the Irish arrived first, they should attempt to hold the Yanks at the bridge."

Before Matthew could respond, a volley of shots rang out. The men glanced at each other and immediately increased their pace, the street dust billowing from under their pounding feet. They rushed onward until the church was finally in sight. Yanks armed with weapons stood at each corner of the building. One of them yelled out a warning and leveled his rifle as Matthew and Liam approached.

Liam's face was lined with concern. "It appears the Yanks crossed the bridge and took siege of the church before the Irish even arrived."

Matthew nodded. "It would appear that way," he said as they neared the church. "Thomas Lambert, you'd best aim that weapon somewhere besides my belly," Matthew shouted.

"Don't you get in the middle of this, Matthew!" the man hollered back.

Liam and Matthew slowed their pace but continued moving closer to the church. "What's going on here?" Matthew asked.

"Nothin' that we can't handle without interference by the Corporation," Lambert replied.

In front of the church, men's voices mingled with the sound of breaking stone. "I'm going in there," Matthew defiantly announced. "And you'd best not attempt to stop me, Thomas."

Immediately Thomas moved to block the door. "I wouldn't . . ."

Matthew pushed him aside. "Quit acting like a fool, Thomas," he growled. "Come with me, Liam."

Liam followed, his shoulders squared and head high. He wondered if Thomas Lambert would shoot him in the back. "What are we doin'?" Liam whispered.

"Getting these men out of the Acre before there's a bloody battle," Matthew replied.

It took a silver tongue, along with several threats, to finally convince the men to leave. Liam wasn't certain whether it was Matthew's words or the realization there was nothing of value hidden in the church that dislodged the men, but at last they began filing out of the building. Unfortunately, at that same time the inhabitants of the Acre began to descend upon the church with picks, shovels, rocks, and rifles in hand.

"Matthew!" Liam shouted. He pointed in the direction of the crowd.

"Do you see Hugh among them?"

"Not yet, but I'll try and stop them," Liam replied. He rushed toward the crowd, waving his arms above his head. "Hold up! I need to talk to ya!" he shouted as he drew closer.

"Out of the way or we'll trample ya," a voice in the crowd cried out.

"Hugh! Hugh Cummiskey! Are you among these men?" Liam shouted.

"Right here," Hugh replied, waving a rifle in the air.

Liam rushed alongside Hugh, explaining Matthew was with the Yanks. "It appears everything is under control," Liam said. "Ya need to stop the men before they confront the Yanks, or there may be bloodshed. I know ya don't want that to happen, Hugh."

Hugh held up his arm and halted the men not far from the church. "If they've damaged our church, and I suspect they have, the Yanks had best get busy with repairs," Hugh told Liam. "What's your stake in this matter? You sidin' with the Yanks?"

Liam held his anger in check. "Ya'd be knowin' better than that, Hugh. I'd rather see this resolved peaceably. Surely ya feel the same."

Hugh nodded. "I do, but the Yanks started this fight, and they need to pay for their actions."

"You're the voice of reason for the Irish, Hugh. Tell them to settle themselves and listen to what Matthew has to say. Matthew knows it's not the Irish that have caused this upheaval, and he'll not be speakin' ill of them."

Hugh hesitated for a moment, then spoke to the men. There were a few murmurs of dissent, but the majority of the men appeared relieved they'd not have to do battle this night. They moved forward with Hugh and Liam in the lead until they stood opposite the Yankees.

Matthew stood on the top step of the church, looking down upon the segregated groups and then turned his attention to his fellow Yankees. "You men have embarrassed yourselves this night with your irrational behavior. I don't know who or what convinced you to act in such a manner, but I'd appreciate some insight."

The men glanced back and forth among themselves until finally one of them confessed that they had expected to find gold and weapons hidden in the church.

"And why on earth would you believe such nonsense? Why would these people be amassing weapons?" Matthew questioned.

"We heard talk that the Irish were storin' up weapons and money in order to attack Lowell and take over the mills," one of the men reported.

"Does that really seem plausible? Knowing that almost all of these men send money back to Ireland to help support their extended families, just how much gold do you think they could accumulate? Someone planted an evil seed among you, and you embraced it. In fact, you watered it and watched it take root. There's no denying the differences between our people, but attacking one another, destroying property, and believing the worst of each other is not God's design for us."

"You don't know what they're capable of," one of the men called out from the Yank side of the group. "They perform sacrifices and all manner of evil. That's probably what happened to their missing girls."

This created an angry surge of comments from the Irish.

"Ya don't know what ya're talkin' about, Yank."

"Ya're daft in the head. That's the kind of talk that gets men killed."

Matthew raised his hands to calm the crowd. "You know, you fellows remind me of a story. Once there was a farmer who had a jack mule and a gelding bay. He found it necessary, for the sake of plowing his field, to yoke the two animals together. Each morning he took the animals to the field, where they steadily pulled the plow, until one day he started experiencing problems. The mule wanted to pull left and the gelding wanted to pull right. Try as he might the farmer couldn't get them to work together. With his field unplowed, the farmer had no choice but to quit for the night and hope he might have better luck the next morning.

"In the meanwhile, the mule and the gelding had their own conversation. The mule told the gelding that he was a horse and horses were notoriously uppity and full of self-regard. The mule said he wasn't about to work with anyone who lived in a fancy barn and ate from a fancy trough.

"The horse was equally offended. 'You're just a lazy mule. You lay about the field all day, eating here and there, never making yourself useful at all until the master actually puts a yoke on you and forces you into work. You're dirty and smelly and totally useless.'

"The next day, the farmer tried again to put the mule and horse together, but neither one would have any part of it. They bucked and brayed, whinnied and kicked. Finally the farmer had no choice but to take the jack mule back to the barn and then proceed to plow the field with the gelding alone. The horse labored under the strain, and by noon he was spent and the farmer exchanged him for the mule. By night the mule, too, was exhausted."

Liam saw that Matthew had the attention of every man in the audience. "When the mule and horse came together, they realized that their stubbornness had caused them to bear the entire burden of responsibility on their own. There was no one else to share the load, so they pulled the plow alone. And all because they refused to work as a team."

"Are you saying the Irish are mules?" a man called out.

Liam couldn't tell if it had been an Irishman or a Yank who'd asked the question. Matthew chuckled. "Not at all. My father used to tell this story to my brother and me whenever we fought. The whole point I want to make here is that we need not let our cultures and backgrounds separate us. Neither should our religious beliefs and worship practices. If we allow issues to separate us, we'll be just like the mule and the horse—pulling the full weight of responsibility all alone. We aren't perfect and neither is religion. God alone is perfect, and He calls us to be at peace with one another. To love our neighbor as ourselves."

Liam saw the men around him relax a bit, their expressions conveying a certain understanding. Matthew was smart—Liam had to give him that. He approached these people by bringing something bigger than themselves to the table. Matthew Cheever didn't bother with threats of the supervisors or the Boston Associates, however. He went straight to the heart of it. He went to God.

"God would see His people work together—to encourage and lift each other up. The Bible says that we should esteem others as better than ourselves. Would you men deny the Word of God—reject its truth?"

The audience remained completely silent. Matthew nodded. "I thought not. Now I'd like for all of you to return to your homes. There's no cache of guns or gold. There are no plans to ruin the church. Go home and sleep off your anger."

One by one the crowd dispersed until only Liam, Matthew, and Hugh remained.

"I didn't think you'd manage to keep the peace here, but I'm glad you did," Hugh commented. "I'll bid you good-night and see to it the rabble-rousers get to bed instead of the pub."

Liam waited until Hugh had gone before he turned to Matthew. "It seems that you hold great stock in this issue of God and what He wants for His people."

Matthew smiled. "I do indeed."

"And ya're believin' that God truly cares about the people on earth—that He'd be listenin' to our prayers?"

"I do."

Liam shook his head. "Why? What has God ever done to prove this to ya?"

"He's answered my prayers," Matthew replied. "He's not always said yes when I'd have liked Him to, but He's blessed me in many ways, and I honestly believe this is the result of His love and concern for me as an individual."

"But why would God be givin' us any more consideration than He gives the beasties in the field?"

Matthew smiled. "I believe the Bible when it says we're made in God's image. I believe He did that because He desired fellowship with us, Liam. I believe God desires our love and adoration, our worship and praise. I believe we're here on this earth to serve Him first and foremost, and the best way we can do that is by serving each other."

The words made more sense to Liam than his mother's superstitions and his church's threats. "I'd like to be thinkin' on this for a time. Do you suppose we might be discussin' it again?" Liam questioned.

Matthew grinned. "I'd like that very much."

28

Addie's cheeks were flushed bright pink as she tucked a damp wisp of graying hair behind her ear and hurried from her warm kitchen to the front door. The pounding at the front door was continuous.

"Patience! I'm coming!" she called, unable to hide her irritation as she pulled open the door. "Yes?"

A small woman with doelike eyes stood clinging to the arm of a stout, dour-appearing man. "We're Mr. and Mrs. Wilson—Ruth's parents," the man said.

"Adelaide Beecher. Pleased to make your acquaintance," Addie replied. "Please excuse my appearance; I've been busy in the kitchen." She stepped aside and gestured them into the foyer. "We can visit in the parlor," she said, leading the way.

The couple perched side by side on the larger of the two overstuffed settees and stared at Miss Addie. Then Mr. Wilson cleared his throat and leaned forward, his forearms resting upon his bulky thighs. "What time will our daughter return from the mill?" he asked.

Addie's mouth involuntarily dropped open, and it took a moment for her to regain her deportment. "The girls will be home in less than an hour. I was busy preparing supper when you arrived," she replied. "Did someone from the mill contact you?" Addie haltingly inquired.

"From the mill? No. Why should someone from the mill contact us? We're here to fetch Ruth home," Mr. Wilson explained.

Addie stared at them, suddenly unsure how to proceed. Truth was always best, but it was obvious Mr. and Mrs. Wilson were ill prepared for the news she would soon give them. "Did Ruth write that she wanted to come home?" Addie hedged.

"No. Her letters were always quite happy—content, you might say," Mrs. Wilson answered. "But I need her at home right now. I wrote and told her we'd be coming so she could give her proper notice at work."

"I see," Addie replied. She prayed God would give her words to ease the pain these unsuspecting parents would soon feel. "There is no easy way to tell you this . . ." she began.

Like a guard dog hearing an intruder, Mrs. Wilson perked to attention.

"Has something happened to our daughter?"

"Ruth has disappeared," Addie replied in a hoarse whisper. "We thought, rather, we wanted to believe that Ruth had returned home. Obviously we were wrong. Ruth has disappeared."

Mrs. Wilson's eyes grew wide. She pounced across the room and grasped Addie's hand in a death grip. "What do you mean? How could she disappear?" she quizzed, her voice abruptly warbling into a high-pitched squeal. But before Addie could answer, the harried woman bounded back across the room to her husband's side. "I told you something was wrong." Her accusatory words permeated the room. Mr. Wilson's stern expression faded in the wake of his wife's indictment.

"Perhaps you could give us more particulars," Mr. Wilson suggested. He encircled his wife's shoulder and shushed her as though she were a small child.

Addie nodded. Her gaze remained fixed on Mrs. Wilson as she recounted the few details surrounding Ruth's disappearance. It seemed a paltry bit of information to give two devastated parents who had come seeking a reunion with their oldest daughter, yet there was nothing more she could add. She said it all in a few brief sentences.

Mr. Wilson's cold, hard exterior appeared shattered by the details, or lack of them—Addie wasn't certain which. Mrs. Wilson sat coiled beneath her husband's protective arm, her eyes glazed with grief.

"Has anyone contacted the police or sheriff?" Mr. Wilson questioned.

Addie glanced at Mrs. Wilson. The woman appeared fragile, as though one more gloomy report would shatter her delicate exterior. "They talked to us, but it is their opinion Ruth ran off with a gentleman friend," Addie replied hesitantly.

Mrs. Wilson slid from under her husband's protective wing. "Ruth has a beau? She never mentioned a man in any of her letters."

"Well, I didn't think it was anything serious. He's a young salesman who called on her when he was in Lowell on business. I believe they went to dinner on a couple of occasions and he visited with her here in the parlor. They may have attended a few church functions, though I'm not altogether certain. I've questioned all of the girls who live here. Ruth hadn't mentioned that she had any plans to elope or that she was even interested in marrying the young man. I told the police I didn't believe Ruth had run off with him. She's a bright girl with a good head on her shoulders. Besides, I don't think she would intentionally worry you."

"Nor do I," said Mrs. Wilson. "Perhaps we need to go and talk to the police," she suggested to her husband.

"I think you should stay here and rest. I'll go," Mr. Wilson replied. "I'm sure Miss Beecher wouldn't mind if you rested in the parlor until I return."

"Of course," agreed Addie. "You're more than welcome."

"No," Mrs. Wilson adamantly replied. The feather decorating her outdated hat danced overhead as she shook her head back and forth. "I'll be overly anxious if you insist I remain behind."

"As you wish," her husband replied. "Thank you for your kindness, Miss Beecher."

"Will you return after talking with the police? I'd appreciate knowing of any progress."

"Yes, we'll be certain to return," Mrs. Wilson agreed.

Addie fidgeted with her handkerchief as she walked Mr. and Mrs. Wilson to the front door. "Would you like me to pack Ruth's belongings so that you may take them home with you?" She couldn't bear to look at Mrs. Wilson while awaiting an answer. "I hope you'll forgive me. I realize my question appears insensitive, but the Corporation has advised me they'll be sending Ruth's replacement to board with me. The new girl will need space for her belongings."

Mr. Wilson glanced toward his wife. "Thank you for your offer, but we don't want to impose. We can pack her things," he said.

"Tell you what—if there's time before you return, I'll do my best to have things prepared. If not, I'll help you when you return."

"Fair enough," Mr. Wilson replied.

Mrs. Wilson's dark brown eyes were wet with tears. "Taking her belongings makes it seem like we're never going to see her again."

"I don't think that's true," Addie quickly replied. "I'm sure Ruth will be in touch with us soon."

"I pray she will," Mrs. Wilson whispered.

Addie watched the Wilsons walk down the street, her gaze turning heavenward when they turned the corner and were out of sight. The clouds were hanging low and gray, hiding any patch of blue from sight. It might rain after all, she decided, closing the front door and then scuttling off to the kitchen. She'd best hurry or supper wouldn't be on the table when the girls arrived home.

Working with diligence, Addie carved generous pieces of ham and arranged them on a platter. Fortuitously, she'd placed the kettle of potatoes to boil over a low fire before the Wilsons' arrival and had set the table after the noonday dishes had been washed and dried, a timesaving trick Lilly Cheever had taught her years ago. It wouldn't take long to cream the potatoes with some nice fresh peas she'd shelled early this morning, and she'd open several jars of her canned apples. The girls liked them sprinkled with a dash of cinnamon and nutmeg.

Addie finished slicing loaves of freshly baked bread and was carrying large serving platters of ham to the table as she heard the familiar sound of the girls coming in the front door.

"I'm a bit off my schedule. Just give me a minute," she said before rushing back to the kitchen.

"Did Miss Mintie come visiting this afternoon?" one of the girls inquired with a chuckle as Addie carefully carried a large platter of ham into the dining room.

"No, but I did have visitors. Ruth's parents arrived in Lowell this afternoon," she told the girls.

Silence. For just a moment it was as though all of them had stopped breathing, but an endless barrage of questions immediately followed the short-lived quietude. They wanted details of Ruth and her parents. Addie wished there were more she could tell them, wished she could say that Ruth had merely gone home for an unexpected visit and was now back, safely in the fold. But she couldn't.

"There's nothing much to report. Ruth's parents haven't heard from her, either, and they've gone to talk to the police. They promised to stop back after supper. Perhaps they'll have something more to tell us upon their return," Addie replied before returning to the kitchen to retrieve two brimming bowls of creamed potatoes and peas.

The girls moved on to other topics as the meal progressed, and it wasn't until the Wilsons arrived later in the evening that the subject of Ruth once again became fresh. The girls surrounded the Wilsons, all of them interested to hear any shred of news. Addie feared the sight of Ruth's housemates would overwhelm Mrs. Wilson. It appeared, however, she found some sense of comfort seeing their youthful faces filled with anticipation.

"I expected to be back earlier, Miss Beecher," Mr. Wilson said as he took the steaming cup of coffee Miss Addie offered. "Our visit with the police was of little assistance. They were dismissive, telling us they didn't believe there was any foul play surrounding Ruth's disappearance. I confronted them with the fact that we knew some Irish girls were missing. He suggested that perhaps Ruth had gotten into trouble—in a family way—and didn't want us to know."

Mrs. Wilson nodded in agreement as her husband spoke. "I was disquieted by their lack of interest in Ruth's disappearance, but the police are even less concerned about the Irish girls. The policeman said the Irish girls were never officially reported missing. He even went so far as to say the girls were probably just hiding from a heavy-handed father and now they're even more afraid to return home. I find their attitude appalling," she added.

"Yes, it's pitiable," Addie agreed. "And so you are no further along than when we parted earlier today?"

"It appears the police have done nothing to find Ruth. However, just as we were preparing to leave our meeting with the police, a lady came in and reported a missing boarder. It seems this girl worked at the Hamilton Mill. She had gone out alone last evening and was seen purchasing some ribbon in town.

Later in the evening she was seen by some girls who said they'd observed her walking toward home, but the keeper said she never arrived."

"Dear me!" Miss Addie exclaimed. "I'm going to want to keep my girls under lock and key. Did the police appear alarmed by this latest report?"

"They said they would look into it, but somehow I didn't believe them, so I asked if they had talked with anyone from the mills regarding Ruth. One of the policemen mentioned a man named Matthew Cheever. I located his address and took the liberty of calling upon him at his home," Mr. Wilson explained.

The idea of Mr. and Mrs. Wilson calling at the Cheever home, uninvited, took Addie by surprise. "Were you kindly received by Mr. Cheever?" she inquired.

Mrs. Wilson nodded her head up and down. "Oh yes, and he has a lovely wife. She was most sympathetic to our plight."

"When I mentioned the new report of a girl missing from the Hamilton, Mr. Cheever appeared quite alarmed. He was on his way to the police station when we departed his home. I told him that we couldn't remain in Lowell."

"We have other children at home and the farm to look after," Mrs. Wilson quickly interjected.

"He's promised to keep us informed and said that if the police are reluctant to investigate further, he will hire a private investigator. He's going to go talk with a man named Hugh Cummiskey in the Irish part of town and see if any of the Irish girls have reappeared. I believe he will keep his word," Mr. Wilson added.

"Mr. Cheever is a good man," Addie concurred. "I'm glad he's agreed to move forward with the investigation. Will you folks be leaving soon?"

"Early tomorrow morning. We're staying at the Wareham Hotel tonight," Mr. Wilson said.

"Two of Ruth's friends helped me gather her belongings. I've put them in my parlor. If you'd rather wait until morning . . ."

"No, we'll take her things tonight," Mr. Wilson replied. "I left our address with Mr. Cheever. He's promised to contact us the moment there's any word, although he didn't expect any immediate results."

Addie led them across the hallway to the parlor and then, for the second time in one day, bid Mr. and Mrs. Wilson farewell.

Addie remembered only after they'd gone she had unfinished business with Taylor Manning. The very thought of him stepping out of line with one of her girls was enough to fuel her with newfound energy.

"I'll return shortly," she told Margaret.

"Aren't you afraid of going out alone? Maybe one of us should go with you," Margaret suggested.

"No," Addie replied, putting on her bonnet. "I'm not worried that some-one will attack an old woman like me." After all, she was forty-eight. With that she picked up her shawl and exited the house. The less said the better—for Bella's sake and for her own.

John's house wasn't all that far, only a matter of blocks. The walk in the night air gave Addie strength for the words she had to say. She had thought Taylor might stop by the boardinghouse as he'd done the day he'd returned the picnic basket. *Oh, if only I'd known his actions then,* she fumed, *I would have set that young man straight then and there.*

She approached the house, and seeing that a light shone from the parlor window, she knocked. *Lord, help me to deal with this boy in a reasonable but firm manner. Let him see the error of his ways.*

The door opened and a rather ragged-looking Taylor Manning stared back at her. "Miss Addie?"

"Taylor, we need to talk. There is the none-too-small matter of the liber-ties you took with Miss Newberry."

Taylor paled. "Come in. I figured that sooner or later Bella would tell someone."

Addie stepped into the house. "Taylor, how could you? Your uncle told me of your philandering ways, but how could you take liberties with a girl such as Bella? She's made her opinions of you very clear."

Taylor shrugged. "I suppose that was part of the attraction, but believe me, Miss Addie, I've been wracked with guilt. I know what I did was wrong, and for once I really care about it—but I don't know what to do."

Addie softened, feeling sorry for the young man. "Taylor, women and their feelings are not to be trifled with. You know better than most, having grown up in England, where the women have few choices but to take a hus-band or labor as someone's slave. Here young women are encouraged to make a living for themselves, and the girls who work for the mills are the lucky few who enjoy such freedom.

"Still," she continued, "you knew that Bella had no interest in hunting a husband and yet you pursued her."

"I know," Taylor said, pushing back his blond hair. "But there's something about her."

"Forbidden fruit?"

"No, it's more than that. Bella has a spirit to her that seems more open and honest than other women. Perhaps it's because she's the first woman I've ever met who didn't play games with me and fall at my feet when I offered her a soft word and appreciative glance."

"But relationships are built on far more than that," Addie answered. "Bella has been deeply wounded by the men in her life, and you've done nothing but perpetuate that problem."

"I honestly didn't mean to, Miss Addie. I kissed her and would have done nothing more. Please believe me. I wouldn't have pressed her for anything."

Addie nodded. "I suppose I do believe you. Still, you hurt her, and you need to make amends."

"But how? She won't see me."

"I think you'd better start with a reckoning of your soul. Taylor, you wouldn't even begin to act in such a manner if God were guiding your heart. I'd rather not have to be so bold on this issue, but Taylor, every man and woman is called to account before God. Without an acceptance of Jesus Christ as Savior, they will make that accounting alone." Taylor said nothing, so Addie pressed home her point. "Jesus died for your sins long before you were even born, Taylor Manning. He longs for you to come to Him and to seek forgiveness and rightness before Him. You're the only one who can make that choice. John can't do it for you, although he would in a heartbeat if only he could. I can't choose that way for you and neither can Bella. But, Taylor, mark my words: by rejecting what I'm saying—by rejecting Christ—you're making your choice. And that choice will only lead to certain destruction."

~ 29 ~

Matthew had seen the look Lilly leveled in his direction as the Wilsons detailed the plight of their missing daughter and then began telling of an additional missing girl who worked at the Hamilton Mill. Instantly, he knew there would be no peace in his household without another visit to the police station. Truth be told, he believed Ruth Wilson would return to Lowell on the arm of her salesman with a wedding ring on her finger. And the same could likely be said about the recently reported missing girl from the Hamilton. However, he wasn't about to further upset the Wilsons—or Lilly. Knowing there could be no delay, Matthew abandoned the rest of his leisurely evening for the company of policemen who likely would become offended when he began questioning their inability to solve the puzzle of Ruth's disappearance.

He entered the small brick building that sported two small iron-barred cells, an unpleasant reminder of the consequences associated with the town's growth. Martin Hensley waved him forward. "I sincerely hope you've not come to discuss missing girls," he warned. "I've had enough of that nonsense for one evening."

"I'm afraid that's exactly why I'm here, Martin. What makes you believe it's all nonsense?" he asked, hoping Martin would give him something tangible to support his argument.

"Aw, come on, Matthew. These girls take a fancy to some fellow, and next thing you know they skedaddle out of town, get married, and have themselves a passel of babies. What's so different about these girls? We know the Wilson girl had a beau. I'm checking on the gal from the Hamilton, but it'll probably be the same thing."

"What's her name—the one that works at the Hamilton?"

"Hilda Beckley. Don't know much else. Figure I'll go over there come morning. With a little luck maybe she'll have returned."

"Don't get your hopes up, Martin. I understand there are several Irish girls missing. What information do you have on them?"

"None. Nobody ever came in and talked to me. Far as I'm concerned, there aren't any girls missing from the Acre."

"But you know there are—and people are beginning to get a little apprehensive with all this talk of disappearing girls. I think you'd best make some effort so folks settle a bit. It will affect the local businesses if the girls are afraid to leave the boardinghouses. I'd like to have your word you'll treat these disappearances as abductions rather than runaways."

Martin grunted. "I'll see what I can do," he said and immediately went back to cleaning his gun.

Obviously Matthew had been dismissed. He clicked open his pocket watch and then walked out of the building, deciding he'd pay a visit to the Acre before heading home. Perhaps Hugh would be at the pub. If not, their visit would wait until morning. It was certainly too late to go calling at Cummiskey's home.

Wending his way through the mucky streets of the Acre, Matthew arrived at the pub shortly after nine o'clock. The shouts and laughter of drinking men overflowed into the street long before he arrived at the door. But surprisingly, there were few patrons at the bar. Instead, they appeared to be congregated toward the back of the room, most of them circling one table and hollering out instructions.

"Appears you've got some entertainment going on back there," Matthew commented to the barkeep.

The man nodded. "Arm wrestlin'. What's your pleasure?"

"I'm looking for Hugh Cummiskey. Does he happen to be here?"

The barkeep eyed him critically. "Who wants to know?"

"I'm Matthew Cheever—a friend."

The barkeep emitted a grunt before pointing toward the table. "He's back there with the rest of 'em."

Matthew thanked him and moved toward the crowd. Circling the outer perimeter of men, Matthew edged a bit closer. Two men were battling each other in a fierce arm-wrestling match. A pile of gold coins lay on the table awaiting the victor. Matthew ceased searching the crowd as his gaze fell on one of the participants. Before him sat a shirtless, sweating, seemingly drunk William Thurston fighting to take down the arm of another man.

Astonished by the sight, Matthew found it impossible to look away. Thurston was hurling insult upon insult while attempting to push his opponent's arm to the table. Matthew felt himself being shoved toward the action as the crowd tightened. He was now standing to one side of Thurston, the man's beefy arm in full view. Matthew's breath caught in his throat as he stared at a prominent mushroom-shaped birthmark on William Thurston's right arm.

Without warning, someone grabbed his shoulder. "Now, what would you be doing in the Acre at this time of night?"

"Hugh," he said, relief flooding his being. "I came to talk to you. The barkeep said you were amongst the crowd," he explained.

"Come on over here," Hugh said, pushing several men aside to make a path. "There's plenty of tables available with everyone crowded over there to watch William Thurston make a fool of himself."

"Seems William's in the Acre every time I make a visit," Matthew commented, looking back toward the table. "Is that J. P. Green over there? I wonder what in the world he would be doing here."

"I don't know. Mr. Green has begun coming down here occasionally. Mostly when Thurston is sniffin' about. They appear to be on friendly terms. Now, Thurston is another story. He spends a great deal of time in and about the Acre. For a man who hates the Irish, he certainly seems to find something that pulls him back here all the time. What problem is it that brings you here?" he asked.

"Why do you think there's a problem?"

"Come now, Matthew. You wouldn't be in the Acre at this time of night unless there was some kind of problem brewin'."

Matthew nodded. "You're right, of course. I was hoping you could fill me in on any information you might have regarding some missing girls—missing Irish girls. The police tell me no one has filed a complaint with them, but it seems to be common knowledge around town."

Hugh nodded. "I went and talked to the police after the first ones disappeared. They said the girls probably ran off to get married or were hiding out somewhere in the Acre because they feared their drunken fathers. I've finally accepted the fact that they're not going to do anything, and so I haven't reported any disappearances beyond the first three. Personally, I think they're pleased to hear when our numbers decrease."

Matthew's eyes grew wide. "First three? How many have disappeared?"

"Seven so far—at least seven that I know about. There may be more."

His stomach lurched. "Seven! And none of these girls' parents can explain why their daughters are missing?"

"No, although they were all comely lasses—at least that's my opinion. I don't know that the police would agree with that view."

Matthew remained silent. Now that he was armed with more information, he wasn't sure what to do. He could feel Hugh's gaze upon him. Finally he looked up and met the Irishman's stare. "I'll do something, Hugh. I don't know how or what, but we've got to get to the bottom of this and find these girls. Bring me a list of the girls' names, along with the names of their parents, tomorrow morning."

"Thank you, Matthew. I appreciate your willingness to help. I'll get the list to you first thing in the morning."

Matthew pushed back from the table, stood, and shook Hugh's hand.

"Not interested in watching the remainder of the wrestling match? It's best out of five," Hugh said with a lopsided grin.

"I think I'll pass on that offer. To be honest, I find William's behavior rather disgusting."

Hugh gave a resounding laugh. "So do I. However, I enjoy watching him lose his money," Hugh said as he walked with Matthew to the door. "I'll stop by your office with a list of names in the morning."

Matthew nodded his agreement and stepped out into the street. An angry-sounding dog barked in the distance as he hurried out of the Acre. Slowing his pace, Matthew considered what Hugh had told him. Seven girls. What could have happened to them? It couldn't possibly be a coincidence. And now Yankee girls were disappearing. Certainly there was a greater risk attached to these latest abductions. Since the Irish girls had been kidnapped without causing any stir from the police, it was little wonder the abductions had continued. He needed to devise a plan, and it was obvious the police weren't going to be helpful.

His thoughts shifted to William Thurston sitting at the marred wooden table with his sweating hefty arm exposed—and that birthmark, an exact replica of the birthmark Lewis, Lilly's brother, had described to Lilly as he lay dying. Why, Matthew wondered, did William Thurston spend so much time in the Acre? It made no sense that a man who constantly denigrated the Irish would languish in their company. Unless he had a mistress . . . and not just any mistress, but an Irish mistress. And if he had a mistress, might he have a child? And if he had a child, might that child have a mushroom-shaped birthmark? Could the child whom Lewis spoke of be William Thurston's child rather than Lewis's progeny?

Matthew attempted to remember exactly what Lewis had related to Lilly. He'd said there was a baby boy and that he was alive. He'd said the words *Paddy camp* and that the child had a mushroom birthmark on his arm. Lewis had been a handsome man who'd always had women falling at his feet—American women. Why would he have gone to the Acre to find companionship with a woman? William Thurston, however, was another story. Thurston would want to hide any illicit relationship from his wife. What better place than in the Acre? And yet, would William Thurston, a man who held an innate hatred for the Irish, take an Irishwoman as his mistress?

Matthew wondered what Lilly would say to his thoughts. She desperately wanted to find the mysterious child. But would she want to continue the search if there was a possibility the boy was not her nephew? Knowing Lilly, it would be difficult to convince her the child could possibly belong to another man. Even confronted with evidence of Thurston's matching birthmark, it was doubtful whether Lilly would concede that she had misunderstood Lewis's deathbed confession.

He sprinted up the steps leading to his front door. "Lilly, I'm home!" he called out, greeting her with a smile as she rounded the corner of the parlor and walked toward him.

He quickly weighed his options. Lilly would want to take immediate action; likely she'd expect to march into the Acre, inspect William's arm, and confront him regarding the mysterious child. But at this time he couldn't be sure the child's birthmark and Thurston's were alike. *I must find the child,* he decided. *There's no other way to be certain.*

~ 30 ~

September 1831

Seotember was a fine month for dedicating the new Catholic church. Matthew and Lilly were pleased to see the large turnout, and the bishop appeared surprised at the sizeable congregation that gathered. After the official blessing, he commented to Matthew that he'd underestimated the growing Catholic community. Lilly knew Matthew would have liked to have believed the man's interest was because of the souls who would need guidance and direction. Instead, he'd already told her that the man saw a large congregation as a means of milking money out of those who were already dirt poor.

To Lilly's surprise, Miss Addie and Taylor Manning had also decided to attend the celebration. Other than the four of them, there were no other non-Irish to be seen. Addie appeared astonished by the conditions of the Acre and the people around her, but she said nothing. Lilly, too, eyed the surroundings with disdain. Here was an expensive church, yet another monument to God . . . and all around the area children went to bed hungry, unclothed, and without so much as a pillow to lay their heads upon.

"What are you considering?" Matthew asked softly. "You're scowling."

Lilly shook her head. "Sorry. I was just concerned with the conditions. I've seen so many little children who have no shoes and who are caked in dirt. Does the Corporation care nothing for them?"

"They care," Matthew replied. "They care that they're here—instead of in Ireland. The Corporation would just as soon sweep them under the rug. They were never intended to be here. The Associates wanted only those big strapping men who could dig from dawn till dusk. Children and women were never part of the arrangement."

"But now that they're here, surely Kirk Boott and the others see the need of helping them to live in a proper manner."

"Lilly, you're positively radiant," Addie said, coming to embrace her friend.

Matthew smiled at Taylor and extended his hand. "Well, there were times when I wondered if this church would get built, but here it is."

"Looks as though it's built to stay," Taylor replied. "I suppose you're surprised to see us here, but we promised John we'd attend and tell him all the details."

"I didn't know John was all that interested in the Irish or their church," Matthew stated.

"He's made friends among the men and I think he sees it as a duty of friendship to see to the matter. But that aside, Mr. Cheever, I wondered if we might talk of other business—briefly. I realize it's the Sabbath, but I want to ask you about some designs we're having trouble with."

Matthew looked to his wife. "Would you spare me for a moment?"

Lilly nodded. "Of course. Addie and I will visit. Why don't you walk us back to the carriage and we can wait for you there. Afterward we can give them a ride home." She turned to Addie. "Unless you drove also?"

"No, we walked. A ride home would be lovely," Addie said as Matthew guided Lilly toward the carriage.

Once they'd been secured in the carriage and the men had stepped away several feet, Lilly turned to Addie. "What have you heard from John?"

"I'm afraid not very much. I so long for a letter from him, but he's much too busy to write," Addie explained.

"I suppose he is. I'm sure he's pining for you just as much as you're pining for him," Lilly said, patting Addie's hand.

Addie smiled and motioned toward the church. "Such opulence in the midst of poverty. Can you believe the conditions here? I had heard stories—some I didn't believe—but now I'm beginning to wonder. Taylor says there isn't much to be done about it because most of the Yanks would just as soon see the Irish perish. He told me of one man who commented that he didn't care if the children starved or froze to death this winter, so long as it eliminated more Irish from the face of the earth."

"How awful," Lilly said, shaking her head. "Surely there is something we might do to help them. Perhaps we could start some sort of aid society."

"I doubt you'd find too many who feel as we do," Addie declared. "I've heard negative comments even among my girls. Prejudice is such an ugly thing."

Lilly considered this a moment. "You know, Matthew has mentioned scraps, even bolts, of cloth—flawed cloth. . . . Do you suppose we might get the Association to let us have those?"

"Not if they know they're for the Irish."

Lilly smiled and raised a brow. "Well, what if they're for the Lowell Ladies Society, a collection of like-minded women who desire to make quilts for the poor?"

Addie grinned. "We just won't mention who the poor are."

"Exactly."

Addie, Daughtie, Bella, and Lilly Cheever were gathered in Lilly's parlor, each diligently stitching on a square that would eventually be quilted and fashioned into a coverlet of embroidered lambs and daisies for Lilly's expected child.

"I'm so pleased you invited us to spend the evening with you," Addie commented as she knotted a piece of pale blue thread.

"I thought it would be prudent to put some structure to our organization," Lilly explained. "I know you've spoken to Daughtie and Bella about the society. Are you girls in agreement that it doesn't matter who will receive our finished quilts?"

Bella nodded. "I think it's a marvelous idea. I'd like to mention it at the regular meeting of our mill girls' organization. I believe there might be many there who would lend their skills to helping to make quilts."

"So long as they don't question where the articles we make actually go. We can't risk having Kirk Boott refuse to give us seconds and scraps just because the items are going to bless the Irish."

"Did Matthew believe that would be Mr. Boott's response?" Addie questioned.

"Matthew said that Kirk would see this as yet another issue the community would fight about. However, if we give quilts, clothes, and whatever else we choose to make to more than just the Irish, then the community as a whole will benefit. My heart is in seeing that the poor have something warm to get them through the winter."

"Maybe next year we could plant a vegetable garden and raise food for the poor, as well!" Daughtie exclaimed.

"I like that idea very much," Lilly replied. "Matthew's parents have a great portion of land that wasn't sold to the Boston Associates. I wouldn't be surprised if they would allow us a nice plot of land. If the girls agreed to help with the work, we might plant several acres in vegetables."

"This ladies' aid society is getting off to quite a start," Addie said with a smile. "Who knows what we might accomplish."

They had worked for nearly an hour when Lilly stretched and put her sewing aside. "Would you like to see the baby's room?"

"Indeed we would," Miss Addie replied.

Bella was enchanted as Lilly led them up the wide staircase and into a small bedroom adjoining the one she and Matthew shared. The baby's room was equipped with a beautifully carved maple cradle and matching chest. A rocking chair had been strategically placed near the lace-curtained window that overlooked Lilly's small flower garden.

"It's a lovely room," Bella said as she peeked out the window. "And what a lovely view. The children's dormitory in Canterbury overlooked a flower garden. I always found great joy watching the flowers bloom each spring."

"Did you spend a great deal of time with the little children?" She inquired, seating herself in the rocking chair.

Bella nodded her head. "We rotated our duties, but Daughtie and I always looked forward to our time with the children, didn't we, Daughtie?"

"Oh yes," Daughtie agreed. "It was such fun teaching them. Bella and I would take the little ones into the garden and read and sing. The children always lifted my spirits."

Lilly's eyebrows furrowed. "The Shaker community does require celibacy, doesn't it? So how do they have young children?" she inquired, a slight blush tingeing her cheeks.

"Most belong to families who join the Society. Others are left because a mother or father can no longer care for them and the parents believe the child will be safe among the Shakers. Sometimes they return for their children, but most of the time they don't," Bella explained.

"How devastating it must be for those parents to leave a child with complete strangers," Lilly commented.

Bella watched as Lilly's eyes clouded. "I'm sorry. It wasn't my intention to upset you with such talk," Bella said. "You'll never be in a position where you must even think of such a thing."

"Perhaps not that particular situation, but I know what it's like to lose family, and I've almost lost hope of ever finding my brother's child," Lilly replied.

"Now, dear, you mustn't upset yourself," Addie said, taking Lilly's hand in her own. "Your husband won't want you inviting us back to visit if he sees our conversation has given you cause for concern."

"Matthew knows there isn't a day that goes by that I don't think about Lewis's son. I fear he's given up on the search. He doesn't appear to share my longing to find the boy."

"Now, Lilly, I'm sure he has overturned every stone. I think it's likely he doesn't want you to build false hope. Finding one small child when you have no idea what he looks like or where he might be is a daunting task," Addie replied.

Bella observed the exchange between the two women, intrigued by the topic of the missing little boy. She'd overheard a snippet of conversation between Miss Addie and Lilly during the tea at Lilly's several months ago, but she had soon forgotten the conversation. It now appeared this would be the perfect opportunity to hear more.

"So your nephew has disappeared?" Bella ventured.

"Yes. However, I didn't even know of the child's existence until my brother was on his deathbed. Lewis was in dreadful pain and gave only sketchy information about the child. I've never seen him and have no idea where he is, although Lewis mentioned the Acre. Matthew and I agree that the boy's mother is probably Irish."

"With the Acre nearby, it seems you'd be able to easily locate the boy,"

Bella commented, then instantly wished she could snatch back the words as she watched sadness etch itself upon Lilly's face.

"You would think so, wouldn't you? However, my husband says he's expended great effort with no success. I'm not sure he's been completely forthright," she replied.

Addie wagged her head back and forth. "Surely you don't believe Matthew would lie to you, dear. You must keep in mind that the Irish folks keep to themselves. I'm certain the mother wouldn't want to give up her child, and if she's gotten wind that someone is looking for him, she's probably doing her best to keep the boy hidden."

"You forget that Lewis said the mother was dead. I have no idea how she might have died, but I believe Lewis told me about the boy so that I could provide him with a better life. I wouldn't attempt to take him away from his mother's family, if that's indeed who is caring for him now. But what if they don't want him now that Lewis is dead?"

"You can't spend your life worrying about 'what ifs,' " Addie admonished. "You're unduly upsetting yourself, and the child is probably doing remarkably well."

"Perhaps," Lilly halfheartedly agreed.

"Did your brother give you any other information?" Bella inquired.

Addie leveled a look of disapproval at her. "I think we should change the subject. Why don't we go back downstairs and resume our sewing?"

"Bella isn't upsetting me, Miss Addie. I want to discuss the boy. It's Matthew who attempts to squelch any conversation about the child." Lilly turned her gaze toward Bella. "The boy would be close to four years old now. I have no idea about his appearance except that he has a birthmark in the shape of a mushroom."

Bella's gaze immediately shifted to Daughtie. Her friend was staring back at her, eyes wide and mouth agape.

"Could it possibly be?" Daughtie croaked.

Lilly looked back and forth between the girls. "What? Could what possibly be?" Lilly asked in a frantic voice. "Tell me! Do you know something?"

Bella glanced toward Miss Addie, who was obviously upset over the turn of events. Bella raised her eyebrows and gave the woman a questioning look.

"It appears you'd best finish what you've begun, but I do hope that whatever you have to say won't cause Lilly pain," Addie chided.

Bella certainly didn't want to upset Lilly, yet her heart fluttered with excitement at the prospect of offering any valuable information. "During one of my assignments to work in the office at Canterbury a few years ago, I remember an Irishwoman bringing a little boy and signing him over to the Shakers. She avowed the child was not hers. She related to Eldress Phoebe that the boy had been born out of wedlock to her sister and the sister had met with an untimely death. When Eldress Phoebe asked about the father, the woman said he was a Yank who had no interest in the boy."

Lilly gasped and placed her handkerchief over her mouth. "You don't suppose?"

"Don't get yourself overly excited, Lilly. Those few facts don't mean that much," Addie replied.

The older woman stared at Bella, her lips set in a tight line and her eyes creased into narrow slits as she waggled her head back and forth.

Bella chose to ignore the warning. This was a matter of enormous importance, she decided. And so she forged ahead. "The little boy had a birthmark on his arm. I saw Eldress Phoebe examine the mark, and she had me write the information in the boy's paper work. She told me to write that the boy had a mushroom-shaped birthmark on his arm, the color of an underripe plum."

"It must be Lewis's child!" Lilly proclaimed. "Is he still in Canterbury?"

~ 31 ~

I n the privacy of the parlor, Bella eyed Taylor with apprehension, not certain whether she should believe his words. She wanted to accept his apology and trust that Miss Addie's talk had given him pause to consider his unseemly behavior.

"What more can I say that will cause you to give me another chance?" Taylor asked in a pleading voice. "Surely Miss Addie told you of her lecture regarding my behavior," he submitted with a lopsided grin. "We had a long conversation once she completed her reprimand. She made me see that the behaviors I've been exhibiting will not serve me well if I am truly interested in pursing a relationship with a young lady named Bella Newberry."

Bella felt the blood rush to her cheeks. Such talk made her more than a little uncomfortable, and she wasn't certain how to respond.

"Doesn't the church teach forgiveness?" Taylor asked.

Bella felt a twinge of indignation. "Why is it that people who have no use for God or the church attempt to use them as a weapon against those of us who do?"

"I never said I didn't have any use for God or the church," Taylor argued. "I believe in God. It's just that . . . well, it embarrasses me to say this, but I enjoyed the life I was living. And I certainly didn't want to attend church and be confronted with biblical teachings that wouldn't permit me to continue making those same choices. It wasn't until Miss Addie explained that if I ever hoped to call upon you again—and if I ever hoped to be right before God— I would have to change my ways."

Bella folded her arms across her chest and gave him a sidelong glance. "And after all these years of enjoying your carousing lifestyle, it took merely a word or two from Miss Addie to cause this dramatic change?"

"No, Bella. It took meeting you and realizing what I was missing," he replied. "Miss Addie simply pointed out the reasons why it would be impossible for me to win your love until I made significant changes in my life."

Once again she was unsure of herself. "I'm not certain I can believe you," she simply stated. And even if she did believe him, did she want the relationship he was suggesting? She looked at him standing there, hat in hand, his expression so full of hope.

"I understand," he replied, "but will you at least give me an opportunity to prove that I'm speaking the truth? That's all I'm asking for—just a chance. Surely you wouldn't deny me that."

Taylor's hair had fallen forward across his forehead. If she could look directly into his eyes, it would be much easier to evaluate the truthfulness of his words. Bella longed to reach across the distance between them and push the errant strands away from his face. Of course, she would never presume to do such a thing. Instead, she'd be forced to give him an answer without the benefit of seeing what his eyes might tell her.

"I will give you another chance, but should you do anything to make me regret my decision, I will be loath to forgive you again. Please don't disappoint me." Her final words were but a whisper—more a supplication than a request.

"Thank you, Bella. I won't disappoint you," he promised. "And now I want to share some news I think you will find most pleasing."

Bella sighed with relief. She had feared the remainder of the evening would be filled with idle chatter to fill the awkward silences that were certain to follow their earlier discussion. "What is it?"

"It has become evident that having women on the selection committee has already proved extremely beneficial. Last night the men voted to have female representatives assist with the lecture series—but only if they decide they'd like to be involved," he hastened to add.

"Of course they'll want to," she replied. "How wonderful! And did you play a role in this decision?"

"I'd like to say it was all my idea, but it wasn't. I did speak in favor of the proposal, but that's as much credit as I can take in the matter."

"I'm sure your influence helped sway the vote. This is wonderful news. I can hardly wait to tell the other girls," she said, giving him a winsome smile.

"Don't rush me out the door just yet. I have more to tell you."

She could barely contain her enthusiasm. "I can't imagine there's anything else that will excite me any more than what you've already shared."

"Perhaps not, but I know how interested you've been in the new schools. It seems that in spite of the fact that Mr. Boott has withdrawn himself from membership at St. Anne's, construction will soon begin on the first of the new graded schools."

"So Reverend Edson refuses to give in to Mr. Boott's threats? I admire the good man's tenacity. It's truly sad that Mr. Boott would use his position in the church in an attempt to force Reverend Edson to change his stance on the school issue. Let's hope his actions haven't created a cause for his termination."

"Since Mr. Boott has left the church, I doubt there will be a problem. The majority of the membership appeared to be in favor of the new schools."

Bella knew what Taylor said was true, but she also knew that people could become fickle when matters took an unexpected turn—especially when that unexpected turn wasn't advantageous to them.

"Yes, but since Mr. Boott has promised to withhold all of the money both he and the Corporation had been contributing to the church, some of those church members may change their minds," she rebutted.

Leaning back into the cushioned settee, Taylor gave her a grin. "And what good does all this worrying accomplish?"

"You're right. I'll stop," she agreed.

Several loud knocks sounded at the front door. Miss Addie bustled from the kitchen at full tilt, calling out, "I'll answer the door."

Bella heard the scraping of wood and then listened to Miss Addie warmly greet Matthew Cheever. She looked toward Taylor. "I wonder why Mr. Cheever has come calling," she said as Addie and Matthew walked into the room.

"Mr. Cheever would have a word with you, Bella," Miss Addie said. "Why don't you accompany me to the kitchen, Taylor? You can help me prepare some tea. If we're extremely fortunate, I may find some apple cake to serve you."

Miss Addie led the way, and Bella momentarily watched Taylor follow along behind the older woman. She then turned her attention to Mr. Cheever.

"Your wife is doing well?" Bella inquired as Matthew seated himself in a chair opposite the settee.

"Yes, quite well, thank you. In fact, we're preparing for a short journey. That's why I'm here."

Bella's eyes widened at the remark. "Oh?" She didn't know how to respond to his statement.

"It seems you know of a child in the Shaker village that bears a birthmark similar to the one described by Mrs. Cheever's late brother."

"Yes," Bella tentatively agreed. "I did mention such a child to your wife. Are you angry?" she hastened to ask.

"No, not angry—concerned. Lilly is insisting upon journeying to Canterbury to find the little boy. I have concern about Lilly traveling. The doctor says she's in good health but he'd rather not see her travel this late into her pregnancy. Added to that, I'm apprehensive about the outcome of the visit. Even if the boy is the one we're seeking, there's no way of being certain he is Lewis Armbruster's child."

"Perhaps you'll find there's a family resemblance," Bella suggested.

"Perhaps, but I think making the journey is folly. Lilly believes she's going to locate the boy and bring him home. She's already decided the boy is Lewis's child. I'm not as convinced of that fact. However, she is determined to go to New Hampshire, and that is what brings me here. We plan to leave for Canterbury the day after tomorrow, and quite frankly, we need you to accompany us. I doubt we'd be able to secure any information without you."

"No! I don't want to go," she blurted without thinking how her words would sound. Mr. Cheever appeared stunned by her pronouncement.

"I've already made arrangements for your absence from work, and I'll reimburse you for your lost wages. It is imperative that you make the journey, Miss Newberry. You're the one who told Lilly about the child. I implore you to reconsider your answer."

How could she face Eldress Phoebe and the other Sisters? Mr. Cheever didn't realize she had run away from the Society under the darkness of night and that she would be less than welcome.

"Let me explain, Mr. Cheever," she said.

When she had at last revealed the circumstances of her departure, Bella gave him a beseeching look. "And so you can now understand why I can't return."

He nodded. "I understand that returning to the Shakers will be uncomfortable for you. However, I beseech you to join us—for Lilly's sake."

Matthew's earnest plea on behalf of his wife touched Bella's heart, and she knew she could not reject his request. Like it or not, the time had come to face her fears. Her stomach churned as she met his gaze and whispered, "If you believe my presence is absolutely necessary, then I'll go."

"Thank you, Bella."

She closed her eyes momentarily and gave a faint nod. There was no taking back her words. She soon would be returning to Canterbury.

~ 32 ~

Liam settled himself in a chair by the fireplace in the Flynns' tidy home and picked up a newspaper. "I see Mrs. Byrne's been here to visit," he said, picking up one of the outdated newspapers from the stack placed on a wooden footstool.

Mrs. Flynn's cheeks were pink from the heat of the fire. Her plump figure jiggled as she laughed at Liam's remark. "Mrs. Byrne believes she's doin' her good deed by sharin' the papers, Liam, and stale though the news may be, 'tis better than none at all."

"And for sure you speak the truth," he replied, turning the page of last week's paper and reading announcements of newly arrived dry goods that most likely had already been sold out. "Now, here's something interesting," he said. "There's a big advertisement askin' for any information regardin' the girls who have been listed as missing from Lowell."

"Is that a fact?" Mrs. Flynn inquired, taking up a position behind his chair and reading over his shoulder. "Well, would ya look at that," she said, reaching in front of Liam. "They've even listed the lasses who are missin' from the Acre. Now, that's a real surprise, isn't it?"

"That it is," Liam replied as he scanned down the list. There was something familiar about the names—not the names of the Yankee girls, but certainly those of the Irish lasses. Where had he seen them before?

Mrs. Flynn clucked her tongue and shook her head back and forth. " 'Tis a sad day when a mother sees her daughter disappear without a trace. I knew every last one of those Irish lasses, and there wasn't a bad one among them. Sweet girls—pretty, too," she added. "And now some Yankee girls are missin', too. Soon it won't be safe to go out of the house after sunset," she lamented.

Liam continued staring at the list, irritated that he was unable to jog his memory. "It appears the Corporation is beginnin' to take the disappearances seriously."

"One has to wonder if they would have ever taken the matter seriously if the Yankee girls hadn't started vanishin'," Mrs. Flynn commented as she peeled and quartered another potato and placed it in the pot.

"I'd like to think so, but either way, perhaps someone will come forward. It seems they're offerin' a reward," Liam said as he continued reading.

"If the promise of a few gold coins doesn't spawn some interest, I don't know what will. Folks will be scurryin' into that police station like mice after a piece of cheese," she said with a hearty laugh. "I don't suppose ya saw Mr. Flynn on your way home this evenin'?" she ventured.

Liam shook his head. "No, can't be sayin' that I did."

"I'm sure he's busy conductin' business down at the pub," she retorted. "If he isn't home soon, he'll be eatin' his supper cold."

"Ya say that every night, Mrs. Flynn, and every night Mr. Flynn walks in the door just as ya're setting his supper on the table."

"Rather amazin', isn't it?" she asked, her lips curving into a bright smile.

"Indeed," he said, continuing with his reading.

Just as Liam had prophesied, Thomas Flynn walked through the front door while his wife was placing supper on the table. Liam and Mrs. Flynn exchanged a look and laughed aloud.

Mr. Flynn glanced back and forth between them. "I'm pleased to see I've been the cause of a bit of cheer for the two of ya," he announced, sitting down at the table.

Mrs. Flynn gave her husband a loving pat. "Ya've given me a bit o' cheer every day since I married ya," she replied, giving him a quick peck on the cheek.

Supper with the Flynns reminded Liam of his parents' home in Ireland. His parents had always enjoyed a special relationship, one that he hoped to emulate with a wife of his own someday. Not that he was apt to soon find a wife. Liam wanted a wife, all right. He just didn't want to spend time finding her, which was a matter that hadn't gone unnoticed by Mrs. Flynn from the first day of his arrival. She had now taken it upon herself to invite a different young lady for a cup of tea several evenings during the week. When a knock sounded at the door, Mr. Flynn and Liam would exchange a wink as they awaited a view of Mrs. Flynn's latest candidate.

"Do tell Thomas about that piece in the paper, Liam," Mrs. Flynn urged.

"Seems the Corporation is finally concerned about those missing girls. They've run an ad listin' their names and asked for anyone with information to talk to the police. They're even offerin' a reward."

"Well, I'm pleased to hear someone's finally takin' this seriously," Thomas replied. "I hope the reward will loosen a few tongues. Doesn't seem possible that all these girls could disappear without somebody seeing or hearing somethin'," he said, pushing away from the table and picking up his pipe.

Liam joined Mr. Flynn in front of the fire, retrieving the paper and once again reading over the names of the girls. Leaning his head back against the chair, he closed his eyes and gave thought to where he might have read those names before. Without warning, he jumped up from his chair.

"What's the matter, boy? Ya 'bout scared the life out of me," Mr. Flynn exclaimed.

"I'm sorry. I happened to think of somethin'. Excuse me, would ya?"

Liam didn't wait for an answer before taking the few steps to the cordoned-off area where he slept. He opened the small trunk and pulled out the sheaf of papers he'd salvaged from J. P. Green's fireplace months ago, the ones containing names he'd been unable to make sense of. Slowly, he ran his finger down the column of names, comparing them to the list in the newspaper. They matched—at least the names of the girls who'd been missing since before he'd snatched the papers from the fireplace. Beside each name was a column listing an amount of money. What could it mean? He sat on the edge of the bed, staring at the page and permitting his memory to carry him back to the home of J. P. Green.

Liam remembered the opulent house with its serpentine-shaped tables of mahogany, intricately carved mirrors, elaborate tapestries, and highly wrought wool carpets. And then he remembered something else. He'd been working late one evening while Mr. Green's family was away visiting relatives. There had been a noisy upheaval in the foyer when two coarse sounding men had come seeking Mr. Green. Before Green finally got them out of the house, there'd been a terrible commotion.

Immediately after hearing the front door close, Mr. Green had come into the library where Liam was working and questioned him, asking if the ruckus had disturbed him. Liam lied and said he'd disregarded the matter and assumed it was some of Green's associates who were in their cups. Green appeared satisfied by Liam's response and said nothing further. But Liam had heard a portion of the argument. He'd heard Green threaten to horsewhip the men if they ever brought another girl to his home. And he'd heard one of the men repeating over and over that he was afraid they'd been followed. Green had finally screamed at the man to shut up, and when the men were finally quiet, he'd instructed them to take the girl down to the warehouse at the wharf.

The conversation Liam had overheard was now taking on a frightening new meaning. In spite of the chill in the house, beads of sweat formed across Liam's forehead and upper lip. Could J. P. Green possibly be involved in abducting young women and selling them? Surely not! And yet, like a complex puzzle, the pieces were now coming together to form a picture, a horrifying mosaic of unspeakable crimes.

He must talk to someone, Liam decided—someone he could trust. Perhaps Hugh Cummiskey. But what could Cummiskey do about the likes of J. P. Green? This matter needed the attention of someone who wielded power in the community. Kirk Boott or . . . perhaps Matthew Cheever. Yes, that was it! He'd talk to Matthew Cheever—after all, he had talked to him several times since that day at the bridge. Each time had given him more reason to believe that Matthew was sincere and honest when he said that all men were equal in the eyes of God and that because of this, Matthew worked to make sure they were equal in his sight, as well. Perhaps Matthew had even been responsible for the advertisement in the paper. Yes, Liam felt he could trust Matthew with this information. He didn't seem the type to hide the details of a crime simply because one of his own social class was responsible.

Liam gathered the remainder of the papers from his trunk and grabbed his coat from the peg near his chest. "I'll be goin' out for a while," he announced to the Flynns as he shoved the papers inside his jacket.

"Tomorrow's a workday—don't tip too many or ya'll be havin' a big head come mornin'," Mr. Flynn replied with a laugh.

"Right you are," Liam called over his shoulder as he hurried out of the house with purpose in his step, his collar pulled high around his neck to ward off the damp chill in the fall evening air. He approached the Cheever house with uncertainty. What would Matthew Cheever think of a lowly Irish stonemason calling at his home?

"I'll soon find out," he murmured, running up the front steps and knocking on the door.

Matthew Cheever answered the door, a smile on his face as he greeted Liam. "What a surprise. Come in, Liam," he offered, leading the way into the parlor. "Let me take your coat."

Liam reached inside his jacket and pulled out the folded papers before removing his coat. "I hope I'm not interruptin' ya."

"Not at all. In fact, my wife has gone to visit my mother this evening, and I had planned to do a bit of reading. The opportunity to visit with you will be much more enjoyable, I'm sure."

Liam gave him a tired smile. "I'm not certain it will be enjoyable, but I didn't know who else to come to."

"This sounds intriguing. I thought you'd come to discuss religious beliefs. Am I wrong?"

Liam unfolded the sheaf of papers and pressed them flat with his hand. "I'm afraid so. I've come to talk to you about these."

"Perhaps we should sit at the table. It may be easier if we can spread out your papers," Matthew suggested.

Liam separated and stacked the papers on the ornately carved mahogany table. "What I've got here are papers that I retrieved from J. P. Green's fireplace when I was workin' at his home," Liam stated. "Coming from a people who can't afford to waste anythin', I noticed only one side of the paper had been used. I decided I could use the other side for writin' letters home, so I removed the papers and put them in me satchel."

Matthew's eyebrows knit together in obvious confusion.

"I'm tellin' you this only so ya'll understand that I didn't steal the papers—

they were in the fireplace, obviously discarded."

"Go on," Matthew encouraged.

"I never looked at the papers until the day I moved in with the Flynns—ya may recall that's the day after you visited the church with Hugh Cummiskey."

"Yes, I remember," Matthew replied.

"In goin' over the papers and the figures listed there, I discovered that Mr. Green has been keeping two sets of books. This set," he said, pointing to one stack of papers, "that shows the actual amount of money received by Appleton & Green and this one," he continued, while pointing to another stack of papers, "that shows the company makin' much less money. The difference between the two is what he's deposited in this account, which appears to be in his name only. It appears as if he's falsifyin' the records and stealin' money from the shippin' business."

Liam glanced at Matthew, hoping to gauge his reaction to the revelation. He didn't want to proceed if Mr. Cheever appeared in any way affronted by the information. Matthew didn't appear upset. In fact, he was carefully studying the papers and nodding his head.

Finally he looked at Liam. "Several months ago Nathan Appleton talked to Kirk and me when we were in Boston. He expressed some concern that J. P. might be stealing from the company. He was certain it had to be making more money than J. P. was depositing into the business account. I fear his suspicions are not only correct but that the thievery has been going on much longer than even he suspected. Having these papers gives me pause to wonder about something else, however," Matthew said, a thoughtful look etched upon his face.

"What's that?" Liam inquired.

"J. P. told us about a robbery at his home. He appeared unduly upset and spoke of missing papers of great importance. He went so far as to say it would be disastrous for him if the papers fell into the wrong hands. I'd wager these are the papers that concerned him."

Liam felt as though he'd taken a strong blow to the stomach. "Ya think I robbed Mr. Green? Is that what ya're sayin'?"

Matthew appeared startled by Liam's words. "No, of course not. If you had stolen from Mr. Green, you wouldn't have come here tonight. Besides, Liam, I think too highly of you to immediately assume you would ever consider doing such a thing. I'd guess that the thief pulled the valuables from the safe, considered the papers of no value, and tossed them in the fireplace. You went to work the next morning and, seeing the papers, assumed Mr. Green had discarded them and placed them in your satchel."

"What ya've said makes sense. However, I'm guessin' that Mr. Green is even more concerned about these papers than the ones I've already shown you," Liam said, picking up the remaining sheets. "I happened upon an old newspaper this evenin' and noticed an ad for the missing girls. I was pleased to see someone was finally taking their disappearance seriously."

Matthew nodded. "The Corporation agreed to pay for the ad. I had hoped it would yield some information. Unfortunately, it's done us no good thus far."

"Until now," Liam replied, handing the papers to Matthew. He watched while Matthew read one column and then another until at last he finished.

Matthew gave Liam a steely gaze. "So much for my trip to New Hampshire. Who else have you told about this?" he demanded.

33

Have you decided?" Bella asked as she plopped down on the bed beside Daughtie. "We leave in the morning, and you'll need to pack if you're going to return."

"I've decided I'm going to remain in Lowell," Daughtie triumphantly announced.

Bella reached around her friend's shoulder, pulling her into a warm hug. "I'm so glad. I hope it's because you truly want to stay and not because you fear Eldress Phoebe."

"I must admit that the thought of a confrontation with some of the Sisters was a bit of a deterrent," Daughtie said, giving a nervous giggle. "I've prayed very hard about my decision, Bella, and I believe I'm supposed to stay here. Not that I received a startling revelation like some members of the Society, but I've felt a kind of tugging in my heart as I've prayed. I don't seem to receive as much clarity as some of the Sisters, but then, I never did."

"That doesn't mean God isn't leading you or answering your prayers, Daughtie. I believe He speaks to each of us in different ways."

Daughtie gave her a halfhearted smile. "Do you think the Sisters will treat you awfully?" Her voice was a mixture of sadness and fear.

"I doubt they'll be pleased to see me, but I've prayed God will give me the strength to face them so that I may overcome my fears. Besides, Mrs. Cheever needs me, and I can't bring myself to tell her I won't help by going with her."

Daughtie nodded. "Will you tell Sister Mercy I send my love to her?"

"You know I will. She's the only one I want to see."

"What about your father? Will you not make an effort to talk to him?"

Bella simply shook her head. "Let's go downstairs. I promised Miss Addie I'd visit her before I went to bed."

The two girls bounded down the stairs, and Bella tapped on the door as they walked into her parlor. The older lady sat at her desk staring intently at a sheet of paper lying before her. She glanced up as Bella and Daughtie entered the room and clapped her hands in obvious delight.

"Oh, good," she exclaimed. "You've saved me from writing a letter. Come sit down," she said, beckoning them farther into the room. "Are you prepared for your journey? I do wish I were going along."

"I wish I could stay here and you could accompany the Cheevers. I dread going back to Canterbury."

"You'll do just fine. Daughtie and I will be praying for you the whole time. You'll be back in no time at all. It will be a pleasant diversion, especially since Taylor is going along."

"What? Why would you ever think such a thing? Taylor has no interest in any of this," Bella replied.

"You haven't talked to Lilly, have you?"

Bella shook her head back and forth. "No."

"I called on her today. I wanted to wish her well on the journey," Addie explained. "While we were having tea, Lilly told me that Matthew has decided to remain in Lowell. It seems he's had an unexpected problem arise within the Corporation and he can't leave Lowell at this time. He suggested they wait until after the baby is born and then make the trip, but Lilly wouldn't hear of it. Finally he agreed to find someone who would drive the carriage and escort you and Lilly to Canterbury."

Bella sank back in her chair. She had forgiven Taylor for his improprieties, but she didn't want him as her escort on the trip to Canterbury. The choice of a young single man accompanying them would certainly create a flurry among the Shakers and give them yet another reason to find fault with her. She found it impossible to concentrate on Miss Addie's chattering and finally asked to be excused, saying she must get a good night's sleep.

Sleep, however, did not come easily. When the first bell sounded the next morning, she forced herself out of bed and began preparations for the day. The other girls were already working at the mill when a knock sounded at the front door. Bella's breath caught in her throat as she walked to the hallway to answer the knock. Perhaps Mr. Cheever's problem had been solved and when she opened the door he would be standing there to greet her . . . but he wasn't.

The journey was long and tiring for Lilly, with her condition necessitating frequent stops as they traversed the wending, bumpy roads to Canterbury, yet Taylor remained patient and thoughtful. Even when Lilly insisted they seek lodging for the night by midafternoon, Taylor had pleasantly acquiesced. Throughout the journey, Bella had critically observed his behavior, expecting to see him revert to his caddish manners. At the very least, she had anticipated he would attempt to kiss or embrace her when they were alone, but surprisingly, he had done neither. Instead, he had exhibited the epitome of gentlemanly behavior. Perhaps Taylor's declaration that he had changed his ways was true. But then again, she decided, perhaps he was merely using this trip to his advantage and would return to his old habits when she least expected it.

The inn they chose was small but clean. Lilly gave Taylor money and had him arrange for two rooms. When he returned to help with the luggage, Lilly told them both she intended to lie down for an hour or two. Taylor agreed it was a good idea, but Bella thought otherwise. She would be sharing a room with Lilly and she wasn't in the leastwise prepared to nap. That meant that other than sitting quietly in the room, Bella would have to find some other diversion for herself while Lilly slept.

Deciding a walk might be in order, Bella saw to Lilly but then decided this might be an excellent opportunity to broach the subject of Thaddeus Arnold.

"If it wouldn't overly tax you, Mrs. Cheever, I was wondering if I might discuss a matter with you. I promise to be brief," Bella quickly added.

Lilly lowered herself onto the bed. "If you don't mind if I lie down while you talk; my back is aching," she said while massaging her lower back in small circular motions.

Bella plumped one of the pillows. "Of course not. Please make yourself comfortable."

Lilly leaned back. "Ah, this feels much better." She closed her eyes. "I won't fall asleep until you finish talking. Sit down here on the side of the bed and tell me what concerns you."

Bella found it a bit discomfiting to talk to someone whose eyes were closed but decided she'd best seize this chance. It might be a long time before another opportunity would present itself. "Well, you may recall my friend Ruth, the one who is missing?"

"Mm-hmm," Lilly murmured. "I'm hoping she'll be safe and sound by the time we get home."

"As am I," Bella replied. "Anyway, the night Ruth disappeared I awakened. I thought I was having a nightmare, and although I couldn't remember what occurred in the dream, I remembered hearing noises. As it turned out, it was those noises and not my dreams that awakened me. The noises were coming from next door—at the Arnolds'."

Lilly's eyes opened wide. "What kind of noises?" she inquired, her full attention now riveted upon Bella.

"Thumping, slapping, and the sounds of a woman crying. Then I heard the muffled sounds of a man's voice telling the woman to be quiet. I'm quite sure it was Mr. Arnold. However, Ruth's disappearance drew my attention away from the happenings next door. But I felt I had to do something to help Mrs. Arnold before she or the little girl suffered injury."

Lilly nodded in agreement. "I'm glad you've told me. I thought this matter was resolved a couple of years ago. It appears that Mr. Arnold may have returned to his old habits."

"Do you think there's some other possibility? Perhaps I've jumped to conclusions because of Virginia's comment, but I certainly would never forgive myself if something happened to Mrs. Arnold or that sweet little girl," Bella said, her words tumbling forth in a flurry.

Lilly took Bella's hand and patted it. "Don't give this matter another thought, Bella. You've done the proper thing by telling me. I'll take care of it, and Mr. Arnold will be none the wiser as to how I've once again unearthed his despicable behavior." She gave Bella a sleepy-eyed gaze. "Even after hearing this unsavory news, I can't seem to keep my eyes open. I'm sorry, Bella, but I fear I must take a nap."

Bella nodded her head and rose from the side of the bed, hoping she'd done the proper thing. She then headed for the door. "I think I'll take a walk while you sleep," she offered. "I won't go far, so don't worry."

Lilly yawned and nodded. "I'm too tired to worry."

Bella slipped from the room and headed for the stairs just as Taylor came from his room.

"Running away, Bella?" he asked with a smile.

"I wasn't tired—at least not tired in the sense of wanting a nap. I'm a bit sore and road weary, so I thought a walk would do me good."

"May I join you?"

This was a different side of Taylor Manning. Asking instead of demanding. Bella shrugged. "If you must." Besides, having Taylor's company would keep her from dwelling on her conversation with Lilly Cheever.

He laughed and followed her down the stairs. "We haven't really had a chance to talk since coming on this journey. I suppose you were surprised to see me in Mr. Cheever's stead."

"Yes, I suppose I was."

"I was secretly glad Mr. Cheever couldn't accompany you," Taylor said, taking hold of her elbow as they exited the inn. "I'm glad for any extra time I can have to convince you of my sincerity."

Bella considered his words for a moment, then paused under a large chestnut tree. "Taylor, you mentioned not having much to do with God because He would get in the way of your lifestyle. Has that changed?"

Taylor let go of his hold on her and paced back and forth alongside her. With his hands clasped behind his back, Bella thought he looked more like a great orator about to speak than a young man making confessions of faith.

"I have to say that certain things Miss Addie shared have profoundly affected my soul. She told me every man and woman would be called to reckon for his actions. I remember my mother saying the same thing when I was a boy. I didn't take it very seriously," he said, pausing to meet her gaze, "but now I do."

"Because of what Miss Addie said?" Bella questioned softly. She was suddenly humbled by his declaration. Miss Addie had shared the Gospel with Taylor and had called him to account. Bella had only argued with Taylor. She hadn't concerned herself at all with the condition of his soul.

"Partly because of Miss Addie, but also because of you."

"Me? Why me?"

Taylor straightened and unclasped his hands. "You are unlike other girls. You didn't pursue me—you would scarcely even talk to me." He grinned. "I saw in you a gentle spirit yet a bold and courageous one. Miss Addie told me of your deep religious convictions shortly after I first met you. She told me about the Shakers and their strict beliefs."

"But I don't believe as they believe," Bella replied. "That's part of the reason I wish I weren't making this journey." She was astounded by the open manner in which she'd just spoken. Even so, it felt so very right.

"Are you afraid they'll hurt you—demand you return? I won't let anyone harm you—you must believe that."

"They can't hurt me physically," Bella replied, "but there are worse pains than those delivered by physical blows."

Taylor came to her and took hold of her gloved hands. "Bella, I promise you, they won't harm you. I won't let them."

Bella smiled at his sincerity. Maybe God *had* begun a good work in Taylor's heart. Yet it was so hard to trust—to believe. Not only that, but Taylor had no idea of the manner in which the Shakers could heap on guilt and punishment without ever raising a hand. This trip was going to test everything she'd come to understand. There was no hope that Taylor could comprehend that. "Thank you," she finally said, pulling her hands away from his. "I'm sure you'll do your best."

By the time they reached Concord, Bella's stomach was churning. She gave a fleeting thought of a brief stop at her Aunt Ida's, but Lilly was anxious to reach their destination, so she withheld the suggestion. Besides, Aunt Ida would most likely be embarrassed to entertain unknown guests in the dilapidated rented rooms on Franklin Street.

"The closer we get, the more excited I become. I hope there will be no problems and we can bring the boy home with us. You said the Shakers named him David?"

Bella nodded.

"I wonder what his mother and Lewis named him," Lilly commented.

"I don't remember, but it is common practice for names to be changed when children are left at the Village. The Sisters pick a name they think more suitable."

Lilly's brows furrowed. "Really? It seems that would be confusing to children, especially when they've already been placed in unfamiliar surroundings without their parents. Was your name changed, Bella?"

"No, but both my parents remained at the Village with me. My mother wouldn't permit a name change."

Bella gave Taylor directions as the coach rolled onto the road leading to the Trustees' Building. "We'll stop at the large stone building on your right, Taylor," she said, the words tumbling out as her stomach continued churning. She wondered if she might faint.

Taylor held out his hand to assist her down from the coach. She stared at him, willing herself to move, yet she could not. Her body remained frozen in the seat.

"Bella?"

She heard him say her name. His voice seemed to echo in the distance; then she felt his arms lifting her out of the carriage and her feet touching the ground—ground that belonged to the Believers. She shivered and heard Taylor's voice asking if she was ill. She looked up into his sapphire blue eyes and saw his apprehension.

"I'll be fine. It's just this place—seeing the people, knowing they'll be judging me, and knowing I must listen to their recriminating words. I can't explain how difficult it is for me to be here," she whispered. "I told Mr. Cheever I didn't want to come back, but he wouldn't listen," she said, her voice cracking with emotion.

Taylor lifted her chin with one finger, forcing her to look into his eyes. "Remember what I said. I'll not let anything happen to you, Bella. If they speak ill of you, they'll suffer my wrath. You've done nothing wrong, and you have nothing to fear. We'll go in there, make our inquiries, hopefully gain control of the little boy, and be on our way home. Do you believe me?"

She nodded her head. "Yes," she whispered.

Taylor left her side momentarily and assisted Lilly down from the carriage. Bella held her breath as the three of them walked through the front door of the Trustees' Building. Brother Justice was situated behind the curved wooden counter where business was conducted and visitors received.

He glanced up from his paper work. "Sister Bella? Is that really you, or do my eyes deceive me?" he inquired as he rose to his feet.

Returning his smile, Bella approached the counter. "It's me, Brother Justice. It's good to see you." The tall, broad-shouldered Brother leaned on the counter, his shock of white hair neatly combed and his familiar smile a welcome sight. "I'm guessing Brother Jesse is not with you," he said, his pale blue eyes gazing expectantly toward the door.

"No," she softly replied. "I've come with two friends, Brother Justice. Mr. Taylor Manning and Mrs. Matthew Cheever. Mrs. Cheever has reason to believe the little boy known as David is her brother's child. She wishes to see him."

The smile on Brother Justice's face was now erased. "I can't assist you with that request, Sister Bella. You must talk to one of the elders. Eldress Phoebe is in the upstairs office. I'll fetch her."

Bella's heart dropped. Seeing Brother Justice had been one matter. But Eldress Phoebe was quite another. Bella quickly explained to Lilly and Taylor that a meeting with the Elders would be required. Neither appeared concerned or intimidated at such a proposal. She, on the other hand, was once again feeling light-headed at the prospect of such a confrontation.

The muted sound of voices could be heard from upstairs, and soon Brother Justice descended the staircase. "Eldress Phoebe will meet with you. I know I shouldn't ask, but is Jesse well?"

"I haven't seen him in some time, Brother Justice, but I'm sure he's fine. He's living in Concord, working for a cooper. The last I heard he was to be married to the granddaughter of his employer," she told him.

Brother Justice nodded. "He was the most talented young man that ever apprenticed with me in the woodworking shop. It broke my heart when he left. We all thought the two of you . . ." He looked at her with a questioning look in his eyes.

"Marriage was not my reason for leaving this place," Bella replied.

"And how is Sister Daughtie?"

"Daughtie is fine. She's living in Lowell with me—at a boardinghouse. We work at one of the mills," she hastily replied.

"It's good to know you are both well. I'm sure Brother Franklin is going to be pleased to see you."

"I have no plans to see him, Brother Justice. We'd best go upstairs. I don't want to keep Eldress Phoebe waiting."

"Yes, of course. You remember where the office is?"

She smiled and nodded. "I haven't been gone so long that I would forget."

"No, I suppose you haven't. It just seems a long time since I've had Jesse working alongside me in the shop."

There was a pang of sorrow in his voice that saddened Bella, but she realized there was nothing she could say to ease his pain. Jesse's absence created a void in the life of Brother Justice that only his return would fill. Regretfully, she doubted whether her own father missed her nearly so much.

She turned to Lilly and said, "This way," and then led them up the wide staircase to Eldress Phoebe's formidable office.

She hesitantly knocked on the closed door and waited until Eldress Phoebe's familiar voice bid them come in. After casting a worried look in

Taylor's direction, she turned the knob and entered the room with Taylor and Lilly following close behind. The Eldress turned her attention away from the papers on the birch fall-front desk and peered over her spectacles. She gazed at them as though they were some form of foreign creature that had inadvertently entered her domain.

"I believe my eyes must be playing tricks on me," she said, her dark eyes riveted on Bella. "Could this girl in her shameful clothing and unadorned head be Shakeress Arabella Newberry? Surely she would not dress herself in the gaiety of Babylon and come back among her former people. Such blasphemy!" she proclaimed, rising from the low-backed birch chair.

Already things were going worse than even Bella had imagined. She silently censured herself for not wearing her Shaker gown but quickly changed her thoughts. To have done so would have been hypocrisy, she decided. Eldress Phoebe's disapproving eyes seared her very soul, and now she was glaring at Lilly and Taylor, obviously prepared to vilify them, too.

"And who are these invaders of my sanctuary?"

Taylor stepped forward. "We've not invaded you nor your office. The gentleman downstairs announced our presence and informed us we were to come to this room."

"Taylor, please," Bella whispered. "Let me talk."

He gave her a feeble smile and stepped back. "Mr. Manning is our escort, and this," she said, pulling Lilly forward, "is Mrs. Matthew Cheever."

Eldress Phoebe leveled a look of disdain in Lilly's direction. "Brother Justice tells me you've come asking questions on Mrs. Cheever's behalf—about David."

"Yes. Mrs. Cheever believes David may be her nephew. The son of her deceased brother," Bella explained.

"Lewis Armbruster," Lilly added.

Eldress Phoebe ignored Lilly and kept her eyes focused on Bella. "And what did you expect? That I was going to summon David here and permit you to take him off to the world, where he will be condemned to hell?"

"We came because Mrs. Cheever wanted to examine the ledgers to see if the child's mother or father were listed."

Without a word, Eldress Phoebe returned to the desk, pulled open the upper drawer, and removed a ledger. She opened the book and began tracing her bony finger down the pages. "Here it is," she said, tapping her finger on the page. "Cullan O'Hanrahan—an obviously unacceptable name for the child," she mused before turning her attention to Lilly. "You don't look or sound Irish, and your name certainly is not O'Hanrahan," she accused.

"No. I believe the mother was Irish, but my brother—the father—was not. My brother is now deceased," she replied. Lilly was obviously no longer able to remain silent. She moved a few steps closer, eyed a chair, and asked, "May I sit down?"

"Yes, sit down," Eldress Phoebe replied. "All of you," she begrudgingly offered.

Lilly seated herself and immediately besieged Eldress Phoebe with the story of Lewis's untimely death and his dying declaration regarding the little boy. "The combination of facts—the birthmark, the Irish heritage, and the age of the child—makes me believe this boy is my nephew."

"The father is listed as unknown, the mother is listed as deceased, and I have a signed contract waiving all rights to the child," Eldress Phoebe proudly announced.

"Who signed the contract?" Lilly inquired. "May I see the paper?"

Eldress Phoebe appeared either offended or angry—Bella wasn't sure which. But she pulled the contract from a wooden file drawer and handed it to Lilly.

"Noreen Gallagher. She lists her address as Lowell, Massachusetts. This is the child's aunt?"

"That's what she told me. There was no reason to doubt her word, and we will not consider releasing the child to your custody," Eldress Phoebe responded forcefully. She placed the paper back in the drawer, pulled a set of keys from her pocket, and locked both the file drawer and her desk. "If there's nothing else, our meeting is concluded," she announced.

"May I at least see the boy?"

"Absolutely not!"

"But Eldress Phoebe, if she sees the child and there's no resemblance to her family, it could mean the end of this matter. Otherwise, I'm sure Mrs. Cheever will return with a lawyer or papers from a judge to support her request to inspect the child."

"It's obvious you've quickly become one of them—quick to use threats and the law to win your way," Eldress Phoebe charged. She pointed a bony finger at Taylor. "Go downstairs and tell Brother Justice I wish to see him."

A short time later, an uncomfortable silence filled the room. Brother Justice had been ordered off to retrieve the child while the three of them sat waiting in the office.

"What's become of Daughtie and Jesse?" Eldress Phoebe asked, breaking the silence.

"Daughtie is in Lowell. We work at the mills and live in a boardinghouse. Jesse is living in Concord, and I believe he has now married the granddaughter of the cooper he works for."

Her lips curled in disdain and she shook her finger at Bella. "You were always a willful girl. I told your father years ago you'd come to no good end."

"Don't you talk to her like that," Taylor warned.

Bella turned and gave him a feeble smile. "Don't bother, Taylor. This is her world, and she is speaking her opinion. However, it counts for nothing anymore."

"Well, I never! Brother Franklin is going to be devastated to see what a turn you've taken."

"Brother Franklin? My father? Why would he be devastated? He didn't care about me when I lived among you. Why would he care now that I'm gone? Talk of my father will not cause me to turn back to the Shaker ways, Eldress Phoebe, nor will your caustic words."

"Sister Bella!" David cried as he raced across the room and flung himself into her arms.

"Hello, David. You've grown," she said, giving him a bright smile. "I've brought some people to meet you. This is Mr. Manning and this is Mrs. Cheever," she said, turning him to face Lilly.

"Hello, David," Lilly said. "You're quite a fine young man."

David nodded his head in agreement.

"I'll wager you have big muscles. Could you roll up your sleeve and show me?" Taylor asked.

David nodded in agreement as Bella helped him roll up his shirtsleeves. Lilly gave a small gasp as the birthmark came into view. David turned and smiled at her. "You're surprised my muscles are so big, aren't you?"

"Exactly," Lilly replied. "I don't know if I've ever seen such fine muscles on a little boy. You must work very hard."

"I do, don't I, Brother Justice?"

"Indeed you do. Will that be all, Eldress Phoebe?" Brother Justice inquired.

"Yes, you may take him back."

"But I want to stay with Sister Bella," David whined.

"David!"

Eldress Phoebe's one-word command said all that was necessary. The child bid them good-day, grasped Brother Justice's extended hand, and quietly walked out of the room.

"Well?" Eldress Phoebe said, her gaze fixed upon Lilly.

"He doesn't look anything like my brother—or any other member of our family as far as I could tell. But the birthmark and his age together with the fact that an Irishwoman brought him here from Lowell all lead me to believe David must be Lewis's child."

"So you'll not let the matter rest?"

Lilly stood. "I'll discuss the boy with my husband and seek his counsel."

"If you plan to return here, I suggest you send a letter prior to your arrival. Otherwise, we'll not meet with you." Eldress Phoebe's words held an unmistakable note of finality.

"And you, Arabella, should not heap difficulties upon us. Unless you should decide to repent of your ways and return to the Society, please don't return."

Bella nodded. "As you wish, but I'll be stopping at my mother's grave before we leave the grounds."

Eldress Phoebe wagged her head back and forth. "You still insist on grieving over Sister Polly when she's gone to a better place. You never did successfully break your ties from her."

"I never believed it was a part of God's plan to split families or for children to look upon their parents with no higher degree of love and concern than for the other members of this sect. You'll have to count me as one of your failures, Eldress Phoebe. I always loved my mother much more than anyone else in this community." She paused. "Some of you I didn't love at all. Farewell," she added, feeling as though a terrible burden had suddenly been lifted.

When they reached the top of the stairs, Bella turned to face Taylor. Something about his defense of her had endeared him a bit. "Thank you for attempting to come to my rescue with Eldress Phoebe. It's been a long time since I've had anybody willing to fight for my cause."

"You're welcome, Bella. I only wish I could have done more," Taylor replied softly.

There was something surprising in the way he made that pronouncement—his words weren't filled with the old cockiness she'd come to expect from him in the past. Instead, she heard a new sincerity. It pleased her.

Brother Justice met them at the bottom of the stairs. "I told Brother Franklin you were here," he whispered to Bella. "He asked that I tell you he is praying that you will return and keep your covenant with the Believers."

"I think not," Bella replied. "This world is his choice, not mine."

34

The sound of the front door opening caused Matthew to jump to his feet. "Lilly, I'm so glad you're home safe and sound. How are you feeling?" he questioned, pulling her into a warm embrace.

"I feel fine, just tired."

Matthew released her, studying her face momentarily. "Are you certain? I've been very worried about you." He spied Taylor bringing up Lilly's bag. "Here, I'll take that," he said, reaching for Lilly's satchel. "Did you have a good journey?"

"I'm afraid not. We must talk immediately," Lilly said, moving toward the parlor.

Taylor stood in the hallway, anxiously moving toward the door. "I'm going to take Bella back to the boardinghouse, and then I'll deliver your horse and carriage to the livery, Mr. Cheever."

Matthew grasped Taylor's hand in a firm handshake. "Yes, that would be of great assistance, and thank you for making the journey in my stead, Taylor."

"My pleasure. Good day, Mrs. Cheever."

"Good-bye, Taylor, and thank you again," Lilly called out from the parlor.

Matthew hastened back to his wife's side and took her hand in his own. "Now, then, what is it that requires immediate attention?"

Lilly sat down, wiggling a bit in an obvious effort to make herself more comfortable, her brow furrowed in a look of concern. "Before I begin recounting the problems in Canterbury, there is another matter we must discuss," she said. Cutting straight to the heart of the matter, Lilly related the information Bella had shared at the inn. "Thaddeus Arnold must be dismissed from the Corporation, Matthew. He was given his opportunity to change. He'll end up either killing or permanently injuring his wife or their child."

Matthew stared at his wife, stunned by the revelation. "I'll talk to him, Lilly. However, I can't fire him without first giving the man opportunity to defend himself against these allegations."

"Really, Matthew! You know he's up to his ghastly behavior once again. However, if you insist on talking to him, you must promise you won't mention Bella's name. I gave my word I wouldn't divulge where I received the information."

Matthew gave his wife a faint smile. "Of course. I wouldn't want to place Bella in harm's way, either. Now, tell me about your trip to New Hampshire," he urged.

Lilly sank back into the overstuffed settee and began recounting their misadventure in Canterbury.

"I can certainly understand why Bella and Daughtie were anxious to leave the place," Matthew replied. "Eldress Phoebe sounds like a bit of a fusspot."

"She's more than that, Matthew. She's a scheming fanatic, and she adamantly refuses to release the child to me."

"You must calm yourself, Lilly. All of this upset can't be good for you or the baby."

"I'll calm myself once we have Lewis's child here in Lowell with us. It's imperative we return for him, Matthew. Had you been with me, I know the boy would be with us now. You wouldn't have let that controlling Eldress Phoebe turn us away empty-handed. I think we should plan to leave by the week's end."

"Lilly, there's someone you must talk to. I believe you may change your mind about returning to Canterbury."

"I can't imagine what would cause me to change my mind," she replied before giving her husband a look of surprise. "And why are you home at this time of day, Matthew?"

"I arranged to meet Liam Donohue here at the house. In fact, it's Liam I want you to talk to regarding the little boy."

Moving to find a more comfortable position, Lilly leveled a look of confusion in Matthew's direction. "Why are you holding business meetings at the house? And what information would Liam Donohue have regarding Lewis's son?"

Before Matthew could answer, there was a knock at the front door. "That must be Liam now," he said.

Only moments later, Matthew escorted Liam into the parlor. Although Matthew had spoken of Liam from time to time, Lilly had never been properly introduced to the stonemason. With as little ceremony as possible, Matthew made the perfunctory introductions. "I was just telling Lilly I wanted her to speak to you about the child you mentioned."

Liam hesitated a moment and gave Matthew a questioning look. "Noreen's sister's child? Ya want me to tell her now?"

Matthew nodded his assent, and Lilly turned her attention to the Irishman.

"Well, Mrs. Cheever, yar husband was tellin' me about the child ya'd gone seekin' in New Hampshire," he began. "For sure, he mentioned the fact that the lad you were seekin' had a mushroom-shaped birthmark on his arm."

"Yes," Lilly interjected, now obviously anxious to hear what this man had to say.

"When I first arrived in Lowell I boarded with a woman named Noreen Gallagher for a short time. Noreen had the gift of gab, especially when she'd had too much to drink," he explained. "There were several occasions when Noreen spoke about a young lad, her nephew, who bore such a birthmark."

Lilly's hands were shaking. "Yes, yes. Noreen Gallagher is the woman who signed the papers Eldress Phoebe presented to us when we were in Canterbury." She turned to look at her husband, excitement etched upon her face. "You see, Matthew, it's all coming together. We must leave tomorrow."

"Wait, Lilly. Liam's not finished."

She gave Liam a nervous smile. "I'm sorry. Go on, Mr. Donohue," she said.

"Noreen told me the child's father was one of the Boston Associates. I later heard from several men in the pub that William Thurston and Kathryn O'Hanrahan had been involved in a . . . umm . . ." Liam stammered and looked to Matthew.

"Liaison," Matthew said.

"Yes. And these men mentioned that Kathryn had a child by this William Thurston."

"No! He's Lewis's child," Lilly objected.

Matthew moved to Lilly's side. "Lilly, William Thurston has a birthmark exactly like the one on the child."

"Why would Lewis mention a child on his deathbed if it wasn't his?"

Liam cleared his throat. "For sure I'm not knowin' anything about yar brother, ma'am, but I did ask Noreen why she hadn't kept the lad with her—not that he'd have been well cared for under that woman's wing. Anyway, she told me she feared for the lad's life and was sure he would come to some harm by his father's hand. She decided it would be best to give him up to the Shakers rather than have him suffer possible harm. Perhaps your brother possessed that same knowledge and was merely issuin' a warnin' to protect the wee lad."

Matthew pulled Lilly close. "I know you want to believe the boy is related to you, Lilly, but this evidence proves otherwise. You know that Lewis was involved with William Thurston to some extent. Thurston could have told him about the woman and boy. Remember, also, that Mrs. Gallagher says the father was one of the Boston Associates. That information further implicates William as the father, not Lewis. We must think this through. I wouldn't be able to live with myself if we brought that child to Lowell and he came to some harm."

Pulling a lace-edged handkerchief from her pocket, Lilly dabbed one eye and then the other. "I think I must rest, Matthew. This is all too much for me right now. If you'll excuse me, I believe I'll go upstairs and lie down."

"Of course, my dear. I think that's wise. You're tired from your journey and there's much information to consider. I'll come up once Liam and I have concluded our business."

Matthew escorted his wife to the bottom of the wide oak stairway. "Try to get some sleep, Lilly," he said, brushing her cheek with an affectionate kiss. He waited until she had ascended the stairs before returning to the parlor.

"I'm sorry me words caused yar wife such grief," Liam apologized.

Matthew placed his hand in a reassuring manner on Liam's shoulder. "You spoke only the truth. There's nothing to apologize for, Liam. I appreciate your willingness to help me sort out this whole issue of the boy. I don't know if Lilly will want to talk to Noreen Gallagher—I pray not. But should she insist, would you be willing to arrange for them to meet?"

"For sure I would, although I'd avoid such a meetin' if at all possible. Noreen's not the type ya'd want to have come callin'. And she might try to put the touch on ya for some money, too."

Matthew smiled and nodded. "I'm hopeful Noreen's presence won't be necessary. Now, have you been able to scrape up any more information regarding J. P. or the missing girls?"

Liam nodded and leaned forward, resting his forearms on his muscular thighs. A shock of dark hair fell forward across his brow, and he absently ran his fingers through the mass of thick black waves in an attempt to shove it back into place. "I've taken into my confidence an old Irishman who spends most of his time in the pub. Haven't told him why I want information, of course, but told him I'd stand good for some ale if he'd keep a listenin' ear directed toward J. P. and his cronies any time they're in the pub."

"Do you think you can trust him?"

Liam nodded. "I do. He dislikes havin' Yanks come into the pub—says they should keep to their own part of town since they expect the Irish to stay in the Acre. He spends most of his time at the pub. His son brought him over from Ireland, and he lives with his son's family in the Acre. Probably spends his time in the pub to stay out of the way at home. He says he's old but his hearin' is sharp," Liam explained with a hearty laugh.

"But has he come by any information that's helpful? I believe we've got to produce something even more substantial than those papers of J. P.'s before we go to the police. I'm afraid he'll refute the ledgers, insisting they were altered after being stolen from his safe."

"Seems the old man heard a conversation a few days back. Green and a couple scalawags were talking about needin' more high-quality merchandise right away."

"But that doesn't really tell us much," Matthew cut in.

"For sure, but as they continued talkin', one of the men said something about not likin' the idea of going after the Yankee girls. He said it was drawin' too much attention and mentioned the ad in the paper. J. P. told him he didn't care whether he liked it or not—he was bein' paid to do a job, and they needed at least three beauties to take down the canal very soon."

"Down the canal? They must travel by canal to Boston and then ship the girls out of the harbor," Matthew said, running a hand across his forehead. "The fact that this bartering in human flesh is taking place right here in Lowell sickens me. The families of the mill girls give approval for their daughters to come here and work because they believe they'll be safe. It won't take long until we'll have frightened girls rushing back home and disastrous results as we attempt to find their replacements."

"I'm supposin' that's true enough. If we've a bit o' luck on our side, perhaps they'll discuss when they plan to be takin' the girls to Boston."

Matthew looked up and met Liam's gaze. "I doubt we'll be that fortunate. Most likely their schedule revolves around whenever they're able to abduct the girls rather than a set timetable. Let's hope we're able to bring this whole ugly business to a stop before they're able to seize another girl."

Taylor slowed the horse a bit as the boardinghouse came into view. "I'm sure you're weary from all this traveling."

"Not really, although I must admit it seems odd to be riding about Lowell at midafternoon on a workday," Bella responded. "I do hope Miss Addie is home. I'm anxious to visit with her about our journey."

"I trust you plan to tell her that you've a growing admiration for me," he said, giving a somewhat embarrassed laugh. "I'd hate to bring on another of her lectures."

Bella graced him with a bright smile. "I plan to tell her that I believe your behavior was praiseworthy and that I was most pleasantly surprised with the changes I saw."

"Do those changes merit enough admiration that you'll grant me permission to call on you?"

A slight blush colored her cheeks. "Perhaps. It would depend on your intentions."

"My intentions are completely honorable, I assure you. However, I fear if I said more you'd consider me forward. So for now, I'll settle for the privilege of escorting you to your meeting at the Mechanics Association this evening."

Bella decided she best not question him further about his intentions unless she wanted to be completely embarrassed. "I'd completely forgotten we had a meeting this evening."

"Then I may call for you?"

"Yes, that would be fine," she replied. "Look! Isn't that Mr. Farnsworth's carriage in front of the boardinghouse?"

"Uncle John must have concluded his business down South ahead of schedule. I wasn't expecting him until next week." Taylor pulled the horses to a halt behind John's carriage and then assisted Bella down.

"Bella! You're home," Miss Addie greeted from her parlor. "Come in and visit with us. You, too, Taylor—and look who's here! Aren't you surprised?"

Miss Addie was beaming, obviously unable to contain her excitement over Mr. Farnsworth's return to Lowell.

"Indeed I am. Welcome home, Uncle John. I wasn't expecting you until next week."

John grasped Taylor's hand in a firm handshake. "Fortunately our negotiations went more smoothly than anticipated, permitting my early return. It is good to be home among family and friends. I hear from Addie that you've been on a journey of your own."

"Yes, although I don't believe we were as successful on our mission."

Miss Addie gave Taylor an encouraging smile. "Sit down and tell us all about it."

Taylor shook his head back and forth. "I'll leave the telling to Bella. I've got to take Mr. Cheever's horses and carriage to the livery. Glad you're home, Uncle John."

"Thank you, my boy. I'll be home shortly."

Taylor turned his gaze to Bella before leaving. "And I'll see you this evening, Bella." Bella smiled and nodded in agreement. Once Taylor had closed the front door, she took her cue from Miss Addie and began to relate the events of their journey.

"My, my," Miss Addie lamented as she wagged her head back and forth when Bella had finally recounted the tale. "Tell me, dear, did you have an opportunity to see your father or Sister Mercy?"

"I didn't see my father. He elected to send word to me that he was praying I would return to the Society and honor my covenant. However, I did have an opportunity to see Sister Mercy. We stopped at the cemetery as we were leaving, and there she was, waiting by my dear mother's small tombstone. I think Brother Justice told her of my arrival, and she knew I wouldn't leave without visiting my mother's grave."

"It sounds as though Brother Justice is a very kind man. I'm delighted you were able to visit with Sister Mercy. I know Daughtie is anxious to hear your report. She's been in a dither anticipating your return."

"I only wish we could have brought the little boy back with us. Mrs. Cheever was quite upset over the situation and even talked of returning with Mr. Cheever and a lawyer."

"There is no end to the measures Lilly will take if she believes that child is her blood relative," Addie replied.

"Well, if you'll excuse me, I believe I'll go upstairs and unpack and prepare for this evening. I'm to talk to members of the Mechanics Association regarding the prospect of teaching an English literature class."

"You go right ahead, my dear. I'm sure you've lots to accomplish," Addie replied.

Bella picked up her satchel and walked up the stairs to her room while silently enumerating the many changes in her life since she'd left Canterbury. Most of them were good, yet she'd given thanks for very few of them. In fact, she hadn't been diligent in her prayer time or Bible study of late, always putting God off until later, and still she'd been abundantly blessed. Instead of pulling out her notes on the literature class, Bella opened her Bible and began to read. God's Word spoke to her of His relentless love and everlasting grace, which were two topics that had not been included in her lessons among the Shakers.

She'd chided Taylor in the past for ignoring God, but she now found herself just as guilty. "I don't mean to be so fickle or unfaithful," she murmured in prayer. "I know I'm sorely lacking when it comes to doing things as I should." She glanced to the ceiling. "But I want to do right in your eyes. I want to yield the hardness of my heart and put aside the past.

"At the village, I felt so angry and bitter for the things they'd done—for the things my father had done. Lord, it's hard to just let go and put it aside. Sister Mercy said we were to look forward in our walk, not even glancing behind. Now I read in your Word that we are to actually forget what is behind us and press on toward the goal. But, Father . . . I don't seem to have any goals."

Love me. Serve me. Trust me. Let these be your goals.

The words were stirred from somewhere deep in her heart. Was God truly speaking to her heart? Was this what He'd been trying to tell her all along?

~ 35 ~

Although he dreaded a confrontation with Thaddeus Arnold, Matthew decided it was best to address the situation without further delay. Arriving at the mill, he sent a message requesting Arnold's presence in his office.

A short time later a knock sounded at Matthew's door. "Come in," he called.

Thaddeus Arnold entered the office, closing the door behind him. "You wanted to see me?" he asked. In spite of the cool temperature, beads of perspiration had formed on Arnold's forehead and damp half-moons now circled his underarms.

Matthew pointed toward a chair. "Sit down, Mr. Arnold," he offered and then waited until Thaddeus seated himself. "I've received some distressing information regarding your behavior. From the accounts I've heard, it appears that you've returned to your past behaviors—behaviors, as you well know, the Corporation will not tolerate."

Thaddeus pulled a checkered handkerchief from his pocket and wiped his brow. "I suppose I need not attempt to defend myself—I'm certain you'll never believe me over those who have made these accusations."

Matthew leaned forward and rested his arms atop his desk. "On the contrary. I'm hopeful you can shed light on this matter. If you have a defense, by all means, let me hear it."

Thaddeus shook his head back and forth. "No. I'll not honor such vicious lies with a defense. But remember, Mr. Cheever, if you terminate my employment, my wife will suffer more from your actions than she has from my hand."

Matthew stared across the expanse between them in disbelief. Too late, Thaddeus realized the full weight of his words. "You've condemned yourself, Mr. Arnold. I'll escort you back to your living quarters so that you may pack your belongings. As for your wife and child, I'll not see them punished for your behavior. Mrs. Arnold will be given opportunity to remain in the house and take in boarders to support herself, should she desire."

Thaddeus's complexion turned a shade of purplish red. "Why is it that men such as you can't seem to understand women need to be kept in their place? Give them too much freedom and they consider themselves our equals. I'll not tolerate such behavior from my wife or any of those uppity girls you hire to work in the spinning room," he spat.

Standing up and walking around his desk, Matthew opened the office door. "Then it appears I've done you a service, Mr. Arnold. You'll no longer have to contend with either the mill girls or your wife. Shall we go?"

Bella stood in the foyer awaiting Taylor's arrival. She had prepared a few notes after supper and then decided she would extract additional information from the attendees. Surely some of them had specific titles or authors they hoped to study. Perhaps she would take a vote and they would make their choice based upon the majority decision. Yes, she decided, the class would benefit from assisting her with the selection.

Deciding upon what she would wear to the meeting had taken a bit of thought, even though she had few choices. After considering her options, Bella had chosen her plaid dress of myrtle green and black. She'd purchased the fabric quite reasonably and fashioned the style after one of the gowns Lilly Cheever had given her. With a few minor alterations to the pattern, the dress had taken on a unique appearance.

Taylor arrived in his uncle's wagon and immediately upon greeting her at the door complimented her on the gown. A good choice, she decided, giving him a warm smile.

"I thought perhaps Daughtie would be going with us."

"So did I, but she decided to walk with the other girls instead."

"I'm sorry to have the buckboard. I had hoped to have Uncle John's carriage this evening. Unfortunately, he's using it himself. He has a meeting with Mr. Boott and Mr. Cheever and then plans to visit Miss Addie again this evening."

Taylor held her books and papers as Bella donned her gray woolen cape. "She's so delighted to have him back in Lowell. She tells me your uncle John had a letter waiting for him from his father in England when he arrived home, stating he'd moved to London," she said as he assisted her up into the wagon.

"Yes, and the move appears to have been an excellent decision. Apparently Grandpa Henry—that's Uncle John's father—found a doctor in London who can better treat his medical condition."

"Miss Addie said the doctor required Mr. Farnsworth's father move to London so he would be close at hand for the treatments."

"Exactly. As luck would have it, Grandpa Henry was able to lease his house in Lancashire to a distant cousin. So it appears to have worked out well for all concerned. I know Uncle John holds out hope that his father's health will one day improve enough to bring him to Massachusetts. In fact, he tells me Miss

Addie has been very supportive of his desire to bring Grandpa Henry to the United States."

Bella glanced into a shop window as they passed by. "That doesn't surprise me. Miss Addie is such a generous, loving person. They do complement each other, don't you think?"

"Indeed. I wouldn't be surprised to see them marry soon—if Miss Addie's willing to give up the boardinghouse."

"It would be difficult if she were to leave the house—nobody could take her place. And yet I would very much like to see her snatch this opportunity for happiness."

"I'm certain it would please Uncle John," he agreed. "After we parted this afternoon, I took Mr. Cheever's carriage back to Mr. Kittredge's livery as he had requested."

Bella's eyebrows arched. "Yes?"

"Mr. Kittredge asked if I'd mind delivering a message to Mr. Cheever before I returned home. Of course I told him I'd be happy to do so. After delivering the message to Mr. Cheever, he told me there had been important developments in regard to the little boy in Canterbury."

"David?"

Taylor nodded. "Yes. Perhaps it was a good thing we didn't gain custody of the boy. It seems he may not be Mrs. Cheever's blood relative after all. Mr. Cheever said the child might be the son of a well-known Bostonian. And if that's true, there's even concern the father would do the child harm."

Bella listened carefully as Taylor outlined the latest revelation, her mind reeling with the information. "Then it could be dangerous for David to live in Lowell?"

"Absolutely. Mr. Cheever asked that we keep this information between us. He said he wanted to share it with you and me since we had made the journey to Canterbury with Mrs. Cheever."

"And Mrs. Cheever? How did she take the news? Did she accept this information as truth?"

"Mr. Cheever said he's attempting to convince her to put the child out of her mind."

"I'm sure the poor woman is distraught—especially in her condition. I'm certain this news is very disturbing to her. We should both remember the Cheevers in our prayers."

Taylor gave her a sidelong glance. "I'm not much into praying yet, Bella. I'm just now becoming accustomed to actually listening in church."

Bella gave him a smile. "I'm pleased to hear you're beginning to find the services enlightening. As to the praying, just talk to God as if you were talking to me. He doesn't require special words, Taylor."

"Seems a bit strange—just talking, that is—but I suppose I can give it a try," he said as he pulled open the door of the Mechanics Association meeting room. "Here we are. I'm looking forward to your class."

The class, Bella decided, might prove more difficult than anticipated. She'd never previously conducted a meeting where both men and women were in attendance. She now questioned her ability to teach such a group. And her idea of having the participants make a choice had been cause for great debate. The women's interests proved opposite to the men's. After much debate, they'd finally agreed upon Ivanhoe, deciding it would provide something for both the male and female readers. By meeting's end, she wanted nothing more than a quick retreat to the boardinghouse.

She had tied on her bonnet and had been waiting for at least fifteen minutes when Taylor finally approached. "Sorry for the delay, but I want to remain a little longer and visit with several of the men on another matter," he told her. "And incidentally, I think you may need to develop a higher level of skill in these combined meetings. Some of the men thought you gave more consideration to the women's requests."

His words punctured her already-wounded spirit. But instead of quietly retreating and reflecting upon his suggestion, she quickly rebutted.

"Consideration is obviously not at the top of your list, either. If it were, you would have advised me beforehand that you would be remaining late. I'm exhausted, and our meeting went much longer than I'd expected. I'd prefer to leave now."

"I'm sorry, Bella. It wasn't my intent to upset you. Surely you know by now that I'd not intentionally hurt your feelings. I promise to have you home by curfew. After all, I wouldn't want to tarnish the name of the woman I plan to marry."

Bella ignored his apology, unwilling to succumb to his charms. "That's unacceptable. I've already waited longer than necessary. All of the other girls have already left for home."

"I'll tell the men we need to move swiftly. Please sit down and wait in the main meeting room."

She didn't answer. Instead, she waited until he'd gone back to his meeting and then walked out the door. In any case, it wasn't as if she didn't know the way home by herself! Clutching her reticule in one hand and her paper work in the other, Bella strode off with purpose in her step. She realized it was later than she usually ventured out at night, especially unaccompanied, yet she was surprised to find the streets nearly deserted. Bella gave momentary consideration to Mr. Cheever's warning that the women of Lowell should not walk alone at night but quickly pushed the thought aside. She was weary. Besides, Taylor should be escorting her home!

A gust of wind whipped at her cape, and she clutched it more tightly around her. A puddle of crisp fallen leaves swirled around the hem of her dress, and the moon's light cast silhouettes of dancing tree branches in front of her. The breeze grew stronger and Bella glanced over her shoulder, certain that she'd heard something behind her. Probably the wind—or Taylor had realized she was gone and was following her. Her lips curved into a smile at the thought. He did care enough to leave the meeting. She gave thought to waiting for him but decided he could catch up quickly enough. However, she slowed her pace ever so slightly as she turned the corner. After all, she had spoken rather sharply, and differences were more easily resolved before they'd simmered for days on end.

Her heart quickened at the sound of the approaching footsteps. She began to turn and greet Taylor when, without warning, a rough hand slammed over her face. Before she had opportunity to struggle, a cloth was stuffed into her mouth and two large hands were wrenching her arms behind her. She could feel a coarse rope being twisted around her wrists while another set of hands was pushing aside the hem of her dress and tying her ankles with such force that the cord was cutting deep into her flesh. It was impossible to fight against the brute force of the men as they rolled her into a carpet and then hoisted her up. Her body was now tightly wound in the rug, and she struggled to breathe. Horror engulfed her. Why hadn't she waited for Taylor? Instead of pushing her self-importance aside, she'd let emotion control her actions—and her life.

Taylor's attempts to hasten the meeting proved futile, so it was nearing ten o'clock when the men finally decided to adjourn. Stealing a quick glimpse at the walnut case clock, he hurried from the meeting room. He could have Bella home by curfew if they hurried, and perhaps he'd still have time to set things aright. Rushing back to the small room where he'd left her, Taylor glanced in the doorway. Where was she? He pushed his way back through the sea of men exiting the building and momentarily felt as though he were swimming against a strong tidal wave that was going to suck him under. Finally making his way through the departing men, he hurried about the building, checking every nook and cranny, but Bella was nowhere to be found.

Taylor quickly realized it was going to take more than a few pleasant words to make amends, and there certainly wasn't time tonight. Her absence spoke volumes. Pondering the idea of whether a small gift might aid his cause, Taylor exited and locked the front door. After work tomorrow, he'd stop in town and find something Bella might like. Once again he chastised himself for not mentioning his need to remain late this evening. But he hadn't expected Bella's intense reaction. She had spunk—of that he was now certain. He went home, then thought better of the situation. It would be wise to at least go to the boardinghouse and make sure she'd returned safely. He turned the wagon around and headed back down the street. At least this would show Bella how much he cared. When he reached Miss Addie's house, however, he noted that all the lights had been extinguished. There was no sound coming from within—no doubt they had all retired. He couldn't disturb them now. With a sigh, he headed back to John's house.

"I'll see her tomorrow," he murmured as he made his way home.

With the sound of the first bell, Taylor groaned and rolled over. He hadn't slept well and now longed to remain abed for another hour or two, but such a luxury was impossible. Lifting the hand-painted pitcher of water, Taylor poured several inches into the matching china bowl and then splashed it on his face. Glancing into the mirror hanging above the oak chest, he shook his head in disgust. Dark circles rimmed his eyes, which gave him the appearance of a weary raccoon.

John stood near the bottom of the stairway, ready to leave for the mill. "You're looking none too chipper this morning."

"I didn't sleep well."

"That much is obvious. I'm wondering what caused your insomnia," John remarked as he pulled open the door, a smile playing on his lips. "Surely not problems with young Bella."

Taylor began recounting the evening's events as the men walked down the front steps. They had walked only a short distance when they turned toward the frantic sound of a young woman calling out their names.

Daughtie skidded to an abrupt halt only inches before plowing into Taylor's broad chest. Her eyes were panic-filled as she called out, "Where's Bella?"

"No need to scream, Daughtie. I'm right here." He gave her a guarded smile. "I haven't seen Bella since last night."

Daughtie grasped his arm, her fingers penetrating the thick wool of his jacket and digging into his flesh with a death grip. "She never came home!"

His terror merged with a surging panic before it actually plunged Daughtie's words into the depths of his consciousness. A choked guttural cry escaped his lips.

Taking hold of Taylor's shoulder, John said, "Calm yourself, boy! You've got to remain calm. Now tell me, when did you last see Bella?"

Moments passed before Taylor could quiet his jumbled thoughts. Finally he composed himself enough to speak coherently. "That's what I was beginning to tell you. I thought she was going to wait for me to escort her home after my second meeting, but she had already gone when we adjourned for the night. It was close to ten o'clock—she was angry with me. I thought she went home. Dear God in heaven, what have I done?" His mind reeled with possibilities. He turned and grasped John by the shoulders. "What if she's been abducted like those other girls?"

"Come on," John commanded. "We'll get over to the Appleton. Matthew can surely be of assistance. You've got to keep a level head, Taylor. Anything you can remember will surely help. Come along, Daughtie. Your supervisor won't excuse you if you're tardy."

The three of them rushed off toward the mill with Taylor taking the lead and Daughtie and John close on his heels. As they neared the mill yard, Daughtie grasped John's arm and begged him to send word of any news. When he had agreed, she bid the men farewell and scurried toward the stairwell.

Taylor spotted Lawrence Gault standing near the countinghouse as they grew nearer and waved to the older gentleman. "Is Mr. Cheever in his office?"

"He is, but—"

"Good!" Taylor shouted in return, not waiting for any further information before bursting into Matthew Cheever's office. His mouth fell open at the sight. The outer room was already filled with several mill girls and Liam Donohue, and Miss Addie was sitting opposite Matthew's desk. Mr. Cheever's full attention was directed toward the older woman, but Taylor was undaunted by the sight. He strode past the others waiting in the outer office and into Matthew's office while saying, "I'm sorry, but this can't wait."

Matthew looked up as Taylor neared the desk. "Taylor, I'm—"

Miss Addie turned in her chair. "Oh, Taylor, I'm glad you're here. Where is Bella?"

"I don't know. That's why we've come. We need to organize a search party, and Uncle John thought this would be the place to get folks organized."

"Oh, John, this is terribly frightening," Addie said, rising from her chair. "I fear something dreadful has happened."

"Why don't you go on back home, Addie? You've done everything you can," John suggested. He took her arm and led her toward the door. "I'll keep you apprised of any news."

"Ask Liam to step in, would you, John?" Matthew requested.

Taylor turned his attention to Matthew. "What's Mr. Donohue got to do with Bella's disappearance? Do you think the Irish are involved in these abductions?"

"No, but Liam has furnished me with some helpful information regarding the abductions—or at least we're hoping it's going to be helpful," Matthew explained before turning his attention to Liam. "I'm sure you've heard enough of our conversation to realize we have another missing girl. I think we should get down to the canal. The locks begin operating at daybreak, and if they're going to attempt transporting the girls to Boston, we'll want to search any suspicious-looking boats or cargo."

John cleared his throat rather loudly. "I don't mean to be a spoiler, Matthew, but don't you think this is something the police should be called in on?"

"Absolutely. In fact, I've talked with them at some length, and they're aware of our concerns. However, since there are only two of them, it's impossible for them to lend much assistance. They requested our help at the waterway. I'll explain more fully if you like, but we'd best get down to the docks. Any of you on horseback?"

Liam gave a hearty laugh. "I don't think anyone in the Acre owns a horse."

"We're afoot, also. Taylor can fetch my horses from the livery if you think we'll need them," John offered. "It won't take long."

Matthew shook his head back and forth. "No. My horse is tied out back, so I'll ride ahead. The rest of you follow as quickly as possible," he said before moving to the outer office, where two girls still sat waiting. "Unless you have a missing person to report, you'll need to return later in the day. We've an emergency to tend to right now," Matthew told the mill girls as he opened the front door. He turned back toward the men. "I'll meet you near the loading dock by the millpond. It will probably take all four of us to inspect the boats preparing for departure."

Taylor was filled with a sense of mounting distress as they hurried off toward the wharf. He forced himself to take a deep calming breath. If he was going to find Bella, he needed clarity of thought, he decided as they finally approached the millpond. Without warning, he put voice to unbidden words that had mysteriously exploded in his mind. "I think we should pray."

The other three men stopped, turned, and stared at him as though he'd spoken in some unknown tongue.

He wondered if his words had been offensive. When none of them replied, he hastened to add, "If that would be all right with you."

John reached out and placed an arm around Taylor's shoulder. "You make me ashamed of myself, Taylor. I should have suggested prayer immediately. Yet it gives me great pleasure to know that you are beginning to place your trust in God rather than man. Gentlemen?"

Taylor silently communicated his own prayer for Bella as his uncle prayed aloud. The supplication took only a minute—it was a simple plea for help— yet Taylor felt more at peace. Bella's faith was strong, and surely she must be praying, too. Perhaps with the unification of their utterances, God would pause and assist them. A childish thought, perhaps, but it gave him added hope. He momentarily considered bartering with God but then decided God might frown upon such a concept. Bella would have an opinion on that idea. He'd discuss it with her once she was safely home.

"Taylor, you can go ahead and search this boat. Liam, you take that one,"

Matthew ordered while pointing where they were to go. "I'm going to talk to George West. He's in charge of the canal and locks this morning."

"Whadd'ya think you're doing? Get off this boat," a rough-looking man hollered as Taylor jumped aboard his boat.

"Nothing to be concerned about. We have permission to search all boats carrying cargo or passengers to Boston."

The man ran a dirty hand through his greasy unkempt hair before arching a stream of tobacco juice into the air that landed directly on Taylor's right shoe. "Since when?"

The other man working on the boat gave a snort.

Taylor looked down at his foot in disgust. Rolling his hand into a fist, he used his thumb to point toward Mr. West. "If you've got a problem, take it up with the man in charge. He says we've got permission, and so do the police. Now, you want to get out of my way? 'Cause if you don't, I'm going to guess it's because you've got something on this boat that ought not be here and you figure I'm going to find it. Could that be the problem, mister?"

"You talk mighty big. We'll see how big you are when you're alone in town someday."

Taylor knew the threat was intended to intimidate him, but it served only to make him angrier than he already was. "Why wait? You think you're man enough to take me on, then let's get to it."

"Taylor! We're not here for pugilistic entertainment," John called out. "Get busy and search that cargo. There are three more boats already loaded."

His uncle was right. They couldn't afford to waste time. Bella's life could be at risk, and he was acting like a schoolboy who needed to impress the other children in the play yard. He turned away from the man and began moving among the crates and barrels, moving them about and prying off lids while the two men spat curses in his direction.

The second man was following Taylor closely, hammering lids back down where needed and attempting to direct his path, or so it seemed to Taylor. Finally the man appeared to have lost all patience. "Look here, mate, you've gone through everything and found nothing out of order. Now get off the boat and let us be on our way."

Taylor surveyed the boat and glanced toward the center of the boat, where the one mast stood ready to hoist a sail when needed. "I've not gone through the goods stowed over there by your sail."

"Ain't nothing but some of the same what you've already seen."

Taylor gave the man an unswerving stare. "Then you've got nothing to be concerned about. The quicker we get done, the quicker you can be on your way," he said while tugging to move the deflated canvas sail.

Just then the first man rushed toward him. "Hey! Don't mess with that sail!" the man commanded as he shoved Taylor off balance, causing him to fall backward. He landed heavily on a row of rolled-up carpets, immediately thankful it hadn't been the pitchforks he'd found a short time earlier. He slowly began to lift himself up, then shook his head in wonder as two of the carpets appeared to wriggle back and forth.

"Seems to be a bit of turbulence in the water. Things is jostling about."

Taylor stared up at the man. "We're sitting dead still in a millpond. The only turbulence is right here in these carpets." He began to tug the edge of one of the rugs and heard a muffled noise.

"Uncle John! Over here!"

The scruffy boatman yanked at Taylor's arm. "Get away from there! You've got no right."

Taylor pulled free and yanked at the carpet. He saw two feet and then rope-bound ankles. Bella! It must be her. He looked up at his uncle, who was holding one of the men at bay while Liam held on to the other. Matthew rushed forward to help him. A torso appeared and then two bound arms— and then a face. But it wasn't Bella's face.

Working feverishly, they loosened the gag around the girl's head and then unbound her arms and legs. She flung about like a fish let loose on dry ground. "And for sure, I thought I was gonna die." The words spurted out in short gasps. "I could barely breathe with that carpet rolled about me." Her red hair flew about wildly as she lunged toward one of her abductors.

Matthew and Taylor let the other two men contend with the Irish girl and her temper. They unfurled carpet after carpet. They had now released seven girls, each one gasping for air and flailing for freedom as her bindings were loosed. Taylor stared down at the last roll of carpet. *Please, God, let it be Bella,* he silently prayed.

The two men tugged on the edge of the rug until they saw evidence of one more girl, whose feet and wrists were bound just as they had seen with the others. But this time the girl didn't shout with relief when her gag was loosened; this time the girl didn't flail about or jump to her feet. This time the girl lay perfectly still; this time the girl was Bella.

This time Taylor screamed in agony.

~ 36 ~

L illy Cheever grasped the fullness of her skirts, lifting the hem from the muck that lined the narrow winding path. She took careful steps, attempting to secure her footing in the slimy mess. Her walking boots were already covered with filth, and now a wiry-haired dog was yapping and nipping at her skirts as it circled her at a dizzying pace. Unfortunately, her attempts to shoo away the dog had only caused the animal to bark more incessantly.

A stooped old woman with a tattered shawl wrapped around her bent shoulders hoisted a bucketful of waste into the street, barely missing Lilly as she passed by. "What ya doin' in this part o' town?" The woman's voice was laced with a heavy Irish brogue. Piercing blue eyes that seemed strangely out of place were set deep in the ancient leathery face that had been marked with the countless creases of a hard life.

Lilly stopped and turned to face the woman, feeling out of place in her fur-collared mantle and morning dress of floral challis. "I'm looking for Noreen Gallagher's home. I was told it was down this path to the left. Is that correct?" She gave the woman a gentle smile. "I'd be willing to pay for the information."

The woman's eyes seemed to cut to her soul as she appraised Lilly for a moment before answering. "Hold to the left at the fork. Third door on the right," she replied and then held out her withered hand for payment.

Lilly dug into her lozenge-shaped velvet reticule and pulled out a coin. The woman's eyes brightened at the sight of the money as Lilly placed it in her hand. She clasped her bony fingers around the coin and then quickly disappeared behind her door as though she feared Lilly would snatch the money away from her.

The fork in the road was only a short distance away, and the mangy dog had now departed to chase after a wandering chicken rather than her skirts. She continued onward, picking her way through the litter-strewn pathway until she stood in front of Noreen Gallagher's door. *What kind of reception awaits me behind that dilapidated door?* she wondered. Fear would win if she remained there any longer.

She knocked—three firm raps—and waited. The door scraped open, the bottom of the board digging into the dirt floor before revealing an unkempt woman with matted hair and yellowed broken teeth. "Noreen Gallagher?" Lilly ventured.

"And who'd be wantin' to know?"

"I'm Lilly Cheever, and I wondered if I might have a word with you."

The woman fidgeted for a moment, running her fingers through her reddish-brown mass of greasy hair before answering. "What for? I ain't done nothin' to bring the likes of ya into the Acre."

"I've come to inquire about Kathryn O'Hanrahan's child."

Noreen's fingers immediately locked around Lilly's wrist. "Who says Kathryn ever had a child?" she hissed. The woman's eyes reflected a jittery mix of surprise, fear, and curiosity as she pulled Lilly forward into the hovel.

Lilly swallowed down her fear and croaked, "Liam Donohue."

"Liam!" The woman loosened her grip on Lilly's arm. "That traitorous man. Did he tell ya he wasn't possessed of enough manhood to tell me to me face that 'e was movin' out? And now it seems he's taken to spreadin' false rumors."

The smell inside was putrid, a farrago of every foul odor Lilly could imagine. She pulled a handkerchief from her pocket but then thought the better of placing it over her nose and mouth. Most likely the woman would take offense. "Your sister didn't have a child? Oh, please, this is very important."

Noreen held up an empty bottle. "How important?"

"I'm willing to pay for the information, and I promise no harm will come to you nor the child."

Noreen's lips curled into a wicked grin, her broken yellow teeth resembling the ruins of a city wall. "If I should be decidin' to tell ya anythin', there best be nothin' but good come from the use o' me words. Otherwise, I'll place a curse on ya that'll take the life of that child ya're carryin' in yar belly."

Lilly shivered at the threat. "If I tell you why I have an interest in the child, perhaps you'd be reconciled to helping me."

Noreen nodded and pointed at a broken-down wooden chair. "We'll see. Sit down."

Lilly carefully lowered herself into the chair, not certain it was capable of holding her weight without collapsing to the floor. Once seated and somewhat assured that the chair was stable, Lilly began to carefully explain the events surrounding her brother's untimely death. She told of his dying declaration concerning the existence of a child, a boy with a mushroom-shaped birthmark, and her determination to find the boy, although she remained silent regarding her journey to Canterbury.

"Yar brother's name?"

"Lewis. Lewis Armbruster."

Noreen slowly wagged her head back and forth. "Me sister never mentioned anyone by the name o' Armbruster to me. 'Course, that's not to say she didn't know 'im, 'cause I can't say that for sure. But Cullan is not yar brother's child. He was sired by William Thurston, and of that there is no doubt. For reasons I never understood, me sister believed that one day Thurston would leave 'is wife and marry 'er. Such nonsense! I told her so, too, but she wouldn't listen. William Thurston did nothin' but use her, and 'e was angry as a bull seein' red when Kathryn told 'im she was givin' him a babe—like he had nothin' to do with it."

"Did he accept the boy as his offspring?"

The Irish woman's lips curled in disgust. "He didn't like it none, but when he saw the birthmark, 'e knew. Besides, whether he wanted to admit it or not, he knew Kathryn hadn't been with other men. Kathryn said sometimes 'e was kind to the boy, but mostly not. I think Kathryn knew he'd never accept the lad. In fact, she told me should anything ever 'appen to her, she feared for the child's life. When she died, I figured Cullan would be safer outside of the Acre."

Lilly nodded. "And you took him to the Shaker Village in Canterbury."

Noreen jumped up from her chair and was leaning over Lilly. "How'd ya know that?"

"Purely coincidence, Mrs. Gallagher, but I've been to Canterbury to see the boy. They named him David but mentioned he had been known as Cullan."

Noreen's face softened slightly. "Is 'e well? How'd 'e look?"

"He appeared very well. He was neat and clean, obviously well nurtured—a fetching child," Lilly related. "I'm curious why you took him to Canterbury. You're obviously not of the same religious beliefs."

Noreen cackled and clapped her hands. "No. I doubt ya'll find many Irish among them Shakers. Odd sort of people, what little I saw of 'em, but I told Kathryn when the lad was born that if anything ever 'appened to her, I'd make certain the babe didn't come to any harm. I didn't think he'd be safe with me—figured if William Thurston heard tell I had a young boy living with me, he'd figure out soon enough the child was his and come after 'im."

Lilly remained silent, her gaze fixed upon Noreen's rough hands, the dirty fingers laced together as if in prayer. She didn't want to believe this woman's story. Lilly had fought against the idea the child could belong to anyone other than Lewis since she'd heard Liam Donohue's tale. But Matthew had willingly believed every word he'd been told. And as far as Lilly's husband was concerned, the matter was resolved—not that she hadn't attempted to resurrect the topic at every given opportunity. But Matthew always managed to change the subject. Today, she'd had no choice but to take matters into her own hands.

"Farfetched as my idea may seem, don't you think we should explore this matter more deeply? What if Lewis really is the boy's father? Wouldn't you want to know?"

"Me? I already know the truth. William Thurston's the boy's father, and there ain't nothin' ya can dig up that'll change that fact. I figure I could lie to ya. I might even make meself some money in the tellin'. Who would be the wiser? But the fact is Cullan might end up dead because of it. There ain't much I wouldn't do for a few coins, and folks here in the Acre would tell ya that's a fact. But I won't break a promise to me dead sister. If ya go and bring that lad back to Lowell, ya best be ready to accept the fact that yar actions will likely kill him. Are you so stubborn that ya're willing to see the lad die?"

"I'm stubborn enough to want him to have a better life, a life with his true family."

Noreen shook her head back and forth. "You ain't his kin, Mrs. Cheever. I don't know what else I can be sayin' to convince ya. But I'll tell ya this much—if ya have a speck of sense, ya'll leave this house and forget the lad."

Lilly knew she had been dismissed. There was, after all, nothing else to say. Reaching into her reticule, she pulled out several shiny coins and extended them to Noreen.

"Keep yar money. Just do as I've asked—forget the lad." Noreen's lips were set in a tight, hard line as she stood and looked down at Lilly. "Go back to yar fancy house, have a nice healthy baby of yar own, and pretend none of this ever 'appened."

Lilly stood, nodded, and dropped the coins into a metal cup as she slowly walked out of the shack. She remembered little of her journey out of the Acre. If there had been stares or whispered remarks, she'd been unaware. If there had been a yapping dog or an old woman pitching waste, it had gone unnoticed. So focused were her thoughts that she was surprised to find herself walking up the front steps to her home.

The first step was easy, but the second was halted as pain ripped through her abdomen and spread into her back. Gasping, Lilly put a hand to her stomach and tried to ignore the pain. In a moment it passed and she was able to reach the house. Drawing a deep breath, she knew her time had come. Now she would have to see about reaching Matthew and the doctor before the baby was born without them.

Bella coughed, then sputtered, carpet fibers invading her airways as she strained to fill her lungs with fresh air. A voice somewhere in the distance instructed her to breathe slowly and relax. Yet she couldn't. Her body ached for oxygen. And so she fought for air—in short panicky gasps until her body finally responded and the distant voice became clearer, saying her name and instructing her to remain calm and open her eyes.

Fingers cradled her head, and she could feel the warmth of someone's breath on her face. She struggled to open her eyes. They felt heavy, as though a weight had been placed upon them, sealing them tight. Once again she heard someone calling her name in the distance. Her eyelids fluttered momentarily and then languidly opened to reveal a face that was nearly touching her own. Startled, Bella lurched upward and struck Taylor's forehead with her own. The force of the blow caused her to drop back onto the boat's deck.

Taylor moved to her side, his hand now rubbing his forehead. "Are you all right? I was so worried."

Bella focused upon Taylor's face and watched as a small bump began to rise on his brow. She gave him a faint smile. "I believe I've injured you."

"Don't concern yourself with me. Try to sit up," he encouraged, taking her hand. "How do you feel?"

Loosened strands of hair fell across her face as she lifted herself into a sitting position. Instinctively, she brushed the hair behind one ear. "I think I'm fine. The other girls, are they injured? Where is Ruth?"

Ruth moved closer, with the other girls following her lead. "I'm right here, Bella."

Bella glanced toward Hilda. "And you, Hilda, did they hurt you?"

Hilda gave her a bright smile. "I'll be fine once we get back home."

Turning her gaze to Taylor, Bella said, "Hilda works at the Hamilton. And poor Ruth, they've been holding her longer than any of us. We had given up all hope of being found."

Ruth nodded her head. "I was certain I'd never see my family again. Several times they said I was being sent to Boston."

"Where have you been all this time, Ruth?"

"I wish I could tell you, but I truly don't know. They blindfolded me and put me in the back of a wagon. I have no idea where we went, but I think it was somewhere out of town. I was kept in one room with no windows, and then they brought the other girls, one by one," Ruth explained, her gaze now shifting to Hilda and the Irish girls. "But they never brought Bella. We didn't see her until they moved us to the warehouse here at the millpond. Of course, we didn't know it was the millpond, but we could hear water and boats. We knew we were near water and that we were going to be shipped off somewhere."

Bella glanced toward Matthew and Liam. Both of them appeared to be listening intently as Ruth related her story. The two men in charge of the boat shifted about, obviously growing more and more uncomfortable as Matthew glared down at them. "I'm not going to waste much time on the two of you," Matthew growled. "You know we've already sent for the police. If you have any hopes of leniency, I suggest you cooperate and tell us everything you know about this illegal business you're conducting. Otherwise, I'm going to tell the police you both deserve as much punishment as can possibly be meted out by the judge."

"Now, wait a minute," one of them objected, "this wasn't our idea. We're being paid to haul cargo to Boston—nothing more."

Matthew grunted. "Don't lie to me. You two men kidnapped these girls and knew what was going to happen to them."

The other man stroked the bristly stubble along his jawline. "Well, yeah, that there is true, but we was following orders. It was them or us. If we didn't do what we was told, we'd find ourselves taking a bullet or floating in the river. I'm too young to die."

"Then you'd best tell us who put you up to this whole thing. I want names—all of them, starting with yours."

The two men exchanged a look before the second one continued. "My name is Jake Wilson and this here's Rafe Walton. But you ain't gonna believe me when I tell you who set this up."

"Try me. You may be surprised what I'll believe."

"William Thurston's the one in charge. Him and J. P. Green. They put us up to this whole thing, and they're the ones getting rich, not us. But I doubt you want to hear it's some of your fancy Associates dealing in human flesh. You don't believe me, do ya?"

"Unfortunately, I do. Have you left out any names? Is there anybody else involved?"

Rafe slowly moved his head back and forth. "If there is, they never told us. Thurston and Green are the only ones we ever met with, and I doubt they wanted to share their profits with anyone else."

"Me too. They wasn't paying us hardly anything," Jake said before turning his attention to the girls on the other side of the boat. "You tell 'em we never did you any harm."

Taylor jumped to his feet and took three long strides to where Jake was sitting and glared into the man's face. "What do you mean you didn't do them any harm? You tore them away from their homes against their will, kept them as prisoners—and you almost killed her," he shouted while pointing toward Bella. "And if we hadn't stopped you, they would be bound for the slave market in New Orleans. I'd say you did plenty of harm."

Bella gasped. "Slave market? They were going to sell us as slaves? Is that what you've discovered, Taylor?"

Her words brought him back to her side. "It's a long story, but Matthew discovered these men have gotten into the business of abducting girls when they are out alone at night. It appears as if they were waiting until they had a goodly number of you before making the journey to Boston."

The words struck fear in her heart. Foolish pride had nearly caused her ruin. She didn't want to imagine what would have happened had Taylor and the other men not arrived. Bella looked across the boat to where Matthew and Liam had now secured Rafe and Jake. "One of them said they were taking us to Boston and from there we would be taken south; he mentioned New Orleans. He said there was no need for concern—that we'd have lovely new homes. I inquired why he didn't advertise for girls to work in these homes if these were desirable positions, pointing out the fact that the Corporation advertises in the newspaper for mill girls. He quickly told me to shut up and labeled me a troublemaker. But the thought of slavery never entered my mind."

Taking her hands in his own, Taylor gently warmed her cold fingers. "It's best you don't dwell on what might have happened, Bella. You're safe and that's what really matters."

She couldn't believe his kindness. "After the way I acted, I'm surprised you would even bother to look for me."

"Don't be foolish. A few misspoken words can't drive me away from you, Bella. I realize my behavior last night upset you—and rightfully so. I should have told you I needed to remain for another meeting. I must admit I was surprised when I realized you'd left for home, but it wasn't until very early this morning that I discovered you had never arrived back at the boardinghouse. Miss Addie sent Daughtie to inquire about your whereabouts, and that's when our search began," he explained. "I would have never stopped looking for you, Bella. I love you . . . and I never want to lose you again. It's my desire that one day you'll feel the same way. I can't make you trust me, but I hope you'll come to believe that I will never abandon you."

His words were filled with warmth and compassion. She wanted desperately to believe him, to once again feel the safety of another's love and protection. Yet dare she let him into her heart? Could she withstand rejection if he should one day decide she was no longer worthy of his love? Bella wasn't certain, yet she knew Taylor deserved a reply. Before she could form a response, Dr. Fontaine jumped onto the boat, his medical bag swinging from one hand.

"John tells me someone down here needs a doctor."

"Over here," Taylor called out. "Bella was having difficulty breathing. However, I believe she's much better now that she's gotten some fresh air."

Dr. Fontaine quickly moved to her side. "Let's take a look, young lady."

Bella held up a hand in protest. "I don't need a doctor. I'm fine. They've brought you down here unnecessarily."

The doctor gave her a paternal smile. "Since I'm the one with medical training, why don't you let me decide whether you need me or not?"

There was no sense in arguing; it was obvious she wouldn't win. "As you choose, but I'm certain you'll find me a healthy specimen."

All of them turned to look as a rider came galloping toward the dock, shouting and waving in their direction. "Doc, you're needed at the Cheever house. You'd best be coming, too, Matthew. I've been told your wife's about to have her baby." The rider jumped down from his horse. "You can take my horse, Doc," the man offered.

Matthew looked helplessly from Liam to Taylor. "I've got to go. John should be back with the police soon. Can you handle this?"

"For sure we can. Ya be gettin' yarself home," Liam said, giving Matthew a hearty laugh. "I've no doubt that yar wife might not be too forgivin' if ya don't get home to her right now."

"I'll return your horse once Uncle John gets back," Taylor promised as Matthew stepped out of the boat.

Matthew waved and called out over his shoulder, "And by that time, I hope to have a son or daughter to introduce."

Matthew's words brought a smile to Bella's face. "I pray that this baby will fill the void in Mrs. Cheever's life. I'm certain she's been distraught since hearing that the child in Canterbury isn't her nephew. I know this baby won't replace her parents or brother—or even the place she'd set aside for little Cullan—but certainly a new life will bring affirmation that her family lives on through the baby. Family is very important to her."

Taylor gazed into her eyes. "And to you, I believe."

A faint smile played upon Bella's lips as she stared into Taylor's intense blue eyes. "Yes, family is very important." At the sound of pounding horses' hooves, they both turned toward the road. "It appears your uncle John has arrived with the police."

"It seems to me that every time I'm able to engage you in a serious conversation, someone interrupts us," Taylor lamented. "Once we finally have this kidnapping issue resolved, I want time alone to discuss our future."

"Our future?"

Taylor put his arms around Bella and helped her to her feet. "Yes, our future . . . as Mr. and Mrs. Taylor Manning."

"I'm not sure—"

He placed a finger to her lips. "Wait until we have time to talk before you say anything more."

"Lilly!" Matthew called to his wife as he took the front porch steps two at a time. He knew the doctor would be on his heels and left the front door wide open as he bounded into the house. "Lilly!"

"I'm right here, dear," she said softly.

He found her sitting in the front room. "Why are you here? Why aren't you in bed?"

"I didn't feel like going to bed. Not yet, anyway. I sent for the doctor."

Matthew nodded. "I know. He was with me when the rider came."

"Why was the doctor with you?" she asked curiously.

"It's a long story. But it has a happy ending. We found many of the missing girls, Lilly. I'll tell you all about it after I help you to bed. The doctor should be here any minute." He knelt beside her and lifted her skirt slightly. "Here, let me take off your shoes. I'm sure—" He stopped in midsentence. "Your shoes are caked in mud . . . manure, too, from the smell of them. Where have you been?"

She gave him a weak smile. "I've been to see Noreen Gallagher."

Matthew momentarily forgot about his wife's labor and barely controlled his anger. "You went to the Acre?" He stared in silence for a moment before regaining his composure. "Surely my wife would not do such a thing. Tell me this is an ill-thought-out hoax, Lilly. Please."

"I'm sorry, Matthew, but it's true. I needed to talk with her, to somehow be convinced that the boy in Canterbury is not Lewis's child."

"And did you see her?"

Lilly nodded her head.

"And were you convinced?"

"Well . . ."

"I knew it!" he exclaimed. "What will it take to convince you, Lilly? Lewis is dead. The boy's mother is dead. Who is left that can make you see the truth?"

"I don't know."

"Obviously there is no one. You're even willing to bring on the premature birth of our child in this futile effort to convince yourself the boy is somehow related to you."

"That's not true. I would never harm our child. The baby may be coming a bit sooner than we expected, but that happens to a lot of women."

Matthew stopped pacing and leveled his gaze her way. "Lilly, you placed both yourself and our child in jeopardy the minute you walked into the Acre. I'm surprised you weren't knocked down and robbed. You certainly extended an invitation, dressed in fur and velvet and, if my guess is right, carrying a reticule in plain sight."

"How was I to know?"

"That's exactly my point, Lilly."

"I knew you'd refuse me. Every time I attempt to talk about the boy, you change the subject."

"Don't make this my fault, Lilly. I would have permitted a talk with Noreen. In fact, I had already mentioned the possibility to Liam Donohue. But I certainly wouldn't have sent you to the Acre. I would have brought Noreen here, to our home, where the possibility of danger would have been nonexistent."

Lilly lowered her head. "Nothing happened. We're both safe. I promise I'll not go back there again. Am I forgiven?" Her voice was little more than a whisper.

Matthew lowered himself into the chair opposite her and took her delicate hands into his own. "Of course you're forgiven, Lilly. I love you more than you can possibly imagine. It grieves me to know how deeply affected you've been by the boy and yet you believed I was unapproachable. Because I believed without doubt that the child was William Thurston's, I assumed that you, too, would be convinced. I was wrong."

"In my heart I know you're right. And even if I still harbored hope, Noreen has convinced me the boy's life would be in danger were he returned to Lowell. I can't take such a risk. I could never live with myself if he came to harm because of my selfish actions. Yet I maintain this deep longing for a continuation of my family."

He lifted her chin until their eyes met. "You do have a continuation of your family—the baby and me. God has blessed us, Lilly, and although your parents and brother are gone, they'll live on through you and our child."

"I know you're right, Matthew, but it's difficult letting go of the hope."

"You must never lose hope, Lilly. I'd never ask such a thing, but perhaps you could redirect your hope—reassign those dreams to the future of our child and our family."

She smiled up at him and whispered, "Perhaps I could." Her smile faded as she doubled in pain. "The baby!" she gasped.

"Did I hear tell there was a baby to be born today?" the doctor questioned as he came into the house.

Matthew lifted Lilly into his arms. "I was just getting her upstairs. She's the stubborn type, you know. Sometimes you just have to impose your will on her."

The doctor laughed and followed them upstairs. "No doubt the baby will impose his or her will on you both. Parenting is no easy chore."

After dealing with the police, Liam saw the Irish girls home while Taylor took care of Ruth and Bella and Hilda. Walking back to the boardinghouse, Bella glanced up hesitantly. "Why do you keep talking of marriage to me? You scarcely know me."

"I know enough," Taylor replied, grinning. "I know you're spirited and full of life. I know you believe in righting wrongs and standing your ground when you believe you're right." He paused on the walkway and took hold of her hands, turning her to face him. "I know that the thought of living without you is something I do not want to contemplate."

Bella swallowed hard, trying to push down the lump of emotion that had risen from within. "Taylor, you've been the most important person in your life for so long; why should I believe that would change now?"

"Because God can change anyone's heart. At least that's what Uncle John told me, and I believe you've said much the same. I did a great deal of thinking while searching for you, and I know I've been wrong to push God away. My mother brought me up to love the Scriptures and to esteem God. But losing her . . ." His voice grew soft. He straightened his shoulders and drew a deep breath. "It was so hard. I saw my father fail every day after her death. They were one in every sense, and when she died, he couldn't go on. That terrified me. I decided then and there I would never love a woman as my father had loved my mother."

"What changed your mind?"

He smiled. "You."

Bella shook her head. "Surely there was more."

"Oh, I suppose I was impressed with Uncle John and Miss Addie. I would come away from our meetings feeling emptiness in light of what they had. I would remind myself of Father's pain, but it didn't seem to matter." Taylor met Bella's gaze. "Then I came to realize it wasn't Miss Addie and Uncle John's situation that brought about this feeling, but rather you. When I first met you, I knew you were different . . . I knew you were unique."

"I'm not unique in any real sense," Bella replied. "I also know I'm not without my faults. I suppose I should thank you for bearing with my errors so graciously."

He laughed. "Bella, we are both troublesome creatures. We have much to learn and a long way to go toward a complete understanding of marriage and love, but I want to educate myself in those things with you by my side. I'm not asking you to marry me tomorrow—I'm just seeking a pledge that you will be my wife . . . someday."

Bella felt her knees tremble and fought to steady herself without giving notice to Taylor. During the entire ordeal of being kidnapped, Taylor had been all she could think of. She had already determined that she loved him—faults and all—but she wanted very much to be certain about this momentous step.

"I didn't come to Lowell with the thought of getting married."

He nodded. "I know, and that's what made you exactly the right woman for me. All the others threw themselves at me. I could give them a wink or a nod, and they were totally devoted to me."

"Yes, well," Bella said, feeling her anger ignite, "I witnessed enough of that to last me a lifetime." She pulled away from him and began walking again.

"Bella, those girls meant nothing to me then, and they mean nothing now. Don't you hear me? I know that toying with their affections was the wrong thing for me to do. I know I'm a sinful man, but, Bella . . . I love you."

She stopped and turned, seeing the sincerity in his expression. "We'll probably fight all the time," she murmured.

He grinned. "But then we can make up."

"I have a temper."

He walked slowly toward her. "So I've noticed."

Bella bit her lower lip. She felt a surge of excitement as he stopped only inches from her. "I find it difficult to trust—especially men."

"I don't care if you ever trust other men; just trust me. That's all I'm asking."

"I still believe in the equality of men and women. I still believe in education for females as well as males," she said, thinking it best to throw out everything and give him time to rethink his proposal.

"So do I, Bella," he said, taking hold of her shoulders. They stood there for several moments, neither one saying a word.

With a startling certainty, Bella knew her heart. She loved Taylor Manning and didn't want to go through life without him.

"And God must come first in our home," Bella finally added.

He pulled her into his arms. "Yes," he breathed against her lips.

"Yes," she murmured as he captured her mouth in a tender yet passionate kiss.

He pulled away. "Was that yes for me?"

She nodded.

He grinned in his self-assured manner. "Good. So long as we have that matter taken care of." He pulled her along toward the boardinghouse. "Now we must tell Miss Addie that you're safe and that Mrs. Cheever is having her baby."

Bella felt dazed but happy. "I suppose we might also tell her that we plan to marry in a few years."

Taylor stopped dead in his tracks. "A few years? I thought maybe next week."

Bella shook her head. "We need time, Taylor. Being engaged for, say . . . five years could be very prudent in our situation. You know that as well as I. We both need to reaffirm our hearts to God and to allow His guidance in this matter. Our love for each other will only grow stronger—if it's real."

Taylor shook his head and guided her up the walkway to Miss Addie's. "I've never known anything more real—and I never want to." He paused with a grin before opening the door and added, "And I'm not waiting five years."

❧ EPILOGUE ❧

Christmas 1831

Lilly, she's positively perfect," Addie said as she beheld the newest member of the Cheever family.

"Her father certainly thinks so," Lilly replied. "Would you like to hold her?"

"Oh, please," Addie replied.

Lilly handed her daughter to Addie, then nodded to Bella. "You, too. You can share her for a moment, and then I'm going to put her down for her nap and we shall have our Christmas punch and exchange our gifts."

Addie cuddled the baby momentarily before giving her up. Bella thought her heart would melt into a puddle on the floor as she took the baby into her arms. Violet Cheever looked up at her with large dark eyes. She yawned a tiny baby yawn and made sucking noises as she closed her eyes.

Bella gently touched her downy soft hair and smiled. "She's perfect."

"You look very natural holding her. You and Taylor should have a whole houseful of children," Lilly said, reaching out to take Violet. "I'll be back momentarily. Why don't you both join the men in the music room?"

Addie linked her arm with Bella. As they crossed from the parlor to the music room, Addie stated, "I'd imagine holding Violet makes you want to speed up your wedding plans."

Bella grinned. "Just don't tell Taylor that or he'll start pestering me all over again."

"Don't tell Taylor what?"

Bella looked up to find Taylor at her side. "Never mind," she said. "Some things are better left unsaid."

"Since when? I've always known you to speak your mind and make certain that everyone knows your thoughts," Taylor teased.

Bella smiled as Miss Addie left her with Taylor and joined John and Matthew across the room by the fireplace. "You are purposefully trying my patience in the hope that I will tell you what I do not wish to share."

He laughed and pulled her close. "I can be most persuasive, Miss Newberry. Would you like me to show you how?" He gently caressed her cheek with his fingertips, then trailed the touch down to her lips.

Bella trembled. "Hmm, yes, actually . . . I think that might be a nice diversion."

Taylor roared with laughter and kissed her soundly. Bella wrapped her arms around his neck and sighed. Maybe putting the wedding off for five years would be too long. Maybe three would make better sense.

Their kiss deepened as they completely ignored the other people in the room. Maybe, Bella reconsidered, a year would be enough time to wait.

These
TANGLED
THREADS

I object to this marriage—the woman is not free to wed!" The indictment reverberated off the walls and then plummeted to the slate floor of St. Anne's Episcopal Church. The wedding guests craned their necks, a few murmuring and shifting in their pews before finally retreating into a cocoon of silence.

Arabella Newberry whirled toward the voice, her bridal satin rippling in waves behind her. "What are *you* doing here?" she cried out, her strained words slicing through the hushed quietude of the sanctuary.

Franklin Newberry edged out of a pew near the rear of the church, moved to the center of the aisle, and squared off with his daughter. Raising a paper into the air like a flag, he waved it above his head. "I hold proof of my words," he avowed, continuing to brandish the paper overhead while moving down the aisle toward Bella. "She is bound by contract to the United Society of Believers in Christ's Second Appearing." His voice boomed through the church.

Bella reached out and clutched Daughtie's hand, pulling her friend close. "How did he know? You wrote to him, didn't you?" she accused, staring into Daughtie's doe-eyed gaze.

"N-n-n-no," Daughtie stammered. "How could you even think such a thing?"

There was no time to answer Bella's claim, for Franklin Newberry was now upon them, pushing Bella to one side as he thrust the document atop Reverend Edson's open Bible.

"See for yourself!" He stepped back a pace after issuing his command.

Theodore Edson stared at the document lying before him. Quickly scanning the contract, he glanced at Bella's ashen face and graced her with a look of compassion before turning his attention to Franklin Newberry. "I don't believe this document to be of legal consequence. It appears to have been signed by Miss Newberry when she was still a child of tender years—and she's female. I'm not a lawyer, but I don't believe a judge would find she had capacity to contract."

"She had capacity among the Shakers. She was old enough to understand the gravity of her decision, and the Shakers believe in equality between the sexes. She held the same ability to contract as any man and she is bound." Franklin reached out and grasped his daughter's wrist.

Bella tugged against his hold and winced as her father's fingers tightened. Her creamy white skin quickly turned red and was now beginning to resemble the bluish-purple shade of an overripe plum. She wiggled her fingers. Pinpricks ebbed through her hand, and she pumped her fingers in and out, praying the action would permit a smidgen of blood to pass through her father's constricting grasp.

"You're hurting me. Turn loose my wrist." The words hissed from between her clenched teeth.

Disregarding the plea, he gave her an icy stare, one that would freeze the warmest of hearts. She willed herself to maintain a steady gaze. Should she look away, her father would believe he had the advantage. "You are coming with me." His voice was cold, void of emotion.

Bella ignored the ripple of fear flowing through her body and with an air of determination jutted her chin forward. "No! I intend to marry, and nothing you say or do will prevent this wedding from taking place. Create a scene if you must, but when I leave this church, my name will be Mrs. Taylor Manning."

"Indeed it will," Taylor agreed. His chest puffed out a bit. "I think you'd best leave," he said, raising his voice loud enough for the entire congregation to hear.

Bella shot him a look of gratitude. She was beginning to think he'd lost his ability to speak.

Franklin turned his frosty stare upon Taylor. "*You're* the one who invited me. Now that I've arranged to be present, you want me to leave? I'll depart right now, so long as my daughter accompanies me."

Bella leaned around her father's large frame in order to see Taylor. "*You?* You invited my father to attend our wedding? How could you do such a thing without asking me?"

"I was hoping the two of you could resolve your differences and mend your relationship. What better time to apologize and grant forgiveness than on this happy occasion?"

"Apology? You think I owe this disrespectful, vow-breaking girl an apology?" Franklin Newberry's voice once again boomed through the church.

"Forgiveness? I don't need *his* forgiveness." Bella's voice was no match for her father's, but she knew he heard her words, and that was all that mattered. She looked at Taylor. "Did you truly invite him?" Her voice was now soft and filled with disbelief.

Taylor nodded and gave her a feeble smile. "My intentions were honorable."

"Indeed they were," Franklin agreed. "Who can say what it cost him to send a coach to Canterbury in order to have his man deliver an invitation. A noble gesture."

Reverend Edson cleared his throat. "If this discussion is going to continue, I would suggest we move to another place outside the hearing of the wedding guests. Perhaps we could request they excuse us for a short time," he suggested.

"I've nothing to say that can't be heard by these people. You asked openly if there was an objection to this marriage, and I've voiced my protest for all to hear. Why should we move elsewhere? If Bella truly believes she has a right to marry, let her defend herself in front of her invited guests," Franklin replied.

Taylor directed his gaze toward Bella. "Had your father sent a response agreeing to attend, I would have told you he was expected. But he sent no reply with the coach driver, nor did he respond later. Consequently, I assumed he would not attend." Taylor hesitated a moment and arched his eyebrows. "I expected him to follow proper etiquette."

Her father's hold loosened, and Bella shook off his hand. "You thought my father would adhere to the rules of etiquette? The only rules he follows are those that take him down a path of ease. That's why he joined the Shakers—to escape the responsibilities of a wife and daughter. Isn't that correct, *Brother* Franklin?" She spoke quietly, her words audible only to Reverend Edson and Taylor. "You were an adult who broke your marriage vows to my mother—vows you made before God. You have no right to speak to me of broken contracts. Your words are fouled by your own behavior. Please leave this place."

The minister turned his gaze from Bella to her father. "I don't want to have you forcibly removed, Mr. Newberry. Either take a seat or quietly leave this church. Please."

Bella watched as her father tugged at his indigo blue surtout and meticulously fitted each cloth-covered button through its buttonhole. Then, with head high and lips twisted in a tight line, he turned on his heel and walked down the aisle, the click of his shoes coldly tapping out his farewell. She squinted against the sunshine that streamed through the arched doors of the foyer, momentarily encircling Franklin Newberry with a dazzling light. Once again her father was turning his back on her.

Bella swallowed hard against the sudden urge to call him back. He hadn't wanted her years ago when he'd decided to join the Society of Believers, and he still didn't want her. Why couldn't he love her for who she was? Why couldn't her earthly father offer the same unconditional love she'd found in Jesus?

Reverend Edson lightly touched Bella's arm and brought her back to the present. "Bella? You look pale. Do you want to proceed or shall we wait?" The pastor's words were a hushed whisper.

Bella glanced at Taylor. He met her gaze, his eyes filled with concern. "We should proceed," she replied, turning toward the pastor. "But," she continued, turning her attention back to Taylor, "we need to discuss this entire matter after the ceremony."

"We don't want your marriage to begin on a sour note. Perhaps a short interlude *would* be best," Reverend Edson encouraged.

Bella gently adjusted the pleats along the waistline of her ivory satin gown. "No need to delay, Reverend Edson. Our marriage will survive the brief discussion of today's events," Bella replied with a sweet smile. "Nothing has changed my love for Taylor."

"Very well. We'll proceed from where I left off," he told the congregation.

"Let's begin *after* the part where you asked for objections," Taylor suggested.

Nervous laughter followed by warnings of *shh* drifted through the sanctuary, eliciting a faint smile from the minister. "Repeat after me," he instructed Taylor.

Bella listened as Taylor recited his vows and then slipped a gold band onto her trembling finger while he pledged his love. She followed with her own vows before looking up to receive his kiss. Her face tinged scarlet as they turned to face their smiling guests. Tugging at Taylor's arm, she propelled him forward, down the steps, and out of the church.

"I didn't realize you were so anxious to be alone with me. I believe we were at a full trot coming down the aisle," he teased while helping her into their awaiting carriage.

She turned to face him, ready to defend her actions, but burst into laughter when he began imitating their quick escape from the sanctuary. She patted the seat beside her. "Come along. If we hurry, we'll have a few minutes alone before the guests arrive."

"Yes, my dear," he said, giving her a mock salute. "I'll fortify myself for the tongue-lashing I'm about to receive for my boorish behavior." He slapped the reins, sending the horses into motion.

She giggled at his remark. "You do realize you almost ruined our wedding."

"*Almost.* That's the key word, my love. Even with my lack of common sense, we still managed to become husband and wife. And having you as my wife is all that matters."

She gave his arm a playful slap. "How can I remain angry when you're so willing to be reprimanded?"

"Because I know I was wrong," he said, his voice suddenly becoming serious. "I realize my actions were foolhardy, and I apologize for taking such liberty without first consulting you, Bella. I give you my word: it won't happen again. With both of my parents deceased and the remainder of my family in

England, and with your mother deceased, I thought it would be nice if your one remaining parent could be in attendance. My genuine wish was for you to experience reconciliation with your father. I foolishly thought our wedding might provide an opportunity for the two of you to make amends. Little did I realize your father would use such an important event to wreak havoc."

"The wedding gave him a perfect opportunity to return the embarrassment I caused him when I ran off from the Shaker village to work at the mill. I'm sure he viewed my departure from Canterbury as a personal affront rather than what it truly was—an unwillingness to embrace the Shaker beliefs and way of life he had chosen for our family. I only wish my mother could have lived to see me happily married."

Taylor's expression filled with concern. "Bella dear, I didn't mean to make you sad with all of this talk. I had simply hoped your father would come for the right reasons, such as wanting to resolve differences . . . and to see his lovely daughter in her wedding gown," Taylor added.

Bella looked heavenward. "If seeing me in my gown was his intent, he could have done so without causing a scene. Instead, he brought along my contract with the Shakers; he obviously desired a confrontation."

"You're right. I suppose I wanted to give him the benefit of the doubt," Taylor said while pulling back on the reins and drawing the horses to a stop. "I'll be pleased when we're able to move into our own house, and with a bit of luck, it should be finished by the time we return from our wedding trip to England," he said, helping her down from the carriage and escorting her up the steps of John and Addie Farnsworth's house.

"Perhaps if you hadn't insisted on all the intricate stonework, the house would already be completed," she said, gracing him with an engaging smile.

"Uncle John is the one who insisted upon having Liam Donohue design and build the fireplaces and decorative stonework. When I objected, he said I couldn't refuse him since he considered it our wedding present—over and above the gift of our journey to England."

"Yes, but had you not gone on and on about the new fireplaces and beautiful stonework Matthew Cheever had Liam complete in his house, I doubt whether your uncle John would have hired Mr. Donohue. However, I find his choice a unique and wonderful gesture, one we'll enjoy for years to come."

Taylor gave her a broad smile. "I certainly hope so. And here I thought we had hastened back to the house so you would have time to chastise me before our guests arrived."

Her face grew serious at his comment. "Chastising my husband in public is not something I plan to do. However, I *would* like you to promise you won't contact my father again without first discussing such an invitation with me."

"You have my word *and* my apology, Mrs. Manning," he replied, pulling her into his arms and kissing her soundly.

"That was a thoroughly delightful kiss," Bella whispered before disengaging herself from Taylor's hold around her waist. He attempted to once again pull her close. "Taylor, we have guests arriving," she said in her most prim and proper tone.

Taylor glanced toward the procession of horse-drawn carriages now moving down the road toward the house and emitted a loud guffaw. With a swoop of his arm, he pulled Bella back into his arms. "You're my wife, Bella. It's perfectly acceptable for me to kiss you," he replied, holding her close.

Taylor released her from his embrace before the entourage pulled into the driveway, but Bella's cheeks remained flushed a deep ruby red long after he'd turned her loose. "It may be acceptable to kiss me, but it's hardly appropriate to do so in the middle of the street."

"We are nowhere near the middle of the street, my love."

Addie and John Farnsworth hurried up the steps to the house, their carriage the first to arrive. Addie looked at Bella with definite concern. "You're overheated. Look at your face—all red and flushed. Come along upstairs and I'll tend to you," she ordered, taking Bella by the hand. Addie had been mothering Bella since Bella came to work for the mills and resided at the boardinghouse she ran. Now, as a newly married woman herself, Mrs. Addie Farnsworth clearly didn't intend to neglect her duties.

"I'm not overheated," Bella protested while following Addie upstairs. "It's downright cool outdoors."

Addie touched Bella's cheek. "Your cheeks are warm—you're sick."

Bella giggled. "I'm not sick, Miss Addie. Taylor embarrassed me and I blushed," she explained.

Addie nodded, her eyebrows furrowed in concern. She went to a pitcher and poured water into a bowl. "You need to understand that Taylor was attempting to present you with a wonderful gift—the opportunity for a restored relationship with your father."

"Yes, we've . . ."

"Now don't interrupt, dear. I want to finish my explanation. Granted, Taylor should have given the matter thorough consideration before inviting your father. It would have been wise for him to seek out his uncle's advice or gain your permission, but his intentions were admirable. I pray you won't overly fault him," Addie rattled on. She wrung a cloth in the water and continued to fuss. "He truly is a good and thoughtful man. Don't let the sun go down on your anger." She dabbed the cool wet towel on Bella's face.

Bella reached up and pulled the cloth away. "I'm not sick, Miss Addie, and I've already forgiven Taylor."

Addie's eyebrows arched and her mouth dropped open. "You have? Well, why didn't you tell me? I've been going on and on when I should have been downstairs seeing to our guests."

"I tried, Miss Addie. You told me not to interrupt," Bella explained.

"You're right, I did." Addie chuckled and pulled Bella into a hug. "And you must remember I'm no longer a boardinghouse keeper that you refer to as Miss Addie nor the wife of John Farnsworth that you address as Mrs. Farnsworth; I'm now your aunt."

"Yes, *Aunt* Addie," Bella replied, the words sounding foreign though delightful to her ears. "I'll try to remember."

"Good. Now let's go downstairs and greet your guests."

Bella leaned close and whispered to Daughtie and Ruth, "Come upstairs and help me change into my traveling dress. I want to spend a little time alone with the two of you before we leave for England. We can sneak off and go up the back stairway without being detected."

The three girls wended their way through the crowd, coming to a halt several times to respond to a guest or answer a question before reaching the stairway. They giggled in delight when they finally entered the bedroom upstairs.

"Let me help you with the buttons," Daughtie offered. "I couldn't believe your father actually appeared at the wedding today," she confided while helping her friend out of her gown.

Bella nodded. "I could barely believe my eyes or ears. I knew it was my father's voice, but I couldn't believe he was actually in the church. The whole ordeal with my father is like a bad dream."

Ruth sat down on the edge of the bed and ran her hand over the smooth satin fabric of Bella's wedding gown. "Didn't Taylor realize you and your father weren't on good terms?"

"That's exactly why he invited him. Taylor hoped the wedding might be a way to bring us together. Unfortunately, he didn't realize the depth of my father's anger. Even though my father willingly relinquished his claim to parenting me when he became a Shaker, he still believed he had the right to force his will upon me. Taylor didn't realize the only reason my father would attend the wedding was if he thought he could force me to return to Canterbury. Taylor was distressed by my father's behavior," Bella explained.

Ruth cast her gaze downward. "Perhaps I ought not complain about my family quite so much."

Daughtie held up the fitted jacket of Bella's carriage dress. "This emerald green print is perfect with your blond hair, Bella."

"Thank you," she replied, a faint blush rising in her cheeks. "I'm going to miss both of you so much, but I want you to know I've been praying an agreeable new roommate will arrive to take my place at the boardinghouse."

Ruth bounded off the bed. "Tell her our news, Daughtie."

Daughtie hesitated a moment and then gave Bella a faint smile. "We're going to move out of number 5. Mrs. Arnold next door has a bedroom open that Ruth and I are going to share. The room had been rented to two sisters, but they've returned home to Vermont. Isn't that the best of news?"

Before Bella could respond, a knock sounded at the bedroom door. "May I come in?" Lilly Cheever inquired while peeking into the room.

"Of course; please join us," Bella replied.

"I hope I'm not interrupting."

"No, not at all. Actually, you may be able to lend some insight to this conversation. We were just discussing the fact that Daughtie and Ruth have decided to move into Mrs. Arnold's house. Based upon Mr. Arnold's past behavior, I have some concerns about their decision. What do *you* think?" Bella asked, taking Lilly by the arm and drawing her toward a chair.

Lilly seated herself in the upholstered walnut rocker and seemed to briefly contemplate her reply before speaking. "Well, it's obvious Mr. Arnold isn't likely to change his ways. After all, he received ample warning from his supervisors to correct his behavior with both the mill girls and his wife. Although his conduct improved for a period of time, he ultimately returned to his unseemly actions. However, it isn't as though he's living here in Lowell any longer—nor does anyone expect him to ever return."

Bella's gaze remained fixed upon Ruth and Daughtie while Lilly spoke. She had hoped Lilly would caution her friends against such a move. Unfortunately, it appeared both Daughtie and Ruth had been comforted by Lilly's statements. Crossing her arms, Bella plopped down on the bed and faced Daughtie. "He's a despicable man. Once he discovers the two of you have moved in, I believe he'll enjoy coming to the house and nosing about. And with his terrible temper, I'm concerned for your safety. Besides, isn't there a rule that girls can't be assigned to Mrs. Arnold's house unless the other boardinghouses are full? After all, that house wasn't designed to be a boardinghouse, was it, Mrs. Cheever?"

"The other houses *are* full. A new girl has already moved in to take your place and there are two more girls arriving who will move into number 5 as soon as we move out," Daughtie interjected. "You do think it's safe, don't you, Mrs. Cheever?"

Lilly glanced back and forth between Daughtie and Bella. "I don't know which question to answer first," Lilly replied, giving the girls a broad smile. "You're correct, Bella. The Arnold house wasn't designed as a boardinghouse. The houses at the end of the rows were built specifically for the overseers and their families, with a common wall joining them to the boardinghouses. The Corporation gave Mrs. Arnold special permission to remain in the house and board two girls because of her difficult circumstances and because the new overseer wasn't married. It worked out well because he preferred to remain a boarder at Miss Mintie's boardinghouse." She leaned in as if to share a secret.

"I think he's completely gone over Miss Mintie's cooking." The girls giggled.

Ruth picked up a tortoise-edged comb and began fashioning Bella's hair into long curls. "Why did they limit Mrs. Arnold to only two boarders? There's certainly space for additional girls in the house."

"The house would have required remodeling to become a true boarding-house. While the Associates desired to help Mrs. Arnold, they didn't want to make structural changes to the dwelling, for they realize that another overseer and his family will eventually occupy the house."

A lock of Bella's thick blond hair was tightly wrapped around Ruth's finger as she turned toward Lilly. "You mean Mrs. Arnold will eventually be forced from the house?"

"No, I don't think that's going to happen, Ruth. But when her child becomes older, Mrs. Arnold may decide to go to work in the mills herself or become a keeper, should a position become available at one of the regular boardinghouses," Lilly replied.

Bella tugged on Ruth's hand. "You're pulling my hair, Ruth." With an apologetic smile, Ruth released her hold and handed Bella the comb. "It's the reappearance of Mr. Arnold that most concerns me," Bella said. "Surely he returns to visit his daughter. What if he becomes abusive on one of those visits? Daughtie or Ruth could become the subject of his rage. Furthermore, I don't like the idea of my friends being anywhere near that unscrupulous man."

"Well, I think you're borrowing trouble," Daughtie replied. "Besides, I'm looking forward to being around little Theona. You know how much I enjoy children, Bella."

Bella nodded. "Daughtie was always requesting assignment to the children's dormitory at the Shaker village," she told Lilly and Ruth.

Ruth grimaced. "I spent enough years at home looking after younger brothers and sisters. What attracts me is having a bedroom we won't have to share with four or five other girls—and there will only be four of us around the table for meals. Won't that be delightful?"

Lilly nodded. "I understand completely, Ruth—about living with fewer people. Although I must admit I'm like Daughtie when it comes to children. Having a little girl in the same house *is* most agreeable. Our little Violet has truly brought joy into my daily routine," Lilly replied, a faint smile touching her lips at the mention of Violet's name. "I truly doubt there's any need to worry about Mr. Arnold. I think he would fear being placed in jail should he cause a ruckus. Now, why don't we turn to a more pleasant topic. I understand you and the Farnsworths are sailing for England in only a few days, Bella."

"Yes. Taylor and I are taking the *Governor Sullivan* to Horn's Pond, where we'll spend the night before going on to Boston tomorrow. Then John and Addie will join us in Boston later in the week. Can you imagine anything more exciting? I've never even been to a city the size of Boston, much less traveled to another country. Having the opportunity to meet Taylor's family makes the trip even more wonderful. He's quite anxious to see his grandfather Farnsworth and grandmother Manning. I'm certain his grandmother must be a wonderful lady. She graciously moved to London in order to help care for Taylor's grandfather Farnsworth when his physical ailments worsened. Considering they're only related through the marriage of their children, I find her actions commendable. Taylor's younger sister, Elinor, is now nine years old, and she writes Taylor the most endearing letters. We'll be visiting her, of course. However, it's still uncertain whether there will be sufficient opportunity to meet his older brothers and sister," she explained.

"Bella! Here you are. Taylor was beginning to fear he'd lost his bride," Addie said while entering the bedroom. She gave the younger ladies a bright smile. "I dislike being the one to break up this little gathering. However, Bella, you really must come bid your guests good-bye. It's nearly time for you and Taylor to depart for Horn's Pond. You're due at the canal within the hour."

Bella stood and turned for Addie to inspect her outfit. "Do you think Taylor will like my dress?"

"Taylor Manning will be pleased with anything you choose to wear, whether it be coarsely loomed cotton or this beautiful printed challis." Addie quickly adjusted the neckline pleats and gave a nod of approval. "He is quite smitten with you; of that there is no doubt."

Taylor made his way through the garden and then surveyed both the parlor and dining room. Bella was nowhere to be seen. He glanced at his pocket watch. Perhaps Addie was correct—perhaps she'd gone upstairs to change into her traveling apparel. Though they'd been married only a few hours, Taylor wanted Bella close by his side. His misstep of inviting Mr. Newberry had given him a fleeting glimpse into a future without Bella. What foolishness! Why he had ever considered such a notion now astounded him. Certainly his plan had been well intentioned, but he should have realized there was a potential for failure, a calamity that could cause his bride embarrassment and pain. He didn't deserve the gentle forgiveness Bella had extended.

Taylor startled as Matthew Cheever slapped him on the back and observed, "It appears as if the womenfolk have deserted us. Best get used to these unexpected disappearances. Isn't that right, John?"

John Farnsworth gave Matthew a nod. "Indeed. I'm constantly looking about for Addie. She's generally fluttering about the kitchen rather than enjoying herself with our guests. But I suppose that's one of the things I love about her. She's more concerned about others being cared for than being cared for herself."

"We can only hope that Taylor has been as fortunate in his choice of a wife as we've been," Matthew replied. "Kirk and Anne asked me to extend their apologies. Anne wasn't feeling well, and they were forced to make an early departure."

John gave a hearty laugh. "I doubt it was Mrs. Boott's health that caused the early departure. When I last saw her, she appeared to be enjoying herself. I fear attending Taylor and Bella's wedding was a huge concession for our Mr. Boott. I don't think he'll soon forgive Bella for her public arguments in favor of the new school system. After all, a man willing to withdraw his membership from a church named after his wife is one who doesn't easily forgive those who take a stand against him."

Matthew's lips turned upward into a broad smile. "You're probably correct, John. I'm sure Anne nudged him into attending the wedding, but I doubt it took much effort. Let's not forget that he values both you and Taylor. He knows you've contributed immeasurably to the success of the mills. It was appropriate for him to be here even though Kirk is not overly comfortable in these social settings."

"Especially when he's unsure how some of the guests feel about *him*," Taylor replied with a grin.

"Well, you must admit you have quite a variety of social classes represented today," Matthew said.

John nodded. "Ah, Matthew, but that's the joy of a wedding. It's acceptable to force the socially elite to mingle among us commoners."

"You're no commoner, John. You hold a position of high esteem in this community. Look at this home the Corporation built for you. Why, I'd venture to say you live better than I do," Matthew replied with a grin. "I know you're paid better."

Patting Matthew on the shoulder, John said, "I'm a man of the working class, Matthew. My position in this town was elevated because I hold valuable knowledge and ability needed by the Corporation. That asset has proved beneficial to all of us, and I'm most grateful. But the fact remains that my social class remains with the laborer, and I'm delighted to have them in attendance. It pleased me immensely to see Hugh Cummiskey and Liam Donohue make an appearance here today. And if all these mill girls hadn't attended, why, Bella and Addie would have been devastated."

"Don't forget—I'm married to a young woman who once worked in the mills, also," Matthew replied. "I have no problem with anyone who's here today. However, I think some of those in attendance came as a surprise to Kirk."

"And hastened his departure," John promptly added.

"Perhaps," Matthew said, "but he did want me to advise you against taking any unnecessary actions while the four of you are in England. Kirk and I both fear there are still those in England who would like to see you brought to justice for what they consider treason."

"We plan to keep to ourselves," John said while waving off the remark. "I seriously doubt anyone in England remembers I ever worked for the mills, much less cares if I ever return for a visit."

Matthew shook his head. "Don't discount what I'm saying, John. We both know danger could befall you. The English economy has suffered greatly because we've been able to duplicate their machinery."

Several girls moved closer, their laughter and animated chatter infiltrating the men's conversation. John nodded toward the library, and the three men moved into the unoccupied, inviting room before continuing their discussion.

John seated himself in front of an alcove lined with shelves of leather-bound books. "If memory serves me, it was your man, Francis Cabot Lowell, who stole the plans for the machinery. They hold *him* responsible for that particular act, not me. My part in the growth of the mills is minuscule. Had I not assisted with the improvement of your printworks, someone else would have soon done so. I doubt the English still bear a grudge."

Matthew took a seat opposite John. "I'll not argue with you, John, but you and I both realize you are in some danger. We can't be certain how much, but I would ask that you give your word you'll be careful."

"If it makes you feel better, you have my word. Weather permitting, we may journey to Portsmouth, but other than that, the majority of our time will be spent in London. I've no plans to visit Lancashire. With my family all re-located in London, there's no reason to venture anywhere near the mills."

"I understand, but I'm sure there are mill owners who visit London, just as members of the Associates travel between Boston and Lowell."

"Those men of importance didn't know who John Farnsworth was even when he worked for them. I doubt they'll remember me or bear a grievance after five years."

"Some wounds take a long time to heal, especially when they affect the financial investments of powerful people," Matthew warned. "Remember, I have a stake in your welfare, too. I'm the one who convinced the Associates we could do without you and Taylor for this extended period. If you'll not consider cautious behavior essential to your own well-being, then consider it a favor to me."

John leaned toward Matthew and rested his forearms on his thighs. "If it will cease your worrying, then you have my word I'll remain alert."

"Thank you, John. And on a more pleasant note," Matthew said, now turning his attention toward Taylor, "I wanted to let you know Kirk and I will be attending a meeting of the Associates next week in Boston. I plan to present your new designs, Taylor. I find them very exciting. I'm certain the owners will be impressed and eager to begin production of them once you've returned from England."

Taylor attempted to hide his pleasure, not wanting to appear portentous. He had spent a great deal of time on the drawings, discussing them with his uncle as he proceeded to ensure the machinery could be adjusted to accommodate the patterns. When both Addie and Bella had given their delighted approval to the designs, he had finally believed the plans were ready for production. He had anxiously awaited approval, but when none came, he believed they had been determined unacceptable.

"I'm pleased you like them. I only hope the Associates will share your opinion."

John smiled broadly and rose from his chair. "I told you there was nothing to worry over. Those new designs are wonderful, innovative. They can't help but like them—and if they express concern, Matthew, you need only call upon their wives to change their minds."

Matthew gave a hearty laugh. "I showed them to Lilly and she was enchanted, so I know you're correct on that account, John. If need be, Kirk and I will insist upon interrupting the women in their music room and asking for their opinion," he agreed.

"If you'll excuse me," Taylor said, rising from his chair, "I believe I'll see if I can locate my bride. We really need to make our departure or we'll miss our boat."

"Certainly, my boy. You don't want to do that or you'll be stuck here at home with us old folks."

Taylor gave his uncle a lopsided grin before leaving the men to continue their exchange. Stepping into the hallway, he glanced over his shoulder. The two men were once again deep in discussion, his uncle's brows furrowed and his lips set in a narrow, tight line. Perhaps his uncle John was more concerned about their journey than he'd indicated earlier.

Bella's voice pulled him away from his thoughts, and he glanced up the stairway. She was a beautiful vision with her creamy yellow hair tucked under a bonnet trimmed in the same emerald green that was woven into the fabric of her dress. Suddenly spotting Taylor, she graced him with a bright smile as their guests gathered around. Upon reaching the final step, Taylor leaned forward and placed a tender kiss on her cheek. She blushed uncontrollably, and Taylor knew he would love her forever. John and Matthew joined the crowd, and Taylor's glance momentarily rested upon his uncle's face. His thoughts returned to their earlier discussion, and a wave of concern overcame him. Surely this journey wouldn't put any of them in jeopardy. He attempted to push thoughts of danger from his mind, but Matthew's words of caution would not be silenced. Taylor looked back at his wife's smiling face. He fervently prayed this journey would not place Bella in any peril.

❦ 3 ❧

Boston, Massachusetts

Tracy Jackson leveled a scowl directed at everyone in the room. Matthew Cheever shifted his gaze to Kirk Boott in an attempt to gauge Boott's reaction. Tracy was obviously intent on imposing his will upon the other Associates. Kirk's expression was indecipherable; however, Matthew was certain the stoic mask was a facade, for Kirk's passion regarding anything that affected Lowell and its paternalistic operation was legendary.

"Comments, gentlemen? Nathan? Josiah? Kirk—surely *you* have something to say," Jackson urged.

Swirling the small amount of port remaining in his glass, Kirk shook his head. "I'll defer." He tipped the glass to his lips and finished his drink.

Josiah Baines cleared his throat. "Well, I vote to remain practical and move slowly. You all know I believe in the railroad, but I certainly don't think we need to consider steam locomotion. We're talking about transporting goods between Boston and Lowell. We can use horse-drawn wagons pulled on rail just as effectively."

"Now, why would we even want to consider such a proposition, Josiah?" Tracy rose from his chair and gave Baines an icy stare before turning toward the other men. "Could we all consider being a little more forward thinking?"

"There's no need to become offensive, Tracy. You asked for our opinions, but it's obvious you really don't want them unless they concur with your own. Well, I for one, have always believed in carefully calculating my risks and not taking unnecessary chances investing money."

"I haven't noticed any unwillingness to share in the vast profits that have come from any of my previous suggestions or proposals, Josiah. You're always against me in the vote but first in line for your money."

"Now, now, gentlemen," Nathan Appleton interrupted, "let's remain civilized. We can discuss this without coming to odds among ourselves. I understand your excitement over the prospect of using steam locomotion, Tracy. However, some of us aren't as informed and enlightened. A calm examination of ideas will be much more helpful than exchanging barbs, don't you think?"

The cue was obvious to all in attendance, and Tracy nodded his agreement. "My apologies, Josiah. As you know, I tend to be overzealous when I'm trying to make a point."

"Apology accepted," Josiah replied. "Anyone else care to voice an opinion? Surely some other member of this group has a view he'd wish to share."

Nathan rubbed his jaw and nodded. "You say Robert Stephenson had good results with the steam engine on the Liverpool and Manchester Railroad, and I don't doubt your word, Tracy. But you must admit that making the huge financial investment required for steam locomotion is a bold stand, especially on an invention that hasn't proven the test of time. I'm having difficulty justifying the capital outlay based upon the population and commerce of Lowell. We can't compare the cities of Boston and Lowell to Manchester and Liverpool. Such a concept would be foolhardy, for our numbers are vastly dissimilar, both in trade and inhabitants."

"Our primary concern is to have reliable transportation during the winter months when the canals are frozen," Thomas Clayborn commented.

Tracy poured himself another glass of port before turning his attention to Clayborn. "We need to think beyond today's needs. If we don't make plans for the future before it arrives, we'll never be the forerunner, the one to set the standard. I, for one, prefer taking the lead rather than playing catch-up."

"Come now, my good man. We're hardly a bunch of backward bumpkins. Look at what we've accomplished over the past few years. I think you'll have to agree that all of us have willingly cooperated with most anything you've presented. You ought not take us to task the first time we question a major decision," Clayborn rebutted.

Matthew glanced out the tall, narrow window where a golden autumn sun now rested upon the distant horizon. He wondered if an amicable agreement could possibly be reached among the members, and although he had a definite stance, the only opinions that mattered here were those of the Associates. Matthew's stomach emitted a loud growl and he quickly pressed a hand to his midsection, hoping to silence the noise.

Kirk shifted in his seat. "I'm going to weigh in on Tracy's side this time. Personally, I believe his concept will transform Lowell from a mercantile community to an industrial powerhouse—and create extraordinary wealth in the process. This is no time for diffidence. If we move forward with the railroad, we'll no longer need to depend upon navigability of the canals. There's no doubt steam is the direction of the future. I don't see how we can decide against Tracy's proposal and continue to think of ourselves as capitalists."

Clayborn rubbed the back of his neck as though the massaging motion would clear his head. "You're probably correct, Kirk, but I think I'm going to need some additional time to decide. Tracy, if you could supply us with some definitive costs, it would be helpful."

"I think I can manage that within the next few weeks. Again, I apologize to those of you who think I've been overly aggressive with my proposal."

"Well, at least we haven't been subjected to William Thurston's legendary ranting about the Irish and their blight upon the town. I'd much rather listen to your fresh ideas than one of Thurston's tirades. That man's absence as a member of the Associates is refreshing as far as I'm concerned," Josiah replied. A murmuring of agreement and a few guffaws followed the remark.

"I concur with your assessment, but I would certainly like to see that man brought to justice," Nathan stated. "Who would have ever thought someone as inept as William Thurston could have eluded the police and kept them at bay for this long? Rather unfair, I think, that J. P. Green is in jail while Thurston is probably involved in some other illegal scheme."

Josiah nodded. "However, with Thurston's egotistical nature, there's no telling when he might reappear and attempt to do further harm to the Corporation. My poor wife still can't believe William was in the business of kidnapping and selling Yankee and Irish girls into the slave market. Of course, I didn't reveal all of the unpleasant details, nor did I tell her that he hadn't been captured. I fear she would have taken to her bed."

Henry Thorne scratched his head and grinned. "I think all this talk of William Thurston is nonsense. He associated with thugs and ruffians and has likely come to an early death. I'd guess he's probably rotting in a shallow grave somewhere. Besides, even if he has escaped harm, I doubt if he'd be foolish enough to show his face in Lowell again."

Kirk selected a cigar from the box that was being passed and carefully clipped the end. He inhaled deeply on the imported extravagance before expelling a large cloud of grayish-blue smoke. Lips pursed into a tight pucker, he watched in obvious satisfaction as the haze lifted toward the ceiling. "Let's don't forget the matter of the doctor," he reminded the others.

"Thank you, Kirk. The matter had slipped my mind," Nathan replied. "For those of you who may not know, Dr. Ivan Ketter has accepted our offer to set up his practice in Lowell the first of the year. With Dr. Fontaine's departure some months ago and now Dr. Barnard retiring at the end of the year, the town will be without a physician. Dr. Ketter seems a good choice, and Matthew has agreed to find suitable accommodations. We had hoped he could commence his duties immediately. Unfortunately, he's advised me he can't accept the position until January."

"I take it Dr. Ketter isn't interested in purchasing Dr. Barnard's house?" Josiah inquired.

Kirk flicked the ash from his cigar. "Dr. Barnard isn't interested in selling. He plans to remain in Lowell. There *are* those of us who prefer Lowell to Boston," he replied with an amused grin.

"My apologies. The question wasn't meant to be offensive," Josiah replied.

"No offense taken. Why don't we adjourn? I'm famished," Kirk said as he snuffed out his cigar.

4

England
October 5, 1833

Bella quivered, unable to contain her excitement. After weeks at sea, the sails of the *Sea Sprite* were now finally furled and the passengers were jostling each other for a better view of England's sights. A sharp elbow in her ribs and a heavy foot coming down upon her stamped kid shoe caused Bella to grimace and then move closer to Taylor's side. He glanced down and gave her a broad smile.

As a cool ocean breeze swirled across the deck of the boat, Taylor encircled her waist with his arm, pulling her close. "I can't believe we've finally arrived. It seems an eternity since I left England and my family," he said. "Of course, with Rowland and Edward off at sea and Beatrice now married to a Scotsman and living in the north, it leaves only my grandfather Farnsworth, grandmother Manning, and Elinor for you to meet."

"If we're very fortunate, one of your brothers may be home between voyages, and perhaps your grandmother has written your sister Beatrice and she'll come for a short visit while we're here."

Taylor gave her a faint smile. "You are an optimistic young woman. I suppose anything is possible, but I'm not holding out much hope of seeing them. I fear Elinor will have to suffice."

A sigh of exasperation escaped Bella's lips, and she gave him a look of mock indignation. "You should be every bit as anxious to see your little sister as your other siblings," she lectured.

"Elinor can be a pesky child, constantly vying for attention. Unless she's changed—which I seriously doubt—I'm certain you'll soon come to share my opinion."

"Little girls are known to adore their older brothers. You should feel honored. And she *has* grown older. Her letters to you have been enchanting."

Taylor made a snorting sound and then pointed toward the shoreline as the small ship drew closer to town. "I can hardly wait to show you the sights in London. Some of my fondest memories are the yearly visits to London with Uncle John. The summer each of us turned ten and every year thereafter, he would treat my brothers and me to a few days in London. What fun we would have."

"And your sisters? Were they ever included?"

A chuckle escaped his lips. "You're going to give me your equality speech again, aren't you?"

"No, but just remember—when we have our daughters, I'll expect equal treatment for each of them."

"Each of them? I didn't realize you were planning such a large family. However, since you are, I'd like to put in my bid for *several* boys."

"What's this I hear, young man? You're already expecting to father several sons?" John asked while maneuvering Addie close to Bella on the deck.

"To be honest, it was more a discussion on equality that somehow took a turn," Taylor admitted. "Thankfully we've finally arrived and can call a cessation to this conversation."

John laughed and slapped his nephew on the back. "I'd think that procreation is a topic you'd be happy to discuss with your wife."

"John! Such talk." Addie gave him a stern look of admonition.

Her husband smiled. "Well, we're all married, and there's . . ."

Addie's eyebrows arched and her lips formed a tight line. She moved her head back and forth in a quick, definitive movement. The conversation ceased.

Bella stood beside Addie as they waited patiently while the men located their trunks. John motioned them forward, having wasted no time securing transportation to his father's residence. Once the trunks were loaded, John gave the driver the address and settled down beside Addie.

"I'm so excited I can hardly contain myself," Bella said, gazing out the window. "I keep thinking of all the places you've told me about."

Taylor nodded but couldn't get a word in edgewise as Addie took over the conversation. "John has shared so many descriptions of places. I just want to see them all."

The men chuckled as Bella adamantly agreed. "Yes. It hardly seems there will be time enough for everything."

"Then we'll simply have to come back at a later time," Taylor said, patting Bella's hand, "for a person can do only so much in a day."

The carriage driver maneuvered them through the busy traffic while Bella and Addie continued to chatter and look for anything that matched the descriptions their husbands had given during their storytelling. Addie leaned forward and peeked out of the carriage. "Oh, look! That's St. Paul's Cathedral, isn't it?" She looked to John for confirmation. He followed her gaze and nodded.

Addie clapped her gloved hands together. "This is so exciting. I must pen a letter to Mintie and let her know we've arrived safely and that I've already had a view of this glorious cathedral."

John emitted a loud guffaw. "The poor woman will likely keep herself in a state of distress the entire time you're here in England."

"Now, John, it's not kind to laugh at her. After all, Mintie *is* my sister," Addie replied.

"I know, I know. But you'd think the woman would finally accept the fact that the United States and England are no longer at war. She continues to see spies and traitors at every turn. Such nonsense!"

"She's gotten better. After all, she attended *our* wedding even though she had been certain you were a spy back when you were living at her boarding-house," Addie replied with a chuckle.

"You see? That's exactly what I mean. The minute Mintie realized I had recently arrived from England, she was certain I was in the country to spy on behalf of the English. Besides, we both know that if she could have talked you out of our marriage, she'd have done so. She conceded only after she realized you wouldn't change your mind," he reminded her.

"True, but at least Mintie accepted the defeat graciously," Addie said as the carriage came to a halt in front of a row of Georgian town houses. The white panel door, lined on either side by pillar-type facades, offered a cheery welcome behind the walkway's wrought iron gate. Addie was already on the edge of her seat.

"Oh, do hurry and help us down, John."

The men quickly complied, alighting the carriage in short order. Taylor stepped aside to allow John to help Addie down.

"This is just lovely, John. I had no idea it would be such a pretty place," Addie noted. John reached up to help Bella down before Taylor could protest.

"It costs a pretty price, so it should be," John answered, smiling at Bella.

The front door opened and a dimple-cheeked girl bounded out, her nut-meg brown hair flying loose behind her. Taylor fell backward against the carriage as the girl enveloped him in a tackling embrace. "Elinor," he said while attempting to gain his footing, "you've grown considerably."

"Yes," she agreed. "I'm already taller than Grandmother. Do hurry up—she's quite anxious to see you."

"Though not quite so anxious as you," he said with a chuckle. "Elinor, this is my wife, Arabella—Bella. She's been eager to meet you."

Elinor gave a quick curtsy. "Pleased to meet you, Bella."

Bella graced Elinor with a charming smile. "The pleasure is mine," she said before turning toward Taylor. "You didn't tell me she was such a beautiful young lady."

Elinor beamed. "That's because he thinks I'm still a little girl."

John strode toward Elinor and pulled her close. "You *are* a little girl. Now come over here and you can meet *my* wife. Elinor, this is Adelaide Beecher Farnsworth, and I'm certain she's going to be delighted to have you address her as Aunt Addie."

"Pleased to meet you, Aunt Addie. Grandfather Farnsworth is *very* anxious to meet you," Elinor said while dropping into an exaggerated curtsy. "All these weddings," she mused. "I do wish I could have come to see them. I'm sure they were grand."

Addie's face had visibly paled at the child's remark, and Bella went quickly to her side. "I'm sure John's father is anxious to meet you in the very best of ways," Bella whispered while squeezing the older woman's hand. "I, too, am feeling a bit nervous over meeting our new relatives."

"Are you attempting to frighten my wife into leaving before we've even gotten settled, Elinor?" John asked with a chuckle. "See if your brother would like some help."

Elinor hurried back to her brother, who was now wrestling a large hump-backed trunk. She eyed him momentarily and then grasped Bella's hand. "I'll show you inside," she offered.

Though her stomach lurched at the prospect of being scrutinized by Taylor's family, Bella nodded her agreement and took hold of Elinor's hand. What if Taylor's grandmother didn't like her? She followed the younger girl up the steps and into the house, with Elinor tugging upon her hand each time she attempted to lag behind. Stopping to admire a quaint hand-loomed rug inside the front door, Bella grinned at Elinor before finally surrendering to the child's insistent yank.

"Come on. Grandmother Cordelia is in the parlor," Elinor urged, pulling her forward. "Here she is, Taylor's wife," the girl announced with a beaming smile.

Bella felt as though she were a prize animal placed on display for approval and possible purchase. She glanced back and forth between the older woman and the gentleman who had now risen from his chair, his few wisps of white hair falling forward as he nodded his head into a bow.

"I'm Jarrow Farnsworth, Taylor's grandfather on his mother's side of the family, although I'm sure you've already come to that conclusion. And this is your husband's grandmother on his father's side, Cordelia Manning. Come have a seat," he said while directing her to the tapestry-covered settee. "Go on, sit down," he encouraged. "We'll not bite."

Bella forced herself to smile at the remark and seated herself across from Cordelia Manning. The older woman was obviously appraising her. "The others will be in shortly. Elinor insisted I come ahead," she stammered, looking to Grandfather Farnsworth as he took a seat once again.

"Elinor can be very insisting," Jarrow said with a hint of amusement in his tone.

"I hope you're a woman of high moral fiber. Taylor was always drawn to the wrong type of women when he lived in England. Ever since he sailed for the United States, I've prayed he'd find a good God-fearing woman who would steer him onto the straight and narrow," Cordelia said.

A loud thud, followed by the sound of footsteps, echoed from the hallway. "I wasn't sure where you wanted me to put the trunks," Taylor said as he strode into the parlor. Moving directly to his grandmother, he pulled her into a warm embrace and kissed her on the cheek. "You look beautiful, as always," he flattered.

The admiration brought a faint smile to Cordelia's lips. "You always did have a way with words," she remarked.

"At least with the women," his grandfather interjected.

"*You're* still quick with a rebuttal, Grandfather," Taylor replied as he grasped his grandfather's hand in a warm handshake.

Jarrow winked. "It's my body that's the problem, not my mind."

As if prompted by his words, Cordelia leaned to the right and tucked the lap robe more tightly around the old man's legs. "Now, then, tell us about your bride," she said.

Taylor smiled at Bella as he dropped down beside her. "Your prayers have been answered, Grandmother. I know Bella will meet your every expectation."

Cordelia folded her hands and then rested them in her lap. "We shall see," she murmured.

Bella gazed at Cordelia, uncertain what was meant by the older woman's response. Perhaps Taylor's grandmother had some personal test in store for her. However, John and Addie's appearance in the parlor forestalled any immediate discussion of the matter.

Jarrow's lips turned upward into a broad smile, and his blue eyes twinkled. "John! It is so good to see you. And this must be Adelaide," he said. "Very pleased to meet you. I suppose you realize you've snagged yourself a fine husband," he continued with an exaggerated wink.

"Indeed I do," Addie replied, returning his smile.

"I'm the fortunate one in this marriage. Addie has the patience of Job and the kindness of an angel."

Jarrow gave a hearty laugh. "I'm certain you're right on that account, John," he replied.

Bella smiled, enjoying the verbal exchange between the Farnsworths. It appeared the elder Mr. Farnsworth was pleased with John's choice for a wife. She wasn't, however, so certain about Cordelia Manning's feelings toward her. Perhaps Mrs. Manning thought her grandson deserved someone prettier or perhaps a woman of higher social standing. Elinor sidled closer and then carefully wedged herself between Bella and the arm of the settee.

"We're anxious to hear about life in Massachusetts, but I would guess the ladies would like to freshen up while I make some tea," Cordelia said. "Jarrow insisted on making arrangements for dinner at the Bloomsbury."

"It appears as if we're going to be treated like royalty our first night home. The restaurant is located in a hotel by the same name. Quite nice—and good food, too," Taylor explained to Bella and Addie.

"Hurrumph," Cordelia snorted. "I told Jarrow you'd probably prefer to relax here at home and have a nice mutton stew. Besides, he ought not be out and about in the cool night air. But, of course, he wouldn't listen."

Jarrow narrowed his eyes and shook his head. "I wanted to celebrate the arrival of our family. They can eat mutton stew tomorrow night, and I'll feel no worse outdoors than I do sitting inside this house."

"Waste of good money, and say what you will, your health will suffer," Cordelia muttered before turning her attention to her granddaughter. "Elinor, you can show the ladies to their rooms and then promptly return and help me in the kitchen."

Elinor wrinkled her nose at the request, her behavior drawing an immediate reprimand from Mrs. Manning.

"Sorry, Grandmother," the girl meekly apologized. "Follow me, ladies," she said, motioning Addie and Bella up the wooden staircase.

Once Addie had been directed into her room, Elinor led Bella to another bedroom at the end of the hallway. "Don't permit Grandmother to frighten you. She's really quite nice, and I think she likes you. She'll question you severely once she gets you alone, so you'd best be prepared," Elinor confided.

"I'm not nearly as convinced she's fond of me—and why would she want to question me privately?" Bella inquired.

Elinor wiggled onto the bed. The child waited until Bella finished pouring water from the china pitcher into the matching bowl before replying. "I'm not supposed to tell. It's a secret."

"Then you ought not tell me," Bella replied. "I wouldn't want to be the cause of your breaking a confidence."

"It's not really a confidence because I didn't give my word not to tell," she retorted. "I overheard Grandmother say she's going to see if you and Taylor will take me back to Massachusetts when you leave."

The comment rendered Bella momentarily speechless. She stared at the girl, who was now peering back at her in wide-eyed anticipation.

"You mustn't tell anyone—not even Taylor. And when Grandmother brings up the topic, you'll appear surprised, won't you? She doesn't think I know a thing about her plan, and she'll think I was eavesdropping on her conversation."

"Weren't you?"

"Not really. I happened home early and she was talking to Grandfather. They didn't hear me come in the house."

Bella arched her eyebrows. "Once you realized they were discussing a matter that wasn't meant for your ears, did you announce your presence?"

Elinor wagged her head back and forth.

"Then you *were* eavesdropping."

"Well, I suppose just a little. But *please* act surprised. And I do hope you'll agree to her request. I truly want to go to America, and even though Taylor would probably consider me a nuisance, I'm hopeful you'd find my presence to your liking."

Elinor's words had rushed out like a torrent of rain, and Bella couldn't help but smile. "All of this is quite a surprise. Right now I think you'd best hurry down and help your grandmother with tea. Otherwise, she may be required to come looking for you."

Elinor jumped down from the bed. "You won't tell, will you?"

"I won't volunteer any information, but I won't lie, either. If I'm asked a direct question, I must tell the truth. That's the very most I can promise."

"That will do just fine. Thank you," Elinor said, flashing Bella a bright smile before scurrying off.

Bella stared at her reflection in the oval mirror above the walnut commode. The thought of a nine-year-old girl returning home with them was daunting. Yet how could she possibly deny the request? She considered the consequences of Elinor making her home with them until her head ached. *I'm borrowing trouble. No need to worry until I actually know there's a problem,* she decided, rubbing away the furrows that now creased her brow.

⸺◦⸺

Barlow Kent turned and watched as the Farnsworths and Mannings were escorted to an oval table in the main section of the restaurant. Surely his eyes deceived him. He stood just outside the doorway and waited.

"A moment, sir," he said as the waiter returned. "Those people you seated—did they have a reservation?"

The man pursed his lips and sniffed. "Yes, of course," the man replied.

Barlow leaned in close to the waiter. "I believe I recognized one of the men, an old friend named John Farnsworth."

"Yes, Farnsworth," he agreed. Seeing that the man clearly knew the party in question, he became rather talkative. "Mr. Jarrow Farnsworth made the reservation. He said he wanted to have a surprise dinner reunion when his relatives arrived from America with their new wives. Perhaps you'd care to join them for a glass of wine?" he suggested.

Barlow grasped the waiter's arm. "No, absolutely not. I wouldn't want to disrupt their reunion. If I could beg your indulgence, I'd prefer you not tell John I inquired. I'd like to surprise him at a later date."

"Yes, of course. I enjoy a good surprise myself. Your secret is safe with me."

~ 5 ~

Litchfield, New Hampshire
Late October

Thaddeus Arnold reached inside the breast pocket of his greatcoat and retrieved the missive he'd placed there earlier in the day. He wanted an opportunity to relax and read the letter without interruption. Downing a mug of ale, he waited while the alcohol spread its warmth through his chilled body and then pulled the flickering candle closer. Although the tavern was noisy, Thaddeus had strategically chosen a table in a rear corner where he could ignore the din.

He scanned the letter for any urgent message it might contain and then began to read it more carefully. It appeared William Thurston was enjoying himself in England, living on all the money he'd managed to accumulate while selling girls into the slave market and appropriating goods manufactured in the mills for sale to other unscrupulous marketers. Thaddeus imagined Thurston dining in a stylish English hotel, mingling among socially noteworthy people, and imbibing in the finest epicurean delights while Thaddeus remained in New England drinking ale in a seedy tavern. After all, William had committed crimes that far exceeded his own, yet William was enjoying life to its fullest. Thaddeus slumped down in his chair. Nothing had changed—life always treated him unfairly.

"Another mug?" the barkeep inquired.

Thaddeus nodded.

"The men at the table across the room wondered if you might want to join them for a few hands of poker."

Thaddeus leaned to one side in order to gain a better view. "You know any of them?"

"Two of them are locals. Don't know the other one."

"Are they any good at cards?"

"Average—never known 'em to cheat. You want your ale delivered here or over there?" he asked with obvious impatience to move on.

"May as well join them. Perhaps my luck will change," Thaddeus replied, pushing back from the table.

Wending his way through the tavern, Thaddeus moved toward the far table, assessing the men as he approached. He'd never seen any of them before and wondered what could have precipitated their invitation. He nodded before extending his hand. "I don't believe we've been properly introduced. I'm Thaddeus Arnold."

"Right. I'm James Wooner. This here's my brother, Sam, and that's Michael Sidley," James replied while nodding at the men surrounding the table.

"Pleased to make your acquaintance. Any particular reason you asked *me* to join you?"

James glanced at the others before looking back at Thaddeus. "You were the only person alone in the place," he stated simply.

Thaddeus relaxed and seated himself in the empty chair. He hoped the cards would fall in his favor; he could use a few extra coins to tide him over. Unfortunately, William Thurston's letter hadn't mentioned any money coming his way in the near future. He picked up his cards and absently fanned them apart while his thoughts returned to the last time he'd met William Thurston. It had been in this very pub. The only piece of good fortune to have come his way in years, Thaddeus decided.

"You in?" the man named Michael asked.

Thaddeus looked at the hand one final time before snapping the cards together and placing them face down on the table. "Not with this hand." Like it or not, he'd have to play cautiously. He couldn't afford to lose any money.

The men continued their game, but Thaddeus quickly lost interest. What was it William had said when they'd met in the tavern? *"The gods must be smiling on both of us."* Yes, that was it, and the statement had held some truth. Had it not been for that meeting, Thaddeus would have been forced into some sort of manual labor. He loathed the very idea. Working as the supervisor of all those lovely young girls in the spinning room had been idyllic. Had it not been for Lilly Cheever and a few other girls who couldn't keep their mouths shut, he'd still be enjoying his position. There were days when he'd been required to help with machine repairs, but overall, he had enjoyed his time watching the girls as they moved about the room. And they had proved to be such easy prey, most of them afraid to say a word when he'd make advances. In fact, some of them had been more than willing to cooperate when given special privileges. Instinctively, he wet his lips.

Sam slapped his hand on the table. "You don't act like a man wanting to play cards."

Thaddeus startled at the interruption. "I apologize. My thoughts were elsewhere."

"That was mighty obvious," James replied. "Where you hail from, Mr. Arnold? Don't think I've seen you afore."

"I was in Lowell before coming here."

Michael shuffled the deck of cards and began to deal. "Lowell? I hear there's some high-paying wages for womenfolk in that town. I gave a few minutes thought to going down there myself. I figure if they're paying them girls such good wages, I might find *me* a high-paying job. What you think, Mr. Arnold? S'pose there's work for the likes of me in Lowell? What kind of work was you doing?"

Thaddeus couldn't restrain his pride. "I was the supervisor of the spinning room in the Appleton Mill."

"Spinnin' room, huh? That don't sound too hard. Bet I could do that. What'd they pay you?"

Thaddeus took a drink of ale and wiped the back of his hand across his upper lip. "I doubt you would qualify, Mr. Sidley. A thorough knowledge of the machinery is required, not to mention the ability to supervise forty or fifty girls."

Michael emitted a boisterous laugh. "I might not be able to handle the machinery, but I sure could handle the women. How 'bout it, James? You think you could *supervise* a roomful of women?"

"What're you talking about, Michael? You can't even handle your own wife," James replied before turning toward Thaddeus. "How come you left such a good position, Mr. Arnold? I wouldn't think a man would soon give up a job like that."

Thaddeus pretended to be concentrating on his cards while he silently chastised himself. He should have kept his mouth shut. "I had other opportunities," he replied. "Your bid, Sam."

"What opportunity could possibly be better here in Litchfield?"

Obviously, Michael wasn't going to be deterred. "A confidential business venture. Until we're operational, I can't discuss it," Thaddeus replied while pulling out his pocket watch. "I didn't realize it was so late. I'm sorry to pull out of the game so early on, gentlemen, but I really must be on my way."

He didn't wait for a response. Shoving back from the table, he bid the men farewell and exited the tavern. He'd not soon become mired in another situation in which strangers could question him. The evening had proven a failure. Not only had he managed to raise suspicion about himself, but he had come away from the gaming table without so much as a few extra coins. He would pen a letter to Thurston this evening telling him John Farnsworth's nephew had been recently wed. Thaddeus doubted whether he would find the information of great interest, but William *had* promised to pay for any details relating to the mills, its employees, or those highfalutin' Boston Associates. Of course, he couldn't expect much remuneration for such an insignificant morsel. Another journey to Lowell would be necessary to ferret out the latest happenings, he decided.

Mrs. Hobson was peeking from behind the dust-filled draperies that hung like red-clad sentries protecting the front window of her boardinghouse. Thaddeus gave a quick wave of his hand, for he wanted the snooping woman to know he had seen her. Mrs. Hobson was everything he detested in a woman: she was meddlesome, devious, and gossiping. But as far as Thaddeus was concerned, most women filled that description. Her boardinghouse, however, was inexpensive and, as much as he hated to admit it, she did serve a decent meal. He entered the foyer and immediately walked into the parlor, where Mrs. Hobson sat demurely stitching a piece of embroidery.

He leveled a beady-eyed glare in the woman's direction. "Is there some particular reason you were peeking through the draperies, Mrs. Hobson?"

"I heard a rapping noise outside the house and was checking to see if an animal was on the porch."

"I didn't know animals were endowed with the ability to rap," he replied with a sneer.

Mrs. Hobson's cheeks flushed bright pink. Pleased with himself, Thaddeus turned on his heel and marched up the stairs and then down the narrow hallway to his room. After loosening his collar, he seated himself at the small table, took up his pen, and began composing a letter to William Thurston. After embellishing the report as much as he dared, Thaddeus folded the missive and placed it on the chest. He'd post it first thing tomorrow, he decided while disrobing for bed.

A short time later he settled his wiry body beneath the bedcovers, but sleep eluded him. His mind was filled with thoughts of his former wife. Even though he loathed the prospect of once again returning to their former home in Lowell, he relished the discomfort his visits to Lowell caused Naomi. His jaw tightened at the thought of her. He knew when he married her she would require a heavy hand if she were to become a suitable wife. He had attempted to make Naomi into a decent, respectable woman. Unfortunately, he hadn't succeeded in changing her. Their marriage had been a disaster—all because of Naomi's behavior, of course. And yet everyone had taken her side, accusing *him* of mistreatment. Even the management at the mills had aligned themselves with Naomi. Why, Matthew Cheever had even gained corporate consent for Naomi and his daughter to remain in the house their family had occupied while he was supervisor of the spinning floor. Such an occurrence was previously unheard of—and yet Naomi and their daughter, Theona, still remained in the house, an ever-present thorn in his side.

Calling at the house on the pretense of visiting their daughter did, however, give him a valid excuse for his return trips to Lowell. Unfortunately, his former wife hadn't proved the font of information he had hoped for. In fact, she preferred to remain silent while he was in the house. However, one of her boarders would occasionally pass along some interesting scrap—that's how he had discovered Taylor Manning was to be married. In order to garner any information of value on his next visit to Lowell, he would most likely be forced to visit the Acre or at least a local pub. He didn't relish the thought, for too many of the locals remembered the reason he'd been dismissed from the mills. They enjoyed the opportunity to look down their self-righteous noses at him. But one day that would all change.

Taking pleasure in the satisfying thought, Thaddeus pulled the scratchy wool blanket under his chin. Yes, one day those supercilious Associates and the haughty townspeople of Lowell would pay for what they'd done to him.

6

Lowell
November

Daughtie rushed down the stairs carrying a stack of fabric, her navy blue cottage bonnet swinging back and forth from one finger as she made her descent. "I hope everyone is ready, because we're going to be late if we don't hurry," she called out toward the kitchen.

"I'm helping Theona with her cape and then we'll be with you," Mrs. Arnold replied, her voice drifting into the hallway from the rear of the house.

Ruth came through the parlor. "I'm ready," she said while tying the wide green ribbons of her bonnet into a fashionable bow beneath her chin. She nodded toward the fabric in Daughtie's arms. "Do you want me to carry some of that?"

Daughtie loosened her grip, and Ruth gathered half of the cloth into her own arms. "I didn't realize you had accumulated so much fabric since our last meeting," Ruth remarked.

"It's wonderful, isn't it?" Mrs. Arnold said as she led Theona by the hand. "I think we're ready. Do you need some additional help with the cloth?"

Daughtie shook her head. "No, we can manage. You look after Theona. Are you excited to be visiting the Cheevers, Theona?"

The little girl bobbed her head up and down, her dark curls springing about with each nod. "I wike Viowet," she said in her lisping toddler voice.

"I'm certain you do. She's a sweet little girl—just like you," Daughtie said, using her free hand to tug the hood of Theona's cape up over the child's head. "There. It's chilly outside. You'll want to keep your ears warm."

They walked more slowly than usual since Theona's short legs were unable to accommodate the stride of her elders. Finally the child's mother swooped her up. "I think I can carry her the remaining distance," Mrs. Arnold told them.

"We're right on time," Daughtie reassured Mrs. Arnold as they walked up the steps of the Cheevers' front porch and lifted the brass door knocker.

The front door opened and Theona squealed in delight. "Viowet!" The child squirmed for release from her mother's arms.

The women smiled as they watched the two girls nearly fall atop each other while attempting to embrace. "Rowena is going to care for the girls upstairs in Violet's nursery," Lilly told Mrs. Arnold.

"Oh, but that seems unfair. I'm sure she'd rather be downstairs with the other women. I can go up with the girls."

Rowena came out of the parlor in a flurry. "Oh no. *I* get to watch after the girls. My stitching is atrocious, and I utterly detest any type of sewing. My mother considers herself a failure because I can't stitch a straight hem," Rowena confided with a giggle.

Naomi gave Rowena a sweet smile. "If you insist. But if Theona becomes a burden or if she fails to mind properly, please come and get me," she said before turning to Theona and removing the child's cape. "You be a good girl and mind Miss Rowena."

"I will," the child promised, giving her mother a dimple-cheeked smile.

"She's a beautiful little girl," Lilly remarked as the women walked into the parlor.

Naomi nodded. "Yes, sometimes I can't believe she's actually mine. I mean, when you consider the appearance of Thaddeus and me, it's rather difficult to believe we could produce such a beautiful child."

Lilly grasped Naomi's hand in her own. "Nonsense! You're a lovely woman, Naomi, and God's very own creation."

Naomi grinned. "One of His lesser accomplishments, I fear. Now, let's get started with our sewing or we'll not have sufficient time to complete our final quilt this evening."

The women had been working consistently throughout the year at their weekly gatherings and, as time permitted, at home. Lilly Cheever, along with Addie and Mintie Beecher, Bella, Daughtie, and Ruth, had formed a Ladies Aid group that had grown over the past two years. Originally they had organized to stitch a few blankets and garments for the needy residents of Lowell. The number of participants in their group that first year had been limited and production had been meager. But thanks to Lilly Cheever's influence, they had, since the beginning of the year, been able to secure the end pieces of cloth made in the mills. That fact alone had caused the members to enlist the help of additional women. The variety of fabrics now made it possible to create an array of goods rather than the few quilts they'd managed to produce during those first years.

The founders of the group, however, continued to maintain secrecy concerning a portion of the goods that they distributed to the Irish community. "No need to borrow trouble," the women had decided before expanding their membership. It was difficult to determine in advance who might be offended by the prospect of assisting the disadvantaged Irish folks living in the Acre. While the larger group met weekly at the Episcopal church, the original members plus one or two trusted newcomers, such as Mrs. Arnold, had remained intact and continued to meet at the Cheever residence on Thursday evenings.

"I've been wondering about our distribution this year, ladies," Lilly started. "Miss Beecher, Naomi, and I have been attending the weekly gatherings at the Episcopal church during the daytime as well as our Thursday evening group. I think they will agree that production this year far exceeds our expectations. We've even had a number of ladies bringing older clothing to donate. With the exception of those goods going to the Acre, I wonder if we should rely upon the churches to distribute the goods. What do you think?"

"We'd certainly have to determine how much would go to each church. There may be a larger membership at St. Anne's, but the needs of the parishioners aren't as great there, either. I would guess that some of the Baptists and Methodists could use more help," Mintie replied.

"We certainly don't want to offend or humiliate anyone," Daughtie quietly offered. "Could the preachers make an announcement during church services? The preachers could prepare a list of needs for us to fill and then distribute the items. That way the names of the recipients could be kept private—only their pastor would know."

Lilly gave Daughtie's hand a reassuring pat. "That's a wonderful idea, Daughtie. I think folks would appreciate maintaining their privacy."

Mintie's forehead creased in deep lines before she jabbed her needle into the quilt. "Pride! When folks are set on keeping their need private, it's nothing but pride."

"Well, I for one, don't think it's any of our business who receives these items," Mrs. Arnold replied. "It's difficult enough admitting to yourself when you need help. Even if other folks realize you're in dire straits, a person needs to be able to hold her head up in public."

"As I said—pride," Mintie repeated, her pinched features revealing the lines of her age.

"And what foible is it that requires one to know who is the recipient of one's charity? Wouldn't that, too, be a form of pride, Miss Beecher?" Daughtie's voice was barely audible, yet the attention of every woman in the room focused upon her before slowly shifting back to Mintie Beecher.

Mintie's eyes flashed with anger. "Well, I never," she sputtered.

Daughtie gave the older woman a retiring smile and prayed God would provide the perfect words to resolve this situation. "I'm sure you never considered the concept prideful. I am certain a woman of your stature and Christian compassion would never intentionally promote an attitude of pride," she said in a gentle tone. She held her breath, awaiting Mintie's reply.

Mintie twisted her neck, shifting her head upward as though she were attempting to keep her nose above water. "You're absolutely correct, Daughtie. I wouldn't want to act in a prideful manner. Thank you for that kind revelation. I think we should follow Daughtie's suggestion."

Daughtie softly exhaled and returned Mintie's smile. "Thank *you*, Miss Beecher."

"Tut, tut, right is right. Let's finish this quilt or we'll still be stitching come Christmas. I hear tell there's to be an antislavery meeting at the Pawtucket church in December," the older woman noted, skillfully changing the topic of discussion.

Lilly cut a piece of thread and deftly drew it through the eye of her needle. "I'm hoping Matthew will agree to attend, although I'm not certain he'll find it wise."

"Why would your husband find it imprudent?" Naomi inquired.

"Matthew is reliant upon the Corporation for his employment. The Corporation is reliant upon plantation owners for cotton. The plantation owners are reliant upon slaves to cultivate the cotton. It's a vicious circle. However, Matthew doesn't believe in slavery," she added.

"That's what the Associates say when they're in Boston and the other big northern cities, but they tell a different story when they are in the South," Daughtie said. She glanced up from her stitching. The other women were once again staring at her. "At least that's what I'm told," she added.

"And who told you this?" Mintie inquired as she outlined a yellow flower with tiny, evenly spaced stitches.

"It's on the handbills advertising the meeting."

"I read the broadsides and saw no such thing," Mintie countered.

Daughtie shook her head. "That information isn't on the broadsides posted about town, but there are printed circulars being handed out. They give additional information concerning the antislavery movement that's beginning to take root. The paper lists groups that have taken a stand and those that seem to be straddling the fence. That's what they say about the Boston Associates—that they're straddling the fence."

"I wonder if Matthew has seen those circulars," Lilly murmured.

Ruth picked up a pair of scissors and clipped her thread. "I doubt it. The circulars are reserved for those people truly aligned with the antislavery cause. That wouldn't include the mill management."

"What else does this circular say?" Lilly asked.

"Mostly it lists those people who are pro slavery and others, like the Associates, who speak from both sides of their mouths. The handbill contains a little more information about Prudence Crandall, the woman who will be speaking at the meeting. Other than that, the particulars are very similar."

"Oh, and you'll never guess the interesting similarities between Daughtie and Prudence Crandall," Ruth exclaimed.

"They're both antislavery," Lilly replied with a grin.

"Well, yes, but in addition to that," Ruth said with a giggle.

Mintie tapped her forehead for a moment. "Is Prudence Crandall one of those Shakers, too?"

"No, but she's a Quaker."

"Practically the same thing," Mintie said.

"It isn't," Daughtie protested.

"No, but they're both from Canterbury," Ruth interjected delightedly.

Mintie pursed her lips. "You see, I'm right. They're both Shakers."

"No, Miss Mintie. Prudence Crandall is a Quaker, and she lives in Canterbury, Connecticut, whereas Daughtie was a Shaker and lived in Canterbury, New Hampshire. Isn't that astonishing?" Ruth asked.

"Well, it's interesting," Mintie agreed. "It would be more astonishing if they were both *Shakers,*" she insisted. "What does this Prudence Crandall have to say that's so important to the Negroes and the antislavery movement?"

"She is the headmistress at a girls' boarding school," Daughtie replied.

"Well, I would certainly think they could find someone other than the headmistress of a boarding school to speak about the slavery issue."

Daughtie smiled. "It's a boarding school for Negro girls."

"*What?* I've never heard of such a thing," Lilly replied. "And this school is in Connecticut? What do the townspeople say about this?"

"That's what she'll be talking about at the meeting," Daughtie replied. "I can hardly wait to hear what she has to say."

"It does sound interesting. Perhaps Matthew will agree to attend once he hears this information," Lilly replied.

"Did I hear my name mentioned?" Matthew Cheever inquired as he entered the hallway.

"Only briefly, dear. I'll tell you about it later," she replied. "Oh, good evening, Liam," Lilly greeted.

"Evening," Liam replied pleasantly.

"Nice to see all of you ladies," Matthew said to the group of women and then turned back toward his wife. "We'll be in my office should you need me, Lilly."

"Isn't that an Irishman with Matthew?" Mintie inquired.

"Why, yes, Liam Donohue. He's the stonemason who is doing all this marvelous handiwork about town. Liam did our fireplaces," Lilly replied.

"He's obviously talented, I'll give him that," Mintie replied. "But it seems odd Matthew would bring him here—to your home."

Daughtie leaned forward and looked directly at Miss Mintie. "Why is that, Miss Beecher? Because Mr. Donohue is Irish?"

Mintie leaned forward. "Well, they are given to the—" she raised her hand up and down to her mouth for a moment before adding—"drink."

"Surely you don't believe that just because some Irish are given to imbibing that all Irish behave the same way."

Mintie arched her eyebrows and leveled a look of irritation in Daughtie's direction, but before she could speak, Lilly put down her needle and stood. "Would you help me prepare tea, Daughtie?" she asked.

"Of course," Daughtie replied. Lilly had never requested assistance at any of their previous gatherings, and Daughtie silently chastised herself for prodding Mintie. Obviously Lilly was requesting her assistance in the kitchen in order to prevent any further unpleasant conversation among the ladies.

They had barely entered the kitchen when Daughtie spoke. "I apologize for my unpleasant behavior this evening. I've spoken out of turn twice, and I now fear Miss Beecher won't return to our meetings."

Lilly laughed aloud while donning an apron of blue-striped cotton. "It would take more than a few disagreeable comments to keep Mintie away. You think that's why I've asked you to help in the kitchen, isn't it? To reprimand you for your behavior?"

"Isn't it?" Daughtie asked.

"No, of course not. Mintie Beecher is quite capable of defending herself in any circumstance—especially when she has a parasol in her hand. Why don't you arrange these biscuits on the tray while I prepare our tea." Lilly pointed toward a hand-painted china serving platter, and Daughtie immediately set to work. "I did have another reason for requesting you join me, however," Lilly admitted.

Daughtie glanced up from the tray, her interest aroused. "What is it?"

"Would you consider coordinating our gifts for the people in the Acre?"

"But *you've* taken charge of distribution in the Acre ever since we began this project, and it has worked well. Why change now?"

Lilly gave her a tentative smile. "It's clear you have a heart for others, Daughtie. You're a good choice. Matthew asked me to minimize my activities for a while. I haven't been feeling well of late."

"You're ill?" Daughtie's heart began to pulse in quick, heavy thumps against her chest. Her mother had talked the same way when she became ill. Two months later she had died.

"I'm not yet certain, but we may have another child next year. Matthew insists I take care of myself."

Daughtie breathed a sigh of relief. "How very wonderful for all of you. Well, in that event, I'll do my best. But I'll need your guidance. I don't even know anybody in the Acre."

"There's not much involved. You won't actually be required to go into the Acre. In fact, Liam Donohue, the Irishman who came in with Matthew, will be your Irish liaison. Would you like to meet him?"

Daughtie brushed a strand of hair behind one ear. "If you'd like. We won't be interfering with their business, will we?"

"Of course not. Matthew never discourages my interruptions when he's working at home. However, I'm sure he'd be even more welcoming if we took a few of these pastries for them. I've discovered that men are always hungry."

Lilly led the way while Daughtie followed close behind with a plate of biscuits, scones, and marmalade. "Look what we've brought you," Lilly announced as they entered Matthew's library. "You can put their refreshments on the desk," she instructed Daughtie.

"Not the desk," Matthew said, jumping up and taking the plate from Daughtie's hands. "This table will be fine. We have drawings on the desk. I wouldn't want to get food on my paper work," he explained.

Daughtie nodded and glanced toward the desk where Liam Donohue stood hunched over a sheaf of papers, his dark curly hair falling across his forehead. Daughtie watched his arms bulge in muscled strength as he pushed himself into an upright position and nodded in greeting.

"I wanted to introduce Liam and Daughtie since they will be handling the charitable goods for the Acre this year," Lilly said. "Daughtie, this is Liam Donohue, Lowell's illustrious stonemason. And Liam, this is Daughtie Winfield, a fine young lady who works at the Appleton."

Liam smiled and his entire face appeared to soften, his dark eyes sparkling. "Pleased to make yar acquaintance, Miss Winfield," Liam said, reaching for the cup of tea she offered.

His hand encircled hers warmly. She met his gaze and quickly looked away, breathless and unable to speak. He continued to hold her hand, finally giving a tiny squeeze that brought her to her senses. "A pleasure, Mr. Donohue," she croaked, pulling back on her hand.

"I look forward to assistin' you with the distribution," he said.

"What? Oh yes, the distribution. I'm sure it will be an enjoyable experience," she replied. An enjoyable experience? What was she saying? She felt the hot sting of blood rushing to her cheeks.

"I'm certain it will," Liam stoically replied. "I've already begun coordinatin' a list with the priest at St. Patrick's. Ya can send word when the items are ready for delivery."

If he thought she had just made a total fool of herself, he didn't let on, and for that, Daughtie was thankful. She didn't know how she was to send word— she had no idea where he lived—but this wasn't the time or place to inquire. She'd get the necessary information from Lilly Cheever.

Lilly brushed Matthew's cheek with a kiss. "We'd best get back to our sewing."

Daughtie glanced toward Liam. He was staring at her, not a gawking, uncomfortable stare, but one of gentle kindness—as though he'd known her for years. His eyes were filled with a tenderness that somehow made her long to be loved. She looked away, confused by the feelings this man had stirred within her.

"We'd best serve tea to the ladies or they'll think we've deserted them," Lilly said as they left the room.

Daughtie clenched her fists into tight knots and willed them to cease their shaking as she followed Lilly back into the kitchen. Her fingers trembled while she finished arranging the tray of pastries. What was wrong with her? She was acting like a silly schoolgirl who had never before met a man.

"Liam is a very nice man; quite talented, also. Did you like him?" Lilly inquired while preparing the pot of tea.

"I think we will be able to work together quite nicely," Daughtie pleasantly responded.

"Yes, I believe you will," Lilly replied, the hint of a smile tugging at her lips.

Mrs. Arnold looked up from her stitching when they entered the room. "There you are, Lilly. We were just talking about the new doctor who will soon be moving to Lowell. Have you heard any word on exactly when he'll be coming?"

"Matthew did mention the fact that Dr. Ketter's arrival was discussed at the last meeting of the Associates. Although they had hoped he could begin his medical practice the end of the month, he's been detained until the end of the year. Did you tell the others he'll be setting up his office in your house, Naomi?"

Naomi nodded. "Yes, and of course, Ruth and Daughtie knew. The carpenters have already begun making the minimal changes necessary to the downstairs rooms."

"So old Dr. Barnard is finally going to quit practicing. It's about time," Mintie declared. "He can't hear at all, and his eyesight failed him long ago. He should have quit doctoring ten years ago."

Lilly giggled. "We can always depend upon you to speak your mind, can't we, Miss Beecher?"

Mintie gave an affirmative nod of her head. "Absolutely. If there's one thing I've always had, it's an opinion—and a willingness to share it with others. If my sister, Adelaide, were here, she'd give a hearty amen to that admission."

Lilly offered the plate of pastries to Mintie. "Speaking of your sister, I do hope they all have a wonderful time in England. What fun it will be for Addie to meet all of her new relatives and visit the places Mr. Farnsworth speaks of so fondly."

Mintie jabbed her needle in and out of the fabric. "Pshaw! I think all this traveling to England is nonsense. I can't imagine why anyone would want to associate with anyone living in that treacherous country. Believe me, I told Adelaide she'd do better to stay here in Massachusetts than traipse across the ocean. But did she listen? No! Off she went, pretty as you please, without a thought to what I said."

"I doubt there's any reason to fear for her safety. England and the United States are no longer at war, Miss Beecher."

"So they say," Mintie replied, giving her needle a resolute stab. "Tell me more about this new doctor. Where does he hail from? Not England, I hope. I could never utilize his skills if he were trained in England."

Mrs. Arnold took a sip of her tea. "No, I understand he completed his medical training a few years ago and has been doctoring in Vermont the past two years."

"Nothing but a young whippersnapper. I'd guess he prescribed the wrong tonic to one of those Vermont farmers, and now they've run him out of town on a rail," Mintie declared quite seriously. "He'll set up his practice here in Lowell and likely kill us all."

The room fell silent, the women obviously unsure how to react to Mintie's comment, until Lilly laughed aloud. Soon they all joined in, with Mintie appearing to delight in the revelry as much as the rest of them. "Let's at least give him a chance before declaring him incompetent," Lilly said between gasps of laughter.

"If you insist," Mintie replied, trying hard not to appear amused. The group once again burst into laughter.

"You ladies seem to be enjoying yourselves," Matthew genially remarked. He stood in the parlor doorway with Liam at his side.

"To tell you the truth, Mr. Cheever, I don't know *when* I've had such fun," Mintie replied. Matthew shared a surprised glance with Lilly and Daughtie.

"I'm delighted to hear it," he responded with a smile.

Daughtie looked past Matthew and watched Liam shrug his broad shoulders into a dark woolen coat. He suddenly glanced up and met her gaze while tugging his cap tightly onto his head. Before she could turn away, he gave her a broad smile and it appeared as if he winked at her. *Did* he wink? Surely he hadn't been so bold, although she felt a strange tingling sensation at the prospect. Likely he had something in his eye. After all, she shouldn't be hoping a man had winked at her—especially not an Irishman. Yet she couldn't turn her gaze away from him.

7

London

Once he bid the doctor good-night, John Farnsworth stood at the front entryway and momentarily pressed his forehead against the door in a futile attempt to draw strength from the firm, cool wood. He had hoped for better news and now needed time to digest the doctor's prognosis before returning to his father's bedside. Methodically he turned the brass key, locked the door, and entered the parlor. Edging down into an overstuffed chair, he leaned back and rested his head on the cushion before silently reviewing the doctor's words.

"Ah, there you are," his wife said.

Addie stood in the hallway looking in upon him. He straightened in the chair and gave her a cheerless smile. "Come sit down. The doctor left only minutes ago."

"I do hope he gave you a good report on your father."

John shook his head. "I'm afraid not, my dear. In fact, I fear Father is much worse than any of us anticipated. Although the doctor is unable to explain this flare-up, he strongly recommended I cancel my return voyage until . . ." John attempted to hold himself in check. It would serve no purpose to give in to his feelings of despair. He needed to remain positive for his father's sake.

Addie sat down in the chair next to John and clasped his hand. "Of course, my dear. We'll stay as long as necessary."

John leaned over and kissed her cheek. "Thank you, Addie. I know you wanted to be home before Christmas, and I'm certain remaining here is going to cause Mintie no end of worry on your behalf." He forced a smile. "She'll no doubt believe you to have been kidnapped by English spies."

Addie offered him a tender smile. "I'll write her a letter. Once she knows your father has taken a turn for the worse, she'll understand. Mintie has her faults, but she believes family should be together in their time of need."

"I'll need to pen a missive to Kirk and Matthew, also. I'm certain they'll be less than pleased with this turn of events."

Patting his hand, Addie encouraged, "They'll have no choice but to understand. In any case, these circumstances aren't of your own making. What exactly did the doctor say?"

"That's part of my dilemma. Dr. Adams says he doesn't understand what has occurred. Father was making excellent progress until this sudden turn for the worse, and the doctor can find no reason for the change. Therefore, he hesitates to change the medical regimen. He'll return tomorrow, but if Father doesn't begin a turnaround within a few days, he fears the worst. Of course, he was quick to add that he has no way of being certain when any change may actually occur. That's why he suggested we postpone our voyage."

Addie nodded. "We'll abandon our plans and leave our return date open, John. I'll have the opportunity to experience an English Christmas," she cheerily replied.

He smiled and rose from the chair with a little of his old sparkle returning. "And somehow we'll make it a very merry Christmas. In fact, we'll go out and do some Christmas shopping tomorrow. Our gifts may arrive in Lowell on time if we can get them on a ship very soon. What do you say? We ought to find at least a gift or two for Mintie and perhaps something for Matthew and Lilly. We'll take Bella and Taylor along and make a nice day of it. Cordelia will be here to look after Father. And, of course, we'll invite Elinor to join us."

Addie frowned, her brow furrowing into deep wrinkles. "Do you think we dare spend the day out in public? Up until this point, you've wanted to remain somewhat reclusive. After all, you know there are those in England who still consider you a traitor."

"I don't know that for a fact, my dear. I promised the Associates I would be cautious more because of their fears than my own. I truly doubt there's anyone who cares whether I've returned. Besides, London is a large city, and it's not my home. I imagine anyone possibly holding a grudge against me would be in Lancashire, not London," he explained. "It will be good for us to get out. Taylor and Bella are the only ones who have had much fun since our arrival."

"Well, it *is* their honeymoon. They should be going to see the sights and having fun," Addie replied. "I do know Bella has been completely agog over the places they've visited thus far. She told me all about seeing St. Paul's Cathedral. Oh, and she had a marvelous time strolling past a place called Buckingham House. They're in the process of converting it into a palace for the king."

"This excursion hasn't been fair to you, what with all this worry about keeping myself secluded. Well, from this point forward, we're going to find a spark of enjoyment amidst this gloom."

"I've not been unhappy, John. We've been able to share time with your father and each other. And I know you've finished several books you've been eager to read."

"That's true enough. But who knows if we'll ever be back in England again. You need to see London before we sail. We can plan a list of places you'd like to see, but first I'll go and visit with Father. I know he's anxious to hear the doctor's report. Thank you, Addie. I now feel as though I can keep focused while talking to Father," John replied. He leaned down and gave her a kiss before leaving the room. He turned to face her once he'd reached the bottom of the stairway. "You warm my soul, Addie Farnsworth."

"Thank you, John."

He nodded, continued up the stairs, and inhaled a deep breath before opening his father's bedroom door. "Father? Are you awake?" he whispered.

"Come in, son," his father replied in a weakened voice. He lifted a hand to wave John forward. The veins in his father's hand were a cloudy bluish-green against his aged, fragile skin. "What did Dr. Adams have to say?" He paused, looking intently at John. "I'm dying, aren't I? How much longer do I have?"

John pulled a straight-backed chair close to his father's bedside and sat down. "The doctor can't tell us much as he's not sure what has happened. However, he doesn't want to change his treatment—at least until he has a better idea of what's occurring. He'll be back tomorrow. In the meantime, he thinks you should continue to rest and take your medicine."

His father gave him a feeble smile. "I don't have much choice about that, now, do I? And what of your departure?"

"I talked with Addie before coming upstairs to visit with you. We've decided we'll stay until you're stronger. Besides, Addie assures me she would like to observe Christmas in England. This will be the perfect opportunity," John replied, hoping the note of cheerfulness in his voice would forestall any questions his father might raise.

"Having you home for Christmas will be very special." He paused for a moment and then said, "I think I'd like to rest awhile, and I'm sure you're hungry. Why don't you go downstairs and partake of the noonday meal with your wife while I take a nap?"

John gently patted his father's hand. "You rest, then, and I'll be back later this afternoon."

"Oh, I've simply had the most marvelous day," Addie said as their carriage came to a stop.

"I'm glad to hear it," John replied as he stepped from the carriage and turned to assist his wife. "I fear we've traveled enough ground to have ridden all the way back to America."

Addie pulled her wool cape close. "You didn't mind too much, did you, dear?"

John smiled. "Not at all. Just seeing how happy it made you is enough to cause me to do it all again tomorrow if that would be your wish."

Addie laughed. "I never could have imagined the grandeur of it all." She looked up at the building in front of them. "Oh, a teahouse. How lovely. Could we stop in?"

John took hold of her arm. "It was exactly what I had in mind. It's time for proper genteel folk to have their high tea. This teahouse has been highly recommended to me—by one Mrs. Arabella Manning."

"Well, if it passed Bella's scrutiny, it must be wonderful."

John opened the door and escorted his wife into the small shop. Without delay they were shown to a lovely linen-covered table.

"Oh, it's so charming. Warm and cozy and not at all pretentious," Addie exclaimed. John helped her out of her wrap, taking care to seat her before tending to his own coat and hat.

It wasn't long before they were presented with a steaming pot of tea and a platter of tiny sandwiches and cakes, fruit tarts, and scones. A bowl of jam and clotted cream rounded out the offering.

Addie sampled a bit of each thing, feeling contented and not at all embarrassed by her enthusiasm. "I suppose you must think me quite out of step with propriety," she told John, watching him for any sign that he did indeed feel that way.

John merely laughed. "Addie, you can be out of step with propriety any time you like, but I see nothing wrong with a woman enjoying herself at the table."

"Mintie would be aghast. She has always chided me about my plump waist. If she saw me with clotted cream, she would never let me hear the end of it."

John reached over to gently touch Addie's arm. "You must never concern yourself with such things. I find you perfectly sized and delightful company." He touched his hand to her cheek, causing Addie to feel flushed at the public display.

"John, you shouldn't. People will think we're lovers instead of husband and wife."

At this John laughed with an abandonment Addie hadn't seen since their arrival in London. Several of the other patrons looked their way and Addie felt her cheeks burn.

"John!"

He glanced over his shoulder and smiled at those who watched him. Then he quickly turned his attention back to Addie. "You are such a delight."

Addie calmed and returned her focus to the pastries on her plate. "I want to do some more Christmas shopping if there is time. I'd like to find something special for your father, as well as Daughtie and Bella and Lilly."

"Sounds as though we'll have to buy another trunk, as well," John teased.

"For how else will we be able to transport all of the things you purchased for Mintie, as well as these new gifts?"

Addie frowned. She hadn't thought of the cost. She'd been guilty of spending John's money quite freely, in fact. "Oh, I am sorry, John. I hadn't considered the extravagance of it all."

"I'm not chiding you for your choices, my dear. I'm teasing you. We will purchase whatever your heart desires. Even if we need to buy ten trunks to haul it all back. I have made my fortune and am quite capable of providing for you."

"But your generosity is beyond anything I've ever known." Addie gave her husband a smile. "Even the Judge didn't spoil Mintie and me as much as this." The thought of her departed father reminded her again of Jarrow Farnsworth's own impending death. "What do you suppose your father would enjoy as a gift?"

"I do believe there are some wonderful new books available in the shop just around the corner from the house. I was down there the . . ." John fell silent. Addie watched as he slowly turned.

"What is it?" she asked.

"I don't know." He turned back around, shaking his head. "I just felt a chill run up my spine—as if someone were watching me."

"Oh, John, you don't suppose . . ."

He smiled and lifted his cup. "It's nothing. Someone probably opened the door, then changed their mind about coming in. That's all."

"Still, perhaps we should return home. We've been gone a long time."

John looked as though he might refuse but then nodded. "Perhaps you're right." He quickly paid the bill and collected their coats.

They said nothing as they exited the teahouse, but John continued to look over his shoulder. "Do you mind if we just walk?" he asked.

Addie couldn't help but notice the edge to his voice, but she made no comment. Nodding, she looped her arm through John's. His body was unyielding, almost rigid. Something wasn't right, but she could see he didn't want to discuss it. Forcing a smile, she pulled him along. "Look, it's starting to snow."

John glanced to the lead gray skies overhead and back to Addie. "Yes. It's grown colder—we'd best hurry."

8

Lowell

Irresistible excitement captured Daughtie's imagination as she thought of the note she'd received earlier that day. She quickly gathered the goods to be distributed in the Acre, anxious to be on her way. Over these past weeks, her routine had not varied. Each Tuesday evening she would take the items completed by the Ladies Aid to the storage room in the circulating library. But tonight was different. Tonight Liam Donohue was to meet her and load the boxes into his wagon for delivery to the Catholic priest, who would distribute the items to the Acre's Irish residents. Weeks had passed since she'd last seen Liam. She thought of the wink he'd leveled in her direction at the Cheevers' house. Once again, she pulled the scrap of paper from her skirt pocket and read it.

I look forward to seeing you this evening. Liam Donohue

Daughtie's lips curved into a faint smile while considering these words. He could have simply written *I'll arrive at eight o'clock*. Instead, his message revealed he was looking forward to seeing her. Her heart quickened at the thought. Then Daughtie chastised herself. She was likely reading more into his message than he'd intended. Liam was simply being polite, she decided. Yet there had been no need for him to send her a note at all. He knew Lilly Cheever was going to advise her of his arrival. Perhaps he *was* looking forward to seeing her. She packed the last hand-stitched quilt into the box and bounded down the stairs, a bright smile on her face.

Ruth was seated in the parlor and glanced up from the book she was reading. "You appear cheerful this evening," she remarked.

Daughtie pulled her cloak from one of the wooden pegs that lined the wall beside the front door. "I always enjoy working at the library. I'll talk to you when I get home if you're still awake."

"If you happen to see a book I might enjoy, would you sign it out for me? I've only a few pages to read before I'll be finished with this one."

"I'll inspect the shelves for any new offerings," Daughtie promised before hurrying out the door. She didn't want Ruth to draw her into a lengthy conversation. Even though it was early, Daughtie didn't want to run the risk of missing Liam.

The weight of the box had caused her steps to slow, but the library clock revealed she was still a half hour early. "Good evening, Mrs. Potter," she called out while placing the heavy box on the floor just inside the front door.

"Good evening, Daughtie," the older woman greeted, rounding one of the bookshelves and walking toward the front of the store. She glanced toward the clock above the checkout desk. "You're early this evening."

Daughtie nodded. "If you'd like to get home a few minutes early, I don't mind if you leave now."

"Only if you're certain it wouldn't be an inconvenience. I haven't been overly busy today. In fact, I was dusting shelves to keep myself occupied."

"The new books we ordered haven't arrived, have they?"

Mrs. Potter shuffled through the papers on top of the desk. "We received a partial shipment the day before yesterday, but I've already cataloged and shelved them, and I've posted the past due notices."

"No wonder you're dusting shelves," Daughtie replied with a grin. "I'll have to hope there are a lot of people anxious to borrow books this evening if I'm to keep myself busy."

Mrs. Potter fastened her cape and then removed a small reticule from the bottom drawer of the desk. "Well, I'll be off. You're on the schedule for next week," she reminded Daughtie while pointing toward the list atop the desk.

Once Mrs. Potter had exited the building, Daughtie picked up the list of recently purchased books. Making her way up and down the aisles, she pulled a number of volumes from the shelves and carried them to the front desk. Surely among all these selections she could find something intriguing for Ruth.

The clock above the desk slowly ticked off the minutes. Several girls came in looking for specific titles, a few girls returned books they had borrowed, and one or two sheepishly returned overdue books and quickly paid their fines. Mrs. Potter would be pleased. Daughtie carefully drew a line through the names posted on the past due notice and once again returned to the volumes she'd pulled from the shelf. The bell over the front door jingled, and Daughtie glanced up from her reading. Liam Donohue was pulling off his cap as he approached the desk.

"Good evenin', Miss Winfield."

"Good evening, Mr. Donohue. I was beginning to wonder if you had forgotten," she said, giving him a sweet smile.

He stood directly in front of her, looking down into her eyes. "I'd never be forgettin' something so important as comin' here tonight."

The odd sensation she'd experienced when she last saw Liam returned in full force, once again taking her by surprise. However, she wasn't certain if Liam meant he wouldn't forget something as important as picking up the items for the Acre or if he meant he wouldn't forget coming to see her. She hoped it was the latter yet felt embarrassed to admit such a thing—even if only to herself.

"Is it this box here?" he asked while pointing toward the items she'd carried into the library earlier in the evening.

"No. Well, yes—but that's not everything."

He gave her a hearty laugh. "I was wonderin' why I'd be needin' my wagon if there was only this one box to be hauled off. Have you been keepin' yarself busy this evenin'?"

"Not too busy. I've been glancing through a few of these books to pass the time."

"Perhaps I should be seein' if you 'ave a book on how to fancy up a house. Do you have a book such as that?" His Irish lilt delighted her senses.

"A home decorating book? You want something that explains how to enhance the beauty of your home?"

Liam grinned and nodded. "Aye. The construction of me house has finally been completed. I'm generally pleased with the outer appearance, but the inside lacks a woman's touch."

"Oh—that's the most exciting part—decorating the interior. Of course, flower gardens can also provide a challenge," she quickly added. "The Shakers believed in stark simplicity, which I found boring. I believe God wants us to create and enjoy beauty. Lilly Cheever has decorated her home with simple elegance, don't you think? She must have found such pleasure in beautifying their home."

"I'm thinkin' my house could best be described as Spartan tawdriness," he said with a chuckle. "If ya'd like to be tryin' your hand at some decorating, I'd be happy to employ you to give mine a bit o' that simple elegance."

"Truly?" Daughtie could barely contain her excitement. "When can I begin?"

"Whenever you like. You pick out the items ya'll be needin'. Just go to the shops, have them record the purchases against me name for payment, and let me know when ya're ready to begin."

Daughtie hesitated for a moment. "I'd best see the house first, don't you think? I'd hardly know how to decorate it until I've seen the rooms."

Liam laughed. "And for sure ya're right. A tour of the house would likely be helpful. How about Saturday evenin'? You get off work early on Saturdays, don't ya?"

"Yes, I can come immediately after work if you'll give me directions."

He paused for a moment, a frown crossing his expression. "Ya don't think people would be condemnin' ya if ya were to be alone with me?" His Irish intonations were more prominent as he voiced this new concern.

"I truly don't care what other people think, Mr. Donohue. Besides, this isn't Boston. Lowell is much more open to women moving about and doing things on their own. After all, if they allow us to sweat and toil at the mills, they must give us time to move about and tend to business. They call us progressive here, but I simply believe it's just as the good Lord intended."

Liam studied her a moment and smiled. "Well, then, let us not hinder progress."

Liam took the paper she offered, penned his address, and drew a simple map. "If I'm not there by the time you arrive, just be lettin' yarself in. The key is under the flagstone to the right of the front door. Now that I've resolved my decoratin' problems, I suppose I should get busy loadin' the boxes," he said.

"The other items are in the storage room. I carried them with me each week when I came to work. There's more room for storage here at the library than at Mrs. Arnold's house," she explained. "Back here," she said, stepping from behind the desk and directing him to the rear of the library.

"*All* of these?" he asked, glancing into the room and then back at Daughtie.

"Yes," Daughtie replied. "And those along the wall, also."

"*Now* I understand the need for a wagon," he said, folding his cap in half and tucking it into the back pocket of his work trousers. He stacked several boxes on top of one another and hoisted them into his arms. Daughtie followed his lead and began to lift one of the parcels. "You needn't be liftin' these heavy boxes," he quickly said. "If you'll just take care of openin' and closin' the door, I'd be most appreciative. I don't want to be lettin' all that cold air blow in here."

Daughtie hurried ahead of him to open the front door. She watched him in fascination as he made trip after trip. When the last boxes had been loaded, Liam returned inside. "I'm guessin' that's everythin'?"

Daughtie bobbed her head up and down. However, she didn't want him to leave so soon. "Will you be delivering the parcels this week?" she asked.

He moved away from the door and drew closer. "That's up to Father Rooney to decide. I told him I'd be bringing the boxes by later tonight. I'll leave them with him for distribution. I'm thinkin' he's goin' to be mighty pleased. I doubt he was expectin' so much."

"I'm glad we can help. There are so many people who need help and so few willing to lend a hand. Don't you think?"

Liam raked his fingers through the mass of dark curls, pushing them back off his forehead. "That's a fact. And I know for certain there's plenty o' needy folks down in the Acre that appreciate *any* help they can get."

"I grew up among the Shakers, where everyone was cared for and none of us lived any better than the other. We shared in the work as well as the fruits of our labor. Living in the world is much different. I hadn't realized there was such an immense division between classes of people. Bella tried to explain to me before we left—she'd lived in the world before her family joined the Shakers. But, of course, I couldn't completely understand the concept. Are you planning to attend the antislavery meeting?"

Liam had a puzzled expression on his face. "My, but you do go jumpin' from one topic to another very quickly, don't you? I'm not certain what a Shaker is, and now you're askin' about the antislavery meetin'," he said with a broad smile.

She cocked her head to one side. "No, I don't suppose you would know about the Shakers. It's a religious sect. The United Society of Believers in Christ's Second Appearing organized in England, and the group has now become commonly known as Shakers. I don't know if any of them made their way into Ireland, but they were run out of England," she added.

"I see. Well, there appear to be any number of those in this country. It's difficult for a person to decide what to believe."

Daughtie snapped to attention. "You don't know what you believe?"

"Oh, I believe in God," he replied. His tone was noncommittal. "But I think it's a wee bit late in the evenin' to be gettin' into a religious discussion. We'll save that for another time when I don't have to make a delivery. But in answer to your earlier question, I *am* plannin' on attendin' the antislavery meeting."

"Would you like to go with me? I mean, since you're going and I'm going, we could attend together," she stammered.

He twisted his cap with both hands and looked her straight in the eyes. "Do ya not realize that a lass such as yarself ought not be seen in public with the likes o' me? Ya'll be shunned by yar own kind for such behavior. It would not be good for either of us." Again, his Irish brogue thickened with every word.

"I don't understand. Obviously you didn't see a problem with my helping decorate your home. Why is attending a meeting with me any different?"

"Ah, but it is. I'm employin' ya to work in my home. Now, I realize most Irish can't even afford to own a home, much less hire someone to adorn it. I am very fortunate. But all of that doesn't change the fact that I'm Irish. People will likely be understandin' if ya're workin' for me, but anything beyond work would be considered unacceptable behavior."

"As I mentioned earlier, what others think has never been of great importance to me. I've always been more concerned about God's opinion regarding my conduct. We're both His creatures, and I doubt He'd frown upon the two of us attending an antislavery meeting together."

Liam shook his head. "Ya've led a sheltered life, Miss Daughtie Winfield, of that there's little doubt. I'll not come calling at yar door, but I'd be pleased to sit beside ya should there be a vacant seat when I arrive," he replied with a grin. Tugging his cap down on his forehead, he went to the door, turned back toward her . . . and winked.

The bell over the front door jingled, and Liam jumped aside, barely avoiding the heavy door as Ruth thrust it open. Daughtie watched Ruth edge past him while drawing her cloak close about her, as though touching Liam might somehow contaminate her.

Liam tipped his cap. "Good night to you, Miss Winfield," he said and then was gone.

Ruth stared at the door momentarily and then turned her attention back to Daughtie. "What is an Irishman doing in the library? I'd think if he wanted to borrow a book, he'd go to the Mechanics Association library before he'd come here and bother you. I doubt he can even read." Her words were filled with utter disdain.

"That was Liam Donohue. Didn't you recognize him? He came to collect the items going to the Acre, Ruth. And what's wrong with the Irish using this library? They have a right to improve their minds the same as anyone else, don't they?"

Ruth shuddered, a look of dismay etched upon her face. "You know I'm willing to help with making goods and donating old clothing to the down-trodden, and I'm in favor of lending our assistance to the Irish. But the Irish belong in their part of town, and we belong in ours. I don't go into the Acre, and it's probably best if they don't come into our part of town."

Daughtie wagged her head back and forth, as though the movement might somehow clear the invisible cobwebs gathering in her mind. "I thought you were *against* slavery and segregation."

"Of course I'm against slavery. What has slavery to do with the Irish? They're free men and women, paid for their work, and able to come and go at will."

"Are they? If we don't want them anywhere but the Acre, are they truly free? Isn't the blood that runs through the veins of an Irishman the same as ours?"

"Oh, Daughtie, let's do not get into one of your philosophical discussions. Sometimes I think those Shakers filled your head with extremely odd ideas."

"I don't see anything odd about believing in the equality of *all* people—men and women, black and white . . ."

"Irish and Chinese," Ruth said with a giggle.

Daughtie nodded enthusiastically. "Absolutely!"

Ruth eyed her with obvious curiosity. "You've developed an interest in this Liam Donohue, haven't you? I can see it in your eyes when you talk about him."

"Don't be foolish. I've seen him on only two occasions. That's hardly enough time to develop an interest in someone. Although I shall be seeing more of him since he has employed me."

Ruth's eyebrows arched high on her forehead. "*What?* Employed you? To do what? And exactly how is it an Irishman has money to employ anyone?"

"He's an extremely talented man, Ruth, specifically chosen and brought to Lowell in order to design and lay the stonework at St. Patrick's. His talent has taken him into the finest homes in Boston and Lowell—and other cities in Ireland, I suspect. He's built a home and has asked for assistance with the interior decorations. He offered to employ me and I agreed, although I don't intend to take pay for the service. The opportunity to be creative will be payment enough."

"I can't believe my ears. I think you've lost your senses, Daughtie Winfield."

"And your attitude is small-minded and downright annoying," Daughtie replied, unable to keep her mouth closed. "I've invited Liam to attend the antislavery meeting with me," she added with a note of defiance.

Ruth was stunned into momentary silence. When she opened her mouth to speak, her lips quivered as though she would cry. "I don't believe you. Do you realize that if you're seen in public with an Irishman, no respectable man will ever call on you? Your reputation will be completely ruined. You absolutely must reconsider. Don't do it, Daughtie!"

"If it helps to assuage your fears, Liam refused to call for me at the boardinghouse. He seems to share your concern about my reputation."

"Well, at least he has a modicum of common sense, even if you don't," Ruth rebutted.

Daughtie chose to ignore the remark, returning to the desk with her paper work in hand. "I found you a book. I've already signed it out in your name," she said, handing Ruth the volume. "It will be a while before I finish my work. You needn't wait for me."

"Remember what I've said, Daughtie. That Irishman will be your ruination—stay away from him." Faint red stains accentuated Ruth's pronounced cheekbones. Other than her blushing cheeks, there was no indication she considered her words ignoble in the least. With her head tilted upward in a haughty position, she tucked the book beneath her arm and walked out.

The reverberating jingle of the bell above the door permeated the stillness of the room long after Ruth's departure. The echoing sound seemed to quietly repeat Ruth's admonition: *Don't do it. Don't do it.* Defiantly, Daughtie slapped the book she was holding upon the thick wooden desktop and murmured, "I *will* do it. He's a good man who happens to be Irish. I don't care what anyone thinks—especially Ruth Wilson!"

Liam washed his hands and glanced for the fifth time at the clock. It wouldn't be long before Miss Winfield would be coming. He could still see her dark eyes staring up at him in wonder, her dark curls dancing soft on her shoulders. She was a fine figure of a woman—delicate in appearance, yet sturdy in design. And it was clear she wasn't afraid of hard work.

With Daughtie on his mind, Liam put water on for tea and forced himself to think of something other than the petite woman. He thought of his homeland and all that he'd left behind. His family . . . his mother. He missed Ireland sometimes; missed the rich green hills and stone fences, missed the thatched cottages and the lively music that spilled out from the pubs.

He'd lived differently than most Irishmen. He'd trained early as a stoneworker, learning the skills and designs of setting stone and creating a masterpiece. His skills were famous in his homeland. Why, he'd even been approached by a traveling English architect to come work in London—something he'd not even considered for a moment. He'd never do anything to aid the English. They were harsh masters—landowners who came where they weren't invited and stole what was never theirs to own.

It was this rage toward the injustices heaped upon his people that had caused Liam to come to America in the first place. He knew he could never make the kind of money in Ireland that was possible in America. Here, stonemasons were fewer and whether Irish, English, or something else, they were afforded a bit of respect.

Daughtie had told him she'd been taught to respect all mankind, regardless of race or gender. How could it be that a handful of . . . what did she call them? Ah, yes, Shakers. How could it be that a handful of Shakers could understand the need to give respect and value to each human life, but it somehow eluded the rest of the English-speaking race?

The kettle whistled, steam pouring from its spout. Liam glanced at the clock again and smiled. She'd be here soon and she would share his company—share his tea. The thought brought a liveliness to his step and a hope to his heart.

———◆———

The tower bell dutifully tolled the dismissive clangs releasing the mill workers for another day. Daughtie pushed her straight-backed wooden chair away from the drawing-in frame and stood up. Setting aside the long metal hook used to draw warp threads through the harness and reed, she donned her indigo blue Shaker cape and tied her bonnet strings in place before scurrying down the circular stairwell taking her out of the mill.

She'd barely made it to the edge of the mill yard when Ruth's words sliced through the crisp air. "Daughtie! Wait for me."

Daughtie hesitated. Much as she desired to hurry on and ignore Ruth's request, she came to a halt. Half of the girls in the mill yard had turned in Ruth's direction. Daughtie could scarcely claim that she alone had been unable to hear Ruth calling out her name.

"Where are you hurrying off to? Why didn't you wait for me?" Ruth panted, the words spurting out in short, explosive puffs.

The wind whipped at Daughtie's cloak and swept across her body, chilling her to the bone. "I have an errand and won't be going directly to the boardinghouse," she said, pulling her woolen cape more tightly around her body and beginning to walk away.

"I'm in no hurry to get home," Ruth said, quickening her pace to match Daughtie's stride. "I'll walk along with you."

"I'd rather you didn't." Daughtie's words were simple and to the point.

Ruth stopped midstride. "Why!" It was more accusation than question.

"Because I prefer to be alone." Daughtie continued walking.

"Oh, *now* I remember," Ruth called after her. "You're going to meet *him,* aren't you?" she quizzed, hastening her steps until she came alongside Daughtie. "Aren't you?" She seized Daughtie's arm and pulled her to a stop. "Answer me!" she demanded.

Daughtie yanked free of Ruth's grasp. "Quit acting like an overly protective parent, Ruth. What I do is not your concern. Go home," she exclaimed with a note of finality in her voice.

"Don't go there. You're making a mistake," Ruth cautioned. "It's not proper that you should be alone with any man, much less someone like him!"

Daughtie turned and walked away, though Ruth's disdainful attitude served to dampen her spirits. She glanced toward the sky. The air had now turned cold and appeared to be threatening snow showers. Likely a dismal forecast of things to come, she decided. Trudging onward through the shopping district and then toward the outskirts of town, Daughtie turned at the fork in the road but then stopped short, her gaze suddenly focused upon the house that surely must belong to Liam Donohue. Surrounded by trees and perched alone on a small rise, the house was centered by a gabled flagstone entry with an extension on each side. The structure appeared to rise up and lengthen itself in a welcoming gesture, much like an open-armed lover awaiting the return of his sweetheart. There was an inviting warmth about the dwelling that seemed to beckon her forward.

Hurrying up the steps leading to the front door, Daughtie lifted the iron knocker and waited, a smile now on her face. The door opened, and the hallway lamp cast a dim light behind Liam, haloing his raven hair with an auburn hue. Daughtie's breath caught at the sight of him. "Good evening," she croaked, her voice sounding foreign to her ears.

"Good evening," he greeted, stepping aside to permit her entry. "Please come in." He pushed the door closed behind her and then gave it an extra thump with his broad hand. "It sometimes doesn't latch well. I'll be needin' to plane it just a trace," he explained. "May I take your cape?"

"Yes, thank you," Daughtie replied, thankful her voice had returned to its normal pitch. A crackling fire burned in the Rumford fireplace. She moved into the parlor, her gaze locked on the granite mantelpiece.

"Your fireplace—it's, it's . . ." she stammered, unable to think of words to express herself.

"Granite."

"No. Beautiful," she contradicted in a soft, contemplative tone. "Honestly. It's more than beautiful, but just now I can't think of a word to adequately describe the workmanship."

His head tilted at an angle, and he gave a hearty laugh. "Thank you. I'm quite fond of it myself. However, it *is* granite."

She moved closer and, drawing near, ran her hand across the smooth, charcoal-black facade. Tracing one finger around the outline of the etched eagle in flight that embellished the center of the arch, she whispered, "It's lovely. Your carving shows such strength, yet the delicate wings make the bird appear almost vulnerable. Why did you choose an eagle?" she inquired, looking up into his dark eyes.

"The eagle is a part of the Donohue family coat of arms. I didn't want to carve the entire coat of arms, so I decided to extract one portion for the fireplace."

"You have a family coat of arms? How impressive."

"My people were once powerful and influential. At least in Ireland."

"What happened?"

Liam gave her a sad smile. "The British happened."

She hated having led him into sad memories. "So you carved only part of the coat of arms. Still, it seems quite perfect."

"I doubt my mother would approve of the idea. She'd be tellin' me I've disgraced our heritage."

"You might be surprised. I don't see how she could find this carving anything other than compelling artistry."

Liam pushed the dark curls off his forehead and grinned. "You *do* have a way with words, Miss Winfield. Still, I believe my mother would take one look at this fireplace and ask when I was going to carve the greyhounds."

"Greyhounds? Dogs?"

Liam nodded his head. "Aye. There are two of them that make up a portion of the Donohue coat of arms. Now, if the beasts were lying there peaceful and cozy, I might 'ave considered adding them. But the greyhounds that are pictured in the Donohue coat of arms are standin' on their hind legs and appear to be dancin' with each other more than anythin' else."

Daughtie giggled. "Well, I think you've made a wonderful choice," she replied, finally looking away from the fireplace and permitting herself to observe more of the house.

"I told the truth—I've done little to fix up the inside. Would you like to see the rest of the house?"

"Yes, of course. But you must tell me which rooms you want adorned."

He glanced over his shoulder and gave her a grin. "All of them."

"All?"

He nodded his head. "As my mother used to say, 'No need in doin' anything halfway.'"

"I see. Well, that may take a little more time than I anticipated—and money," she added.

"Money's not an issue. As I said, just tell the merchants to keep a tally. And if it's yar own wage that's causing concern, I'll be glad to pay ya whenever ya say—right now, if that's what ya prefer."

Daughtie could feel the heat rising in her cheeks. "No, I'm not worried about myself. I consider it a privilege to have this opportunity. I expect no payment, but we'll need to discuss how much you're willing to spend."

"Right you are. But for now, ya needn't worry about the money issue. Just go ahead and buy what ya need to make the inside of this place look as respectable as the outside," he instructed while walking her through the dining room, kitchen, and the room he referred to as his office. "I'll not need ya fixing up my office, I don't suppose," he added. "So there's at least one room you can take off the list. Oh, and not too many lacy frills—except in the guest bedroom. Ya can use ruffles and the like in that one, I suppose."

The mention of the bedrooms caused her to swallow hard. She knew she was risking her reputation simply by being alone with a man—much less an Irishman. And now he was talking about bedrooms and showing her around his house . . . all alone. Daughtie quickly covered her nervousness with a chuckle. "I'll attempt to keep the lacy frills to a minimum, but I hope you won't object to some color—not overly bright," she quickly added.

They made their way downstairs, returning to the parlor. Liam stood before her, his feet planted a short distance apart and arms folded across his chest. "As ya can see, I've not purchased any furniture, except the wood pieces I had specially made. You can choose any colors ya like for the overstuffed furniture. Except for bright pink. I'm thinkin' that would be a little too womanly for a single man. 'Course, I don't plan on stayin' single all my life, but until then, I think it might be best to use another color."

Daughtie gave him a solemn nod of agreement. "I agree. Pink won't even be considered. Unless I should find something absolutely irresistible, that is."

Liam turned back in her direction, nearly snapping his neck. He stood before her in stunned silence, gazing down into her eyes.

Daughtie giggled at him. "I was teasing, Mr. Donohue."

"Please don't address me as Mr. Donohue. Liam. My name is Liam," he cordially replied. "And I certainly *hope* you were teasing."

A clock chimed in the hallway, signaling nine o'clock. "I really must be going. It's getting late, and your house is quite a distance from where I live."

"Oh, I'll be takin' ya in the wagon. I wouldn't consider letting you walk home alone after dark. Besides, I'm sure it's gotten a mite colder since you arrived. I'll deliver you close to the boardinghouse and then watch until you get to your doorway. Probably best we're not seen together, especially after dark."

"I believe you worry overmuch, Mr. Dono—Liam."

"Trust me. Living in the Shaker village has left you inexperienced in the ways people think," he said while fetching her cloak. He slipped the woolen wrap over her shoulders. "I'll only be a moment. I'll bring the wagon around front. The horses are still hitched."

As soon as Daughtie heard the rear door close, she moved to the front porch and waited until the team of horses came clopping and snorting around the side of the house. Once the wagon came to a halt, she hurried down the steps. "No need to get down, Liam. I can make it up by myself."

"Not likely I'd permit such a thing," he said, jumping down from the wagon and hurrying to the other side.

"Thank you," she said as he handed her up. "I see you've already delivered all of the goods to the Acre."

Liam flicked the reins and the horses moved off toward the lane. "Indeed. And Father Rooney was more than a little happy to receive every last article. He was still busy sifting through the lot of it when I finally left 'im the other night."

"I'm glad he was pleased."

"Not nearly as pleased as the folks that'll be keeping warm under those quilts this winter," he said with a smile. "It's a fine thing you ladies have done."

"Not nearly enough, I'm sure," she whispered. "There's always someone needing help. The children, those are the ones we need to be helping the most."

"True enough, but remember you're only one person; you can't lend a hand to everyone."

"I suppose, but I believe the Bible commands us to do our utmost to help those in need, to share our bounty, so to speak."

"You've a good heart, Miss Daughtie Winfield. So do ya think I should be givin' away my money to the poor instead of livin' in a big house and fixin' it up with nice furniture and the like?"

Daughtie gave him a pensive look. "I think you should do whatever your heart tells you to do."

Liam leaned back against the wooden seat of the wagon and gave a hearty laugh. The moon reflected down upon them while his gaze moved from her eyes and then settled upon her lips. "If I did what my heart's telling me to do at this very moment, I'm afraid I'd find myself in more trouble than an Irishman could handle."

~ 9 ~

Thaddeus Arnold looked down into the Merrimack Valley as the rickety old wagon in which he was riding rumbled down the dirt road nearing the outskirts of Lowell. "Stop here, if you don't mind," he requested pensively.

The wagon driver complied and Thaddeus thanked him before donning his black beaver hat. He patiently waited until the wagon was out of sight, a malicious grin playing upon his lips. He'd had no difficulty convincing the old man to give him a ride. A simple lie about a dying child was all that had been necessary. The gullible old fool had even refused the paltry few coins Thaddeus had offered. *His stupidity is my gain,* he thought while walking briskly down the road toward the house occupied by Naomi Arnold.

Digging deep into his pocket, Thaddeus slid his fingers around the old pocket watch his father had given him on his sixteenth birthday. He glanced down and noted the time before snapping the lid closed and shoving the time-piece back into place. Nearly five o'clock. A disgusted grunt escaped his lips. He had hoped to arrive earlier, but the old man wouldn't lay a whip to his horse. Naomi would be busy preparing dinner for those girls she boarded in the house that *he* had acquired through his overseer position. No matter that the house belonged to the Corporation. Naomi's possession of the dwelling had come through *his* effort, not hers. But the Corporation had elected to grant Naomi the privilege of remaining in the house. The thought still rankled him, yet he needed an excuse to return to Lowell. His wife and daughter provided justification for those visits.

Tugging at his jacket, he brushed out the wrinkles while approaching the front door of what had once been his home. It chafed him to knock, but he yielded and did so. Three loud raps. The front door opened as he began to once again lower his fist against the door.

Naomi stood before him, wiping her hands on a checkered towel, a flour-covered apron tied about her waist. "I wasn't expecting you." Her expression made it obvious she was neither anticipating nor pleased by his visit.

He gave her an insolent grin. "No need to look so dour. You should be pleased to see your husband. Isn't that what they teach you in that church you've been wagging off to every Sunday?"

Her jaw went slack at the question. "I'm no longer your wife, Thaddeus.

And who told you I've been attending church?"

Pushing his way past her into the entryway, he removed his hat and wool coat, then meticulously hung them on the same pegs he'd used while living in the house. He turned and faced her. "I'm aware of *everything* you do, Naomi. The fact that I live in New Hampshire doesn't preclude me from knowing your every move." She shuddered visibly at the remark. He rubbed his hands together, enjoying her discomfort. "You know I don't want Theona's mind glutted with nonsensical religious babble."

Naomi straightened her shoulders and met his stare with what appeared to be a modicum of defiance. "Theona *needs* God in her life. Besides, attending church gives her the opportunity not only to learn she has a heavenly Father who loves her but also to observe men modeling that same type of love for their families. I want her to know there are such men so that one day when she's considering marriage, she'll seek a man who loves and serves the Lord. I don't want Theona marrying a man she can't love and respect."

Thaddeus felt his anger rise. "A man like me—is that what you're saying?" he growled, clasping her face, his thumbs pushing hard into her hollow cheeks.

She pulled back from him, pushing his arms away. "Why are you here? You knew Theona would be napping and I'd be busy preparing supper."

He bit the inside of his cheek, forcing himself to remain calm. He wanted to slap her until she said aloud that he was a wonderful man, worthy of her love, but he knew he dared not. Naomi turned away and took a step toward the kitchen before he caught her by the arm. "Don't you ever walk away from me when I'm talking," he said, jerking her forward until her body was against his. Grasping her chin in a rough hold, he lowered his face to hers. Too soon she realized his intent and pulled away. "I'm entitled to my rights as a husband," he snarled.

"You're entitled to nothing in this house, Thaddeus. You're no longer my husband. If your abusive behavior continues, I'll be forced to report you to the Corporation and the judge. You're only permitted to visit Theona in this house based upon the judge's order and the Corporation's agreement. And, if you'll recall, the judge was concerned about your temper in Theona's presence. I doubt he would look favorably upon your behavior today."

Thaddeus backed away, his anger seething inside him. He knew, however, he had to make her believe he was contrite.

"I apologize. It's just that I miss you and Theona so much, and when I come back here, I become angry realizing all that I lost with my foolhardy behavior," he lied.

Naomi gave him a sidelong glance. "You have a strange way of showing your remorse. Now if you'll excuse me, you may wait for Theona in the parlor. I must finish preparing supper."

He silently chastised himself for his boorish behavior. If he was going to succeed in extracting information from Naomi, he needed to hold his temper in check. His very existence depended upon discovering some morsel of gossip to pass along to William Thurston. "Is there anything I can do to help?"

Naomi stopped midstep. "You? Help in the kitchen?"

He stifled the urge to spew what he was truly thinking and instead said, "Certainly there must be something I could manage to do without ruining the meal."

"You could set the table," she curtly replied before walking off toward the kitchen. "The dishes and utensils are out here," she called over her shoulder.

There was a hint of mistrust in her tone, but he forced himself to appear unperturbed. Following along behind, he grimaced and replied, "I'll do my best."

Naomi pointed toward the dishes and picked up a wooden spoon. She gave the ham and bean soup a quick stir, then scooped a measure of cornmeal into a large bowl. Thaddeus grabbed the dishes, quickly placed them on the table, and returned to the kitchen. "It appears the mills are continuing to operate in fine fashion," he ventured.

"Did you assume your departure would shut down the Corporation?"

He gritted his teeth. "I was merely attempting to make polite conversation. I thought the mills would be a neutral topic we could discuss." It took all the determination he could muster to maintain a note of civility in his tone.

"I hear little of what goes on in the mills, and what I do hear, I soon forget. Most of it has little effect upon my life or Theona's."

He stood staring at her back while she poured the corn bread mixture into an iron skillet. "Since your home and livelihood are dependent upon the Corporation, I'd say what goes on there does affect you."

"Umm, perhaps," she murmured, obviously more intent on her baking than carrying on a conversation.

The sound of Theona's voice drifted into the kitchen, and Naomi quickly rushed off to fetch her. The child came hurrying into the room but stopped short at the sight of her father.

"Aren't you going to give me a hug?" Thaddeus held his arms open in a welcoming gesture and waited until the child hesitantly moved toward him. He pulled her into an embrace but quickly released his hold when she began squirming. "She seems to grow taller every time I see her."

Naomi nodded. "That tends to happen with children."

A short time later the front door slammed, followed by the sound of female voices. "Good evening, Mrs. Arnold," someone called out.

"Good evening, Daughtie; good evening, Ruth. Supper will be on the table by the time you wash up."

"Thank you," the girls replied in unison.

Thaddeus pushed his pride aside and said, "Am I invited to supper?"

"I suppose, but please don't make a habit of arriving at mealtime. I can't afford to feed you."

Digging into his pocket, Thaddeus pulled out a coin and slapped it on the table. "I wouldn't want it bantered about that I'm begging food from your table."

He watched as Naomi took the coin and slipped it into her apron pocket. After managing to save coach fare for his journey, he now found himself paying to eat in his own home. The gall of the woman! He silently followed her into the dining room, where the two girls were already seated at the table entertaining Theona.

"Mr. Arnold will be joining us for supper, girls."

They looked at him with the same suspicion and wariness he'd observed only moments earlier in his own daughter's eyes. It was obvious Naomi had kept the gossip about him uppermost in their minds. "Good evening, ladies. Ruth and Daughtie, if memory serves me correctly," he said in his most gentlemanly fashion. "How are you this fine evening?"

"I'm doing very well, Mr. Arnold," Daughtie responded. "Are you visiting Lowell for long?"

Brazen girl, he thought, but he gave her a pleasant smile. "I'm hoping to depart this evening if all goes well."

"Did you injure yourself, Mrs. Arnold? There are red marks on your face. In fact, there's one along the left side of your face that appears to be turning blue. I hope you didn't meet with an accident this afternoon," Daughtie said, pointing toward Naomi's jaw.

Thaddeus came to attention at the comment. "You always were a bit clumsy, weren't you, my dear?" Thaddeus dismissively questioned before quickly shifting his attention back to Daughtie. "Tell me, Miss Winfield, have there been any changes occurring at the Appleton? Even though I no longer work for the Corporation, I still maintain an avid interest in the mills."

"I'm unaware of anything that would interest you, Mr. Arnold. I merely go to work, perform my labor, and return home. If there were plans for change, I'm guessing that the mill girls would be the last to know. Did I mention I received my first letter from Bella, Mrs. Arnold?"

"No. How exciting. Did she say if they encountered any problems on their voyage?" Naomi asked.

Thaddeus perked to attention, his gaze fastened upon Daughtie as he anxiously awaited any details she might reveal.

"She said the ship was quite beautiful, and they met with rough waters on only one occasion. Her missive detailed that the captain was extremely capable and maneuvered their ship through the storm with relative ease. I know Bella must have been relieved. Before they sailed, she expressed grave concern over becoming seasick. I told her I would be praying for smooth waters."

"I'm certain that must be what calmed the seas," Thaddeus replied, unable to keep the sarcasm from his tone. "Where did your friend's voyage take her?"

"England," Daughtie curtly answered. She shifted in her chair, turning her back toward Thaddeus. "She said that she and Taylor had attended a concert, but the letter was written only a few days after their arrival. The missive was certainly filled with joy and excitement. I can hardly wait to hear all the details of the journey upon her return."

"And Mr. Farnsworth's father—how is he faring?" Naomi questioned.

"Apparently his move to London was a wise decision. Bella says that the day they arrived, he was in fine spirits and appeared much improved. The family believes his regular visits to the doctor have been helpful."

"So the Mannings and Farnsworths are in England? I'm surprised John Farnsworth would return to his motherland," Thaddeus commented offhandedly.

"Why is that?" Ruth asked as she helped herself to another piece of corn bread.

Thaddeus peered down his long, thin nose. "Men skilled in the art of fabric printing were valued in England. In addition, the English certainly didn't want their secrets shared with the mill owners in this country."

Ruth's dead-eyed stare affirmed what Thaddeus had always known: women had no comprehension of the business world. It was obvious the silly girl hadn't begun to grasp the seriousness of his words and so he continued in his attempt to explain. "If English printers came here and worked for the mills in this country, the English mill owners knew it wouldn't be long until we'd no longer need to import their cloth. Their profits would be drastically reduced. And that's exactly what has occurred. Consequently, men like John Farnsworth are considered traitorous in some circles." He enunciated each word, his voice taking on a singsong tone as though he were talking to Theona rather than a grown woman.

Ruth's head began bobbing up and down. "Oh, I see. Well, I don't think Mr. Farnsworth would ever place his wife or Taylor and Bella in jeopardy. Besides, their visit was a surprise so I doubt any of those English mill owners will know they've visited until long after they've returned home."

"You're probably correct," Thaddeus agreed with a glint in his eyes. "And when *will* your friends be returning to the fair city of Lowell?"

"I'm not certain. I think their return depends upon the health of Mr. Farnsworth's father. However, since he's making good progress, they may return soon. I certainly hope that's the case," Daughtie replied. "I'm hoping for another letter from Bella. Perhaps they've already boarded a ship for their return."

Thaddeus cringed at the thought. He was certain this news would interest William Thurston, but only if he could get word to him before John Farnsworth departed from England. Snatching up his napkin, he quickly swiped it across his mouth and shoved his chair away from the table. "I hate to rush off and leave such excellent company, but I've just remembered a matter that needs my immediate attention. Thank you for dinner, Naomi, and do be careful. I'd hate to see you suffer any other bruises. No need to see me to the door. I know my way out."

He shrugged his wiry frame into the wool coat and grabbed his hat from the peg before rushing out the front door. He would hurry to the stationer's shop for supplies and pen a letter to Thurston this very night.

10

London

William Thurston stared into the mirror while fastening his collar. He took a moment to brood over his reflection, rather disturbed he now bore the receding hairline and long protruding brow that were both lineaments of his heritage. He had always hoped to avoid the strong familial resemblance to his father.

His dull gray eyes stared back from the mirror and reminded him of his dreary wife and the marriage they had shared for nearly twenty years—utterly lifeless. Shortly after his departure from the United States, William had realized certain advantages flowed in his direction solely because he was a fugitive. The greatest of these benefits was being inaccessible to his wife, who continued to live in Massachusetts, ignorant of his whereabouts. Another was the opportunity to mingle with true bluebloods, a feat he would accomplish within the hour.

It mattered little that his presence wasn't truly desired at tonight's gathering; he had managed to wangle an invitation from Chauncy Fuller, and he *would* attend, tipping his nose up in the air along with the rest of the gentry. He'd make them believe he was one of them. No one would be the wiser. This little get-together could provide access to some of the greatest fortunes in England. These men were the backbone of England's industrial wealth. He smiled into the mirror. The Boston Associates paled in comparison to the men with whom he would dine this evening.

Thurston walked down the stairs, a shiver of delight coursing through his body. Nathan Appleton, Kirk Boott, and the other Associates who so freely despised him would be amazed to find him mingling among the elite of English industry. He stepped out the front door of the small boarding-house where he'd rented a room when he had first arrived in England. A coach and driver awaited him. William considered the cost of hiring the carriage and driver to be an investment in his future and willingly paid the fee. To be seen arriving afoot could cause questions regarding his suitability to attend tonight's gathering.

The ride was bumpy and the driver was careless in handling the horses, but William remained silent. He kept his mind focused upon the evening that lay ahead. "You can park and wait with the other drivers," he instructed while clambering down from the carriage. The driver tipped his hat and flicked the reins, urging the horses forward, moving off toward the end of the circular driveway.

William squared his shoulders and walked up the steps of the Fuller mansion. A butler, with silver tray in hand, stood guard at the front door, artfully extending the scallop-edged plate as each guest entered the front door. Placing his card in the center of the tray, William patiently waited until the butler returned and beckoned him forward. At the door of the main drawing room, the butler stepped aside and nodded. William walked into the room with its gilded walls and flickering candles, the shimmering light dancing down upon the Fullers' jewel-bedecked female guests.

His gaze flitted about the room, finally resting on Chauncy Fuller, who was standing alongside two women greeting the guests. William made his way toward the group and anxiously awaited his host's acknowledgment. Chauncy nodded and welcomed William rather off-handedly with a slight bow.

"Good evening," he said, introducing him neither to the women nor to any of the gentlemen who stood nearby.

Knowing he had never achieved anything in life by adhering to strict social mores, William realized he could ill afford to begin now. Edging his way into the circle of men, he stood listening attentively until the topic of American industry began seeping into the otherwise lackluster dialogue.

William took a deep breath, infusing himself with courage. "I'd not talk too harshly against the textile industry in America. If their progress continues, they'll soon be selling their cloth here in England."

A hush fell over the group as the men turned to face him. A tall, elegantly dressed gentleman stroked his mustache and narrowed his eyes. "You speak with an American accent." The blistering words jabbed through the silence like a thrusting rapier.

William nodded. "I was born in Massachusetts, although I come from a long line of fine Englishmen. My heart and loyalty are to the motherland, not America."

"Your words sound as though you have more belief in the ability of the Americans than the English. We've had years of industrialization in this country. The United States will not easily usurp our power," the gentleman argued.

William held out his hand to the man. "I'm William Thurston. I don't believe we've met."

"Reginald Archer. I own a controlling interest in several cotton mills in Lancashire."

"I don't mean to offend any of you fine men, but the fact remains the Americans are moving forward by leaps and bounds in the textile industry. Surely you've already experienced a decline in sales. I know they now import very little from England."

Archer nodded his head. "Of course. But they'll never achieve the quality of our cloth. There are Americans who will still demand cloth woven in England."

"I'm not as certain as you, Mr. Archer. The mills in Lowell are now weaving every imaginable type of cloth, even carpets for American and foreign markets."

Archer glanced about the circle of men and then eyed William suspiciously. "How is it that you are privy to information that permits you to speak with such authority on the topic of the American textile industry?"

Chauncy Fuller had drawn closer and now placed his hand on Archer's shoulder. "Mr. Thurston is personally acquainted with some of the *industrial giants* of America."

Several of the men sniggered while casting glances at one another. "*Industrial giants,*" one of them guffawed.

"The Americans have never had an original idea. Everything they've accomplished has been developed by the English. The only achievement those American capitalists can claim is thievery," Reginald asserted.

William nodded in agreement. "That's a fact, Mr. Archer. Oh, they may have refined a thing or two, but Francis Cabot Lowell relished telling how he had visited the homeland and managed to finagle an invitation to tour the mills. Of course, I must give the man credit. He possessed an exceptional memory, and it served him well. He died a wealthy man while causing a dip in profits for the rightful owners of the design living here in England."

A lanky bespectacled man moved closer, his eyebrows knit into a tight line above his wire-rimmed eyeglasses. "Just how did you come by this information that you're so willing to share with us, Mr. Thurston?"

"I was a member of the Boston Associates."

A gasp could be heard from somewhere among the group. Thurston peered around the circle, wishing the uncomfortable silence would soon end.

"Well, that's quite a revelation," Chauncy finally remarked.

The lanky gentleman removed his spectacles and leveled a beady-eyed stare in William's direction. "Indeed! And you left the financial security of your membership in the Boston Associates because you suddenly have an abiding love for the motherland. Is that what you expect us to believe, Mr. Thurston?"

The man's accusatory tone sent a ripple of irritation flowing through William. "It would appear you find difficulty accepting my explanation, sir."

The man nodded, a smirk etched upon his lips. "Any sane man in this room would find it difficult to believe a man would leave a thriving investment merely because he's suddenly decided he loves the motherland—especially when he's never even lived here before."

William rested his chin in one hand and gave the man a look of contemplation. "You're right. Were the circumstances reversed, I'd probably harbor at least an iota of disbelief. I can't force you to accept the truth of what I've said. However, I think that you'll find all of my information verifiable. In fact, the Associates were busy spreading ugly rumors about me before I ever sailed for England. Feel free to contact any of them. I'm sure they'll tell you all manner of lies about me. They consider my departure nothing short of a crime—in fact, sources tell me they've accused me of any number of criminal deeds since my departure. They're fearful I'll somehow undermine their plan to overtake England as the leading industrial nation." He leaned forward and lowered his voice to a hoarse whisper. "And, in fact, gentlemen, that is exactly what they're planning—to send England into a spiraling business slump—a depression, so to speak."

"Depression?" The word spread among the men like a flame licking its way through dry kindling.

William gestured for quiet. "Gentlemen, gentlemen. There's no need for concern—at least not yet. Armed with information and a few good men, we'll be able to outsmart the Americans at their own game. I have sources in America who are willing to, shall we say, *share* information for a small price. There's no reason we can't *borrow* information and use it here in England."

"I'm not certain we want to stoop to their level. After all, we can't prove what they've done is illegal—at least not all of it," Fuller stated.

Thurston plucked a glass of port from the tray of a passing servant. "If you don't stoop to their level, you'll soon find yourselves swept aside by the industrial tidal wave in America. I don't think any of you want to suffer the kind of financial disaster such inaction will reap, but of course, I wouldn't consider forcing your decision."

William peered over the rim of his glass, taking great satisfaction in the manifestation of fear that had already etched itself upon all the faces now staring back in his direction. "To your health and good fortune, gentlemen," he said while lifting his glass into the air.

"How reliable is your information?" one of the men called out.

"Reliable enough to know that all of your printing designs have been copied and are presently being sold in the United States. In fact, they've expanded upon your printing technology through several Englishmen who sold out to the Americans. When I left Massachusetts, the Associates were developing new print designs that surpassed anything I've seen in England. Any of you familiar with John Farnsworth?"

Reginald Archer hoisted his cigar into the air. "I am. He was my employee in Lancashire. Good man, talented. I hated to lose him, but he said he had an opportunity that would provide him a more substantial lifestyle than he could make in the mills."

"Perhaps Mr. Farnsworth meant to say he had an opportunity that would provide him more money than he could make in the *Lancashire* mills. He left

England and is working in Massachusetts for the Boston Associates. He spoke the truth about a substantial lifestyle. He's managed to make himself invaluable and is handsomely paid," William divulged.

"Treason!" Archer shouted. "Employees of the mills are forbidden to divulge trade information to foreign powers. It's difficult to believe John Farnsworth would behave in such a self-seeking manner. I thought his allegiance to the crown was above reproach."

A surge of delight swept over William. His plan was working. "Money is a treacherous master, Mr. Archer. John Farnsworth has obviously bowed to its power. Not only that, but he later sent for his young nephew, Taylor Manning. Granted, the young man had no previous experience, but Farnsworth has taught him everything he knows, and his nephew appears to have a natural talent for design. I understand that between Farnsworth's mechanical prowess and the nephew's artistic design, they're developing what will be undeniably beautiful fabric."

Discordant murmurs sifted throughout the room. "Gentlemen, gentlemen. We'll not resolve any of this tonight; in fact, I've already received several disapproving looks from my wife. Perhaps we should agree to meet in another setting. I believe we'll soon be going in for dinner," Chauncy advised.

"We can meet in my London office if you like," Reginald Archer offered. "When are you available, Mr. Thurston? Your attendance is imperative."

William attempted to hide his feeling of smug satisfaction. "My priority is to assist you gentlemen in any way possible. You decide what time and date will work for all of you, and I'll be present."

Chauncy Fuller escorted William to the door, confirmed their meeting for the following Wednesday, and returned to the drawing room, where Barlow Kent, his wife's pitiable cousin, was obviously attempting to gain his attention. Chauncy's wife had recently begun inviting Barlow to their social functions, obviously hoping to somehow cheer her distant relative. Since his wife's untimely death several years ago, Barlow had been wallowing in self-pity. But although Chauncy dearly loved his wife, her relatives were another matter altogether. They were a beggarly lot, not one of them ever amounting to much, and Barlow was a prime example.

The half-crazed man continued to wave a lit cigar overhead until Chauncy finally reached his side. "Put that thing down before you set someone's hair afire," he warned.

"Let's step outside for a few minutes. We need to talk," Barlow said.

"Outside? It's freezing outdoors. If it's privacy you want, we can go to my library," Chauncy replied, leading the way down the hallway and into the room. Firmly closing the door, he turned to face Barlow. "What's so important?"

"I heard what that Thurston man had to say, but John Farnsworth is in London at this very moment. I've seen him."

"What are you talking about, Barlow? You don't even *know* John Farnsworth. It was Reginald he worked for down in Lancashire." Chauncy gave the man a sympathetic look, fearing Barlow's grief had finally caused him to become delusional.

"I'm not crazy, Chauncy. John Farnsworth and I worked together for a number of years—before Reginald hired him. I know it was Farnsworth whom I saw going in and out of several shops and the museum last week. I followed him. He was with four or five people—relatives, I surmise. Then a few days ago, I happened upon him at a teahouse. I kept out of sight and followed him back to his father's house. Look, I know John left England to help the Americans. He told me as much when he quit his position with Reginald. There's no doubt in my mind he's returned to gather more information and seek out our latest innovations to take back to the Americans."

"You're certain about this?"

"Absolutely."

Chauncy hesitated, wondering if he should trust Barlow's rationality, yet a sense of urgency gripped him. He knew they must act. "Then we must put together a plan to stop Farnsworth. I'll contact the authorities first thing in the morning."

"No! I don't think that's wise. The police will want to investigate, and they'll scare him off. Worse yet, he may complete his espionage and leave the country before they arrest him. We can take care of this ourselves. Once we've formulated and carried out our plan, we can turn him over to the Crown and he can be tried for treason, but we don't want to let him get out of the country. You know how the authorities tend to mishandle the simplest of matters."

"Perhaps you're right," Chauncy conceded. "I'm to meet with William Thurston next Wednesday. Would you feel comfortable confiding in him? Possibly we could join forces with him to bring Farnsworth down."

Barlow nodded. "I would rather talk to Thurston than the authorities, and with his knowledge of the United States and his obvious disdain for the Boston Associates, he may prove useful."

"Well, then, let's set this matter aside until Wednesday. I really must return to my guests," Chauncy said. "Perhaps you should get some rest, Barlow. You look exhausted."

"I think I will excuse myself if you won't think me an ungrateful guest."

"Not at all," Chauncy replied. "I'll send the butler for your coach."

Barlow raised his hand in protest. "No. I'll see to it. You attend to your guests. I've already taken too much of your time."

Chauncy flinched as Barlow Kent grasped his hand in a death grip and pumped his arm up and down. Barlow would bear close scrutiny.

11

Lowell

Daughtie tied her bonnet and impatiently waited at the bottom of the steps. "Come on, Ruth, or we'll be late," she called out while intently watching the stairway.

Daughtie didn't want to be delayed this evening. Over the past several weeks, she had been growing increasingly annoyed at Ruth's persistent tardiness. Thus far, Daughtie had been able to hold her tongue, but it was becoming increasingly difficult. She waited, tapping the toe of her shoe on the shining hardwood floor and watching the hands of the mantel clock march onward.

"Ruth! I'm leaving right now."

Ruth appeared at the top of the steps and cast a look of disdain in Daughtie's direction. "I'm doing my best. We have plenty of time."

"I want a good seat where I can see and hear everything. I specifically told you I wanted to leave early."

Ruth raced down the steps at breakneck speed and came to a skidding halt directly in front of Daughtie. "Well, here I am. *Let's go*," she said, holding the door open.

Daughtie frowned at the remark. Ruth's tone made it sound as though she'd been ready and waiting for hours instead of the other way around. "We're leaving, Mrs. Arnold," Daughtie called out. "Are you certain you don't want to attend the meeting?"

Naomi Arnold came from the kitchen, wiping her damp hands on a frayed white dishcloth. "I'd love to hear Miss Crandall speak, but I don't want to keep Theona out after bedtime, and I fear the meeting will run late. You girls go along. I'll look forward to hearing everything when you return—if it's not too late. I may be in bed," she added with a smile.

"If you're not up when we return, I'll be sure and set aside some time before I go to the library tomorrow evening," Daughtie promised.

The girls walked in silence for several minutes, the cold December wind whipping at their cloaks. "It's cold. Let's walk a little faster," Ruth said, picking up the pace. "I wish they were having the meeting at one of the churches here in town."

"You know that would have caused trouble for certain. There are too many folks who would object to Miss Crandall being permitted to use one of the bigger churches. It's better this way—maybe the folks who disagree with her views will just stay away."

A coach and several wagons rumbled down the street past them. "As cold as it is, maybe *everyone* will stay away," Ruth retorted.

"I doubt that. After all, *we'll* be in attendance, and I know there are a lot of others planning to be present."

"You lasses care for a ride?"

Both girls looked up toward the driver as he pulled back on the reins, bringing the team of bays to a halt alongside them.

"Yes," Daughtie delightedly replied.

"No!" Ruth responded while tugging at Daughtie's arm. She leaned in close to Daughtie's side. "We can't ride with *him*."

"You can walk if you want, but I'm going to ride. As you pointed out only a few minutes ago, it's cold." Daughtie accepted Liam's outstretched hand and allowed him to assist her up. "Are you walking or riding, Ruth?"

"Riding," Ruth grumbled while reluctantly accepting Liam's assistance. She settled beside Daughtie and whispered, "This is a mistake and you know it."

Daughtie chose to ignore the comment. Liam gave a slap of the reins, the horses moved out, and the wagon lurched forward, jostling her closer to Liam. Ruth jabbed Daughtie in the ribs, motioning her to scoot away from him. Instead, she held fast and made no effort to move. In fact, Ruth would be appalled if she knew just how much she was enjoying Liam's nearness, Daughtie decided.

"From the look of all those wagons, it appears there'll be a good crowd this evenin'," Liam said as the churchyard came into view. Wagons, coaches, and saddled horses filled the area that surrounded the small country church. He pulled into a spot between two coaches and helped the girls down from their perch before moving to the front of the wagon to secure the horses.

"Come on, Daughtie," Ruth urged, grasping Daughtie's hand.

Daughtie tugged back, freeing herself from Ruth's hold, squared her shoulders, and stood firm. "I'm waiting for Liam," she replied.

"Liam? You call him by his first name? I'm worried about you, Daughtie. What's going on up there?" Ruth asked while pointing a finger toward her head.

"I'm just fine, and nothing's gone awry with my thinking. I'm going to sit beside Liam at the meeting, and if you don't want to be seen with us, then you go ahead in and take a seat. I'll be careful not to sit beside you. I wouldn't want to cause you any embarrassment."

"Fine!" Ruth retorted, and Daughtie watched her roommate march off toward the front door of the church.

"I'm guessin' yar friend is a wee bit worried about being seen in public with an Irishman," Liam said as he approached Daughtie. "And ya should be, too. Why don't ya go on and join her?"

"Because I don't want to. I've given this a great deal of thought over the weeks, and I feel like a hypocrite every time I avoid you. I'm not embarrassed, and if folks don't like it, that's their problem. I'm not going to permit narrow-minded people to interfere in my life."

"I don't know that ya'll be gettin' a choice in the matter," he said, walking alongside her into the church.

Daughtie took the lead and found a pew near the front with only a few occupants. She edged her way into the row, seated herself, and patted the space beside her. Liam lowered his gaze and seated himself as far from her as space permitted, hugging the end of the pew.

"Liam! Good to see you." Matthew and Lilly Cheever were standing at the end of the pew. "May we join you?"

"Certainly," Liam replied while standing to permit the Cheevers entrance into the row.

Matthew seated himself and then leaned forward to meet Liam's gaze. "Did we interrupt something?"

"No, 'course not. Miss Winfield and Miss Wilson were afoot, and I offered them a ride in me wagon. There were only a few seats remaining when we arrived," he hurried to explain.

"Well, I'm pleased there's a good crowd. I had to twist Matthew's arm to get him here," Lilly replied before turning her attention to Daughtie. "Have you received any correspondence from Bella or Addie since their arrival in England? I'm anxious to hear how they're doing."

"Yes, I had a letter from Bella, and they had a safe voyage," Daughtie replied. She glanced toward Matthew and then lowered her voice to a whisper. "Did you discover Mr. Cheever is pro slavery after all? Is that why you had difficulty getting him to attend the meeting tonight?"

"Pro slavery? No—but as I explained at our Ladies Aid meeting, he must be very careful where he places his allegiance, what with the mills and all. I'm sure you understand."

"No, I'm not certain I do understand. Why would he let his position in the mills affect his stand on slavery?"

Lilly leaned closer. "As I explained at the meeting, the mills are dependent upon cotton, and cotton is raised in the South. Without slaves, the Southern plantation owners say they are doomed for failure."

Daughtie nodded her head. "I see. So it's not a matter of what's right or wrong but what's economically in the best interest of the Southerners?"

"Not exactly. You may have twisted my words just a bit. However, it's the economic future not only of the Southern plantation owners but all of us that would be affected if slavery were abolished. However, I don't know how much serious thought has been given to the total impact abolition would have upon the country. Don't misunderstand—I'm an abolitionist through and through."

"Well, I think we'll all be called to make sacrifices if slavery is ever to be abolished. It will require a commitment to place others ahead of our personal economic security. I'm extremely eager to hear Miss Crandall speak this evening. From what I've been told, she's a very brave woman, and she's been forced to make difficult decisions. One can't help but applaud her willingness to model a lifestyle that exemplifies the cause she so capably champions."

Reverend Walters moved to the lectern and rapped with a wooden gavel several times before the assembled crowd turned their attention to the front of the church.

"If I could have your attention," Reverend Walters said. "Miss Crandall has arrived, and we'll begin as soon as the room quiets."

The sound of murmurs and shuffling feet subsided, and Reverend Walters cleared his throat. "Because Miss Crandall must leave for Connecticut early in the morning, I'll reluctantly forego the urge to spend at least an hour telling you of her bravery and fine accomplishments. Instead, I'm hoping she'll include the many details of her struggle over the past year, and I believe what she says tonight will heighten your awareness of the bigotry and hatred that sometimes occurs when a person takes a stand for egalitarianism."

Reverend Walters turned to his right and motioned Miss Crandall forward. The speaker's long fawn-colored hair was swept into a decorative coil that framed her face and added fullness to her long, narrow features. Her piercing blue eyes and the white bodice of her russet dress accentuated the porcelain fairness of her skin. She gazed into the audience as though taking account of each person in attendance before uttering a word.

"Thank you for braving the cold in order to attend this meeting. I come to speak to you about a matter of grave concern, and I pray you will give consideration to what I say this evening. I believe each of us will one day be required to take a personal stand on the issue of slavery. Now, I'm not talking about whether we're from the North or the South and what the general opinion of that locale may be; I'm talking about deep down inside our beings, what you as an individual believe. I tell you this because you may be required to put your convictions to the test. Unfortunately, I have already been forced to take a stand. Little did I realize I would be met with such hostility and anger—and this type of behavior was from people who profess to be abolitionists. I find there are many who say they oppose slavery, yet few of them believe in equality for the Negro. I say that the Negro must be given his freedom *and* treated as an equal to the white man. There is a mighty chasm between freedom and equality. What I am about to tell you is proof of that statement."

Daughtie gave Miss Crandall her rapt attention, anxious to hear the unfolding story.

"This whole affair began through no instigation on my part. In 1831 I was approached by a number of families residing in Canterbury who valued my Quaker upbringing. They'd heard I was an experienced teacher and encouraged me to open a school for their daughters, who had already completed their primary education requirements. I made arrangements with the bank to purchase a home on the Canterbury Green, a house large enough to accommodate the girls who would be boarding with me. Everything progressed nicely. The residents of Canterbury were pleased, enrollment soon reached capacity, and from all appearances, opening the school was a sound decision that worked to the benefit of all concerned.

"However, in 1833 Miss Sarah Harris, a young lady of color who was living with her parents in Canterbury, approached me. Miss Harris had attended the district schools in Norwich, Connecticut, and dreamed of becoming a teacher herself. This fine young lady believed that once she received additional education at my academy, she would be equipped to teach people of her own race. Naturally, I applauded her desire and agreed that she could attend classes. She remained at home with her parents and merely came to the school each day for classes. Nonetheless, once word spread about town that I had admitted Miss Harris, the residents of Canterbury were outraged."

A smattering of murmurs could be heard throughout the church. Daughtie wasn't certain if folks were whispering their approval or displeasure over Miss Crandall's actions. Daughtie, however, was in awe of Miss Crandall's moral fiber and was anxious to hear every word the woman uttered.

"Needless to say," Miss Crandall continued, "I was surprised and saddened by the attitudes and behaviors with which I was confronted. All of my white students withdrew from the school, for their parents were unwilling to accept a Negro girl being educated beyond the boundaries of the district schools. Realizing that I would soon be destitute, yet unwilling to bow to the demand of ejecting Miss Harris, I consulted with several abolitionists. After much thought-provoking discussion and prayer, I made the decision to reopen my school. However, this time I organized it as a school for the education of young ladies of color. I began recruiting pupils throughout the Northeast for the first boarding and teacher training school for young women of color."

Miss Crandall hesitated for a moment and gazed about the church. "I was astounded when the people of Canterbury immediately retaliated by sending representatives to the Connecticut General Assembly. The Assembly quickly passed a law prohibiting the education of out-of-state Negroes in private schools. Although there was no doubt the law was specifically aimed at closing my school, I have defied that ill-conceived law and continue to operate. I have been arrested, spent the night in jail, endured one trial, and will soon suffer the disruption of another, yet I plan to fight on for the equality of educating these fine young ladies. Many of those who oppose my school also say they oppose slavery. Perhaps they do; I am not their judge. However, I believe *all* people must be treated with the same equality and opportunity. So on this cold winter's night, I come to tell you that if you stand for abolition, you may be forced to bear some discomfort. But if you believe in equality, be prepared—for you will surely suffer.

"My students and I continue to be bullied and harassed, but we will withstand as long as humanly possible. Should the safety of the girls become a factor, and I fear one day it shall, I may be forced to reevaluate my position. But for now, I stand resolute in my determination to educate any young woman desiring an education, regardless of color."

Applause filled the church, though not as boisterously as when Miss Crandall had taken the podium earlier in the evening. Several people left the building before the question-and-answer session began, while others, obviously pro slavery, stayed and queried her unmercifully. Daughtie watched with admiration as Miss Crandall patiently responded to the inquiries without evidence of anger.

A tall, well-dressed man stood near the back of the church. "In case you people of Lowell don't remember what's needed to keep this town operating, let me remind you that it's cotton," he called out. "It takes slaves to raise that cotton. If we're to survive, these mills need to operate. Without cotton, the mills will fail and you'll be without jobs. Before you adopt Miss Crandall's ideology, you'd best decide if you can survive with the ramifications of such a decision."

"Thank you, sir. I concur with your last remark," Miss Crandall stated. "I'm not encouraging anyone to blindly follow along with my beliefs. Each person in this room needs to prayerfully evaluate the truth that God speaks to his or her heart and be prepared for the consequences of the decision, whether for or against slavery. I'm well aware this town is dependent upon the cotton raised in the South. I disagree, however, that the only way to raise cotton is through the use of slaves. Granted, those wealthy plantation owners may suffer some losses if they're required to pay wages, but cotton *can* be raised without slavery."

The man wagged his head in obvious disagreement. "Just remember, folks, if the plantation owners are required to pay wages, the price of cotton will increase, which means the cost of production increases, so the cost of cloth will increase. If folks can buy imported cloth cheaper, production will dwindle and your wages will decrease—if you're able to maintain a job at all."

"That makes sense," another man agreed. "And I can't afford to lose my job."

"Yeah, and what if those Negroes move up here and are willing to take lower wages for our jobs? We'd have them *and* the Irish to deal with!"

A sense of anger rose within Daughtie, and she stood to her feet. "People need to have a willingness in their hearts to do what's right no matter what the personal cost. Wouldn't you want the Negroes to sacrifice for you if the situation were reversed and *you* were held in bondage?" With legs trembling, she plopped down on the pew, her meek nature having returned full force.

"They could all go back to Africa and be free. They wouldn't be competing for our jobs thaddaway," another man remarked.

"You gonna pay their passage, Emil?" someone called out. A few chuckles followed, and an embarrassed-looking Emil Kramer sat down.

There was more Daughtie wanted to say, but the few words she had spoken earlier left her feeling drained and inadequate. She listened as members of the audience continued to speak and, on several occasions, clenched her fists in anger at the comments being made. Yet she knew little would be accomplished through hostility and brash words and was relieved when Reverend Walters finally called the meeting to a close.

The moment the crowd was dismissed, Daughtie rushed forward, determined to speak with Miss Crandall. For a short time she was forced to move against the crowd, much like a fish swimming upstream, but finally she freed herself from the other attendees and waved her handkerchief in the air. "Miss Crandall! May I have a moment?" she called out, hoping her voice could be heard over the din.

Miss Crandall turned in her direction and then motioned Daughtie forward.

Breathless, Daughtie rushed up the two steps to the stage and came to a halt in front of the speaker. "Thank you for waiting. I'm Daughtie Winfield," she said, almost feeling as though she should curtsy.

Miss Crandall's face warmed in a bright smile. "Prudence Crandall. I'm pleased to meet you, Miss Winfield. What may I do for you?"

"I wanted to personally express my admiration for you and the work you're doing. I was hoping we could discuss in more detail what might be done to overcome the attitudes opposing equality for all races. I agree with everything you've said this evening, especially your words that we must not only free the slaves but also have a willingness to embrace them as equals. I find some of the people in this community unwilling to treat the Irish as equals, and that attitude causes me to question the sincerity of their stand for abolition. Do you believe they can treat the Negroes as equals when they won't do that much for the Irish immigrants?"

Miss Crandall patted Daughtie's hand. "Or women, for that matter," Miss Crandall said. "Based upon my own experience, I seriously doubt the black man will be considered an equal when he is finally freed, but that doesn't mean we should blindly accept such an attitude. Change will not occur if we silently agree to whatever the majority imposes upon us."

"I apologize for interrupting, but we really must leave, Miss Crandall," Reverend Walters said.

"Of course," she replied and then turned back to Daughtie. "Above all, pray for guidance, my dear. I'm sorry we don't have more time to visit, but should you feel so inclined, you may write to me."

"Oh, thank you. Corresponding with you would give me immeasurable satisfaction."

"Then by all means, please do so. I promise to answer each and every letter," Miss Crandall said while pulling on her doeskin gloves. She fastened her gray woolen cape, then bid Daughtie good-bye before following Reverend Walters out the back of the church.

Ruth was waiting outside the door and quickly latched on to Daughtie's arm. "Where have you been? We'd best hurry if we're going to make it back to the house before curfew."

"Matthew and I will take you home, won't we?" Lilly offered as she glanced up at her husband, who was conversing with Liam Donohue. "It's too cold to walk all that distance."

Daughtie glanced toward Liam, but he said nothing. Why didn't *he* offer to take her home? Instead, he pulled up his collar against the cold, bid the Cheevers good-night, and after nodding in her direction, hurried off toward his wagon.

"What did you think of Miss Crandall?" Lilly inquired after they were seated in the carriage with warm woolen blankets tucked around their legs.

Ruth squirmed forward. "I was very impressed with what she said. Her courage is remarkable, and I completely agree with what she said regarding equality. It truly does little good if the slaves are freed and then prevented access to the same opportunities as their white brothers."

"Which white brothers?" Daughtie asked, meeting Ruth's surprised gaze.

Ruth's mouth gaped open in an exaggerated oval. "Why, whatever do you mean, Daughtie?"

"Equality doesn't exist between the 'white brothers.' So I'm wondering if the fairness you speak of would provide Negroes the same equality we give the mill workers and farmers, or would it be the same access we give the Irishmen? The Irish are permitted to dig canals and haul stone, but they're relegated off to the Acre to live in shanties, their children are required to attend separate schools, and they are treated with disdain," Daughtie passionately replied.

"You just want to argue," Ruth responded. "Just because I don't think you should be keeping company with Liam Donohue, you attack everything I say regarding fair and equal treatment of differing people."

"Daughtie has a valid point, Miss Wilson. The Irish are mistreated and underappreciated. They don't receive the same advantages as other white people in this community—or any other, for that matter," Matthew replied. "However, Daughtie, you might want to talk to my wife regarding the sensibility of a courtship with Mr. Donohue. Don't misunderstand; Liam's a fine man and we value his friendship. But I doubt whether the community will harbor the same attitude."

Daughtie gave momentary thought to pinching Ruth's arm. How dare she make such unsolicited remarks about Liam? Even if they were keeping company, it was improper of Ruth to speak of the matter.

Lilly gave Daughtie an enchanting smile. "I think Daughtie has a very sound mind, and I doubt she needs my assistance sorting out the details of her personal life. In fact, I believe she's quite mature and certainly capable of deciding what's best for her future." Lilly reached across the carriage and patted Daughtie's arm. "That isn't to say I wouldn't be happy to discuss the matter, if you desire. However, it's not a topic I would broach should you come for tea."

Daughtie returned Lilly's smile. "Nor is it one I would expect you to solve. Quite honestly, I fear Mr. Donohue is even more concerned than Ruth about the ramifications of such a social relationship—if it's possible to be any more alarmed than Ruth," she added.

Ruth stiffened beside her, and Daughtie felt a modicum of satisfaction. Perhaps Ruth would think twice before attempting to embarrass her again.

"As I said, Liam's a fine man, but right or wrong, there are undeniable prejudices against the Irish. You should be careful," Mr. Cheever warned.

"Daughtie tells me she's had word from Bella, and they're enjoying their time in England," Lilly said, obviously intent on changing the topic of conversation.

"That reminds me, I failed to tell you we received a missive at the mill office just the other day. It was from John—seems his father's health took a downward turn, and with winter setting in, he doubts they'll return until early spring."

Lilly turned to face her husband. "Oh, my. That means they'll be gone over the holidays. I was so hoping they'd be returning any day—before the weather turned any colder. How disheartening . . . yet I'm being selfish. I *am* pleased John and Addie can be with John's father and lend their assistance."

"I know, my dear. I miss them, too."

Thoughts of defending Liam quickly slipped from Daughtie's mind. Bella would be gone until next year. An undeniable pang of despair clutched her heart as the carriage pulled up in front of Mrs. Arnold's house.

"Here we are," Matthew said. He opened the carriage door and assisted both girls down. "We've gotten you home with at least fifteen minutes to spare."

"Thank you for the ride," Daughtie said.

"Do let me know if you hear further from Bella or Miss Addie," Lilly called out before the carriage began to pull away.

"I will," Daughtie called after them.

The house was dark save a burning candle Mrs. Arnold had left for them on the candlestand beside the stairway. While Daughtie removed her cloak and hung it on a peg by the doorway, Ruth grasped the candle and silently led the way to their room.

Once inside, Daughtie closed the bedroom door and began preparing for bed.

"You're angry with me, but I'm only looking out for what's best for you," Ruth said, breaking the heavy silence that permeated the room.

Daughtie seated herself on the bed. "I don't need you to mother me, Ruth. If I want your opinion regarding the choices I make, I shall ask. Your intent to embarrass me in front of Mr. and Mrs. Cheever was obvious. But I'm more angered by your statements regarding equality than by what you said to the Cheevers. I can't imagine how you can say you believe in equality for the Negroes and then, in the next breath, defame me for seeking to befriend an Irishman. Your words and deeds are in opposition."

"I *do* believe in abolition. I don't think people should *own* each other. However, permitting Liam Donohue to court you is a totally different issue. You listen to me, Daughtie Winfield. You stand to lose more than you think if you continue down this path of defiance. It may be a step up the social ladder for Liam Donohue to be seen with you on his arm, but it is certain death to any future marriage plans of yours. Do you think any respectable man is going to escort you, much less marry you, after you've been associated with an Irishman? If you have any sense at all, you'll cease this imprudent behavior immediately."

Daughtie sat momentarily silent, mystified and quite unable to comprehend Ruth's behavior. "I was taught from the time I was a little girl that we all have equal value in the eyes of God. Two Negro women joined the Shakers and lived with us at Canterbury. They were our sisters, treated no differently than anyone else. Nothing more and nothing less was expected of them; the same rules applied to everyone; the same benefits were enjoyed by all. Why must it be so different out here among the world's people?"

"Greed and selfishness, I suppose," Ruth replied simply.

Daughtie nodded. "Life isn't so simple away from the structured existence of the Shakers, where personal belongings are nonexistent. However, I believe change can occur—if we're willing to pay the price."

Liam prepared for bed, thinking all the while of Daughtie Winfield and her passion for equality in mankind.

"For sure she's like no lass I've ever met," he murmured to himself.

And indeed she was unique. Her upbringing seemed to envision a world that Liam was sure could never exist—a world where no one would think twice if Liam were to show up on her doorstep to escort her to a dance or a lecture.

"That world will never exist!" he declared, crawling into bed. "The world would never be seein' the likes of me on the arm of a Yankee girl like her."

It was best to put thoughts of such a nature completely from his mind. Better to concentrate on his work. He was scheduled to begin the creation of a stone staircase for a Mr. and Mrs. Price. Mrs. Price had recently been to England, where she was entertained in the home of some grand lord and lady. Their staircase was of palatial proportions; however, Mrs. Price was confident Liam could recreate the entire thing, on a smaller scale, for her new home. Being an artist, she had made multiple sketches of the stairs, banisters, and newels. They would be paying him a nice tidy sum for the grand stonework they'd described, and he would have a good amount of cash to send home to his mother and family.

Taking a deep breath, Liam blew out the candle on his bed table and closed his eyes. He thought of his boyhood home—of racing across the stone bridge with his playmates, of learning to jump his mare over rock walls and streams. Those were the moments he'd been most happy as a child. Life had seemed quite simple then. He had enough food to fill his belly and a warm bed in which to sleep. Every night his mother would come to tuck him in, bending over to gently kiss his forehead and bid him pleasant dreams.

But memories of his mother soon faded, replaced by Daughtie Winfield's dark-eyed gaze. He could see her clearly enough in his mind that if he'd wanted to, he could have etched her in stone. Her face was almost heart-shaped, with huge brown eyes that seemed to take in every detail of life. Her nose was pert, turned up just a bit at the end, and her lips . . . He pushed the images aside and rolled over on his stomach.

"My mother would say I'm bewitched," he muttered. "She'd say the fairies had taken my mind, and no doubt she'd have a charm or potion to rid me of such misery and thoughts."

But in truth, he didn't want to stop such thoughts. In fact, he'd just as soon lose himself in dreams of what could never be.

～ 12 ～

London

Bella's lips formed a contented smile. She stared into the blazing fire, the warmth coloring her cheeks a rosy pink. "This was a lovely Christmas," she whispered, her fingers reaching to touch the cameo pin at her neckline while snuggling against Taylor's chest. With Grandfather Farnsworth asleep in his bed and the others out enjoying a short visit with their friends, Bella and Taylor were alone for the first time in days.

Taylor pulled her closer, then leaned down to place a kiss atop her head. "I know you would have preferred celebrating Christmas in Massachusetts, but you've been a good sport about all of this. Even though I haven't said so before, I hope you realize I'm very thankful for your sweet attitude. Had you been in a dour mood about remaining in England, I don't know what I would have done," he confessed.

"You need to be here with your family, especially now that your grandfather's health is no longer improving. I fear I've done little other than lend moral support. I wish there were more I could do."

Taylor placed a finger beneath her chin and, tilting her head upward, gazed into her eyes. "You have been an immense help, especially with Elinor. I don't know what we would have done without you. Somehow you've miraculously managed to keep her entertained and out from underfoot. Believe me, that is quite an accomplishment. Grandmother has been ailing herself, and keeping up with Elinor takes more energy than she can muster."

"Elinor is a sweet girl. I find she uses her misbehavior to gain attention. Whenever I lend an ear to her woes or provide a bit of entertainment, she immediately settles. She's even begun reading with me each day," Bella replied.

Taylor nodded. "When I saw her sitting and stitching while you read to her the other day, I could hardly believe my eyes. Quite frankly, I didn't think Elinor had any idea how to use a needle."

Bella giggled. "She didn't. There were quite a few pricked fingers and several screams of pain before she mastered the technique. However, she's taken quite a liking to needlepoint. I'm going to see if I can interest her in tatting over the next few weeks."

"From what I saw of Grandmother's Christmas gift, you're quite the teacher. I'm not sure who was more excited over the gift, Elinor or Gran."

"We used to make sewing kits in the Shaker Village and sell them to the townsfolk or give them as gifts to visitors. They were one of our bestselling items. Elinor is quite interested in the Shakers—she's been quizzing me incessantly."

Taylor's laughter filled the room. "I can't imagine our Elinor interested in the strict communal life of a Shaker. She can't even discipline herself to come to the dinner table on time. How would she ever survive?"

Bella joined his laughter. "You'd be surprised how quickly Eldress Phoebe could change bad habits. A hickory switch to the legs and extra laundry duties usually made an impression upon us. Of course, I'd never want to see Elinor forced into such a situation. A child needs the freedom to enjoy her early years without fear of constant reprimand. I'm ever so thankful I have memories of life with my parents before going to live in Canterbury. Poor Daughtie spent her entire life among the Shakers until we ran off."

"And I'm still surprised she agreed to leave with you," Taylor remarked.

Bella smiled and nodded. "I don't think she regrets her decision. Ever since she secured the drawing-in position at the Appleton, she's been content."

"Did she say anything in her last letter about finding a beau?" Taylor inquired.

"No. I am a bit concerned, however. She mentioned Liam Donohue several times in her letter. I'm beginning to fear that her interest in him goes beyond friendship."

"Liam's a fine man. Not many Englishmen could match his work ethic, and his talent is without challenge."

"A fine man, yes. But he's Irish. We both know such a relationship is unacceptable. Daughtie would be shunned by the entire town."

"You're worrying unnecessarily, my dear. I doubt either one of them would enter into such a thorny situation."

Bella gave him a sidelong glance. "Once love begins to bloom, people tend to forget the difficulties of 'thorny situations.' I do hope Daughtie will guard herself against heartache."

"Pen her a letter and speak of your concerns. After all, you're the closest to family she's ever known, and I'm certain she values your opinion."

"Perhaps I'll write her tomorrow while Elinor works on her stitching."

Taylor turned to face Bella and then clasped her hands in his own. "I'm truly pleased you and Elinor have been getting on so well, because Gran has approached both Uncle John and me about Elinor's future. She's asked that we consider taking Elinor back to Massachusetts with us. I told them I didn't feel we could undertake such a responsibility. After all, we're newlyweds not yet adjusted to marriage, and a nine-year-old is quite a handful, but Gran said to pray about it and talk to you."

Bella swallowed hard before speaking. "What did your uncle John say?

Perhaps he and Aunt Addie would be the better choice to raise Elinor."

"Exactly what I thought. But Uncle John pointed out that we would be much better suited than he and Aunt Addie since we're young and would be more capable of keeping pace with a girl Elinor's age."

"Oh, pshaw! Aunt Addie was managing a boardinghouse filled with young women not long ago, and her health hasn't deteriorated one iota since marrying your uncle. Don't misunderstand—I think your grandmother has a valid concern, but what about your older sister, Beatrice, and her husband? They're in Scotland, and that would be in closer proximity if Elinor wanted to return and visit your grandmother from time to time. Surely Elinor would be happier with her own sister."

Taylor's laughter was tinged with disdain. "Don't expect Beatrice to step forward and offer assistance. She's always been one to shirk any responsibility that happened her way, and I don't expect she's changed a jot. Besides, if Beatrice and that Scot she calls a husband *did* agree to rear Elinor, they'd expect the child to arrive with a pocketful of coins to pay for her keep and then require Gran to send money at every turn. They'd bleed Gran for every farthing she's managed to save. In addition, Elinor would likely run off before she'd ever agree to live with Beatrice. They can't seem to abide each other for more than a few minutes at a time."

Bella refused to panic. They would be in London until early spring. By winter's end, they would surely arrive at an agreeable solution. "Well, then, we'll do as your grandmother has requested. We'll pray that the Lord will provide a solution."

Taylor silently stared into the fire, his hands, fingertip to fingertip, forming a small pyramid. Finally, he turned toward her. "Yes, surely by spring we shall have an answer."

Just then a ruckus sounded at the front door. Taylor got up to see what was the cause and Bella followed him into the vestibule just as Elinor burst into the house.

"Oh, Bella, you missed the best fun. There was dancing and storytelling, and Uncle John even sang for us."

John assisted Addie and Cordelia through the door as Elinor made this announcement. He laughed and released the women. "A mistake I won't be repeating."

Bella smiled. "I'm sure your offering was as fine as could be had."

"If you heard me and still thought so," John said, helping Cordelia from her coat, "I would have to assume you to be tone deaf."

Taylor laughed and pulled his wife close. "Uncle John doesn't lie. He sounds rather like a hound to the fox."

Bella elbowed Taylor and moved to Uncle John's side. "Don't listen to him. He's just jealous because he can't carry a tune."

John winked. "It's a family curse."

"Not so," Addie threw in, "for Elinor sang like a bird. She has a sweet voice."

The girl beamed under the praise. "I love to sing."

"See there," John replied, pointing to the girl, "she's inherited all of the family talent."

"Come now," Cordelia stated stiffly, "let us go into the parlor and warm up. I'm certain in spite of the hour we can still have a cup of tea and some refreshments."

Bella remembered her arrangements with the cook. "Indeed we can, for I had such thoughts earlier in the evening. I've already arranged for tea and some other goodies. Just come in by the fire and I'll see to it."

Cordelia eyed Bella for a moment, and then with a look of approval she nodded and motioned the family to the parlor.

Taylor followed Bella to the kitchen. "You've made points with her for sure. My grandmother is not easily won over, but I believe you have her in the palm of your hand."

"I hope she doesn't think me simply trying to impress."

"I'm sure she recognizes your good nature and ability to think ahead. She values sensible people," Taylor replied, halting Bella before she entered the kitchen. He pulled her into his arms. "And I value the warmth of your lips and the sweetness of your kiss." He lowered his mouth to hers.

"I see some of us are getting our refreshment sooner than others," John Farnsworth said, surprising them both.

Bella jumped back, feeling her face grow hot, while Taylor only laughed. "I couldn't help myself, sir." He threw Bella a look of pure mischief. "She insisted."

Bella gasped. "Taylor Manning! How dare you tell such falsehoods—and on Christmas!"

The men roared with laughter while Bella turned back for the kitchen. She couldn't help the smile that spread across her lips.

~❧ 13 ❧~

Lowell
January 1834

Church was over and the noonday meal completed. Ruth, Daughtie, Naomi, and little Theona sat in the parlor, the four of them primly lined up on the settee and chairs with their hands folded, poised, as if waiting to be cued into action. However, when a knock on the front door finally sounded, they all startled.

"I'll go," Mrs. Arnold announced, standing and pressing the wrinkles from her skirt with the palm of her hand while moving toward the front door.

Daughtie and Ruth leaned forward as the door hinges squeaked, straining to hear the exchange of voices or perhaps catch a glimpse of the doctor who would be depriving Mrs. Arnold of a portion of the house. Being hired as a physician for employees of the mills granted Dr. Ketter the right to occupy the greater portion of the first floor. Mrs. Arnold's voice sounded more animated than usual as she offered welcoming words. Moments later, the older woman returned to the parlor with the new doctor in tow.

Daughtie noted he was a slim, smallish sort of man with a narrow face and aquiline nose. His dark brown hair and eyes were his better attributes, she decided, for while he was not an ugly man by any account, neither was he truly handsome.

"Dr. Ivan Ketter, I'd like to introduce Miss Daughtie Winfield and Miss Ruth Wilson. And this," she said, taking Theona's tiny hand in her own, "is my daughter, Theona."

Dr. Ketter gave a slight bow. "It's a pleasure to meet you. When I was told of the disruption my arrival would cause, I became concerned that perhaps I should find another place to set up my practice. However, Mrs. Arnold's letter set me at ease. I want to thank all of you for your willingness to accept these changes."

They'd really had no choice in the matter, but Daughtie wouldn't embarrass him with that tidbit of information. The Corporation had declared Dr. Ketter would board with Mrs. Arnold, using the downstairs rooms for his living quarters and medical practice, with the exception of the kitchen and the dining area. Those two rooms would remain under Mrs. Arnold's authority. The parlor would be rearranged as a waiting room for his patients; the bedroom Mrs. Arnold and Theona had shared would become an examination room. Daughtie lamented the fact that there would be no parlor for entertaining guests or reading by the fireplace on a cold winter's evening, but Mrs. Arnold was at the mercy of the Corporation. Of course, the Associates *had* been generous in granting their permission for her to remain in the house after her husband's discharge from the Appleton. She could ill afford to be less than receptive to their recent announcement, but moving to an upstairs bedroom with little Theona would certainly make her life more difficult.

Obviously the changes would be most difficult for Mrs. Arnold and Theona, so Daughtie attempted to hide her irritation over the newest boarder. After all, she shouldn't make this any more difficult for Mrs. Arnold. *Besides,* she reasoned, *bearing a grudge against the doctor would be unfair: it isn't his fault the Corporation foisted him upon Mrs. Arnold.*

And so she smiled and gave a small curtsy in response to his welcoming gesture before glancing upward. As she met his eyes, he stared deep into hers. The boldness of his gaze caused her to quickly look away.

"I'm sorry," he murmured, appearing surprised by her discomfiture. "Daughtie. Is that a nickname for Dorothy?" he inquired, obviously hoping a bit of cordial conversation would set matters aright.

"No. I was told that my parents were certain they would have a son. Because of their confidence, they had not chosen a girl's name. My father called me Daughter, and my mother decided to shorten Daughter to Daughtie—at least that's what Sister Mercy told me." The doctor's face appeared to cloud with confusion, but Daughtie ignored the questioning gaze and directed him to Ruth. "Ruth, step forward and meet Dr. Ketter."

The doctor briefly greeted Ruth but immediately turned his attention back toward Daughtie. "I'm going to want to hear more about you, Miss Winfield."

"Perhaps you should get settled, Dr. Ketter. I'm certain your journey was tiring, and Mrs. Arnold has your rooms prepared—don't you, Mrs. Arnold?"

"Indeed. And I hope you're going to be comfortable with the way I've arranged the rooms. I thought you could use the parlor as your waiting room, and I've made very few changes. You may want to purchase some additional seating, for when word spreads that you've arrived, I'm certain there will be many townsfolk who wish to avail themselves of your services."

"Well, of course those employed by the Corporation will receive priority, but I do hope my practice will expand to include other residents of the community. I enjoy keeping busy," he replied as Mrs. Arnold led him toward his new office.

"He appears quite taken with you," Ruth whispered, envy etched upon her face as she glanced first at Daughtie and then over her shoulder toward the doctor.

Daughtie grasped Ruth's arm and pulled her toward the stairway. "If you'd quit acting so shy and talk to him, he'd likely be much more interested in you."

"I'll see you at supper, Miss Winfield?" Dr. Ketter inquired.

Ruth's eyebrows arched. She gave Daughtie a smug grin before racing up the stairs.

Daughtie turned toward Dr. Ketter. "I'm present for three meals a day, just like Ruth, Theona, and Mrs. Arnold," she advised before making a hasty retreat.

She ran up the stairs and into the bedroom. Ruth was already sitting on the bed, her gaze fixed upon a book she obviously wasn't reading. "That book is *much* easier to read when it's turned right side up," Daughtie remarked with a smile.

Ruth snapped the book closed and whacked it down on the bed.

Daughtie plopped down beside Ruth. "Please don't be angry with me, Ruth. I did nothing to encourage Dr. Ketter's attention. You know I'm not interested in him. Besides, he was only being cordial. He's probably got a fiancée back home."

"Strange that *you* were chosen as the sole recipient of his conviviality," Ruth retaliated.

Daughtie sighed and leaned back against the wooden headboard. "I promise to direct all the conversation to you at supper tonight. *Now* will you forgive me?"

"I never said I was angry with you."

"There's more frost inside this room than out on the front steps."

Ruth giggled. "I'm sorry for my unseemly behavior. I suppose I did feel jealous when Dr. Ketter appeared interested in you. Instead, I should be encouraging you to befriend him. After all, if you direct your attention toward Dr. Ketter, perhaps you'll stop making a fool of yourself with that Irishman."

Daughtie attempted to hold back the anger that suddenly rose in her chest. "When I want your opinion, I'll ask for it."

Ruth crossed her arms over her chest and gave a smug grin. "Now who's caused the chill in this room?"

"Arguably, I could say it's *you*. You're the one determined to make disparaging remarks about Mr. Donohue," Daughtie replied before stomping out of the room, down the steps, and directly into the arms of a surprised-looking Dr. Ketter. Instinctively, she flailed about to steady herself before finally gaining her balance.

She looked up and was greeted by Dr. Ketter's chocolate brown eyes, which were now sparkling with amusement. His head was tilted at a slight angle, and his full lips were turned up in a broad smile that caused his cheeks to plump.

"Excuse me! I lost my balance. I guess you realize that," Daughtie stammered, pulling out of the doctor's grasp.

"Well, I've heard tell of girls throwing themselves at eligible men, but having never been the recipient of such activity, I wasn't quite certain if this was to be my first encounter. Now you've gone and dashed my hopes," he said while maintaining his wide grin.

Daughtie felt the heat rise in her cheeks. "I had no intention of throwing myself at you. I tripped on the stairs."

Dr. Ketter laughed. "I realize you stumbled, Miss Winfield. I was merely teasing you and certainly didn't intend to cause you further embarrassment. Mrs. Arnold tells me you lived in the Shaker community in Canterbury, New Hampshire," he said, leaning back against the wall and crossing his arms. "Moving to Lowell must have posed innumerable difficulties for you."

"I doubt if I've had more difficulties to overcome than any of the other girls. After all, most of the mill girls left families behind. At least I didn't have to leave my parents and siblings, wondering if and when I might see them again," she replied while attempting to inch off toward the kitchen.

He reached out and gently grasped Daughtie's elbow, directing her into the parlor. "Why don't we sit down? I'd appreciate the opportunity to visit with you."

Daughtie stiffened. She didn't want to spend the remainder of the afternoon being questioned by Dr. Ketter. "I have some mending to complete" came her feeble excuse.

"That's quite all right. Why don't you fetch it, and we can talk while you stitch? I'll feel as though I've returned home. My mother used to sit by the fire and stitch while I worked on my school lessons years ago."

Daughtie knew she was trapped. Dr. Ketter was one of those people who would have a remedy for any excuse she might toss in his direction. "I'll get my sewing," she mumbled before retracing her steps to the bedroom.

"Back so soon?" Ruth inquired, looking up from her book.

"Yes. Dr. Ketter has requested company in the parlor. I came to fetch my sewing *and* you. I didn't want to fritter away the afternoon and not have my mending completed come morning," she replied. "Come along."

"How kind of Dr. Ketter to include me," Ruth said while they were descending the staircase. "Perhaps he *is* interested in me."

Daughtie cringed. She hoped that nothing would be said to lay blame on her for stretching the truth. After all, she hadn't told a blatant lie. That thought helped salve her nagging conscience for only a brief moment, for the instant they entered the room, Ruth flashed a smile in the doctor's direction.

"Thank you so much for inviting me to join your conversation," she said, fluttering her eyelashes with a wild abandon that caused her to appear absurd.

Dr. Ketter leveled a questioning glance at Daughtie before replying. "You are most welcome, Miss Wilson. I'm sure you will lend tremendous insight to our discussion."

Daughtie breathed a sigh of relief and aimed a grateful, albeit fleeting, smile in Dr. Ketter's direction before taking out her mending.

"Tell me, Miss Winfield, how did you happen to leave the Shaker community? I didn't think anyone ever left their communes."

Daughtie could feel Ruth's cold stare. "Oh, people leave from time to time for various reasons. I left with a friend in order to see what life was like among the world's people. Ruth grew up in New England and knows all about the farming communities in the area, don't you, Ruth?"

Ruth bobbed her head up and down. "Indeed. But I'm sure Dr. Ketter finds life among the Shakers much more intriguing, don't you?"

"Since I know little about the Shakers, I do find the topic of genuine interest."

Ruth leaned back in her chair and stared at Daughtie with a look of irritated satisfaction crossing her face.

"Well, that proves my point exactly. I've always been interested in hearing about Ruth's life—and I'm interested in hearing about yours," Daughtie hastened to add. "We're always interested in the unknown, aren't we?"

"Exactly!" Dr. Ketter replied, slapping a hand to his knee.

"Perhaps the solution would be for each of us to tell a little about our background," Ruth ventured.

"That's a marvelous idea, isn't it, Dr. Ketter?"

"Yes, I suppose it is. But I'm going to insist that you ladies call me Ivan. If we're going to be living in the same house, we should be less formal, wouldn't you agree?"

"By all means," Ruth agreed. "You may call me Ruth."

"And *you,* Miss Winfield? May I address you as Daughtie?" Dr. Ketter inquired.

Daughtie didn't immediately reply. She preferred to keep things as they were—more formal and distant. Yet a refusal would make her appear haughty, so she nodded her reluctant agreement. "I suppose that would be acceptable, although highly unusual. After all, we are hardly peers."

"But of course we are," Ivan replied. He allowed his gaze to linger on Daughtie, causing her to grow very uncomfortable.

"Why don't you begin by telling us about yourself?" Ruth requested, leaning forward and giving the doctor her undivided attention.

"I fear you'll find my life to date rather boring. However, I'm hoping that will change now that I've completed my studies. I wanted to excel in school and consequently didn't enjoy much social life, I fear."

"Where did you grow up?" Ruth inquired, her enthusiasm almost contagious.

"My family owns a fishing business in Maine. I grew up along the coast, enjoying the ocean and the seafaring life. My father determined early on that I'd best receive an education if I was going to support myself. My mother worried about the dangers at sea. In fact, I had to sneak aboard my father's boat in order to fish with him, and then when we'd return home, Mother would give me a tongue-lashing and sulk about for at least a week," he said with a grimace.

Ruth chuckled at his antics. "And who decided you should go to medical school?" she inquired.

"Medicine was my choice. My mother and father briefly mentioned studying law, but I thought I was more suited to medicine. I've not regretted my choice. I found medical school much to my liking, although there were times I longed to put away the books and get on with healing patients."

"I think medicine is an admirable calling," Ruth agreed.

"*Was* your decision to enter the medical profession a calling?" Daughtie inquired.

"I don't know that I'd say it was a calling, but I do want to help people. Does that count?"

"The question wasn't meant as a test. I merely asked because I believe the finest doctors are called to the profession."

"And upon what theory or study do you base your conclusion?" Dr. Ketter inquired.

"None—other than personal observation, that is. Throughout my life at the Shaker village, I worked alongside two different doctors and numerous Sisters who acted as nurses. It was a simple matter to identify those who were truly called to the medical field and those who were merely performing a task."

"And which were *you*, Daughtie?"

"My calling was in the children's dormitory. I found great pleasure working with children, and I'm told I was very good with them. Children enjoyed being around me."

"I can understand why," he replied.

Daughtie blushed and tried to ignore his remark. Ruth glared in her direction, but Dr. Ketter met Daughtie's gaze with an adoring smile.

"Supper is ready," Mrs. Arnold announced from the doorway.

"Prayer answered," Daughtie murmured. She jumped up from her chair and hastened into the dining room, strategically placing herself beside Theona. "Sit here beside me," Daughtie said while beckoning Ruth toward the chair to her left.

Ruth ignored her request and seated herself at the far end of the table, which permitted Dr. Ketter access to the seat beside Daughtie. He walked to the chair and sat down next to Daughtie. Ruth's annoyance was obvious, yet she'd done nothing to prevent the situation. Her actions were akin to those of a spoiled child, Daughtie decided.

Mrs. Arnold fluttered into the room with a bowl of fried potatoes in one hand and a platter of boiled chicken in the other. "Would you give thanks, Dr. Ketter?" she inquired after setting the bowls atop the table and sitting down.

"I'd be honored," he replied, reaching out to grasp hands with Mrs. Arnold and Daughtie. The rest of them followed his lead and joined hands. "This was a custom in my family at meal times. I hope you don't mind."

"Of course not," Mrs. Arnold replied. "It's a very nice custom."

Daughtie wondered if Dr. Ketter had intentionally squeezed her hand upon completion of his prayer but then decided she was likely overreacting. Reaching for the buttered turnips, she scooped a serving onto her plate and passed the bowl to Dr. Ketter.

"Has Daughtie told you of her excellent medical background?" Mrs. Arnold asked while placing a piece of chicken on Theona's plate. "Why, if it hadn't been for Daughtie's nursing skills, Theona would probably still be fighting a fever."

"Not at all," Daughtie explained. "I merely sat with her so you could get some rest, Mrs. Arnold. And Ruth certainly took her turn at Theona's sickbed, also."

Mrs. Arnold nodded in agreement. "Yes, although I don't believe Ruth is quite so comfortable tending to illness, are you, Ruth?"

"No, I'm certainly no match for Daughtie. Now, if you'll excuse me, I'm not very hungry. I think I'll go upstairs and read my book. I feel certain I won't be missed," Ruth replied. The wooden chair legs scraped across the floor, their protest seeming to mirror Ruth's angry emotions.

"I have apple pie, Ruth. I'll call you when we're ready for dessert," Mrs. Arnold offered.

"Thank you, Mrs. Arnold, but please don't bother. Once I've finished reading, I plan to retire for the evening."

"In that case, I'll bid you good-night," she said. "Theona, tell Ruth good-night."

Ruth rushed from the room while Theona and Dr. Ketter were still in the midst of bidding her good-night. They don't realize she doesn't want to go up those stairs at all, Daughtie thought. What Ruth *really* wants is to hear them beg her to remain and tell her the gathering will be of no consequence without her. Instead, each of them wished her an amiable good-night and quickly returned to their food and conversation. Daughtie wondered if she should follow Ruth—if it would make her feel better knowing that only Mrs. Arnold and Theona would be garnering Dr. Ketter's attention. But what plausible reason could she give in order to excuse herself? She could think of none, so she remained, listening to Dr. Ketter's compliments and answering his onslaught of questions with as much brevity as she could manage.

"I would certainly enjoy seeing a bit more of the town. Is there any possibility you would agree to accompany me for a stroll, Daughtie?"

"Oh, absolutely not. I have my mending to complete and several other tasks that need my immediate attention. But thank you for the kind invitation," she added, feeling she must at least exercise proper etiquette.

"Tomorrow night?"

"I work at the library, but I'm certain Ruth would be pleased to accept your invitation. Shall I ask her when I go upstairs?"

"No, thank you. I'll wait until one evening when you're free," he replied, a trace of a smile on his lips.

Dr. Ketter was absent when the girls hurried home from the mill for breakfast the next morning.

"Apparently Dr. Ketter isn't an early riser," Ruth observed, heaping an empty bowl with oatmeal.

"He's already left the house. He's going to be busy throughout the day completing arrangements for the delivery of his office supplies. Some of the items should be arriving today," Mrs. Arnold explained.

The reply brought an obvious look of disappointment to Ruth's face; however, Daughtie was relieved. In fact, she hoped to avoid Dr. Ketter as much as possible since his attention was obviously going to cause difficulties in her friendship with Ruth. In truth, she hoped he would be delayed until after her departure for the library this evening.

When Dr. Ketter failed to arrive at the table for supper that evening, a sense of relief washed over Daughtie. She ate her supper more quickly than was necessary for the last meal of the day, jumped up from the table, and announced she was leaving for the library.

"Surely you have time for dessert," Mrs. Arnold said, attempting to coax her back to the table.

"No, I must be on my way. I'll be home by nine forty-five," she replied, grabbing her indigo blue wool cloak from a peg in the hallway and scurrying out the door.

Mrs. Potter gave a cheery greeting the moment Daughtie opened the front door of the library. "I'm glad you've arrived, my dear. We received a large box of books late this afternoon. They need to be evaluated and shelved. Most of them appear to be in good condition."

"How wonderful! Were they donated?"

"Yes. The wife of one of the Boston Associates heard the mill girls had begun a library, and she boxed up all these books and shipped them from Boston, along with this lovely note," Mrs. Potter said, waving a piece of engraved stationery in the air. "I've been giddy with excitement all day. They're all such treasures. Near the bottom of one box, I found *The Lady of the Lake* as well as *The Fair Maid of Perth,* both Sir Walter Scott offerings that I'm certain girls will enjoy."

"How wonderful!" Daughtie exclaimed, quickly shrugging out of her cape and hastening to reach deep into the box. "I can see I'm going to have a delightful evening," she said, pulling out a leather-bound volume of *Waverley.*

"Indeed. I selfishly wished they had arrived earlier in the day, but alas, I must go home and complete my chores. Please be certain you catalog the books before you place them on the shelves. I don't want to lose any of them."

Daughtie nodded her agreement and began leafing through another book. The hours ticked by, and for once, Daughtie was pleased there had been few patrons throughout the evening. She'd unpacked most of the books and had cataloged and shelved them according to Mrs. Potter's exacting instructions. After assuring herself the whale oil lamps were extinguished, Daughtie doused the embers in the fireplace and then donned her wraps. Exiting the library, she carefully turned the key and then jiggled the handle, assuring herself the library was securely locked.

"I thought you should be closing soon."

Daughtie whirled around and found herself face-to-face with Dr. Ketter. "What are you doing here?" she snapped.

"I frightened you—I apologize. I asked Mrs. Arnold for directions, hoping you might enjoy some company on your way home," he replied.

A wagon lumbered up the street and came to a halt in front of the library. "Good evenin', Miss Winfield. I was comin' by to see if ya had any additional boxes that needed to be delivered to the church and thought you might need a ride home on this cold night. But I see ya've already closed up the library, and it appears you have an escort to see you home, so I'll bid ya good-night," Liam Donohue said. Without waiting for a reply, he flicked the reins and was gone.

Daughtie turned and glared at Dr. Ketter. The one night when Liam Donohue materialized, asking to escort her home, Ivan Ketter had to emerge on the scene. She wanted to thrash the good doctor. Instead, she hiked off toward home without so much as a word, Ivan Ketter following close on her heels.

~ 14 ~

Boston

Tracy Jackson moved behind the large desk and bellowed into the conversation-filled room, "Gentlemen! If I could have your attention, we really must begin. Otherwise, I fear we'll still be discussing matters at midnight."

Josiah Baines emitted a sigh. "The sky was threatening snow when I arrived. I certainly want to get home before we have a major storm."

"I don't think there's any need to worry, Josiah. It's looked like snow for the past two weeks, and we haven't seen so much as a flurry," Henry Thorne replied. "You'd best get comfortable. I'm certain there's going to be a great deal of discussion once I've completed my report."

"Then why don't we begin with Henry's report?" Josiah questioned.

Matthew Cheever observed Tracy as he closed his eyes momentarily and shook his head in obvious frustration. "If everyone will take a seat, we'll begin the meeting. We'll get to Henry's report in due time, Josiah. I believe Nathan would prefer to conduct the meeting in the same orderly fashion he's utilized in the past. Nathan, would you like to begin?"

Boott leaned toward Matthew. "I'm thankful Nathan agreed to take charge this evening. I'm guessing tonight's agenda will make for heated discussion," he said in a hushed voice.

Matthew nodded his agreement but remained silent. He wasn't quite so convinced the meeting would be lengthy. He doubted the agents were going to argue at length for the mill girls, but he kept his opinion to himself, anxious to observe the unfolding drama.

Nathan Appleton moved to Tracy's side and picked up a sheaf of papers. "Gentlemen, as we discussed at our last meeting, the profits have dropped considerably, and urgent steps are needed if we're to protect our investment. With all of the directors in attendance earlier this month, we voted to decrease the mill girls' wages by twenty-five percent. This proposal was discussed with the supervisors at the mills. They asked to meet with us in order to expound upon their ideas and concerns."

"Excuse me, Nathan, but wouldn't it expedite matters if Kirk spoke on behalf of the supervisors? After all, he attended their meeting as well as our previous meeting. *And* he's here tonight," Josiah said with a flourish while giving Kirk a broad smile.

Nathan turned toward Kirk Boott. "Would you like to respond to Josiah's question?"

"You're in charge of the meeting, Nathan," Kirk replied. He settled into his chair and glanced around the room from under hooded eyelids. Either he was attempting to avoid the smoke from his cigar or he didn't want any supposition regarding his thoughts. Matthew surmised it was the latter.

Turning his attention back toward Josiah, Nathan said, "As I believe you all know, Kirk is a director of the Boston Associates and owns an interest in the Corporation. While he has his finger on the pulse of Lowell, the supervisors and agents are in an entirely different position. Although they have a vested interest in our success due to their employment, they don't own any shares in the Corporation. If Kirk were to speak for them, it could be said his suggestions and ideas were tainted by his monetary investment. You see—"

"Oh, all right, Nathan. I'm not a complete dolt. You don't need to go into further detail. I understand," Josiah interrupted. "Let's just get on with the meeting, shall we?"

"I would be delighted," Nathan replied with sarcasm dripping from each word. "Mr. Meanor, I believe the agents and supervisors have delegated you as spokesman for their group. Please step up here so that we may all hear what you have to say."

Matthew glanced toward Robert Meanor. He knew the man well. He was a good agent who capably managed the Tremont Mill and was respected by both workers and the other supervisors and agents. Both groups generally accepted his opinions with favor, and Matthew suspected that was why he had been chosen. The other agents hoped Robert could influence the Associates.

Robert took his place at the desk, the sheet of paper he held visibly shaking as he began to speak. "Thank you for giving us this opportunity to present our views," he began. "You asked that the agents meet and discuss your proposal for a twenty-five percent reduction in wages and respond to you. All agents are in agreement that a twenty-five percent reduction would be disastrous. We believe you would suffer irreparable damage by such a large reduction. If you move forward with this idea, the climate will be unfavorable for the procurement of good help in the future, and we believe there will be a mass migration homeward of many employees. Such an exodus will only lead to a further downward spiral. We need dependable, hardworking, trained employees if we are to keep production at the present output and maintain the current marginal profit."

"What do you suggest, Mr. Meanor?" Tracy Jackson inquired.

"The agents have proposed you consider nothing greater than ten percent."

"Oh, but that is preposterous. At that rate, we'll continue our losses without any hope of recovery. We need a change that will make a difference," James Babcock replied.

"What we need is for John Farnsworth to return home with additional new and exciting patterns for the print shop. Something that will send the women scurrying to buy our cloth and make it desired in every country around the world. And we need Taylor to return so he can begin production on the new prints we've already approved," Josiah replied. "We haven't been able to gain a large enough foothold in the foreign market."

"Those statements may be true, but we need relief right now. The only way I see that happening is a reduction in wages," Tracy replied.

"A wage reduction is an easy answer as we sit here tonight, gentlemen, but I do believe there will be repercussions if you continue down this road. I doubt whether the operatives will remain silent," Robert countered.

Nathan adjusted his collar and looked about the room. "There may be a few that quit and go home, but the majority have grown accustomed to earning a wage. Given time and thought, they'll adjust to the idea. After all, if we don't turn a profit, the mills will close and they'll have no jobs at all."

"The entire country is in total disruption with that scoundrel Andrew Jackson at the helm. As president he is surely causing more damage than good," Tracy began. "His ideas regarding the Bank of America and its dissolution are enough to create mass panic in the streets. Surely other businesses across the nation will find it necessary to cut expenses."

"Yes, but their cuts might well have less of a national effect than those of the textile industry," Babcock threw out. "It's just a collection of women, after all. They have no head for business or knowledge of the way our banking system is teetering on the edge of disaster."

Mr. Meanor cupped his chin in one hand and cast his gaze downward. "Forgive me for being so bold, sir, but most of you men have distanced yourselves from Lowell. I believe you may get more of a fight than you've bargained for. That collection of women you refer to has gone out of their way to educate themselves. Just last week a banking expert from Philadelphia came to lecture them. You might be surprised at what they have a head for. But either way, I'll follow your instructions."

"Perhaps we should test the waters. Why don't we have broadsides posted that explain there will be a decrease in wages beginning the first day of March? We can suggest that the amount may be as high as twenty-five percent. If we see the need, we can always rescind the proposal," Kirk suggested.

"Excellent idea, Kirk. It's no wonder we hired you to manage the city," Nathan replied. "What do you think, gentlemen?"

Agreement came quickly, and Mr. Meanor and the other agents who had accompanied him were soon dismissed with orders to post broadsides at each of the mills as soon as they could be printed. Any reactions were to be reported to Matthew, who was charged with investigating the seriousness of any agitation.

"Kirk, you can decide if we need to reconvene. If a meeting is necessary, send word to me," Nathan instructed. "Let's move on to Henry's report, and after that, I think we can adjourn. I'm certain Josiah will want to hurry home, but for any of you who care to remain, there's a fine bottle of port awaiting us in the drawing room."

London

William Thurston walked up the stairs to his small room and removed his woolen greatcoat before seating himself at the small desk. He had decided on his way home he would pen a letter to Thaddeus Arnold. He longed to feel the surge of delight caused by sharing his schemes with another. Writing a letter to Thaddeus would not give him the same heightened pleasure, but it would have to suffice. He dared not trust anyone else in England.

The last letter he'd received from Thaddeus was tucked into a small drawer. William withdrew the missive and reread the letter before carefully folding and returning it to the drawer. Thaddeus would be pleased to know the information he had supplied regarding John Farnsworth had proved correct.

Picking up his pen, William dipped the nib into a small bottle of ink and began to write. Thaddeus would be delighted to hear of his success this evening. The meeting with Barlow Kent and Chauncy Fuller, although brief, had exceeded William's expectations. Chauncy had completed some investigating on his own and was quick to tell William he and Barlow agreed that Farnsworth was likely in England to pilfer additional information for the Americans. Much to Thurston's pleasure, they had agreed the authorities should not be involved. Little did they realize that their announcement had eliminated William's greatest fear. Surprisingly, Barlow Kent had made the statement and Chauncy had quickly voiced his agreement that they should be able to handle the Farnsworth matter on their own. In fact, the two men said they'd nearly completed a plan to ensure John Farnsworth would never return to America, and once the arrangements were in place, they would contact Thurston. Although he preferred the role of leader to that of follower, he knew his power was limited. If these men wanted to take charge, he'd adhere to their pronouncements—as long as their decisions concurred with his own.

With his lips curved in a self-satisfied smile, William continued with his letter.

15

Daughtie slumped into the thick-cushioned chair and folded her arms. "I wish you hadn't invited a whole group of girls," she complained. "Did you ask Dr. Ketter's permission to use his waiting room?"

"*Yes*," Ruth replied, her irritation obvious. "And even though I specially requested his permission, you may recall that Dr. Ketter told us we could use this room as a parlor on Sundays."

"Strange you can remember what Dr. Ketter said about the parlor, yet you can't seem to recall I wanted to have a private discussion about the turnout."

"Why does everything have to be on *your* terms, Daughtie? I'd rather have the opinions and ideas of several people. That way we'll have a well-balanced viewpoint. Besides, nobody's forcing you to sit in that chair. You can go upstairs if you don't want to be involved."

"I'll stay and listen, but I doubt whether I'll add much to the conversation. I barely know these girls, and they could be some of the very ones who have been reporting information back to the supervisors."

Ruth gave her a look of disdain. "You're overreacting. There is nothing preventing you from merely sitting there like a bump on a log and listening to what the others have to say. You can weigh the information and still have plenty of time to decide if you want to support a strike before the first of March arrives," Ruth replied before hurrying off to answer a knock at the door.

With Dr. Ketter having granted permission to use the parlor and Mrs. Arnold and Theona gone visiting for the afternoon, there was little doubt Ruth was planning on several hours of lively discussion. When Ruth returned with ten girls in tow, Daughtie knew there would be no shortage of opinions.

The introductions were brief. Two of the girls were employed at the Appleton; the remainder worked at the Lawrence, Tremont, and Suffolk mills. Daughtie recognized the girls from the Appleton, for they both worked on the spinning floor. However, she had never seen the others and carefully scrutinized each one as introductions were made. "I'm Daughtie Winfield. I work at the Appleton. I recognize you girls from the Appleton, but I don't believe I've seen any of you other girls before, *even at the library*," she remarked. There was an edge to her voice.

"I don't have time for reading," one of the girls replied. "And I've never seen you, either," another remarked, returning Daughtie's condescending gaze.

"You should *make* time to expand your mind," Daughtie rebutted.

Ruth sighed. "We're not here to discuss library usage and mind expansion. We're here to discuss the merits of a turnout the first of March. If you want to discuss these other matters, I suggest we schedule another get-together for that purpose. Now, why don't we begin? Who would like to make a statement against turning out?"

One of the girls from the Suffolk raised her hand. "I'm afraid to go on strike. I need my job, and what if they find replacements to take our place? They could blackball us and never let us return to work at any of the mills. They do things like that, you know!"

"If we sit back and let them decrease our wages, they'll take it as our approval to do the same thing the next time they claim that their profits are going down. We can't idly sit by and let them get away with this," Marjorie, a girl from the Lawrence mill, replied.

Several girls nodded in agreement.

Jane Rinemore from the Suffolk shifted in her chair. "Perhaps we could circulate a petition setting forth our opposition to the lowering of wages. If we gathered enough signatures, the owners would see that we disapprove of their actions, yet we could continue working."

"A page full of signatures won't stop them from lowering the wages. Are you willing to do nothing but sign a protest and then smile and accept your wages being decreased?" Marjorie inquired.

Jane shrugged her shoulders. "I don't believe I have a choice. My family depends upon the money I send them."

"Well, your family will have less to count on come the first of March unless we do something," Marjorie countered.

"The Bible tells us that we honor Christ by submitting to each other. Wouldn't it then be a mark of faith if we acted in love and obedience to Christ's teachings and merely accepted the Corporation's offer?" Jane asked while surveying the room.

Marjorie's lips tightened into a knot. "Well, if you're referring to Ephesians 5:21, you've completely misinterpreted the passage. *That* passage means Christians shouldn't create disturbances within the church with their stubborn behavior."

"But what *is* the church if it's not the believers? The mills are owned by Christian men, aren't they? I certainly don't think that verse is speaking of a church building," Jane replied with authority. "And if you disagree with that Scripture, Ephesians also says that Christians should submit to their employers."

Ruth patted Marjorie's arm. "I don't think we need to discuss this matter based upon biblical truths, Jane. Our decision is purely related to right and wrong within our workplace. Don't the rest of you agree?"

There were nods of agreement around the room, except for Jane and Daughtie.

"Your remark makes absolutely no sense, Ruth. We may disagree over interpretation of the Scripture, but the Bible is *exactly* where we should look for our answers. If you're saying our behavior at work shouldn't reflect Biblical principles, I heartily disagree. I concur with Jane; I think a turnout is improper behavior," Daughtie said, having regained her composure.

"I should have known," Ruth murmured before squaring her shoulders and leveling a look of disdain at her roommate. "Your Shaker upbringing is surfacing."

Several of the girls giggled.

Daughtie observed the group for a moment and then stood. "I thought this was to be an exchange of thoughts and beliefs—an open discussion. However, it appears I misunderstood the intent of the meeting. Please excuse me. I'm going upstairs, since it appears those opposing the majority opinion will gain only hurt feelings."

"Daughtie! Wait for me," Ruth called.

Daughtie hesitated and then stopped. She wanted to continue on her way without a confrontation with Ruth. They hadn't spoken since the meeting yesterday, but there wasn't time to resolve their differences now.

Ruth hastened toward her. "Could we clear the air? I don't want us to quarrel."

"We can talk later if you like. I'm not going back to the boardinghouse right now. I've already told Mrs. Arnold not to expect me for supper."

"Would you like some company? I'd be happy to accompany you—or help with whatever is needing your attention."

"No, thank you. I don't need any help, and I prefer to be alone."

"How long are you going to continue pouting? I'm trying to apologize, but you're determined to make me suffer even longer, aren't you?"

"Don't be silly. I'm not pouting, and my prior arrangements have nothing to do with you or yesterday's meeting. I'm sorry if you're offended, but I really must be on my way," Daughtie replied before turning and hurrying out the mill yard gate. She could feel Ruth staring after her, but she continued onward without glancing back until she reached Whidden's Mercantile on Gorham Street.

The bell over the door jingled, announcing her presence as she walked into the store. "Good evening, Mrs. Whidden," she greeted. "I came back to pick up the fabric swatches."

The older woman smiled and motioned her back toward the rear of the store. "I have them all ready for you," she said while reaching beneath the counter and pulling out a bundle wrapped in brown paper and tied with cord. "Here you are. Be certain your measurements are exact. We wouldn't want to order incorrectly," she cautioned.

Daughtie nodded. "I'll make sure the dimensions are correct. Thank you for your assistance, Mrs. Whidden."

"You're welcome. I hope your customer is pleased with the choices."

Daughtie scurried from the store with the package tucked under her arm. She'd been awaiting the arrival of the fabrics and was anxious to see Liam's reaction to the prints. She hadn't had an opportunity to visit with him since he'd seen her with Dr. Ketter outside the library. By the time she reached Liam's house, her fingers were cold and stiff inside her knitted mittens. She knocked, her knuckles aching as they struck the hard wood of the front door. A pair of the Shakers' coonskin mittens would be a welcome delight, she decided when a rush of cold air swept across the front porch.

Liam pulled open the door, and a gentle draft of heat rose up to warm her face. She opened her mouth to greet him, but instead her teeth chattered incessantly. Try as she would, even with her mouth clamped tightly shut, the clicking sound continued. Her jaw was jiggling like a freshly opened jar of grape jelly.

Liam smiled and quickly moved aside. "Come in before ya freeze to death."

"Th-th-th-thank you," Daughtie finally chattered.

"Let me take yar cloak," he said, assisting her with the garment. "Go in by the fire and warm yarself."

Daughtie didn't offer to wait for him. She scurried into the parlor and yanked a wooden chair in front of the fireplace. Plopping down, she leaned forward, stretching toward the pleasant warmth of the fire.

"This is yar package?" Liam inquired, carrying the paper-wrapped parcel in his large callused hands.

Daughtie remained in her extended position while nodding her head. "Yes. Open it."

Liam sat in a nearby chair, carefully untied the cord, and pulled back the paper. "Are ya goin' to make a bedcover from all these pieces of cloth?" he inquired.

Daughtie giggled. "No. These are pieces of different fabrics we can choose from." It was obvious he was confused by her remark. "For your draperies and furniture," she explained.

He smiled and nodded. "Oh, I see! From the mills. Ya've brought me samples o' cloth from the mills."

"No—I ordered these from a book at Whidden's Mercantile. Most of them are from England. Once we make our decision, I'll order the fabric."

Liam appeared dumbstruck.

"I know it's going to be difficult to choose. There's such a lovely variety, and then attempting to envision the fabric on the furniture or hanging at the windows is an overwhelming task. I'd be happy to share my first choices if you like," she offered, a winsome smile turning up the corners of her pink lips.

"No." Liam placed the pile of fabric on the settee.

"'No' you don't want my opinion, or 'no' you can't come to a decision right now?" Daughtie questioned.

"No, I'll not be wantin' any of these fabrics."

"What? Why not? Just look at this claret damask. It would be beautiful for your bedroom windows. And please notice that I didn't bring you any pink." She graced him with a bright smile while holding the piece of plum-colored fabric in her outstretched hand.

Liam shook his head. "I'm thinkin' it best to use fabric produced at the mills here in Lowell. Buyin' cloth made in this city is the proper thing to do. Besides, I'm not for spendin' any money in England; goes against my beliefs."

Daughtie leaned back in her chair. "Well, I wish you would have mentioned that fact before I put Mrs. Whidden to all the trouble of ordering these samples. I don't know how I'll ever explain."

Liam rested his ankle across his opposing knee and produced a hearty chuckle. "Just tell her the truth. Ya're workin' for a hardheaded Irishman who won't give in to buyin' from the English."

Daughtie was silent for a moment, contemplating Liam's edict. "You're absolutely right," she finally agreed. "Residents of the community *should* support the industrial efforts right here in Lowell. I don't know why I didn't think of that."

"Ya were merely attemptin' to give me more choices. Don't be hard on yarself."

"Instead of rushing off to Whidden's to select fabric, I should have prayed about my new assignment. Perhaps then I would have had a similar thought about the fabric."

Liam grinned at her, his eyes sparkling in the firelight. "And do you go prayin' about *everythin',* Miss Daughtie Winfield?"

"Are you laughing at my beliefs?"

Liam held up his hand as though to ward off an attack. "I would never be laughin' at your beliefs. I think prayin' is laudable. Much good has been wrought through prayer."

"Do you speak from personal experience?"

"I'm afraid not. 'Tis one of my mother's famous quotes. Though I'm not opposed to prayer," he hastened to add.

"I can't explain very well, but my life goes more smoothly when I pray about things."

He scooted down into his chair in a relaxed manner and gave her his full attention. "And since you weren't prayin' about the decoratin' of me house, what have you been prayin' about lately?"

She felt comfortable with his easy manner and returned his smile. "My position at the mill. The Corporation has posted broadsides informing us that our wages are going to be cut. They're proposing a twenty-five percent decrease in our wages. The very day the announcement was made, the girls began talk of a turnout. Girls from all of the mills are urging a strike."

"And you, Daughtie? What do *you* believe is best?" Liam asked, his gaze unwavering.

"I believe we should continue working. I know a loss of wages is difficult to accept, especially for the girls who are helping support their families, but I fear that if we go against the Corporation, the Associates may vote to close the mills entirely. In my opinion, closing the mills would cause irreparable harm to the whole community. Besides, I don't believe a turnout is the Christian thing to do."

"And what do the girls who favor the strike argue?"

"They say that if we agree to a pay cut, there's nothing to stop the owners from continuing down this path of decreasing our income. Ruth called a meeting last night, and most of the girls favor the turnout for that particular reason. Of course, they believe the Corporation is acting in an unchristian manner and therefore they feel no responsibility to respond in a fair and prudent manner."

Liam nodded his head but said nothing.

"You disagree with me?"

"I didn't say that. I don't believe I have enough information to agree or disagree about a strike, but I do admire yar willingness to base yar decisions on what the Bible has to say. 'Course, people tend to argue about what the Bible says, too. My mother was always at loggerheads about the Scriptures."

"Your parents are still in Ireland?"

"Aye. They promised to come to America once I had a steady job; then my mother postponed, sayin' I should be buildin' a house first. Now she says it needs to be properly furnished. Once it's furnished, she'll be findin' another excuse to remain at home. Yet she'll be pleased because she can be tellin' all the women in the village that her Liam has a good job, a large house, and fine furniture," he said with a laugh.

"And are your parents Christians?"

With his eyebrows arched, Liam gazed heavenward for a moment. "I'm not certain that's a word I'd use to describe them. My father doesn't speak of his beliefs or faith. He goes to church with my mother from time to time, mostly to stop her incessant nagging, I think. My mother's beliefs are a puzzlement to me. As far as I can tell, she goes shiftin' back and forth between the church and witchcraft . . . or maybe it's idolatry. I quit tryin' to figure her out."

Daughtie smiled in understanding. "And you, Liam? What do you believe?"

"To be honest, I'm not certain. O' course I went to catechism and attended church every week when I was growin' up. My mother wouldn't have had it any other way, but like me da, I quit going. Seems as though people in this country have some different ideas about religion and God—not the Irish over here in the Acre, but the rest of ya."

"Maybe you never noticed the differences in Ireland because people in your village didn't talk about their faith," Daughtie suggested. "Who have you been talking to since you arrived in Lowell?"

"About what? My belief in God?"

She cupped her chin in one hand with an elbow perched upon her knee. "Yes."

"Mostly just to Matthew Cheever, although John Farnsworth and I have had a conversation or two. I first talked to Matthew back when I was working on the masonry at St. Patrick's Church. That was shortly after I'd come to Lowell. We talked a little about the stonework I was doin' in the church, and then Matthew said he'd be likin' to get together again and continue our discussion. I laughed at the thought of it—Matthew Cheever associatin' with a lowly Irishman. I'm tellin' ya, I was surprised when he did just that. We've spent some fine times talkin' about God. I'm not sayin' he's convinced me just yet, but I'd say I'm a lot closer to believin' than I was when I stepped foot in this country. Matthew's a good man and he has strong beliefs—like you and your friends."

"Not all of my friends share my beliefs. In fact, one of the reasons there are so many churches is because people disagree about interpretation of the Scriptures and then rush off to start a church of their own. I disagreed with some of the Shaker beliefs, and that's one of the reasons I left the community," she explained.

His eyes grew wide at her reply. " 'Course, ya didn't go startin' your own church . . . or did ya?" he asked with a grin.

"No. But I suppose I get as opinionated as the next person. Sometimes I wonder just what God thinks of all of us running around down here on earth acting the fool over petty matters."

"Thing is, it's a petty matter only if it doesn't go against what ya believe, right?"

"I suppose you have a valid point, and I do believe some things are blatantly unscriptural. In that event, and if you know the beliefs are not going to change, I think it's better to leave than cause problems within the group. The

Bible says we're not to cause disruption within the body of believers. I knew the Shakers would not change, and that is part of the reason I left the Society. I truly prayed for guidance. Once I felt my prayers were answered, I didn't have time to look back," she said, giving him a wistful smile. "Clearly, my decision was for a mixture of reasons. My friend Bella was determined to leave, and from the time she came to the Shaker village in Canterbury, we were the best of friends. I didn't think I could bear the pain of losing her friendship. I had grown to love many of the Sisters; I still miss some of them. On the other hand, there were two or three Sisters I could barely abide. I spent much time in prayer about how to love those particular Sisters. I'm somewhat ashamed to make that admission," she said, giving him a sheepish grin.

He laughed at her remark. "And now ya have no regrets, even though yar friend has married and left you alone?"

"Bella will be back from England soon. Besides, I'm not alone. I have other friends," she defended.

"And I hope ya'll be countin' me as one of them."

There was an intensity in Liam's words that caused her face to warm at his remark. "Yes, that would be nice." Suddenly the fact that they were alone seemed very noticeable. Daughtie cleared her throat. "Now, about the fabrics? I suppose I'd best go back and have a talk with Mrs. Whidden."

"My talk of friendship has embarrassed ya. I apologize. I'd never overstep me bounds. You know that, don't ya?"

Impulsively, Daughtie reached across the chasm between them and touched Liam's hand. "I'm honored that you consider me a friend, and you need not worry about overstepping boundaries. Surely you know I don't choose friends based upon where they were born or the color of their skin. *That* is one principle of the Shakers to which I gladly conform," she said, finally gaining the courage to look into his eyes. Liam's gaze, however, was fixed upon her hand resting atop his own. Daughtie's eyes followed his gaze, and she immediately found herself overwhelmed with the impropriety of her own behavior. She snatched her hand away quickly, as if she'd been jabbed with a hot poker. Scooting back in her chair, she primly wove her fingers into a prayerful pose.

Liam laughed aloud. "Ya jumped like ya were being attacked by a band of leprechauns. There's no need to go concernin' yarself—I didn't mistake your warmth for anything more than the kindness of a friend. And since I do count ya as a friend, and because I know how ya feel about the slavery issue, there's a matter of confidence I was hoping we could be discussin'."

Daughtie nodded in agreement, pleased to discuss anything other than her recent conduct.

"I've given me name as a contact for runaway slaves," he said.

Daughtie stared at him in stunned silence.

"Did ya hear me? I said—"

"I heard you. I'm just, just—amazed. Of all the things you could have possibly said, I never expected to hear those words."

"Why? Do ya think I have no sympathy for a people torn from their homeland and forced into slavery?"

"No, that's not what I think, not at all," Daughtie immediately replied. "You're a compassionate man. It's just that we've talked little of the slavery issue since Prudence Crandall's visit. Your announcement came as a total surprise. When did you arrive at this decision?"

"I went back and talked with several of the men who accompanied Miss Crandall to the meeting. They told me there's a need for safe houses for runaways trying to get to Canada and assured me that once the slaves 'ave made their way this far north, the owners have generally given up on tryin' to get them back. I don't think there's much danger. Besides, I have this big house and the barn out back. Not many folks have as much space to offer, and it's only me I'd be puttin' in any danger."

Daughtie began wringing her hands, a habit for which she'd been soundly rebuked as a child in the Shaker village. "I admire your willingness to help, but I fear the assurances you've been given may be overstated. We had a Sister join the Society. She was a runaway who had escaped from a cruel owner, and by the time she reached Canterbury, the Elders doubted whether anyone would continue searching for her."

"What happened?"

Daughtie's eyes glazed. The long-forgotten memory returned anew. "It was a few weeks after Sister Bessie arrived. We were in Sunday meeting. As usual, a group of spectators had entered the church to observe our worship. Everything progressed normally—we had begun to dance—when a man pointed toward Sister Bessie and began yelling out he'd found his runaway slave. He had two other men with him—big burly men. With total disregard, all three of them bullied their way through the sanctuary and dragged poor Sister Bessie out of the room. I can still hear her screaming for help."

"And no one tried to stop the men?"

"The Brothers and the other spectators tried. But two of the men pointed their weapons and threatened to shoot the first person who made any further move toward them. They said if anyone followed them, they'd return and burn down our buildings. I suppose it does sound quite cowardly that we all stood staring after her, doing nothing. I thought so at the time. I wept and told Sister Mercy there wasn't one soul among us that deserved a heavenly reward. She hugged me close until I quit crying and then explained that either Sister Bessie or someone else in the church would have been killed had the Shaker men continued their pursuit. I suppose she was correct, but I lay awake many a night thinking about Sister Bessie, wondering if she'd been beaten and what had become of her." Daughtie raised her head and met his concerned gaze. "So you see, there are slave owners who will pursue their runaways even farther north than Lowell. I doubt what I've told you will change your decision, but you should have accurate information. You could be placing yourself in serious danger."

"So ya think I've made a bad choice?"

"No, I think you've made a courageous decision. I applaud your willingness to help, but I want you to understand that there could be danger involved. I'm honored you would take me into your confidence."

Liam gave her a broad smile. "I don't know if anythin' might ever arise so that I'd need help, but if I did . . ."

"Just send word, and I'll do anything I can," she said. "Anything."

"I knew I could be countin' on you," he said, slapping an open palm on his knee. "But from the way the men talked, I'm not expectin' I'll ever be needed. Seems as though they try to find people willin' to help in every town they visit."

"That makes sense. It's wise to have a solution before a problem settles on your doorstep. Perhaps you should do the same."

His forehead creased in concern. "What do ya think I should do?"

"If runaways arrived tonight, would you be prepared to care for them and help them move on? Think about what items are necessary to feed and clothe them. You may need to offer some medical care. Where would you hide them? Is the area safe for men, women, children, and babies? You never know who may arrive or how many. Would you use the house for some and the barn for others? If so, you'll need provisions in both places and good hiding places in the event unexpected visitors arrive."

Liam scratched his head and laughed aloud. "Appears I'll be needin' your help with more than just decoratin' this house."

~ 16 ~

Dr. Ketter stood poised in the doorway to his office as Daughtie and Ruth returned home from work late Saturday afternoon. Daughtie cast a sidelong glance in Ruth's direction. Her friend appeared pleased to see the doctor, but there was something more—a look that passed between them—almost as if Ruth expected Dr. Ketter to be awaiting their arrival.

"Good afternoon, ladies," he greeted. A gust of cold air whisked across the threshold. The doctor rubbed his hands together and shivered. "Seems as though it hasn't warmed up outside."

Daughtie pushed the door closed before removing her cape and gloves. "If you're chilled, perhaps you should move back into your office. That way you'll be out of the draft."

"If you'll join me, I'll do exactly that. It's at least an hour before supper."

Not even taking time to contemplate the request, Daughtie moved toward the stairway. "I'm sorry, but I have several matters I wish to accomplish before supper. If you'll excuse me—we can talk during the evening meal."

She had taken two steps up the staircase when Dr. Ketter's words stopped her. "I have a patient I wish to discuss, and I don't think the conversation would lend itself to mealtime, especially with a child present. I'm hoping your knowledge of herbs may be helpful."

Turning, she retraced her steps and he led the way to his office. "What is it you wish to talk about?" Daughtie inquired from just inside the doorway.

"Do sit down," he encouraged, gesturing toward a chair.

"No, thank you. How may I help?"

Dr. Ketter gave her an embarrassed smile. "I hope you'll forgive me, but I've actually gotten you into my office under false pretenses."

"Truly? So you don't need my assistance?"

"Not with a patient, but I did want the opportunity to speak with you privately."

"What is it you want to discuss, Dr. Ketter?"

"I've been told that there is a ball March 21, the Blowing Out Ball. I was hoping you would attend with me."

With her eyes wide, Daughtie stared at him. "You wanted to invite me to a dance? Is *that* your important question?"

"Yes," he replied, his face suddenly taking on a red tinge.

"I think the Blowing Out Ball may be an uncertainty this year given the fact that the girls are threatening a turnout. Who knows? The mills could be closed down five or six weeks from now," she replied tersely.

Dr. Ketter's crimson complexion paled. "Do you truly believe a strike is possible? I set up practice in Lowell because the Corporation said there was security and that I wouldn't have to rely upon farmers paying me with produce or animals. If the mills close—even one or two of them—it could adversely affect the whole community. Surely the girls will consider the impact their actions could have upon the rest of us. Such behavior would be completely irrational."

Dr. Ketter's outburst annoyed Daughtie. He seemed not concerned about the workers or the city of Lowell; instead, his fretfulness was for himself and the inconvenience a strike might cause in the plans he'd made for a flourishing medical practice. For the first time since she'd heard talk of a turnout, Daughtie considered siding with the girls who favored the strike.

"I believe a turnout is highly possible, though it will depend upon the supporters rallying enough workers to their cause," she replied.

"A bright girl like yourself doesn't favor the plan, do you?"

"I haven't given it my support, as yet. I believe much depends upon how the Corporation presents its final offer regarding the cutback of wages. If they remain determined to lower wages by the full twenty-five percent, there's no doubt many of the girls will strike in opposition."

"But a level-headed woman like yourself could be the voice of restraint. You're educated and articulate. You could sway many of the undecided."

Daughtie gave him a faint smile. "It's up to each girl to determine the merits and vote her own conscience. They've all listened to the positive and negative aspects of a walkout. There have been many meetings over the past two weeks. I'm surprised you aren't more aware of the goings-on in the town, especially since you express a strong desire to remain in Lowell."

"I've been so busy—I haven't had an opportunity to talk with many of the businessmen in town or become involved in community activities."

His tone was defensive, and Daughtie knew her words had hit the mark. "Priorities, Doctor," she said, turning to leave the room. "It would appear that becoming involved in the community could yield some of those benefits you seem to value and currently enjoy. Now if you'll excuse me, I really must go upstairs."

"Wait," he said, grasping her arm. "If there is a ball, will you do me the honor of attending with me?"

"I don't—"

He held up a hand to stave off her answer. "Perhaps I should do as you suggested earlier. I'll wait to see if the Associates will be hosting the celebration."

Daughtie gave a nod of her head and ran up the stairs. Just as she reached the bedroom, she heard a knock at the front door—likely an ailing patient needing the doctor's assistance. She'd let him answer.

Ruth perked to attention when Daughtie entered the room. "Did you and Dr. Ketter have a nice visit?"

"You knew he was going to ask me, didn't you?"

"Ask you what?"

"To accompany him to the Blowing Out Ball. Don't try to act innocent. The two of you arranged that entire encounter, didn't you?"

"You two are perfect for each other. With all you have in common, you're an ideal match. He's a doctor, and you know so much about medicine. I know I was a bit jealous at first, but honestly, you should consider him a fine match. Together, you could do so much good—and be so happy. My mother says that a husband and wife need to have common goals."

"Husband and wife? If you think Dr. Ketter would be a perfect husband, why don't *you* attend the ball with him?"

"Because it's you he's interested in," Ruth snapped. "Besides, you need to focus your attention on a *decent* man."

"Does that mean you think I'm paying attention to an indecent man?"

"Liam Donohue is certainly an inappropriate suitor for anyone except, perhaps, one of his own kind," Ruth replied.

A fount of righteous indignation rose up within Daughtie and then spilled over. "How *dare* you speak ill of Liam Donohue! He's a fine man with outstanding principles. Dr. Ketter would be hard-pressed to exhibit the kind of moral fiber I've seen in Liam Donohue."

"Truly? And exactly what display have you seen from Mr. Donohue?"

After realizing she'd spoken out of turn, Daughtie hesitated, attempting to regroup her thoughts. "He attended the antislavery meeting, and he's done a good deal to help the struggling Irish in the Acre. He cares deeply for the less fortunate."

"And you think Dr. Ketter doesn't? I haven't heard you say anything about Mr. Donohue that couldn't apply equally to Dr. Ketter. Certainly you should be considering the fact that Dr. Ketter has chosen a profession in which he is constantly helping others."

"So long as they pay for the service," Daughtie countered. "His biggest concern right now is whether the mills will strike. And do you know why that concerns him? Not because he fears the workers are being ill treated, not because he fears others will suffer if there's a strike, not even because he's concerned for the investment of the Associates. Oh no! Your fine Dr. Ketter is worried because he was promised a flourishing medical practice, and should the workers strike and a mill or two close down, the number of patients would decrease and his income would suffer. His concern is his own livelihood. I don't think Dr. Ketter is the humanitarian you make him out to be."

"You can't fault a man for being concerned over his own welfare. He has expenses to pay like any of us." She lowered her voice momentarily. "He might even have debts. I'd think less of him if he *weren't* concerned about making a living. The way you continually defend Liam Donohue makes me wonder if there isn't more going on between you two than meets the eye. If it's nothing more than friendship, why would you turn down Dr. Ketter's invitation to the ball? I'm beginning to think you're less than forthright about Mr. Donohue."

The smug look on Ruth's face was more than Daughtie could bear. There was little doubt that Ruth would soon be spreading false rumors. "If going to the ball with Dr. Ketter will serve to convince you I'm telling the truth, then so be it. In reality it proves nothing except that I've tired of this debate."

Ruth jumped up and clapped her hands together. "So you *will* go with him?"

"If there's a ball, I'll go with him—but not because I've any romantic interest in the good doctor. My agreement is given solely to silence your nagging."

"And you'll tell him you accept his invitation?"

Obviously the reasoning behind Daughtie's agreement mattered little to Ruth. "Yes, I'll tell him. But not this evening."

"Well, when?" Ruth whined.

"Once there's an actual announcement by the Corporation that the ball is going to be held. And don't you say a word to him, either. If you do, I'll take it all back and stay at home."

"Oh, all right, but I do wish you'd reconsider. I know it would make him ever so happy to have your acceptance this evening."

"Ruth! Not another word about this subject. I'm going to need headache powders if you don't cease this bothersome behavior."

A short time later, Daughtie rounded the doorway and skidded to a halt. "Mr. Arnold! I didn't realize you were here," she said, backing away. His beady-eyed stare caused her to give an involuntary shiver.

A wicked smirk tugged at his lips. "No harm done. In fact, it's a shame you stopped short of reaching my arms. I rather like the thought of holding you in a warm embrace."

"What did you say, Thaddeus?" Mrs. Arnold inquired while carrying a heaping platter of roasted pork into the dining room. "I wasn't able to hear you out in the kitchen."

"Nothing. I was merely admiring Miss Winfield's charm and grace. She is a lovely young lady, isn't she?"

Mrs. Arnold's gaze shifted between her former husband and Daughtie. "Yes, she's quite lovely," she replied before retreating to the kitchen.

"Why did you say such a thing?" Daughtie hissed.

"You *are* lovely, my dear," he said, drawing nearer and stroking her arm.

Instinctively, Daughtie pulled away and hurried across the hallway. "Aren't you coming to supper, Dr. Ketter?"

Ivan looked up from his papers and gave her a broad smile. "Yes, of course. How kind of you to remind me of the time."

Daughtie slipped her hand through the crook of his arm and permitted him to escort her back across the hall to the dining room. Thaddeus Arnold appeared amused by the sight, Mrs. Arnold surprised, and Ruth—Ruth's face was etched in delight.

Thaddeus speared a slice of roast pork and looked toward Dr. Ketter. "Are you enjoying the hospitality of my house, Dr. Ketter?"

Ivan appeared taken aback by the question. "It's my understanding this house belongs to the Corporation, Mr. Arnold. However, I do find the accommodations to my liking."

"I'm certain you find more than the accommodations to your liking," Thaddeus retorted as he eyed the three women. "Having the pleasure of dining with these lovely women each night is certainly enough to make me envious." He leisurely wet his lips with the enjoyment of a cat licking the last droplet of cream from its whiskers, leaned back in his chair, and awaited Ivan's reply.

"I find the company as pleasurable as the accommodations," Ivan simply stated.

Thaddeus gave a wicked laugh. "Don't become too comfortable in your new surroundings, Dr. Ketter. Women can be a fickle lot—telling lies and causing all manner of problems."

Daughtie ceased eating, carefully watching the exchange. It was obvious Thaddeus was toying with Ivan, enjoying the doctor's obvious discomfort, while Mrs. Arnold fidgeted with Theona in an understandable attempt to draw her husband's attention away from Dr. Ketter.

Uncertain whether it was sympathy for Mrs. Arnold and Dr. Ketter or a distinct dislike for Thaddeus Arnold that caused her boldness, Daughtie said, "I was taught at an early age that good digestion is dependent upon pleasant table conversation. I'm certain we can find something more enjoyable to discuss."

Thaddeus squeezed his face into a condescending mask of tolerance and pointed his fork in Daughtie's direction. "If you'd rather change topics, why don't you tell me about work at the Appleton? I continue to miss the pleasure my duties at the mill afforded me."

Neither Mr. Arnold's smirk nor the evil glint in his eye was lost on Daughtie. How a kind woman such as Naomi Arnold could have ever chosen to marry him was beyond Daughtie's comprehension. "Work at the mills continues as usual," Daughtie replied.

Ruth twisted in her chair and leveled a look of amazement in Daughtie's direction. "Daughtie! How can you make such a remark? The Corporation is threatening to lower wages by twenty-five percent, the operatives are organizing for a turnout, and you say everything is normal?"

Thaddeus arched his neck in Ruth's direction. "A decrease in wages, you say? Profits must be down, which means sales have decreased and production, of course, has increased. I know someone who projected this is exactly what would happen. They've expanded too rapidly for their own good. And you say the operatives are going to strike?"

Ruth came to attention. "Yes, they—"

"Merely talk, nothing more," Daughtie interrupted. "I doubt whether this topic is any better for the digestion than your earlier discussion of women's foibles, Mr. Arnold."

"Quite the contrary, Miss Winfield. I find the discussion excellent for my digestion. Tell me, Miss Wilson, have the girls organized? I find that organization is the key to efficiency in all things."

"I absolutely agree. We began organizing the day the broadsides were posted. Since then, we've been holding meetings in an attempt to persuade all of the operatives to join those of us who have already committed to the cause."

"Good, good," Thaddeus encouraged, nodding in agreement, "and when will you strike?"

"We're awaiting a final decision on the amount of the wage decrease. The Associates want twenty-five percent. However, we've been told Mr. Boott and Mr. Cheever, along with other members of management here in Lowell, have requested the amount be reassessed."

"No matter the amount, the wages should not be lowered. You must rally the operatives and explain they must stand their ground," he replied with a thump of his fist on the table.

"For a man who no longer works at the mills, you appear to be keenly interested in this difficulty," Dr. Ketter suggested.

Thaddeus ignored the remark and remained focused upon Ruth. Her eyes had widened at Mr. Arnold's impassioned declaration, and she glanced toward Daughtie.

"Don't look to Miss Winfield for advice. You're obviously a young woman of vision and leadership. I have no doubt you can convince the other workers they should strike. And the sooner, the better. You must send a clear and concise message to the Associates that the workers will not tolerate their greedy actions. Those men in their fancy mansions will continue to live in the lap of luxury, no matter the consequence to the lowly mill workers. They care little whether there's a crust of bread in your mouth."

"I think your statement is somewhat melodramatic, Mr. Arnold," Daughtie said in a lighthearted tone, hoping to ease the tension permeating the room. "Our discussion is not going to resolve the problems in the mill, and I'm certain your former wife and daughter would find another topic much more edifying."

"Don't attempt to tell me what will or will not interest Naomi or Theona, Miss Winfield. They'll listen to whatever I care to present."

Daughtie wanted to continue the argument, but one look at Mr. Arnold's ashen complexion convinced her to reevaluate her position. He might hold his temper in check during dinner, yet Daughtie knew afterward it would be Mrs. Arnold and Theona who would suffer the brunt of his anger. She should have known better than to provoke him, but in a momentary lapse of memory, she'd forgotten his detestable behavior. Well, she'd not leave Mrs. Arnold and Theona alone with Thaddeus this evening, of that she was certain.

"Please accept my apology, Mr. Arnold. I didn't mean any offense," she replied in a conciliatory tone.

His chest swelled slightly, obviously pleased by her act of contrition. "As I was saying, Miss Wilson, you should make due haste in gaining support. Is there no word from management as to when you can expect a decision?"

Ruth cast a sidelong glance at Daughtie before replying. "We're told the first of March, but some say it may be later."

"Have the supervisors met with you and set forth exact reasons for this callous behavior?"

"It's as you stated earlier. Profits have diminished."

"And you poor girls are going to be the Corporation's scapegoats, suffering the disastrous effects of their inept ability to manage their assets. Disgraceful!"

Daughtie stared in disbelief. When had Thaddeus ever cared about the girls in the mills? For that matter, when had he ever cared about anyone other than himself? And why was he still so interested in the mills? He quizzed them every time he came to visit, obviously anxious for any morsel he might acquire. His behavior made no sense. The moment Ruth began to spoon-feed him the information he so desperately desired, his wrath subsided. Still, she wouldn't leave Mrs. Arnold alone in his presence. The man was a chameleon, altering his behavior at every twist and turn.

Pushing away from the table, Thaddeus crooked his finger and beckoned Ruth. "Let's finish our discussion in the parlor—or, should I say, Dr. Ketter's waiting room? You don't mind if we use your waiting room, do you, Doctor? Come, come, my dear," he urged. "We have important matters to discuss."

17

London

William Thurston threaded his way through the shoppers and sightseers lining the streets, careful to keep John Farnsworth and his group within sight. If he grew too close, he feared one of them might see his reflection in a store window. He attempted to edge past a group of elderly women moving at a snail's pace, obviously more intent upon their own conversation than the fact that they were blocking the path of others.

He inadvertently brushed the shoulder of one woman as he passed by. "Well, I *never*! You might excuse yourself," she scolded. When William didn't respond, she thumped him soundly with her cane. "I *said* you need to excuse yourself!"

William turned and tipped his beaver top hat. "My apologies. I'm in a hurry."

"That much is obvious," the old woman called after him.

William ignored the remark and rushed onward, now concerned John Farnsworth might disappear from sight. "Foolish old woman," he muttered, scanning the crowd. Spotting Farnsworth, he breathed a sigh of relief.

He waited outside each time they entered a shop until his gloved fingers grew numb from the cold. When they entered a large establishment, he pulled up his collar and followed them inside. The freezing temperatures had forced him to discontinue his observations outdoors.

Moving down an adjacent aisle, he wended his way through the shelves and counters until he found a spot within listening distance of the group, where he heard John mention their dinner reservations were for seven o'clock at the Blue Boar.

Relieved when the group finally completed its shopping expedition, William retraced his steps back toward his boardinghouse. If luck was on his side, he'd be seated somewhere near the Farnsworth dinner party this evening.

William's lips turned upward in a smile of satisfaction. Citing his dislike of large groups, he had convinced the waiter to place a small table in a secluded area behind an ornate marble column near the Farnsworth table—close enough to overhear their conversation, yet concealed enough to remain undetected.

He sipped a glass of deep red port and watched as the Farnsworth party was seated, enjoying the surreptitious infringement his location would afford him throughout the evening. "It's almost as though they've invited me to their little party," he muttered in self-satisfaction.

"I do believe we're privileged to have the most beautiful women in the room seated at our table," John commented to Taylor.

Taylor nodded in agreement. "I believe Bella spent more time fashioning Elinor's hair than her own."

"And well worth the effort, I might add. You look beautiful, Elinor," John said. "And you, my dear, are too lovely for words."

"Enough of this drivel," William mumbled.

"Excuse me? Did you want something, sir?"

William glanced up to see a waiter standing in attendance at his table. "No, just thinking aloud. I'll wait until later to place my order," he replied, turning his attention back to the conversation that was taking place on the other side of the stone pillar.

"I'm not sure that's wise, John. I think we should wait until the first of the month before making a final decision. After all, Taylor has been able to locate those new print ideas to take back to Mr. Boott, and he seems to have reconnected with some of his old acquaintances. Haven't you, Taylor?" Addie inquired.

"Absolutely. Believe me, we know that what we're doing here in England is necessary. Bella and I are committed to staying until Uncle John is certain there is enough information to return home with confidence."

William's eyes widened, and he strained closer to listen.

"I appreciate your willingness to remain in England. The fact that you both realize the importance of this visit means a great deal to me. I know you've put your future on hold, but I promise you'll be rewarded for your efforts."

"No need for that, Uncle John. You're family—we do whatever we can for family. Right, Bella?"

Bella smiled and nodded. "Yes, for your family, we're pleased to help wherever and however needed."

"I still think it wise to check on passages home. If things go as we're hoping, we still may be able to sail by early March," John replied.

"As you wish, my dear. Whatever will make you most contented," Addie replied.

William startled at the remark, nearly toppling over his glass of port. The conversation at the other table swirled through his mind. Manning had said he wanted Farnsworth to return home with enough information to feel confident. *No doubt he's made promises to the Associates that he'll produce valuable information. If Farnsworth returns to Massachusetts without anything of real value, he'll appear the fool and, more importantly, lose stature with the Corporation,* William decided. And the fact that Farnsworth had the total agreement of his entire family to assist him in this sabotage was even more baffling.

Certainly *he* would never have confided any business information to his wife, yet both of the women appeared fully informed, entering into the conversation as though they were equals in the decision making. William's wife would never have agreed to help him, much less keep her mouth shut. The idiocy of these men astounded him! But, he reasoned, both of the women had worked for the Corporation. Perhaps they felt some overwhelming loyalty to the mills—or perhaps it was merely an allegiance to their husbands.

The fact that Farnsworth and his family might soon be returning to America was most disconcerting. Having all but promised to deliver Farnsworth and proof of his espionage activities, there was now a strong possibility Thurston might lose his foothold with the British aristocracy. Tomorrow he would follow Farnsworth to the ticket offices at the wharf; perhaps the ticket agent would be forthcoming. If not, a few coins would likely loosen his tongue. On Wednesday he would follow Taylor Manning to find out how he was stealing fabric patterns.

William stroked his chin in absolute delight. What more could he have asked for? A recent letter from Thaddeus telling him of a possible strike in the Lowell mills, coupled with the information he'd assembled about John Farnsworth and his family over the past week, should raise his stature a notch or two with Chauncy Fuller and his pompous English associates. He ordered ale and watched the front door of the pub.

Barlow Kent and Chauncy Fuller entered the Ale House. William waved the men toward his table and then rose to greet them. "Exactly on time," he said.

"I personally abhor tardiness," Barlow replied while signaling to the barkeep.

Chauncy pulled a gold watch from his pocket and checked the time. "Since the topic of time seems to be of the utmost importance to both of you, I'd best mention that I have only an hour to spare before my next meeting."

Thurston clenched his jaw. However, he didn't want Chauncy to discern his irritation. "Then we'd best move along swiftly, as I have much to report." He hesitated for a moment, assuring himself he had their full attention—he *deserved* their full attention. "Since our last meeting, I have been engaged in numerous activities, all of them garnering valuable information. I began my quest for additional facts by following John Farnsworth on numerous occasions. My first piece of significant information was gained through secreting myself at dinner—"

"I'm sorry to interrupt, my good man, but if we're to accomplish anything today, you'd best cut to the chase. As I said, I've only an hour," Chauncy cautioned impatiently.

Unable to hide his irritation, William leaned across the table and met Chauncy's gaze. "I spent innumerable hours in the freezing cold gathering this information, and now you want me to hurry along so that you may attend to other business? I think not! Perhaps you need to reevaluate your priorities."

Chauncy didn't appear offended, yet he didn't waver from his proclamation. "Tell the information at your own pace, but the fact remains that I must leave in an hour. Unlike you, I have more than one matter that beckons my attention."

William inwardly flinched at the remark but gave no visible sign he was offended. Instead, he offered a perfunctory nod. "In that case, I assume you're even more grateful for my assistance. As I was saying, I followed the Farnsworth family to numerous locations and, through my observations, became privy to information that Taylor Manning, Farnsworth's nephew, may have discovered a way to steal print designs, and the group may be departing England in the very near future."

Chauncy's eyebrows arched. "If they're leaving and none of the mills has reported espionage problems, what makes you certain designs have been stolen or anything has gone amiss? Perhaps they were here for the obvious reasons— to visit family and spend the holidays in England."

William wagged his head back and forth, clearly enjoying the moment. "I assume you're playing devil's advocate since I know you're already convinced Farnsworth is up to no good. The information I've uncovered will prove exactly that—Farnsworth is a traitor. And please remember that the earlier espionage committed by the Americans was not detected until their mills were already operating in Massachusetts."

"That's true. He has a valid point," Barlow agreed.

William flashed a glance at Barlow Kent. At least he'd succeeded in convincing Kent there was reason for concern. Twisting in his chair, William focused his attention upon his enthusiastic supporter. "As it turns out, Farnsworth didn't book passage; instead, he merely inquired when ships were scheduled to depart in the months of March, April, and May. The ticket agent has agreed to send word to me when Farnsworth actually books passage. As I expected, it took a few coins to persuade him to cooperate. However, by the time I left his office, I had secured his complete cooperation."

Barlow Kent rubbed his hands together, obviously enjoying the revelation.

Leaning forward, he gave William his full attention. "Go on," he encouraged.

William offered an appreciative smile. "The next day, I followed young Taylor Manning. He's the one who has been helping with design work back in Massachusetts. I don't suppose either of you would like to venture a guess where he might have gone, would you?"

"I don't think we have time for guessing games," Chauncy curtly replied.

"He waited outside Armstrong and Talley—the company that designs for the print work mills in Lancashire. He met one of their employees and the two of them walked off together. I followed but could never get close enough to hear their conversation. However, I'm certain the man handed him some papers."

Barlow Kent straightened in his chair. The information had obviously captured his interest. William momentarily basked in the attention before continuing. "You realize, of course, the possibility exists for him to steal any new ideas they may be formulating."

Chauncy still didn't appear convinced. "They may be old friends enjoying a brief opportunity to become reacquainted."

"You've obviously had little experience in the area of industrial espionage, my good man. All these men need is a foot in the door, so to speak. He could be doing something as unassuming as meeting an acquaintance, but mark my words, he'll find a way to secure any scrap of information that will assist the Americans."

"I think you may be overreacting."

"I concur with Thurston, Chauncy. I think William is correct in his assumptions. These men have already hoodwinked us once. Are we going to permit them to do it again?" Barlow Kent asked.

Chauncy rubbed his forehead and glanced across the table. "I agree they must be stopped. I've already conceded that point, but I think we need to be absolutely certain of their plans. We don't want to make fools of ourselves."

"Nor do we want to miss the opportunity to thwart this espionage. It appears their return will depend upon Manning's ability to steal the design plans. Why else would Farnsworth be checking on so many alternate dates for their return?"

"Didn't you say Jarrow Farnsworth is ill? They may be awaiting medical advice," Chauncy suggested.

William took a drink from his tankard and settled back in his chair. "That's all a ploy. I'm beginning to doubt whether the old man is even sick. Likely his illness is a ruse to keep us at bay."

"You may be right," Chauncy replied. "I suppose those who would willingly turn traitor against the motherland would also manipulate and exploit their own families. Perhaps I should have a visit with Wilbur Talley. He's a business acquaintance and family friend. Once we tell him of our suspicions,

I'm certain he'll be pleased to assist with investigating young Mr. Manning."

"Excellent! I was hoping you might have a contact at Armstrong and Talley. If you'd be willing to write a letter of introduction, I'd be pleased to meet with Mr. Talley—since you're so busy with other matters," William added. "If he's willing to cooperate, we could plot out a plan of action. I certainly wouldn't want to disrupt his business or upset his valued employees."

Chauncy hesitated for only a moment. "Since I can't possibly meet with him for at least a week, I believe I'll take you up on your offer. I'll write a letter for you later today. You can stop by my office at your convenience."

"Any word from your contacts in Massachusetts?" Fuller inquired.

"As a matter of fact, I have," William replied, pulling Thaddeus Arnold's missive from his breast pocket. "You'll be pleased to hear there is talk of a turnout among the working class."

A glint of pleasure shone in Barlow's eyes. "Do tell! That *is* pleasurable news. Apparently all this talk of their happy employees working in a utopian existence is little more than propaganda."

Chauncy drew closer. "If the employees are striking, it's because their wages are being lowered or their workload is being increased without an offer of additional wages. Lower wages could mean production has dropped off and their profits are down, which would be excellent news for us. However, if the Corporation is wanting to increase the workload without an increase in wages, it could mean they're receiving more orders than they can fill and they see this as an opportunity to recoup their investment in rapid fashion."

William nodded. "My informant states that orders have remained steady; however, with the increased number of mills in operation, they need to see an increasing market if they're to operate with a profit. The easiest way to increase their profit margin is to lower wages."

"What have they proposed to their employees?" Barlow inquired.

"Twenty-five percent."

Chauncy exhaled a deep breath between his teeth that culminated in a long, low whistle. "I can see why they may be faced with a strike."

"Apparently a final decision hasn't been made—at least it hadn't at the time this letter was written. By now the workers may already be on strike."

"And wouldn't that be grand news for us? If they remain on strike for any length of time, our orders could double by spring," Chauncy rejoiced. "Barkeep! Another round," he called out. Suddenly his two o'clock appointment seemed not quite so important.

18

Lowell

Escaping to the library again this evening?" Ruth inquired, her voice distant and cold.

Daughtie tightened her jaw. She wasn't going to engage in another verbal contest over the turnout. "Not escaping—merely helping shelve books," she replied.

"You can run out of the house, but tomorrow morning you'll be forced to make your final decision for all to see, Daughtie. You'd do better to sit here and discuss the merits of both sides and make a choice tonight. Or have you already decided and you're merely afraid to tell me?"

"Why would I fear *you,* Ruth? *I'm* the one who must live with my choice. I'm seeking what God would have me do in this matter. My decision doesn't reflect upon what you or anyone else is supposed to do, only what I believe *I* am supposed to do. So, you see, further discussion with you will be of little assistance. Now, if you'll excuse me, I really must be going."

Daughtie pulled on her cloak and hurried out the door without looking back. She could feel the cold stares of Ruth and the other girls, and she knew they thought her cowardly. Well, perhaps Mrs. Arnold didn't harbor such views, but certainly Ruth and the others who had gathered at the house shortly after supper believed she was weak and indecisive. She pulled her cape tight against the cold, damp wind until she reached the welcoming warmth of the circulating library.

"Daughtie! Dear me! Where is my mind? I should have sent word to you. I completed shelving all the books earlier today and have two other girls scheduled to work. I'm afraid there will be little to keep you busy. Of course, there are books to read," Mrs. Potter said with a bright smile. "I hope you'll forgive me. I doubt you wanted to be out on this cold night."

Rubbing her hands together near the fire, Daughtie gave Mrs. Potter an easy smile. "No need to concern yourself. There are some new fabrics being produced at the Tremont. I understand they've been stocked at Whidden's Mercantile. I'll go and take a look at those."

"If you'll wait just a minute, I'll accompany you as far as Gorham Street."

Daughtie nodded. "Certainly. I'd enjoy your companionship."

Several minutes passed while Mrs. Potter issued instructions and donned her coat and muff. When they were finally on their way, the older woman looped her arm through Daughtie's. "I've overheard talk of a strike. But I'm hoping it's merely idle gossip," she said with a note of expectancy in her voice.

"It appears as if there are many girls who support a turnout. However, it's impossible to know what will actually occur until the time arrives for them to make their choice. A part of me wonders if those who are speaking so favorably about a strike will, at the last moment, change their minds. Most of them realize that there's no guarantee they can return to their jobs if they participate in the walkout."

Mrs. Potter nodded. "I hope they'll weigh their decisions carefully. I know many of the girls help support their families, and this situation could prove devastating for them. Now, tell me about these fabrics you're going to inspect at the mercantile. Are you making yourself a new dress?"

"No. I've been hired to assist with choosing some fabrics and furnishings for a new home."

"Really? How exciting. And do you get to make all the choices?" Mrs. Potter asked with a smile.

"No. Mr. Donohue makes the final decisions. In fact, I had chosen fabrics made in England, but he wants to use only textiles produced here in Lowell."

"Mr. Donohue? The stonemason?"

"Yes. Do you know him?" Daughtie inquired.

"He's Irish."

"Yes, I know."

Mrs. Potter stopped midstep. "Is it *his* house you're decorating?"

Daughtie continued walking. "Yes. It's a beautiful home," she replied.

Mrs. Potter hastened to keep in stride, tugging at Daughtie's elbow. "Associating with an Irishman will jeopardize your future. You know that, don't you?"

"My future with whom? I've been told by various well-meaning people that I'll never find a *decent* husband if I'm seen with Liam Donohue. However, I would have no desire to marry a man who didn't consider Liam Donohue his equal. You see, I believe we're all alike in the eyes of God. After all, He created all of us, didn't He? I would find it impossible to respect a man who thought himself better than another merely because his skin color or birthplace differed. Consequently, I'm unwilling to concern myself with what others think of my association with Liam Donohue."

"That's a noble thought for a girl of tender years, but I'm older than you, and I hope you'll give serious consideration to my words. Virtuous deeds won't warm you on a cold winter night, furnish food for your table, or care for you in your old age. We've all made improper decisions in our youth. Most of those choices are forgotten. But socializing with an Irishman is a millstone about your neck that you'll not escape."

Daughtie patted Mrs. Potter's hand. "I do value your opinion and thank you for your concern, but this is merely a task I've been employed to complete."

Mrs. Potter smiled weakly. "You intend to continue down this path of destruction, don't you?"

"I intend to finish what I've already begun. I believe this is where you turn, isn't it?" Daughtie inquired as they reached Gorham Street.

"Yes. You have a pleasant evening, my dear."

"Thank you, and you do the same."

Daughtie stood and watched until Mrs. Potter reached the corner before walking off toward Whidden's Mercantile. She shivered, uncertain whether the involuntary gesture was caused by the freezing temperature or by Mrs. Potter's reproving words. Why were people continually judged by external appearance? Was it not a person's heart that truly mattered?

Pushing open the front door of the store, the warmth beckoned her in like a mother's welcoming smile. "Good evening, Mrs. Whidden."

"Good evening to you, Miss Winfield. Have you come to view more fabric?"

Daughtie nodded. "Yes, but as I told you when I returned the English textiles, only fabrics manufactured here in Lowell. I'm told there are some new offerings from the Tremont Mill."

"Indeed. And they are quite lovely. I'm certain you'll find something to your liking," the older woman replied as she led Daughtie toward the middle of the store. "All of these," she said, pointing toward a long wooden table piled high with folded cloth.

Daughtie approached the table and giggled in delight. "It's hard to believe I have so many choices. These are beautiful." The sight of the gorgeous fabrics was almost enough to erase the painful headache she had suffered throughout the day.

"I thought you might be pleased," Mrs. Whidden remarked while pulling out an especially colorful piece of damask fabric from the bottom of the pile.

Daughtie carefully evaluated the choices, finally limiting her selection to six before glancing at the clock. Eight o'clock. There would be sufficient time to take the samples to Liam for his inspection. Grasping the package of cloth under her arm, she waved good-bye and hurried out the door.

She was nearing Liam's house when the thought of actually seeing him and delivering the fabrics caused an unfamiliar stirring. Was it seeing Liam's reaction to the textiles or purely seeing Liam that was creating her excitement? The thought startled her. She regarded Liam with the same respect and attention she had always afforded others. Why, then, did she feel this strange exhilaration? Her mind raced back to conversations she'd had with Bella when her friend had first fallen in love with Taylor Manning. Daughtie's eyes widened.

Bella had mentioned her heart occasionally fluttering with excitement when she first began to fall in love with Taylor. Was *she* falling in love with Liam Donohue? Yet he was a friend—nothing more, nothing less, she cautioned herself while walking up the steps to his porch.

She reached out and knocked on the door, realizing her hand was trembling! "It's the cold," she said aloud, hoping to convince herself. *It's anticipation over seeing Liam,* a small voice inside her head whispered. A bewildering uncertainty plagued her. Instinctively, she rubbed her throbbing temples, hoping the pressure would ease her distress.

A smile captured Liam's lips the moment he opened the door. "Would you look who's here! Come in, come in."

He stepped aside and waved Daughtie forward. "Let me take yar cape. Ya've chosen a frigid night to be out and about, lassie." He hung her cloak and turned back to his guest. "Don't misunderstand—I'm always delighted to have a lovely lady appear on me doorstep."

Daughtie felt the heat rise in her cheeks. She doubted Liam would notice. Surely the freezing temperature had already colored her complexion to a bright pink. "I stopped by Whidden's," she explained, holding out the package to justify her visit.

"Ah, I see. I'm guessin' this is the fabric," he replied, untying the cord and pulling back the brown paper. "Let's take them in the parlor and see what ya've brought me." He hesitated a moment. "But first, let me show you something else," he said, beckoning her down the hallway.

Daughtie followed behind him, stopping when they arrived in the kitchen. Her eyes widened at the sight. There were barrels and wooden boxes stacked all about the room. "What is all of this?" she quizzed.

"Provisions!" His voice was filled with a joyful pride. "I've been doin' as ya told me, gathering as many provisions as I dared. Mrs. Whidden did question the number of blankets I'd been buyin'," he said with a chuckle. "I told her my family might be coming to visit and they were a cold-blooded lot. She appeared to accept my explanation."

Daughtie stood on tiptoe, peered into several of the boxes, and nodded her approval. "This is wonderful," she said while still lifting lids and eyeing the contents. "However, you must get it put away—hidden from sight. What if someone came in here and saw all of this?"

"Besides myself, ya're the only person that's been in this kitchen since the day I moved in. I'm not expectin' visitors."

"But, Liam, if you're suspected of harboring slaves, they'll go through your entire home. If the authorities should find all of this out in plain sight, there's little doubt of what they would think. They'd never even give you a chance to answer questions before hauling you away."

"I s'pose ya're right about that. Guess I'll be needin' to make me some good hidin' places. I think the men and boys will be safe enough out in the barn, and there's ample space to store some blankets and a few clothes. For sure we can't be storin' any food out there, though—the coons and possums would have it eaten before any runaways arrived. I've made a couple of good places upstairs for any women and their youngsters. I built a false wall in two of the bedrooms. Long as they're quiet, there's no one could detect what I've done," he proudly announced.

"I'm amazed at all you've accomplished. It doesn't appear you need any help with your preparations."

"I sent word me house was ready. Now I just have to wait and see if anyone comes," he said, leading her back down the hallway.

Daughtie patted the folds along the side of her dress. "I have something here to share with you, too," she said, reaching deep inside her pocket and retrieving a letter. "From Prudence Crandall."

"Really? She wrote you a letter?"

"She encouraged me to correspond with her. This is her second letter."

"You never mentioned you intended to write her."

"I know. I feared she wouldn't reply," Daughtie stated simply. "But she seems quite pleased to answer my missives. Listen to this," she said, lowering her voice as though she planned to include Liam in some dark conspiracy.

Seating himself, Liam folded his brawny arms and gave her his full attention. "All right, I'm listenin'."

"I want you to hear this one paragraph," she said before looking back down at the letter. "'The girls and I continue to persevere, although many of the townspeople are steadfast in their determination to see me and all of my girls removed from their community. Their anger grew deeper this week when I enrolled two more girls. The house was pelted with rotten eggs and rocks. Two windows were broken, but I give thanks that none of us were injured. Continue to pray that we'll be protected and that God will soften the hearts of those who persecute us. I will not give in to these tormentors unless I fear for the lives of my charges. They are such capable young ladies, eager to be educated. Each one will make fine contributions to our country, if only given the opportunity.'" Daughtie refolded the letter and tucked it back inside her pocket. "I'm deeply saddened Miss Crandall and the girls must endure such treatment."

"I agree, but 'tis good to know she hasn't given in to the ruffians. She's determined to educate her students, and I believe it will be takin' more than rotten eggs and a few rocks to frighten her off."

"You're right. The best thing we can do is what she's asked: pray."

Instead of responding, Liam jumped up from his chair like he'd been hit by a bolt of lightning and began spreading the pieces of cloth across the cherry dining room table. "These are quite lovely. All from the Lowell textile mills?"

"All from the Lowell textile mills," she affirmed, loving the sound of his lyrical Irish lilt. "You can choose the drapery fabric from among this group, and we'll use your choice of two other favorites for the overstuffed furniture in this room."

"Only two? That may prove difficult."

"We can use some of the others in the bedrooms, dining room, and library," she suggested while seating herself in one of the chairs that would soon be upholstered with fabric. While Liam directed his attention to the cloth, Daughtie began to once again massage her temples.

"Headache?" Liam inquired, turning toward her.

"Yes. I can't seem to rid myself of the pain. It's been a nuisance most of the day."

"Here, let me," he said. Without awaiting her consent, he moved behind the chair and began to gently massage her temples with his broad fingers while gently moving his thumbs in a circular motion at the nape of her neck. The chokehold of pain banding her head began to ease as he continued to massage her head. Her eyes closed in relaxation. She knew she should stop him—but she didn't. His ministrations were much too soothing.

When the throbbing finally began to subside, she raised her hand. "Thank you. I'm feeling much better," she said. "It appears you're a man of many talents."

"My mother suffered with headaches. From the time I was a wee lad, I would massage her head until the pain would leave. It's good to know I haven't lost my touch. Now tell me, what's causin' your muscles to knot up in pain? Is it Miss Crandall's letter?"

"No," she murmured.

"When the muscles get knotted up like this, it's usually caused by worry. You know, keepin' yarself tense, not lettin' the body relax itself. If it's not Miss Crandall's situation that's causin' ya to fret, what is it that's been weighin' so heavy on yar mind?"

Daughtie gave him a forlorn look as he pulled a chair directly in front of her. "It's all the discord at the mills. The turnout's been scheduled for the first of March, and that's only a few days away. Unless the Associates change their minds about the decrease in wages, I fear many of the girls are determined to strike."

Liam nodded. "I thought you'd made up your mind about that issue back when the idea of a turnout was first proposed by Ruth and the others."

"You're right, and I was vocal in my disagreement. Then a few days later, when I refused to sign the petition they were circulating, Ruth wouldn't even speak to me. She gave me the silent treatment for two full days."

"That was probably a blessin' in disguise," Liam said with a chuckle.

"True, for she hasn't stopped nagging me ever since. She presents the petition to me on a daily basis, telling me she knows I'll soon come to my senses."

"And does this petition say ya agree to walk out with them?" Liam inquired.

"It says we've been wronged by the Corporation and cheerfully agree not to enter and work in the mills on the first of March or any time thereafter unless our wages are restored to what we received prior to the date of the turnout."

"And so it's not just an agreement but a *cheerful* agreement they're wantin'?" he asked, his full lips turning up into a wide grin.

"I think the girls want to emphasize to the Corporation that they're happy to go without their wages. I thought Ruth might come to her senses when they dismissed a girl over at the Suffolk Mill, but even that didn't faze Ruth."

Liam's eyebrows arched high on his forehead. "So they've actually fired someone?"

"Yes—Mary Wickert is her name. They said she was holding meetings within the mill during dinner breaks and stirring the operatives into such a state of agitation that by the time they returned to work, the girls couldn't concentrate and production suffered. Of course, Ruth said the charges were totally unfounded. However, Lucinda Seawart works at the Suffolk. She was in the library last night and told me that the accusations were true. She said the supervisor told Mary to cease the meetings at the mill or she'd be terminated. So when Mary met with a group of girls the next day during the dinner hour in the mill yard, they sent the agent to escort her into the office and fired her—they even escorted her to the boardinghouse and waited while she packed her belongings. She was told to never set foot on Corporation property again. Wouldn't you think terminating Mary's employment would give the girls pause to wonder about their own futures?"

Liam nodded. "Aye. But just as we believe helpin' slaves escape is vital, these girls obviously believe their cause is justified. Perhaps it is; I don't be pretendin' to know."

"I don't think you can compare the two, Liam. The slaves didn't choose to leave their homes and become the chattel of white plantation owners. However, these girls made a decision to come here and work in the mills. I realize they thought their income would continue to increase rather than decrease, but the contracts don't even address the issue of a wage reduction."

"I understand, but there are times when people get swept up in the tide of a movement such as this and feel obligated to go along with the crowd. They fear bein' singled out as unsympathetic to the cause. 'Course, I'm not one for signin' things like petitions, so whether I agreed or not, I'd refuse to sign their paper. I believe a man's *word* should be his bond."

"Even if I did agree with the strike, I don't concur with the remainder of what they've tacked on to the petition."

"And what is that?"

"If you sign the agreement and then don't turn out with the others, you're then required to pay five dollars to be used for some benevolent action in the town. Even with that added language, the girls are signing; their anger over Mary's dismissal has caused many more to sign up."

"And has all of this now caused you to change your mind?"

"No, I don't think we should strike. It's just that the actions of Ruth and her supporters leave me feeling alone."

"Surely there are others who stand in opposition, aren't there?"

"Yes, but they don't have to sleep in the same room with Ruth. Besides, with Ruth acting as an organizer at the Appleton, all of those who come to our house favor the walkout."

"Isolation is a difficult thing. You find yourself in a position of bein' so much the same as those around you and yet very different," he said in a soft voice.

She glanced up into his eyes. "You know exactly how it feels, don't you?"

"Yes. I know about loneliness and separation. I've lived with them ever since comin' to this country."

"How have you managed?" she questioned, her voice no more than a whisper.

"I keep busy with me work and me dreams." His voice was low and husky.

Daughtie trembled at his nearness. She held her gaze on his face, unwilling to lose the feeling that was growing within her. The wonder of the moment filled her with awe.

"I'd be thinkin' that prayin' and such might come as a comfort to you," he added.

Daughtie forced her thoughts to reform. "Yes, it does. I rely heavily on God for comfort—especially when I'm . . . particularly . . . discouraged."

He leaned forward and surprised her by taking hold of her hands. "Like now?"

She nodded, almost afraid to speak. "Yes. Like now." She bit at her lower lip to keep Liam from seeing how it quivered. Her stomach did flip-flops, leaving her wavering between wanting to run away from Liam and longing to run to him.

"I know it's hard for you to endure, but I admire your strength. I admire most everything about you."

For a moment Daughtie thought he might kiss her, but the clock chimed the hour and Liam quickly released his hold and sat up straight. "We should be gettin' ya back to the boardinghouse. It's bad enough ya go keepin' company with me like this—with no other womenfolk around to keep things good and proper. But to be comin' home late . . . well, now, there'd be no end of grief for ya." His brogue thickened with the emotion of the moment.

Daughtie took up her things while Liam went quickly to hitch the horses. She floated to the door as if in a dream. There was something about this man . . . something that touched her deep inside.

They rode in silence, the cold pressing them close together in spite of propriety. Daughtie was actually glad to see that Liam was willing to drive her directly to the boardinghouse rather than drop her off at the end of the street.

Liam reined back the horses and fixed the brake before jumping down to help Daughtie. She was in no hurry to leave his company, but a pelting sleet began to blow down from the skies. Liam reached up and took hold of Daughtie's waist as if she were a small child. Setting her down gently, he continued to hold her for just a moment. Then, without warning, he kissed her lightly on the cheek.

Daughtie gave a gasp of surprise and touched her gloved hand to her cheek in wonder. Liam hurried back to the wagon and was gone before Daughtie could even speak. She watched him disappear into the night—suddenly not feeling nearly as alone as she had earlier in the evening.

Daughtie shoved her fist into the pillow, attempting to create the perfect cradle for her throbbing head. But the cruel pounding wore on, mimicking the thumping looms in the weaving room. She rolled to her side and tugged at the covers, longing for the deep, restful slumber of her childhood, when thoughts of a turnout hadn't invaded her sleep. She pulled the covers over her head and attempted to blot out all thoughts of the mill. She tried to focus on Liam and how he had kissed her cheek, but the worry and concern of what events might yet come to pass pushed the memory aside.

It seemed as though she had barely crawled into bed when the pealing of the tower bell startled Daughtie from her restless slumber. Her eyelids drooped heavy with sleep, but she forced herself to remain awake. Edging into a sitting position, she swung her legs over the side of the bed and attempted to stand. Her legs wobbled, protesting the weight she now forced upon them.

"I'm going downstairs," Ruth announced curtly.

Daughtie glanced over her shoulder. Ruth was perched upon the bed, dressed for the day with her hair properly braided and fashioned into a knot atop her head. "How long have you been awake?"

"Probably an hour or so. I woke up and couldn't go back to sleep. I'm meeting with some girls before final bell," she said as she moved toward the door.

"You're meeting here at the house?"

"No, we're going to meet on the weaving floor before Mr. Kingman arrives."

"Oh, Ruth, I don't think that's wise. Mr. Kingman is likely at the mill at least a half hour before any of us. With Mary's dismissal, I think you're taking a foolish risk."

Ruth shrugged her shoulders. "I imagine you do, but if you're not willing to join our ranks, you need not force your opinions upon me."

"I'm not forcing my opinion upon you, Ruth. I'm expressing my concern."

"Well, you don't need to do that, either. I'll be fine."

The anger in Ruth's voice caused a lump to form in Daughtie's throat. "I'll be praying for you," she said while holding back her tears.

There was no reply. Tears flowed down Daughtie's cheeks as she listened to Ruth's footsteps clattering down the stairs.

Daughtie hastened off toward the mill, feeling strangely unsettled. Only on those rare occasions when Ruth was ill did Daughtie walk alone. Her discomfort abated when she peeked in the weaving room and saw Ruth standing by her looms. Ruth glanced in Daughtie's direction but didn't return her wave. No matter—at least there had been no repercussions to the early morning meeting Ruth had attended.

She sat down at her drawing-in frame and permitted herself a mental review of the fabrics she'd taken for Liam's assessment. He hadn't made his final choices by the time they had parted, and now she was hoping he would pick the deep rose damask fabric for the parlor. It would be lovely with the carpet of dark blue, beige, and rose he had chosen. Yet he had said he didn't want pink. Would he consider the rose hue to be a shade of pink? If he decided upon the lighter blue, she would focus his attention upon the shades of rose in the carpeting.

She couldn't help but think of Liam and how kind he had been—gently massaging her head until the pain ebbed, tenderly holding her hands as he spoke to her about loneliness. Along with these thoughts, however, came reminders of Mrs. Potter's negative comments and Ruth's persistence that Daughtie would ruin her life by associating with the Irishman. Daughtie knew that most people would take the same stand as her dear friend. The Irish were despised; they were associated with brawling and papist views. *But Liam's not like that. He's neither a brawler nor a papist. The poor man isn't even sure about God, much less the complications of religious views,* she thought to herself.

Then her musings traveled to those silent moments outside the boardinghouse. *He kissed me.* Her hand went to her cheek again. What did it mean?

Was it just the sweet gesture of a friend?

Drawing the threads through the harness, Daughtie worked with expert speed until her thoughts were interrupted by the sounds of Mr. Kingman's shouts, which could now be heard over the rumbling sound of the looms. Daughtie glanced over her shoulder. Mr. Kingman was moving toward her with Delia Masters following close by his side. Daughtie gazed toward Delia, and a hard knot formed in her stomach. Fear burned bright in Delia's pale gray eyes as she passed by Daughtie's frame.

The sounds from the weaving room began to subside as the looms groaned into a halting silence. Daughtie stared in disbelief as operatives began filing down the hallway and out of the building. "What's happening?" she shouted as Ruth neared.

"Those of us who signed up for the turnout are leaving now. They're discharging Delia, and we're leaving in protest."

"But the turnout isn't scheduled until the first of March," Daughtie argued.

Ruth nodded. "Yes, but when they terminated Mary, we all agreed that if it happened again, we would immediately begin the turnout. I've got to go. I'm supposed to notify the girls at the Tremont that the turnout's begun. Are you going to join us?"

Daughtie bit her bottom lip. "No. I'm not going to participate."

Ruth appeared startled. "But Delia's our friend and she's losing her job. I can understand those girls who have families to support remaining at their machines. But surely *you're* going to support Delia's bravery."

"No, Ruth. You know my position. We've discussed this over and over. I wouldn't expect Delia to compromise her beliefs for me, and I won't change my own on her account," Daughtie replied unwaveringly.

Ruth's searing glare went through her like a sharp knife, and profound sorrow seeped into Daughtie's heart as she picked up her steel hook and once again began pulling threads through the harness. Two hours later, the dinner bell pealed from the tower, and the machinery droned into quietude as the remaining operatives rushed toward the stairway. Daughtie joined them and hurried down the stairs.

As the throng of workers bustled through the mill yard, a procession of girls marched past the entrance, heading off toward the center of town. Daughtie stood watching until the last few demonstrators disappeared around the corner. She should go and eat dinner, but her curiosity nagged like a puppy nipping at her heels. Glancing over her shoulder, she gazed at the girls who were already making their way toward the boardinghouses and their noonday meals. Her stomach growled, and she gave momentary consideration to following them. "I'd rather know what's going on in town than eat," she muttered, lifting her skirts and running down the street.

The sight of Delia standing atop a stack of boxes, her hair blowing free as she waved her calash high into the air, brought Daughtie to an immediate halt. Ruth was standing near her side.

"We must take heed of our rights and prove to the moneyed aristocracy that they cannot trample on the rights of their female employees. I beseech you to sign our resolution vowing to discontinue your labors until terms of reconciliation are made. There are petitions circulating among you as I speak. Sign now and support your sisters in their crusade," Delia shouted to the cheering women.

A young operative tugged at Daughtie's cape and pointed toward Delia. "Isn't she wonderful? I'm going up to sign the petition right now."

The girl didn't wait for an answer. Instead, she rushed off toward one of the petitions Ruth was now waving heavenward like a flag of glory. Sorrow etched Daughtie's face as she bowed her head against the wind and turned toward home.

❧ 19 ❧

J osiah Baines scuttled across the room and threw himself into a chair like an
ill-mannered child. "This turnout at the mills has completely interrupted
my schedule. I thought the agents and supervisors had this matter under control. If they can't handle their employees, why are we paying them?"

Nathan inhaled and then removed an intricately carved pipe from between
his clenched teeth. "If you find the meetings an undue burden, please don't
feel obligated to attend, Josiah. I'd be happy to act as your proxy," Nathan said,
his exhaled smoke mingling with the words and floating off toward the ceiling.

"Which would also ensure an earlier conclusion to the meetings," Tracy
mumbled.

"I take that statement to mean you gentlemen believe I'm the sole cause
of these infernal meetings that last well into the early morning hours. And
where is Kirk?"

"Take it however you choose, Josiah. I'm weary of your petulant attitude.
We all have busy schedules and other business interests that require our attention. Either give me your proxy and take your leave, or permit me to begin
the meeting," Nathan replied. "As to Kirk's whereabouts, he is suffering with
a bout of illness and has sent Matthew to represent him at this meeting."

Nathan turned away from Josiah and focused his gaze upon Matthew.
"Although we wish Kirk could be in attendance, we all realize that the information you relate to us will be directly from his perspective. I know we will
profit much from what you have to tell us, Matthew. Why don't you begin?"

"Thank you, Nathan, for your kind words. Gentlemen, I appreciate your
understanding. Kirk's profound desire was to be here tonight. In fact, he gave
serious consideration to overriding the doctor's warning against travel—until
his wife got wind of his plans."

The room resonated with telltale laughter.

"As you are aware, the turnout is over, most of the operatives are back to
work, and wages have been reduced by ten percent. I wish I could report that
the workers are satisfied with what has occurred. Unfortunately, that is impossible. There are still rumblings of anger from time to time, although to our
knowledge, there are no plans for future strikes."

"It's beyond me how Kirk ever permitted such an occurrence," Josiah growled.

Matthew leveled a thoughtful look in Josiah's direction. "Tell me, good sir, without the ability to leave wages intact, how did you expect Mr. Boott to prevent such an incident? We can hardly lock the employees in the building. And even if we could, how would you propose we force them to operate their machines?"

"Perhaps he should develop a better relationship with the workers so that they value his opinion and accept the decisions of the Corporation as being in their best interests," Josiah retaliated.

"The workers at the Lowell mills are endowed with the same reasoning powers and intelligence God gave you, Mr. Baines. They are not animals we can herd about and prod into submission. We had hoped the workers would not turn out when management agreed to a ten percent reduction rather than the original twenty-five percent. I might add that the agents, supervisors, and Mr. Boott believe that the number of strikers was dramatically decreased due to that very action on your part."

Josiah rose from his chair and began pacing in front of the fireplace. "Well, of course you're going to report there was a decrease in strikers due to our change in percentages because, truth is, there's no way of knowing how many would have walked out if we'd just left it at twenty-five percent."

Matthew nodded. "That's true. But we had reports that there were as many as fifteen hundred threatening to strike when the wage reduction was set at the higher figure. Our final count showed that there were only eight hundred who actually left the mills. I think we should give credit to the supervisors that we lost little in production time through the turnout. They managed to have us at full production within a week while maintaining a continuum of dignity and calm inside the mills."

"Hear! Hear!" Tracy said, raising his glass of port.

"Except for a few of the organizers who were discharged and a handful of others who decided to return to their farms, the employees returned to work and now are adhering to all rules of the Corporation. Quite frankly, it's as though the incident never took place."

"Hah! Do you read newspapers, Mr. Cheever? We're either notorious bandits taking food from the mouths of babes or shrewd businessmen who have perfected the art of coercing these young women to do our bidding."

"You exaggerate, Josiah. I've seen only one report that spoke ill of our tactics," Nathan argued. "Most reports state the girls are highly paid unskilled workers who are unable to comprehend the economics of business, and were their minds able to digest such information, they would be on their knees thanking God above for the kindness of the Corporation."

"He's right, Josiah. You always tend to overstate the negative," Tracy concluded. "Granted, this was an unfortunate event, and we can hope it never recurs. However, should we face these same problems in the future, I hope we will be blessed with the same fine results we've seen this time."

"Well, what else is there to say, then? You gentlemen are all pleased, and I don't see that we have any recourse against the employees. After all, we need them," Josiah replied, once again taking his seat. "So is that it? Are we through for the night?"

Nathan pulled a linen handkerchief from his pocket and mopped his brow. "As I said earlier, you're free to leave at any time. As for the rest of us, I'm planning to discuss plans for the railroad and possibly make some final decisions."

Josiah wriggled back in his chair. "The railroad is going to cost us money that we can ill afford to spend. Since I believe we need to reevaluate this whole railroad idea, I suppose I'll be remaining for the balance of the meeting."

Tracy leaned forward, resting his forearms across his thighs, and met Josiah's gaze. "There's that negative approach rearing its ugly head again, Josiah."

Matthew remained standing near Nathan's desk. "If I could have time for one more issue before you begin your discussion of the railroad?"

"Of course, my boy. I thought you had completed Kirk's report."

"Mr. Boott asked that I make you aware of the fact that farmers who live in proximity to Pawtucket Falls have become increasingly distressed due to the ongoing problems caused by the dam."

"Balderdash! That dam was erected years ago," Josiah responded. "Why is this even being brought up for discussion?"

"If you'll let me finish, Mr. Baines, I'll try to explain," Matthew replied patiently. "During the past couple of years, we've had more rain than usual. To a certain extent, the farms have flooded ever since the dam was erected. However, with the increased rains the past few years, the flooding has caused crop failures that are sending the farmers into ruination. And then there's the problem with the fish. The consistently high waters make it impossible for them to spawn, and we're receiving complaints from not only the farmers and citizens who depend upon the fish in those waters for their own dinner tables or to supplement their income but also the citizens living in Lowell. Kirk is concerned that this problem could escalate if we don't address it and at least attempt to look toward a solution—something we can report to the farmers that will hold them in abeyance or ease their minds."

Josiah grunted. "Hold them in abeyance? What are they planning to do? *They* can't strike. Personally, I don't see the need to appease them. Besides, we need the dam."

Henry Thorne had remained quiet throughout the evening but now raised his hand to be recognized. Nathan nodded. "Yes, Henry?"

"We don't want to be perceived as the villain in all of our dealings. The good people that farmed the Chelmsford soil already believe that they were wronged when the Corporation purchased land for the mills. Now the few farmers who've been able to remain believe their livelihood is being jeopardized. Perhaps we won't suffer financial losses due to this issue, but we do stand to lose the working relationship that's been cultivated with the farmers over the past years."

Nathan nodded. "That's true, Henry, but I don't know what we're to do. We can't release additional water without jeopardizing the operation of the mills."

"I know we can't do that. Has Kirk offered any solution? What about the possibility of increasing the size of the millpond? Is that feasible?" Henry asked.

"Mr. Boott gave me no possible solution to offer you," Matthew said. "I have no idea if it's possible to enlarge the millpond."

"What about having the engineers at the Locks and Canals Division study that prospect and report to Kirk?" Tracy inquired.

"Sounds reasonable," Nathan replied.

"The cost of labor alone to perform such a feat would be prohibitive," Josiah countered. "Let them present their argument to the courts if they think they have legal standing. Are we going to cave in at every whim?"

"Could we agree merely to investigate the possibility?" Tracy inquired. "At least it will give Kirk something he can tell the farmers. Before we begin worrying about the cost, Josiah, let's find out if it's even a possibility to expand."

"I think that's an excellent idea," Henry replied.

"Of course you do," Josiah muttered.

The measure passed, with Josiah casting the only dissenting vote.

"I'll write out instructions to Kirk," Nathan told Matthew. "Was there anything else you wanted to bring before us?"

"We are assuming the Corporation will sponsor the Blowing Out Ball as scheduled?"

"Yes, of course. It's business—and pleasure—as usual," Nathan replied.

Matthew gave a quick nod and took his seat. "Then that's all I have."

"We appreciate your reports, Matthew. Now let's get on with discussing the railroad. Spring is already upon us, and if the railroad is to progress as scheduled, we need to be prepared."

"Good idea, Nathan. I'd like all of you to consider the possibility of opening a machine shop to build locomotives. I believe we have the caliber of men in the Locks and Canals Division who can see this to fruition. We would save money as well as bolster the economy of Lowell and the Corporation," Tracy Jackson said.

Josiah sighed and slumped deeper into his chair. "Is there nothing you men won't think of to bring us into total decline? The *last* thing we should be doing right now is thinking of expansion. We need to rein ourselves in and pay heed to the financial condition of the company and the country. The banks may well all close their doors after Andrew Jackson's through with them. On top of that, there's the fact that steam locomotives are quite untested and unproven as far as I'm concerned. Just because the British are having success with them doesn't mean the same will be true for us. We need to practice caution, but you all seem to want to rush in on a whim."

"It's hardly a whim, Josiah. We are men of vision," Tracy replied frankly. "Men of vision are willing to risk the future on untried creations because, like it or not, it is the new inventions and industries that will take us forward in progress. Even if there are problems and failures, the situation will eventually be mastered and life will be better because of it. Mark my words, the railroad will transform this country. Within the next twenty years we'll see railroads crisscrossing this country as the major form of long-distance transportation."

"Don't be ridiculous," Josiah protested. "Such machinery and the tracks necessary to move them about will be too costly. And, I might ask, who do you suppose is going to be willing to pay the thousands—no, the millions of dollars that it will cost to finance such inventions?"

Tracy smiled rather smugly. "Men of vision, Josiah. Men of vision will finance such inventions."

"Perhaps, but now is hardly the time for foolish investments." Josiah's face reddened as if the strain of the conversation were too much for him. "The mills can ill afford to add this expense. Think of it, gentlemen. We just reduced wages—how can we justify building a locomotive machine shop?"

Matthew listened intently as the discussion wore on. Kirk would expect extensive details of the meeting—especially Tracy's viewpoint—since Boott also favored the locomotive project. In fact, he'd heard discussion between the two men several weeks ago when Tracy had visited Lowell immediately after the turnout, so the topic came as no surprise. By the time Josiah finally convinced the men to reconvene at a later date before making a final decision on the machine shop, it was nearing midnight.

"You planning to remain in Boston for a few days?" Nathan asked as he escorted Matthew to the front door.

"No. I'll be leaving in the morning. I must be back in Lowell to make final arrangements for the Blowing Out Ball. I doubt my wife would forgive me if I were the cause of an improperly planned ball," he replied with a grin.

Nathan gave him a broad smile. "I understand. Please advise Kirk that most of us plan to be in attendance. I'm holding out hope that Josiah will remain at home."

"I heard that remark, Nathan, and I'm sorry to disappoint you, but I plan to attend. I want to have a few words with Kirk. Perhaps he'll listen to a voice of reason and see that this machine shop idea is pure folly. Besides, I might be able to give him a few pointers for handling those irate farmers."

Nathan arched his eyebrows, his lips turning up in a patronizing smile. "You do that, Josiah. I'm sure Kirk will be pleased to have your counsel."

~ 20 ~

Lowell

I wish I hadn't agreed to attend the ball with Dr. Ketter," Daughtie lamented while stitching a row of lace along the neckline of her dress.

Ruth stretched out on the bed and wound a loose thread around her finger. "I was hoping the girls who participated in the turnout wouldn't attend the ball. Instead, they're fluttering around as though dancing with members of the Corporation is the greatest honor they could ever hope for."

"I don't know about dancing with the Boston Associates, but attending the ball is a treat for most folks—at least for those who work in the mills. You ought not fault the girls for wanting to have an evening of enjoyment."

Ruth snorted. "I'll fault them if I want to. When I told Mrs. Arnold I was thinking of staying home, she said it would be unwise, especially for anyone who participated in the strike. She thinks the supervisors may monitor our behavior for a while."

"Mrs. Arnold's probably correct. If anyone knows how these supervisors think, surely she does. After all, she was married to one," Daughtie replied. "Besides, I told Dr. Ketter you would be attending with us."

"*What?* I'm not going with the two of you."

"Oh, yes, you are. After all, it was you that encouraged him to invite me, and don't bother denying it. I know you've been busy playing the matchmaker almost from the day he arrived. If you won't attend with us, then I'm going to tell him I must cancel on my commitment because I won't attend without my dearest friend."

Ruth flipped over on the bed like a salmon floundering on the banks of the Pawtucket. "Well, I'll not dance with those pompous men, I can tell you that much for certain. And should one of them ask, he'd get a firm refusal."

"So long as you're courteous, I doubt whether anyone could fault you for refusing. However, Sarah told me the girls actually line up in order to dance with the men, so I think you need not worry."

"Oh, what does Sarah know? She's never attended a ball," Ruth argued. "You'd best watch what you're doing. You're sewing that lace on crooked." Her brows furrowed into wavy lines of disapproval.

Daughtie poked her needle into the fabric and took another stitch. "My sewing is fine, but you're certainly in foul humor. What are you going to wear to the ball?"

Ruth scooted upward and leaned against the wooden headboard. "If I must go, I'll wear the same dress I wear to church on Sundays. If that's not fancy enough for those self-important men, they can tell me so and I'll give them an earful. I'll be quick to tell them that I can't afford to buy a new dress now that wages have been reduced."

"I believe you'd actually *enjoy* being confronted by one of them."

"Indeed I would!"

"There. I think I'm done," Daughtie said while inspecting her dress. "What do you think?"

"I still think the lace is crooked."

Daughtie giggled. "The lace is not crooked. I'm going out for a while, but I'll be back by nine-thirty. Why don't you go downstairs and visit with Mrs. Arnold and Theona?"

Ruth swung around on the bed, her shoes thumping as they hit the floor. "Where are you going? You're not scheduled to work at the library, and you don't quilt at Mrs. Cheever's home until next week. Are you going to buy something special for the ball? A new comb or reticule, perhaps? I'll go with you."

"No," Daughtie replied a tad too quickly.

Ruth's eyes darkened a shade as she leveled an accusatory look in Daughtie's direction. "You're going to see Liam Donohue! Don't even try to deny it."

Daughtie remained silent as she tucked away the sewing box and carefully returned her dress to a peg on the wall. Retrieving her cape, she walked toward the bedroom door.

"You *are* going to see him!" Ruth's voice was filled with surprise. "Otherwise, you would have denied my accusation."

Daughtie hastened out the door and down the stairway, with Ruth following close on her heels.

"What are you thinking?" Ruth hissed. "You can't keep running off to that Irishman's house."

Peeking into the dining room, Daughtie waved at Theona and Mrs. Arnold. "I'm going out for a while. I'll see you in the morning."

"Have a pleasant evening, dear," Mrs. Arnold said before turning her attention toward Ruth. "Are you going, too?" she asked Ruth, who had nearly appended herself to Daughtie's side.

"I believe I will," she said. "What do you think of *that*?" she asked, giving Daughtie a smug grin.

Daughtie continued fastening her cloak. "If you'd like to join me, I'd be pleased to have your company. Shall I wait while you get your cape?"

Ruth furrowed her brows in obvious confusion. "So you're not going to Liam Donohue's house?" she whispered.

"I don't see what difference it makes. Are you coming or not? I really need to be on my way," Daughtie replied.

"I suppose I'll stay home since you won't divulge where you're going."

Daughtie nodded and walked out the door. A sigh of relief escaped her lips. Taking Ruth along would have ended in catastrophe. Not that Liam would have been inhospitable, but Ruth—well, no doubt she would have acted boorish and aloof.

Daughtie dabbed her nose with an embroidered linen handkerchief. "I believe I'm coming down with something. My throat feels scratchy, and I've had the sniffles for two days."

"It's nothing but the fibers in the air at work. You're not fooling me, Daughtie. You'd best get dressed. Dr. Ketter said we would leave for the ball in less than an hour. I'm still disappointed you didn't accept his invitation to have supper at the Merrimack House."

"If you had your way, I'd spend every free moment with Dr. Ketter. Why would I want to go to supper with him? After all, we dine together twice a day, occasionally three times if he manages to get out of bed early enough for breakfast. Going out to supper with him would be a wasteful expense."

Ruth wagged her head back and forth. "Well, it is his money, and if he wants to take you to a nice restaurant for supper, you should accept. He asked you to accompany him to see *The Heir at Law* when the professional players appeared in Lowell, but I understand you refused that invitation, also."

"And how would you know? Are you and Dr. Ketter conspiring? Have you been acting as his advisor and confidante?" Daughtie asked while fashioning her hair into a pile of cascading curls.

Ruth plopped down on the bed and gave a quick nod. "How do you manage to fix your hair without a mirror?"

"The Shakers believe that staring into a looking glass fosters vanity. There was only one small mirror for use by all of the Sisters, and if you were caught staring into it, you were reprimanded. Accordingly, I grew up styling my hair without a mirror. Of course, we didn't wear our hair in fashionable styles. I've discovered it takes more time to create curls, but I don't find it requires a mirror," she said. "You didn't answer my question. Have you been urging Dr. Ketter to pursue me?"

"I wouldn't say I've *urged* him."

"Just what would you say?"

Ruth tapped her index finger on the bedpost as though the matter took deep contemplation. "Encouraged! I've encouraged him."

Daughtie gave her a sidelong glance. "Well, I'd appreciate it if you'd cease your encouragement. I'm not interested in Dr. Ketter, and he should spend his energy wooing another."

"After tonight, you may change your mind. He has quite an evening planned," Ruth replied with a secretive grin.

Dr. Ketter stood waiting at the foot of the stairs. "You ladies look absolutely lovely," he said, his gaze fixed upon Daughtie. He took her hand in his own and placed a fleeting kiss upon her extended fingers.

Daughtie flinched at his familiarity, but his grip tightened as she attempted to pull away.

"Shall we?" he inquired, pulling open the front door with his free hand while still holding on to Daughtie. Ruth giggled, obviously amused by Daughtie's noticeable discomfort. Dr. Ketter carefully looped Daughtie's arm through his own as though she were his prized possession. "I attempted to hire a carriage, but there were none available when I checked at the livery. However, Ruth tells me you enjoy walking, so I hope you won't mind since it's such a lovely starlit evening."

"Walking is fine," Daughtie replied. "I'm unaccustomed to riding in a carriage."

"Ruth tells me you have quite a talent for sewing and decorating," he said. "Perhaps you could assist me with my living quarters."

"I'm rather busy right now. I've committed to the library and several other matters, and I doubt I'd have adequate time. But Ruth has quite an eye for design herself. Since you two have become such close friends, perhaps she could help you."

"You would be a *much* better choice," Ruth insisted, leveling a glare in Daughtie's direction.

"Daughtie! Ruth!" Amanda Corbett called out. "Wait for us!" A group of six girls, with Amanda in the lead, came scurrying down the street in their best attire, with hair coifed to perfection and cheeks blushing with anticipation. "Isn't this exciting? I can hardly wait to begin dancing," she said, her blond tresses bouncing up and down as she expressed her delight. "And aren't you the most fortunate one of all, Daughtie. You'll be able to dance all of the dances with Dr. Ketter."

"I'm not fond of dancing, so I'm certain Dr. Ketter will be happy to sign all of your dance cards," Daughtie offered as they reached Phineas Whiting's establishment.

"Oh, would you, Dr. Ketter? That would be *so* kind. I understand the girls always outnumber the gentlemen by at least six or seven to one." Amanda thrust her card into Dr. Ketter's hand.

Before Dr. Ketter could assist Daughtie with her cape, he was surrounded by a group of chattering girls, each one vying for his signature. "Could we each have two dances with you?" one of the girls pleaded.

Dr. Ketter handed the cards back and reached around Daughtie's shoulders to assist with her cloak. "I've promised each of you a dance and two dances to Ruth. Surely you wouldn't want me to ignore Daughtie. She'll never agree to accompany me again if I don't designate most of my time to her."

"Oh, I don't want to be selfish. I'm more than willing to share your time and attention," Daughtie replied.

"Dr. Ketter's correct. We're already taking advantage of his time. Let's don't be greedy," Ruth admonished.

Daughtie met Ruth's steely glare with a smug grin. "I see a table that will accommodate all of us," she said, pointing to the left side of the room and leading the way. The others fell in step behind her, and as they settled themselves at the table, Amanda strategically placed herself at Dr. Ketter's left while Daughtie sat to his right.

The musicians were seated along the north wall, and the sound of their stringed instruments filled the room with soft music. Daughtie kept her gaze focused upon the feet of the dancers as they waltzed to the melody. "This is nothing like Shaker dancing. I'm not certain I could dance like that," she whispered to Ruth.

"It's really quite simple. I'm certain you'd be willing to try if *Liam Donohue* was asking to be your partner," Ruth snidely replied.

Daughtie stared at Ruth momentarily and then turned away. The remark didn't deserve a reply, she decided.

"Oh, look! Mr. and Mrs. Cheever have arrived," Amanda said while pointing toward the door. "Doesn't she look exquisite?"

Matthew Cheever led Lilly onto the dance floor as Daughtie turned in their direction. "Indeed!" she replied, unable to think of adequate words to describe Mrs. Cheever's stunning appearance. Lilly Cheever's pale yellow gown was lined with satin the shade of summer daffodils and embellished with sheer ivory lace. Tiny yellow flowers that perfectly matched the dress surrounded her intricately arranged curls. There was little doubt anyone would outshine Mrs. Cheever this evening; she was the epitome of loveliness.

"Did you know they're to have a baby?" Amanda questioned. "I heard it talked about just the other day."

Daughtie nodded, having known for some time that Lilly would give birth to another Cheever heir in July. She noted the woman's beautiful attire and slim figure that was only now starting to thicken at the waist. It was hard to believe Lilly was even expecting.

"I love babies," another of the girls added. "I would love to be a nanny instead of a mill girl."

"Oh, they look so wonderful together," Amanda said with a sigh.

Dr. Ketter leaned toward Daughtie. "I would enjoy the pleasure of this dance," he whispered into her ear. "I think we might look wonderful together, as well."

Daughtie stiffened. "As I explained when you invited me, I'm not accustomed to this type of dancing. Why don't you dance with one of the other girls, and I'll watch until I'm more familiar with the steps."

His lips tightened into a thin line, but he finally nodded in agreement. He moved to the other side of the table and held out his hand to Ruth with a smile on his face. She rose and he escorted her onto the dance floor. As promised, Daughtie watched the couples and attempted to memorize their movements as they twirled around the room. Each time Dr. Ketter returned and gazed in her direction, she signaled to wait just a little longer. After fulfilling his dance card obligations to most of the doting girls who had accompanied them into the hall, Daughtie finally succumbed to his request.

Ivan pulled her into his arms, his lips curved into a broad smile as he began to lead her to the steps of a waltz.

"Let's stay close to the outer perimeter. I don't want my clumsiness to interfere with the other dancers," Daughtie requested, pushing against the pressure of his hand on the small of her back as he attempted to lead her into the crowd.

He acquiesced, and they moved somewhat clumsily, with Daughtie making a valiant attempt to follow Ivan's lead.

She grimaced when her foot came down hard atop his boot. "I'm sorry," she apologized with a weak smile.

"No need to apologize. Practice makes perfect. We'll just keep trying," he replied in a cheery tone.

When the musicians announced the need for a few minutes to refresh themselves, Daughtie sighed with relief. Taking Ivan's arm, she joined the throng of dancers moving back toward their tables. However, Ivan pulled her to a stop when shouting voices and the sound of pounding feet drifted into the room. He drew her close to his side as several men burst through the front door of the Old Stone House.

"Where's Mr. Boott and Mr. Cheever?" one of the men shouted. His eyes glistened in the flickering light cast by the sperm-oil lamps. He gazed about the room, his panic obvious for all to see.

Kirk and Matthew approached the men and began talking in hushed whispers while the partygoers milled about, obviously hoping to overhear some snippet of their conversation. Several minutes passed before Kirk finally requested that the partygoers take their seats. The guests strained forward, watching as he mounted the small platform being used by the musicians.

"I've just received word that there are vandals attempting to destroy the

Pawtucket Dam at this very moment. I need able-bodied men to accompany us, men prepared to block these evildoers by any means necessary. If you have easily accessible weapons, bring them with you. I don't want any bloodshed, but we don't know if these men are armed."

"Who are these miscreants? Do you have any idea, Mr. Boott?" someone called out from across the room.

"We've been told they are farmers from the surrounding area. However, there may be those among them who merely enjoy a fracas. We can't be certain. One thing is clear: this matter requires our immediate attention. Ladies, I apologize for leaving you without dance partners, but perhaps you can remain and enjoy the company of one another as well as the food that's been prepared. I'm hoping we'll soon return and the evening will not be totally spoiled. Gentlemen, please join me," he encouraged, obviously hopeful the men would rally to the cause.

The scraping of chairs echoed throughout the hall, and men scurried toward the door. Daughtie turned toward Ivan, who remained seated beside her. "You'd best get your medical bag and accompany them," she urged. "If the men resort to fisticuffs, they'll need medical aid."

"I suppose you're right," he acknowledged, though still not moving. "But my preference is to remain here with you."

"I imagine the other men would prefer to remain here, too. However, they're already on their way."

He placed an arm across the back of Daughtie's chair and drew near. "But they didn't have the pleasure of escorting *you*. If they had, they'd still be here, too," he whispered.

Daughtie leaned back and met his gaze. Both his words and the look in his eyes caused her discomfort.

Matthew pulled back on the reins and brought the carriage to a halt in front of the Old Stone House. As the men began scurrying out of the building, Matthew directed them to the livery. "Kirk, Nathan, Josiah, and I will meet you at Kittredge's. Mr. Kittredge has two wagons we can use. He's hitching up the teams. It's best we travel as a group," Matthew called after them. He waited until the three men were settled into the carriage and then flicked the reins.

"Seems it's just one problem after another here in Lowell," Josiah complained, grasping Kirk's arm as the carriage wheeled around at breakneck speed. "Could you slow the horses down before this carriage turns over?" he shouted while tapping Matthew on the back with his silver-tipped walking stick. "Is there some sort of management problem, Kirk?"

Nathan turned in his seat and glared at Josiah. "As I recall, you're the one who said we should ignore the farmers' complaints and grumbled because we held a discussion of the issue. And let me see, weren't you the one who voted *against* exploring the possibility of expanding the millpond?"

"No need for sarcasm, Nathan," Josiah replied. "Did you tell the farmers we're attempting to renovate the millpond, Kirk?"

Matthew slowed the carriage as they neared the livery and motioned the men to follow. Both wagons were filled with men, a number of them bearing weapons—either their own or those loaned to them by Mr. Kittredge, Matthew surmised.

Once they were on the road to the dam, Josiah turned his attention back to Kirk. "You didn't answer my question. Did you talk to the farmers?"

"Yes, they've been advised. However, they expressed their dissatisfaction with the idea, saying they weren't going to wait until engineers did a survey and report. Instead, they said they'd handle it in their own way. I suppose this is what they meant. Let's hope they don't have a keg of gunpowder waiting to greet us."

"You actually think they might destroy the dam?"

"That's what I explained at our Boston meeting, Mr. Baines. They want the dam out of there," Matthew called over his shoulder.

The horses raced on, their hooves drumming out a warning of the approaching wagons. "Up there, Kirk!" Nathan shouted, pointing toward the dam. "It looks as though there may be thirty or forty men. Let's pray they don't have weapons leveled in our direction."

The instant Nathan's words had been uttered, Kirk leaned forward and shouted in Matthew's direction, "Stop the carriage. Now!"

Matthew pulled hard on the reins, hoping the wagons behind him would stop in time. "What's wrong?" he shouted to Kirk.

"Nathan's words made me wonder if they might have those men out in the open to entice us onward. There may be an ambush up ahead. I don't want to ride directly into harm's way. Have one or two of the men make their way closer. They can see if there's a trap and discover what's actually happening closer to the dam. Surely the farmers have men watching the road. They've likely heard us coming."

"I'll go," Matthew volunteered.

"No! I forbid it. I'll not have you risking your life. Ask one of the men in the other wagons to go."

Matthew swung about, startled at Kirk's request. "My life is no more valuable than any of those men!"

In the dim moonlight, Kirk's features appeared carved in granite. "Don't question my decisions. Do as you're told." His voice had taken on the harshness of a father reprimanding his errant son.

Matthew stalked off toward the wagons without a word. Anything he wanted to say would be disrespectful. He neared the first wagon. "Any volunteers to see if there's an ambush lying in wait up the road? We need two or three men."

"You afeared to go?" Thomas Getty hollered with a loud guffaw before jumping down from the wagon. Two other men joined Thomas, both of them obviously amused by his remark.

"I volunteered, but Mr. Boott refused my offer."

"Of course he did," Thomas replied, his retort followed by another round of laughter. "Let's get going before Matthew insists upon replacing one of us."

Matthew gazed heavenward. Attempting to defend himself had only made matters worse. "Get your instructions from Mr. Boott before you rush off. And each of you needs to take a weapon," he called after them. One of the men came racing back to the wagon and retrieved a rifle from one of his friends. He nodded at Matthew, his grin still intact as he scurried after the other two men, who were already making their way down the dark roadway.

"That was most embarrassing," Matthew mumbled while climbing back into the carriage.

A volley of gunfire cracked through the dark silence shrouding their carriage. "Better embarrassed than dead. I hope none of them is injured," Kirk matter-of-factly replied. "We need at least one of them to get back here with a report."

Matthew stared in disbelief. As far as he was concerned, Kirk's remarks went beyond callous. They were both self-serving and cruel. "These men volunteered to assist us. I can't believe you feel no distress over their welfare."

Kirk shook his head in disgust. "Distress? What good does it do if I sit here wringing my hands like a frightened child? I spent my early adulthood in England training for the military. Battle requires intelligent tactical decisions and people who carry out orders without question. I'll not apologize for exemplary battlefield behavior."

"But those men are not *soldiers* under your command; they're ordinary citizens," Matthew argued.

"Technically, you're correct, but they are also employees who are dependent upon their positions in the mills. If the dam is destroyed, they'll find themselves without wages until it's reconstructed. They may not be soldiers, but they *are* men fighting for their livelihood."

A rumbling explosion sounded in the distance, and the ground shuddered underfoot. The two men silenced their arguing while all eyes focused upon Kirk and awaited his direction.

"Hold fast!" he called out as Thomas Getty came racing toward them.

Chest heaving and gasping for breath, Thomas clung to the side of the buggy. "We need to advance around the woods to the left. They set off an explosion to block our path, and they're readying to blow up the dam."

Kirk shouted for the wagons to follow, and Matthew grasped Thomas by the arm. "Get in the carriage!" he hollered, assisting Thomas up before cracking the whip and sending the horses into a gallop. "Direct the way!" he shouted to Thomas.

Thomas pointed toward a growth of trees. "You'll need to slow down. We've got to navigate through those tall pines. Horace and Zedediah are waiting for us."

"No injuries, then?" Matthew asked.

"No, we're all fine, but that explosion scared the stuffin' out of Zed," he said with a chuckle. "Lodged a particle of fear in me, but I didn't tell Horace or Zed. They don't think nothing bothers me." As their progress slowed, he stated, "Think we'll do better on foot from here on out. Too hard to get the wagons through the rocks and trees, and some of their men may be scattered about out here. Besides, the wagons make too much noise." Thomas then emitted an eerie hooting sound that brought Zed and Horace running toward them.

"There's more of us than them," Horace reported. "I made it over to the dam. They're getting powder kegs ready to set off, so we need to get moving. Best be careful where you shoot. If we hit one of them kegs, we'll all be blown to kingdom come."

Kirk gathered the men close. "Stay together until I signal. Then separate into four groups," he said, quickly pushing the men into four clusters. "When you hear a single gunshot, I want those of you with weapons to fire them into the air. When they hear gunfire coming from four different directions, I'm hoping they'll believe they're mightily outnumbered and surrounded. If we can frighten them off without bloodshed, I'll be satisfied."

Thomas aligned with one group of the men. "I don't aim to kill no one, but if they start shooting at us, we'll have to return fire. This could turn into a massacre. I don't think none of us want to see that happen, Mr. Boott."

Kirk nodded his agreement. "I don't, either, so let's be cautious and pray for the best," he said, signaling the men to move out.

"Apparently the suggestion of prayer was only a figure of speech," Matthew murmured before silently making his own plea for safety among them and taking his assigned position near the rear.

"Mr. Boott appears confident. If I didn't know better, I'd almost believe he was enjoying himself," one of the men beside Matthew remarked.

"I wouldn't go so far as to say he's enjoying himself. He's likely remembering all those years of military instruction years ago. I'd guess he's surprised to be putting the training into use at a small dam in Lowell," Matthew replied. "There's the signal to break off into our section and head south."

Kirk's lone shot resonated in the distance. The men followed instructions, answering his single blast with a volley of gunfire. The countryside was filled with the sound of gunfire, shouting men, and pounding feet trampling through the woods.

"Hold your fire!" The order echoed down through the ranks in a ripple effect.

When the shadowy wooded area had once again grown silent, Kirk summoned Matthew forward. "They want to talk," he told Matthew. "I want you to go with me. Some of them will recognize you. If we're lucky, they'll still consider you one of their own and be more responsive to us."

"I doubt my presence will aid you, but I'm happy to lend my assistance," Matthew replied.

It took but a few minutes to walk the short distance to a clearing near the dam. No less than twenty angry-looking men, all of them armed, stood waiting as they made their appearance. "We have no weapons," Kirk said. He moved slowly, careful to show the men he truly was unarmed. Matthew, following Kirk's example, moved forward and stood beside him.

Matthew squinted into the darkness. "Simon? Is that you?"

Simon Fenske edged his way forward between two men. "Yep—sure is."

"I'm surprised to see you among these men. I've always known you to be a man of reason, not one who would join forces with a group intent on taking the law into their own hands," Matthew said, moving closer.

"Don't try to influence me with your flattering words, Matthew. I'm here because I support this cause. Not all of us sold out to the Corporation. *We* still earn our living from the land," Simon replied harshly.

"If we're to continue fishing and farming this land, we need this water running free like God intended. Either tear down this dam or we will!" another man shouted.

A chorus of support rang out from the surrounding throng, and soon the men were shouting in cadence: "Tear down the dam! Tear down the dam! Tear down the dam!"

Kirk waited patiently and then slowly waved his arm in the air. "If you'll permit me to speak," he shouted, obviously hoping that his voice would be heard above the chanting men. "Gentlemen! Gentlemen!"

With the metal of his weapon gleaming in the moonlight, Simon Fenske gestured to the crowd. The pulsing mantra ebbed into a deafening silence before he finally spoke. "Let's see what Mr. Boott has to say. We don't have to agree, but we've got nothing to lose by hearing him out."

Reluctant nods and murmurs of uncertain compliance hung in the air like gloomy shrouds begging for elimination.

Kirk cleared his throat, tugged at his waistcoat, and gave Matthew a pat on the back. "This young man is one of your own. He's tilled the soil and loves this land like all of you. We've talked at length about the concerns you've expressed over the dam and how it impacts your land and livelihood. We are deeply grieved that while the dam has created industrialization and progress for many of us, it has caused grief and hardship for others. Our goal is to find a reasonable solution, but we can't accomplish anything in haste."

"We can completely destroy the dam in less than an hour," someone shouted from the rear of the group.

"Demolition of property is not the answer," Kirk replied firmly. "We're reasonable men who can solve this problem without harm to one another or the dam. Would you be willing to appoint one among you to act as a representative to meet with us? Someone you trust to speak and make agreements on your behalf?"

"What do you say, men? Do you want to talk or fight?" Simon bellowed.

"You talk to 'em, Simon," John Wells called out, "but we ain't willing to wait until they have all them fancy-pants fellers come from the city to do a report. There's enough men at the Locks and Canals that can figure out what needs to be done to free up this water."

"You willing to talk with 'em, Simon?" another man shouted.

Simon reached up under his cap and scratched his head. "If that's what you want, I'll meet with them. However, I'll not enter into any agreement without the consent of the group. I'm not looking to lose any friends over this."

"Why don't we meet tomorrow morning? Matthew and I can come out to your farm. And any of you other men who want to be present—please feel free to attend," Kirk said, raising his voice so the entire assemblage could hear the offer.

"Tomorrow's fine," Simon replied.

"Do I have your agreement that nothing further will happen here at the dam until we've talked?" Kirk inquired, extending his hand.

"You have our word," Simon said, shaking hands and sealing the agreement.

Daughtie hurried out of the mill, anxious to eat supper and be on her way to Liam's. "Hurry up, Ruth. You're plodding along like a lazy mule."

"I'm tired. Some of us were up very late last night."

"Don't whine. You chose to remain at the ball and lose sleep. I didn't."

"Oh, don't act so self-righteous, Daughtie. The only reason you left the ball was because you thought Dr. Ketter might return. You didn't fool me one jot with your story of a headache and being tired. Running off was an easy way to escape your obligation."

"Escape my obligation? I fulfilled my duty. I attended the ball. *He's* the one who departed the dance."

"At *your* urging. I heard you tell him there might be injuries and he should go along with the men," Ruth rebutted.

"I was thinking of the men, not myself."

"Of course you were. And that's why you rushed home and prepared for bed the minute the men rode out of town." The sarcasm dripped from Ruth's words like thick oozing syrup.

A deafening silence remained between them until they arrived at the boardinghouse. "I don't want to argue," Daughtie said, turning the knob of the front door.

"Good evening, ladies," Ivan Ketter greeted in an exceedingly cordial tone. He gave a slight bow from the waist with one arm carefully tucked behind his back.

"Good evening," Daughtie replied, glancing into the parlor. "You have no patients waiting to be seen?"

In a grand sweeping gesture, Ivan whisked a bouquet of flowers from behind his back. When Daughtie didn't reach out to accept the offering, he thrust the droopy gift directly in her path. "For you," he said, glancing first at her and then at the wilting arrangement. "With my sincere apologies—to make up for last night. And to ask if you would be my guest at the Merrimack House for dinner this evening."

"I'm sorry, but I've already made plans for this evening," she replied, edging toward the stairs.

"Tomorrow, then?" he asked while still holding the flowers.

"No. I'll be working at the library," Daughtie said. "Now if you'll excuse me, I really must go upstairs." Without waiting for a reply, she raced up the stairs at breakneck speed.

Daughtie was sitting on the bed darning a pair of black lisle stockings when Ruth walked in and dropped the bouquet onto the bed beside her. "You forgot your flowers. Ivan asked me to see that you got them. How could you be so cruel, Daughtie?"

"Would it be kinder to lead him on? I've attempted to convince him I have no interest in a social relationship. Unfortunately, he doesn't appear to believe me. I didn't take the flowers because I don't want to accept his gifts. Such behavior would only serve to encourage him."

Ruth grabbed a book from the shelf before turning back toward Daughtie. "You make no sense. You don't want to accept a dinner invitation from an eligible doctor, yet you'll place your reputation at risk by going to the home of that Irishman." Ruth stalked across the room and grabbed the flowers. "I'll return these for you. I wouldn't want you to keep an unwanted gift."

The door slammed, and Daughtie listened to Ruth's heavy footsteps as she descended the stairs. Prolonging an encounter with Ivan Ketter was going to make a prickly situation even more uncomfortable. Folding the darned stockings, she tucked them into a drawer, summoned her courage, and went downstairs to supper.

21

London

Barlow Kent was waiting when William arrived at Crouch's, a small pub carefully tucked between a tailor's shop and tobacconist's store on Murdock Street.

"Surely I'm not late," William said, snapping open his gold pocket watch.

"No, I arrived early," Barlow replied. "Have a seat."

William pulled a chair away from the table and sat down. "You must be anxious for my report."

Barlow leaned forward, resting his arms upon the table. "I'm *anxious* to hear something of value. For nearly four months you've been spoon-feeding us scraps of information with little substance. It's time to make our move."

"You look dour, Barlow. Did they run out of your favorite whiskey?" Chauncy Fuller asked as he approached the table.

Barlow leveled a glare at Chauncy. "If you had any sense, you'd be annoyed, too. I just told Thurston that I've grown weary of this silly charade. Either we're going to agree to do something about Farnsworth or I'll take care of this matter myself. We've been listening to these incessant reports for months, but we're no closer to making definitive plans than we were back in November. Thurston has appeared more intent on tracking down the comings and goings of Farnsworth's nephew, Taylor Manning, than on reining in Farnsworth."

William held his anger in check and gave Barlow a patronizing smile before replying. "Chauncy thought it imperative the information regarding young Manning be substantiated."

"To be honest, I think with the information you had we could have falsely accused him and no one would have been the wiser. Your continued investigation has only served to corroborate his innocence. What earthly good did that do us?"

"We don't want to be made fools when we bring in the law, Barlow," Chauncy explained as though he were speaking to a child. "And the information regarding young Manning came through *my* friendship with Wilburt Talley. Had we gone off ill-advised as you suggest, it's likely we would have caused a breach between Armstrong and Talley's design business and the Lancashire mills. Such an incident would have proved disastrous. Caution and good sense will bring a sound resolution to this situation."

"I'm weary of both of you. Talk—that's all either of you want to do. Well, I for one, am tired of your incessant chatter!"

"Settle yourself, Barlow. Whether you wish to acknowledge the value of William's information is of little consequence. This matter needs deliberate planning, and the reports we've received from William have been indispensable. I don't understand your constant wish to expedite our undertaking. As I said earlier, if we're to be successful, we must prepare well-thought-out plans using all the information available. We now know young Manning is of no concern, and William has been able to focus his attention entirely upon Farnsworth. It makes this matter simpler knowing Manning is of little consequence to us. It appears you've become obsessed over Farnsworth leaving the country; however, all your worry serves no purpose."

Barlow set his glass down with a thud. "Don't speak to me as though I were an unruly child. You don't necessarily know what's best, and there's no guarantee Farnsworth isn't preparing to board a ship for America as we speak. William's *sources* and his unsubstantiated reports don't ease my concerns in the least. We have no idea who these shady characters are or if their information is correct."

William shifted in his chair and narrowed his eyes as he glared at Barlow. "Point out one bit of information in any report I have given you that has been inaccurate," he challenged.

"Thus far it's been correct—at least the little bit that is of consequence. Most of your reports are drivel. I don't care what's occurring in Boston or Lowell. I have no interest in how much cotton they're importing or what the output is per day in the New England mills."

"Well, you *should* be interested, Barlow. The Americans and the advancement of their industrialization have already caused a weakening of our investment in the English mills. Besides, Farnsworth and his family have been under close surveillance, haven't they, William?" Chauncy inquired.

Thurston nodded, his steely-eyed glare still directed at Barlow.

"And who is keeping watch over Farnsworth right now? He could be purchasing his passage to America, and we'd be none the wiser," Barlow countered.

"Trust me. I'll be immediately notified should he make such a purchase. I've already explained I have a man in the ticketing office—who is being well paid, I might add."

"That's just it, William. I *don't* trust you. I don't trust anyone except myself. The two of you are interested in having Farnsworth tried for treason. But I don't care if he's a spy, and I don't want to make an example of him to the English people. I want him *dead!*"

Chauncy gaped across the table in disbelief. William observed the situation unfold like a three-act play. He was now certain that Barlow's mental problems were spiraling out of control; soon the man would be a raving lunatic.

"You need to control yourself," Chauncy warned. "The last thing we need is Farnsworth showing up dead in some dark passageway. John Farnsworth is the only one who can supply the additional information we hope to gain regarding production and any new concepts they're developing for the New England mills."

William watched Chauncy continue speaking to Barlow in a soothing tone. When Barlow finally quieted and ceased his demands, William said, "Barlow may have a point. Perhaps we *should* do away with Farnsworth."

Chauncy swiveled in his chair, his features etched into an astonished stare. "What? Have you gone mad, too?"

"No, but Farnsworth will never voluntarily talk to us. Force will be required in order to gain any meaningful information. Afterward, we dare not release him, for he'd give our names to the authorities. I believe Barlow is correct: Farnsworth must die."

Barlow rubbed his hands together and leaned forward. "Let *me* do it."

William shrugged. "I don't care who kills him, but a plan is necessary. Once he's abducted, we'll need to convince him that if he doesn't talk to us, we'll use threats against his family. We may be forced to actually harm some member of his family in order to prove to him that we mean business."

"Hold up, gentlemen," Chauncy said. "I'm not opposed to abducting Farnsworth and making a few threats to his family. However, I won't condone murder or the abduction of his family members."

"I didn't realize you were so faint of heart, Chauncy. I'm certain Barlow and I can handle this matter if you'd prefer to place us in charge. However, I could use a suggestion of someplace where we can interrogate him."

"No! I will not agree to murder. I must have your word," Chauncy said.

William glanced toward Barlow and gave a slight nod. "You're right, Chauncy. We'll turn him over to the authorities once he's talked. After all, there are three of us. We can deny any allegations he might make against us."

"Right. It's best we leave it to the authorities," Barlow agreed.

William grinned. Barlow had understood and followed his lead. The two of them would handle Farnsworth any way they pleased; Chauncy would have to live with their decision.

"Good! Since we're all in agreement that the authorities will be called in once we've questioned Farnsworth, I suggest you move ahead with his abduction, William. I have a rather unpleasant room adjacent to my wine cellar that is quite private. He couldn't possibly escape, and there's an outside entrance into the cellar. If you come by my office tomorrow, I'll have a key for you," Chauncy said.

Tapping his fingers along the edge of the table, William hoped he gave the appearance of a man deep in thought. "I'm thinking it may be wise to use Barlow's assistance with the abduction. In spite of his age, John Farnsworth is a powerful man. There's always the possibility he could wrestle free of me, and I wouldn't want that to happen. Another set of hands would provide additional backup should the need arise."

Chauncy's brow creased at the proposal. "I fear Barlow's involvement might cause him undue stress. No offense, Barlow, but you have been troubled of late. I wouldn't want to make matters worse," Chauncy said, glancing toward his wife's cousin.

Barlow grasped Chauncy's arm. "Quite the contrary. Having this challenge will keep my mind off other more distressing situations. Give me this opportunity. You won't regret it—I promise."

Chauncy hesitated for only a moment. "If William wants your assistance and believes you're up to the task, then I'll give my approval."

Barlow's complexion turned ruddy, and he appeared close to tears. "Thank you, Chauncy."

Chauncy nodded and quickly turned back toward William. "Then we're settled. You'll stop by my office in the morning."

"Yes, in the morning," William replied, firmly shaking Chauncy's hand. "I believe we'll remain behind and formulate our plans."

Chauncy nodded his agreement, and the two men watched until he left the pub. "I was pleased to see that you picked up on my veiled message—I didn't know if you'd understand."

Barlow's lips formed a thin line. "Chauncy believes me unstable, but I am completely reliable and understand everything going on around me," he replied solemnly.

"Well, then, let's begin planning, shall we? The fact that John knows both of us presents a bit of a problem. If he should see either one of us, he may become suspicious. Because I've surreptitiously maintained a watchful eye, he's still not aware I'm in England. I'd like it to remain that way until we have him under our control. Perhaps you know a couple of less-than-reputable men who might agree to lend their assistance—for a reasonable fee, of course."

"Yes, I can make arrangements. How soon will we need them?"

"I'm not certain just yet. Tell them they'll be paid to remain available for the next two weeks. They must be accessible both night and day."

"*Two weeks?* I thought we were going to make our move right way."

William leaned forward, his features frozen into a cruel expression. "You listen to me, Barlow. I'm in charge of this maneuver, and if you want to remain involved, you'll do as you're told. If we're not prepared for every circumstance, the plan will fail and Farnsworth will slip out of our grasp. I won't attempt Farnsworth's apprehension until I'm certain we will succeed. Do you understand?"

"Yes," Barlow mumbled. "I'll put two men on alert. Anything else?"

"Outfit them with uniforms worn by the local constables. Is that possible?"

Barlow nodded. "Yes, but it might take a few days."

"Let me know when the men and uniforms are ready."

"And what are you going to be doing?" Barlow asked.

"Maintaining a close surveillance on Farnsworth and his family. If it appears they're going to sail before you've made arrangements, we'll be forced to apprehend him ourselves. I'd prefer that didn't happen, but we must be prepared in either event. Let's make this pub our meeting place. It's not far from where I'm residing, and it's fairly close to Jarrow Farnsworth's home."

"I'm not far from here, either, and I'll find suitable quarters in the vicinity for the men I hire."

"Excellent. I'll meet you here tomorrow evening. Seven o'clock?"

"Seven o'clock will be fine," Barlow replied, retrieving his felt top hat and following William to the door of the pub.

The men parted, Barlow heading off toward his empty house and William to the boardinghouse where he had taken up residence. He longed for someone he could take into his confidence, someone who could enjoy the totality of what he hoped to accomplish. But he dared not trust any of these Englishmen, who already questioned his loyalty and motivation.

He hurried past the parlor and up the stairs to his room, hung his coat, and sat down at the small writing desk. Pen in hand, he began to write:

Dear Thaddeus,

The events of this evening proved more fruitful than even I could have hoped. . . .

22

D aughtie waited outside Mr. Gault's office. She was exhausted and wondered if Mr. Kingman had asked her to deliver his message as retribution
for today's ineptness. Two girls stood in front of her, obviously wanting to
inquire about positions at the mills. Their excited chatter buzzed around her
like bees swarming to the hive. She stared toward the mill yard in a half-dazed
stupor before spotting Ruth coming across the yard. Daughtie waved with as
much enthusiasm as her weary limbs would permit.

Ruth sprinted toward her, the spring breeze whipping at her cape. "Why
are you waiting to see Mr. Gault? Planning to apply for another position?" she
asked with a wry smile.

"Mr. Kingman asked me to deliver a message for him. Nothing seemed to
go right today. Normally I can draw two full beams on Saturdays, and if I'm
having a really good day, I can complete three. However, I struggled to get
even one beam done today. Mr. Kingman came out from the weaving room
several times. His scowls made it abundantly clear he was unhappy with my
lack of progress. I think he decided since I was slow at the frames, he'd find a
way to punish me. What better way than to consume my precious extra time
off on a Saturday afternoon?"

"Don't let Mr. Kingman bother you. All of the weavers were busy today.
Had you completed another beam, one of us would have been forced to work
an extra loom. I'm glad you weren't successful," Ruth sullenly replied.

Daughtie gave her a weary smile. Ever since the day of the turnout, Ruth
had remained irritable. Her words were generally laced with anger, and she'd
become even more opinionated about the working conditions at the mill.
Daughtie remained uncertain if the anger was directed at her or the Corporation. She doubted her refusal to participate in the turnout had been forgiven,
although both girls pretended things were normal. Yet there remained a chasm
between the two of them, especially over matters relating to their work.

"You don't need to wait with me. Go and enjoy your extra time away
from the mill. I overheard you tell Margaret you'd go to the shops with her
before supper. You won't have time if you wait on me. There's Margaret over
there," Daughtie said, pointing across the yard.

Ruth glanced toward the gate and waved at Margaret. "Would you tell Mrs. Arnold I'll be home before supper?"

"Of course. Have fun shopping."

Ruth gave her a patronizing smile. "We're not going shopping; we're meeting with a printer. We're going to see how much it would cost to print pamphlets."

"What kind of pamphlets? What are you up to, Ruth?"

"Nothing that would be of interest to you," she replied before walking off.

"You're determined to get yourself dismissed," Daughtie muttered as she watched Ruth march off with her head held high, resolve in her step.

By the time she'd received her pay and was leaving the mill yard, Daughtie's shoulders were slumped and there was little resolve in *her* step. She merely wanted to get home and put this terrible day behind her.

A dirt-smudged young girl with reddish-brown curls tugged at Daughtie's cloak as she rounded the corner. "Would ya be Daughtie Winfield?" the girl asked.

Daughtie nodded.

"Mr. Donohue said I should give ya this." The child thrust a paper into Daughtie's hand and disappeared before she could say a word.

Daughtie unfolded the paper and read Liam's words: *I must see you this evening. Come after supper and be certain you're not followed.*

The message was intriguing. Was Liam planning something special? Obviously he didn't want her to bring anyone else along. She smiled at the thought. Whom would she even ask to accompany her to Liam's house? Ruth wouldn't consider darkening the doorway of an Irishman's home. She read the note one last time before entering the front door. Her weariness and disillusionment were quickly replaced by an unexpected excitement and energy.

"Good afternoon, Daughtie," Dr. Ketter greeted as she walked in the front door.

"Good afternoon to you," Daughtie replied a little too excitedly.

He brightened at her reply. "You certainly appear to be in fine spirits today. Perhaps I could convince you to join me for a stroll after supper this evening."

Daughtie's enthusiasm waned. "I'm sorry, but I have plans this evening," she replied while removing her cape and hanging it on a peg by the front door. When she turned back toward the hallway, Dr. Ketter was directly in front of her, blocking her path to the stairway.

"Tomorrow afternoon, then? Or perhaps I could escort you to church in the morning, and then we could take a stroll in the afternoon—or a carriage ride. I could go to the livery right now and make arrangements for a horse and buggy. Would you find a carriage ride to your liking?" he inquired persistently.

His enthusiasm likely matched what she had felt after reading Liam's message. She didn't want to injure his feelings, yet accepting his invitation would only give him false hope. "Thank you for the offer, but I can't accept. You're a fine man, and any number of girls would be flattered by your attention. In fact, I'm certain Ruth would find a buggy ride after church much to her liking. Why don't you consider asking *her*?"

Dr. Ketter flinched as though he'd been stuck with a hatpin. "Because I don't want to keep company with Ruth. You've captured my interest, and I know it's only a matter of time before you come to trust me," he replied.

"Trust you? What makes you think I don't trust you?"

He patted her hand. "Please don't be angry with Ruth, but she's told me that you have a problem trusting men. She counseled me to move slowly and take time to build a friendship before I attempt to pursue a romantic relationship with you. However, I have let my heart rule instead of my head. Now I fear I've lost all hope of gaining your trust."

"I'm not certain how Ruth determined I have a problem with trust, but let me assure you, Dr. Ketter—"

He held up a finger. "Ivan—not Dr. Ketter."

"Let me assure you, *Ivan,* that I've never had a problem trusting either men or women—unless they do something to destroy my belief in them."

His lips turned up in a broad smile. "So you trust me?"

"I have no reason not to. But that doesn't mean I want to take a carriage ride tomorrow afternoon. Now if you'll excuse me, I must go upstairs and complete some tasks before dinner," she said, edging her way around him and hurrying toward the stairway.

"She trusts me," he murmured expectantly.

Daughtie advanced up the stairs, pretending she hadn't heard his words. Obviously Ruth had continued to play the matchmaker, assuring Dr. Ketter it would only be a matter of time until Daughtie trusted him, only a matter of time before he could become romantically involved with her. How dare Ruth meddle in her life!

The mood at supper was stilted and uncomfortable. Ruth hadn't returned in time for the evening meal, and Dr. Ketter's attempts to draw Daughtie into conversation made her edgy. She gulped down her meal, excused herself, and rushed from the house, mumbling that she wouldn't return until just before curfew. Tucking her head against the strong wind, she hurried toward Liam's house.

A hand grasped her arm as she rounded the corner toward Worthan Street. "Where are *you* off to?"

Her gaze snapped upward and she met Ruth's questioning stare. "I have some—some errands to attend to," she stammered.

"Errands? Where? You've already passed the library and all the shops."

"Have I? I was so deep in thought, I lost track."

"Come on," Ruth said, placing an arm around her shoulder. "I'm going home. I'll walk back to town with you."

Daughtie glanced at Ruth. "Where were you?"

"After our visit to the printer, Margaret and I had a meeting to attend. Was Mrs. Arnold upset that I missed supper?"

"No. She said she'd keep a plate warm in the oven. Will you be home the rest of the evening?"

Ruth nodded her head. "Why do you ask?"

"When I get home, I'd like to talk with you."

"Why don't we stop at Clawson's Tea and Pastry Shop? We could visit over tea and cake," Ruth suggested, looping her arm through Daughtie's in the first act of amiability since before the turnout.

Panic welled up within Daughtie, threatening to cut off her breath. How was she going to get away from Ruth? Drawing a deep breath into her lungs and then slowly blowing outward, Daughtie relaxed and began to gather her wits. "That would be lovely, Ruth, but I fear Mrs. Arnold will worry if you don't return to eat that dinner she's keeping warm for you."

"Oh! I had completely forgotten. I don't want to worry Mrs. Arnold. Perhaps I shouldn't stop for tea. We can talk when you get home."

"Exactly! We wouldn't want Mrs. Arnold to fret."

A complacent smile crossed Daughtie's lips as Ruth turned and walked toward home. She waited until Ruth rounded the corner and was out of sight before changing directions and heading back toward Liam's house. A slight chill, obviously unwilling to surrender its frosty clutches to the warmth of springtime, clung to the nighttime air. Daughtie bowed her head into the cold breeze and quickened her pace, breathless by the time she reached Liam's front porch.

She lifted the heavy knocker and let it fall from her hand, permitting it to bounce against the iron striker. The silence resonated with a series of metallic thumps before the front door opened. Grasping her arm, Liam yanked her inside and quickly slammed the door.

"Does anyone know ya're here?" His Irish brogue hung thick on the air.

"No."

"And ya're certain ya weren't followed?"

"No—I mean yes, I'm certain I wasn't followed."

"What took ya so long? I was beginnin' to think ya weren't comin'."

His dark eyes sparkled with excitement—or was it fear? She wasn't certain if she should be frightened or joyful. "Why are you acting so strangely, and why do you suddenly care if someone sees me coming into your house?"

Before he could answer there was a mewling sound—weak at first, but now growing stronger. She clasped his arm. "You've baby kittens upstairs, don't you? Oh, let me see them," she begged.

He shook his head. "That's not kittens; it's a baby—two babies. Up there," he said while pointing toward the stairs. "They were born after the mother arrived here. A slave. And for sure, I don't know how she ever made it. She wasn't here more than an hour before they were born. Two boys. The mother needs tendin'—she's in bad condition. That's why I sent for ya."

Daughtie rushed up the steps at breakneck speed, the cries of the babies directing her to the proper bedroom. A young black woman lay on one side, her eyes closed and one arm protectively crooked around the two babies. The infants' cries grew increasingly louder, and Daughtie wondered at their mother's ability to sleep.

Drawing closer, Daughtie kneeled down beside the bed. The babies were so very small. "I've come to help you," she explained while leaning forward to stroke the woman's arm. However, one touch confirmed her worst fears: the woman was dead, and her infant sons would soon follow if they didn't receive nourishment.

Hurrying to the top of the staircase, she called down to Liam, who was perched on the bottom step, "She's dead, Liam, and the babies need milk or they'll die."

"The goat? Will her milk do?"

"Let's hope so. We have no other choice."

"Stay upstairs while I'm out in the barn. Should ya hear anybody knockin' at the door, keep yourself out of sight, and whatever ya do, don't open it," he instructed.

She watched as he turned a key in the lock of the burnished wooden door before striding off toward the back of the house. Daughtie returned to the crying babies and lifted them away from their mother's cold body. Pulling a soft quilt from an oak blanket chest, she wrapped the boys together in the coverlet. Perhaps they could lend each other a bit of the same comfort and warmth they had shared in their mother's womb. Lifting the bundled infants, she began pacing the floor, just as she'd done so many times at the Shaker village. Movement had seemed to work with those babies. But then, *their* bellies had been full.

The infants remained awake. Their lusty cries had turned to pitiful whimpers when she finally heard Liam's footsteps coming up the stairs. A small pail dangled from his broad fingers.

"She wasn't very cooperative," he said, extending the container toward Daughtie.

"They're newborn babies, so they won't eat much at a feeding," she said while eyeing the contents of the bucket. "We'll need a couple of clean handkerchiefs."

Liam strode out of the room and quickly returned with two folded white squares in his palm. "Will these do?"

"Yes, they'll be fine," she said, shaking the folds from each handkerchief and handing one back to him. "Fold over one corner and twist the end," she said while forming a loose knot at one end of the cloth.

"Like this?"

She smiled up at him and nodded. "That's good. Now, dip the knotted portion in the pail," she instructed, plunging her own cloth into the milk. "Once you've got it soaked, hold it to the baby's mouth and let him suck on it."

Liam watched intently as Daughtie offered the milk-soaked rag to one of the infants. "Shall I try with the other babe?" Liam inquired, gazing toward the crying infant lying on the bed.

"Please," Daughtie replied.

The sound of the babies' smacking mouths soon filled the room.

Liam glanced in Daughtie's direction as he once again saturated the cloth with milk. "I'm not sure what to do about their mother. There's a nice place with trees and wild flowers out beyond the barn. Once we've finished feedin' the babes, I could dig a grave and bury her—if ya think that would be proper."

"I don't see that we have any choice. We certainly can't go ask Mr. Livermore to build a casket and buy a plot in the local cemetery."

Liam gave a snort. "That's a fact. Ya're the only one in this room that would receive permission to push up daisies in the Lowell cemetery. They'd turn away an Irishman as quickly as they'd turn away this black girl or her babes. Maybe faster," he added.

"I'm concerned with how you're going to care for these babies by yourself. If I don't return to the boardinghouse before curfew, Ruth is certain to send someone looking for me. There's little doubt she'd have them come here first."

"Don't see as I 'ave much choice but to try and take care of them until ya return tomorrow or the others arrive."

"Others? You expect more runaways?"

He nodded and motioned toward the mother. "She thought they were less than a couple days behind her. They'd been travelin' together, but when she started feelin' poorly, they decided to remain behind as decoys. They didn't want her to be forced to give birth out in the open, with no protection. Their plan was to go spreadin' out and deflect the slave owners and hounds that had been trackin' them. I think she feared some of the other slaves had been re-captured because of her condition. I tried to reassure her as best I could."

"Our best hope is that they arrive soon and that they'll be willing to take the babies with them."

"Willin'? I don't know as I'll be givin' them a choice, lassie. I think I'd have a bit of a problem explainin' how two little black babes arrived on my doorstep," he replied with a grin.

"It's good that you haven't lost your sense of humor," she said while placing one of the babies in one end of an empty drawer. "You can put him at the other end; then if you'd get me some water and towels, I'll get their mother ready for burial."

Liam followed her bidding, fetched the items, and then left to dig the grave. Daughtie prepared the body in silence while the two tiny infants slept nearby, unaware of the fact that their mother had died so they could be born free from the slavery that had bound her.

When Liam returned, the young woman was wrapped in the sheet and blanket Liam had given her. "Are ya comin' with me?"

"No, I'll stay here with the boys and pray—for their health and God's protection over all of you."

He nodded. "Aye. Let's hope yar prayers are answered."

"Liam, I must depart as soon as you return. It's getting late."

"I'll hurry," he replied, lifting the woman's body with a care and respect that touched Daughtie's heart.

Daughtie gathered her Bible and pulled a fresh handkerchief from the oak chest, hoping to escape the room while Ruth was still in the midst of her preparations for church. Exiting the doorway, she hurried down the hall and reached the top of the steps before she heard Ruth's voice.

"Are you going to the Baptist church with the rest of us this morning? All the girls from the weaving room decided to go there today."

Daughtie hesitated a moment. "No. I believe I'll attend services at the Methodist church."

"Why?" Ruth quizzed in a whiny tone. "You're always separating yourself from everyone else. There are some girls who think you're aloof."

Daughtie wasn't going to continue this conversation. No doubt Ruth was attempting to delay her departure until she could have a face-to-face confrontation. "I'm sorry to hear that, but I'm certain you'll set them aright," she called over her shoulder while scurrying down the steps.

Making a turn to the right when she reached the bottom of the staircase, Daughtie walked into the kitchen, where Mrs. Arnold was busy preparing breakfast. "I'm attending the Methodist church this morning, so I'll be leaving—no time for breakfast," she explained.

Mrs. Arnold looked up and gave her a smile. "Take a biscuit or two. You can eat them on the way," she encouraged, wrapping two of the freshly baked offerings into a small cloth napkin.

"Thank you," Daughtie said, giving the older woman a grateful smile. She tucked her Bible under one arm and grasped the biscuit-filled napkin. "I have plans for the day and won't be eating my meals here at the house."

"Going on that picnic and carriage ride with Dr. Ketter after all?"

Surprised by the question, Daughtie jerked her gaze upward and was met by Mrs. Arnold's inquiring stare. In addition to formulating plans with Ruth, it appeared Dr. Ketter was forming an alliance by taking Mrs. Arnold into his confidence. "No, I haven't changed my mind. My plans don't involve Dr. Ketter," she replied before hurrying back toward the hallway.

Daughtie quickly peeked up the stairway. Ruth was nowhere to be seen. Swinging her blue worsted capuchin about her shoulders, she pulled up the hood and adjusted her Bible.

"May I walk with you?"

Daughtie turned with a jolt. Ivan Ketter was standing directly behind her. "No. Not today. I'm busy with other matters," she stammered.

He glanced toward the Bible tucked under her arm. "You're obviously going to church. Is there some reason I can't accompany you?"

"I don't think you'll find my companionship enjoyable today. Besides, I'm not going to the Baptist church," Daughtie explained. She gave a sidelong glance toward the stairway. If he didn't soon release her from this conversation, Ruth would come bounding down the steps, and she'd never get away without additional questions.

He graced her with a broad smile. "I'm willing to attend whatever church you like," he said, removing his hat from a peg and opening the front door.

"Have a nice time, you two," Ruth called from the top of the stairs.

There was no escape—Dr. Ketter was at her side, and Ruth was descending the stairs. "As you wish," she murmured, walking out the door.

Dr. Ketter's voice droned in the background as they walked the short distance to the church. Meanwhile, Daughtie's mind was focused upon Liam. How had he coped with the babies last night? Did he get any sleep? Her concerns had caused her to choose the Methodist church this morning because their services began earlier. The preacher served both the Lowell and Belvedere Methodist churches, which left no choice but to have services earlier in one of the communities. Lowell had drawn the short straw. Daughtie had taken advantage of the schedule with the hope of reaching Liam's house as early as possible. However, if she was going to free herself of Dr. Ketter's company, a plan would be necessary—of that, there was little doubt. Thus far, Dr. Ketter appeared unwilling to accept her rejection.

"Are you going to answer me?" Ivan inquired in a loud voice as they walked up the steps of the white wood-frame church.

"What?" She turned to face him, a puzzled look upon her face.

"You haven't heard a word I've said, have you?"

"I told you I wouldn't be good company," she replied distractedly.

"Obviously you're intent upon proving your point," he said, his tone accusatory.

The two of them stood in the vestibule as the members of the congregation strained to hear the couple's conversation while moving past them on their way into the sanctuary.

"Could you please keep your voice down? I really don't want to share this conversation with every person attending church services this morning," she said from between clenched teeth.

"Perhaps you'd prefer if I just left," he fired back.

"Suit yourself. You're not here at my invitation." She turned on her heel and walked into the sanctuary.

Ivan didn't follow. Although his presence was unwanted, she felt a twinge of guilt for exhibiting bad manners. She abhorred rude behavior. She bowed her head. *I'm asking your forgiveness, Lord. I was rude and behaved like a petulant child,* she silently prayed while the congregation rose and began to sing. "And I promise to apologize to Dr. Ketter," she muttered aloud before joining in to sing the chorus.

The minute services ended, Daughtie darted from her pew and down the aisle. She willed herself to maintain a modicum of restraint as she greeted the preacher in her most cordial voice. Holding her head high, she sauntered out the front door and down the street in a most dignified manner. Rounding the corner and finding the street deserted, she abandoned modesty, hiked her skirt, and bolted off toward Liam's house. She slowed only occasionally to glance over her shoulder, assuring herself she wasn't being followed.

Bounding up the front steps, she hesitated just long enough to catch her breath and then rapped on the front door. It seemed an eternity before Liam peeked out from behind the opaque lace curtain that covered the oval-shaped glass in the walnut door.

He opened the door only wide enough for Daughtie to slip through. "Hurry," he commanded, nearly closing the door on her skirt while pulling her forward. "You weren't followed, were ya?"

"No. I was careful. Besides, folks are still at church."

"You're not," he replied, obviously unwilling to accept her simple explanation.

She pushed back the hood of her cloak and placed her Bible on a small cherrywood table near the foot of the stairs. "The streets were deserted, but I did keep a watchful eye," she said while removing her cloak. The sound of crying immediately captured her attention, and she glanced up the stairway. "Did the babies sleep last night?"

Liam gave her a weary smile. "No—and neither did I. Just as well, though, since the rest of the slaves arrived in the middle of the night. I don't know if I would have heard them had I been sleepin' soundly."

"Wonderful! I'm pleased you had help with the babies."

"Help? Those poor people were so exhausted I couldn't have possibly asked any of them to stay awake with those cryin' babes. I'm thinkin' the twins are sufferin' with what my mother called a sour stomach. Do ya think maybe the goat's milk isn't agreein' with them and that's the cause of all their discomfort?"

"Colic may very well be the problem. Let's have a look at them." Taking the lead, she hurried up the steps, the sound of the babies' cries growing louder as she neared the bedroom. Opening the door, she hurried to the babies and lifted one of them into her arms. "He's drawing his legs up as though he's having stomach pain," she said. "How long since you fed them?"

"About an hour. They shouldn't be hungry."

The muffled sound of a baby's cry in the next room caused Daughtie to turn toward Liam. "Another one?"

He nodded. "The woman that was with them has a babe—a little girl. I'd guess her to be six months old, maybe a little less."

"I think God has answered my prayers. He's sent us a wet nurse for the twins! Where is she?"

Liam nodded toward the door. "The far bedroom—across the hall," he said. "But she's likely tryin' to sleep."

"Well, her baby's awake, so I'm sure she'll be up and about. Do they know about the twins?"

"They questioned whether their friend had arrived. I told them she had and that she'd given birth, but that's all. We didn't talk much. I gave them food, put the men and boys in one bedroom and her in the other. Thought I could be hidin' them better today. I didn't figure anyone would come snoopin' around last night."

"I think those runaway slave hunters come looking any time of the day or night. You're fortunate they didn't appear during the night—or early this morning. It's probably more important the runaways are in a safe hiding place; they can always sleep once they're in a secure place. Why don't you go and instruct the men? I want to talk to the girl. I'll tell her about the twins and see if I can convince her to nurse them. Once she knows her friend has died, I'm certain she'll want to help," Daughtie replied, striding off toward the room with one of the twins in her arm. She tapped on the door and waited a moment before turning the knob and entering.

"Who's you?" the wide-eyed girl asked while shrinking back into one corner of the room. The young woman's ebony skin glistened in the sunlight that now filled the room. A baby lay cradled in her arms, contentedly nursing at her breast.

Daughtie glanced toward the infant in her own arms and pulled the piece of swaddling away from his face. "He's only a day old. He has a brother—twins—born to your friend. I'm sorry to tell you she died after giving birth. Were you close?"

"Sistas. She was my sista," the girl replied, a tear rolling down her cheek. "Can you bring 'im closer?"

Daughtie drew nearer. "We've been feeding the boys milk from Mr. Donohue's goat. It doesn't seem to agree with them. Do you think you could . . ."

The girl nodded and formed her other arm into a cradle for the newborn. "You gonna let us take 'em wid us?"

Daughtie handed over the infant and smiled at the girl. "That's our hope. We were concerned you might not be able to take them. What's your name?"

The dark-skinned girl looked up at Daughtie, her eyes still wet with tears. "Dey call me Florie."

"I'm pleased to meet you, Florie. I'm Daughtie Winfield."

"Thankee, ma'am. Where's de odder one?" she asked, peering down at the baby.

"He's across the hall in Mr. Donohue's room. I don't want to overburden you with three babies. Is there anyone who will help?"

"My husband and my brodder are with de odder men. They'll hep tote 'em. We got a far piece to go 'fore we get to safety?"

Daughtie nodded her head. "It's still quite a ways before you reach Canada, but I'm certain there are excellent safe houses on the remainder of your journey. I know you're going to reach freedom," Daughtie said, giving the girl an encouraging smile.

Florie didn't appear completely convinced as she placed her child on the bed and began nursing her newborn nephew. "Ain't gonna be easy keeping three babies quiet. Appears we gonna need a lot of hep from de Almighty if we gonna make it."

Daughtie gave the girl a gentle smile. "If it's any consolation to you, I'll be praying for all of you, Florie."

~ 23 ~

London

Addie fluttered into the parlor while tucking a wisp of hair behind one ear. "John, I've been sorting through our things, and we really need to finish packing our trunk. Why don't you put down that book and come help me," she urged, a rosy hue coloring her plump cheeks.

Giving his wife a fleeting smile, John enveloped her hand in his own. "I don't believe there's a need to begin this flurry of activity so early in the evening. We'll have ample time later, my dear. Besides, I'm rather enjoying my book. I'd much prefer to have you sit with me and relax for a while."

"Really, John! You men just do not understand the amount of time it takes to properly arrange for a long journey. And then there's Elinor. I need to oversee her preparations. I simply can't wait to complete everything," she explained.

When she sat down beside him, John exclaimed, "Ah, good," and patted her hand as though he were patting the head of his favorite hunting dog.

"I haven't acquiesced, John. I thought perhaps you might reciprocate my altruistic behavior if I sat with you for a while."

"I see," John replied. "It would seem your behavior is less than altruistic, then, isn't it?" he asked with a grin.

"I suppose it is," she replied with a giggle. "But do say I've been successful in gaining your assistance."

"How could I possibly refuse you after such honesty? Just let me finish this chapter, and we'll go upstairs."

Addie leaned her head against his shoulder and compliantly waited while he finished reading, her mind racing with all she must accomplish before they sailed. She jarred to attention the moment John snapped the book together.

"Ready?" he asked.

"Absolutely!" She moved off toward the stairway, glancing back to assure herself he was really following. "I can hardly wait to see Mintie. It seems ages since I've shared a cup of tea with her."

John gave a hearty laugh. "How can you miss the old girl? You receive at least one letter a week telling you every scrap of gossip that's occurring in Lowell. I dare say, I doubt you've missed out on one jot of chitchat since we departed."

"Well, that's true enough, but sitting down and talking over a cup of tea is quite different from receiving a letter. Besides, Mintie's my sister, my only living relative. She can be cantankerous, but I still love and miss her."

"I find it's been easier to accept Mintie's shortcomings since we've been in England. I fear once we set foot in Lowell, your sister's overbearing attitude will become more annoying. What does she say about Lawrence Gault? Is he still calling on her? The man must be a saint—or a fool; I haven't decided which. I can't imagine why he'd put himself through such torture. After all, there's many a woman in Lowell who would treat him like a king."

Addie turned to face John at the top of the stairs. "Mintie has mentioned Mr. Gault from time to time, but she hasn't said enough to make me think he's become a steady suitor. But who knows? She may want to surprise us. She may be wearing a ring by the time we arrive back in Lowell."

John reached up and scratched his head. "For Lawrence's sake, let's hope not."

"That's not a very nice thing to say," Addie chided gently.

"Hmm. Perhaps not, but at least it was truthful. Now, what is it you're expecting to accomplish before bedtime? And what's all that giggling down the hall?"

"I set Bella and Elinor to work before I came downstairs. They're busy sorting through Elinor's belongings. Once they've set things aside, I'll go through them one final time before packing her trunk."

"Seems it would save time to just let her pack. Why do *you* need to go through everything?"

Addie glanced toward the ceiling. How could she possibly make a man understand that a young girl could not be left to her own devices at such an early age? "She'll be packing nothing but bric-a-brac and leaving all her important belongings behind."

John shrugged his shoulders. "She has Bella helping her, and if she forgets something, we can replace it when she gets to Lowell."

She shook her head. "You don't understand—there are some things that can't be replaced, John. It will be best for me to help."

"I suppose that's up to you, but I still think you could save yourself time and effort by allowing them to complete the job they've started. In any event, it sounds as though they're enjoying themselves."

Elinor held up a moth-eaten woolen shawl and giggled. "Shall I take this, Bella?"

Bella laughed at the sight. "I think that wrap has outlived its usefulness."

"We could put it with the pile of belongings to be packed. It would likely prove interesting to hear Aunt Addie's reaction to my choice."

"No need to cause her undue anxiety. She's already worried we won't be prepared in time to sail, and she's most anxious to return home."

"I thought she liked England."

"She does, Elinor, but she misses being in her own home—and I'm sure she's longing to be reunited with her sister. They've never been separated for such a long time."

"Well, she seems rather old to be missing her sister," Elinor whispered.

Bella carefully folded a green plaid dress and placed it on top of several others. "Age doesn't diminish feelings for those we love. In fact, our affection for others usually increases as we grow older."

"Are you anxious to get back to those you love?"

"I suppose you could say that. I long to visit with my friend Daughtie. She's my dearest friend and I miss her."

"Who is it you're missing? Your husband, perhaps?"

Bella turned to see Taylor leaning in the doorway and graced him with a glowing smile. "I'm always pleased to see you, Taylor. However, I was telling Elinor that I miss visiting with Daughtie."

"I'm sure I can't take Daughtie's place, but I'd be pleased to spend the remainder of the evening visiting with you. Surely you two have done enough sorting and folding for one night."

"I doubt Aunt Addie would agree with you, but I can work on my own until bedtime," Elinor replied.

"Do you mind if I leave you?" Bella inquired.

"Taylor will thrash me if I keep you here," she replied, then beamed a smile in her brother's direction.

"I appreciate your willingness to go on without me. Just don't place any more moth-eaten items with the clothes to be packed," Bella warned as she and Taylor exited the bedroom.

Taylor cocked an eyebrow. "What was *that* all about?"

"A little prank Elinor was plotting."

"I trust you discouraged her childish behavior."

Bella's lips turned up in a winsome smile. "We need to remember that she is only a child; she's bound to enjoy a little mischief from time to time. If memory serves me correctly, I participated in my share of childish behavior."

"You? Why, that's difficult to believe," Taylor said with a boisterous laugh. "Now, tell me, what is it you're so anxious to discuss with Daughtie?"

Bella walked to the dressing table and seated herself. "It's her most recent letters," she said, letting down her hair.

"All that business about the walkout?"

"No. Although I must admit I'm anxious to hear all of those details, too," she said, beginning to brush her hair in slow, methodical strokes. "My primary concern is that her letters are filled with talk of Liam Donohue. I had hoped she was going to take an interest in Ivan Ketter, the new doctor. I had a letter from Ruth, who says that Dr. Ketter is quite smitten with Daughtie. However, Daughtie continues to discourage his advances."

"Exactly what is it that concerns you?"

"Daughtie is helping Mr. Donohue furnish his house, choosing the draperies and furniture—that sort of thing. From the tone of her letters, it appears as if her visits to his home are the most important part of her life."

Taylor stroked his chin. "What would you have her write about? Her day-to-day life in the mill? I doubt either of you would find that very interesting. I imagine her jaunts to Liam's house are the bright spot in her life. She merely wants to share that with you."

Bella continued brushing her hair. "She invited him to attend a meeting at the Pawtucket church—and sat beside him."

"She attended a public meeting and sat beside a man. My, that is shameful. You would never have done such a thing, would you?" he asked with a grin.

Turning on her chair, Bella stared up at her husband. "He's an Irishman, Taylor. You understand the ramifications of such a relationship. Daughtie will be ostracized if she begins keeping company with him. Her letters sound as though she's developed feelings for him. It would be better if she directed her interests toward Dr. Ketter."

"I thought she wrote that she was attending the Blowing Out Ball with him."

Bella nodded. "Yes, that's true. Perhaps I am overreacting, but Ruth—"

"Don't take too much stock in what Ruth says. You've told me over and over again what a sensible girl Daughtie is. I doubt there's any more to this than her willingness to assist Liam. She's likely finding pleasure in the diversion. Liam's an honorable man, Bella. He knows Daughtie's unavailable—at least to him."

"But Daughtie believes all people are equal. She's studied her Bible, and since we've been in Lowell, she's forsaken much of the Shakers' doctrine. However, she still holds to their belief that God is the creator of all mankind. If she believes she's living what the Scriptures proclaim, she doesn't care what others think."

"Then why are you so concerned? Daughtie's capable of looking after herself."

"That's my point—she *isn't* capable of knowing exactly what such behavior could mean to her future. She could be fired from her job in the mills; *then* what would she do? I don't want her to ruin her future."

"You're worrying needlessly, my dear. We'll soon be home and you can express your concerns. However, you need to remember that Daughtie must make her own decisions."

"I understand, but I'll still be offering my guidance and— Who can that be?" Bella asked as loud knocks sounded at the front door, interrupting her midsentence.

Taylor shrugged his broad shoulders. "I don't think we were expecting anyone. I'm not certain whether Uncle John is still downstairs," Taylor said, striding toward the hallway. "I'll be back momentarily."

The sound of angry voices drifted up the stairs. Bella moved into the hallway, listened for a moment, and then tentatively edged down the steps. She stopped before reaching the bottom of the stairway, bewildered at the sight of two lawmen threatening to arrest her husband if he didn't immediately produce his uncle John.

"If you men will give me just a moment, I'll see if I can find him. I believe he's already retired for the night," Taylor explained.

"None of your excuses. We're here to arrest him, and we're prepared to search this entire house if necessary."

Bella could listen to no more. "My husband said he would go and fetch his uncle. I think you'll find that solution much more expedient than searching the house. Once you've met with Mr. Farnsworth, I'm certain you'll see there's some mistake."

"There's no mistake. John Farnsworth is guilty of crimes against the Crown. There's ample proof of his treason," one of the men replied before turning back toward Taylor. "Now go and get him, or we'll take matters into our own hands."

Bella watched as Taylor hastened up the stairs. "And what are these charges against Uncle John?" Bella inquired, moving closer.

"We told you—treason," the other lawman answered irritably.

"Yes, but since you've already completed your investigation, I was wondering if you could explain the exact acts of treason of which he stands accused."

The two men glanced at each other. "We're not supposed to give details," one of them replied.

"Why not? Surely a bit of clarification isn't out of line. Who instructed you to withhold details?" Bella persisted.

"Our—our—the one who gives orders," the man stammered.

"The *investigator*," the other interjected while nudging his companion in the side.

"I see. And what reason did he give for this admonition?" Bella inquired.

"He's not required to give a reason. We follow orders, and we were told to arrest John Farnsworth."

"Well, here I am," John said as he walked down the steps. "What's this all about?"

"You're under arrest for treason," one of the officers replied, thrusting several legal documents into John's hand. Without warning, the officer pulled John toward the door.

John swung around, the rapid motion releasing his arm from the hold. "I'm willing to go peacefully, but I want a moment to speak to my wife and nephew before departing. If you'll permit me this small concession, we can then leave."

One of the policemen nodded agreement as Addie came scurrying down the steps. "You're *not* going with them, John. You've done nothing to deserve this shoddy treatment. Tell these men to go away. Surely there are some dishonest scoundrels they should be arresting instead of harassing a decent law-abiding citizen."

"Now, now, my dear. We'll get this matter straightened out in due time," John reassured her as he pulled her into his arms. Reaching out, he drew Bella and Taylor near and lowered his voice to a whisper. "I want you to listen carefully. I want all of you on that ship tomorrow morning whether I'm able to join you or not. Taylor, I want you to take charge of the women should I be delayed."

"I'll not leave without you, John," Addie replied, tears beginning to trickle down her cheeks. "Please don't force me to go," she begged, taking his hand and pressing it to her lips.

"Don't cry, Addie dear. I'm hopeful this can be resolved in short order. If not, I need you to trust that I know what is best. I want you to promise me that you'll abide by my request."

"I feel totally helpless," Addie replied, her shoulders sagging as Bella pulled her into an embrace.

"We're never defenseless, Aunt Addie. We have the Lord, and we have the power of prayer."

John nodded his agreement. "Taylor, I'm not certain the paper work these men have shown me is authentic, but it's imperative you sail with the women as scheduled. Promise me you'll do as I've asked—no matter what happens."

"I promise, although if you haven't been released, I would prefer to remain in England and send the women on without me."

"No. I don't want them traveling across the ocean unaccompanied."

"If you're absolutely certain that's what you want, I'll conform to your wishes."

John patted Taylor on the shoulder. "Thank you, my boy. It appears my escorts are growing anxious to depart. I'd best accommodate them before things become ugly. Bella, take care of Addie for me."

John leaned forward and kissed Addie. "Don't worry. I'll be back before you've time to know I'm gone."

The two lawmen followed John out the front door. He glanced over his shoulder at one of the men. "Which way?"

"To the right and down the alley."

The reply confirmed John's impression of these men. They weren't the police; the police wouldn't be escorting him down a dark alleyway; instead, they would lead him off to the nearest jail, most likely in a police wagon. He didn't know where these men were taking him, but he did know he must flee. If they managed to get him confined somewhere, he'd likely never free himself.

Slowing his gait, John turned toward the men, who were following close behind. "Why don't you take the lead? I'm having difficulty seeing in this shadowy alley."

One of the men grunted, and as he moved forward, John grasped his arm, propelling him into his companion with such force that they both plummeted to the ground. The moment the men were down, John ran off in the opposite direction as his mind scrambled with thoughts of where he might hide. He couldn't possibly return to the house; that would be the first place the men would expect him to hide. Although the homes of several acquaintances were nearby, he knew he dared not place his friends in jeopardy.

He continued running in a chaotic pattern until he finally neared the docks of the Thames. Hesitating only a moment, he surveyed the area and rushed onward. Lowering himself behind a mass of stacked cargo, he placed one hand over his pounding heart and waited until the rhythm slowed. When his breathing had finally returned to normal, John raised himself upward and peered around one of the stacks, his glance focused upon the ship docked nearest to where he stood. It was the *Liberty Queen*—the ship on which he had booked their return passage. Seeing no one in sight, John moved across the open expanse, careful to stay in the shadows. Certain he'd gone undetected, he stole on board the ship, waited momentarily, and then made his way below deck.

Morning came much too soon to suit Taylor. He hurried Bella and Elinor into their clothes, periodically stopping at the window to gaze into the streets below.

"Aunt Addie?" he called as he tapped on her door.

Addie appeared, her eyes red from crying. "Must we leave now? It's not even light."

"We have to go now or we'll never make it on time. The ship won't wait for us."

"But we could change the sailing to another ship—one leaving later," she challenged. But Taylor ignored the woman's pleas that he book passage on a later voyage, holding fast to the promise he'd made.

"We have to go, Addie. I've already arranged for the cab. The luggage is being loaded even now."

She nodded, tears threatening to spill again. "Very well."

It was difficult to convince his grandfather and grandmother that John had been called away unexpectedly and wouldn't be able to return to bid them good-bye. He assured them both, however, that John would be in touch soon and was profoundly sorry for such rude manners. Grandmother Cordelia eyed him suspiciously, making Taylor certain she knew something underhanded was afoot, but she said nothing.

"May God hide you all in the palm of His hand," his grandmother whispered. Taylor pulled away to meet her gaze, seeing by her resolve that she would also save Jarrow Farnsworth from any undue misery. "You will write?" she questioned.

He nodded. "Yes. As soon as I can."

Shafts of sunlight were just starting to glisten through the heavy fog as the party made their way to the awaiting carriage. Two men, who were stationed across the street, turned their backs when Taylor glanced in their direction, but he said nothing to the ladies about their surreptitious presence. He had noticed the men late last night while wandering about the house, unable to sleep. He'd seen that they were still there this morning every time he'd gone to check from the bedroom window. There was actually nothing to be done about it, but it did give Taylor cause to wonder. If the Crown was intent on arresting John, why were they having the house watched? They'd taken John to jail last night.

A thought came to mind that John might have escaped.

"They must be concerned he'll return to the house," Taylor muttered as he climbed the carriage steps.

"Did you say something?" Bella asked.

Taylor took the seat beside her. He momentarily considered explaining the situation, then decided against it. Calling attention to the fact that they were being watched would only serve to alarm Bella or Addie. And saying anything in front of Elinor would likely cause the girl to prattle on incessantly.

Keeping the surveillance issue to himself was judicious, yet he longed for someone to confide in. If John hadn't escaped, why was the family being watched? Since John was already in custody, was it possible the police had decided to arrest *him* for treason, also? Why else would these men continue observing them? He glanced over his shoulder as the carriage neared the docks. The men were nowhere in sight. Perhaps he had overreacted.

"Come along, ladies," he said, leading the three women on board and then, after receiving directions, escorting them to the first of the reserved cabins.

"This is the room Uncle John reserved for the two of you," he told Addie as he opened the door.

Addie glanced about and nodded her approval. "As soon as my trunk is available, I'll begin unpacking."

As Addie entered the room, a shuffling sound was followed by a deep groan. They watched, awestruck, as John unfolded his body from a small cloth-covered nook at one end of the bed, the disheveled piece of cloth hanging from his shoulders like an ill-fitting mantle.

"John!" Addie cried, hurrying forward to embrace her husband. "How did you get here?"

"No time to explain right now," he said while returning her embrace. "I'm guessing my captors are already on board ship searching for me."

"So *that's* why those men were outside watching the house all night," Taylor exclaimed. "I feel certain they followed us to the wharf, although I didn't catch sight of them."

"Men were watching the house and you said nothing?" Bella questioned in anger.

"We'll discuss it later," Taylor insisted. "Right now other matters are more pressing."

John nodded. "There's no time to waste, my boy. Why don't you see if you can search out a hiding place and perhaps find something to help me disguise myself? Then get back here as soon as possible."

"I'll see what I can locate. If you're forced to answer the door, be certain Uncle John is well hidden," Taylor told Addie before motioning toward his sister. "Elinor, you stand in front of that nook with your skirt spread wide to help camouflage the area, should the need arise, and remain calm," he instructed before striding out of the cabin.

Avoiding several deckhands, Taylor made his way through the narrow passages below decks, noting several places where John might safely hide. He paused and glanced about before stealing into a large area that was obviously used by the sailors for sleeping. Stacked beneath the hammocks, he discovered items of worn clothing that likely belonged to the sailors who were now hoisting sails above deck. Choosing a frayed shirt, knitted Monmouth cap, checkered neck square, and a pair of canvas trousers, Taylor slipped the items beneath his arm and hurried back toward the cabin.

He knocked on the door several times. "It's me," he finally announced through the closed door.

Bella opened the door only a crack before peering into the hallway, a questioning look etched upon her face.

"I'm alone," Taylor said.

Opening the door only wide enough to permit her husband entry, Bella took the clothing and handed it to John.

"Why don't you ladies take a stroll down the passageway while I change into these clothes?" John suggested. "Taylor can remain with me in the event someone should appear at the door."

John quickly changed into the garments. "I'll wait until the women return before I depart. Addie will be unhappy if I hurry off without a word. These breeches obviously belong to someone shorter than I," he said while tugging at the waist.

"I'm sorry. It's the best I could do with so little time to choose."

"No need to apologize, my boy. This is excellent," John replied. He was pulling the knitted woolen cap down over his thatch of graying hair when the women returned.

Addie gave her husband an appraising look. "You make a convincing sailor, my dear."

A loud knock sounded, and John nodded for Taylor to open the door. The captain stood centered between two broad-shouldered men dressed as police officers. Taylor immediately recognized them as the men who had been watching the house. "Gentlemen, what can I do for you?" he inquired with a false sense of bravado. Taylor noticed that his uncle had turned his back to the door and busied himself with something.

"We'd like to search this cabin. The police tell me they're looking for John Farnsworth. My manifest shows he and his wife are assigned to this cabin. They'd like to satisfy themselves that he's not here."

Addie stepped forward. "I'm Mrs. Farnsworth. Surely you know that two of your fellow policemen were at the home of my father-in-law last night and took my husband into custody."

One of the officers pushed the captain aside, his gaze darting from person to person as he pressed through the doorway. "Who might you be?" the officer inquired, his gaze resting upon Taylor.

"Taylor Manning, the nephew of John Farnsworth," he replied with a note of pride.

The captain moved forward, the room now filled to capacity. "And what are you doing in here?" the captain inquired of John while the two men in police uniform searched under the bed and in the tiny closet. "I haven't seen you before. Are you Cookie's new helper?"

"We have some special problems with my aunt's diet and asked to speak to the cook," Taylor replied before John could answer. "This man was sent to pass along the information to your cook."

"I'm surprised Cookie is willing to consider a special request. Gauging from past experience, don't be surprised if he immediately dismisses your demands," the captain said, his gaze directed toward Addie. "Of course, a few coins might change his mind."

"I'll find a way to manage if he's unable to accommodate my needs," Addie responded sweetly.

"Well, then, have you finished with him?"

Taylor nodded. "I believe so."

"Then you best get back to the galley. Cookie will be needing your help," the captain ordered John.

"Aye," John replied, edging through the group and making a hasty exit.

Taylor turned his attention to the captain. "If there's nothing further, I'd like to leave my aunt to rest, and I imagine these police officers would like to disembark before we set sail."

The captain glanced toward the two men.

"We'll be going ashore; however, I would ask that you keep a watch out for Farnsworth, Captain. Should he appear, I'd request that you place him in chains and keep him on board until you return to England," one of the men replied.

The captain's forehead creased with his eyebrows knitting into a tight woolly row. "I'll do my best, but I'm not making any promises. I've a ship and passengers that need my attention while we're at sea. If you still believe Mr. Farnsworth is aboard, I'd suggest you purchase passage and seek him out. Then you'll have ample time to search every nook and cranny of the ship," he said with a loud guffaw.

"Since we can't leave our posts, I fear we must rely on you and your men for assistance. Perhaps you'd be willing to inform your men that there will be a tidy bounty offered to the man who brings Farnsworth back to us?"

"And what about the ship's captain? Will there be a reward for him, also?"

"Of course, my good man. We wouldn't expect you to haul a criminal across the ocean without recompense."

"In that case, I'll be certain my men are aware of the possibility that Farnsworth is a stowaway," the captain replied as they turned and walked down the passageway.

All color drained from Taylor's face. He closed the door and waited a moment before turning toward the women. "I'll be back shortly. With the promise of a reward, every man on this ship will be on the lookout for Uncle John. I must get word to him."

~ 24 ~

William Thurston stood beside a stack of crates along the wharf, watching as two of his hirelings, known to him only as Hobbs and Jones, disembarked the *Liberty Queen*. They were alone. He felt the blood rise in his cheeks. Incompetent fools!

The men skulked toward him like two disobedient schoolchildren. "Where's Farnsworth?" he seethed.

"He's nowhere to be found on that ship. We searched it high and low—even had the captain helping us in our attempt to locate him."

"I *know* he's on that ship," Thurston fumed.

"You can go and look for yourself, Mr. Thurston, but you'll not find him, either. The man's vanished into thin air. My guess is that some friend of the family has hidden him, or he may be hiding in his father's house," Hobbs said.

"I'm not interested in what you think. His father's home has been thoroughly searched. Besides, Farnsworth wants to get out of England, and I *know* he's on that ship!" Thurston insisted.

Jones shrugged his shoulders and began to turn away. "Maybe you should go on board and see if you have any better luck finding him. We told the captain you'd pay a reward if anyone was able to find and capture Farnsworth."

William's irritation increased as he watched the two men walk off without another word. "Slackers! I should have saved my money and done the job myself," he muttered as he neared the ship.

"Where d'ya think you're going?" a raggedy-appearing sailor shouted at William when he reached the top of the gangplank and attempted to board the ship.

"Step aside," William commanded.

"Can't let anyone except passengers on board. We'll soon be casting off. Captain's orders."

"I *must* come on board," William insisted.

"Not unless you're a passenger," the sailor repeated.

Making a hasty retreat down the gangplank, William rushed into one of the many shipping offices that lined the wharf. "I need to purchase passage on the *Liberty Queen*," he called out to a clerk sitting at his ledgers.

"Hasn't she sailed yet?" the young man inquired, slipping off his stool and moving toward a window.

William pushed the clerk back to the desk. "No, and I need to purchase passage immediately—before she sails. Hurry!"

The clerk peered across the desk with a look of irritation as he took Thurston's payment. "There'll be no refunds if she sails without you," he called as Thurston hurried out of the office.

William didn't answer. He was certain there would be sufficient time to search the ship, find John Farnsworth, and return to dry land before the ship sailed. He'd worry about recouping his fare when Farnsworth was in his grasp. The same raggedy sailor met him as he attempted once again to board the ship. With a smug grin, he waved his passage papers in the air and pushed past the man.

"We're setting sail any minute now," the sailor called after him.

William turned, his lips curved into a wry grin. "You gave me that same information fifteen minutes ago, and you still haven't set sail," he replied before stalking off to begin his search.

"Don't say you wasn't warned," the sailor bellowed.

William didn't reply, his gaze darting about the ship for some sign of the elusive Farnsworth. He made a wide turn to go down the steps and check the cabins when he spotted a tall man leaning on the ship's railing facing the dock. Farnsworth! He moved forward, his focus steadied upon the tall lean figure with graying hair. As he grew nearer, a young woman with her skirts billowing in the breeze and a small child at her side blocked his path. He could no longer see Farnsworth, and by the time he'd gotten the woman and child out of his way, his quarry had slipped away.

William hurried to the rail, his gaze flitting about as he surveyed the amassed passengers. He caught a glimpse of Farnsworth going below decks and followed at breakneck speed. However, a sailor was coming up the steps as William approached. "Best slow down, sir. The steps are wet and we don't want you falling."

William gritted his teeth. Who did this insolent tar blocking the stairway think he was? He wanted to shove the sailor aside but knew he dared not lose his temper. "I'll do my best," he said, forcing a smile.

The moment the sailor stepped aside, William fled down the stairs. Farnsworth had once again eluded him! He walked through the ship's passageway and then slowly retraced his steps. He heard the orders to cast off, and the ship lurched slightly as it began to move away from the dock. Mounting the steps two at a time, he reached the deck and once again his gaze locked upon Farnsworth at the railing. This time he headed straight for his prey and in a swift, calculated motion, William grasped the man's arm and pulled it back in a painful twisting motion.

Yelling in pain, the man attempted to turn toward his assailant as the ship lurched unexpectedly. Breaking Thurston's hold, the man gave a shove and pinned Thurston against the ship's railing.

The man appeared incredulous. "What are you doing?" he screamed while staring into Thurston's bulging eyes.

"I thought you were someone else," Thurston hoarsely whispered.

The man shoved William away from him. "Next time you decide to accost someone, make sure you've found the proper person."

"My sincere apologies," William said. "If there's anything I can do to—"

"Just stay away from me for the remainder of the voyage," the man said in a warning tone.

"I'm not making the voyage to America. I merely came on board to find a man who's hiding on board—he's done me a grave injustice. In fact, you resemble him, and that's why I acted in such haste. Once again, I do apologize."

The man shook his head. "It appears to me you *will* be making the journey," he said while pointing his thumb toward the dock, which was growing more and more distant as they talked.

Forgetting his apology, Thurston rushed toward the ship's railing. The sailor who'd forced him to purchase passage nodded toward land with a smug look etched upon his face. "Guess you'll be sailing with us, Mate," he said with a snigger.

"I want off this ship," Thurston angrily commanded.

"Unless you plan on swimming for land, I'd say the next time you get off this ship you'll be setting foot in Massachusetts."

"You go and tell the captain I *must* return," William insisted.

The sailor bellowed a loud guffaw. "Tell him yourself, mister."

William watched the sailor walk away, an insolent swagger in his step. "I'll report you to the captain," he hollered.

The sailor pulled his knitted cap from his head and waved it in the air. "You do that. Tell the captain I wasn't willing to bother him with nonsense about dropping anchor for someone who knew we were setting sail. If I know the captain, he'll toss you overboard," he replied in a loud voice.

Many of the passengers had stopped, listening to the barbed exchange, their gazes flitting back and forth between the two men as they argued. William felt the heat rise in his cheeks. He disliked being made the fool in front of one person, much less a crowd.

He glanced about the group and then gave them a dismissive wave. "You'd just as well go on about your business. There's nothing more to see or hear." A few passengers walked away, but most remained, staring at him and waiting for the next lick of excitement he might send their way.

Wending his way through the curious assembly, William's anger continued to mount. *Why won't they just go away!* A seaman was in front of Thurston, but when he didn't move rapidly enough, William gave him a hefty shove and continued off toward the stairway. He held his shoulders straight and head high until he was securely inside his cabin. Then, behind the closed door, he vented his rage, yelling in anguish as he hurled the few unbolted furnishings into the walls.

When his anger had finally subsided, he picked up the husk-filled mattress and threw it back across the ropes attached to the wood frame bolted to the wall. He'd broken the only chair in the room. Disgusted he now had no place to sit, he flung himself onto the bed, weary from a day that had gone amiss at every turn. He was on a ship with little money and no personal belongings, not even a change of clothes. Soon he would be in Boston—a place he dare not be seen. If even one of the Boston Associates should gain knowledge he was back in the country, there would be a manhunt to see that he was placed behind bars. Of that fact, there was no doubt! He would have to carefully lay his plans before the ship docked.

———

A soft knocking at the cabin door caused Taylor to look up from his reading. "I'll answer," he said, placing his book aside. "Uncle John," he uttered as the older man slipped through the open door and then leaned against it, his breathing rapid and his complexion a pasty white. "You look as though you've seen the devil."

John loosed the checkered kerchief from around his neck and wiped the sweat from his brow. "If not the devil, then one of his faithful followers," John replied.

Bella set her stitching aside and stared at John. "You're not making any sense. Whom are you referring to?"

"William Thurston."

"On this ship? Surely not," Taylor replied.

John narrowed his eyes. "I know William Thurston, and he *is* on this ship. He pushed me out of his way only minutes ago."

"He's seen you?" Taylor asked, his voice tinged with concern.

"No. He was too busy attempting to get below decks to his cabin. There's no doubt in my mind he's behind this whole charade of having me arrested by those hooligans who pretended to be police. I'd venture to say that those men with the captain this morning weren't truly policemen, either. They're probably a couple more of Thurston's hired thugs."

Bella frowned. "Exactly what is Mr. Thurston hoping to gain through all of this?"

"I suppose he's seeking to earn himself a place of prestige among propertied Englishmen since he's no longer welcome in America. If Thurston has successfully convinced them I'm a traitor and can hand me over to these men, he'll gain gratitude and respectability."

Taylor nodded. "I agree, Uncle John. He's likely told them a pack of lies in order to persuade them you're a traitor and has probably promised to deliver you as a token of his goodwill. I can just hear him telling all those stiff-necked aristocrats how much he loves the homeland."

"Not to mention the fact that he's probably counting on a tidy sum for capturing a treacherous villain such as I."

"But it appears his plan has gone awry. Surely he didn't plan on sailing to America."

John moved away from the door and seated himself. He had finally regained some color in his cheeks. "You're right, but he waited too long and was unable to disembark. Now he finds himself in a quandary. Taylor, you're going to have to talk with the captain. Explain what occurred back in Massachusetts, including the fact that William Thurston escaped a couple years ago, evading just punishment for his heinous crimes. And since the captain believes those men were truly the police, you'll need to be at your most eloquent."

Taylor smiled broadly. "I'll do my best. Perhaps it would be wise to schedule an appointment with the captain. Arranging a definite time to meet would ensure an adequate period in which to explain our dilemma."

"Excellent! You're already planning a strategy. I believe you'll be able to handle this matter in fine fashion. As for me, I believe I'll go and visit with Addie in our cabin. I'll await word from you."

"No need postponing matters. I believe I'll go and see the captain now. Perhaps he'll have time to visit with me today," Taylor said while straightening his cravat.

Bella picked up her stitching, her lips turned upward in an endearing smile as she gazed at her husband. "I think that's a prudent decision," she agreed.

While mounting the steps and striding toward the captain's quarters, Taylor began formulating his plea. His argument must be incisive, for without the captain's assistance, they would be helpless in gaining control over Thurston and having him placed under arrest once they arrived in Boston. Surely the captain would be willing to assist in bringing his reluctant passenger to justice once he realized the fact that Thurston had been the primary architect of kidnappings and thievery in Lowell.

Taylor knocked on the cabin door and then waited a few nervous moments until the captain shouted for him to enter. "Good day to you, Captain. I'm Taylor Manning, one of your passengers."

"What can I do for you, Mr. Manning?"

Taylor met the commander's gaze. "I'll need an hour or so of your time to totally explain my dilemma," Taylor explained. "I wanted to see if you might have that much free time available today or tomorrow."

The captain cleared his throat and leaned back in his leather-covered chair. "Must be a mighty thorny issue if it's going to take you an hour to state your case."

Nodding in agreement, Taylor said, "It's complex, and I don't want to leave you with unanswered questions."

The captain gave him a lopsided grin. "You've managed to rouse my interest. I've got time right now. Why don't you take a seat over there and begin telling me your story."

Taylor's lips twitched nervously. "Now?"

The captain pointed to the empty chair. "No time like the present. Sit down."

———✦———

"You've already talked to the captain?" John asked in an incredulous tone.

Taylor smiled at his uncle, unable to hide his pleasure. "Yes. And he's agreed to help us."

John pulled Taylor into a husky embrace. "I'm proud of you, my boy. Has the captain secured Thurston in chains?"

"No. He explained that Thurston had taken to his room, and since there was no place for him to go, he'd wait until we docked to take him into custody and place him in irons. If William remains unsuspecting, there should be no problem; at least that's what the captain believes."

"I'd prefer he be placed in shackles right now," John replied.

Taylor nodded. "I attempted to convince the captain. However, he feared the passengers would be unduly upset by the tumult. He thought it best to wait."

"Well, we'll abide by his decision. I'm just thankful you were successful in winning over the captain. You performed admirably."

Taylor beamed. "Thank you, Uncle John."

~ 25 ~

Boston Harbor
May

Taylor moved away from the crowd of passengers beginning to gather on deck. The sun was shining brightly as the *Liberty Queen* neared Boston's harbor. He wanted to ensure William Thurston was detained before the ship docked. The captain clenched an unlit pipe in his fist as he moved about the deck of the ship shouting orders to his crew.

"Good morning," Taylor greeted as he approached the captain. "I was wondering if it might be wise to take Mr. Thurston into custody before we docked."

The captain turned his attention to Taylor. "Glad you reminded me. I had nearly forgotten our unwelcome passenger."

With no more than a nod of his head and a wave of one hand, several sailors scurried to the captain's side. He issued their instructions and soon they were all outside the door of William Thurston's cabin. The captain knocked, waited, and then knocked once again. When there was no sound from within, he unlatched the door.

"He's gone," one of the swabbies announced. He spoke the words as though the others would not realize the cabin was empty without his verbal declaration.

"Search the ship. I want him found," the captain commanded.

Taylor stared after the sailors as they scurried from the cabin. He dreaded taking the news to his uncle, but the older man was awaiting word of Thurston's detainment. No doubt he would grow concerned if Taylor didn't soon return.

He entered John and Addie's cabin and gave his uncle a feeble smile. "It appears Thurston has eluded us. He's obviously hiding on board somewhere, but he's not in his cabin."

John rubbed his forehead while listening to the news. "Just as I feared. That scoundrel should have been placed in shackles when he was first discovered on board."

"We'll hope they locate him before we disembark," Taylor replied.

"I don't hold out much hope they'll be successful," John put in.

"If not, we'll notify the authorities here in Boston when we go ashore.

Perhaps if we offered a reward, the sailors would continue searching for him after we dock," Taylor suggested.

"If the crew doesn't find him before we dock, ask the captain if he'll notify his men we've posted a reward, and if found, Thurston should be delivered to the police," John replied. "I'd much prefer to remain in Boston until he's arrested, but I know the women are going to want to be on the first canal boat to Lowell. Once we've talked to the authorities, we'll depart."

Lowell

Daughtie edged her way down the spiral staircase of the Appleton and into the mill yard, anxious to return home to supper and a quiet evening. Perhaps there would be a letter from Bella waiting for her. During the noonday meal, Mrs. Arnold had mentioned that she would stop and check the afternoon mail. The thought of a letter caused Daughtie's step to quicken as she passed through the gate and turned toward the boardinghouse.

"A message for ya, ma'am." The young Irish girl who had once before come to fetch her now impatiently tugged at Daughtie's arm. The girl's wary gaze darted about in every direction before finally settling upon Daughtie. With deliberate determination, she shoved the piece of paper into Daughtie's hand and hurried off in the direction of Liam's house.

"Was that an *Irish* girl?"

Daughtie startled at the sound of Ruth's voice. "You frightened me. It's impolite to sneak up on people," she chastised while continuing her rapid pace toward home.

"Sneak up? I walk home with you three times a day, six days a week. I would think you'd be expecting to see me," Ruth rebutted. "What did the girl want? I saw her say something to you. She was over here begging, wasn't she? We ought to turn her in to the overseer or tell Mr. Gault down in the office. Those Irish vagrants aren't permitted to come over to this side of town and beg. You didn't give her any coins, did you? If so, she'll be waiting outside the gate for you every day."

"No, I didn't give her anything," Daughtie tersely responded.

"There's no need to become haughty. I was merely looking out for your best interests. I know how you tend to take pity on every pathetic creature you encounter, and I don't want the girl taking advantage of your kind nature."

Daughtie ascended the steps leading to the front door of the boardinghouse. "Thank you, Ruth, but I do believe I can take care of myself. And it's not my nature that causes me to take pity on the less fortunate; it's the love of God. The Bible says we should be kind to one another."

"But she's not one of us," Ruth said sternly as she pushed open the front door. "She's Irish."

"I am quite certain that I've never yet seen a verse in Scripture telling me to be kind to everyone but the Irish."

Both girls were met with the inquisitive stares of half a dozen people. The parlor was filled with Dr. Ketter's patients, all of whom appeared immensely interested in the girls' conversation. Daughtie ignored the obvious interest, her gaze focused instead upon the candle table near the foot of the stairway, where she spotted a letter. Moving quickly, she picked up the missive and read the inscription. It was a letter from Bella.

"Oh, Daughtie, I'm pleased to see you. I'm running behind with my patients. Could you possibly assist me?" Dr. Ketter inquired expectantly.

"I'm sorry, but that's impossible, Dr. Ketter. I'm going to have a quick bite of supper and be on my way—errands. I'm sure Ruth would be most pleased to help, wouldn't you, Ruth?"

Ruth appeared surprised by Daughtie's suggestion. "I thought you planned to stay in and do your mending and read this evening."

"My plans have changed," she replied. "If you'll excuse me, I want to read Bella's letter and be on my way within the hour." Without waiting for a response, she raced up the stairs and unfolded the note delivered by the Irish girl.

As she'd expected, the missive requested she come to Liam's house at the earliest possible moment. Tucking Bella's letter into her reticule, she hurried back down the stairs and into the kitchen, and with Mrs. Arnold's permission, helped herself to a piece of ham and a slice of thick, warm bread.

"Cut yourself a slice of apple pie," Mrs. Arnold instructed considerately.

Daughtie nodded and helped herself to a thick piece of the fruit-filled pastry. "I'll eat it on the way. I promise to return your napkin," she said, folding the checkered square cloth around the pie.

Mrs. Arnold gave her a cheerful smile. "That'll be fine," the older woman replied as Daughtie rushed back down the hallway and out the front door.

Fortunately, Ruth was nowhere to be seen. Either she was in Dr. Ketter's office assisting him, or she'd gone upstairs. Regardless, Daughtie had been able to make her exit without an explanation or argument, and for that she was most thankful. The evening air was warm and thick with the scents of budding lilac and honeysuckle. She breathed deeply to enjoy the spring aroma as she hurried onward. Finally reaching Liam's house, she raced up the front steps and knocked on the door, her heart pounding with excitement and fear.

The door opened and Liam smiled down at her. "Come in."

"More runaway slaves?" she whispered.

He nodded. "Aye, but no babes," he replied with a wan smile. "Only two lasses. The rest were restrained by their owners sometime yesterday."

"How many did they manage to recapture?"

"Six—all men and lads. The girls are thinkin' their owner quit searchin' for them once he had the men back in his possession. They didn't see any sign they were bein' followed last night or today. I've got them hidden in the upstairs room. I was expectin' them to arrive last night and feared something had gone wrong. And for sure, when the girls arrived, they were confirmin' my fears. Doesn't seem many of them are bein' liberated," Liam lamented.

Daughtie could see the anguish in his expression and took his hand in her own. "I understand your feeling of helplessness, but we must remain positive and celebrate the fact that at least some of them are reaching freedom."

"I know ya're right, but those poor girls are worried sick about their friends and family. They know what 'appens to runaways when they're recaptured. And now I must pass along more bad news."

"What do you mean? What's happened?"

"These girls and the rest of their group were expected last night. I was to be deliverin' them to me contact a short distance north of Lowell. When they didn't appear, I met up with me contact to tell him of the situation. He said the group had likely been recaptured."

"And? Didn't he realize they might only have been detained? Did he tell you what to do if they arrived?"

Liam shook his head. "No. I should've been askin', but I wasn't thinkin' straight. He seemed nervous and was anxious to be goin' on his way. Now I don't know what I'm to do with these girls. I don't know the proper route they're to take, and there's no man to travel along with them. The only instructions I've ever had were to either deliver them to their next contact or give instructions to the next safe house."

"Can't you do that? Direct them to the next safe house?"

"The safe houses change frequently. We're given new instructions each time a group is expected. My house isn't used every time runaways come this direction. It would be too risky for them to always move in the same direction and to use the same houses. So I'd be needin' to have some assurance they'll reach safety before I send them on."

"You're right, of course," she said as she began to wring her hands, attempting to contemplate their options. "I think we need to pray."

Liam's eyes widened, apparently startled by her pronouncement. "Pray? Here? Now?"

Her lips curved into a gentle smile. "Yes, here and now."

"Ya're beginnin' to think ya shouldn't be involved in such a thing as this, aren't ya?"

"No, not at all, but I *am* feeling as though we need divine intervention to find a solution. It's clear neither of us knows what to do."

" 'Tis true that a little help from above couldn't hurt. I'm thinkin' ya know more about what God might be wantin' to hear, so you go ahead and pray. I'll listen and agree," he said with a grin.

"There aren't any set rules about prayer, Liam. God wants to hear whatever is in your heart; how we say it doesn't really matter."

"Maybe so, but I'd still prefer you do the talkin'."

She nodded her agreement, bowed her head, and asked God to send them a plan, some resolution that would protect all of them.

"That's it?" he asked when she'd whispered a soft amen.

"Did I forget something?"

Liam wagged his head back and forth. "No. It's just that your prayin' was kind of simple."

"The Shakers taught me to be simple and direct; I carry that same concept into my prayers. I like to believe God appreciates the fact that He doesn't have to sift through all the inconsequential words before getting to the heart of my supplications—not that He doesn't already know my needs," she added.

"So if He already knows what ya're needin', why do ya pray?" Liam inquired.

"Because God's Word instructs us to pray. Even Jesus prayed to the Father."

Liam rubbed his forehead, a confused look in his eyes. "So ya pray in order to let God know ya're doin' what the Bible instructs, which is countin' on Him to solve your problems, even though He already knows what's goin' on before ya pray?"

Daughtie reflected on Liam's statement for a moment. "God is certainly all-knowing. He *could* solve our problems without hearing our prayers, but He created man for communion. Prayer is our way to fellowship with God."

"I can understand the Almighty wantin' to hear from a sweet lady like yarself, but why would He want to hear the blatherin' of an ungodly Irishman?"

"Because He loves you, Liam. It's God's fondest desire that every man love Him in return. God *wants* to bless all of our lives, but many refuse Him. They miss out on the wondrous gift of His love and protection. Isn't that sad?"

"Are ya tryin' to make a point with me, lassie?"

Giving him a gentle smile, Daughtie nodded. "I don't want you to miss *any* of the blessings God has stored up for you, Liam. I know you're a decent man, but doing good deeds and caring about others won't gain you access into God's kingdom."

He appeared puzzled by her words. "I thought that's what godly people were supposed to be doin'—helpin' the poor and downtrodden."

"Yes, of course they are. Good deeds are exactly that—a way of ministering to our fellow man. But that's all they are—charitable acts, not a key to eternity with our Heavenly Father," she explained.

"What more *am* I to do?"

"You must acknowledge that Jesus is the Son of God, confess your sins and ask His forgiveness, and invite Him into your life, Liam," she explained.

He remained silent for a moment and then slowly rubbed his jaw, appearing to contemplate her words. "I'll be thinkin' about what ya've said. Yar beliefs are a far cry from the peculiar ideas my mother adopted. Sometimes it's hard to be knowin' what to believe."

Daughtie nodded in agreement. "Exactly! Rather than accept what I've said here tonight, you need to search out the truth for yourself. Read your Bible. Pray. Seek God. He'll reveal Himself and the truth of His Word to you, and then you can make a sound decision."

"How is it that such a young lass can be so wise?" he asked, his dark eyes reflecting the golden glow of the flames dancing in the fireplace.

For a moment she felt mesmerized, captive to his unyielding gaze. A thump, immediately followed by the sound of breaking china, pulled her attention to the stairway. "The girls?" she inquired, looking back at Liam.

"Sounds as though they're having a bit o' trouble. I'd best be checkin' on them."

"May I go with you?" she asked. "I'd like to meet them."

"Of course," he said, leading the way.

Two dark-skinned girls, both attired in ragged dresses made from the white cotton known as Negro cloth, which was produced in the Lowell mills, were on their knees gathering broken pieces of a hand-painted china bowl and water pitcher. Both gazed upward with a look of terror filling their large chocolate brown eyes.

"It was an accident," the older of the two explained in a shaky voice while inching herself in front of the younger girl. "It were *my* fault, Massa; you can whip me," she continued.

"There won't be any whippin' around this house," Liam replied in a firm tone.

"But I broke—"

The younger girl peeked around from behind her companion. "She din do it—I did. You can whip me, but please don' hurt her," she pleaded.

"I've never seen folks so anxious to take a whippin'. There's nothin' in this house that can't be replaced or repaired, so don't concern yourselves over a broken piece of china. Just be careful you don't cut yourself," he said while pointing toward a shard of the porcelain.

"Thank you, suh," they replied in unison.

Daughtie stepped forward. "I'm Daughtie Winfield, a friend of Mr. Donohue. We're hoping to find a safe place for you girls to call home."

"I'm Minerva, and this here be my sister, Nelly. Ain't we goin' on up north ter Canada?" the older girl asked.

Liam squatted down in front of the girls. "Here's the problem. The two of you can't make it on your own all the way to Canada, and I don't know when another group of runaways may be passin' through that I could be sendin' you with. I can't risk keepin' you here too long, and yet I can't just send you off without havin' a place arranged for you to go."

"Can't we move on ter de next station? We'll keep a lookout fo the signal."

"What signal?" Daughtie asked.

"A single candle in the window," Liam replied before turning his attention back to the girls. "You'd be travelin' at least twenty miles, and even if ya found the signal, I don't know the password. That's what I've been tryin' to explain. We missed our connection last night. We're goin' to try and devise another plan."

Daughtie gave them a confident smile. "We've been praying for God to send us the perfect answer."

"Den we'll pray, too," Minerva said.

"Oh, that would be most helpful. With all of us praying, I'm certain God's going to send us a magnificent solution. You should be careful to remain hidden when Mr. Donohue's gone from the house. Don't answer the door, and don't burn a candle upstairs. Folks around here know Mr. Donohue lives alone," she instructed and then turned back toward Liam, who was grinning at her. "I should take my leave. I'm sure Ruth will be questioning me concerning my whereabouts since I told her I had errands to complete. Why are you grinning at me? Have I said something to amuse you?"

"Your orders to the girls—I gave them all that information when they arrived," he replied, escorting her down the hallway.

"Oh! Would you extend my apologies to them?" she asked, her cheeks flushed red with embarrassment.

"I doubt they were upset over your reminder." A smile tugged at the corner of his lips. "Any special orders for *me*?"

She gave him a sidelong glance, uncertain if he was toying with her. "Be certain you keep to your normal routine so you don't arouse suspicion," she warned. "And pray," she hastily added as he opened the front door for her.

"I think I can remember all of that," he said, a twinkle in his eyes.

"Even if you should forget everything else, don't forget to pray—that's the most important of my instructions." She stared up into his eyes, remembering the night he'd kissed her on the cheek outside the boardinghouse. She wondered now if that had just been a passing kindness—a tenderness because she'd talked of her loneliness. Her own feelings for him seemed to spill out from her heart and into her every thought. If only she could be sure of what he was feeling—thinking.

Liam leaned down, and before she realized his intent, she felt the softness of his lips upon her cheek. "Good night, Daughtie. And thank you for your help."

"You . . . you're welcome," she stammered.

She headed toward home, her fingers touching the spot Liam had kissed, her heart thumping in wild delight.

It was nearly eight-thirty when Daughtie returned home—early enough Ruth ought not quiz her at length, but late enough that Dr. Ketter's patients would be gone. Hopefully he wouldn't see her come in.

"There you are!" Ruth exclaimed.

Daughtie turned toward the parlor, where Ruth sat with her hands neatly folded atop her lap.

"You went sneaking off without so much as a word, and now you've missed all the excitement." There was no mistaking the smugness in Ruth's voice.

"What have I missed?" Daughtie inquired.

"Bella has returned from England and sent word for you to come and visit her tonight. Their ship docked yesterday, and they returned to Lowell by canal boat early this evening."

"Oh, that's marvelous!" Daughtie exclaimed, turning again for the door. "I'll be back after a while."

Daughtie hurriedly made her way to Bella's and knocked at the front door. She waited several anxious moments before it swung open. "Bella!" Daughtie greeted, pulling her friend into a warm hug. "It's so good to see you."

Bella returned the embrace and then led Daughtie into the parlor. "I was beginning to think you weren't coming—or that you hadn't received my message."

Daughtie sat down on the overstuffed settee. "I left the house before your message arrived. I came as soon as I heard you'd returned. I want to hear all about the wonderful places you visited."

Bella giggled. "I haven't enough time to even begin telling you of the wondrous sights we visited in the short time before you must return to the boardinghouse. We'll have to save that for a lengthy visit after church on Sunday. But I couldn't wait to tell you of the excitement that occurred on board ship. However, the story really begins before we left England," she said, taking time to explain about John's kidnapping and William Thurston's connection to the incident.

Daughtie clasped a hand over her mouth. "So William Thurston is alive and well, living in England?"

"He *was*. As I told you, by the time we boarded the ship, Uncle John had already escaped and was hiding on the ship. Then, lo and behold, he spotted William Thurston on board. In fact, Mr. Thurston, whom we believe was searching for Uncle John, pushed John out of the way thinking him to be no one of importance—since he was dressed like a sailor. We set sail before Thurston disembarked."

"Oh, my! What a turn of events!" Daughtie exclaimed.

"And that's not the worst of it. Taylor went to the captain with the arduous task of explaining the situation. Fortunately, the captain believed him and agreed to take Thurston into custody before we docked in Boston."

"I am so *very* thankful to hear that evil man is going to be held accountable for his crimes. And Ruth will be elated to hear the good news. She's always harbored anger that William Thurston was the one who planned all of the kidnappings and yet slipped away before receiving punishment," Daughtie said.

"That's just it—he's escaped once again."

"*What?* How did that happen?"

"When Taylor and the captain went to Thurston's cabin to place him in shackles, he was missing. The sailors searched the ship, but to no avail. John has offered a reward and is hopeful some of the crew will continue the search—at least until they set sail back to England."

"How disappointing. Do you think he's still on board the ship? Surely he would want to return to England rather than remain a hunted man in the United States."

"I'm not certain. Uncle John is hopeful he'll be captured and brought to trial, but I fear he's managed to slip away again. But enough of this gloomy talk. I've more news to share."

"What else happened?"

"We brought Taylor's sister Elinor home to live with us!"

"Truly?"

"Yes. It was getting a bit much for her grandparents to continue to care for her, so they decided we would be the best candidates to raise her."

"Well, that's very exciting and scary all at once, isn't it?"

"It certainly is. I want to introduce you to her and tell you all about our journey. Do say you'll come to church with us on Sunday and join us afterward for the noonday meal."

Daughtie hesitated a moment, her mind racing. "I'll try," she said.

The smile faded from Bella's lips. "*Try?* Have you more important plans?" she asked, obvious disappointment in her voice.

"I may be needed to assist some friends," she hedged.

Bella arched her eyebrows. "You're keeping something from me, Daughtie Winfield. What is it?"

"What makes you think I'm keeping secrets?"

"Because you've been my dearest friend since the day I arrived at the Shaker village in Canterbury. I know you almost as well as I know myself. You may as well take me into your confidence, for you surely realize I'll give you no peace until I know what's going on," Bella replied. And then, as if struck by a bolt of lightning, Bella grasped Daughtie's hands in her own. "Does this have something to do with Liam Donohue?" When Daughtie didn't immediately answer, Bella squeezed her hands. "I've guessed correctly, haven't I? I can see it in your eyes."

Daughtie's voice caught in her throat. "It's not what you think," she argued, her voice raspy.

"Then tell me," Bella insisted. "You know I've always kept your confidences."

"Runaway slaves," Daughtie whispered. "We're helping runaway slaves."

Bella clasped a hand across her mouth. "You're placing yourself in extreme danger."

"Given the opportunity, you'd do the same thing."

"Perhaps," Bella conceded. "Give me the particulars—who else is involved? How did this all begin? All you said in your letters was that you had attended an antislavery meeting."

Daughtie nodded. "Yes, Prudence Crandall came and spoke."

"And your letter said you had invited Liam Donahue," Bella continued. "That was an even greater mistake than helping runaways."

Shifting on the settee, Daughtie met Bella's gaze. "Really? Is that how you truly feel, Bella? That if a person was born in Ireland, that makes him less acceptable than someone born in—shall we say—England?"

"Whether it's what *I* believe or not isn't what matters. People consider the Irish to be less . . ." Bella hesitated, obviously unable to find the right words.

"Less *acceptable*?"

Bella fervently bobbed her head up and down.

"But they're not. They're made of the same flesh and blood as you and me. We all are—the Negroes, the Irish, the English—all of us. Neither the country of our birth nor the color of our skin makes a difference."

"Those things don't matter to you or me, and they shouldn't matter to others, but they do," Bella replied.

"Well, I won't accept that way of life. I believe we're equal—all of us— and that's how I intend to live. I'll not let others dictate the acceptability of a person based upon dark skin or an Irish brogue. I'm thankful I grew up among people who taught me we're all created in the image of God. Sister Mary is Irish—and what about Brother Lemuel? He's black, and he's also one of the finest men God ever placed upon this earth. You loved both of them, didn't you?"

"Your argument isn't with me, Daughtie. I don't disagree with you. But this isn't Canterbury—you're not living in the secluded Shaker village anymore, and the rest of the world doesn't hold to Shaker theology. Besides, you left the Shakers because you didn't agree with their beliefs."

"*Some* of their beliefs—the ones that I couldn't justify with the Scriptures. However, I continue to embrace those tenets of the Society that are irrefutable, and I believe equality is one of those basic truths that is undeniable."

"You know I believe in equality, too, Daughtie, but there are barriers that can't be crossed when you're living among the rest of the world."

"Nothing will ever change unless we promote an attitude of accepting everyone. We can't sit back and remain complacent. Someone must lead the way and cross the barriers. How else will slaves be set free? How will Irishmen ever be permitted to live alongside Englishmen? Or how will equality ever truly exist in this country?"

"Or the Shaker girl be permitted to fall in love and marry an Irishman?" Bella whispered.

Daughtie silently stared back into her friend's questioning gaze.

"You're in love with Liam Donohue, aren't you? That's what all of this is about, isn't it?"

"No. That's not what this is all about. I won't deny my feelings for Liam. However, the slavery issue and mistreatment of the Irish did not evolve out of my feelings for him. Rather, I grew to care for him because he so passionately desires to help those less fortunate, no matter their color, creed, or native land. He's a fine man, deserving of a good wife," she adamantly proclaimed.

Bella stared at her, mouth agape. "You—you're going to marry him?" she finally sputtered.

"No," Daughtie replied calmly.

"Oh, Daughtie, for a moment I was so frightened."

"He hasn't asked me," Daughtie quickly added.

Bella clutched Daughtie's hand. "But you wouldn't accept if he did?"

"Yes, I believe I would. I'd be proud to call Liam Donohue my husband."

Bella leaned against the back of the settee. "I believe I'm going to faint," she announced, blotting her face with a lace-edged handkerchief.

Daughtie grabbed the cloth from Bella's hand and began fanning it back and forth in front of Bella's face. "Dear Bella, *please* don't faint. You should be pleased that I've grown so independent in your absence. Remember how you used to worry about my inability to make decisions?"

"I fear you've learned too well," she said with a weak smile.

"I'm sorry I've upset you first thing upon your return. I've so looked forward to having you back, and now look what I've done!"

"It's not your fault. I insisted you take me into your confidence. Although I fear for your safety and happiness, I'll never betray you. You will always be my dearest friend," Bella replied. "If your other plans don't interfere, will you promise to spend the day with me on Sunday?"

Daughtie smiled. "Of course."

~ 26 ~

Boston

William Thurston hurried through the back streets of Boston, his haste causing him to occasionally stumble on an uneven cobblestone or piece of scattered garbage. Undeterred, he continued onward until he chanced upon a seedy tavern along the alleyway he was traversing. Pushing through the door, he welcomed the darkness that shrouded the interior. He knew immediately this would be his hiding place until the sun set.

He sat down at a rough-hewn table in a rear corner where he had a view of the door. Pushing aside the remnants of an unfinished meal, he ordered a mug of ale and remained silent while the barkeep placed it on the table. He placed a coin on the sticky tabletop before taking a swallow of the brew.

Drinking slowly, he began to take stock of the circumstances that had sent his clever plans plummeting into disaster. Had it not been for the ineptitude of the thugs he'd hired to detain Farnsworth in England, he would now be considered a champion to Chauncy Fuller and his friends. Instead, he was hiding out in a vermin-infested pub in Boston. However, he reasoned, he couldn't take the chance of being spotted by one of the Boston Associates. Worse yet, the wife he'd left behind or one of her voluble matron acquaintances might see him should he wander about town.

The day wore on, and by nightfall, William walked out the door of the tavern, his latest plan firmly in place. He'd spent the day watching and waiting. Now he stood outside the door, pausing until he was certain no one was lurking about. He untied the reins of an agile-looking mare, slipped his foot into the stirrup, and hoisted himself up into the saddle. Waiting until he was only a short distance from the tavern, he then dug his heels deep into the horse's flanks, pleased when the animal responded and raced off at full gallop.

The next morning William was knocking at the front door of the Litchfield, New Hampshire, boardinghouse Thaddeus Arnold now called home.

A thin small-framed woman opened the door. "My rooms are full," she said before William could speak.

"I'm not looking for a room. I'm looking for Thaddeus Arnold. I understand he's one of your boarders."

"He is. Come in and sit down," she ordered, pointing a flour-covered finger toward the parlor. "I'll go and get him. He hasn't yet come down for breakfast."

"Thank you."

"You friend or family?" the woman asked, peering down at him while mounting the steps.

"Friend."

The woman stopped her ascent. "Haven't seen you around here before. Where do you hail from?"

"England."

The woman appeared impressed only momentarily. "You don't sound like an Englishman," she snorted and then continued upward.

The sound of muffled voices could be heard from above, and then the woman reappeared, stopping outside the parlor door. "Mr. Arnold will be down in a minute. He didn't seem to be expecting any visitors from England."

William ignored the remark, keeping his gaze fixed upon the stairway until he spotted Thaddeus peeking through the banister. "It's me, Thurston. Get down here and quit acting like a frightened schoolboy," he ordered.

Thaddeus hurried into the parlor, patting his hair into place as he rounded the corner. "William! What an unexpected surprise. I couldn't imagine who might be here. I've not given my address to anyone—except you, of course. And I certainly wasn't expecting *you* to make an appearance. What brings you back from England?"

"Sit down and I'll explain," William said, attempting to keep his irritation under control.

Thaddeus did as he was told, appearing spellbound while William related how his plot to be accepted among England's elite had gone afoul, causing him to now be sitting in New Hampshire instead of the well-appointed drawing room of Chauncy Fuller's mansion.

"How did you manage to get off the ship undetected?" Thaddeus asked, his eyes glinting with excitement.

"I went into steerage and rummaged through the trunk of a buxom woman when she and her husband were on deck, and I found a dress and a bonnet that had a wide brim to help cover my face."

Thaddeus appeared shocked. "You disguised yourself as a woman?"

"Don't act so appalled. My idea worked, didn't it? The captain had his whole crew looking for a man. I strolled by them in that woman's ill-fitting gown, my own clothes tucked underneath, and not one question was asked. Personally, I felt my performance was a stroke of genius."

Thaddeus bobbed his head in agreement. "So it was. You truly are brilliant."

"I'm certain you realize my unexpected departure from England has left me financially embarrassed. My funds are in England, and I'm going to need money to book a return passage. That's where you come in, my friend. I need to borrow enough money for passage and a little extra to take care of my needs until I sail. Of course, I knew you would be the one person I could count on for such a loan."

"Your request comes at a bad time, William. I was at the gaming tables yesterday and find myself without funds to assist you," Thaddeus replied, his voice a hoarse whisper.

William stiffened, and his gaze narrowed into what he hoped was an icy stare. "Then you need to determine how you're going to get your hands on enough money to help me."

Thaddeus squirmed in his chair for several moments and then slapped his leg, obviously pleased with himself. "I know where I can get the money. Naomi! She was always tight with her money. I'm certain she's tucked away every cent the Corporation has paid her. After all, Naomi expects me to leave her a few coins every time I stop to see Theona. I've always complied because I didn't want her to stop me from visiting," he said. "The visits give me a reason to be in Lowell without questions being asked," he explained.

"Your former wife will loan you the money?"

"No, of course not. I'll steal it from her. If you can pass yourself off as a woman, surely I should be able to pilfer the money from the home of my former wife," he said with a coarse laugh.

"She doesn't keep her money in the bank?"

"Naomi was never one to use the bank. Unless one of those mill girls has recently convinced her to begin using the Thrift Savings where they keep all of their earnings, I'm certain I'll find her money hidden away in the bedroom. The blanket chest was always her favorite hiding place. I'll call on her tomorrow," Thaddeus said.

"Thank you, my friend. Of course, you'll be handsomely rewarded once I return to England."

A sign on the front door advised patients to walk in and be seated. Although Thaddeus wasn't a patient, he walked in the front door and down the hallway of what now served as both Naomi's boardinghouse and Dr. Ketter's office.

"Hello, Naomi," he said, enjoying the opportunity to make a surprise visit upon his wife. He knew she despised having him appear, but that fact made his visit even more appealing.

She whirled around, the apple she was peeling suddenly falling to the floor. "Thaddeus! What are *you* doing here?" Picking up the apple, Naomi rinsed it in a pan of water and sliced it into thin pieces before handing it to Theona.

"Paying a visit to my daughter," he said in an even tone.

The wide-eyed child remained partially hidden behind Naomi's skirt, her round rosy cheeks moving up and down as she chewed the apple. "You were here only days ago. Usually it's at least several weeks between your visits," she replied while giving him a hasty once-over. "I'm merely surprised your visits with Theona are so stimulating that you'd make the journey twice in one week. Are you certain you're not in some kind of trouble?"

Thaddeus beckoned to the child. "Quite the contrary, my dear," he amicably replied before lifting Theona to his lap. "I see you've water boiling over the fire. Would it trouble you too much to prepare a cup of tea?" he asked in his most pleasant tone.

She eyed him suspiciously. "I suppose a cup of tea wouldn't be out of order."

Naomi's wary attitude didn't surprise him. After all, his amiable behavior toward her was utterly out of character, but he needed time if he was going to find a way to get into the blanket chest in her bedroom. Watching as she brewed the tea, he bounced Theona on his knee, hoping to appear the doting father.

Naomi placed his tea on the table beside him. "Won't you join me?" he asked.

She pushed a stray wisp of hair behind one ear. "No, I have laundry to hang," she responded.

"Surely you can take a few minutes," he urged.

She hesitated and then sat down. "You talked as though things are going well for you. Have you found new employment?" she inquired.

"A new business venture," he replied, finding pleasure in divulging the information. He continually hoped to make her regret the fact that they were no longer married.

"Business venture? That sounds risky. I hope it's a sensible investment," she impulsively responded.

He inwardly bristled at her comment, wanting to launch into a verbal assault upon her. How would *she* possibly know anything about business? Her only concern was his ability to pass along a few coins for Theona's care. Forcing himself to remain calm, he gave her an affable smile. "I believe this particular activity will prove extremely beneficial. In fact, one of the primary partners in the venture has been visiting from England only this week. He came specifically to see me and encourage my participation in the undertaking," he boasted.

She leveled a look of skepticism toward him. "An unknown man came all the way from England to talk to *you* about entering into a business enterprise?"

"I didn't say he was unknown," Thaddeus countered.

"Whom do you know in England?" she quizzed.

Without thinking, he blurted out William Thurston's name. Too late, he caught himself, realizing he ought not be speaking of William's whereabouts.

"I don't believe I've ever heard you speak of him," she replied.

Thaddeus breathed a sigh of relief, pleased that while they were married he'd managed to keep his wife at home, well away from the gossip that circulated about Lowell. She'd likely never heard of William Thurston or his involvement in the kidnappings that occurred three years ago. Perhaps she would forget the name as quickly as she'd heard it.

"I must get to my laundry. Theona, stay here with your father while I go outside," she instructed. "I won't be too long," she called over her shoulder while exiting the rear door.

"Take your time. I'll just have another cup of tea," he replied, listening until the door closed and then lifting Theona off his lap. "I'll be right back, Theona. You stay here and finish your apple."

Assuring himself the doctor and his patients would not see him, Thaddeus hurried down the hallway and up the stairs to Naomi's bedroom. Spotting the blanket chest, he moved quietly across the floor, uncertain if sounds from above would alert the doctor. The hinges on the chest squealed in protest as he lifted the lid. He waited a moment—his heart hammering wildly as he listened for the sound of footsteps. Only the sound of murmuring in the office below could be heard. He exhaled deeply as he began rifling through the stored coverlets, pleased when his fingers finally touched upon what he knew was Naomi's leather pouch. Circling his hand around the supple doeskin, he pulled it from between the folded blankets and momentarily savored his victory.

"Theona!"

The child stood in the doorway watching him, her blue eyes wide and unyielding.

"What you doing?" she innocently inquired.

He didn't respond to her question. Instead, he took her by the hand and led her out of the room. "Come along, let's go back downstairs."

"Mr. Arnold! What are you doing upstairs?"

Thaddeus startled at the voice and immediately turned his gaze to the downstairs hallway, where Dr. Ketter stood staring up at him.

Pointing toward his daughter, Thaddeus gave the doctor a cautious smile and nodded. "Just retrieving Theona. I didn't want her falling down the steps," he replied. Taking the child's hand, he descended the stairs and hurried back to the kitchen.

"Come along, Theona," he said to the child, pulling her along toward the rear door.

Pulling open the door, he glanced about, finally spotting Naomi's feet beneath a sheet she was hanging on the line. "I've some business to attend to, Naomi. I really must be going. Shall I send Theona out with you?"

She pulled the sheet aside and gave him a questioning look. "You're leaving already?"

"Yes, I had forgotten a matter that needs my immediate attention," he said.

"Come along, Theona," she said.

With his back toward Naomi, Thaddeus leaned down and placed a kiss upon the child's cheek. "It isn't safe for you to be going upstairs by yourself. You might fall," he said, making certain his words were loud enough to be heard by Naomi.

The child gave him a confused look. Narrowing his eyes, he leveled a menacing glare at Theona. "Yeth, thir," she obediently replied.

He tousled her dark hair. "That's a good girl."

Daughtie placed her cape on the peg inside the front door and then greeted Theona, who stood in the doorway of the kitchen. "Did you have a fine day, Theona?" she asked, walking down the hall.

Theona bobbed her head up and down, her bow-shaped lips turning up in a sweet smile. "Papa come," she said as Daughtie drew nearer.

Daughtie turned and gazed toward Naomi. "Was Mr. Arnold here again today?"

"Yes. It was a strange visit. He came in talking as though he was anxious to spend time with Theona, but he didn't stay long."

"It hasn't even been a week since he last called upon you, has it?"

"No," she replied while pulling a stack of plates from the shelf and then gathering silverware in her other hand.

"Papa upthtairs," Theona said as her mother walked into the dining room to set the table.

Naomi turned on her heel. "No. Papa's gone home. He's not upstairs."

"Papa upthtairs," the child repeated.

"No, Theona! Your papa has gone home."

"She likely means that he was upstairs earlier—before he left the house," Dr. Ketter explained as he helped himself to a sweet pickle.

Naomi turned her attention to the doctor, a startled look etched upon her face. "What? Thaddeus was upstairs?"

Theona's head bobbed again. "Papa upthtairs."

Naomi stooped down in front of the little girl. "Why was Papa upstairs?"

The child gave her mother a winsome smile. "Blankie," she said.

"The blanket chest—my money," Naomi cried, racing toward the stairs. "He's stolen my money. I know it!" she shouted.

Theona whimpered, tears threatening to spill down her cheeks at any moment. Daughtie sat down and opened her arms to the child, lifting her into a warm embrace. Theona snuggled close and rested her plump cheek against Daughtie's chest.

Naomi returned to the dining room, a faraway look in her eyes. "He took all of my money—even the leather pouch."

"You must go to the police," Daughtie encouraged.

"Absolutely. I'll go with you and confirm that I saw him upstairs while you were outdoors," Dr. Ketter said. "I'll get my coat."

"No. Wait. I don't want to go to the police. Let's have dinner."

Daughtie stared at the older woman in disbelief. "But, Mrs. Arnold—"

"No, I'll not go," she interrupted. "I don't want to discuss this any further," she said, casting a glance at Theona.

Daughtie nodded. "As you wish."

"Ruth said she wouldn't be here for supper, so we may as well eat," Mrs. Arnold said. "I'll get the bread."

Except for the sound of clattering dishes and an occasional word from Theona, the four of them ate their meal in silence. Ivan excused himself as soon as he'd finished eating a piece of pie and headed back down the hall to his office.

Daughtie took a sip of tea and glanced over the top of her cup at Mrs. Arnold. "You really should go to the police," she softly urged.

Theona scooted down from her chair, marching off to entertain herself in the other room.

"I haven't forgotten the years of abuse I suffered at his hand. He's a cruel man—no one knows that better than I do. I still bear the scars from his beatings. If I go to the police and he convinces them it's all a lie, he'll retaliate. I'm not willing to take the chance that he'll return and harm Theona."

Daughtie longed for words to comfort Mrs. Arnold, but none came to her. "I understand. You must do what's best for both you and Theona. I hadn't considered that he might strike out against Theona—or you," she said, taking Naomi's hand in her own. "I don't want you or Theona placed in harm's way."

Mrs. Arnold gave her a faint smile. "I don't understand Thaddeus. I never have. It's abundantly clear that he came here to steal from me, yet he spent a great deal of time telling me about a new business venture. He seemed genuinely excited, going into detail about a Mr. Thurston who'd come from England to encourage his participation in this innovative enterprise. None of this makes any sense."

"Thurston? William Thurston?" Daughtie's mind reeled with Bella's tale of William Thurston escaping before the authorities could apprehend him. Apparently he was nearby, possibly in Lowell. She must get word to Bella and Taylor.

～ 27 ～

Daughtie remained in the kitchen with Mrs. Arnold and Theona until the older woman composed herself.

"There's really nothing anyone can do, and there's no need for you to remain here in the kitchen with me," Naomi said. "You go on. I've got dishes and mending I need to complete before bedtime, and Theona's here to keep me company, aren't you, dearest?"

The little girl smiled at her mother while clapping her hands. "I will help," she said.

Theona's sincere offer caused Daughtie to smile. "If you're certain you don't need me, I believe I'll call on Bella and Taylor Manning. We had time for only a short visit last evening," she explained.

"What a pleasant coincidence," Dr. Ketter commented.

Daughtie turned toward Dr. Ketter, who was now standing in the doorway of his office.

"I'm preparing to leave for the Farnsworth residence, also. Taylor and his bride *do* reside with Mr. and Mrs. Farnsworth, don't they?"

"Yes. Their new home isn't completed yet," she replied. "Is someone ill?"

"No, at least not that I'm aware of. They extended an invitation to call, saying they would like to meet me."

"I see. I'm surprised they're entertaining so soon after their arrival home. Perhaps I should call upon Bella some other time."

"Nonsense! Mr. and Mrs. Farnsworth merely wish to become acquainted since they find themselves without a doctor now that Dr. Barnard has retired. I'm sure your friend will be delighted to have you visit, and *I'll* be pleased to have you accompany me," he said with a bright smile. "I was planning on walking because it's such a fine evening, but I could fetch a carriage if you'd prefer."

"I'm accustomed to walking. Besides, this is the first day we've been without rain this week. The spring weather will make for an enjoyable stroll," Daughtie said, unable to think of any excuse to avoid Dr. Ketter's company. After all, it was imperative she inform Bella and Taylor of William Thurston's activity.

Dr. Ketter was smiling profusely as they crossed the street, careful to lead her around several large mud-filled puddles. "I'm pleased to have some time alone with you. Sometimes I wonder if you're intentionally attempting to avoid me," he said, hesitating and obviously hoping she'd reject his idea.

His comment mirrored her feelings, yet she knew to simply agree with his remark would be insensitive. Finally she settled upon a vague reply. "I keep very busy with a number of activities."

"I may consider joining into some of those activities in order to spend time with you," he said with a bright smile.

Clearly Dr. Ketter wasn't easily deterred, and Daughtie wished she had given a more direct reply after all. "The groups to which I belong are for women," she curtly stated.

"I was purely jesting with you. I'm hopeful you won't make it *quite* that difficult for me to call upon you."

"I have no time for gentlemen callers," she answered, attempting to hide her irritation. She wanted the discussion of her free time to end. "You might consider directing your attention toward Ruth. As I've said before, I believe the two of you would have much in common, and she has expressed a keen interest in attending several lectures that will soon be presented in Lowell."

They stopped while permitting an approaching carriage to pass, then began crossing the street to the Farnsworth home. Ivan gazed down at her. "Is it truly your desire that I pursue Ruth, or are you being coy? It's sometimes difficult to discern if women are saying exactly what they mean."

"I cannot speak for other women, but you may take *me* at my word. While you appear to be a fine, upstanding man, I am confident that you and I have very little in common. I have not pursued your interest but rather have tried to make my disinterest more than apparent. I believe if anyone is to blame for this, it is Ruth for her encouragement of your attention toward me. I am certain she had the best intentions, for she worries after me like a mother hen; however, she was misguided in this pursuit and I am afraid we have both suffered for it." She paused, eyeing him quite sternly. "So please be assured, I am not attempting to lure you with game playing. There is no reason for you to continue pursuing me. I will not change my mind."

"Well, that was certainly clear and concise," he replied dejectedly. "I'll keep my distance."

His disappointment was evident in his voice, but Daughtie knew that this time she could show no mercy. One kind word and he would resume his pursuit of her. "Here we are," she said, turning up the steps to the Farnsworth house as he followed close on her heels. Her knock was answered by a young girl with a mischievous grin on her face.

"I'm Elinor. Who are you?" the bundle of energy asked.

"Why, it's so nice to meet you, Elinor," Daughtie answered. "I'm Miss

Daughtie Winfield, and this is Dr. Ivan Ketter. What do you think of America so far?"

"I think it rains all the time!" Elinor laughed as she let the guests into the house and turned to find Addie and John waiting patiently behind her. Bella joined the group, and soon Addie and John whisked Dr. Ketter into the formal parlor for a visit while leaving her to chat with Bella.

A clap of thunder sounded overhead. "What's wrong, Daughtie? Is the storm disturbing to you? You've appeared anxious ever since you arrived this evening," Bella said while pouring a cup of tea.

"It's not the storm that's upset me. I've news to share with you—about William Thurston."

"William Thurston?"

Daughtie startled at the deep male voice that echoed her words. "Oh, Taylor! You surprised me," she sighed.

"I'm sorry, but hearing William Thurston's name certainly captured my attention. You have news of him?"

"Yes," Daughtie said while giving a quick nod of her head. "Thaddeus Arnold was in Lowell earlier today. He said he came to call upon his daughter, Theona. In the midst of Mr. Arnold's visit, he mentioned he had entered into a business venture with someone who had recently sailed from England. As he continued with the story, he mentioned that William Thurston is his newly arrived business partner."

Taylor appeared stunned. "He told you this?"

"No, he told Mrs. Arnold and she passed along the information to me."

"Do you know where Thaddeus makes his home?"

"A village in New Hampshire, but I don't recall the name. I can ask Mrs. Arnold. I think she'll cooperate. However, she's fearful of retribution from Mr. Arnold should she go to the police."

"She should be more fearful of the company her former husband is associating with. Did he tell her anything more?" Taylor inquired.

"I didn't finish my story," Daughtie said. "While Mr. Arnold was at the boardinghouse, he went upstairs to Mrs. Arnold's bedroom and helped himself to her savings. I encouraged her to report the matter, but she wouldn't."

"She's *certain* he absconded with the money?"

"She didn't actually see him with it, but when Dr. Ketter was coming out of his office, he noticed Mr. Arnold upstairs. The rains had abated, and Mrs. Arnold was outdoors hanging laundry. There was no reason for Mr. Arnold to be in her room except to steal," Daughtie declared.

"Did I hear my name mentioned?" Ivan inquired as he entered the room, flanked by Addie and John.

"I mentioned your observation of Mr. Arnold in the upstairs rooms today," Daughtie replied.

"Seems William Thurston may be in New Hampshire or possibly even here in Lowell," Taylor told his uncle as the group joined them.

"Do tell," John said, his face flushed with excitement. "How did you come by this piece of information?"

"Daughtie," Taylor replied. "Tell him what you related to me," he instructed.

Daughtie repeated the story, with Dr. Ketter interrupting to add a piece of information from time to time. John's interest was obviously piqued as she related details of William Thurston's dealings with Thaddeus Arnold.

"I'm not at all certain I understand why you're all so interested in this William Thurston," Dr. Ketter remarked when Daughtie had finished speaking.

"He was a primary participant in thefts and kidnappings that took place here in Lowell three years ago. In fact, he was the instigator who stayed behind the scenes, ordering his henchmen to conduct the reprehensible deeds," John explained.

Daughtie leaned forward, peeking around Bella. "Ruth and Bella were both among those who were kidnapped. Fortunately, they were rescued, thanks in large part to Taylor and Mr. Farnsworth," she said, giving both men a charming smile.

Dr. Ketter appeared aghast at the mention of the kidnappings. "And this Thurston fellow managed to escape before being brought to justice?"

"Quite so. But with a modicum of good fortune and careful planning, we may be able to detain him before he's able to slip out of our grasp. To be frank, I'm astounded he's remained in the country this long. Of course, we alerted the police in Boston. They agreed to assist by checking the manifests of passengers sailing to England. If he became aware of police involvement, he may have decided to wait until activity quiets around the docks," John surmised. "I think we should talk to Mrs. Arnold, learn exactly where Thaddeus resides, and pay him an unexpected visit."

"Exactly!" Taylor agreed. "I'll get my hat."

Daughtie rose from her chair. "Please wait. After today's events, I think your appearance at the door may upset Mrs. Arnold."

"Possibly," John agreed. "And the hour *is* growing late for calling."

Taylor stopped midstep. "Perhaps you could talk to her in the morning, Daughtie. Bella tells me you're attending church with us. You could bring us word when we meet."

"I'll do my best," she cautiously replied.

John nodded. "She may still be up and about when you arrive home. I understand the mills will be closed Monday and Tuesday, possibly longer, if these rains don't subside. With these spring freshets flooding the mill pond, it may be impossible to regulate the waterpower for even longer if we don't soon get some relief from the downpours."

"I didn't know a decision had been made. Mr. Gault sent word to each foreman late today simply advising the possibility of a shutdown existed," she said.

"I should think all of you girls would be pleased to have a little time away from the mill," John commented.

"For some of us the break from work is a blessing; for others, the loss of pay caused by the spring freshets can be most distressing."

Addie nodded in agreement. "Ah, yes. I remember only too well those poor girls who were placed in dire financial straits by the loss of wages. Let's hope they've been able to monetarily prepare themselves for the spring rains."

Daughtie and Dr. Ketter moved toward the door and bid farewell. She then stepped outside, knowing that Ivan Ketter would follow her, yet hoping he wouldn't begin his pursuit anew.

"I've been thinking," he said softly as they headed for Mrs. Arnold's house. "I want you to know it was never my intention to make you uncomfortable. I'm generally not so bold, but I was encouraged."

"Yes, I know," Daughtie replied, uncertain where this conversation was leading.

"I'm not a difficult man," he said in a reflective manner. "I'm sorry that I made you uncomfortable. I would never have pursued your affections had I not believed it all to be part of the ritual."

Daughtie couldn't help but chuckle. "I grew up with the Shakers, Dr. Ketter. Men and women were not allowed to share their affections or play a part of any ritual, as you call it. I'm sorry you felt misled."

"Well, truth be told, I wouldn't mind getting to know Miss Ruth better."

Daughtie looked up at him with a huge smile. "I think I can help arrange that."

He perked up at this. "Truly? You don't think she'll feel the same as you?"

Daughtie shook her head. "No, in fact, Ruth was quite jealous of the attention you showed me those first few days. I do not believe it will be a difficult task at all to win her interest."

"And you would consent to helping me?"

Daughtie laughed. "I hardly believe you'll need my help, Dr. Ketter. I believe Ruth's heart will speak for itself once she realizes you are interested."

They reached the house just then. Daughtie turned at the door. "I'm glad this has been worked out between us. I never wished to make an enemy of you."

"You most assuredly will never be my enemy," Ivan replied.

"Nor you mine," Daughtie answered, glad to have things work out much better than she could have hoped for.

Dr. Ketter opened the door to find Ruth conveniently nearby. "Ah, Ruth. Just the woman I hoped to see."

Ruth appeared rather shocked as she looked past Dr. Ketter to Daughtie. "Me?"

"Indeed. Have you a few moments to join me by the fire?"

Daughtie wanted to giggle at the look on Ruth's face. *Good,* she thought, *let her have some of her own medicine. Let her be the recipient of Dr. Ketter's persistent attention.* Somehow, Daughtie believed Ruth would receive it in a much more welcoming manner.

Daughtie readied herself for church the next morning, now armed with the information Taylor had requested the evening before. She would need to depart early if she was to arrive at the Farnsworth home as scheduled. Hurrying downstairs, she sighed, weary from the night of thunder and lightning that had interrupted her sleep. The rain had subsided a bit, but the clouds overhead appeared ominous as she hastened her steps.

"Psst. Ma'am!"

Daughtie turned toward the sound, surprised to see the Irish girl who had always delivered Liam's messages hiding in the brush along the fence line. The girl glanced about and then hurried toward Daughtie, waving a piece of paper in front of her. She shoved the scrap in Daughtie's direction, obviously anxious to be rid of it and on her way. Unfolding and smoothing the rumpled paper, Daughtie scanned the carefully penned words. Her heart plummeted. How could she possibly handle another complex situation at this time?

In a few moments Daughtie was staring at the front door of the Farnsworth house. In order to help Liam, she'd *have* to place her trust in Bella. She knocked, fervently praying Bella would be the one to answer.

"Daughtie! I told Taylor it would be you," Bella replied. Her blond curls were held in place with a tortoise-shell comb inlaid with green stones that matched her dress.

Grasping Bella's hand, Daughtie pulled her into the parlor, where they couldn't be heard. "Mr. Arnold is in Litchfield, a small hamlet north of Nashua."

"Why are you whispering, and why have you forced me into the parlor?" Bella asked, her pink lips forming a diminutive pout.

"You must make some excuse for my absence today, both at church and afterward."

Bella's pout intensified. "You're not going to be here for dinner and visiting this afternoon?"

"Please don't be angry. I've had a note from Liam requesting I come to the house. He truly must get the girls moved, and I've had a brilliant idea. We may even be able to execute the plan today if we begin immediately."

"Oh, do tell me all about it," Bella replied, smiling as she clasped her hands together in excitement.

"I haven't time right now. Besides, it's better if you don't know. That way you'll not be forced to tell a lie."

Bella's smile faded, and she began tapping her right foot at a rapid tempo. "You know I can maintain a confidence."

"I never questioned your loyalty, but I don't want to put you at risk or cause you any difficulty. Besides, there's no time for discussion—I should already be on my way to Liam's. I must hurry," she said, giving Bella a quick hug.

"You know I wish you well. I'll be praying for you."

"Oh, thank you, dear Bella. You are the very best friend I could ever hope for. We'll need your prayers if the girls are to find safety," Daughtie replied.

Bella nodded. "Is there *nothing* I can do to help?"

Daughtie hesitated. "Perhaps there is. Would you send word to Mrs. Arnold that I've gone to Canterbury? I think I can make good use of this time away from the mill."

"Please send me word when you've returned. Otherwise, I'll continue to worry about your safety. And give my love to Sister Mercy."

"Sister Mercy? Oh, yes. If I see her I'll send your regards," Daughtie replied before making a hasty retreat.

The drizzle continued, and thunder rumbled above as if drumming out a warning that the threatening dark clouds would soon deluge the town with further pelting rainfall. Daughtie bent her head against the wind, thankful her hooded cloak offered a modicum of protection against the onslaught. The glow from a whale oil lamp shone through the curtained window of Liam's house, and she quickened her step, anxious to be out of the miserable weather.

Liam approached in answer to her knock, a look of surprise crossing his face as he pulled open the door. "I didn't expect ya quite so early. How did ya manage to depart the boardinghouse undetected? Won't Ruth be expectin' ya to attend church services?"

Daughtie rubbed her hands together, the rain leaving her chilled. "She knew I was leaving early in order to deliver a message to Bella. She's expecting me to attend services with Taylor and Bella. However, I asked Bella to inform Mrs. Arnold that I would be going to Canterbury."

He frowned as he led her into the parlor. "Canterbury? What would be takin' you back to visit the Shakers?" he asked. "I don't mean to appear single-minded, but I truly need your help with the two slave girls hidin' upstairs."

Daughtie moved in front of the fire, extending her hands toward the warmth. "Not Canterbury, New Hampshire, although that's where Bella surmised I was going, also," she explained. "Canterbury, Connecticut."

He stared at her, his eyebrows furrowed. "Sit down and tell me what you're thinkin', lassie."

"The safety of the girls has been in my prayers since I left here the other evening," she began. "I've prayed that another group of runaways would arrive and the problem would be solved, but that obviously hasn't occurred. However, when I opened my Bible last night, my most recent letter from Prudence Crandall fell to the floor."

Liam nodded and leaned forward. "Aye?"

"As I picked up the letter, I was struck by an idea. The very best place for these girls would be at Prudence Crandall's school in Connecticut," she said, somewhat surprised he needed clarification.

"I see," he said, rubbing his forehead. "With all the problems Miss Crandall's had with the townsfolk, do ya think her school is safe? Would it not be less dangerous to take them to the Shaker village, perhaps? You once spoke of the Shakers takin' in some runaways."

"No," Daughtie replied. "Both Minerva and Nelly have religious convictions that are in opposition to those of the Shakers. To force them into that world would be particularly unfair. Besides, in her latest letter, Miss Crandall was pleased to relate that her difficulties had subsided and there had been no further incidents at the school. In fact, she even mentioned she was going to once again begin seeking new students. Then she went on to say that she believed our prayers were being answered," Daughtie replied.

Leaning forward, Liam rested his arms on his thighs and met Daughtie's intense gaze. "So ya believe this is *God's* plan?" he quietly inquired.

Daughtie nodded her agreement. "Yes, I do. I believe it's His answer— and now that the mills are closed due to the rains, I can go with you and speak to Miss Crandall on their behalf."

"If ya believe God wants us to take them to Miss Crandall's school in Connecticut, then I think we should comply. It won't take long to make preparations."

She peered into his eyes, hoping to assure herself he wasn't scoffing. He appeared sincere. "I'm pleasantly surprised at your desire to follow God's direction. You've apparently given additional thought to our recent conversation," she replied cautiously.

"Aye. I've been spendin' some time readin' the Bible and prayin', but those two girls make quite a proclamation for God, also. Their faith would be an inspiration to any heathen," he said with a grin. "They don't waver from what they believe. In fact, they told me their faith in God is what sustains them durin' difficult times. When she's havin' trouble or feeling sorry for herself, Nelly said she thinks how Jesus suffered in order to grant her the gift of eternal life. We've talked a great deal since they arrived— mostly about their faith," he continued. "It appears I've been surrounded by devout young women who aren't afraid to express their belief in God."

A smile tugged at Daughtie's lips. "Seems as though God's found a way to present His message."

Liam smiled in return. "He's found *three* ways. I guess He figures a hard-headed Irishman needs to hear things more than once."

"I've discovered God is more than willing to use any method necessary in order to gain *my* attention, and it seems He's doing the same with you."

Liam arched his eyebrows, obviously taken aback by her remark. "One thing is certain. I've had plenty to mull over the past few days. Now with your idea that the girls should go to Prudence Crandall's school, it's become obvious to me that God's concerned with the future of these girls. We'd best be prayin' that He remain involved if we're going to get them safely delivered to Connecticut."

"Do you think there's any possibility we might be stopped along the way?" Daughtie asked.

"Perhaps. But since we'll be taking the wagon, I can say I'm going to Connecticut for my stonemasonry business."

Daughtie nodded. "I'll go upstairs and tell the girls we're leaving. We'll gather some food while you hitch the wagon."

"Good, but don't be too long. With these rains, I fear we'll be forced to move slowly. We can hope the weather clears as we move south," he said while moving toward the door. "I don't think there's anyone lurkin' around, but I'll bring the wagon up close to the back o' the house. The three of you can come out the kitchen door."

"We'll be ready," Daughtie said, the sound of her shoes echoing as she clattered down the hallway at full tilt.

28

John greeted Matthew Cheever with a warm handshake while entering the foyer of St. Anne's Episcopal Church. "Good to see you, Matthew. I understand that even after being gone all these months, I still won't be returning to work tomorrow."

Matthew nodded. "These spring rains seem to wreak havoc upon us every year. I received word your ship docked earlier this week. Forgive me for not calling upon you and Miss Addie, but the rain has managed to keep all of us indoors more often than not. And now with the water continuing to rise, it's simply impossible to continue operations until the rain lets up. Needless to say, the Associates are unhappy."

"And when the Associates are unhappy, Kirk Boott is *very* unhappy," John added. "There's no doubt this troublesome weather places an additional burden upon you. Production stoppage isn't good for any of us."

Addie tugged at John's arm. "That's enough talk of the mills for now. Services are about to begin. Did John extend an invitation to join us for dinner?" she asked with a cheery smile.

John's eyes widened. "It appears you've taken care of the assignment for me," he teased.

"John!" A playful look of recrimination was etched upon Addie's face. She took hold of John's arm before turning her attention toward Matthew. "Would you and Lilly consider joining us for dinner after church services—if you don't have other plans? We'd enjoy the opportunity to visit, and I'm certain John wants to hear what's been happening at the mills since our departure."

John moved closer to Matthew. "There's a matter of importance I must discuss with you as soon as possible," he confided.

Matthew beckoned to Lilly, who stood visiting with Bella and Taylor. "Mr. and Mrs. Farnsworth have invited us to join them for dinner this afternoon," he said with mock formality. "I didn't know if you'd be feeling up to it. Have you made prior arrangements?" he questioned.

Lilly Cheever, clearly expecting, patted her rounding stomach. "I made no plans for this afternoon. Your mother has offered to take Violet home for the day. I think dinner and visiting with our dear friends will ease the gloom of this frightful weather and be a delightful way to spend our free time. We would *love* to come," Lilly replied happily.

Addie's lips turned upward in a broad smile. "Good! Now I think we had best get to our pews, or Reverend Edson may be forced to conduct the services out here in the foyer."

John smiled at his wife while leading her down the aisle of the church. "I believe your sister is glowering at us," he murmured, catching Mintie's poignant frown.

"She doesn't approve of making a late entrance," Addie whispered in reply.

"Obviously she believes it's perfectly acceptable to crane her neck and stare down her nose at those of us breaching her rules of etiquette," he mused.

"I've likely hurt her feelings by not rushing to her side as soon as we arrived this morning. She becomes easily wounded by my thoughtless behavior."

"Goodness, Addie. How did Mintie succeed in convincing you you're thoughtless? There isn't an inconsiderate bone in your body."

Mintie pushed open the pew door and gazed up at her sister and brother-in-law. "You're late," she charged, thumping the tip of her umbrella on the hardwood floor for emphasis.

"We're *not* late, Mintie. Services haven't even begun," John curtly replied. "We were in the vestibule."

Mintie arched her thin eyebrows high above the wire-rimmed glasses perched on her beaklike nose. "Visiting, no doubt!" she accused.

"Extending dinner invitations," John brusquely replied while seating himself at the end of the pew.

Leaning across Addie's portly figure, Mintie extended her long neck and leveled a thin-lipped look of disapproval at John. "I don't believe *I* received a dinner invitation."

John gazed into his sister-in-law's stern brown eyes. "Where's Lawrence this morning?" he asked, hoping to soften her a bit.

Mintie glanced to the left as though she momentarily thought Lawrence was beside her. "He's gone to Rhode Island. He decided a short visit with his sister might be in order since the mills will be closed for several days. He left by coach early this morning. I told him the coach would likely be hindered by mud before reaching the outskirts of town, but he thought otherwise."

"He was probably anxious for quietude and pleasant company," John murmured, flinching as Addie's elbow jabbed into his side.

"What?" Mintie asked, cupping one ear. "I couldn't hear you over those chattering girls."

Addie bent toward her sister. "He said Lawrence's sister is probably anxious for some pleasant company."

Mintie gave a curt nod. "I'm certain she is. Lawrence tells me the poor woman is married to a disagreeable sort—rigid and difficult to please."

"Sounds as though she's describing herself," John whispered mischievously.

Addie turned and grinned. "Stop, John," she muttered genially.

"So you're having a dinner party?" Mintie asked.

"No, not a dinner party. I must discuss some business matters with Matthew, and since the mills are closed, I thought it expedient to invite the Cheevers to dinner after church services. We knew you'd be busy preparing dinner for your boarders or we would have included you," John replied. "However, if you'd like to come over later in the afternoon for tea, I'll send a carriage," he offered.

"Well, let me think." She hesitated, her forehead crinkled into deep ridges. "I believe I *could* fit tea into my schedule," she finally replied. "You may send your carriage at three o'clock."

John nodded, leaned back against the pew, and grinned at Addie.

"Thank you, John. That was very kind," she whispered.

"You're welcome, my dear. So long as you realize that I invited her only so she wouldn't press you."

"Ssshhhh!" Mintie hissed, extending her umbrella menacingly in John's direction.

"You keep that umbrella under control, Mintie, or you'll not be joining your sister for tea this afternoon," he warned.

Mintie jerked the umbrella away from his leg and pointed a thin finger toward the pulpit. "Quiet! Church has begun."

John leaned close to Addie's ear. "That woman insists upon having the final word. No wonder Lawrence went to Rhode Island," he muttered.

With dinner completed and the women off to the parlor, John led the way into the small library adjacent to the dining room, where he offered Matthew a cigar.

"No, thank you, John," Matthew said, seating himself on one of the tapestry-covered overstuffed chairs opposite Taylor. "I'm glad both of you have returned, and of course, I'm anxious to hear about your journey. Any new designs or innovative ideas to report?" he inquired.

"There are a few new concepts I'd like to see incorporated, and I believe Taylor has a few ideas to report, also. However, those matters can wait."

Matthew appeared surprised. "Really? I thought that's why you'd invited us to dinner."

"No. What we must discuss is of grave concern and will require your immediate involvement."

Matthew sat up in his chair and tugged at his waistcoat. "You're acting terribly mysterious, John. Is there anything illegal or immoral involved in this situation you wish to discuss?" he asked with a chuckle.

"Thurston—William Thurston. He's returned to the United States."

Matthew jumped to his feet. "You're certain? Where is he? How long have you known?"

"Sit down. It's a lengthy story," he said, waiting until Matthew had settled himself before relating the tale of his own kidnapping and escape in London, William's appearance on the ship, and the information recently divulged by Thaddeus Arnold. "So you see," he concluded, "there's every reason to believe William Thurston may be hiding out somewhere in close proximity to Thaddeus Arnold."

Matthew nodded. "And if not, I'd wager Thaddeus must know how to make contact with Thurston."

"If he's still in the country," Taylor remarked.

Matthew appeared confused. "I'm surprised he didn't immediately board the first ship sailing back to England. Why would he remain in Massachusetts when he knows his only future is in jail?"

"Or worse yet, having the fury of his outraged wife vented upon him," Taylor replied in a jesting tone.

"I imagine Mrs. Thurston would be one of the first to contact the police. In addition to all his other crimes, word has it that William made off with some of her family's gold and jewelry before departing the country."

"I don't doubt it," John replied firmly. "I don't believe that man has a shred of moral fiber in his whole body. So what do you say, Matthew? Shall we head out for New Hampshire in the morning and pay Thaddeus Arnold a visit?"

"I can't think of anything else I'd rather do. If you have no objection, I'd like to pass this information along to Mr. Boott. He may want to accompany us."

"Whatever you decide is fine with me," John replied.

***

A spindly woman answered the door, strands of wiry hair poking out from beneath a white mobcap. She wiped her hands on a stained cotton apron that partially covered her worn print dress. Pointing a thumb toward a wooden sign with faded letters announcing rooms for rent, she wagged her head back and forth. "I'm full up. Never take the sign down—just in case one of my boarders leaves unexpectedly."

"We're not looking for a room. The tavern owner told us Thaddeus Arnold is one of your boarders," John said. "We've come to call on him."

"You friends of his from down in Lowell?" she asked.

John nodded. "We worked at the same mill."

"Hear tell it's been raining hard down that way," she said. "Coach driver said he had trouble making it through. Not that far from Lowell to Litchfield, but we ain't had a drop. You reckon it's heading this way?"

"I think the rain's headed away from the area, so it's not likely you'll be getting much, if any," he replied. "Is Mr. Arnold here?" he asked, hoping to curtail her conversation.

"He's become mighty popular all of a sudden," she remarked. Turning away from the doorway, she beckoned toward the men. "Come on in. I'll fetch him for you."

"We truly would enjoy the pleasure of surprising him, if you don't mind," John whispered, as though taking the woman into his deepest confidence. He put a coin in her palm and smiled broadly.

She grinned in return. "I always did like surprises myself," she said. "You go on up and knock—second door on the left."

"Thank you," John replied while motioning Matthew and Taylor to follow him.

Matthew rapped soundly, and the three men waited silently. The sound of shuffling feet approached on the other side of the door, followed by the squeak of the door as it opened to reveal an obviously stunned Thaddeus Arnold.

"What are *you* doing here?" he gasped, his gaze darting about like a trapped animal seeking escape.

"Let's go in your room and talk," Matthew suggested. "I'm sure you don't want the other tenants or the boardinghouse owner hearing our conversation."

Thaddeus tentatively backed into the room, watching as Taylor closed the door and then firmly leaned his body against it.

"You can sit here," Thaddeus offered while looking at Taylor.

"I prefer to stand," Taylor replied.

"You know why we're here," John said in a menacing tone. "Why don't you just tell us where Thurston is and we'll be on our way."

"Thurston? I don't know what you're talking about. Why do you think *I* know the whereabouts of William Thurston?"

"Because you've been seen together," John bluffed.

"If someone's made such an allegation, he's mistaken. William Thurston's a wealthy man of social standing; he wouldn't keep company with someone like me. Anyway, I heard he left the country and lives in England."

"He does live in England. However, he's currently in Massachusetts, and we're certain you know where to find him. If you don't cooperate with us, we'll see to it that you're arrested for aiding a criminal. And then there's the matter of the funds you stole from your former wife."

"How do you know about Naomi?" he screeched.

"At least you're willing to admit you've wronged Mrs. Arnold. Now, why don't you make a clean slate of matters, admit to your involvement with Thurston, and help us apprehend him. Otherwise, I plan to have Taylor go and fetch the authorities. I'm certain they'll be willing to hold you in the local jail until we can return you to Lowell," John threatened.

Thaddeus slipped a finger between his thin neck and the starched collar. Beads of perspiration formed along his brow and then trickled downward, casting a sheen upon his pallid complexion. "I may be able to help you," he ventured in a warbling voice.

"Now, there's a good fellow," John amicably responded while giving Thaddeus an encouraging smile.

His lips quivered, his uncertainty obvious. "I'm expecting William within the hour," he admitted grudgingly.

"Really? Well, perhaps we should wait for him. Taylor, why don't you see if there's an out-of-the way spot to secure the horses, someplace where William won't catch sight of them when he arrives," Matthew suggested. "While you're taking care of the horses, I believe I'll see about getting some assistance from the police. Do you think you can manage Mr. Arnold by yourself for a short time, John?"

"I don't think we'll have any problems," John replied evenly.

Taylor opened the door and then glanced over his shoulder. "Any place you'd care to suggest for our horses, Mr. Arnold?"

"There's a lean-to out back," he grumbled, watching Taylor and Matthew leave the room.

Speculating Thaddeus would likely attempt an escape, John assumed a position in front of the door, folding his long arms across his chest.

"If only I hadn't changed the meeting time, William would be safe. I'm sure I'll be blamed for this entire fiasco. Bad luck seems to follow me like a thundercloud," he lamented.

"Has it occurred to you that your difficulties are self-imposed, Mr. Arnold? If you behaved in a proper fashion, I doubt you'd find yourself surrounded by these intimidating difficulties."

"Save your sermon—it's too late now."

"It's never too late to turn your life around and receive forgiveness," John replied with certainty.

"Forgiveness? You think that's possible?" Thaddeus asked, his eyes glimmering.

"Of course. If you genuinely seek absolution, God will be faithful to His word and forgive you. However, Thaddeus, you mustn't confuse the forgiveness of God with the forgiveness of man."

A scowl replaced his look of expectation. "In other words, I'm going to jail."

John nodded. "Most likely."

Thaddeus slumped down in the chair, his eyes filled with fiery anger. "Well, if that's the case, I'm not asking God or anyone else to forgive me," he snapped.

"As I thought! You're not seeking forgiveness; you're looking to escape punishment," John replied as the sound of footsteps echoed in the hallway.

A knock sounded at the door. "Uncle John, I've a policeman here with me," Taylor announced.

John opened the door to permit them entry and remained silent as the policeman pulled Thaddeus to his feet. "Turn around," he said.

John and Taylor watched as the officer bound Thaddeus's hands behind his back and then led him out of the room and down the stairway.

"Matthew has gone to fetch more lawmen. He should be back directly. They'll wait across the way until Thurston shows himself," Taylor explained.

Time weighed heavy as the men crouched alongside the boardinghouse, their anticipation rising each time they heard the sound of horses' hooves drawing near. Nearly two hours had passed, and they had almost given up all hope of apprehending Thurston when Taylor announced that another rider was approaching in the distance.

"It's him!"

They watched from their hiding place until Thurston began to dismount his horse, and at the policeman's approach, they descended upon him. With an ease that surprised all of them, the elusive William Thurston was quickly under their control.

"You!" Thurston spat in John's direction. "I should have put a knife through your heart when I had the opportunity. Instead, I waited, giving the English gentry the right to make my decisions regarding your future."

John stared at Thurston in disbelief. "Your hatred of me is obvious, yet I'm at a loss to understand the root of your contempt. You successfully escaped punishment for the unspeakable crimes you committed in this country, and still you're willing to place yourself in harm's way in order to damage me. What unfathomable reasoning causes your reckless behavior?"

Thurston emitted a chilling laugh. "This isn't about *you*! This is about much more: This is about the Boston Associates. Without you, they will suffer irreparable damage. Without the knowledge you stole from England, their expansion will be thwarted. I'm certain you're aware the English want you punished for treason. I promised to deliver you to them," he snarled, his face twisted into a picture of demented torment. "You foiled my plans!" He lunged toward John as a gunshot reverberated from the woods nearby. John stared in alarm as he watched Thurston's body crumple forward and then drop to the ground.

With eyes glazed and lips curled in a menacing contortion, a figure emerged, throwing aside his rifle and reaching for the ivory-handled pistol jutting from his waistband. He waved off Matthew and the police officers. "Put down your weapons and back away. I've no grievance with you." He turned with a sarcastic smirk. "Do you remember me, Farnsworth?" he hollered, brandishing the weapon. "Barlow Kent?"

John nodded. "Of course I remember you, Mr. Kent. You worked at the mill in Lancashire. I'm surprised you've left England," he said, attempting to maintain a calm demeanor.

Barlow glared into John's eyes. "To see you receive the punishment you so richly deserve, I would have sailed to the ends of the earth. You ruined my life, and now I'm going to end your time on this earth."

"*I* ruined your life? How can that be, Mr. Kent? We barely knew each other."

"You had me fired from my position. Do you recall telling my supervisor I should be terminated from my job at the mill in Lancashire?"

"Yes. You were a poor employee who wouldn't take instruction or give an honest day's work for your pay. As I remember, you were given several opportunities to mend your ways, but your behavior never really improved," John detailed precisely.

Barlow appeared dazed, as if he'd not heard a word. "You caused the death of my wife—and unborn child," he accused determinedly.

"What? That's a preposterous allegation. I didn't even know your wife. How could I possibly be responsible for her death?"

A spark of anger once again ignited in Barlow's eyes as he gestured wildly with the gun. "My Nancy died in childbirth. We had no money to pay for a doctor because *you* had me discharged from my employment at the mill. Are you finally beginning to understand, Mr. Farnsworth?"

John's gaze remained fixed upon Barlow while Taylor moved with a quiet, determined step and positioned himself behind the crazed man. The officers and Matthew also inched closer.

"You don't claim any of the responsibility for losing your job?" John quietly inquired, hoping he could maintain Barlow's attention. "Surely you don't blame me for this tragic occurrence in your life. Such an idea is outrageous."

John's words appeared to fan the embers of hatred burning deep inside his assailant, who now leveled the weapon directly at his heart.

"You're going to die," Barlow seethed, his anger at fever pitch.

The words had barely been spoken when Taylor and the others jumped forward. Taylor grasped the attacker's arm, wrenching the gun from his hand. Following his lead, Matthew wrestled Barlow to the ground while the lawmen neatly took matters in hand and arrested the man.

John bent down, placing one knee on the ground beside the collapsed body of William Thurston, and felt for a pulse. He looked first at Taylor and then turned his gaze toward Matthew. "William is dead. I guess Thaddeus finally got the better deal," John said, shaking his head. "He may be in jail for a long time—but at least he'll live to tell about it."

29

Canterbury, Connecticut

Daughtie rapped on the front door of Miss Crandall's School for Young Ladies of Color upon their arrival in Canterbury, Connecticut.

"Good afternoon, my dear," Miss Crandall greeted as she opened the door, her thin lips brightening into a welcoming smile.

"Good afternoon, Miss Crandall. I was wondering if I might have a few words with you concerning a matter of grave importance. You may not remember me, but we've corresponded. I'm Daughtie Winfield of Lowell, Massachusetts."

"Ah, Miss Winfield. I didn't recognize you, but it's an unexpected pleasure to have you call. I was in the midst of a class, but if your visit requires my immediate attention, I can make arrangements," she said, her gaze drifting toward Liam, who was still perched in the wagon. "You can have your driver take the wagon to the barn behind the house," she offered.

"There are four of us," Daughtie whispered. "We have two runaways hidden in the back of the wagon."

Miss Crandall's eyes widened slightly. "After you place the horses and wagon in the barn, the four of you can come in through the back door. I'll be waiting there for you."

"Thank you, Miss Crandall," Daughtie said, warmly clasping the older woman's hands.

"Don't thank me yet. We need to talk."

Daughtie didn't wait for further explanation. The fact that Miss Crandall had said the runaways could come into the school was affirmation enough. She ran to the wagon and hoisted herself up beside Liam. "We're to park around back in the barn," she instructed.

"She said the girls could stay?" he asked.

"She said we could all come in and talk. I didn't go into detail."

Liam's shoulders visibly slumped. "Do ya think she'll be willin' to keep them?"

"I don't know. I haven't asked," she replied more abruptly than she had intended.

"I'm not meanin' to make you angry with my questions," he said, his voice low and calm while he directed the horses into a space near the door of the barn.

"I know, Liam," she said hastily while turning on the seat and pulling back the covers that served to obscure the two girls from view. "Come on, girls."

The four of them moved quickly across the small open area between the house and barn, each walking with a hurried determination.

"Is dis da place you was tellin' us 'bout?" Nelly asked as they neared the back of the house.

"Yes," Daughtie replied simply as she ushered the girls through the door. "Miss Crandall, these are the girls I mentioned. This is Nelly. And this," she said, pulling the other girl forward, "is Minerva, her sister." Turning toward Liam, she gave him a bright smile. "This is my friend Liam Donohue. He's been hiding the girls in Lowell."

"I'm pleased to meet all of you," she said warmly, glancing among them. "Girls, I'd like to have you visit one of my classrooms while I visit with Miss Winfield and Mr. Donohue. Would that meet with your approval?"

Nelly and Minerva glanced at each other, obviously surprised their approval was deemed of any importance. "Yessum," they replied in unison.

Once the girls were ensconced in another room, Miss Crandall returned and led Daughtie and Liam into the parlor. "Please make yourselves comfortable," she said before taking a seat in one of the blue-and-beige upholstered chairs. "Now tell me, what brings you to my school?"

Daughtie's lips twitched in a nervous smile. "The girls. We need a safe place for them. They have no family to rely upon, and they can't possibly make it to Canada on their own. We discussed waiting until another group of runaways arrived at Mr. Donohue's house, but we had no idea when the next slaves might arrive, and we were afraid the girls might be discovered if we waited any longer," she hastened to explain, the words tumbling over each other as she spoke.

Miss Crandall's thin lips tightened until they nearly disappeared. "You never said one word in your letters about aiding runaways. Did someone tell you I was harboring runaway slaves?"

"No, not a soul. But your speech at the Pawtucket church addressed the evils of slavery, as did your letters to me—and, of course, you're operating this school for Negro girls," Daughtie replied. She stared at Miss Crandall, her hands folded and resting in her lap, a look of expectation etched upon her face.

Miss Crandall stared back, her eyes narrowed. "So why would you bring these girls to me?" she asked warily.

"Oh yes. Let me complete my explanation. I had been spending a great deal of time thinking and praying about this situation with the girls and how we might help them, knowing we soon must come to a decision. As I picked up my Bible to see if God's Word might reveal an answer, your last letter to me dropped upon the floor. You'll recall you had written that things here in

Canterbury had grown more peaceful and that you were giving thought to the possibility of enrolling a few new students. Needless to say, your letter appeared to be an answer to prayer. The more I prayed, the more I believed the Lord was directing me to bring the girls here—to your school—a place where they would be safe and could receive an education among people they can trust."

Miss Crandall leaned back in her chair and gave Daughtie a kindly smile. "I believe you're telling me the truth, Miss Winfield. And if I weren't in such financial straits, I would consider admitting the girls. But I simply cannot manage to feed and clothe them. When all of this difficulty began, there were some parents who withdrew their daughters. Consequently, I had to begin charging higher fees. If the parents of my students discovered I was permitting these girls to stay here free of charge, I'd likely have further withdrawals from my enrollment, and I can ill afford to have that occur."

Liam shifted to the edge of the settee. "What if ya received full payment for the girls, Miss Crandall? Would ya have any objection to boardin' them?"

Prudence hesitated a moment. "If they paid for tuition and boarding fees, I would be delighted to have them remain, but since that's impossible, I think we must devise some other plan."

"I'll pay for them," Liam modestly replied.

"I mean no disrespect, Mr. Donohue, but I'm not sure you understand the financial commitment involved."

"I believe I can afford your charges, Miss Crandall. I'll sign a note if ya like, but you'll find my payments will be made as promised. I'll be leavin' funds with ya to purchase some clothes and any other necessaries they might be needin'."

Miss Crandall glanced toward Daughtie with a questioning look in her eyes. "If you're absolutely certain you want to do this, then my answer is yes. But you must remember that if matters should begin to worsen with the townspeople, the school may be closed, and the girls will once again be placed in jeopardy."

"We understand, but they'll be safe with you for now. If problems arise in the future, we'll make other arrangements."

Prudence nodded. "Have you told the girls they'll be staying here?"

"We told them a little about the school. They seemed excited with the thought of receiving an education. I did explain that all the girls in your school are daughters of freemen, and they appeared astonished at the concept. However, I believe they're a bit concerned by our decision to bring them to Connecticut. Liam explained this was the safest possible place for two young runaway girls right now. The men they were traveling with were recaptured, and we truly don't believe we should send them off toward Canada by themselves," Daughtie said.

"I agree with you. I'm doubtful they could make it to the border on their own. There are too many tragedies that could befall two young girls traveling alone. However, they won't be content if they're forced to remain in Canterbury against their will," Miss Crandall replied.

Daughtie glanced at Liam. "I think the girls realize this is the wisest possible choice. Perhaps if you talk to them before making a final decision, you'll feel more assured," Daughtie suggested.

"I think that's an excellent suggestion. I'll emphasize the complications and dangers of sending them off on their own and Mr. Donohue's willingness to pay their fees to remain here and attend school. If they choose to stay, we'll need to begin their instruction separate from the other students. I doubt if they read or write, and I wouldn't want them to feel overwhelmed. I'll have to rely upon the discretion of my girls to keep this matter a secret. However, with the inequity and hurtful behavior heaped upon us by the residents of Canterbury, I'm certain my students will be quick to protect Nelly and Minerva."

Daughtie sighed and gave the older woman a broad smile. "Thank you, Miss Crandall."

"Why don't you two relax for a short time? I'll have the girls come to my office, where we can visit privately, and then I'll be back."

Daughtie watched Miss Crandall exit the room and then turned toward Liam, her eyes revealing a modicum of apprehension.

He placed his hand atop hers for an instant. "No need for worryin', lassie. Let's sit back and let God work out His plan."

As they reached the outskirts of Canterbury, Liam snapped the reins, and the team of horses broke into a trot. "It's been a pleasure havin' the sun shinin' down on us while we've been in Connecticut. Can't say I've missed the rain," he commented.

Daughtie nodded her agreement and settled back on the wooden seat. "I'm relieved the girls decided to remain in Canterbury. They actually appeared happy by the time we left, don't you think?"

Liam remained silent, his lips turned upward in a self-satisfied smile.

Daughtie stared at him, waiting. "Why are you smiling? Did I say something humorous?"

"Ah, lassie, you do make it difficult for me to be trustin' in your Lord," he finally replied with a lilt to his voice.

Daughtie's cheeks flushed. The truth of his words pricked her heart. "You're right, Liam. God provided an answer, but I didn't have faith He would see the plan through to completion. How can I expect others to believe when my own faith is so weak?" she lamented.

"Now, don't go bein' so hard on yourself. God managed things just fine without ya this time. Surely He's willin' to accept a misstep now and again, don't ya think?"

Daughtie smiled and nodded. "Seems as if you've gotten to know quite a bit about God since the arrival of Nelly and Minerva."

"That's true. Those girls have an unwaverin' love for God that's hard for me to understand. Even through the difficulties they've endured, they don't doubt God's love for them and they want everybody to know Jesus. 'Course, both Matthew Cheever and John Farnsworth have talked about their faith with me from time to time. However, while those girls made me long to learn more, it was you who made me aware of what I was really missin' by tellin' me to search the Scriptures for myself and pray." He shifted on the wooden seat and took a deep breath. "Tell me, what do you think of the new doctor?" he asked.

Daughtie gave him a sidelong glance. "Aren't you the man who accused me of abrupt changes in conversation not so very long ago?"

Liam gave a hearty laugh. "Now, don't be avoidin' my question, lassie," he teasingly replied.

Daughtie gave him a faint smile. "Dr. Ketter appears to be quite capable. Why do you ask?"

"I saw him escortin' you to the Farnsworths' the other night. He looked to be enjoyin' your company."

Daughtie's brow furrowed as she thought for a moment. "I didn't see you at the Farnsworths'."

"I know. John asked me to stop by and visit with 'im about some stone-work. I thought I'd stop on me way home, but when I saw you and the doctor goin' up the steps, I figured there was a party or some such thing goin' on, so I went home. That doctor would make a good match for ya."

"Match? As in marriage?"

Liam nodded.

"Why would you even think such a thing? Dr. Ketter will likely make a good husband for some woman, but *I'm* certainly not interested in becoming his wife."

"And why would he be such a poor choice for you?"

Daughtie swallowed down the lump that was rising in her throat. Obviously she had misconstrued Liam's words and actions these past months. What a fool she was! He had merely wanted someone to decorate his home and help him with the runaways, when all the time she had secretly thought he was interested in her affections. Their long discussions, the playful banter, his kisses upon her cheek—they had all been nothing more than brotherly companionship.

Liam gave her a lopsided grin. "Have ya lost your tongue, Daughtie? Never known ya to be so slow to answer," he teased.

Daughtie choked back her tears and inhaled a deep breath of the cool morning air. "Dr. Ketter and I don't share the same values."

"Ya don't? Why, the two of ya go to the same church most of the time, and ya said he's a good man." His brogue thickened.

Why wouldn't Liam let the matter rest? "He is a good man, but he's not the man I want to marry," she replied with finality.

"Ya already told me that much. I'm askin' why he isn't the man for ya."

"And I answered you. Perhaps not to your satisfaction, but I *did* answer you."

"You're soundin' a wee bit ill-tempered, lassie. I'm only tryin' to find out why you don't want to marry this fella."

"Because I don't love him," she snapped.

Liam gave her a broad smile. "Now, *that* was an answer!"

Her eyes flashed with anger. "Can we talk about something else now?"

"I'm guessin' he's in love with you. Has he asked ya to marry 'im?"

She clenched her jaw. "No."

"And ya don't want him to ask ya?"

"*No!*"

"Strange," he mused. "Most girls want to get married. Do ya not want a husband?"

Why wouldn't he quit badgering her with these questions about love and marriage? "Yes, I want a husband."

"So it's just Dr. Ketter ya're not wantin'?" he continued.

"Yes," she sighed in exasperation. "I want to marry a man who has a heart for the downtrodden. Dr. Ketter's a physician, but his interest is directed toward those who can pay for their medical treatment. Even though he possesses the skill, Dr. Ketter's not the type who would go into the Acre and help the sick merely because they are in need. I want to marry a man I love, a man who is willing to sacrifice for others—a man who would be willing to take the type of risks you've taken helping runaways. A man like you."

"Ah, but that could never happen, lassie, for ya know folks would never be acceptin' a fine girl such as yourself takin' up with someone of the lower class. They'd condemn and forsake ya for sure. Now think about it, what kind of life would that be?"

"Two people of differing classes could still have a good marriage and a good life if they didn't put stock in what others thought and believed. Besides, look at what Prudence Crandall has endured for the sake of girls she doesn't even know. Do you think I'd be willing to do less for someone I love? The opinion of others is not what's of importance to me. Besides, if a person truly cares for another, their country of birth should make no difference."

"What if your friend Bella and her fine husband would be havin' nothin' more to do with ya should you marry a man such as meself?" he ventured.

"Are you asking me to marry you, Liam?"

"And if I were askin', what would you be answerin', lassie?"

She looked toward a distant spot in the road. "I'd be required to tell you no—but not because you're Irish," she hastened to explain.

He slowly nodded and hesitated, as if weighing her reply. "I'm almost afraid to ask this next question, but if it's not because I'm Irish, and you're unafraid of retribution from your friends, then why?"

Daughtie nervously straightened the pleats in her yellow muslin dress. "You still haven't told me exactly where you stand in your relationship with God. You've hinted that you've read the Scriptures and mentioned you've been praying, and although I would marry an Irishman, I could never marry a man who hasn't avowed his belief in Jesus and accepted Him as his Savior. I fear such a match would lead to nothing but disaster and heartache," she replied, her voice barely above a whisper.

Liam had leaned in close, obviously eager to hear every word. As soon as Daughtie finished speaking, he straightened and shifted back against the wagon seat. A deep sigh escaped his lips.

She turned to face him. "What does that mean?"

"I think ya're looking for an excuse! If ya can't see how much I've changed and grown in my beliefs, well, I doubt I could convince ya by any words I would say. Why, my poor mother would be horror-struck if she knew the changes I've gone through since movin' to America."

"What kind of changes?" she asked, squelching her instinct to argue against his comment about excuses.

"Changes such as discoverin' that what I've needed all my life is to know Jesus—and that I've been able to go through the steps of transformin' my life by acceptin' Him as my Lord and Savior. Not only would she be dumb-founded by the statement, she'd likely believe I've lost my mind."

"And have you lost your mind, Liam?"

He reined back on the horses. "No," he replied softly. "But I have lost my heart."

Daughtie trembled. "Oh?"

"I, too, want to be marryin' for love, but I fear my desire might never be fulfilled."

Daughtie stiffened and lifted her chin ever so slightly. "Well, of course it won't be fulfilled if you don't ask her the question."

Liam raised a brow. "And what question would that be, lass?"

She maintained her serious demeanor and leaned closer. "Will you marry me?"

Liam looked at her for a moment and then began to smile. "Of course I will," he replied. Then with a flick of the reins he put the horses into motion.

"Besides," he added, "I'll have to be doin' somethin' to keep yar reputation from bein' ruined after us bein' alone like this."

Daughter giggled and then began to laugh even harder. "Oh, Liam."

He stopped the horses again, looking at her with grave concern. "What madness has taken ya now?"

She shook her head and wiped tears from her eyes. "You're worried about marrying me to keep my reputation intact."

He looked at her as if she were daft. "And what's wrong with that?" he asked, his voice taking on an indignant tone.

"There's nothing wrong with it, except marrying you isn't going to exactly save my reputation."

From the grin on his face, Daughtie realized he finally understood. "Well, if the town's goin' to be up in arms over ya, then we may as well give them plenty to be up in arms about. This way will make me a whole lot happier than the other." He reached out and pulled Daughtie close.

Daughtie looked up, knowing he would kiss her. She longed for his kiss—his touch—like nothing she had ever longed for before. Reaching up, she toyed with the black curls at the nape of Liam's neck.

"I think I've loved you for a very long time, my handsome Irishman," she whispered.

He pressed his mouth to hers in a very gentle, tender kiss. Daughtie tightened her arms around his neck and sighed as the kiss deepened and she seemed to melt against him.

He pulled away, pushing back a loose wisp of her hair. "I love you, my darlin'. But lovin' ya won't make others accept us together as man and wife. I want ya to think long and hard about this. I want ya to be sure before we make our vows."

Daughtie straightened and reluctantly left Liam's hold. "I am certain, but I'm quite willing to pray on it." She smiled and folded her hands in her lap. "But don't ya go thinkin' to get out of yar agreement to marry me," she said, trying hard to imitate Liam's Irish brogue. "I'll not be havin' it."

~ 30 ~

"Isn't that ten feet?" Daughtie questioned as Liam shoveled yet another load of dirt onto the tarp. They'd connected a pulley to the tarp in order to bring the dirt out of the hole and still it was an exhausting process.

"Not quite. It's close, but not quite ten," he said, looking at the small area.

Liam had gotten the brilliant idea to dig a hiding place for the slaves. Here in the barn, they could easily conceal it, and if anyone should find it, they would simply say they'd dug a root cellar. The plan was quite simple. The dimensions were to be eight by ten and seven feet deep, with shelves on the wall for supplies and a hidden airway near the wall of the barn. They'd been working on the hiding place since late summer, as time permitted. Daughtie thought the process was taking too long, but Liam assured her they were doing just fine.

"It's not going to be very light down here and they won't be able to burn a lantern," Daughtie said as she surveyed the room. "The air will quickly grow bad."

"Aye, but 'tis only goin' to be used for emergencies," Liam reminded her. "A place to hide them away in case the house is searched or they arrive when no one is to home."

"I know. It just seems . . . well . . . almost like a grave."

He stopped what he was doing and pulled her close. "Daughtie, my darlin', you worry too much." He turned her toward the ladder. "Let's get this dirt out of here and go have some tea."

Daughtie nodded. She hiked her skirts and climbed to the top, knowing Liam would finish tying the tarp to the pulley rope. It was only a moment or two before he bounded up the ladder to join her. He took hold of the rope and heaved the heavy weight ever upward. Daughtie's job was to guide the mass once it cleared the hole and pull it to the side, where Liam would deposit it.

Reaching out, she pulled the tarped bundle toward her, but just as she had the bundle in place the load shifted. Daughtie lost her footing and fell backward onto the straw-covered floor—landing with surprising impact despite the cushioning. Liam quickly lowered the load and hurried to her side.

"Are ya hurt?"

She laughed and rubbed her backside as he helped her to her feet. "Only me pride, luv." They laughed at her mimicking Irish.

"Well, for sure ya have straw in yar hair," Liam said, allowing his brogue to become heavy.

"And for sure, ya have straw in yar hair, too," Daughtie said, reaching down to grab a handful to sprinkle over Liam's head.

He laughed and lifted her in his arms. "Ah, my darlin'—my wife," he murmured between kisses.

Daughtie reached up to take hold of his face as he stared down at her. "I am so very happy to hear you call me that." She thought back to the difficulty they'd had in finding someone to marry them. No one wanted to allow a Yankee girl to marry an Irishman. The prejudices were strong—even among men of God who should have been able to see each man as God's child. They'd finally been forced to drive several miles to another town, where Liam managed to convince the Methodist preacher that they were both of age and in love. Daughtie had remained quiet except for an occasional reply in her attempted brogue. The preacher had seemed hesitant until Liam had added that they weren't Catholic and because of this, the Catholic Church would not marry them. The man then took pity on them and performed a hasty ceremony.

"I love—"

"Shhh!" Liam declared, putting his finger to Daughtie's lips. "Someone's coming."

They got to their feet quickly, dusting off the straw as best they could. "Sounds like the entire town is coming," Daughtie said, hurrying to the barn door with Liam following behind.

"Looks like at least three wagons—maybe four," she said, peeking from the narrow opening in the door. She glanced back with apprehension toward the hole in the floor.

"Relax. If someone questions it, we'll just tell 'em we're puttin' in a root cellar. There's no need to be afraid."

Daughtie nodded. "I know, but we didn't want anyone knowing about it. The whole idea was to hide it away after we completed it."

"Aye, and for sure ya're right. Let's just go on outside and greet whoever it is and hope they'll not be wantin' to come to the barn."

Daughtie knew it was the sensible thing to do, but a part of her was still afraid. What if the visitors had come to do them harm? People had not been happy to learn of their union. Daughtie was still snubbed whenever she went into town, and more than once she'd been turned away when a storeowner pointed to a sign that strictly forbade Irish to enter.

Taking a deep breath, she opened the door and stepped outside. The sunlight was warm on her face and hard on her eyes. She squinted and shielded her eyes with her hand. "Oh, it's Bella and Taylor!" she squealed in excitement. "And I do believe that's Miss Addie and John Farnsworth behind them."

Liam took hold of her hand, and together they walked to the front of the house. Taylor brought his wagon to a stop just beyond the front walkway. Bella was already waving in anticipation.

"Hello, Daughtie—Liam! We've brought you some gifts."

John and Addie pulled their carriage up alongside the wagon, while Matthew and Lilly Cheever came up behind them.

Daughtie turned to Liam as the party dismounted. "Oh, my. I had no idea they were coming. Did you?" She frantically tried to check her dress for dirt.

"No, to be sure I didn't."

After Taylor helped Bella to the ground, she came rushing to see Daughtie. "I feel like you've been gone forever. We decided it was time to come for a visit."

"Absolutely," Addie said, coming to join them. "The Ladies Aid Society has missed you at the sewing circles, but they sent along some little gifts to remind you to join us again soon."

Daughtie looked to her husband and then to the ladies. Lilly Cheever had now joined them. "I didn't think . . . well . . ." Daughtie paused and looked again to Liam. She didn't want to hurt him. "I didn't know if I'd be welcome to come sew with the ladies . . . now that I've married."

"Pshaw!" Addie said with a wave of her hand.

Lilly reached out to take hold of Daughtie's hand. "I second that. You are always welcome in my home. If the other ladies have a problem with that, then it is something they will have to deal with. Not you."

"We feel the same way, Liam," John Farnsworth declared as he joined the party. Matthew and Taylor were at his side. They nodded in complete agreement.

"I must be sayin' this comes as some surprise. I didn't think any of ya approved," Liam said, speaking his mind.

"Well, we must admit," Taylor began, "there was concern because of the situation being what it is. We know you've not been treated well at times, Liam. And you aren't even poor Irish. You have money and a good job skill. Still people ostracize you."

"We didn't want that for either you or Daughtie," Lilly Cheever threw in. "However, now that the deed is done and we were cheated out of a wedding, we've decided to come and celebrate with you. We've brought supper, gifts, and a few surprises."

"Surprises?" Liam questioned.

"Definitely," Matthew said, grinning.

Daughtie looked beyond them to the wagon and carriages. "Where are your children, Mrs. Cheever? I must admit I've been quite longing to see that new baby. Has he grown very big?"

Matthew laughed, but it was John who spoke. "Michael Cheever is a fine specimen of a young man. He will no doubt rival his father in height and intelligence."

"He's definitely worth the trip to see," Addie teased.

"Yes, you must come," Lilly agreed. "Maybe you and Liam would take dinner with us after church tomorrow."

Daughtie looked to her husband. Liam nodded. "That sounds quite nice."

"What does Violet think of her new little brother?" Daughtie asked. She began to relax a bit in the circle of friends.

"She is completely delighted—spends her afternoons mooning over him," Matthew declared.

"Say there, is that straw in your hair?" Bella questioned, reaching up to pluck a piece from Daughtie's hair.

Daughtie looked at Liam, who instantly looked away, as if embarrassed. He attempted to casually run his hand through his own hair while Daughtie stammered to answer. "I . . . well, we were . . ." She didn't know how to finish the sentence. The group began to laugh uproariously until John Farnsworth finally put an end to it.

"Well, in spite of what we may have interrupted, I think we need to unload the wagon, gentlemen."

"I'll take care of this," Liam whispered in Daughtie's ear. "You visit with your friends." He turned to the men. "Let's go. Oh, by the way, how did that uprising with the farmers at the Pawtucket dam turn out?"

"Well," Matthew began while striding toward the wagon, "it's under control for now. We don't anticipate any more problems for the time."

Daughtie watched as they walked away talking and enjoying the news to be had. She felt silly for the way Liam's absence from her side was almost a loss. They spent so much time together of late, it was as if they were two sides of the same coin.

"I hope we didn't come at a bad time," Bella said, interrupting Daughtie's thoughts.

"No, not at all. Since it's Saturday evening we were working to get some of our chores done. These September evenings have been quite pleasant." She paused and offered them all a smile. "I'm so touched that you would come here today," she told her friends. "I know this is difficult. I know the world doesn't think highly of what I've done, but . . ." She paused as the men moved past them with various parcels and crates. "But I love him and I know he is the man God gave me to marry."

Bella nodded and wiped at a tear in her eye. "I'm sorry we weren't more supportive. I spoke with Ruth the other day and she was so very ugly about the entire matter. The things she said were echoes of some of the very things I had spoken to you of, but coming from her mouth they seemed so much harsher—less Christian. I suppose I let my fears for you cloud my judgment. Please forgive me."

Daughtie hugged Bella close. "Of course."

They pulled away, this time laughing at each other's tears. "Here this is a happy occasion," Daughtie sniffed.

"It is a happy occasion," Lilly declared. "We want to celebrate and set things off on the right foot." Addie nodded in agreement.

Daughtie reached out to hug all three women. "Oh, I'm so grateful to have good friends like you."

The men made one more trip to empty the wagon and disappeared into the house. Daughtie pulled away and smiled. "So shall we join the men in the house?"

"I think that would be splendid," Addie declared. "We can . . ." Her words faded as the sound of yet another carriage came from far down the lane.

"Who could that be?" Daughtie asked, straining to see.

"Well, I'll be," Addie said with a gasp of surprise. "It's Lawrence and Mintie."

"Oh my," Lilly Cheever said softly.

"Whatever is she doing here?" Bella asked.

The carriage pulled up and a very prim and proper Miss Mintie allowed her escort to help her from the carriage. Her walking-out suit of dark burgundy seemed almost flamboyant on the woman who rarely wore anything more lively than blue.

"Mintie, I didn't think you were going to come here today," Addie said as her sister and friend joined them. "Hello, Mr. Gault." He gave a slight bow. Addie turned back to Mintie for an explanation.

Daughtie wondered if the old woman had come to criticize her choice of husbands. Mintie Beecher had been known for her hatred of the British. Did she feel the same way about the Irish?

"I told you that I couldn't be ready by four. I did not say that I wouldn't come," Mintie announced. She turned to Daughtie, her pinched features as stern as ever. "So they tell me you have married."

Daughtie stiffened. "Yes. Yes, I have. His name is Liam Donohue."

"I see," Mintie said, eyeing the girl as though weighing each word. "So you *did* marry the Irishman."

"Sister!"

Lilly started to protest. "Miss Beecher, that's hardly—"

"Silence!" Miss Mintie declared. "I'm speaking with Mrs. Donohue."

Daughtie swallowed hard. Miss Mintie could be most difficult to deal with, and this occasion was certainly no exception. "Yes," she finally answered. "I married an Irishman."

Mintie hurrumphed and nodded. "Well, it's better than marrying an Englishman."

"But John's English!" Addie protested.

"No," Mintie said quite stoically, "he's an American."

For a moment there was no sound, but only for a moment. After that, Bella began to snicker and Addie to laugh with a great wheezing gusto. Lilly bent double in laughter, while Daughtie and Mintie faced off like two lionesses over a kill.

Slowly Mintie and Daughtie looked to the others. "A great bunch of ninnies," Mintie declared.

Daughtie looped her arm through Mintie's. "I quite agree, Miss Beecher. I think we should leave them here and let them laugh themselves silly."

The old woman looked up to meet Daughtie's gaze. She gave the slightest hint of a grin and declared, "On that matter, my dear, we are already too late."

As they approached the house, Daughtie and Mintie were nearly knocked aside by the men. They bounded out the front door holding Liam high in the air. Liam, kicking and hollering, seemed not at all impressed with their revelry.

"What are you doing?" Lilly questioned from behind Daughtie.

Matthew called over his shoulder, "We're celebrating with the groom. We'll be back shortly—after we've dunked his highness in the pond."

The men laughed and Lawrence Gault hurried to join the fun.

Liam called out as they passed, "Don't ya dare be givin' 'em even a spot of tea. They've come to make mischief on this house—I'm thinkin' they're all leprechauns in the guise of our good friends." And then they were gone, disappearing behind the barn on their journey to the cattle pond.

Daughtie got over her surprise and gave a contented sigh. She knew exactly what this kind of camaraderie meant to her husband. Turning to Mintie, she smiled. "Would you care to take tea with an Irishman's lady?"

Mintie straightened and gave a very curt nod. "I have come with no other idea in mind."

Daughtie felt the warmth of the old woman's approving words. To imagine Miss Mintie offering her support was more than she could have ever hoped for. If Miss Mintie and her sister and Lilly Cheever and Bella could all accept her marriage to Liam, then maybe others would come around in time. And if not, then these ladies were sufficient to bless Daughtie with enough friendship and love to last the rest of time.